*A Treasury of*

# GREAT
# RUSSIAN SHORT STORIES

THE MACMILLAN COMPANY
NEW YORK • CHICAGO
DALLAS • ATLANTA • SAN FRANCISCO
LONDON • MANILA

IN CANADA
BRETT-MACMILLAN LTD.
GALT, ONTARIO

# A Treasury of

# GREAT

# RUSSIAN SHORT STORIES

## Pushkin to Gorky

*Edited by*

AVRAHM YARMOLINSKY

NEW YORK

THE MACMILLAN COMPANY

1958

# ACKNOWLEDGMENTS

THANKS are due to the following publishers for permission to reprint the stories specified on which they hold copyright:

Random House, New York, for "The Undertaker" and "The Queen of Spades" from *The Poems, Prose and Plays of Alexander Pushkin*, selected and edited by Avrahm Yarmolinsky.

Oxford University Press, New York, for "Sevastopol, December, 1854" and "How Much Land Does a Man Need?" from the *Works of Leo Tolstoy*, Centenary Edition.

Dodd, Mead & Company, Inc., New York, for "After the Ball" from *Father Sergius, The Forged Coupon, Miscellaneous Stories, by Lev N. Tolstoy*, edited by Hagbert Wright; and for "Makar's Dream" from *Makar's Dream and Other Stories*, by Vladimir Korolenko.

Adelphi Company, New York, for "Gambrinus," from *Gambrinus and Other Stories*, by Alexander Kuprin.

Henry Holt & Company, Inc., New York, for "Twenty-six Men and a Girl," "Birth of a Man," "Going Home," "Lullaby," from *A Book of Short Stories*, by Maxim Gorki, edited by Avrahm Yarmolinsky and Baroness Moura Budberg.

Some of the translations have been revised by the editor.

# NOTE

UNLESS otherwise indicated, the year placed at the end of each piece refers to the date when it was first published.

# INTRODUCTION

RUSSIAN literature passed out of the awkward age with the writings of Pushkin, matured in the work of the major novelists, declining with Chekhov, and, when the hour of revolution struck, coming to an end which was a new beginning. The scope of the present collection coincides with this grand cycle and so with the better part of the century that preceded the new era; the volume opens with a story dated 1835 and closes with one first published in 1917. Soviet writing does not come within the purview of this book.

Every piece included is complete in itself. Here is nothing to offend those who share the editor's distaste for literary scraps and gobbets, for excerpts torn from their organic context. Fortunately for the anthologist, nearly all the important Russian authors cultivated the art of the short story, and indeed, for Chekhov and those who came after him it was the chief medium, so that such a collection as this is something in the nature of an epitome of Russian fiction.

The function and range of literature were broader in prerevolutionary Russia than in the rest of the western world. The sentiments and opinions that men were forbidden to set forth in the public prints, from the rostrum, even from a club chair, found their way into imaginative writing, as did the impulses that elsewhere expressed themselves in civic activities, thus giving fiction a quasi-political cast and charging it with social implications. The narratives in this volume do not often exhibit the neat plot, the suspense, the severe economy to which the skillfully wrought product of contemporary storytellers has accustomed the public. They are to be read rather for their warm humanity, for their penetrating insights into character, for their musings and speculations on first and last things, and not least for their picture of Russian society, a world that cannot be visited otherwise, and one in which Soviet life is rooted.

i

The two stories with which the book opens are straightforward tales about matters of perennial interest. "The Undertaker" is a genre picture with a touch of the macabre; and the subject of "The Queen of Spades," which is spiced with the supernatural, is gambling. In both, the characters are drawn with a light pencil, but neatly and clearly. Moreover, one finds in these pages for the first time the simplicity and homeliness that Pushkin felt to be more suitable to the Russian tongue than "European finicalness and French refinement." The shorter tale exemplifies the fond perception of the details of daily life that was to become the distinguishing trait of so much Russian writing. There are firm realistic touches in "The Queen of Spades," too, for all its fantasy, and in spite of the fact that the Russified German villain is a man out of the common run. And as this Hermann in his reasoned criminality and thirst for power is the remote prototype of the hero of *Crime and Punishment*, so Lizaveta, the old lady's ward, is the ancestress of the suppressed and humiliated girls in later Russian prose. The man who brought Russian verse to an unmatched excellence did pioneering work when, at the end of his stormy youth, he was constrained, in his own phrase, "to stern prose."

If Pushkin laid the foundations of the realism that dominates Russian fiction, the superstructure was built by men who for the most part lacked his serene objectivity, his healthy, graceful acceptance of life. The first of these builders, Nikolay Gogol, though something of a fantast and not without a latent mystic and moralizing strain, established the naturalist tradition, with its emphasis on the more sordid aspect of the commonplace. He himself spoke of his mind, which he considered typically Russian, as inductive rather than inventive: his imagination needed the support of exact and ample knowledge. Yet the result of his close observations was not a sober likeness, but something exaggerated, comic, monstrous, like a Daumier caricature. His was the deliberate laughter of a morbidly melancholy man, and indeed he echoed Villon's "Je ris en pleurs." This is less evident in "Old-World Landowners," where the picture of a vegetative existence is presented with a nostalgic, half-humorous tenderness, than in "The Overcoat." In the story of the pathetic, dreadful little copyist there is pity for the victim and indignation at the circumstances that have made him what he is, although these sentiments are concealed under a cloak of humor.

"We've all come out of 'The Overcoat,' " said Dostoevsky. And indeed, with this story "the little man" as a figure inspiring social protest entered the province of Russian fiction and became firmly established there. Dostoevsky himself owed a great debt to Gogol. His early stories are in the naturalist vein that his senior opened up. They deal with poor folk, petty clerks, down-at-heel intellectuals, drunken derelicts—as in "An Honest Thief"—men and women so crushed and cowed, so starved in body and spirit that they are seen not merely as victims of an inhuman system but as psychopathological cases; and it was indeed this aspect of them that chiefly interested Dostoevsky. From the first he was fascinated by the abnormal. The situation in "An Unpleasant Predicament" is one of pure comedy, such as might have been grist for Gogol's mill. He could not, however, have conceived the sadistic father of the bride, a character who faintly adumbrates the "antihero" of "Notes from the Underground."

The "Notes" had nothing of the conventional. Here was something new under the sun. This huge, sprawling soliloquy is a "confession" that sometimes masquerades as a spluttering, angry argument. It reads not unlike the monologue of a man who has reluctantly dragged himself into a psychoanalyst's office. The speaker is a miserable nonentity, a solitary, and an outcast, brooding over his frustrations; but he differs from the daydreamers of the early stories in being full of venom and protest.

The monologue opens with discursive pages of explanation and debate, yet these confused, stammering dialectics reveal the anatomy of the undergroundling only less nakedly than does the unforgettable story that follows. Here is a thwarted ego, sore from the batterings of circumstance, asserting itself by tearing at its own wounds and sucking a perverse pleasure from the pain. The undergroundling lashes out at all that is mechanical, all that is rational, particularly utilitarian ethics, at whatever is final in the laws of man and nature, because he sees them as so many attempts upon the inviolability of the self. One aspect of his tragedy is that while he is unwilling to act rationally, he is too full of intellectual pride to obey his natural instincts. The inwardness with which Dostoevsky presents his "antihero" gives these pages unexampled power. The drama enacted between the undergroundling and the prostitute, his posturings before her, his shame, his passion, his hideous revenge upon her for the humiliation that her love inflicts upon him, all this shows that the man's soul-sickness is rooted in a jealous clinging to his self-will, and that this is what cuts him off from "the living life."

Dostoevsky unquestionably shared the undergroundling's distrust of reason and his horror of the determinist philosophy. He was built upon the belief in the sacredness of the self, in man's freedom to choose between good and evil as the token and seal of his humanity. But he held no brief for the principle of self-will. Only love freely given could make for personal salvation and unite men in a true commonwealth. A society that was a Church was Dostoevsky's ideal, and he believed that its consummation would be brought about by the spirit of Russian Christianity. This theocratic, messianic doctrine is central to his work. His most effective writing, however, is that which pictures man with all his evil impulses, with his divided nature, his backsliding and weakness, fitfully striving after grace. It has been suggested that the underground, with its elements of degradation, rancor, and revolt, loomed so large in Dostoevsky's work because he was writing in and about a society that for centuries had breathed the air of oppression. In any event, the "Notes" may be regarded as a subtle and powerful cartoon for his great canvases, and in a measure a clue to them.

## ii

The autobiographic sketch with which the selection from Dostoevsky's writings concludes illustrates a leading trend in Russian thought. The child, frightened by an imagined wolf, clings to the peasant's smock, and that uncouth, strong, earth-stained figure takes on for the grown man the lineaments of the Savior. The populist theme, assuming in turn a mystic, a positivist, a political guise, runs like a crimson thread through the texture of Russian literature. This was largely the product of men whose forebears had been exploiting the peasants for generations and who themselves, however remorsefully, were living on the labor of the masses. Their idealization of the peasantry was in no small measure an expression of the sense of guilt that possessed the more sensitive members of a class that had had its day. In any case, "the people" remained the hub around which so much of Russian writing revolved.

The sober-minded and Europeanized Turgenev entertained no illusions as to the mystic virtues of the muzhik. But the peasant problem was a matter of deep concern to him both as a citizen and as a writer. In his youth he took what he called his "Hannibal's oath" not to rest until serfdom was destroyed. *A Sportsman's Sketches*, the work with which his literary career opened, was in effect a fulfillment of his vow. But if the book was in effect an abolitionist tract, it was a tract with a difference. Here was not a propagandist turning fiction to his own ends, but a story-teller whose human sympathies went out to the underdog. For this reason the book, as the three stories taken from it bear witness, has retained its freshness long after the cause that it served became ancient history. "Moomoo," which he might well have included with the *Sketches*, written as it was about the same time and on an allied theme, comes closer than most of them do to attacking the institution of serfdom. Here too the immense pathos of the situation as Turgenev presents it lives on undiminished. The reminiscential "Old Portraits," a product of the novelist's last years, has something of the quality of the *Sketches*. It is an admirable pendant to Gogol's "Old-World Landowners," but the nostalgia for the placid past is far less emphatic here, and, significantly enough, the piece sounds a harsh note before it closes with explicit if mild condemnation of the ancestral order.

Turgenev admitted that he, along with many of his compatriots, lacked the English writers' gift for contriving a plot. The germ of his story was always a face, an individual man or woman, whose features he studied until he could read the individual's history there. His imagination, like Gogol's, was inductive. What triumphs this method permitted him may be seen in such a piece as "A Lear of the Steppes." One sees in his smaller pieces no less than in his novels how the moral grows out of the situation, the situation out of the characters, and how all, closely observed, sensitively apprehended, are set down with a natural felicity.

As Henry James pointed out, his "distinguished friend" Turgenev held to the belief that the only duty of a work of fiction was "to be well written; that merit included every other of which it was capable." Not that Turgenev was the aesthete, whose effort was concentrated on fine writing, but rather that he felt himself to be a spectator of the human scene, peculiarly equipped to make his vision present to others, and convinced that the moral meaning of that vision lay in the penetration of his insight and the integrity with which he conveyed it.

At no time in his long life did Turgenev's greater contemporary, Leo Tolstoy, see eye to eye with him in this matter. His outlook shifted with the years, but the moralist always stood at the writer's elbow and not seldom his shadow fell across the page. Tolstoy was a genuinely religious man, with the puritan's strong rationalist streak. How to live according to the dictates of conscience and reason was the problem that never ceased to harass him, and this preoccupation colored nearly everything he wrote. In his later years he insisted that a writer of fiction needed "a clear and firm conception of what is good and what is bad in life," that a narrative was held together not "by the unity of characters and situations" but by the cement of the author's "moral attitude toward his subject." A similar statement occurs in an entry in his Diary made when he was twenty-five. The author of *War and Peace*, with his great gusto, with all the variety and richness of his experience, with his marvelous ability to project himself into the lives of others—be it a young girl at her first ball or an old peasant on his deathbed—for all his mastery of his medium, was perpetually intruding on his reader his ethical concern. He had an endless interest in the world, the flesh, and the devil, and he was able to make them wonderfully real; but he was repeatedly waylaid by his desire to reform the world, subdue the flesh, and cast out the devil. If this sometimes reduced his stature as a writer, it only added in the public eye to his stature as a man.

A selection from shorter writings is less apt to do justice to Tolstoy's powers than to those of either Turgenev or Dostoevsky. Many of his tales were written after the artist had placed himself at the service of the preacher, and are in effect parables written in the simple language with which he hoped to reach the hearts of the multitude. A typical instance is that lesson on greediness: "How Much Land Does a Man Need?" The story, "After the Ball," written in his old age, holds a moral that as a young man he had formulated in a letter to a friend: "Truly the State is a conspiracy for the purpose not only of exploiting the citizens but of demoralizing them as well." But even such didactic tales are redeemed by the author's perception alike of the concrete detail and the psychological nuance. In his early work he is less apt to wag a minatory finger at his readers. These stories carry their moral burden more lightly and have a greater amount of what James calls "felt life" in them. This applies to "Polikushka," where the sketches of the serfs help to round out the picture of a slave society that one gets from Gogol and Turgenev.

Tolstoy's moral preoccupation is least obtrusive in his *Sevastopol Tales,* the first of which is included in this volume. Although he participated in the defense of the city against the French and the British, Tolstoy offers an objective, factual account of what he saw that might have been the work of a supremely gifted "special correspondent." The candor with which he depicts the scene strips war of its glamour; yet his later pacifist bias is not evident here. If any of his convictions enters into the story it is that virtue is in the keeping of the simple: the hero of the drama for him is the common soldier. "The principal thought you have brought away with you," he says, after visiting the Fourth Bastion, one of the most dangerous spots in the besieged city (the words might have been written today), "is a joyous conviction of the strength of the Russian people." In "Three Deaths," too, the common people gain by contrast with their betters, and it is a tribute to the basic unity of Tolstoy's thinking that one of the last stories to come from his pen was "Alyosha," that apotheosis of the meek simpleton, the selfless, obedient peasant lad, who, however mistreated by God and man, never talks back.

An interest in the unsophisticated, as well as a religious orientation, form a link between Tolstoy and a remarkable if much less famous writer who belatedly became his disciple: Nikolay Leskov. His story "The Sentry" celebrates the courage and humility of the simple peasant in a fashion that Tolstoy would have approved, though with a light touch alien to that humorless genius. Leskov's drollery takes on a grotesque quality in the other example of his eccentric art presented below. *Chertogon* affords a glimpse of a little known corner of old Russian life, that of the comfortable, solid merchant class. While himself not the pillar of the existing order that the liberals imagined him to be, Leskov was a conservative in the sense that the world represented in his writings appears to have stability and permanence. In this respect at least his work differs from the main body of Russian fiction, which is instinct with portents of dis-integration and renewal.

### iii

It is customary to consider that the great period of Russian prose, lasting nearly half a century, came to an end in the eighties with the death of Dostoevsky and Turgenev and the conversion of Tolstoy. And indeed, the successor of these giants, Anton Chekhov, did not have so large a grasp as theirs. He was not ambitious to plunge so deep or to strain so high. While they were novelists who also culti-vated the shorter form, Chekhov, except for his excursions into drama, confined himself to the short story. Yet in that genre his mastery is unexcelled, as the varied selection from his work in this volume should indicate. One feels in reading him not the limitations of the medium, but its opportunities.

That the short story is a peculiarly modern form may be related, as Stephen Spender has pointed out, to our increased recognition of the fragmentary nature of experience. Certainly Chekhov did not try to see the world steadily and see it whole; but he looked into so many corners of it with so searching and sympathetic an eye that in the end he offered a remarkably full and sober and sensitive view of the Russian scene, chiefly through the human beings who people it and who, he makes plain to us, are much like human beings everywhere.

He began as a writer of humorous sketches, some of them the merest anecdotes; but in his mature work all that remains of the comic spirit is an occasional flash of fun and a vein of irony that crops out now and then. Avoiding alike the solemnity of Tolstoy and the nightmarish quality of Dostoevsky's imaginings, the tone of his later stories is generally serious and often somber. He writes about villagers and factory hands, and to a large degree about people be-longing to the several strata of the middle class. His preoccupation is with men and women whose lives are drab, empty, narrow, and help-less. They may dream of, even passionately long for, something that would bring color, depth, and meaning into their existence, but they lack the requisite strength of will, the capacity for sustained effort. The typical situation that he presents is one in which a man, a woman, or a child is trapped, imprisoned, facing a blind alley. They are perhaps the victims of circumstance, or, more often, of their own inadequacy, or of a combination of the two. In any case, the stories, with few exceptions, move toward no solution of the problem, no emergence from the impasse. Not for nothing was the better part of his work produced in a period of political reaction and cultural quietism, a period marked by failure of nerve. This started with the ebb of the revolutionary tide after the assassination of Alexander II, and lasted until the rise of a new wave of radical activity that culminated in the upheaval of 1905, which Chekhov did not live to see.

Watching the spectacle of futility and heartbreaking frustration, he is as much perplexed as saddened. There is no morbid reveling in gloom. He has been able to make the physician's knowledge and attitude count in his fictions, and indeed some of them have the dry objectivity of clinical studies. Yet he has an immense fund of sympathy. From this the inwardness of his portraiture in great part derives. Whether he is writing about a peasant wench, a disappointed schoolteacher, a tormented adolescent, a middle-class derelict, an unsatisfied bourgeoise, his characters are a permanent addition to our self-knowledge, and in some instances, such as the "darling" or the "man in a case," have become a byword. Each individual is firmly placed within his social context, as also against the physical background of his daily life. Chekhov is as sparing of landscape as he is of description generally, and one is reminded of Turgenev by the way in which he makes the natural scene support and enhance the mood of his story. Above all, his art, with its abhorrence of the mechanical, its revealment of the irregular, complex, unfinished nature of experience, gives the very quality of living: the immediacy of physical sensation, the paradoxes of feeling, the contradictions of behavior.

He was the least doctrinaire of men, but on at least one occasion he stated his credo, which bears a striking likeness to Turgenev's. The elder author had declared: "I am, above all, a realist, and chiefly interested in the living truth of the human face; to everything supernatural I am indifferent, and I don't believe in absolutes and systems; I love freedom better than anything." Chekhov, in a letter to a friend, after a similar rejection of "absolutes and systems," confessed: "My holy of holies is the human body; health; intelligence, talent, inspiration; love; and perfect freedom—freedom from force and falsehood no matter what shape they may take." The allegiance of both men was not to any party or program or church, but to those human values which could be served in accordance with the personal vision of what Chekhov fondly called "the free artist."

He was not politically minded; he remained aloof from the labor movement; the only reform in which he was interested was prison reform; he did not believe in the possibility of a revolution in Russia. Only occasionally his people dream of a distant time when reason, decency, and justice will come into their own. In one of his later stories he presents most sympathetically a man in a fit of impatience with gradualism, and elsewhere one of his characters declares that, if life is ruthless in its conservatism, we must be equally ruthless in our fight for freedom. But such passages stand out from the body of his work. What this gives is a picture of Russian society that helps to explain the course of the hurricane when it arrived: the slave mentality of the peasants, the gulf between them and the middle class, the futility of the intellectuals, the ignorance and black poverty in which the masses were sunk, and their incredible endurance.

Chekhov liked to insist that he did not take sides—that he remained, as a writer should, the impartial observer, the witness, in duty bound to testify honestly only to the little that he knew. But, for all his protestations, he was nevertheless a witness emotionally involved in the cases on which he was testifying. That he hated hypocrisy, meanness, slovenliness, stupidity, whatever balks or soils or stifles genial, rational living and decent human relations, his stories as well as his plays make sufficiently plain. His work is informed with the spirit of compassion. "There ought to be, behind the door of every happy, contented man, someone standing with a hammer, continually reminding him with a tap that there are unhappy people." Thus a character in one of his grimmest stories. In a sense, more truly than any of his predecessors, Chekhov was the man with the hammer.

## iv

When Chekhov died, the year before the upheaval of 1905, the era of which he had been the voice was coming to a close. Fresh currents were in the air, a new buoyant spirit was making itself felt. The literary scene, over which the venerable figure of Tolstoy still towered, was lively and varied. At the turn of the century a "mod-

ernist" trend had come to the fore and was now finding expression
chiefly in esoteric verse and sophisticated, fragile prose. At the same
time a number of talented writers were working the traditional vein
of socially minded realism. Prominent among them was Chekhov's
contemporary, Vladimir Korolenko, a man who in the midst of reaction and demoralization had kept his idealism awake and never abandoned his populist faith. His literary gift was not great, but such a
story as "Makar's Dream" illustrates his capacity for close observation, his incomparable warmth and humor, and shows too the reaching out for justice tempered with mercy that is at the heart of
Russian writing, from Gogol onward.

Korolenko's great prestige was based on his activities as a radical
publicist at least as much as on his literary work. As a whole this
reflected the uneasy temper of the times less clearly than did the
fictions of his younger confrere, Alexander Kuprin. "Gambrinus,"
with its glimpses of the revolution of 1905 and its tribute to the
unconquerable spirit of man, is a fair example of the work of this
full-blooded, masculine story-teller. It is, however, the performance
of Maxim Gorky that most truly represents the troubled quarter-
century preceding the fall of the empire.

Chekhov was a well established author when Gorky, a graduate
of the university of the streets, burst upon the literary scene. The
two men became friendly, but as writers they were poles apart.
Gorky's early stories dealt largely with the vagrants and unskilled
workers among whom he had grown up, and were written with a
rough frankness that carried defiance of the existing order. His
portrayal of the lower depths of society fed the will to revolt; and
the bright colors and rousing rhetoric of his pages were like a banner
and a bugle call to a generation preparing to give battle. The later
work of this stormy petrel of the revolution was impaired by a
strain of didacticism. In good time he became the dean of Soviet
letters and the acknowledged spokesman of the new regime. Nevertheless, while urging the young men to deal with Soviet life and the
promise it held out, he was in his own writings reminiscential: he
wrote about the past that he knew most intimately. His performance
is uneven, yet his autobiography, one or two of his plays, a handful
of short stories, may be ranked with the finest work of his contemporaries. The pieces by which he is represented here show a

searching tenderness, an ability, which seems specially to lie in the gift of his countrymen, to find in the most debased and battered creature a spark of humanity. They also exhibit the gusto for living, the simple courage, the invincible strength of the Russian people, to which these days so emphatically testify.

On one occasion Chekhov pointed out that great writers captivate us because at the heart of their work there is some generous purpose, some goal toward which they move, taking us with them, so that, even when they depict life as it is, as the best of them are apt to do, the picture carries an implicit dissatisfaction with the harsh actuality and a sense of life as it could be. Certainly the authors represented in this book looked at their world realistically, were critical of what they saw, and wrote out of their longing for a life they could barely imagine. The stories included here would be less fascinating and less stirring did they show the dream clearly. But if they have little to say about the shape of things as they ought to be, they quicken the imagination with a sense of the enterprise upon which mankind is stubbornly engaged.

# CONTENTS

*A Treasury of*

GREAT

RUSSIAN SHORT STORIES

# Alexander Pushkin . . . 1799–1837

RUSSIA'S major poet was descended on the maternal side from an African, possibly Ethiopian, princeling, and on his father's side from an ancient Russian family. He was educated at an aristocratic boarding school, where he earned a reputation for light verse, leaping into print at fifteen. He graduated three years later and settled in the capital with a nominal government appointment; but in 1820, as punishment for wielding a wicked and subversive pen, he was transferred to the South. During this disguised exile Pushkin fell in with some of the noblemen who were to participate in the Decembrist conspiracy, but he was occupied mainly with love-making and literature. It was at this period that he began his chief work, the novel in verse, "*Eugene Onegin*," at which he was to labor, on and off, for eight years. Having failed to mend his ways, the poet was ordered to his family estate in the province of Pskov, where he lived under police surveillance.

When, in 1826, he was permitted to return to Petersburg (Leningrad), he continued to suffer from an oppressive censorship, and the giddy life of the capital gave him little leisure for writing. He made the most of brief interludes spent on the family estate. It was there that he composed some of his finest lyrics, several plays, and, in 1830, *The Tales of Belkin*—a collection of prose pieces, which included "The Undertaker," printed below.

Pushkin was a man of thirty-two and debt-ridden when he married a young girl whose social ambitions spurred him to more intensive efforts. For her sake he secured a court appointment, which interfered further with his creative work; yet he went on writing feverishly and, despite all distractions, produced in the years following his marriage some of his finest verse and a good deal of prose, including "The Queen of Spades." A shot received in a duel with his wife's brother-in-law brought Pushkin's harassments and his epoch-making activities to an abrupt end.

# THE UNDERTAKER

Are coffins not beheld each day,
The gray hairs of an aging world?
—DERZHAVIN

THE last of the effects of the undertaker, Adrian Prohorov, were piled upon the hearse, and a couple of sorry-looking jades dragged themselves along for the fourth time from Basmannaya to Nikitskaya, whither the undertaker was removing with all his household. After locking up the shop, he posted upon the door a placard announcing that the house was for sale or rent, and then made his way on foot to his new abode. On approaching the little yellow house, which had so long captivated his imagination, and which at last he had bought for a considerable sum, the old undertaker was astonished to find that his heart did not rejoice. When he crossed the unfamiliar threshold and found his new home in the greatest confusion, he sighed for his old hovel, where for eighteen years the strictest order had prevailed. He began to scold his two daughters and the servants for their slowness, and then set to work to help them himself. Order was soon established; the icon-case, the cupboard with the crockery, the table, the sofa, and the bed occupied the corners reserved for them in the back room; in the kitchen and parlor were placed the master's wares —coffins of all colors and of all sizes, together with cupboards containing mourning hats, cloaks and torches.

Over the gate was placed a sign representing a plump Cupid with an inverted torch in his hand and bearing this inscription: "Plain and colored coffins sold and upholstered here; coffins also let out on hire, and old ones repaired."

The girls retired to their bedroom; Adrian made a tour of inspection of his quarters, and then sat down by the window and ordered the samovar to be prepared.

The enlightened reader knows that Shakespeare and Walter Scott

2

have both represented their gravediggers as merry and facetious individuals, in order that the contrast might more forcibly strike our imagination. Out of respect for the truth, we cannot follow their example, and we are compelled to confess that the disposition of our undertaker was in perfect harmony with his gloomy métier. Adrian Prohorov was usually sullen and pensive. He rarely opened his mouth, except to scold his daughters when he found them standing idle and gazing out of the window at the passers-by, or to ask for his wares an exorbitant price from those who had the misfortune—or sometimes the pleasure—of needing them. And so Adrian, sitting near the window and drinking his seventh cup of tea, was immersed as usual in melancholy reflections. He thought of the pouring rain which, just a week before, had commenced to beat down during the funeral of the retired brigadier. Many of the cloaks had shrunk in consequence of the downpour, and many of the hats had been put quite out of shape. He foresaw unavoidable expenses, for his old stock of funeral apparel was in a pitiable condition. He hoped to compensate himself for his losses by the burial of old Truhina, the merchant's wife, who for more than a year had been upon the point of death. But Truhina lay dying in Razgulyay, and Prohorov was afraid that her heirs, in spite of their promise, would not take the trouble to send so far for him, but would make arrangements with the nearest undertaker.

These reflections were suddenly interrupted by three masonic knocks at the door.

"Who is there?" asked the undertaker.

The door opened, and a man, who at first glance could be recognized as a German artisan, entered the room, and with a jovial air advanced toward the undertaker.

"Pardon me, good neighbor," said he in that Russian dialect which to this day we cannot hear without a smile; "pardon me for disturbing you. . . . I wished to make your acquaintance as soon as possible. I am a shoemaker, my name is Gottlieb Schultz, and I live across the street, in that little house just facing your windows. Tomorrow I am going to celebrate my silver wedding, and I have come to invite you and your daughters to dine with us."

The invitation was cordially accepted. The undertaker asked the shoemaker to seat himself and take a cup of tea, and thanks to the open-hearted disposition of Gottlieb Schultz, they were soon engaged in friendly conversation.

"How is business with you?" asked Adrian.

"So, so," replied Schultz; "I can't complain. But my wares are not like yours; the living can do without shoes, but the dead cannot do without coffins."

"Very true," observed Adrian; "but if a living person hasn't anything to buy shoes with, he goes barefoot, and holds his peace, if you please; but a dead beggar gets his coffin for nothing."

In this manner the conversation was carried on between them for some time; at last the shoemaker rose and took leave of the undertaker, renewing his invitation.

The next day, exactly at twelve o'clock, the undertaker and his daughters issued from the wicket-door of their newly purchased residence, and went to their neighbor's. I will not stop to describe the Russian caftan of Adrian Prohorov, nor the European toilettes of Akulina and Darya, deviating in this respect from the custom of modern novelists. But I do not think it superfluous to observe that the two girls had on the yellow hats and red shoes which they were accustomed to don on solemn occasions only.

The shoemaker's little dwelling was filled with guests, consisting chiefly of German artisans with their wives and apprentices. Of the Russian officials there was present but one, Yurko the Finn, a constable, who, in spite of his humble calling, was the special object of the host's attention. Like Pogorelsky's postman, for twenty-five years he had faithfully discharged his duties. The conflagration of 1812, which destroyed the ancient capital, destroyed also his little yellow booth. But immediately after the expulsion of the enemy, a new one appeared in its place, painted gray and with little white Doric columns, and Yurko again began to pace to and fro before it, *with his ax and armor of coarse cloth.* He was known to the greater part of the Germans who lived near the Nikitskaya Gate, and some of them had even spent Sunday night beneath his roof.

Adrian immediately made himself acquainted with him, as with a man whom, sooner or later, he might have need of, and when the guests took their places at the table, they sat down beside each other. Herr Schultz and his wife, and their daughter Lotchen, a young girl of seventeen, did the honors of the table and helped the cook to serve. The beer flowed in streams; Yurko ate like four, and Adrian in no way yielded to him; his daughters, however, stood upon their dignity. The conversation, which was carried on in German, gradually grew more and more noisy. Suddenly the host requested a moment's attention, and uncorking a sealed bottle, he said loudly in Russian:

"To the health of my good Louise!"

The imitation champagne foamed. The host tenderly kissed the fresh face of his partner, and the guests drank noisily to the health of the good Louise.

"To the health of my amiable guests!" exclaimed the host, uncorking a second bottle; and the guests thanked him by draining their glasses once more.

Then followed a succession of toasts. The health of each individual guest was drunk; they drank to Moscow and to a round dozen of little German towns; they drank to the health of all guilds in general and of each in particular; they drank to the health of the masters and apprentices. Adrian drank with assiduity and became so jovial, that he proposed a facetious toast himself. Suddenly one of the guests, a fat baker, raised his glass and exclaimed:

"To the health of those for whom we work, our customers!"

This proposal like all the others, was joyously and unanimously received. The guests began to salute each other; the tailor bowed to the shoemaker, the shoemaker to the tailor, the baker to both, the whole company to the baker, and so on.

In the midst of these mutual congratulations, Yurko exclaimed, turning to his neighbor:

"Come, little father! Drink to the health of your corpses!"

Everybody laughed, but the undertaker considered himself insulted, and frowned. Nobody noticed it, the guests continued to drink, and the bells had already rung for vespers when they rose from the table.

The guests dispersed at a late hour, the greater part of them in a very merry mood. The fat baker and the bookbinder, whose face seemed as if bound in red morocco, linked their arms in those of Yurko and conducted him back to his booth, thus observing the proverb: "One good turn deserves another."

The undertaker returned home drunk and angry.

"Why is it," he argued aloud, "why is it that my trade is not as honest as any other? Is an undertaker brother to the hangman? Why did those heathens laugh? Is an undertaker a buffoon? I wanted to invite them to my new house and give them a feast, but now I'll do nothing of the kind. Instead of inviting them, I will invite those for whom I work: the Orthodox dead."

"What is the matter, master?" said the servant, who was engaged at that moment in taking off his boots: "why do you talk such nonsense? Make the sign of the cross! Invite the dead to your new house! What nonsense!"

"Yes, by God! I will invite them," continued Adrian, "and that, too, for tomorrow! . . . Do me the favor, my benefactors, to come and feast with me tomorrow evening; I will regale you with what God has sent me."

With these words the undertaker turned into his bed and soon began to snore.

It was still dark when Adrian was roused out of his sleep. Truhina, the merchant's wife, had died during the course of that very night, and a special messenger was sent off on horseback by her clerk to carry the news to Adrian. The undertaker gave him ten copecks to buy brandy with, dressed himself as hastily as possible, took a droshky and set out for Razgulyay. At the gate of the house in which the deceased lay, the police had already taken their stand, and the tradespeople were busily moving back and forth, like ravens that smell a dead body. The deceased lay upon a table, yellow as wax, but not yet disfigured by decomposition. Around her stood her relatives, neighbors and domestic servants. All the windows were open; tapers were burning; and the priests were reading the prayers for the dead. Adrian went up to the nephew of Truhina, a young shopman in a fashionable jacket, and informed him that the coffin, wax candles, pall, and the other funeral accessories would be immediately delivered in good order. The heir thanked him in an absentminded manner, saying that he would not bargain about the price, but would rely upon his acting in everything according to his conscience. The undertaker, in accordance with his custom, swore that he would not charge him too much, exchanged significant glances with the clerk, and then departed to commence operations.

The whole day was spent in passing to and fro between Razgulyay and the Nikitskaya Gate. Toward evening everything was finished, and he returned home on foot, after having dismissed his driver. It was a moonlight night. The undertaker reached the Nikitskaya Gate in safety. Near the Church of the Ascension he was hailed by our acquaintance Yurko, who, recognizing the undertaker, wished him good night. It was late. The undertaker was just approaching his house, when suddenly he fancied he saw some one approach his gate, open the wicket, and disappear within.

"What does that mean?" thought Adrian. "Who can be wanting me again? Can it be a thief come to rob me? Or have my foolish girls got lovers coming after them? It means no good, I fear!"

And the undertaker thought of calling his friend Yurko to his assistance. But at that moment, another person approached the wicket and was about to enter, but seeing the master of the house hastening toward him, he stopped and took off his three-cornered hat. His face seemed familiar to Adrian, but in his hurry he was not able to examine it closely.

"You are favoring me with a visit," said Adrian, out of breath. "Walk in, I beg of you."

"Don't stand on ceremony, sir," replied the other, in a hollow voice; "you go first, and show your guests the way."

Adrian had no time to spend upon ceremony. The wicket was open; he ascended the steps followed by the other. Adrian thought he could hear people walking about in his rooms.

"What the devil does all this mean!" he thought to himself, and he hastened to enter. But the sight that met his eyes caused his legs to give way beneath him.

The room was full of corpses. The moon, shining through the windows, lit up their yellow and blue faces, sunken mouths, dim, half-closed eyes, and protruding noses. Adrian, with horror, recognized in them people that he himself had buried, and in the guest who had entered with him, the brigadier who had been buried during the pouring rain. They all, ladies and gentlemen, surrounded the undertaker, with bowings and salutations, except one poor man lately buried gratis, who, conscious and ashamed of his rags, did not venture to approach, but meekly kept to a corner. All the others were decently dressed: the female corpses in caps and ribbons, the officials in uniforms, but with their beards unshaven, the tradesmen in their holiday caftans.

"You see, Prohorov," said the brigadier in the name of all th[e] honorable company, "we have all risen in response to your invit[a]tion. Only those have stopped at home who were unable to co[me] who have crumbled to pieces and have nothing left but flesh[less] bones. But even of these there was one who hadn't the patien[ce] remain behind—so much did he want to come and see you. . . ."

At this moment a little skeleton pushed his way through the crowd and approached Adrian. His skull smiled affably at the undertaker. Shreds of green and red cloth and rotten linen hung on him here and there as on a pole, and the bones of his feet rattled inside his big jackboots, like pestles in mortars.

"You do not recognize me, Prohorov," said the skeleton. "Don't you remember the retired sergeant of the Guards, Pyotr Petrovich Kurilkin, the same to whom, in the year 1799, you sold your first coffin, and a deal one at that, instead of oak, as agreed?"

With these words the corpse stretched out his bony arms toward him; but Adrian, collecting all his strength, shrieked and pushed him away. Pyotr Petrovich staggered, fell and crumbled to pieces. Among the corpses arose a murmur of indignation; all stood up for the honor of their companion, and they overwhelmed Adrian with such threats and curses, that the poor host, deafened by their shrieks and almost crushed to death, lost his presence of mind, fell upon the bones of the retired sergeant of the Guards, and swooned away.

For some time the sun had been shining upon the bed on which the undertaker lay. At last he opened his eyes and saw before him the servant attending to the samovar. With horror, Adrian recalled all the incidents of the previous day. Truhina, the brigadier, and the sergeant Kurilkin, rose vaguely before his imagination. He waited in silence for the servant to open the conversation and inform him of the events of the night.

"How have you slept, Adrian Prohorovich!" said Aksinya, handing him his dressing-gown. "Your neighbor, the tailor, has been here, and the constable also called to inform you that today is his name-day; but you were so sound asleep, that we did not wish to wake ʾu."

"Did anyone come for me from the late Truhina?"

"ʾhe late? Is she dead, then?"

"ʾat a fool you are! Didn't you yourself help me yesterday to ʾe things for her funeral?"

"ʾou taken leave of your senses, master, or have you not ʾfrom the effects of yesterday's drinking-bout? What ʾe yesterday? You spent the whole day feasting at ʾthen came home drunk and threw yourself upon the bed, and have slept till this hour, when the bells have already rung for mass."

"Really!" said the undertaker, greatly relieved.

"Yes, indeed," replied the servant.

"Well, since that is the case, make tea as quickly as possible and call my daughters."

1830

# THE QUEEN OF SPADES

## I

When bleak was the weather,
The friends came together
To play.
The stakes, they were doubled;
The sly ones, untroubled,
Were gay.
They all had their innings,
And chalked up their winnings,
And so
They kept busy together
Throughout the bleak weather,
Oho!

THERE was a card party at the rooms of Narumov of the Horse Guards. The long winter night passed away imperceptibly, and it was five o'clock in the morning before the company sat down to supper. Those who had won, ate with a good appetite; the others sat staring absently at their empty plates. When the champagne appeared, however, the conversation became more animated, and all took a part in it.

"And how did you fare, Surin?" asked the host.

"Oh, I lost, as usual. I must confess that I am unlucky: I never raise the original stakes, I always keep cool, I never allow anything to put me out, and yet I always lose!"

"And you have never been tempted? You have never staked on several cards in succession? . . . Your firmness astonishes me."

"But what do you think of Hermann?" said one of the guests, pointing to a young engineer: "he has never had a card in his hand in his life, he has never in his life doubled the stake, and yet he sits here till five o'clock in the morning watching our play."

"Play interests me very much," said Hermann: "but I am not in the position to sacrifice the necessary in the hope of winning the superfluous."

"Hermann is a German: he is prudent—that is all!" observed Tomsky. "But if there is one person that I cannot understand, it is my grandmother, the Countess Anna Fedotovna."

"Why? How?" cried the guests.

"I cannot understand," continued Tomsky, "how it is that my grandmother does not punt."

"What is there remarkable about an old lady of eighty not gambling?" said Narumov.

"Then you know nothing about her?"

"No, really; haven't the faintest idea."

"Oh! then listen. You must know that, about sixty years ago, my grandmother went to Paris, where she created quite a sensation. People used to run after her to catch a glimpse of 'la Vénus muscovite.' Richelieu courted her, and my grandmother maintains that he almost blew out his brains in consequence of her cruelty. At that time ladies used to play faro. On one occasion at the Court, she lost a very considerable sum to the Duke of Orleans. On returning home, my grandmother removed the patches from her face, took off her hoops, informed my grandfather of her loss at the gaming-table, and ordered him to pay the money. My deceased grandfather, as far as I remember, was a sort of butler to my grandmother. He dreaded her like fire; but, on hearing of such a heavy loss, he almost went out of his mind; he calculated the various sums she had lost, and pointed out to her that in six months she had spent half a million, that neither their Moscow nor Saratov estates were near Paris, and finally refused point blank to pay the debt. My grandmother slapped his face and slept by herself as a sign of her displeasure. The next day she sent for her husband, hoping that this domestic punishment had produced an effect upon him, but she found him inflexible. For the first time in her life, she condescended to offer reasons and explanations. She thought she could convince him by pointing out to him that there are debts and debts, and that there is a great difference between a Prince and a coachmaker. But it was all in vain, grandfather was in revolt. He said 'no,' and that was all. My grandmother did not know what to do. She was on friendly terms with a very remarkable man. You have heard of Count St. Germain, about whom so many marvelous stories are told. You know that he represented himself as the Wandering Jew, as the discoverer of the elixir of life, of the philosopher's stone, and so forth. Some laughed at him as a charlatan; but Casanova, in his memoirs, says that he was a spy. But be that as it may, St. Germain, in spite of the mystery surrounding him, was a man of decent appearance and had an amiable manner in company. Even to this day my grandmother is in love with him, and becomes quite angry if anyone speaks disrespectfully of him. My grandmother knew that St. Germain had large sums of money at his disposal. She resolved to have recourse to him, and she wrote a letter to him asking him to come to her without delay. The queer old man immediately waited upon her and found her overwhelmed with grief. She described to him in the blackest colors the barbarity of her husband, and ended by declaring that she placed all her hopes in his friendship and graciousness.

"St. Germain reflected.

" 'I could advance you the sum you want,' said he; 'but I know that you would not rest easy until you had paid me back, and I should not like to bring fresh troubles upon you. But there is another way of getting out of your difficulty: you can win back your money.'

" 'But, my dear Count,' replied my grandmother, 'I tell you that we haven't any money left.'

" 'Money is not necessary,' replied St. Germain: 'be pleased to listen to me.'

"Then he revealed to her a secret, for which each of us would give a good deal . . ."

The young gamblers listened with increased attention. Tomsky lit his pipe, pulled at it, and continued:

"That same evening my grandmother went to Versailles *au jeu de la Reine*. The Duke of Orleans kept the bank; my grandmother excused herself in an offhanded manner for not having yet paid her debt, by inventing some little story, and then began to play against him. She chose three cards and played them one after the other: all three won at the start and my grandmother recovered all that she had lost."

"Mere chance!" said one of the guests.

"A fairy tale!" observed Hermann.

"Perhaps they were marked cards!" said a third.

"I do not think so," replied Tomsky gravely.

"What!" said Narumov, "you have a grandmother who knows how to hit upon three lucky cards in succession, and you have never yet succeeded in getting the secret of it out of her?"

"That's the deuce of it!" replied Tomsky: "she had four sons, one of whom was my father; all four are desperate gamblers, and yet not to one of them did she ever reveal her secret, although it would not have been a bad thing either for them or for me. But this is what I heard from my uncle, Count Ivan Ilyich, and he assured me, on his honor, that it was true. The late Chaplitsky—the same who died in poverty after having squandered millions—once lost, in his youth, about three hundred thousand roubles—to Zorich, if I remember rightly. He was in despair. My grandmother, who was always very hard on extravagant young men, took pity, however, upon Chaplitsky. She mentioned to him three cards, telling him to play them one after the other, at the same time exacting from him a solemn promise that he would never play cards again as long as he lived. Chaplitsky then went to his victorious opponent, and they began a fresh game. On the first card he staked fifty thousand roubles and won at once; he doubled the stake and won again, doubled it again, and won, not only all he had lost, but something over and above that . . .

"But it is time to go to bed: it is a quarter to six already."

And indeed it was already beginning to dawn: the young men emptied their glasses and then took leave of one another.

## II

—Il paraît que monsieur est décidément pour les suivantes.
-Que voulez-vous, madame? Elles sont plus fraîches.

*—Society Talk*

The old Countess X. was seated in her dressing-room in front of her looking-glass. Three maids stood around her. One held a small pot of rouge, another a box of hairpins, and the third a tall cap with bright red ribbons. The Countess had no longer the slightest pretensions to beauty—hers had faded long ago—but she still preserved all the habits of her youth, dressed in strict accordance with the fashion of the seventies, and made as long and as careful a toilette as she would have done sixty years previously. Near the window, at an embroidery frame, sat a young lady, her ward.

"Good morning, *grand'maman*," said a young officer, entering the room. "*Bonjour, Mademoiselle Lise. Grand'maman*, I have a favor to ask of you."

"What is it, Paul?"

"I want you to let me introduce one of my friends to you, and to allow me to bring him to the ball on Friday."

"Bring him direct to the ball and introduce him to me there. Were you at N.'s yesterday?"

"Yes; everything went off very pleasantly, and dancing kept up until five o'clock. How beautiful Mme. Yeletzkaya was!"

"But, my dear, what is there beautiful about her? You should have seen her grandmother, Princess Darya Petrovna! By the way, she must have aged very much, Princess Darya Petrovna."

"How do you mean, aged?" cried Tomsky thoughtlessly; "she died seven years ago."

The young lady raised her head and made a sign to the young man. He then remembered that the old Countess was never to be informed of the death of any of her contemporaries, and he bit his lip. But the Countess heard the news with the greatest indifference.

"Died!" said she; "and I did not know it. We were appointed maids of honor at the same time, and when we were being presented, the Empress. . . ."

And the Countess for the hundredth time related the anecdote to her grandson.

"Come, Paul," said she, when she had finished her story, "help me to get up. Lizanka, where is my snuff-box?"

And the Countess with her three maids went behind a screen to finish her toilette. Tomsky was left alone with the young lady.

"Who is the gentleman you wish to introduce to the Countess?" asked Lizaveta Ivanovna in a whisper.

"Narumov. Do you know him?"

"No. Is he in the army or is he a civilian?"

"In the army."

"Is he in the Engineers?"

"No, in the Cavalry. What made you think that he was in the Engineers?"

The young lady smiled, but made no reply.

"Paul," cried the Countess from behind the screen, "send me some new novel, only pray not the kind they write nowadays."

"What do you mean, *grand'maman?*"

"That is, a novel, in which the hero strangles neither his father nor his mother, and in which there are no drowned bodies. I have a great horror of them."

"There are no such novels nowadays. Would you like a Russian one?"

"Are there any Russian novels? Send me one, my dear, please send me one!"

"Good-bye, *grand'maman:* I am in a hurry. . . . Good-bye, Lizaveta Ivanovna. What, then, made you think that Narumov was in the Engineers?"

And Tomsky withdrew from the dressing-room.

Lizaveta Ivanovna was left alone: she laid aside her work and began to look out of the window. A few moments afterwards, from behind a corner house on the other side of the street, a young officer appeared. A deep blush covered her cheeks; she took up her work again and bent her head over the frame. At the same moment the Countess returned completely dressed.

"Order the carriage, Lizaveta," said she; "we will go out for a drive."

Lizaveta arose from the frame and began to put away her work.

"What is the matter with you, my dear, are you deaf?" cried the Countess. "Order the carriage to be got ready at once."

"I will do so this moment," replied the young lady, and ran into the anteroom.

A servant entered and gave the Countess some books from Prince Pavel Alexandrovich.

"Tell him that I am much obliged to him," said the Countess. "Lizaveta! Lizaveta! where are you running to?"

"I am going to dress."

"There is plenty of time, my dear. Sit down here. Open the first volume and read aloud to me."

Her companion took the book and read a few lines.

"Louder," said the Countess. "What is the matter with you, my dear? Have you lost your voice? Wait—give me that footstool—a little nearer—that will do!"

Lizaveta read two more pages. The Countess yawned.

"Put the book down," said she: "what a lot of nonsense. Send it back to Prince Pavel with my thanks. . . . But where is the carriage?"

"The carriage is ready," said Lizaveta, looking out into the street.

"How is it that you are not dressed?" said the Countess: "I must always wait for you. It is intolerable, my dear!"

Liza hastened to her room. She had not been there two minutes, before the Countess began to ring with all her might. The three maids came running in at one door and the valet at another.

"How is it that you don't come when I ring for you?" said the Countess. "Tell Lizaveta Ivanovna that I am waiting for her."

Lizaveta returned with her hat and cloak on.

"At last you are here!" said the Countess. "But why such an elaborate toilette? Whom do you intend to captivate? What sort of weather is it? It seems rather windy."

"No, Your Ladyship, it is very calm," replied the valet.

"You always speak thoughtlessly. Open the window. So it is: windy and bitterly cold. Unharness the horses. Lizaveta, we won't go out—there was no need for you to deck yourself out like that."

"And that's my life!" thought Lizaveta Ivanovna.

And, in truth, Lizaveta Ivanovna was a very unfortunate creature. "It is bitter to eat the bread of another," says Dante, "and hard to climb his stair." But who can know what the bitterness of dependence is so well as the poor companion of an old lady of quality? The Countess X. had by no means a bad heart, but she was capricious, like a woman who had been spoilt by the world, as well as avaricious and sunk in cold egoism, like all old people who are no longer capable of affection, and whose thoughts are with the past and not the present. She participated in all the vanities of the great world, went to balls, where she sat in a corner, painted and dressed in old-fashioned style, like an ugly but indispensable ornament of the ballroom; the guests on entering approached her and bowed profoundly, as if in accordance with a set ceremony, but after that nobody took any further notice of her. She received the whole town at her house, and observed the strictest etiquette, although she could no longer recognize people. Her numerous domestics, growing fat and old in her antechamber and servants' hall, did just as they liked, and vied with each other in robbing the moribund old woman. Lizaveta Ivanovna

was the martyr of the household. She poured tea, and was reprimanded for using too much sugar; she read novels aloud to the Countess, and the faults of the author were visited upon her head; she
accompanied the Countess in her walks, and was held answerable for
the weather or the state of the pavement. A salary was attached to
the post, but she very rarely received it, although she was expected
to dress like everybody else, that is to say, like very few indeed. In
society she played the most pitiable rôle. Everybody knew her, and
nobody paid her any attention. At balls she danced only when a
partner was wanted, and ladies would only take hold of her arm
when it was necessary to lead her out of the room to attend to their
dresses. She had a great deal of *amour propre,* and felt her position
keenly, and she looked about her with impatience for a deliverer to
come to her rescue; but the young men, calculating in their giddiness,
did not condescend to pay her any attention, although Lizaveta
Ivanovna was a hundred times prettier than the barefaced and cold-
hearted marriageable girls around whom they hovered. Many a time
did she quietly slink away from the dull and elegant drawing-room,
to go and cry in her own poor little room, in which stood a screen, a
chest of drawers, a looking-glass and a painted bedstead, and where
a tallow candle burnt feebly in a copper candlestick.

One morning—this was about two days after the card party described at the beginning of this story, and a week previous to the
scene at which we have just assisted—Lizaveta Ivanovna was seated
near the window at her embroidery frame, when, happening to look
out into the street, she caught sight of a young officer of the Engineers, standing motionless with his eyes fixed upon her window. She
lowered her head and went on again with her work. About five minutes afterward she looked out again—the young officer was still
standing in the same place. Not being in the habit of coquetting with
passing officers, she did not continue to gaze out into the street, but
went on sewing for a couple of hours, without raising her head.
Dinner was announced. She rose up and began to put her embroidery
away, but glancing casually out of the window, she perceived the
officer again. This seemed to her very strange. After dinner she went
to the window with a certain feeling of uneasiness, but the officer
was no longer there—and she thought no more about him.

A couple of days afterwards, just as she was stepping into the
carriage with the Countess, she saw him again. He was standing close

to the entrance, with his face half concealed by his beaver collar, his black eyes flashing beneath his hat. Lizaveta felt alarmed, though she knew not why, and she trembled as she seated herself in the carriage.

On returning home, she hastened to the window—the officer was standing in his accustomed place, with his eyes fixed upon her. She drew back, a prey to curiosity and agitated by a feeling which was quite new to her.

From that time on not a day passed without the young officer making his appearance under the window at the customary hour. A spontaneous relationship was established between them. Sitting in her place at work, she would feel his approach; and raising her head, she would look at him longer and longer each day. The young man seemed to be very grateful to her for it: she saw with the sharp eye of youth, how a sudden flush covered his pale cheeks each time that their glances met. By the end of the week she smiled at him. . . .

When Tomsky asked permission of his grandmother the Countess to present one of his friends to her, the young girl's heart beat violently. But hearing that Narumov was not an engineer, but in the Horse Guards, she regretted that by her indiscreet question, she had betrayed her secret to the volatile Tomsky.

Hermann was the son of a Russified German, from whom he had inherited a small fortune. Being firmly convinced of the necessity of ensuring his independence, Hermann did not touch even the interest on his capital, but lived on his pay, without allowing himself the slightest luxury. Moreover, he was reserved and ambitious, and his companions rarely had an opportunity of making merry at the expense of his excessive parsimony. He had strong passions and an ardent imagination, but his firmness of disposition preserved him from the ordinary errors of youth. Thus, though a gambler at heart, he never touched a card, for he considered his position did not allow him—as he said—"to risk the necessary in the hope of winning the superfluous," yet he would sit for nights together at the card table and follow with feverish excitement the various turns of the game.

The story of the three cards had produced a powerful impression upon his imagination, and all night long he could think of nothing else. "If only," he thought to himself the following evening, as he wandered through St. Petersburg, "if only the old Countess would reveal her secret to me! if she would only tell me the names of the three winning cards! Why should I not try my fortune? I must get

introduced to her and win her favor—perhaps become her lover. . . .
But all that will take time, and she is eighty-seven years old: she
might be dead in a week, in a couple of days even! . . . And the
story itself: is it credible? . . . No! Prudence, moderation and work:
those are my three winning cards; that is what will increase my
capital threefold, sevenfold, and procure for me ease and independence."

Musing in this manner, he walked on until he found himself in
one of the principal streets of St. Petersburg, in front of a house of
old-fashioned architecture. The street was blocked with carriages;
one after the other they rolled up in front of the illuminated entrance.
Every minute there emerged from the coaches the shapely foot of a
young beauty, a spurred boot, a striped stocking above a diplomatic
shoe. Fur coats and cloaks whisked past the majestic porter.

Hermann stopped. "Whose house is this?" he asked the watchman
at the corner.

"The Countess X.'s," replied the watchman.

Hermann trembled. The strange story of the three cards again
presented itself to his imagination. He began walking up and down
before the house, thinking of its owner and her marvelous gift.
Returning late to his modest lodging, he could not go to sleep for a
long time, and when at last he did doze off, he could dream of nothing but cards, green tables, piles of bank-notes and heaps of gold
coins. He played card after card, firmly turning down the corners,
and won uninterruptedly, raking in the gold and filling his pockets
with the notes. Waking up late the next morning, he sighed over the
loss of his imaginary wealth, then went out again to wander about the
streets, and found himself once more in front of the Countess's house.
Some unknown power seemed to draw him thither. He stopped and
began to stare at the windows. In one of these he saw the head of a
black-haired woman, which was bent probably over some book or
handwork. The head was raised. Hermann saw a fresh-cheeked face
and a pair of black eyes. That moment decided his fate.

## III

Vous m'écrivez, mon ange, des lettres de quatre pages plus vite que je ne puis les lire.

—A Correspondence

Lizaveta Ivanovna had scarcely taken off her hat and cloak, when the Countess sent for her and again ordered the carriage. The vehicle drew up before the door, and they prepared to take their seats. Just at the moment when two footmen were assisting the old lady into the carriage, Lizaveta saw her engineer close beside the wheel; he grasped her hand; alarm caused her to lose her presence of mind, and the young man disappeared—but not before leaving a letter in her hand. She concealed it in her glove, and during the whole of the drive she neither saw nor heard anything. It was the custom of the Countess, when out for an airing in her carriage to be constantly asking such questions as: "Who was that person that met us just now? What is the name of this bridge? What is written on that signboard?" On this occasion, however, Lizaveta returned such vague and absurd answers, that the Countess became angry with her.

"What is the matter with you, my dear?" she exclaimed. "Have you taken leave of your senses, or what is it? Do you not hear me or understand what I say? . . . Heaven be thanked, I am still in my right mind and speak plainly enough!"

Lizaveta Ivanovna did not hear her. On returning home she ran to her room, and drew the letter out of her glove: it was not sealed. Lizaveta read it. The letter contained a declaration of love; it was tender, respectful, and copied word for word from a German novel. But Lizaveta did not know anything of the German language, and she was quite delighted with the letter.

For all that, it troubled her exceedingly. For the first time in her life she was entering into secret and intimate relations with a young man. His boldness horrified her. She reproached herself for her imprudent behavior, and knew not what to do. Should she cease to sit at the window and, by assuming an appearance of indifference toward him, put a check upon the young officer's desire to pursue her further? Should she send his letter back to him, or should she answer him in a cold and resolute manner? There was nobody to whom she could turn in her perplexity, for she had neither female friend nor adviser. . . . At length she resolved to reply to him.

She sat down at her little writing-table, took pen and paper, and began to think. Several times she began her letter, and then tore it up: the way she had expressed herself seemed to her either too indulgent or too severe. At last she succeeded in writing a few lines with which she felt satisfied.

"I am convinced," she wrote, "that your intentions are honorable, and that you do not wish to offend me by any imprudent action, but our acquaintance should not have begun in such a manner. I return you your letter, and I hope that I shall never have any cause to complain of undeserved disrespect."

The next day, as soon as Hermann made his appearance, Lizaveta rose from her embroidery, went into the drawing-room, opened the wicket and threw the letter into the street, trusting to the young officer's alertness.

Hermann hastened forward, picked it up and then repaired to a confectioner's shop. Breaking the seal of the envelope, he found inside it his own letter and Lizaveta's reply. He had expected this, and he returned home, very much taken up with his intrigue.

Three days afterward, a bright-eyed young girl from a milliner's establishment brought Lizaveta a letter. Lizaveta opened it with great uneasiness, fearing that it was a demand for money, when suddenly she recognized Hermann's handwriting.

"You have made a mistake, my dear," said she: "this letter is not for me."

"Oh, yes, it is for you," replied the pert girl, without concealing a sly smile. "Have the goodness to read it."

Lizaveta glanced at the letter. Hermann requested an interview.

"It cannot be," said Lizaveta Ivanovna, alarmed both at the haste with which he had made his request, and the manner in which it had been transmitted. "This letter is certainly not for me."

And she tore it into fragments.

"If the letter was not for you, why have you torn it up?" said the girl. "I should have given it back to the person who sent it."

"Be good enough, my dear," said Lizaveta, disconcerted by this remark, "not to bring me any more letters in future, and tell the person who sent you that he ought to be ashamed. . . ."

But Hermann was not the man to be thus put off. Every day

Lizaveta received from him a letter, sent now in this way, now in that. They were no longer translated from the German. Hermann wrote them under the inspiration of passion, and spoke in his own language, and they bore full testimony to the inflexibility of his desire and the disordered condition of his uncontrollable imagination. Lizaveta no longer thought of sending them back to him: she became intoxicated with them and began to reply to them, and little by little her answers became longer and more affectionate. At last she threw out of the window to him the following letter:

"This evening there is going to be a ball at the X. Embassy. The Countess will be there. We shall remain until two o'clock. This is your opportunity of seeing me alone. As soon as the Countess is gone, the servants will very probably go out, and there will be nobody left but the porter, but he, too, usually retires to his lodge. Come at half-past eleven. Walk straight upstairs. If you meet anybody in the ante-room, ask if the Countess is at home. If you are told she is not, there will be nothing left for you to do but to go away and return another time. But it is most probable that you will meet nobody. The maid-servants all sit together in one room. On leaving the ante-room, turn to the left, and walk straight on until you reach the Countess's bed-room. In the bedroom, behind a screen, you will find two small doors: the one on the right leads to a study, which the Countess never enters; the one on the left leads to a corridor, at the end of which is a narrow winding staircase; this leads to my room."

Hermann quivered like a tiger, as he waited for the appointed time. At ten o'clock in the evening he was already in front of the Countess's house. The weather was terrible; the wind was howling; the sleety snow fell in large flakes; the lamps emitted a feeble light, the streets were deserted; from time to time a sledge, drawn by a sorry-looking hack, passed by, the driver on the look-out for a belated fare. Hermann stood there wearing nothing but his jacket, yet he felt neither the wind nor the snow.

At last the Countess's carriage drew up. Hermann saw two foot-men carry out in their arms the bent form of the old lady, wrapped in sables, and immediately behind her, clad in a light mantle, and with a wreath of fresh flowers on her head, followed Lizaveta. The door was closed. The carriage rolled away heavily through the yielding snow. The porter shut the street-door; the windows became dark.

Hermann began walking up and down near the deserted house;

at length he stopped under a lamp, and glanced at his watch: it was twenty minutes past eleven. He remained standing under the lamp, his eyes fixed upon the watch, impatiently waiting for the remaining minutes to pass. At half-past eleven precisely, Hermann ascended the steps of the house, and made his way into the brightly-illuminated vestibule. The porter was not there. Hermann ran up the stairs, opened the door of the anteroom and saw a footman sitting asleep in an antique soiled armchair, under the lamp. With a light firm step Hermann walked past him. The reception-room and the drawing-room were in semidarkness. They were lit feebly by a lamp in the anteroom.

Hermann entered the bedroom. Before an icon-case, filled with ancient icons, a golden sanctuary-lamp was burning. Armchairs up-holstered in faded brocade, and sofas, the gilding of which was worn off and which were piled with down cushions stood in melancholy symmetry around the room, the walls of which were hung with China silk. On the wall hung two portraits painted in Paris by Madame Lebrun. One of them represented a plump, pink-cheeked man of about forty in a light-green uniform and with a star on his breast; the other—a beautiful young woman, with an aquiline nose, curls at her temples, and a rose in her powdered hair. In all the corners stood porcelain shepherds and shepherdesses, clocks from the workshop of the celebrated Leroy, boxes, roulettes, fans and the various gewgaws for ladies that were invented at the end of the last century, together with Montgolfier's balloon and Mesmer's mag-netism. Hermann stepped behind the screen. Behind it stood a little iron bed; on the right was the door which led to the study; on the left—the other which led to the corridor. He opened the latter, and saw the little winding staircase which led to the room of the poor ward. . . . But he retraced his steps and entered the dark study.

The time passed slowly. All was still. The clock in the drawing-room struck twelve; in all the rooms, one clock after another marked the hour, and everything was quiet again. Hermann stood leaning against the cold stove. He was calm; his heart beat regularly, like that of a man resolved upon a dangerous but inevitable undertaking. The clock struck one, then two; and he heard the distant rumbling of carriage-wheels. In spite of himself, excitement seized him. The car-riage drew near and stopped. He heard the sound of the carriage-step being let down. All was bustle within the house. The servants were running hither and thither, voices were heard, and the house was lit up. Three antiquated chambermaids entered the bedroom, and they were shortly afterwards followed by the Countess who, more dead than alive, sank into an armchair. Hermann peeped through a chink. Lizaveta Ivanovna passed close by him, and he heard her hurried steps as she hastened up her staircase. For a moment his heart was assailed by something like remorse, but the emotion was only transitory. He stood petrified.

The Countess began to undress before her looking-glass. Her cap, decorated with roses, was unpinned, and then her powdered wig was removed from off her white and closely-cropped head. Hairpins fell in showers around her. Her yellow satin dress, embroidered with silver, fell down at her swollen feet.

Hermann witnessed the repulsive mysteries of her toilette; at last the Countess was in her nightcap and nightgown, and in this costume, more suitable to her age, she appeared less hideous and terrifying.

Like all old people in general, the Countess suffered from sleeplessness. Having undressed, she seated herself at the window in an armchair and dismissed her maids. The candles were taken away, and once more the room was lit only by the sanctuary-lamp. The Countess sat there looking quite yellow, moving her flaccid lips and swaying from side to side. Her dull eyes expressed complete vacancy of mind, and, looking at her, one would have thought that the rocking of her body was not voluntary, but was produced by the action of some concealed galvanic mechanism.

Suddenly the deathlike face changed incredibly. The lips ceased to move, the eyes became animated: before the Countess stood a stranger.

"Do not be alarmed, for Heaven's sake, do not be alarmed!" said he in a low but distinct voice. "I have no intention of doing you any harm, I have only come to ask a favor of you."

The old woman looked at him in silence, as if she had not heard what he had said. Hermann thought that she was deaf, and, bending down toward her ear, he repeated what he had said. The old woman remained silent as before.

"You can ensure the happiness of my life," continued Hermann, "and it will cost you nothing. I know that you can name three cards in succession——"

Hermann stopped. The Countess appeared now to understand what was asked of her; she seemed to be seeking words with which to reply.

"It was a joke," she replied at last: "I swear it was only a joke."

"This is no joking matter," replied Hermann angrily. "Remember Chaplitsky, whom you helped to win back what he had lost."

The Countess became visibly uneasy. Her features expressed strong emotion, but she soon lapsed into her former insensibility.

"Can you not name me these three winning cards?" continued Hermann.

The Countess remained silent; Hermann continued:

"For whom are you preserving your secret? For your grandsons? They are rich enough without it; they do not know the worth of money. Your cards would be of no use to a spendthrift. He who cannot preserve his paternal inheritance, will die in want, even though he had a demon at his service. I am not a man of that sort; I know the value of money. Your three cards will not be wasted on me. Come!" . . .

He paused and tremblingly awaited her reply. The Countess remained silent; Hermann fell upon his knees.

"If your heart has ever known the feeling of love," said he, "if you remember its rapture, if you have ever smiled at the cry of your newborn child, if your breast has ever throbbed with any human feeling, I entreat you by the feelings of a wife, a lover, a mother, by all that is most sacred in life, not to reject my plea. Reveal to me your secret. Of what use is it to you? . . . Maybe it is connected with some terrible sin, the loss of eternal bliss, some bargain with the devil. . . . Consider—you are old; you have not long to live—I am ready to take your sins upon my soul. Only reveal to me your secret. Remember that the happiness of a man is in your hands, that not only I, but my children, grandchildren, and great-grandchildren, will bless your memory and reverence it as something sacred. . . ."

The old woman answered not a word.

Hermann rose to his feet.

"You old witch!" he exclaimed, clenching his teeth, "then I will make you answer!"

With these words he drew a pistol from his pocket.

At the sight of the pistol, the Countess for the second time exhibited strong emotion. She shook her head and raised her hands as if to protect herself from the shot . . . then she fell backward and remained motionless.

"Come, an end to this childish nonsense!" said Hermann, taking hold of her hand. "I ask you for the last time: will you tell me the names of your three cards, or will you not?"

The Countess made no reply. Hermann perceived that she was dead!

## IV

7 mai, 18—<br>
Homme sans mœurs et sans religion!<br>
—A Correspondence

Lizaveta Ivanovna was sitting in her room, still in her ball dress, lost in deep thought. On returning home, she had hastily dismissed the sleepy maid who reluctantly came forward to assist her, saying that she would undress herself, and with a trembling heart had gone up to her own room, hoping to find Hermann there, but yet desiring not to find him. At the first glance she convinced herself that he was not there, and she thanked her fate for the obstacle which had prevented their meeting. She sat down without undressing, and began to recall to mind all the circumstances which in so short a time had carried her so far. It was not three weeks since the time when she had first seen the young man from the window—and she already was in correspondence with him, and he had succeeded in inducing her to grant him a nocturnal tryst! She knew his name only through his having written it at the bottom of some of his letters; she had never spoken to him, had never heard his voice, and had never heard anything of him until that evening. But, strange to say, that very evening at the ball, Tomsky, being piqued with the young Princess Pauline N., who, contrary to her usual custom, did not flirt with him, wished to revenge himself by assuming an air of indifference: he therefore engaged Lizaveta Ivanovna and danced an endless mazurka with her. All the time he kept teasing her about her partiality for officers in the Engineers; he assured her that he knew far more than she could have supposed, and some of his jests were so happily aimed, that Lizaveta thought several times that her secret was known to him.

"From whom have you learnt all this?" she asked, smiling.

"From a friend of a person very well known to you," replied Tomsky, "from a very remarkable man."

"And who is this remarkable man?"

"His name is Hermann."

Lizaveta made no reply; but her hands and feet turned to ice.

"This Hermann," continued Tomsky, "is a truly romantic character. He has the profile of a Napoleon, and the soul of a Mephistopheles. I believe that he has at least three crimes upon his conscience. . . . How pale you are!"

"I have a headache. . . . But what did this Hermann—or whatever his name is—tell you?"

"Hermann is very much dissatisfied with his friend: he says that in his place he would act very differently. . . . I even think that Hermann himself has designs upon you; at least, he listens not indifferently to his friend's enamored exclamations."

"But where has he seen me?"

"In church, perhaps; or promenading—God alone knows where. It may have been in your room, while you were asleep, for he is capable of it."

Three ladies approaching him with the question, *"oubli ou regret?"* interrupted the conversation, which had become so tantalizingly interesting to Lizaveta.

The lady chosen by Tomsky was the Princess Pauline herself. She succeeded in effecting a reconciliation with him by making an extra turn in the dance and managing to delay resuming her seat. On returning to his place, Tomsky thought no more either of Hermann or Lizaveta. She longed to renew the interrupted conversation, but the mazurka came to an end, and shortly afterward the old Countess took her departure.

Tomsky's words were nothing more than the small talk of the mazurka, but they sank deep into the soul of the young dreamer. The portrait, sketched by Tomsky, agreed with the picture she had formed in her own mind, and that image, rendered commonplace by current novels, terrified and fascinated her imagination. She was now sitting with her bare arms crossed and her head, still adorned with flowers, was bowed over her half-uncovered breast. Suddenly the door opened and Hermann entered. She shuddered.

"Where have you been?" she asked in a frightened whisper.

"In the old Countess's bedroom," replied Hermann: "I have just left her. The Countess is dead."

"My God! What are you saying?"

"And I am afraid," added Hermann, "that I am the cause of her death."

Lizaveta looked at him, and Tomsky's words found an echo in her soul: "This man has at least three crimes upon his conscience!" Hermann sat down by the window near her, and related all that had happened.

Lizaveta listened to him in terror. So all those passionate letters, those ardent demands, this bold obstinate pursuit—all this was not love! Money—that was what his soul yearned for! She could not satisfy his desire and make him happy! The poor girl had been nothing but the blind accomplice of a robber, of the murderer of her aged benefactress! . . . She wept bitter tears of belated, agonized repentance. Hermann gazed at her in silence: his heart, too, was tormented, but neither the tears of the poor girl, nor the wonderful charm of her beauty, enhanced by her grief, could produce any impression upon his hardened soul. He felt no pricking of conscience at the thought of the dead old woman. One thing only horrified him: the irreparable loss of the secret which he had expected would bring him wealth.

"You are a monster!" said Lizaveta at last.

"I did not wish her death," replied Hermann—"my pistol is not loaded."

Both grew silent.

The day began to dawn. Lizaveta extinguished her candle: a pale light illumined her room. She wiped her tear-stained eyes and raised them toward Hermann: he was sitting on the window-sill, with his arms folded and frowning fiercely. In this attitude he bore a striking resemblance to the portrait of Napoleon. This resemblance struck even Lizaveta Ivanovna.

"How shall I get you out of the house?" said she at last. "I thought of conducting you down the secret staircase, but in that case it would be necessary to go through the Countess's bedroom, and I am afraid."

"Tell me how to find this secret staircase—I will go alone."

Lizaveta arose, took from her drawer a key, handed it to Hermann and gave him the necessary instructions. Hermann pressed her cold, unresponsive hand, kissed her bowed head, and left the room.

He descended the winding staircase, and once more entered the Countess's bedroom. The dead old woman sat as if petrified; her face expressed profound tranquillity. Hermann stopped before her, and gazed long and earnestly at her, as if he wished to convince himself of the terrible reality; at last he entered the study, felt behind the tapestry for the door, and then began to descend the dark staircase, agitated by strange emotions. "At this very hour," thought he, "some sixty years ago, a young gallant who has long been moldering in his grave, may have stolen down this very staircase, perhaps coming from the very same bedroom, wearing an embroidered caftan, with his hair dressed à *l'oiseau royal* and pressing to his heart his three-cornered hat, and the heart of his aged mistress has only today ceased to beat. . . ."

At the bottom of the staircase Hermann found a door, which he opened with the same key, and found himself in a corridor which led him into the street.

## V

That night the deceased Baroness von W. appeared to me. She was clad all in white and said to me: "How are you, Mr. Councilor?" —SWEDENBORG

Three days after the fatal night, at nine o'clock in the morning, Hermann repaired to the Convent of ——, where the burial-service for the deceased Countess was to be held. Although feeling no remorse, he could not altogether stifle the voice of conscience, which kept repeating to him: "You are the murderer of the old woman!" While he had little true faith, he was very superstitious; and believing that the dead Countess might exercise an evil influence on his life, he resolved to be present at her funeral in order to ask her pardon.

The church was full. It was with difficulty that Hermann made his way through the crowd. The coffin stood on a sumptuous catafalque under a velvet baldachin. The deceased lay within it, her hands crossed upon her breast, and wearing a lace cap and a white satin gown. Around the catafalque stood the members of her household: the servants in black caftans, with armorial ribbons upon their shoulders, and candles in their hands; the relatives—children, grandchildren, and great-grandchildren—in deep mourning.

Nobody wept; tears would have been *une affectation*. The Countess was so old, that her death could have surprised nobody, and her relatives had long looked upon her as not among the living. A famous preacher delivered the funeral oration. In simple and touching words he described the peaceful passing away of the saintly woman whose long life had been a serene, moving preparation for a Christian end. "The angel of death found her," said the preacher, "engaged in pious meditation and waiting for the midnight bridegroom."

The service concluded in an atmosphere of melancholy decorum. The relatives went forward first to bid farewell to the deceased. Then followed the numerous acquaintances, who had come to render the last homage to her who for so many years had participated in their frivolous amusements. After these followed the members of the Countess's household. The last of these was the old housekeeper who was of the same age as the deceased. Two young women led her forward, supporting her by the arms. She had not strength enough to bow down to the ground—she was the only one to shed a few tears and kiss the cold hand of her mistress.

Hermann now resolved to approach the coffin. He bowed down to the ground and for several minutes lay on the cold floor, which was strewn with fir boughs; at last he arose, as pale as the deceased Countess herself, ascended the steps of the catafalque and bent over the corpse. . . . At that moment it seemed to him that the dead woman darted a mocking look at him and winked with one eye. Hermann started back, took a false step and fell to the ground. He was lifted up. At the same moment Lizaveta Ivanovna was carried into the vestibule of the church in a faint. This episode disturbed for some minutes the solemnity of the gloomy ceremony. Among the congregation arose a muffled murmur, and the lean chamberlain, a near relative of the deceased, whispered in the ear of an Englishman who was standing near him, that the young officer was a natural son of the Countess, to which the Englishman coldly replied: "Oh!"

During the whole of that day, Hermann was exceedingly perturbed. Dining in an out-of-the-way restaurant, he drank a great deal of wine, contrary to his usual custom, in the hope of allaying his inward agitation. But the wine only served to excite his imagination still more. On returning home, he threw himself upon his bed without undressing, and fell into a deep sleep.

When he woke up it was already night, and the moon was shining into the room. He looked at his watch: it was a quarter to three. Sleep had left him; he sat down upon his bed and thought of the funeral of the old Countess.

At that moment somebody in the street looked in at his window, and immediately passed on again. Hermann paid no attention to this incident. A few moments afterward he heard the door of the ante-room open. Hermann thought that it was his orderly, drunk as usual, returning from some nocturnal expedition, but presently he heard footsteps that were unknown to him: somebody was shuffling softly across the floor in slippers. The door opened, and a woman dressed in white, entered the room. Hermann mistook her for his old nurse, and wondered what could bring her there at that hour of the night. But the white woman glided rapidly across the room and stood before him—and Hermann recognized the Countess!

"I have come to you against my will," she said in a firm voice: "but I have been ordered to grant your request. Three, seven, ace, will win for you if played in succession, but only on these conditions: that you do not play more than one card in twenty-four hours, and that you never play again during the rest of your life. I forgive you my death, on condition that you marry my ward, Lizaveta Ivanovna."

With these words she turned round very quietly, walked with a shuffling gait toward the door and disappeared. Hermann heard the street-door bang, and he saw someone look in at him through the window again.

For a long time Hermann could not recover himself. Then he went into the next room. His orderly was asleep upon the floor, and he had much difficulty in waking him. The orderly was drunk as usual, and nothing could be got out of him. The street-door was locked. Hermann returned to his room, lit his candle, and set down an account of his vision.

## VI

> "Attendez!"
> "How dare you say attendez to me?"
> "Your Excellency, I said: 'Attendez, sir.'"

Two fixed ideas can no more exist together in the moral world than two bodies can occupy one and the same place in the physical world. "Three, seven, ace" soon drove out of Hermann's mind the thought of the dead Countess. "Three, seven, ace" were perpetually running through his head and continually on his lips. If he saw a young girl, he would say: "How slender she is! Quite like the three of hearts." If anybody asked, "What is the time?" he would reply, "Five minutes to seven." Every stout man that he saw reminded him of the ace. "Three, seven, ace" haunted him in his sleep, and assumed all possible shapes. The three bloomed before him in the form of a magnificent flower, the seven was represented by a Gothic portal, and the ace became transformed into a gigantic spider. One thought alone occupied his whole mind—to make use of the secret which he had purchased so dearly. He thought of applying for a furlough so as to travel abroad. He wanted to go to Paris and force fortune to yield a treasure to him in the public gambling houses there. Chance spared him all this trouble.

There was in Moscow a society of wealthy gamblers, presided over by the celebrated Chekalinsky, who had passed all his life at the card-table and had amassed millions, accepting bills of exchange for his winnings and paying his losses in ready money. His long experience secured for him the confidence of his companions, and his open house, his famous cook, and his agreeable and cheerful manner gained for him the respect of the public. He came to St. Petersburg. The young men of the capital flocked to his rooms, forgetting balls for cards, and preferring the temptations of faro to the seductions of flirting. Narumov conducted Hermann to Chekalinsky's residence.

They passed through a suite of magnificent rooms, filled with courteous attendants. Several generals and privy counselors were playing whist; young men were lolling carelessly upon the velvet-covered sofas, eating ices and smoking pipes. In the drawing-room, at the head of a long table, around which crowded about a score of players, sat the master of the house keeping the bank. He was a man of about sixty years of age, of a very dignified appearance; his head was covered with silvery-white hair; his full, florid countenance expressed good-nature, and his eyes twinkled with a perpetual smile. Narumov introduced Hermann to him. Chekalinsky shook him by the hand in a friendly manner, requested him not to stand on ceremony, and then went on dealing.

The game lasted a long time. On the table lay more than thirty cards. Chekalinsky paused after each throw, in order to give the players time to arrange their cards and note down their losses, listened politely to their requests, and more politely still, straightened out the corners of cards that some absent-minded player's hand had turned down. At last the game was finished. Chekalinsky shuffled the cards and prepared to deal again.

"Allow me to play a card," said Hermann stretching out his hand from behind a stout gentleman who was punting.

Chekalinsky smiled and bowed silently, as a sign of acquiescence. Narumov laughingly congratulated Hermann on ending his long abstention from cards, and wished him a lucky beginning.

"Here goes!" said Hermann, writing the figure with chalk on the back of his card.

"How much, sir?" asked the banker, screwing up his eyes. "Excuse me, I cannot see quite clearly."

"Forty-seven thousand," replied Hermann.

At these words every head in the room turned suddenly around, and all eyes were fixed upon Hermann.

"He has taken leave of his senses!" thought Narumov.

"Allow me to observe," said Chekalinsky, with his eternal smile, "that that is a very high stake; nobody here has ever staked more than two hundred and seventy-five rubles at a time."

"Well," retorted Hermann; "do you accept my card or not?"

Chekalinsky bowed with the same look of humble acquiescence.

"I only wish to inform you," said he, "that enjoying the full confidence of my partners, I can only play for ready money. For my own part, I am, of course, quite convinced that your word is sufficient, but for the sake of order, and because of the accounts, I must ask you to put the money on your card."

Hermann drew from his pocket a bank-note and handed it to Chekalinsky, who, after examining it in a cursory manner, placed it on Hermann's card.

He began to deal. On the right a nine turned up, and on the left a three.

"I win!" said Hermann, showing his card.

A murmur of astonishment arose among the players. Chekalinsky frowned, but the smile quickly returned to his face.

"Do you wish me to settle with you?" he said to Hermann.

"If you please," replied the latter.

Chekalinsky drew from his pocket a number of bank-notes and

paid up at once. Hermann took his money and left the table. Narumov could not recover from his astonishment. Hermann drank a glass of lemonade and went home.

The next evening he again appeared at Chekalinsky's. The host was dealing. Hermann walked up to the table; the punters immediately made room for him. Chekalinsky greeted him with a gracious bow.

Hermann waited for the next game, took a card and placed upon it his forty-seven thousand roubles, together with his winnings of the previous evening.

Chekalinsky began to deal. A knave turned up on the right, a seven on the left.

Hermann showed his seven.

There was a general exclamation. Chekalinsky was obviously disturbed, but he counted out the ninety-four thousand roubles and handed them over to Hermann, who pocketed them in the coolest manner possible and immediately left the house.

The next evening Hermann appeared again at the table. Everyone was expecting him. The generals and privy councilors left their whist in order to watch such extraordinary play. The young officers jumped up from their sofas, and even the servants crowded into the room. All pressed round Hermann. The other players left off punting, impatient to see how it would end. Hermann stood at the table and prepared to play alone against the pale, but still smiling Chekalinsky. Each opened a new pack of cards. Chekalinsky shuffled. Hermann took a card and covered it with a pile of bank-notes. It was like a duel. Deep silence reigned.

Chekalinsky began to deal; his hands trembled. On the right a queen turned up, and on the left an ace.

"Ace wins!" cried Herman, showing his card.

"Your queen has lost," said Chekalinsky, sweetly.

Hermann started; instead of an ace, there lay before him the queen of spades! He could not believe his eyes, nor could he understand how he had made such a mistake.

At that moment it seemed to him that the queen of spades screwed up her eyes and sneered. He was struck by the remarkable resemblance. . . .

"The old woman!" he exclaimed, in terror.

Chekalinsky gathered up his winnings. For some time Hermann

remained perfectly motionless. When at last he left the table, the room buzzed with loud talk.

"Splendidly punted!" said the players. Chekalinsky shuffled the cards afresh, and the game went on as usual.

## CONCLUSION

Hermann went out of his mind. He is now confined in room Number 17 of the Obuhov Hospital. He never answers any questions, but he constantly mutters with unusual rapidity: "Three, seven, ace! Three, seven, queen!"

Lizaveta Ivanovna has married a very amiable young man, a son of the former steward of the old Countess. He is a civil servant, and has a considerable fortune. Lizaveta is bringing up a poor relative.

Tomsky has been promoted to the rank of captain, and is marrying Princess Pauline.

1833

# Nikolay Gogol . . . 1809–1852

BORN into a family of small gentry of Ukrainian origin, Gogol grew up in the patriarchal atmosphere of a manor in southern Russia. Such schooling as he had, he received in a provincial institution where the emphasis was placed on the humanities. At nineteen he went to Petersburg to seek his fortune, with the manuscript of a long narrative poem in his luggage. For a short time he held a minor position in the civil service and he also tried his hand at teaching. Meanwhile he continued to write, and before long was devoting himself wholly to literature.

Between 1831 and 1835 he published three volumes, made up chiefly of short stories. Of these a few had the northern capital for their setting, while the greater number evoked with humor and sentiment the life, the lore, the history of his native Ukraine. The last of the three volumes included among other tales the historical romance "Taras Bulba," and "Old-World Landowners." The touching old couple portrayed in the second were largely modeled upon Gogol's grandparents. These books won him a considerable reputation, which was further enhanced with the staging, in 1836, of his comedy "The Inspector-General," a social satire that time has not withered nor custom staled. Its reception by the conservatives, however, so disconcerted the author that he left Russia.

The dozen years that followed, he spent largely abroad, working on his novel "The Adventures of Chichikov," better known as "Dead Souls"—his major contribution to literature. He also wrote two or three more comedies and several short stories, notably "The Overcoat." The first part of "Dead Souls" was published in 1842. In the decade that remained to him, he was occupied with the second part of the novel, but remained deeply dissatisfied with the results. In 1847 he brought out a volume of essays, purporting to be excerpts from his private correspondence, which outraged the liberal portion of his public. The following year he made a trip to the Holy Land in a vain search for spiritual illumination.

His last years were passed under the shadow of a morbid asceticism, the saddest aspect of which was his growing conviction that it was sinful for him to indulge in literary work. Ten days before his death he burned for the second time the manuscript of the second part of "Dead Souls." He seems to have lost completely the will to live, and after a few days' fast, the end came.

# OLD-WORLD LANDOWNERS

I AM VERY fond of the modest manner of life of those solitary owners of remote villages, who in Little Russia are commonly called "old-fashioned," who are like tumbledown picturesque little houses, delightful in their simplicity and complete unlikeness to the new smooth buildings whose walls have not yet been discolored by the rain, whose roofs are not yet covered with green lichen, and whose porch does not display its red bricks through the peeling stucco. I like sometimes to enter for a moment into that extraordinarily secluded life in which not one desire flits beyond the palisade surrounding the little courtyard, beyond the hurdle of the orchard filled with plum and apple trees, beyond the village huts surrounding it, lying all aslant under the shade of willows, elders and pear trees. The life of their modest owners is so quiet, so quiet, that for a moment one is lost in forgetfulness and imagines that those passions, desires and restless promptings of the evil spirit that trouble the world have no real existence, and that you have only beheld them in some lurid dazzling dream. I can see now the low-pitched little house with the gallery of little blackened wooden posts running right round it, so that in hail or storm they could close the shutters without being wetted by the rain. Behind it a fragrant bird-cherry, rows of dwarf fruit trees, drowned in a sea of red cherries and amethyst plums, covered with lead-colored bloom; a spreading maple in the shade of which a rug is laid to rest on; before the house a spacious courtyard of short fresh grass with a little pathway trodden from the store-house to the kitchen and from the kitchen to the master's apartments; a long-necked goose drinking water with young goslings soft as down around her; a palisade hung with strings of dried pears and apples and rugs put out to air; a cartful of melons standing by the store-house; an unharnessed ox lying lazily beside it—they all have an inex-pressible charm for me, perhaps because I no longer see them and because everything from which we are parted is dear to us.

Be that as it may, at the very moment when my chaise was driv-ing up to the steps of that little house, my soul yielded to a wonder-fully sweet and serene mood; the horses galloped merrily up to the steps; the coachman very tranquilly clambered down from the box and filled his pipe as though he had reached home; even the barking set up by phlegmatic Rovers, Pontos and Neros was pleasant to my ears. But more than all I liked the owners of these modest little nooks —the little old men and women who came out solicitiously to meet me. I can see their faces sometimes even now among fashionable dress-coats in the noise and crowd, and then I sink into a half-dreaming state, and the past rises up before me. Their faces always betray such kindness, such hospitality and singleheartedness that un-consciously one renounces, for a brief spell at least, all ambitious dreams, and imperceptibly passes with all one's heart into this humble bucolic life.

To this day I cannot forget two old people of a past age, now, alas! no more. To this day I am full of regret, and it sends a strange pang to my heart when I imagine myself going some time again to their old now deserted dwelling, and seeing the heap of ruined huts, the pond choked with weeds, an overgrown ditch on the spot where the little house stood—and nothing more. It is sad! I am sad at the thought! But let me turn to my story.

Afanasy Ivanovich Tovstogub and his wife Pulherya Ivanovna Tovstogubiha, as the surrounding peasants called her, were the old people of whom I was beginning to tell you. If I were a painter and wanted to portray Philemon and Baucis on canvas, I could choose no other models. Afanasy Ivanovich was sixty. Pulherya Ivanovna was fifty-five. Afanasy Ivanovich was tall, always wore a camlet-covered sheepskin, used to sit bent up, and was invariably almost smiling, even though he were telling a story or simply listening. Pulherya Ivanovna was rather grave and scarcely ever laughed; but in her face and eyes there was so much kindness, so much readiness to regale you with the best of all they had, that you would certainly have found a smile superfluously sweet for her kind face. The faint wrinkles on their faces were drawn so charmingly that an artist would surely have

stolen them; it seemed as though one could read in them their whole
life, clear and serene—the life led by the old typically Little Russian,
simple-hearted and at the same time wealthy families, always such a
contrast to the meaner sort of Little Russians· who, struggling up
from making tar and petty trading, swarm like locusts in the law
courts and public offices, fleece their fellow-villagers of their last
farthing, inundate Petersburg with pettifogging attorneys, make their
pile at last and solemnly add *v* to surnames ending in *o* [by way of
giving them a Great Russian aspect]. No, they, like all the old-fashioned primitive Little Russian families, were utterly different from
such paltry contemptible creatures.

One could not look without sympathy at their mutual love. They
never addressed each other familiarly, but always with formality.
"Was it you who broke the chair, Afanasy Ivanovich?" "Never
mind, don't be cross, Pulherya Ivanovna, it was I." They had had no
children, and so all their affection was concentrated on each other.
At one time in his youth Afanasy Ivanovich was in the service and
had been lieutenant-major; but that was very long ago, that was all
over, Afanasy Ivanovich himself scarcely ever recalled it. Afanasy
Ivanovich was married at thirty when he was a fine young fellow and
wore an embroidered waistcoat; he even eloped rather neatly with
Pulherya Ivanovna, whose relations opposed their marriage; but he
thought very little about that either now, at any rate he never spoke
of it.

All these far-away extraordinary adventures had been followed
by a peaceful and secluded life, by the soothing and harmonious
dreams that you enjoy when you sit on a wooden balcony overlooking the garden, while a delicious rain keeps up a luxurious sound,
pattering on the leaves, flowing in gurgling streams and inducing a
drowsiness in your limbs, while a rainbow hides behind the trees and
in the form of a half-broken arch gleams in the sky with seven soft
colors—or when you are swayed in a carriage that drives between
green bushes while the quail of the steppes calls and the fragrant grass
mingled with ears of corn and wild flowers thrusts itself in at the
carriage doors, flicking you pleasantly on the hands and face.

Afanasy Ivanovich always listened with a pleasant smile to the
guests who visited him; sometimes he talked himself, but more often
he asked questions. He was not one of those old people who bore

one with everlasting praises of old days or denunciations of the new: on the contrary, as he questioned you, he showed great interest and curiosity about the circumstances of your own life, your failures and successes, in which all kind-hearted old people show an interest, though it is a little like the curiosity of a child who examines the seal on your watch at the same time as he talks to you. Then his face, one may say, was breathing kindliness.

The rooms of the little house in which our old people lived were small and low-pitched, as they usually are in the houses of old-world folk. In each room there was an immense stove which covered nearly a third of the floor space. These rooms were terribly hot, for both Afanasy Ivanovich and Pulherya Ivanovna liked warmth. The stoves were all heated from the outer room, which was always filled almost up to the ceiling with straw, commonly used in Little Russia instead of firewood. The crackle and flare of this burning straw made the outer room exceedingly pleasant on a winter's evening when ardent young men, chilled with the pursuit of some pretty brunette, run in, clapping their hands. The walls of the room were adorned with a few pictures in old-fashioned narrow frames. I am convinced that their owners had themselves long ago forgotten what they represented, and if some of them had been taken away they would probably not have noticed it. There were two big portraits painted in oils. One depicted a bishop, the other Peter III.; a flyblown Duchesse de La Vallière looked out from a narrow frame. Round the windows and above the doors there were numbers of little pictures which one grew used to looking upon as spots on the wall and so never examined them. In almost all the rooms the floor was of clay, but cleanly painted and kept with a neatness with which probably no parquet floor in a wealthy house, lazily swept by a sleepy gentleman in livery, has ever been kept.

Pulherya Ivanovna's room was all surrounded with chests and boxes, big and little. Numbers of little bags and sacks of flower seeds, vegetable seeds, and melon seeds hung on the walls. Numbers of balls of different colored wools and rags of old-fashioned gowns made half a century ago were stored in the little chests and between the little chests in the corners. Pulherya Ivanovna was a notable housewife and stored everything, though sometimes she could not herself have said to what use it could be put afterwards.

But the most remarkable thing in the house was the singing of the doors. As soon as morning came the singing of the doors could be heard all over the house. I cannot say why it was they sang: whether the rusty hinges were to blame for it or whether the mechanic who made them had concealed some secret in them; but it was remarkable that each door had its own voice; the door leading to the bedroom sang in the thinnest falsetto and the door into the dining-room in a husky bass; but the one on the outer room gave out a strange cracked and at the same time moaning sound, so that as one listened to it one heard distinctly: "Holy Saints! I am freezing!" I know that many people very much dislike this sound; but I am very fond of it, and if here I sometimes happen to hear a door creak, it seems at once to bring me a whiff of the country: the low-pitched little room lighted by a candle in an old-fashioned candlestick; supper already on the table; a dark May night peeping in from the garden through the open window at the table laid with knives and forks; the nightingale flooding garden, house, and far-away river with its trilling song; the tremor and rustle of branches and, my God! what a long string of memories stretches before me then! . . .

The chairs in the room were massive wooden ones such as were common in old days; they all had high carved backs and were without any kind of varnish or stain; they were not even upholstered, and were rather like the chairs on which bishops sit to this day. Little triangular tables in the corners and square ones before the sofa, and the mirror in its thin gold frame carved with leaves which the flies had covered with black spots; in front of the sofa a rug with birds on it that looked like flowers and flowers that looked like birds: that was almost all the furnishing of the unpretentious little house in which my old people lived. The maids' room was packed full of young girls, and girls who were not young, in striped petticoats; Pulherya Ivanovna sometimes gave them some trifling sewing or set them to prepare the fruit, but for the most part they ran off to the kitchen and slept. Pulherya Ivanovna thought it necessary to keep them in the house and looked strictly after their morals; but to her great surprise many months never passed without the waist of some girl or other growing much larger than usual. This seemed the more surprising as there was scarcely a bachelor in the house with the exception of the houseboy, who used to go about barefoot in a gray tail coat, and if he were not eating was sure to be asleep. Pulherya

Ivanovna usually scolded the erring damsel and punished her severely that it might not happen again.

A terrible number of flies were always buzzing on the window-panes, above whose notes rose the deep bass of a bumblebee, sometimes accompanied by the shrill plaint of a wasp; then as soon as candles were brought all the swarm went to bed and covered the whole ceiling with a black cloud.

Afanasy Ivanovich took very little interest in farming his land, though he did drive out sometimes to the mowers and reapers and watched their labors rather attentively; the whole burden of management rested upon Pulherya Ivanovna. Pulherya Ivanovna's house-keeping consisted in continually locking up and unlocking the store-room, and in salting, drying and preserving countless masses of fruits and vegetables. Her house was quite like a chemical laboratory. There was everlastingly a fire built under an apple tree; and a caldron or a copper pan of jam, jelly, or a sweetmeat made with fruit, honey, sugar and I don't remember what else, was scarcely ever taken off the iron tripod on which it stood. Under another tree the coachman was for ever distilling in a copper retort vodka with peach leaves, or bird-cherry flowers or centaury or cherry stones, and at the end of the process was utterly unable to control his tongue, jabbered such nonsense that Pulherya Ivanovna could make nothing of it, and had to go away to sleep it off in the kitchen. Such a quantity of all this stuff was boiled, salted and dried that the whole courtyard would probably have been drowned in it at last (for Pulherya Ivanovna always liked to prepare a store for the future in addition to all that was reckoned necessary for use), if the larger half of it had not been eaten up by the serf-girls who, stealing into the storeroom, would overeat themselves so frightfully that they were moaning and complaining of stomach-ache all day.

Pulherya Ivanovna had little chance of looking after the tilling of the fields or other branches of husbandry. The steward, in conjunction with the village elder, robbed them in a merciless fashion. They had adopted the habit of treating their master's forest-land as though it were their own; they made numbers of sledges and sold them at the nearest fair; moreover, all the thick oaks they sold to the neighboring Cossacks to be cut down for mills. Only on one occasion Pulherya Ivanovna had desired to inspect her forests. For this purpose a chaise was brought out with immense leather aprons which, as soon as the coachman shook the reins and the horses, who had served in the militia, set off, filled the air with strange sounds, so that a flute and a tambourine and a drum all seemed suddenly audible; every nail and iron bolt clanked so loudly that even at the mill it could be heard that the mistress was driving out of the yard, though the distance was fully a mile and a half. Pulherya Ivanovna could not help noticing the terrible devastation in the forest and the loss of the oaks, which even in childhood she had known to be a hundred years old.

"Why is it, Nichipor," she said, addressing her steward who was on the spot, "that the oaks have been so thinned? Mind that the hair on your head does not grow as thin."

"Why is it?" the steward said. "They have fallen down! They have simply fallen: struck by lightning, gnawed by maggots—they have fallen, lady." Pulherya Ivanovna was completely satisfied with this answer, and on arriving home merely gave orders that the watch should be doubled in the garden near the Spanish cherry trees and the big winter pears.

These worthy rulers, the steward and the elder, considered it quite superfluous to take all the flour to their master's granaries; they thought that the latter would have quite enough with half, and what is more they took to the granaries the half that had begun to grow moldy or had got wet and been rejected at the fair. But however much the steward and the elder stole; however gluttonously everyone on the place ate, from the housekeeper to the pigs, who guzzled an immense number of plums and apples and often pushed the tree with their snouts to shake a perfect rain of fruit down from it; however much the sparrows and crows pecked; however many presents all the servants carried to their friends in other villages, even hauling off old linen and yarn from the storerooms, all of which went into the ever-flowing stream, that is, to the pothouse; however much was stolen by visitors, phlegmatic coachmen and flunkies, yet the blessed earth produced everything in such abundance, and Afanasy Ivanovich and Pulherya Ivanovna wanted so little, that all this terrible robbery made no perceptible impression on their prosperity.

Both the old people were very fond of good fare, as was the old-fashioned tradition of old-world landowners. As soon as the sun had risen (they always got up early) and as soon as the doors set up their varied concert, they were sitting down to a little table, drinking coffee. When he had finished his coffee Afanasy Ivanovich would go out into the porch and, shaking his handkerchief, say: "Kish, kish! Get off the steps, geese!" In the yard he usually came across the steward. As a rule he entered into conversation with him, questioned him about the field labors with the greatest minuteness, made observations and gave orders which would have impressed anyone with his extraordinary knowledge of farming; and no novice would have dared to dream that he could steal from such a sharp-eyed master. But the steward was a wily old bird: he knew how he must answer, and, what is more, he knew how to manage the land.

After this Afanasy Ivanovich would go back indoors, and going up to his wife would say: "Well, Pulherya Ivanovna, isn't it time perhaps for a snack of something?"

"What would you like to have now, Afanasy Ivanovich? Would you like lard cakes or poppy-seed pies, or perhaps salted mushrooms?"

"Perhaps mushrooms or pies," answered Afanasy Ivanovich; and the table would at once be laid with a cloth, pies and mushrooms.

An hour before dinner Afanasy Ivanovich would have another snack, would empty an old-fashioned silver goblet of vodka, would eat mushrooms, various sorts of dried fish and so on. They sat down to dinner at twelve o'clock. Besides the dishes and sauce-boats, there stood on the table numbers of pots with closely-covered lids that no appetizing masterpiece of old-fashioned cookery might be spoilt. At dinner the conversation usually turned on subjects closely related to the dinner. "I fancy this porridge," Afanasy Ivanovich would say, "is a little bit burnt. Don't you think so, Pulherya Ivanovna?" "No, Afanasy Ivanovich. You put a little more butter to it, then it won't taste burnt, or have some of this mushroom sauce; pour that over it!" "Perhaps," said Afanasy Ivanovich, passing his plate: "Let us try how it would be."

After dinner Afanasy Ivanovich went to lie down for an hour, after which Pulherya Ivanovna would take a sliced watermelon and say: "Taste what a nice melon, Afanasy Ivanovich."

"Don't you be so sure of it, Pulherya Ivanovna, because it is red in the middle," Afanasy Ivanovich would say, taking a good slice. "There are some that are red and are not nice."

But the melon quickly disappeared. After that Afanasy Ivanovich would eat a few pears and go for a walk in the garden with Pulherya

Ivanovna. On returning home Pulherya Ivanovna would go to look after household affairs, while he sat under an awning turned towards the courtyard and watched the storeroom continually displaying and concealing its interior and the serf-girls pushing one another as they brought in or carried out heaps of trifles of all sorts in wooden boxes, sieves, trays and other receptacles for holding fruit. A little later he sent for Pulherya Ivanovna, or went himself to her and said: "What shall I have to eat, Pulherya Ivanovna?"

"What would you like?" Pulherya Ivanovna would say. "Shall I go and tell them to bring you the fruit-dumpling I ordered them to keep on purpose for you?"

"That would be nice," Afanasy Ivanovich answered.

"Or perhaps you would like some jelly?"

"That would be good too," Afanasy Ivanovich would answer. Then all this was promptly brought him and duly eaten.

Before supper Afanasy Ivanovich would have another snack of something. At half past nine they sat down to supper. After supper they at once went to bed, and a universal stillness reigned in this active and at the same time tranquil home.

The room in which Afanasy Ivanovich and Pulherya Ivanovna slept was so hot that not many people could have stayed in it for several hours; but Afanasy Ivanovich, in order to be even hotter, used to sleep on the platform of the stove, though the intense heat made him get up several times in the night and walk about the room. Sometimes Afanasy Ivanovich would moan as he walked about the room. Then Pulherya Ivanovna would ask: "What are you groaning for, Afanasy Ivanovich?"

"Goodness only knows, Pulherya Ivanovna; I feel as though I had a little stomach-ache," Afanasy Ivanovich would say.

"Hadn't you better eat something, Afanasy Ivanovich?"

"I don't know whether it would be good, Pulherya Ivanovna! What should I eat, though?"

"Sour milk or some dried pears stewed."

"Perhaps I might have just a taste, anyway," said Afanasy Ivanovich.

A sleepy serf-girl went off to rummage in the cupboards, and Afanasy Ivanovich would eat a plateful, after which he commonly said: "Now it does seem to be better."

Sometimes, if it was fine weather and rather warm indoors,

Afanasy Ivanovich being in good spirits liked to make fun of Pulherya Ivanovna and talk of something.

"Pulherya Ivanovna," he would say, "what if our house were suddenly burnt down, where should we go?"

"Heaven forbid!" Pulherya Ivanovna would say crossing herself.

"But suppose our house were burnt down, where should we go then?"

"God knows what you are saying, Afanasy Ivanovich! How is it possible that our house could be burnt down? God will not permit it."

"Well, but if it were burnt down?"

"Oh, then we would move into the kitchen. You should have for the time the little room that the housekeeper has now."

"But if the kitchen were burnt too?"

"What next! God will preserve us from such a calamity as both house and kitchen burnt down all at once! Well, then we would move into the storeroom while a new house was being built."

"And if the storeroom were burnt?"

"God knows what you are saying! I don't want to listen to you! It's a sin to say it, and God will punish you for saying such things!"

And Afanasy Ivanovich, pleased at having made fun of Pulherya Ivanovna, sat smiling in his chair.

But the old couple seemed most of all interesting to me on the occasions when they had guests. Then everything in their house assumed a different aspect. These good-natured people lived, one may say, for visitors. The best of everything they had was all brought out. They vied with each other in trying to regale you with everything their husbandry produced. But what pleased me most of all was that in their solicitude there was no trace of unctuousness. This hospitality and readiness to please was so gently expressed in their faces, was so in keeping with them, that the guests could not help falling in with their wishes, which were the expression of the pure serene simplicity of their kindly guileless souls. This hospitality was something quite different from the way in which a clerk of some government office who has been helped in his career by your efforts entertains you, calling you his benefactor and cringing at your feet. The visitor was on no account to leave on the same day: he absolutely had to stay the night. "How could you set off on such a long journey at so late an hour!" Pulherya Ivanovna always said. (The guest usually lived two or three miles away.)

"Of course not," Afanasy Ivanovich said. "You never know what may happen: robbers or other evil-minded men may attack you."

"God preserve us from robbers!" said Pulherya Ivanovna. "And why talk of such things at night? It's not a question of robbers, but it's dark, it's not fit for driving at all. Besides, your coachman . . . I know your coachman, he is so frail, and such a little man, any horse would be too much for him; and besides he has probably had a drop by now and is asleep somewhere." And the guest was forced to remain; but the evening spent in the low-pitched hot room, the kindly, warming and soporific talk, the steam rising from the food on the table, always nourishing and cooked in first-class fashion, was compensation for him. I can see as though it were to-day Afanasy Ivanovich sitting bent in his chair with his invariable smile, listening to his visitor with attention and even delight! Often the talk touched on politics. The guest, who also very rarely left his village, would often with a significant air and a mysterious expression trot out his conjectures, telling them that the French had a secret agreement with the English to let Bonaparte out again in order to attack Russia, or would simply prophesy war in the near future; and then Afanasy Ivanovich, pretending not to look at Pulherya Ivanovna, would often say: "I think I shall go to the war myself; why shouldn't I go to the war?"

"There he goes again!" Pulherya Ivanovna interrupted. "Don't you believe him," she said, turning to the guest. "How could an old man like him go to the war! The first soldier would shoot him! Yes, indeed he would! He'd simply take aim and shoot him."

"Well," said Afanasy Ivanovich, "and I'll shoot him."

"Just hear how he talks!" Pulherya Ivanovna caught him up. "How could he go to the war! And his pistols have been rusty for years and are lying in the cupboard. You should just see them: why, they'd explode with the gunpowder before they'd fire a shot. And he'd blow off his hands and disfigure his face and be wretched for the rest of his days!"

"Well," said Afanasy Ivanovich, "I'd buy myself new weapons; I'll take my sabre or a Cossack lance."

"That's all nonsense. An idea comes into his head and he begins talking!" Pulherya Ivanovna interrupted with vexation. "I know he is only joking, but yet I don't like to hear it. That's the way he always talks; sometimes one listens and listens till it frightens one."

But Afanasy Ivanovich, pleased at having scared Pulherya Ivanovna a little, laughed sitting bent up in his chair. Pulherya Ivanovna was most attractive to me when she was taking a guest in to lunch. "This," she would say, taking a cork out of a bottle, "is vodka distilled with milfoil and sage—if anyone has a pain in the shoulder blades or loins, it is very good; now this is distilled with centaury— if anyone has a ringing in the ears or a rash on the face, it is very good; and this now is distilled with peach stones—take a glass, isn't it a delicious smell? If anyone getting up in the morning knocks his head against a corner of the cupboard or a table and a bump comes up on his forehead, he has only to drink one glass of it before dinner and it takes it away entirely; it all passes off that very minute, as though it had never been there at all."

Then followed a similar account of the other bottles, which all had some healing properties. After burdening the guest with all these remedies she would lead him up to a number of dishes. "These are mushrooms with wild thyme! These are with cloves and hazelnuts! A Turkish woman taught me to salt them in the days when we still had Turkish prisoners here. She was such a nice woman, and it was not noticeable at all that she professed the Turkish religion: she went about almost exactly as we do; only she wouldn't eat pork; she said it was forbidden somewhere in their law. And these are mushrooms prepared with black currant leaves and nutmeg! And these are big pumpkins: it's the first time I have pickled them in vinegar; I don't know what they'll be like! I learnt the secret from Father Ivan; first of all you must lay some oak leaves in a tub and then sprinkle with pepper and saltpeter and then put in the flower of the hawkweed, take the flowers and strew them in with stalks uppermost. And here are the little pies; these are cheese pies. And those are the ones Afanasy Ivanovich is very fond of, made with cabbage and buckwheat."

"Yes," Afanasy Ivanovich would add, "I am very fond of them; they are soft and a little sourish."

As a rule Pulherya Ivanovna was in the best of spirits when she had guests. Dear old woman! She was entirely given up to her visitors. I liked staying with them, and although I overate fearfully, as indeed all their visitors did, and though that was very bad for me, I was always glad to go and see them. But I wonder whether the very air of Little Russia has not some peculiar property that promotes digestion; for if anyone were to venture to eat in that way here, there is no doubt he would find himself lying in his coffin instead of his bed.

Good old people! But my account of them is approaching a very melancholy incident which transformed for ever the life of that peaceful nook. This incident is the more impressive because it arose from such an insignificant cause. But such is the strange order of things; trifling causes have always given rise to great events, and on the other hand great undertakings frequently end in insignificant results. Some military leader rallies all the forces of his state, carries on a war for several years, his generals cover themselves with glory, and in the end it all results in gaining a bit of land in which there is not room to plant a potato; while sometimes two sausage-makers of two towns quarrel over some nonsense, and in the end the towns are drawn into the quarrel, then villages, and then the whole kingdom. But let us abandon these reflections: they are out of keeping here; besides I am not fond of reflections, so long as they get no further than being reflections.

Pulherya Ivanovna had a little gray cat, which almost always lay curled up at her feet. Pulherya Ivanovna sometimes stroked her and with one finger scratched her neck, which the spoilt cat stretched as high as she could. I cannot say that Pulherya Ivanovna was excessively fond of her, she was simply attached to her from being used to seeing her about. Afanasy Ivanovich, however, often teased her about her affection for it.

"I don't know, Pulherya Ivanovna, what you find in the cat: what use is she? If you had a dog, then it would be a different matter: one can take a dog out shooting, but what use is a cat?"

"Oh, be quiet, Afanasy Ivanovich," said Pulherya Ivanovna. "You are simply fond of talking and nothing else. A dog is not clean, a dog makes a mess, a dog breaks everything, while a cat is a quiet creature: she does no harm to anyone."

Cats and dogs were all the same to Afanasy Ivanovich, however; he only said it to tease Pulherya Ivanovna a little.

Beyond their garden they had a big forest which had been completely spared by the enterprising steward, perhaps because the sound of the axe would have reached the ears of Pulherya Ivanovna. It was wild and neglected, the old tree stumps were covered with over-grown hazel-bushes and looked like the feathered legs of trumpeter pigeons. Wild cats lived in this forest. Wild forest cats must not be confounded with the bold rascals who run about on the roofs of houses; in spite of their fierce disposition the latter, being in cities, are far more civilized than the inhabitants of the forest. Unlike the town cats the latter are for the most part shy and gloomy creatures; they are always gaunt and lean, they mew in a coarse uncultured voice. They sometimes scratch their way underground into the very storehouses and steal bacon; they even penetrate into the kitchen, springing suddenly in at the open window when they see that the cook has gone off into the high grass.

In fact they are unacquainted with any noble sentiments; they live by plunder, and murder little sparrows in their nests. These cats had for a long time past sniffed through a hole under the storehouse at Pulherya's Ivanovna's gentle little cat and at last they enticed her away, as a company of soldiers entices a silly peasant girl. Pulherya Ivanovna noticed the disappearance of the cat and sent to look for her; but the cat was not found. Three days passed; Pulherya Ivanovna was sorry to lose her, but at last forgot her. One day when she was inspecting her vegetable garden and was returning with fresh green cucumbers plucked by her own hands for Afanasy Ivanovich, her ear was caught by a most pitiful mew. As though by instinct she called, "Puss, puss!" and all at once her gray cat, lean and skinny, came out from the high grass; it was evident that she had not tasted food for several days. Pulherya Ivanovna went on calling her, but the cat stood mewing and did not venture to come close; it was clear that she had grown very wild during her absence. Pulherya Ivanovna went on still calling the cat, who timidly followed her right up to the fence. At last, seeing the old familiar places, she even went indoors. Pulherya Ivanovna at once ordered milk and meat to be brought her and, sitting before her, enjoyed the greediness with which her poor little favorite swallowed piece after piece and lapped up the milk. The little gray fugitive grew fatter almost before her eyes and soon did not eat so greedily. Pulherya Ivanovna stretched out her hand to stroke her, but the ungrateful creature had evidently grown too much accustomed to the ways of wild cats, or had adopted the romantic principle that poverty with love is better than a palace, and, indeed, the wild cats were as poor as church mice; anyway, she sprang out of a window and no one of the house-serfs could catch her.

The old lady sank into thought. "It was my death coming for me!" she said to herself, and nothing could distract her mind. All day she was sad. In vain Afanasy Ivanovich joked and tried to find out why she was so melancholy all of a sudden. Pulherya Ivanovna made no answer, or answered in a way that could not possibly satisfy Afanasy Ivanovich. Next day she was perceptibly thinner.

"What is the matter with you, Pulherya Ivanovna? You must be ill."

"No, I am not ill, Afanasy Ivanovich! I want to tell you something strange; I know that I shall die this summer: my death has already come to fetch me!"

Afanasy Ivanovich's lips twitched painfully. He tried, however, to overcome his gloomy feeling and with a smile said: "God knows what you are saying, Pulherya Ivanovna! You must have drunk some peach vodka instead of the decoction you usually drink."

"No, Afanasy Ivanovich, I have not drunk peach vodka," said Pulherya Ivanovna. And Afanasy Ivanovich was sorry that he had so teased her; he looked at her and a tear hung on his eyelash.

"I beg you, Afanasy Ivanovich, to carry out my wishes," said Pulherya Ivanovna; "when I die, bury me by the church fence. Put my gray dress on me, the one with the little flowers on a brown ground. Don't put on me my satin dress with the crimson stripes: a dead woman has no need of a dress—what use is it to her?—while it will be of use to you: have a fine dressing-gown made of it, so that when visitors are here you can show yourself and welcome them, looking decent."

"God knows what you are saying, Pulherya Ivanovna!" said Afanasy Ivanovich. "Death may be a long way off, but you are frightening me already with such sayings."

"No, Afanasy Ivanovich, I know now when my death will come. Don't grieve for me, though: I am an old woman and have lived long enough, and you are old, too; we shall soon meet in the other world."

But Afanasy Ivanovich was sobbing like a child.

"It is a sin to weep, Afanasy Ivanovich! Do not be sinful and anger God by your sorrow. I am not sorry that I am dying; there is only one thing I am sorry about"—a heavy sigh interrupted her words for a minute. "I am sorry that I do not know in whose care to leave you, who will look after you when I am dead. You are like a little child. You need somebody who loves you to look after you."

At these words there was an expression of such deep, such distressed heartfelt pity on her face that I doubt whether anyone could have looked at her at that moment unmoved.

"Mind, Yavdoha," she said, turning to the housekeeper for whom she had purposely sent, "that when I die you look after your master, watch over him like the apple of your eye, like your own child. Mind that what he likes is always cooked for him in the kitchen; that you always give him clean linen and clothes; that when visitors come you dress him in his best, or else maybe he will sometimes come out in his old dressing-gown, because even now he often forgets when it's a holiday and when it's a working day. Don't take your eyes off him, Yavdoha; I will pray for you in the next world and God will reward you. Do not forget, Yavdoha, you are old, you have not long to live—do not take a sin upon your soul. If you do not look after him you will have no happiness in life. I myself will beseech God not to give you a happy end. And you will be unhappy yourself and your children will be unhappy, and all your family will not have the blessing of God in anything."

Poor old woman! At that minute she was not thinking of the great moment awaiting her, nor of her soul, nor of her own future life: she was thinking only of her poor companion with whom she had spent her life and whom she was leaving helpless and forlorn. With extraordinary efficiency she arranged everything, so that Afanasy Ivanovich should not notice her absence when she was gone. Her conviction that her end was at hand was so strong, and her state of mind was so attuned to it, that she did in fact take to her bed a few days later and could eat nothing. Afanasy Ivanovich never left her bedside and was all solicitude. "Perhaps you would eat a little of something, Pulherya Ivanovna," he said, looking with anxiety into her eyes. But Pulherya Ivanovna said nothing. At last, after a long silence she seemed trying to say something, her lips stirred—and her breathing ceased.

Afanasy Ivanovich was absolutely overwhelmed. It seemed to him so uncanny that he did not even weep; he looked at her with dull eyes as though not grasping the significance of the corpse

The dead woman was laid on the table dressed in the gown she had herself fixed upon, her arms were crossed and a wax candle put in her hand—he looked at all this apathetically. Numbers of people of all kinds filled the courtyard; numbers of guests came to the funeral; long tables were laid out in the courtyard; they were covered with masses of funeral rice, of homemade beverages and pies. The guests talked and wept, gazed at the dead woman, discussed her qualities and looked at him; but he himself looked queerly at it all. The coffin was carried out at last, the people crowded after it and he followed it. The priests were in full vestments, the sun was shining, babies were crying in their mothers' arms, larks were singing and children raced and skipped about the road. At last the coffin was put down above the grave, he was bidden approach and kiss the dead woman for the last time. He went up and kissed her; there were tears in his eyes, but they were somehow apathetic tears. The coffin was lowered, the priest took the spade and first threw in a handful of earth; the deep rich voices of the deacon and the two sacristans sang "Eternal Memory" under the pure cloudless sky; the laborers took up their spades and soon the earth covered the grave and made it level. At that moment he pressed forward, everyone stepped aside and made way for him, anxious to know what he meant to do. He raised his eyes, looked at them vacantly and said: "So you have buried her already! What for?" He broke off and said no more.

But when he was home again, when he saw that his room was empty, that even the chair Pulherya Ivanova used to sit on had been taken away—he sobbed, sobbed violently, inconsolably, and tears flowed from his lusterless eyes like a river.

Five years have passed since then. What grief does not time bear away? What passion survives in the unequal combat with it? I knew a man in the flower of his youth and strength, full of true nobility of character. I knew him in love, tenderly, passionately, madly, fiercely, humbly; and before me, and before my eyes almost, the object of his passion, a tender creature, lovely as an angel, was struck down by merciless death. I have never seen such awful depths of spiritual suffering, such frenzied poignant grief, such devouring despair as overwhelmed the luckless lover. I had never imagined that a man could create for himself such a hell with no shadow, no shape, no semblance of hope. . . . People tried not to leave him alone; all weapons with which he might have killed himself were hidden from him. A fortnight later he suddenly mastered himself, and began laughing and gesting; he was given his freedom, and the first use he made of it was to buy a pistol. One day his family were terrified by the sudden sound of a shot; they ran into the room and saw him stretched on the floor with a shattered skull. A doctor, who happened to be there at the time and whose skill was famous, saw signs of life in him, found that the wound was not absolutely fatal and, to the amazement of everyone, the young man recovered. The watch kept on him was stricter than ever. Even at dinner a knife was not laid for him and everything was removed with which he could have hurt himself; but in a short time he found another opportunity and threw himself under the wheels of a passing carriage. An arm and a leg were broken; but again he recovered. A year after that I saw him in a roomful of people; he was sitting at a table saying gayly "petite ouverte," as he covered a card, and behind him, with her elbows on the back of his chair, was standing his young wife, turning over his counters.

At the end of the five years after Pulherya Ivanovna's death I was in those parts and drove to Afanasy Ivanovich's little farm to visit my old neighbor, in whose house I used at one time to spend the day pleasantly and always to overeat myself with the choicest masterpieces of its hospitable mistress.

As I approached the courtyard the house seemed to me twice as old as it had been: the peasants' huts were lying completely on one side, as no doubt their owners were too; the palisade and the hurdle round the yard were completely broken down, and I myself saw the cook pull sticks out of it to heat the stove, though she need have only taken two steps further to reach the faggot-stack. Sadly I drove up to the steps; the same old dogs, by now blind or lame, barked, wagging their fluffy tails covered with burdocks. An old man came out to greet me. Yes, it was he! I knew him at once; but he stooped twice as much as before. He knew me and greeted me with the old familiar smile. I followed him indoors. It seemed as though everything was as before. But I noticed a strange disorder in everything, an unmistakable absence of something. In fact I experienced the strange feelings which come upon us when for the first time we enter the house of a widower whom we have known in old days inseparable from the wife who has shared his life. The feeling is the same when we see a man crippled whom we have

always known in health. In everything the absence of careful Pulherya Ivanovna was visible: at table a knife was laid without a
handle; the dishes were not cooked with the same skill. I did not
want to ask about the farm, I was afraid even to look at the farm
buildings. When we sat down to dinner, a maid tied a napkin round
Afanasy Ivanovich, and it was well she did so, as without it he
would have spilt sauce all over his dressing-gown. I tried to entertain
him and told him various items of news; he listened with the same
smile, but from time to time his eyes were completely vacant, and
his thoughts did not stray, but vanished. Often he lifted a spoonful
of porridge and instead of putting it to his mouth put it to his nose;
instead of sticking his fork into a piece of chicken, he prodded the
decanter, and then the maid, taking his hand, brought it back to the
chicken. We sometimes waited several minutes for the next course.

Afanasy Ivanovich himself noticed it and said: "Why is it they
are so long bringing the food?" But I saw through the crack of the
door that the boy who carried away our plates was asleep and
nodding on a bench, not thinking of his duties at all.

"This is the dish," said Afanasy Ivanovich, when we were handed
curd-cakes with sour cream. "This is the dish," he went on, and I
noticed that his voice began quivering and a tear was ready to drop
from his leaden eyes, but he did his utmost to restrain it. "This is
the dish which my . . . my . . . dear . . . my dear . . ." And all
at once he burst into tears; his hand fell on the plate, the plate turned
upside down, slipped and was smashed, and the sauce was spilt all
over him. He sat vacantly, vacantly held the spoon; and tears like
a stream, like a ceaselessly flowing fountain, flowed and flowed on
the napkin that covered him.

"My God!" I thought, looking at him, "five years of all-destroying
time—an old man already apathetic, an old man whose life one would
have thought had never once been stirred by a strong feeling, whose
whole life seemed to consist in sitting on a high chair, in eating dried
fish and pears, in telling good-natured stories—and such long, such
bitter grief! What is stronger in us—passion or habit? Or are all the
violent impulses, all the whirl of our desires and boiling passions
only the consequences of our ardent age, and is it only through
youth that they seem deep and shattering?"

Be that as it may, at that moment all our passions seemed like
child's play beside this effect of long, slow, almost insensible habit.

Several times he struggled to utter his wife's name, but halfway through the word, his quiet and ordinary face worked convulsively and his childish weeping cut me to the very heart. No, those were not the tears of which old men are usually so lavish, as they complain of their pitiful position and their troubles; they were not the tears which they drop over a glass of punch either. No! they were tears which brimmed over uninvited from the accumulated rankling pain of a heart already turning cold.

He did not live long after that. I heard lately of his death. It is strange, though, that the circumstances of his end had some resemblance to those of Pulherya Ivanovna's death. One day Afanasy Ivanovich ventured to take a little walk in the garden. As he was pacing slowly along a path with his usual absent-mindedness, without a thought of any kind in his head, he had a strange adventure. He suddenly heard someone behind him pronounce in a fairly distinct voice: "Afanasy Ivanovich!" He turned round but there was absolutely nobody there; he looked in all directions, he peered into the bushes—no one anywhere. It was a still day and the sun was shining. He pondered for a minute; his face seemed to brighten and he brought out at last: "It's Pulherya Ivanovna calling me!"

It has happened to you doubtless some time or other to hear a voice calling you by name, which simple people explain as a soul grieving for a human being and calling him, and after that, they say, death follows inevitably. I must own I was always frightened by that mysterious call. I remember that in childhood I often heard it. Sometimes suddenly someone behind me distinctly uttered my name. Usually on such occasions it was a very bright and sunny day; not one leaf in the garden was stirring; the stillness was deathlike; even the grasshopper left off churring for the moment; there was not a soul in the garden. But I confess that if the wildest and most tempestuous night had lashed me with all the fury of the elements, alone in the middle of an impenetrable forest, I should not have been so terrified as by that awful stillness in the midst of a cloudless day. I usually ran out of the garden in a great panic, hardly able to breathe, and was only reassured when I met some person, the sight of whom dispelled the terrible spiritual loneliness.

Afanasy Ivanovich surrendered completely to his inner conviction that Pulherya Ivanovna was calling him; he submitted with the readiness of an obedient child, wasted away, coughed, melted like a candle and at last flickered out, as it does when there is nothing left to sustain its feeble flame. "Lay me beside Pulherya Ivanovna" was all he said before his end.

His desire was carried out and he was buried near the church beside Pulherya Ivanovna's grave. The guests were fewer at the funeral, but there were just as many beggars and peasants. The little house was now completely emptied. The enterprising steward and the elder hauled away to their huts all that was left of the old-fashioned goods and furniture, which the housekeeper had not been able to carry off. Soon there arrived, I cannot say from where, a distant kinsman, the heir to the estate, who had been a lieutenant, I don't know in what regiment, and was a terrible reformer. He saw at once the great slackness and disorganization in the management of the land; he made up his mind to change all that radically, to improve things and bring everything into order. He bought six splendid English sickles, pinned a special number on each hut, and managed so well that within six months his estate was put under the supervision of a board of trustees.

The sage trustees (consisting of an ex-assessor and a lieutenant in a faded uniform) had within a very short time left no fowls and eggs. The huts, which were almost lying on the earth, fell down completely; the peasants gave themselves up to drunkenness and most of them ran away. The real owner, who got on, however, pretty comfortably with his trustees and used to drink punch with them, very rarely visited his estate and never stayed long. To this day he drives about to all the fairs in Little Russia, carefully inquiring the prices of all sorts of produce sold wholesale, such as flour, hemp, honey and so on; but he only buys small trifles such as flints, a nail to clean out his pipe, in fact nothing which exceeds at the utmost a rouble in price.

1835

# THE OVERCOAT

In the department of . . . But I had better not mention in what department. There is nothing in the world more readily moved to wrath than a department, a regiment, a government office, and in fact any sort of official body. Nowadays every private individual considers all society insulted in his person. I have been told that very lately a petition was handed in from a police-captain of what town I don't recollect, and that in this petition he set forth clearly that the institutions of the State were in danger and that its sacred name was being taken in vain; and, in proof thereof, he appended to his petition an enormous tome containing some sort of romance in which a police-captain appeared on every tenth page, occasionally, indeed, in an intoxicated condition. And so, to avoid any unpleasantness, we had better call the department of which we are speaking a certain department.

And so, in a certain department there was a government clerk; a clerk of whom it cannot be said that he was very remarkable; he was short, somewhat pockmarked, with rather reddish hair and rather dim, bleary eyes, with a small bald patch on the top of his head, with wrinkles on both sides of his cheeks and the sort of complexion which is usually associated with hemorrhoids . . . no help for that, it is the Petersburg climate. As for his grade in the service (for among us the grade is what must be put first), he was what is called a perpetual titular councilor, a class at which, as we all know, various writers who indulge in the praiseworthy habit of attacking those who cannot defend themselves jeer and gibe to their hearts' content. This clerk's surname was Bashmachkin. From the very name it is clear that it must have been derived from a shoe (*bashmak*); but when and under what circumstances it was derived from a shoe, it is impossible to say. Both his father and his grandfather and even his brother-in-law, and all the Bashmachkins without exception wore boots, which they simply resoled two or three times a year. His name was Akaky Akakyevich. Perhaps it may strike the reader as a rather strange and farfetched name, but I can assure him that it was not farfetched at all, that the circumstances were such that it was quite out of the question to give him any other name. Akaky Akakyevich was born towards nightfall, if my memory does not deceive me, on the twenty-third of March. His mother, the wife of a government clerk, a very good woman, made arrangements in due course to christen the child. She was still lying in bed, facing the door, while on her right hand stood the godfather, an excellent man called Ivan Ivanovich Yeroshkin, one of the head clerks in the Senate, and the godmother, the wife of a police official, and a woman of rare qualities, Arina Semyonovna Belobryushkova. Three names were offered to the happy mother for selection—Moky, Sossy, or the name of the martyr Hozdazat. "No," thought the poor lady, "they are all such names!" To satisfy her, they opened the calendar at another place, and the names which turned up were: Trifily, Dula, Varahasy. "What an infliction!" said the mother. "What names they all are! I really never heard such names. Varadat or Varuh would be bad enough, but Trifily and Varahasy!" They turned over another page and the names were: Pavsikahy and Vahtisy. "Well, I see," said the mother, "it is clear that it is his fate. Since that is how it is, he had better be called after his father, his father is Akaky, let the son be Akaky, too."

This was how he came to be Akaky Akakyevich. The baby was christened and cried and made wry faces during the ceremony, as though he foresaw that he would be a titular councilor. So that was how it all came to pass. We have recalled it here so that the reader may see for himself that it happened quite inevitably and that to give him any other name was out of the question. No one has been able to remember when and how long ago he entered the department, nor who gave him the job. However many directors and higher officials of all sorts came and went, he was always seen in the same place, in the same position, at the very same duty, precisely the same copying clerk, so that they used to declare that he must have been born a copying clerk in uniform all complete and with a bald patch on his head. No respect at all was shown him in the department. The porters, far from getting up from their seats when he came in, took no more notice of him than if a simple fly had flown across the vestibule. His superiors treated him with a sort of domineering chilliness. The head clerk's assistant used to throw papers under his nose without even saying "Copy this" or "Here is an interesting, nice little case" or some agreeable remark of the sort, as is usually done in well-behaved offices. And he would take it, gazing only at the paper without looking to see who had put it there and whether he had the right to do so; he would take it and at once set to work to copy it. The young clerks jeered and made jokes at him to the best of their clerky wit, and told to his face all sorts of stories of their own invention about him; they would say of his landlady, an old woman of seventy, that she beat him, would enquire when the wedding was to take place, and would scatter bits of paper on his head, calling them snow. Akaky Akakyevich never answered a word, however, but behaved as though there were no one there. It had no influence on his work even; in the midst of all this teasing, he never made a single mistake in his copying.

Only when the jokes were too unbearable, when they jolted his arm and prevented him from going on with his work, he would bring out: "Leave me alone! Why do you insult me?" and there was something strange in the words and in the voice in which they were uttered. There was a note in it of something that aroused compassion, so that one young man, new to the office, who, following the example of the rest, had allowed himself to mock at him, suddenly stopped as though cut to the heart, and from that time forth, everything was, at it were, changed and appeared in a different light to him. Some unnatural force seemed to thrust him away from the companions with whom he had become acquainted, accepting them as well-bred, polished people. And long afterwards, at moments of the greatest gaiety, the figure of the humble little clerk with a bald patch on his head rose before him with his heart-rending words: "Leave me alone! Why do you insult me?" And in those heart-rending words he heard others: "I am your brother." And the poor young man hid his face in his hands, and many times afterwards in his life he shuddered, seeing how much inhumanity there is in man, how much savage brutality lies hidden under refined, cultured politeness, and, my God! even in a man whom the world accepts as a gentleman and a man of honor. . . .

It would be hard to find a man who lived in his work as did Akaky Akakyevich. To say that he was zealous in his work is not enough; no, he loved his work. In it, in that copying, he found a varied and agreeable world of his own. There was a look of enjoyment on his face; certain letters were favorites with him, and when he came to them he was delighted; he chuckled to himself and winked and moved his lips, so that it seemed as though every letter his pen was forming could be read in his face. If rewards had been given according to the measure of zeal in the service, he might to his amazement have even found himself a civil councilor; but all he gained in the service, as the wits, his fellow-clerks expressed it, was a buckle in his buttonhole and a pain in his back. It cannot be said, however, that no notice had ever been taken of him. One director, being a good-natured man and anxious to reward him for his long service, sent him something a little more important than his ordinary copying; he was instructed from a finished document to make some sort of report for another office; the work consisted only of altering the headings and in places changing the first person into the third. This cost him such an effort that it threw him into a regular perspiration: he mopped his brow and said at last, "No, better let me copy something."

From that time forth they left him to go on copying forever. It seemed as though nothing in the world existed for him outside his copying. He gave no thought at all to his clothes; his uniform was—well, not green but some sort of rusty, muddy color. His collar was very short and narrow, so that, although his neck was not particularly long, yet, standing out of the collar, it looked as immensely long as those of the plaster kittens that wag their heads and are carried about on trays on the heads of dozens of foreigners living in Russia. And there were always things sticking to his uniform, either bits of hay or thread; moreover, he had a special art of passing under a window at the very moment when various rubbish was being flung out into the street, and so was continually carrying off bits of melon rind and similar litter on his hat. He had never once in his life noticed what was being done and going on in the street, all those things at which, as we all know, his colleagues, the young clerks, always stare, carrying their sharp sight so far even as to notice any one on the other side of the pavement with a trouser strap hanging loose—a detail which always calls forth a sly grin. Whatever Akaky Akakyevich looked at, he saw nothing anywhere but his clear, evenly written lines, and only perhaps when a horse's head suddenly appeared from nowhere just on his shoulder, and its nostrils blew a perfect gale upon his cheek, did he notice that he was not in the middle of his writing, but rather in the middle of the street.

On reaching home, he would sit down at once to the table, hurriedly sup his cabbage-soup and eat a piece of beef with an onion; he did not notice the taste at all, but ate it all up together with the flies and anything else that Providence chanced to send him. When he felt that his stomach was beginning to be full, he would rise up from the table, get out a bottle of ink and set to copying the papers he had brought home with him. When he had none to do, he would make a copy expressly for his own pleasure, particularly if the document were remarkable not for the beauty of its style but for the fact of its being addressed to some new or important personage.

Even at those hours when the gray Petersburg sky is completely overcast and the whole population of clerks have dined and eaten their fill, each as best he can, according to the salary he receives and his personal tastes; when they are all resting after the scratching of pens and bustle of the office, their own necessary work and other people's, and all the tasks that an overzealous man voluntarily sets himself even beyond what is necessary; when the clerks are hastening to devote what is left of their time to pleasure; some more enterprising are flying to the theater, others to the street to spend their leisure, staring at women's hats, some to spend the evening paying compliments to some attractive girl, the star of a little official circle, while some—and this is the most frequent of all—go simply to a fellow-clerk's flat on the third or fourth story, two little rooms with an entry or a kitchen, with some pretentions to style, with a lamp or some such article that has cost many sacrifices of dinners and excursions—at the time when all the clerks are scattered about the little flats of their friends, playing a tempestuous game of whist, sipping tea out of glasses and munching penny rusks, sucking in smoke from long pipes, telling, as the cards are dealt, some scandal that has floated down from higher circles, a pleasure which the Russian can never by any possibility deny himself, or, when there is nothing better to talk about, repeating the everlasting anecdotes of the commanding officer who was told that the tail had been cut off the horse on the Falconet monument—in short, even when everyone was eagerly seeking entertainment, Akaky Akakyevich did not give himself up to any amusement. No one could say that they had ever seen him at an evening party. After working to his heart's content, he would go to bed, smiling at the thought of the next day and wondering what God would send him to copy.

So flowed on the peaceful life of a man who knew how to be content with his fate on a salary of four hundred roubles, and so perhaps it would have flowed on to extreme old age, had it not been for the various calamities that bestrew the path through life, not only of titular, but even of privy, actual, aulic and all other councilors, even those who neither give council to others nor accept it themselves.

There is in Petersburg a mighty foe of all who receive a salary of four hundred roubles or about that sum. That foe is none other than our northern frost, although it is said to be very good for the health. Between eight and nine in the morning, precisely at the hour when the streets are full of clerks going to their departments, the frost begins giving such sharp and stinging flips at all their noses indiscriminately that the poor fellows don't know what to do with them. At that time, when even those in the higher grade have a pain in their brows and tears in their eyes from the frost, the poor titular councilors are sometimes almost defenseless. Their only protection lies in running as fast as they can through five or six streets in a wretched, thin little overcoat and then warming their feet thoroughly in the porter's room, till all their faculties and qualifications for their various duties thaw again after being frozen on the way. Akaky Akakyevich had for some time been feeling that his back and shoulders were particularly nipped by the cold, although he did try to run the regular distance as fast as he could. He wondered at last whether there were any defects in his overcoat. After examining it thoroughly in the privacy of his home, he discovered that in two or three places, to wit on the back and the shoulders, it had become a regular sieve; the cloth was so worn that you could see through it and the lining was coming out. I must observe that Akaky Akakyevich's overcoat had also served as a butt for the gibes of the clerks. It had been deprived of the honorable name of overcoat and had been referred to as the "dressing jacket." It was indeed of rather a strange make. Its collar had been growing smaller year by year as it served to patch the other parts. The patches were not good specimens of the tailor's art, and they certainly looked clumsy and ugly. On seeing what was wrong, Akaky Akakyevich decided that he would have to take the overcoat to Petrovich, a tailor who lived on a fourth story up a back staircase, and, in spite of having only one eye and being pockmarked all over his face, was rather successful in repairing the trousers and coats of clerks and others—that is, when he was sober, be it understood, and had no other enterprise in his mind. Of this tailor I ought not, of course, to say much, but since it is now the rule that the character of every person in a tale must be completely drawn, well, there is no help for it, here is Petrovich too. At first he was called simply Grigory, and was a serf belonging to some gentleman or other. He began to be called Petrovich from the time he got his freedom and began to drink rather heavily on every holiday, at first only on the chief holidays, but afterwards on all church holidays indiscriminately, wherever there is a cross in the calendar. On that side he was true to the customs of his forefathers, and when he quarreled with his wife used to call her "a worldly woman and a German." Since we have now mentioned the wife, it will be necessary to say a few words about her too, but unfortunately not much is known about her, except indeed that Petrovich had a wife and that she wore a cap and not a kerchief, but apparently she could not boast of beauty; anyway, none but soldiers of the Guards peeped under her cap when they met her, and they twitched their mustaches and gave vent to a rather peculiar sound.

As he climbed the stairs, leading to Petrovich's—which, to do them justice, were all soaked with water and slops and saturated through and through with that smell of spirits which makes the eyes smart, and is, as we all know, inseparable from the backstairs of Petersburg houses—Akaky Akakyevich was already wondering how much Petrovich would ask for the job, and inwardly resolving not to give more than two roubles. The door was open, for Petrovich's wife was frying some fish and had so filled the kitchen with smoke that you could not even see the black-beetles. Akaky Akakyevich crossed the kitchen unnoticed by the good woman, and walked at last into a room where he saw Petrovich sitting on a big, wooden, unpainted table with his legs tucked under him like a Turkish pasha. The feet, as is usual with tailors when they sit at work, were bare; and the first object that caught Akaky Akakyevich's eye was the big toe, with which he was already familiar, with a misshapen nail as thick and strong as the shell of a tortoise. Round Petrovich's neck hung a skein of silk and another of thread and on his knees was a rag of some sort. He had for the last three minutes been trying to thread his needle, but could not get the thread into the eye and so was very angry with the darkness and indeed with the thread itself, muttering in an undertone: "It won't go in, the savage! You wear me out, you rascal." Akaky Akakyevich was vexed that he had come just at the minute when Petrovich was in a bad humor; he liked to give him an order when he was a little "elevated," or, as his wife expressed it, "had fortified himself with brandy, the one-eyed devil." In such circumstances Petrovich was as a rule very ready to give way and agree, and indeed, invariably bowed and thanked one. Afterwards, it is true, his wife would come wailing that her husband had been drunk and so had asked too little, but adding a single ten-copeck piece would settle that. But on this occasion Petrovich was apparently sober and consequently curt, unwilling to bargain, and the devil knows what price he would be ready to lay on. Akaky Akakyevich perceived this, and was, as the saying is, beating a retreat, but things had gone too far, for Petrovich was screwing up his solitary eye very attentively at him and Akaky Akakyevich involun- tarily brought out: "Good day, Petrovich!" "I wish you a good day, sir," said Petrovich, and squinted at Akaky Akakyvich's hands, trying to discover what sort of goods he had brought.

"Here I have come to you, Petrovich, do you see . . . !"

It must be noticed that Akaky Akakyevich for the most part expressed himself by prepositions, adverbs, and particles which have absolutely no significance whatever. If the subject was a very difficult one, it was his habit indeed to leave his sentences quite unfinished, so that very often after a sentence had begun with the words, "It really is, don't you know . . ." nothing at all would follow and he himself would be quite oblivious, supposing he had said all that was necessary.

"What is it?" said Petrovich, and at the same time with his solitary eye he scrutinized his whole uniform from the collar to the sleeves, the back, the skirts, the buttonholes—with all of which he was very familiar, they were all his own work. Such scrutiny is habitual with tailors, it is the first thing they do on meeting one.

"It's like this, Petrovich . . . the overcoat, the cloth . . . you see everywhere else it is quite strong; it's a little dusty and looks as though it were old, but it is new and it is only in one place just a little . . . on the back, just a little worn on one shoulder and on this shoulder, too, a little . . . do you see? that's all, and it's not much work. . . ."

Petrovich took the "dressing jacket," first spread it out over the table, examined it for a long time, shook his head and put his hand out to the window for a round snuffbox with a portrait on the lid of some general—which precisely I can't say, for a finger had been thrust through the spot where a face should have been, and the hole had been pasted up with a square bit of paper. After taking a pinch of snuff, Petrovich held the "dressing jacket" up in his hands and looked at it against the light, and again he shook his head; then he turned it with the lining upwards and once more shook his head; again he took off the lid with the general pasted up with paper and stuffed a pinch into his nose, shut the box, put it away and at last said: "No, it can't be repaired; a wretched garment!" Akaky Akakyevich's heart sank at those words.

"Why can't it, Petrovich?" he said, almost in the imploring voice of a child. "Why, the only thing is it is a bit worn on the shoulders; why, you have got some little pieces . . ."

"Yes, the pieces will be found all right," said Petrovich, "but it can't be patched, the stuff is quite rotten; if you put a needle in it, it would give way."

"Let it give way, but you just put a patch on it."

"There is nothing to put a patch on. There is nothing for it to hold on to; there is a great strain on it, it is not worth calling cloth, it would fly away at a breath of wind."

"Well, then, strengthen it with something—upon my word, really, this is . . . !"

"No," said Petrovich resolutely, "there is nothing to be done, the thing is no good at all. You had far better, when the cold winter weather comes, make yourself leg wrappings out of it, for there is no warmth in stockings, the Germans invented them just to make money." (Petrovich was fond of a dig at the Germans occasionally.) "And as for the overcoat, it is clear that you will have to have a new one."

At the word "new" there was a mist before Akaky Akakyevich's eyes, and everything in the room seemed blurred. He could see nothing clearly but the general with the piece of paper over his face on the lid of Petrovich's snuffbox.

"A new one?" he said, still feeling as though he were in a dream; "why, I haven't the money for it."

"Yes, a new one," Petrovich repeated with barbarous composure.

"Well, and if I did have a new one, how much would it . . . ?"

"You mean what will it cost?"

"Yes."

"Well, three fifty-rouble notes or more," said Petrovich, and he compressed his lips significantly. He was very fond of making an effect, he was fond of suddenly disconcerting a man completely and then squinting sideways to see what sort of a face he made.

"A hundred and fifty roubles for an overcoat," screamed poor Akaky Akakyevich—it was perhaps the first time he had screamed in his life, for he was always distinguished by the softness of his voice.

"Yes," said Petrovich, "and even then it's according to the coat. If I were to put marten on the collar, and add a hood with silk linings, it would come to two hundred."

"Petrovich, please," said Akaky Akakyevich in an imploring voice, not hearing and not trying to hear what Petrovich said, and missing all his effects, "do repair it somehow, so that it will serve a little longer."

"No, that would be wasting work and spending money for nothing," said Petrovich, and after that Akaky Akakyevich went away completely crushed, and when he had gone Petrovich remained standing for a long time with his lips pursed up significantly before he took up his work again, feeling pleased that he had not demeaned himself nor lowered the dignity of the tailor's art.

When he got into the street, Akaky Akakyevich was as though in a dream. "So that is how it is," he said to himself. "I really did not think it would be so . . ." and then after a pause he added, "So there it is; so that's how it is at last! and I really could never have supposed it would have been so. And there . . ." There followed another long silence, after which he brought out: "So there it is! well, it really is so utterly unexpected . . . who would have thought . . . what a circumstance . . ." Saying this, instead of going home he walked off in quite the opposite direction without suspecting what he was doing. On the way a clumsy sweep brushed the whole of his sooty side against him and blackened all his shoulder; a regular hatful of plaster scattered upon him from the top of a house that was being built. He noticed nothing of this, and only after he had jostled against a constable who had set his halberd down beside him and was shaking some snuff out of his horn into his rough fist, he came to himself a little and then only because the constable said: "Why are you poking yourself right in one's face, haven't you the sidewalk to yourself?" This made him look round and turn homeward; only there he began to collect his thoughts, to see his position in a clear and true light and began talking to himself no longer incoherently but reasonably and openly as with a sensible friend with whom one can discuss the most intimate and vital matters. "No, indeed," said Akaky Akakyevich, "it is no use talking to Petrovich now; just now he really is . . . his wife must have been giving it to him. I had better go to him on Sunday morning; after the Saturday evening he will be squinting and sleepy, so he'll want a little drink to carry it off and his wife won't give him a penny. I'll slip ten copecks into his hand and then he will be more accommodating and maybe take the overcoat. . . ."

So reasoning with himself, Akaky Akakyevich cheered up and waited until the next Sunday; then, seeing from a distance Petrovich's wife leaving the house, he went straight in. Petrovich certainly was very tipsy after the Saturday. He could hardly hold his head up and was very drowsy: but, for all that, as soon as he heard what he was speaking about, it seemed as though the devil had nudged him. "I can't," he said, "you must kindly order a new one." Akaky Akakyevich at once slipped a ten-copeck piece into his hand. "I thank you, sir, I will have just a drop to your health, but don't trouble yourself about the overcoat; it is not a bit of good for anything. I'll make you a fine new coat, you can trust me for that."

Akaky Akakyevich would have said more about repairs, but Petrovich, without listening said: "A new one now I'll make you without fail; you can rely upon that I'll do my best. It could even be like the fashion that has come in with the collar to button with silver claws appliqué."

Then Akaky Akakyevich saw that there was no escape from a new overcoat and he was utterly depressed. How indeed, for what, with what money could he get it? Of course he could to some extent rely on the bonus for the coming holiday, but that money had long ago been appropriated and its use determined beforehand. It was needed for new trousers and to pay the cobbler an old debt for putting some new tops to some old boot-legs, and he had to order three shirts from a seamstress as well as two specimens of an undergarment which it is improper to mention in print; in short, all that money absolutely must be spent, and even if the director were to be so gracious as to assign him a gratuity of forty-five or even fifty, instead of forty roubles, there would be still left a mere trifle, which would be but as a drop in the ocean beside the fortune needed for an overcoat. Though, of course, he knew that Petrovich had a strange craze for suddenly putting on the devil knows what enormous price, so that at times his own wife could not help crying out: "Why, you are out of your wits, you idiot! Another time he'll undertake a job for nothing, and here the devil has bewitched him to ask more than he is worth himself." Though, of course, he knew that Petrovich would undertake to make it for eighty roubles, still where would he get those eighty roubles? He might manage half of that sum; half of it could be found, perhaps even a little more; but where could he get the other half? . . .

But, first of all, the reader ought to know where that first half was to be found. Akaky Akakyevich had the habit every time he spent a rouble of putting aside two copecks in a little locked-up box with a slit in the lid for slipping the money in. At the end of every half-year he would inspect the pile of coppers there and change them for small silver. He had done this for a long time, and in the course of many years the sum had mounted up to forty roubles and so he had half the money in his hands, but where was he to get the other half, where was he to get another forty roubles? Akaky Akakyevich pondered and pondered and decided at last that he would have to diminish his ordinary expenses, at least for a year; give up burning candles in the evening, and if he had to do anything he must go into the landlady's room and work by her candle; that as he walked along the streets he must walk as lightly and carefully as possible, almost on tiptoe, on the cobbles and flagstones, so that his soles might last a little longer than usual; that he must send his linen to the wash less frequently, and that, to preserve it from being worn, he must take it off every day when he came home and sit in a thin cotton-shoddy dressing-gown, a very ancient garment which Time itself had spared.

To tell the truth, he found it at first rather hard to get used to these privations, but after a while it became a habit and went smoothly enough—he even became quite accustomed to being hungry in the evening; on the other hand, he had spiritual nourishment, for he carried ever in his thoughts the idea of his future overcoat. His whole existence had in a sense become fuller, as though he had married, as though some other person were present with him, as though he were no longer alone, but an agreeable companion had consented to walk the path of life hand in hand with him, and that companion was no other than the new overcoat with its thick wadding and its strong, durable lining. He became, as it were, more alive, even more strong-willed, like a man who has set before himself a definite aim. Uncertainty, indecision, in fact all the hesitating and vague characteristics vanished from his face and his manners. At times there was a gleam in his eyes, indeed, the most bold and audacious ideas flashed through his mind. Why not really have marten on the collar? Meditation on the subject always made him absent-minded. On one occasion when he was copying a document, he very nearly made a mistake, so that he almost cried out "Ow" aloud and crossed himself.

At least once every month he went to Petrovich to talk about the overcoat, where it would be best to buy the cloth, and what color it should be, and what price, and, though he returned home a little anxious, he was always pleased at the thought that at last the time was at hand when everything would be bought and the overcoat would be made. Things moved even faster than he had anticipated. Contrary to all expectations, the director bestowed on Akaky Akakyevich a gratuity of no less than sixty roubles. Whether it was that he had an inkling that Akaky Akakyevich needed a greatcoat, or whether it happened so by chance, owing to this he found he had twenty roubles extra. This circumstance hastened the course of affairs.

Another two or three months of partial fasting and Akaky Akakyevich had actually saved up nearly eighty roubles. His heart, as a rule very tranquil, began to throb. The very first day he set off in company with Petrovich to the shops. They bought some very good cloth, and no wonder, since they had been thinking of it for more than six months before, and scarcely a month had passed without their going to the shops to compare prices; now Petrovich himself declared that there was no better cloth to be had. For the lining they chose calico, but of a stout quality, which in Petrovich's words was even better than silk, and actually as strong and handsome to look at. Marten they did not buy, because it certainly was dear, but instead they chose cat fur, the best to be found in the shop—cat which at a distance might almost be taken for marten. Petrovich was busy over the coat for a whole fortnight, because there were a great many button-holes, otherwise it would have been ready sooner. Petrovich asked twelve roubles for the work; less than that it hardly could have been, everything was sewn with silk, with fine double seams, and Petrovich went over every seam afterward with his own teeth imprinting various figures with them.

It was . . . it is hard to say precisely on what day, but probably on the most triumphant day of the life of Akaky Akakyevich that Petrovich at last brought the overcoat. He brought it in the morning, just before it was time to set off for the department. The overcoat could not have arrived at a more opportune time, for rather sharp frosts were just beginning and seemed threatening to be even more severe. Petrovich brought the greatcoat himself as a good tailor should. There was an expression of importance on his face, such as Akaky Akakyevich had never seen there before. He seemed fully conscious of having completed a work of no little moment and of having shown in his own person the gulf that separates tailors who only put in linings and do repairs from those who make up new materials. He took the greatcoat out of the pocket-handkerchief in which he had brought it (the pocket-handkerchief had just come home from the wash), he then folded it up and put it in his pocket for future use. After taking out the overcoat, he looked at it with much pride and, holding it in both hands, threw it very deftly over Akaky Akakyevich's shoulders, then pulled it down and smoothed it out behind with his hands; then draped it about Akaky Akakyevich with somewhat jaunty carelessness. The latter, as a man advanced in years, wished to try it with his arms in the sleeves. Petrovich helped him to put it on, and it appeared that it looked splendid too with his arms in the sleeves. In fact it turned out that the overcoat was completely and entirely successful. Petrovich did not let slip the occasion for observing that it was only because he lived in a small street and had no signboard, and because he had known Akaky Akakyevich so long, that he had done it so cheaply, but on the Nevsky Prospect they would have asked him seventy-five roubles for the work alone. Akaky Akakyevich had no inclination to discuss this with Petrovich, besides he was frightened of the big sums that Petrovich was fond of flinging airily about in conversation. He paid him, thanked him, and went off on the spot, with his new overcoat on, to the department. Petrovich followed him out and stopped in the street, staring for a good time at the coat from a distance and then purposely turned off and, taking a short cut by a side street, came back into the street and got another view of the coat from the other side, that is, from the front.

Meanwhile Akaky Akakyevich walked along with every emotion in its most holiday mood. He felt every second that he had a new overcoat on his shoulders, and several times he actually laughed from inward satisfaction. Indeed, it had two advantages, one that it was warm and the other that it was good. He did not notice the way at all and found himself all at once at the department; in the porter's room he took off the overcoat, looked it over and put it in the porter's special care. I cannot tell how it happened, but all at once everyone in the department learned that Akaky Akakyevich had a new overcoat and that the "dressing jacket" no longer existed. They all ran out at once into the porter's room to look at Akaky Akakyevich's new overcoat, they began welcoming him and congratulating him so that at first he could do nothing but smile and afterwards felt positively abashed. When, coming up to him, they all began saying that he must "sprinkle" the new overcoat and that he ought at least to stand them all a supper, Akaky Akakyevich lost his head completely and did not know what to do, how to get out of it, nor what to answer. A few minutes later, flushing crimson, he even began assuring them with great simplicity that it was not a new overcoat at all, that it was just nothing, that it was an old overcoat.

At last one of the clerks, indeed the assistant to the head clerk of the room, probably in order to show that he was not proud and was able to get on with those beneath him, said: "So be it, I'll give a party instead of Akaky Akakyevich and invite you all to tea with me this evening; as luck would have it, it is my name-day." The clerks naturally congratulated the assistant head clerk and eagerly accepted the invitation. Akaky Akakyevich was beginning to make excuses, but they all declared that it was uncivil of him, that it was simply a shame and a disgrace and that he could not possibly refuse. However, he felt pleased about it afterwards when he remembered that through this he would have the opportunity of going out in the evening, too, in his new overcoat. That whole day was for Akaky Akakyevich the most triumphant and festive day in his life. He returned home in the happiest frame of mind, took off the overcoat and hung it carefully on the wall, admiring the cloth and lining once more, and then pulled out his old "dressing jacket," now completely coming to pieces, on purpose to compare them. He glanced at it and positively laughed, the difference was so immense! And long afterwards he went on laughing at dinner, as the position in which the "dressing jacket" was placed recurred to his mind. He dined in excellent spirits and after dinner wrote nothing, no papers at all, but just took his ease for a little while on his bed, till it got dark, then, without putting things off, he dressed, put on his overcoat, and went out into the street.

Where precisely the clerk who had invited him lived we regret to say that we cannot tell; our memory is beginning to fail sadly, and everything there is in Petersburg, all the streets and houses, are so blurred and muddled in our head that it is a very difficult business to put anything in orderly fashion. However that may have been, there is no doubt that the clerk lived in the better part of the town and consequently a very long distance from Akaky Akakyevich. At first the latter had to walk through deserted streets, scantily lighted, but as he approached his destination the streets became more lively, more full of people, and more brightly lighted; passers-by began to be more frequent, ladies began to appear, here and there, beautifully dressed, beaver collars were to be seen on the men. Cabmen with wooden trelliswork sledges, studded with gilt nails, were less frequently to be met; on the other hand, jaunty drivers in raspberry colored velvet caps with varnished sledges and bearskin rugs appeared, and carriages with decorated boxes dashed along the streets, their wheels crunching through the snow.

Akaky Akakyevich looked at all this as a novelty; for several years he had not gone out into the streets in the evening. He stopped with curiosity before a lighted shop-window to look at a picture in which a beautiful woman was represented in the act of taking off her shoe and displaying as she did so the whole of a very shapely leg, while behind her back a gentleman with whiskers and a handsome imperial on his chin was putting his head in at the door. Akaky Akakyevich shook his head and smiled and then went on his way. Why did he smile? Was it because he had come across something quite unfamiliar to him, though every man retains some instinctive feeling on the subject, or was it that he reflected, like many other clerks, as follows: "Well, upon my soul, those Frenchmen! It's beyond anything! If they try on anything of the sort, it really is . . . !" Though possibly he did not think even that; there is no creeping into a man's soul and finding out all that he thinks. At last he reached the house in which the assistant head clerk lived in fine style; there was a lamp burning on the stairs, and the flat was on the second floor. As he went into the entry Akaky Akakyevich saw whole rows of goloshes. Amongst them in the middle of the room stood a samovar hissing and letting off clouds of steam. On the walls hung coats and cloaks, among which some actually had beaver collars or velvet revers. The other side of the wall there was noise and talk, which suddenly became clear and loud when the door opened and the footman came out with a tray full of empty glasses, a jug of cream, and a basket of biscuits. It was evident that the clerks had arrived long before and had already drunk their first glass of tea. Akaky Akakyevich, after hanging up his coat with his own hands, went into the room, and at the same moment there flashed before his eyes a vision of candles, clerks, pipes, and card tables, together with the confused sounds of conversation rising up on all sides and the noise of moving chairs. He stopped very awkwardly in the middle of the room, looking about and trying to think what to do, but he was observed and received with a shout and they all went at once into the entry and again took a look at his overcoat. Though Akaky Akakyevich was somewhat embarrassed, yet, being a simple-hearted man, he could not help being pleased at seeing how they all admired his coat. Then of course they all abandoned him and his coat, and turned their attention as usual to the tables set for whist. All this—the noise, the talk, and the crowd of people—was strange and wonderful to Akaky Akakyevich. He simply did not know how to behave, what to do with his arms and legs and his whole figure; at last he sat down beside the players, looked at the cards, stared first at one and then at another of the faces, and in a little while began to yawn and felt that he was bored—especially as it was long past the time at which he usually went to bed. He tried to take leave of his hosts, but they would not let him go, saying that he absolutely must have a glass of champagne in honor of the new coat. An hour later supper was served, consisting of salad, cold veal, a pasty, pies, and tarts from the confectioner's, and champagne. They made Akaky Akakyevich drink two glasses, after which he felt that things were much more cheerful, though he could not forget that it was twelve o'clock and that he ought to have been home long ago. That his host might not take it into his head to detain him, he slipped out of the room, hunted in the entry for his greatcoat, which he found, not without regret, lying on the floor, shook it, removed some fluff from it, put it on, and went down the stairs into the street.

It was still light in the streets. Some little general shops, those perpetual clubs for house-serfs and all sorts of people, were open; others which were closed showed, however, a long streak of light at every crack of the door, proving that they were not yet deserted, and probably maids and menservants were still finishing their conversation and discussion, driving their masters to utter perplexity as to their whereabouts. Akaky Akakyevich walked along in a cheerful state of mind; he was even on the point of running, goodness knows why, after a lady of some sort who passed by like lightning with every part of her frame in violent motion. He checked himself at once, however, and again walked along very gently, feeling positively surprised himself at the inexplicable impulse that had seized him. Soon the deserted streets, which are not particularly cheerful by day and even less so in the evening, stretched before him. Now they were still more dead and deserted; the light of street lamps was scantier, the oil was evidently running low; then came wooden houses and fences; not a soul anywhere; only the snow gleamed on the streets and the low-pitched slumbering hovels looked black and gloomy with their closed shutters. He approached the spot where the street was intersected by an endless square, which looked like a fearful desert with its houses scarcely visible on the further side.

In the distance, goodness knows where, there was a gleam of light from some sentry-box which seemed to be standing at the end of the world. Akaky Akakyevich's lightheartedness grew somehow sensibly less at this place. He stepped into the square, not without an involuntary uneasiness, as though his heart had a foreboding of evil. He looked behind him and to both sides—it was as though the sea were all round him. "No, better not look," he thought, and walked on, shutting his eyes, and when he opened them to see whether the end of the square were near, he suddenly saw standing before him, almost under his very nose, some men with mustaches;

just what they were like he could not even distinguish. There was a mist before his eyes and a throbbing in his chest. "I say the overcoat is mine!" said one of them in a voice like a clap of thunder, seizing him by the collar. Akaky Akakyevich was on the point of shouting "Help" when another put a fist the size of a clerk's head against his very lips, saying: "You just shout now." Akaky Akakyevich felt only that they took the overcoat off, and gave him a kick with their knees, and he fell on his face in the snow and was conscious of nothing more. A few minutes later he came to himself and got on to his feet, but there was no one there. He felt that it was cold on the ground and that he had no overcoat, and began screaming, but it seemed as though his voice could not carry to the end of the square. Overwhelmed with despair and continuing to scream, he ran across the square straight to the sentry-box, besides which stood a constable leaning on his halberd and, so it seemed, looking with curiosity to see who the devil the man was who was screaming and running towards him from the distance. As Akaky Akakyevich reached him, he began breathlessly shouting that he was asleep and not looking after his duty not to see that a man was being robbed. The constable answered that he had seen nothing, that he had only seen him stopped in the middle of the square by two men, and supposed that they were his friends, and that, instead of abusing him for nothing, he had better go the next day to the district officer and that he would find out who had taken the overcoat.

Akaky Akakyevich ran home in a terrible state: his hair, which was still comparatively abundant on his temples and the back of his head, was completely disheveled; his sides and chest and his trousers were all covered with snow. When his old landlady heard a fearful knock at the door she jumped hurriedly out of bed and, with only one slipper on, ran to open it, modestly holding her shift across her bosom; but when she opened it she stepped back, seeing what a state Akaky Akakyevich was in. When he told her what had happened, she clasped her hands in horror and said that he must go straight to the police inspector, that the district officer would deceive him, make promises and lead him a dance; that it would be best of all to go to the inspector, and that she knew him indeed, because Anna, the Finnish girl who was once her cook, was now in service as a nurse at the inspector's; and that she often saw him when he passed by their house, and that he used to be every Sunday at church too, saying his prayers and at the same time looking good-humoredly at every one, and that therefore by every token he must be a kind-hearted man. After listening to this advice, Akaky Akakyevich made his way very gloomily to his room, and how he spent that night I leave to the imagination of those who are in the least able to picture the position of others.

Early in the morning he set off to the police inspector's, but was told that he was asleep. He came at ten o'clock, he was told again that he was asleep; he came at eleven and was told that the inspector was not at home; he came at dinnertime, but the clerks in the ante-room would not let him in, and insisted on knowing what was the matter and what business had brought him and exactly what had happened; so that at last Akaky Akakyevich for the first time in his life tried to show the strength of his character and said curtly that he must see the inspector himself, that they dare not refuse to admit him, that he had come from the department on government business, and that if he made complaint of them they would see. The clerks dared say nothing to this, and one of them went to summon the inspector. The latter received his story of being robbed of his overcoat in an extremely strange way. Instead of attending to the main point, he began asking Akaky Akakyevich questions, why had he been coming home so late? wasn't he going, or hadn't he been, to some house of ill-fame? so that Akaky Akakyevich was over-whelmed with confusion, and went away without knowing whether or not the proper measures would be taken in regard to his overcoat. He was absent from the office all that day (the only time that it had happened in his life).

Next day he appeared with a pale face, wearing his old "dressing jacket" which had become a still more pitiful sight. The tidings of the theft of the overcoat—though there were clerks who did not let even this chance slip of jeering at Akaky Akakyevich—touched many of them. They decided on the spot to get up a subscription for him, but collected only a very trifling sum, because the clerks had already spent a good deal on subscribing to the director's portrait and on the purchase of a book, at the suggestion of the head of their depart-ment, who was a friend of the author, and so the total realized was very insignificant. One of the clerks, moved by compassion, ventured at any rate to assist Akaky Akakyevich with good advice, telling him not to go to the district police inspector, because, though it might happen that the latter might be sufficiently zealous of gaining the approval of his superiors to succeed in finding the overcoat, it would remain in the possession of the police unless he presented legal proofs that it belonged to him; he urged that far the best thing would be to appeal to a Person of Consequence; that the Person of Consequence, by writing and getting into communication with the proper authorities, could push the matter through more successfully. There was nothing else for it. Akaky Akakyevich made up his mind to go to the Person of Consequence. What precisely was the nature of the functions of the Person of Consequence has remained a matter of uncertainty. It must be noted that this Person of Consequence had only lately become a person of consequence, and until recently had been a person of no consequence. Though, indeed, his position even now was not reckoned of consequence in comparison with others of still greater consequence. But there is always to be found a circle of persons to whom a person of little consequence in the eyes of others is a person of consequence. It is true that he did his utmost to increase the consequence of his position in various ways, for instance by insisting that his subordinates should come out onto the stairs to meet him when he arrived at his office; that no one should venture to approach him directly but all proceedings should be by the strictest order of precedence, that a collegiate registration clerk should report the matter to the provincial secretary, and the provincial secretary to the titular councilor or whomsoever it might be, and that business should only reach him by this channel. Every one in Holy Russia has a craze for imitation, every one apes and mimics his superiors. I have actually been told that a titular councilor who was put in charge of a small private office, immediately partitioned off a special room for himself, calling it the head office, and set special porters at the door with red collars and gold lace, who took hold of the handle of the door and opened it for every one who went in, though the "head office" was so tiny that it was with difficulty that an ordinary writing table could be put into it.

The manners and habits of the Person of Consequence were dignified and majestic, but not complex. The chief foundation of his system was strictness, "strictness, strictness, and—strictness!" he used to say, and at the last word he would look very significantly at the person he was addressing, though, indeed, he had no reason to do so, for the dozen clerks who made up the whole administrative mechanism of his office stood in befitting awe of him; any clerk who saw him in the distance would leave his work and remain standing at attention till his superior had left the room. His conversation with his subordinates was usually marked by severity and almost confined to three phrases: "How dare you? Do you know to whom you are speaking? Do you understand who I am?" He was, however, at heart a good-natured man, pleasant and obliging with his colleagues; but the grade of general had completely turned his head. When he received it, he was perplexed, thrown off his balance, and quite at a loss how to behave. If he chanced to be with his equals, he was still quite a decent man, a very gentlemanly man, in fact, and in many ways even an intelligent man, but as soon as he was in company with men who were even one grade below him, there was simply no doing anything with him: he sat silent and his position excited compassion, the more so as he himself felt that he might have been spending his time to incomparably greater advantage. At times there could be seen in his eyes an intense desire to join in some interesting conversation, but he was restrained by the doubt whether it would not be too much on his part, whether it would not be too great a familiarity and lowering of his dignity, and in consequence of these reflections he remained everlastingly in the same mute condition, only uttering from time to time monosyllabic sounds, and in this way he gained the reputation of being a very tiresome man.

So this was the Person of Consequence to whom our friend Akaky Akakyevich appealed, and he appealed to him at a most unpropitious moment, very unfortunate for himself, though fortunate, indeed, for the Person of Consequence. The latter happened to be in his study, talking in the very best of spirits with an old friend of his childhood who had only just arrived and whom he had not seen for several years. It was at this moment that he was informed that a man called Bashmachkin was asking to see him. He asked abruptly, "What sort of man is he?" and received the answer, "A government clerk." "Ah! he can wait, I haven't time now," said the Person of Consequence. Here I must observe that this was a complete lie on the part of the Person of Consequence: he had time; his friend and he had long ago said all they had to say to each other and their conversation had begun to be broken by very long pauses during which they merely slapped each other on the knee, saying, "So that's how things are, Ivan Abramovich!"—"There it is, Stepan

Varlamovich!" but, for all that, he told the clerk to wait in order to show his friend, who had left the service years before and was living at home in the country, how long clerks had to wait in his ante-room.

At last after they had talked, or rather been silent to their heart's content and had smoked a cigar in very comfortable armchairs with sloping backs, he seemed suddenly to recollect, and said to the secretary, who was standing at the door with papers for his signature: "Oh, by the way, there is a clerk waiting, isn't there? Tell him he can come in." When he saw Akaky Akakyevich's meek appearance and old uniform, he turned to him at once and said, "What do you want?" in a firm and abrupt voice, which he had purposely practiced in his own room in solitude before the looking-glass for a week before receiving his present post and the grade of a general. Akaky Akakyevich, who was overwhelmed with befitting awe beforehand, was somewhat confused and, as far as his tongue would allow him, explained to the best of his powers, with even more frequent "ers" than usual, that he had had a perfectly new overcoat and now he had been robbed of it in the most inhuman way, and that now he had come to beg him by his intervention to correspond either with his honor the head policemaster or anybody else, and find the overcoat. This mode of proceeding struck the general for some reason as taking a great liberty. "What next, sir?" he went on as abruptly. "Don't you know the way to proceed? To whom are you addressing yourself? Don't you know how things are done? You ought first to have handed in a petition to the office; it would have gone to the head clerk of the room, and to the head clerk of the section, then it would have been handed to the secretary and the secretary would have brought it to me . . ."

"But, your Excellency," said Akaky Akakyevich, trying to collect all the small allowance of presence of mind he possessed and feeling at the same time that he was getting into a terrible perspiration, "I ventured, your Excellency, to trouble you because secretaries . . . er . . . are people you can't depend on. . . ."

"What? what? what?" said the Person of Consequence. "Where did you get hold of that spirit? Where did you pick up such ideas? What insubordination is spreading among young men against their superiors and betters." The Person of Consequence did not apparently observe that Akaky Akakyevich was well over fifty, and therefore if he could have been called a young man it would only have been in comparison with a man of seventy. "Do who know to whom you are speaking? do you understand who I am? do you understand that, I ask you?" At this point he stamped, and raised his voice to such a powerful note that Akaky Akakyevich was not the only one to be terrified. Akaky Akakyevich was positively petrified; he staggered, trembling all over, and could not stand; if the porters had not run up to support him, he would have flopped upon the floor; he was led out almost unconscious. The Person of Consequence, pleased that the effect had surpassed his expectations and enchanted at the idea that his words could even deprive a man of consciousness, stole a sideways glance at his friend to see how he was taking it, and perceived not without satisfaction that his friend was feeling very uncertain and even beginning to be a little terrified himself.

How he got downstairs, how he went out into the street—of all that Akaky Akakyevich remembered nothing, he had no feeling in his arms or his legs. In all his life he had never been so severely reprimanded by a general, and this was by one of another department, too. He went out into the snowstorm, that was whistling through the streets, with his mouth open, and as he went he stumbled off the sidewalk; the wind, as its way is in Petersburg, blew upon him from all points of the compass and from every side street. In an instant it had blown a quinsy into his throat, and when he got home he was not able to utter a word; with a swollen face and throat he went to bed. So violent is sometimes the effect of a suitable reprimand!

Next day he was in a high fever. Thanks to the gracious assistance of the Petersburg climate, the disease made more rapid progress than could have been expected, and when the doctor came, after feeling his pulse he could find nothing to do but prescribe a fomentation, and that simply that the patient might not be left without the benefit of medical assistance; however, two days later he informed him that his end was at hand, after which he turned to his landlady and said: "And you had better lose no time, my good woman, but order him now a deal coffin, for an oak one will be too dear for him."

Whether Akaky Akakyevich heard these fateful words or not, whether they produced a shattering effect upon him, and whether he regretted his pitiful life, no one can tell, for he was all the time in delirium and fever. Apparitions, each stranger than the one before, were continually haunting him: first, he saw Petrovich and was ordering him to make a greatcoat trimmed with some sort of traps for robbers, who were, he fancied, continually under the bed, and he was calling his landlady every minute to pull out a thief who had even got under the quilt; then he kept asking why his old "dressing jacket" was hanging before him when he had a new overcoat, then he fancied he was standing before the general listening to the appropriate reprimand and saying, "I am sorry, your Excellency," then finally he became abusive, uttering the most awful language, so that his old landlady positively crossed herself, having never heard anything of the kind from him before, and the more horrified because these dreadful words followed immediately upon the phrase "your Excellency." Later on, his talk was a mere medley of nonsense, so that it was quite unintelligible; all that could be seen was that his incoherent words and thoughts were concerned with nothing but the overcoat. At last poor Akaky Akakyevich gave up the ghost.

No seal was put upon his room nor upon his things, because, in the first place, he had no heirs and, in the second, the property left was very small, to wit, a bundle of goose-feathers, a quire of white government paper, three pairs of socks, two or three buttons that had come off his trousers, and the "dressing jacket" with which the reader is already familiar. Who came into all this wealth God only knows, even I who tell the tale must own that I have not troubled to inquire. And Petersburg remained without Akaky Akakyevich, as though, indeed, he had never been in the city. A creature had vanished and departed whose cause no one had championed, who was dear to no one, of interest to no one, who never even attracted the attention of the student of natural history, though the latter does not disdain to fix a common fly upon a pin and look at him under the microscope—a creature who bore patiently the jeers of the office and for no particular reason went to his grave, though even he at the very end of his life was visited by a gleam of brightness in the form of an overcoat that for one instant brought color into his poor life—a creature on whom calamity broke as insufferably as it breaks upon the heads of the mighty ones of this world . . . !

Several days after his death, the porter from the department was sent to his lodgings with instructions that he should go at once to the office, for his chief was asking for him; but the porter was obliged to return without him, explaining that he could not come, and on the inquiry "Why?" he added, "Well, you see, the fact is he is dead, he was buried three days ago." This was how they learned at the office of the death of Akaky Akakyevich, and the next day there was sitting in his seat a new clerk who was very much taller and who wrote not in the same upright hand but made his letters more slanting and crooked.

But who could have imagined that this was not all there was to tell about Akaky Akakyevich, that he was destined for a few days to make a noise in the world after his death, as though to make up for his life having been unnoticed by anyone? But so it happened, and our poor story unexpectedly finishes with a fantastic ending. Rumors were suddenly floating about Petersburg that in the neighborhood of the Kalinkin Bridge and for a little distance beyond, a corpse had taken to appearing at night in the form of a clerk looking for a stolen overcoat, and stripping from the shoulders of all passersby, regardless of grade and calling, overcoats of all descriptions—trimmed with cat fur, or beaver or wadded, lined with raccoon, fox and bear—made, in fact, of all sorts of skin which men have adapted for the covering of their own. One of the clerks of the department saw the corpse with his own eyes and at once recognized it as Akaky Akakyevich; but it excited in him such terror, however, that he ran away as fast as his legs could carry him and so could not get a very clear view of him, and only saw him hold up his finger threateningly in the distance.

From all sides complaints were continually coming that backs and shoulders, not of mere titular councilors, but even of upper aulic councilors, had been exposed to chills, owing to being stripped of their greatcoats. Orders were given to the police to catch the corpse regardless of trouble or expense, alive or dead, and to punish him in the cruelest way, as an example to others, and, indeed, they very nearly succeeded in doing so. The constable of one district police station in Kiryushkin Lane grabbed a corpse by the collar on the spot of the crime in the very act of attempting to snatch a frieze overcoat from a retired musician, who used in his day to play the flute. Having caught him by the collar, he shouted until he had brought two other comrades, whom he charged to hold him while he felt just a minute in his boot to get out a snuffbox in order to revive his nose which had six times in his life been frostbitten, but the snuff was probably so strong that not even a dead man could stand it. The constable had hardly had time to put his finger over his right nostril and draw up some snuff in the left when the corpse sneezed violently right into the eyes of all three. While they were putting their fists up to wipe them, the corpse completely vanished, so that they were not even sure whether he had actually been in their hands. From that time forward, the constables conceived such a horror of the dead that they were even afraid to seize the living and confined themselves to shouting from the distance, "Hi, you there, be off!" and the dead clerk began to appear even on the other side of the Kalinkin Bridge, rousing no little terror in all timid people.

We have, however, quite deserted the Person of Consequence, who may in reality almost be said to be the cause of the fantastic ending of this perfectly true story. To begin with, my duty requires me to do justice to the Person of Consequence by recording that soon after poor Akaky Akakyevich had gone away crushed to powder, he felt something not unlike regret. Sympathy was a feeling not unknown to him; his heart was open to many kindly impulses, although his exalted grade very often prevented them from being shown. As soon as his friend had gone out of his study, he even began brooding over poor Akaky Akakyevich, and from that time forward, he was almost every day haunted by the image of the poor clerk who had succumbed so completely to the befitting reprimand. The thought of the man so worried him that a week later he actually decided to send a clerk to find out how he was and whether he really could help him in any way. And when they brought him word that Akaky Akakyevich had died suddenly in delirium and fever, it made a great impression on him, his conscience reproached him and he was depressed all day. Anxious to distract his mind and to forget the unpleasant impression, he went to spend the evening with one of his friends, where he found a genteel company and, what was best of all, almost everyone was of the same grade so that he was able to be quite free from restraint. This had a wonderful effect on his spirits, he expanded, became affable and genial—in short, spent a very agreeable evening. At supper he drank a couple of glasses of champagne—a proceeding which we all know has a happy effect in inducing good-humor. The champagne made him inclined to do something unusual, and he decided not to go home yet but to visit a lady of his acquaintance, one Karolina

Ivanovna—a lady apparently of German extraction, for whom he entertained extremely friendly feelings.

It must be noted that the Person of Consequence was a man no longer young, an excellent husband, and the respectable father of a family. He had two sons, one already serving in his office, and a nice-looking daughter of sixteen with a rather turned-up, pretty little nose, who used to come every morning to kiss his hand, saying: *"Bonjour, Papa."* His wife, who was still blooming and decidedly good-looking, indeed, used first to give him her hand to kiss and then would kiss his hand, turning it the other side upward. But though the Person of Consequence was perfectly satisfied with the kind amenities of his domestic life, he thought it proper to have a lady friend in another quarter of the town. This lady friend was not a bit better-looking nor younger than his wife, but these mysterious facts exist in the world and it is not our business to criticize them.

And so the Person of Consequence went downstairs, got into his sledge, and said to his coachman, "To Karolina Ivanovna," while luxuriously wrapped in his warm fur coat he remained in that agreeable frame of mind sweeter to a Russian than anything that could be invented, that is, when one thinks of nothing while thoughts come into the mind of themselves, one pleasanter than the other, without the labor of following them or looking for them. Full of satisfaction, he recalled all the amusing moments of the evening he had spent, all the phrases that had set the little circle laughing; many of them he repeated in an undertone and found them as amusing as before, and so, very naturally, laughed very heartily at them again. From time to time, however, he was disturbed by a gust of wind which, blowing suddenly, God knows whence and wherefore, cut him in the face, pelting him with flakes of snow, puffing out his coat-collar like a sack, or suddenly flinging it with unnatural force over his head and giving him endless trouble to extricate himself from it. All at once, the Person of Consequence felt that someone had clutched him very tightly by the collar. Turning round he saw a short man in a shabby old uniform, and not without horror recognized him as Akaky Akakyevich. The clerk's face was white as snow and looked like that of a corpse, but the horror of the Person of Consequence was beyond all bounds when he saw the mouth of the corpse distorted into speech and, breathing upon him the chill of the grave, it uttered the following words: "Ah, so here you are at last! At last I've . . . er . . . caught you by the collar. It's your overcoat I want, you refused to help me and abused me into the bargain! So now give me yours!"

The poor Person of Consequence very nearly died. Resolute and determined as he was in his office and before subordinates in general, and though anyone looking at his manly air and figure would have said, "Oh, what a man of character!", yet in this plight he felt, like very many persons of athletic appearance, such terror that not without reason he began to be afraid he would have some sort of fit. He actually flung his overcoat off his shoulders as fast as he could and shouted to his coachman in a voice unlike his own: "Drive home and make haste!" The coachman, hearing the tone which he had only heard in critical moments and then accompanied by something even more rousing, hunched his shoulders up to his ears in case of worse following, swung his whip and flew on like an arrow. In a little over six minutes the Person of Consequence was at the entrance of his own house. Pale, panic-stricken, and without his overcoat, he arrived home instead of at Karolina Ivanovna's, dragged himself to his own room and spent the night in great perturbation, so that next morning his daughter said to him at breakfast, "You look quite pale today, Papa." But her papa remained mute and said not a word to any one of what had happened to him, where he had been, and where he had been going. The incident made a great impression upon him. Indeed, it happened far more rarely that he said to his subordinates, "How dare you? Do you understand who I am?" and he never uttered those words at all until he had first heard all the rights of the case.

What was even more remarkable is that from that time the apparition of the dead clerk ceased entirely: apparently the general's overcoat had fitted him perfectly, anyway nothing more was heard of overcoats being snatched from any one. Many restless and anxious people refused, however, to be pacified, and still maintained that in remote parts of the town the ghost of the dead clerk went on appearing. One constable in Kolomna, for instance, saw with his own eyes a ghost appear from behind a house; but, being by natural constitution somewhat feeble—so much so that on one occasion an ordinary, well-grown pig, making a sudden dash out of some building, knocked him off his feet to the vast entertainment of the cabmen standing round, from whom he exacted two copecks each for such rudeness—he did not dare to stop it, and so followed it in the dark until the ghost suddenly looked round and, stopping, asked him: "What do you want?" displaying a fist such as you never see among the living. The constable said, "Nothing," and turned back on the spot. This ghost, however, was considerably taller and adorned with immense mustaches, and, directing its steps apparently towards Obuhov Bridge, vanished into the darkness of the night.

1842

# Ivan Turgenev . . . 1818–1883

THE SCION of wealthy gentlefolk, Turgenev spent his childhood on the family estate in the province of Orel, and in Moscow. There he received his early education and attended the university, later studying philosophy in Berlin. He had been taken to visit western Europe even as a boy, and the man was to make it his second home. He began scribbling early, and at twenty-five broke into print with a narrative poem. The same year, 1843, in Petersburg, he met Pauline Viardot, the singer, to whom he was to offer a lifetime's devotion and for the sake of whom he was often thereafter to stay abroad. He was in France from 1847 to 1850, the most fertile period of his literary career, in the course of which he wrote several plays, as well as most of the pieces that go to make up *A Sportsman's Sketches.*

An overly eulogistic obituary of Gogol, who died early in 1852, earned Turgenev a short stay in prison, during which he wrote the story, "Moomoo." His incarceration was followed by a period of confinement to his own estate. He was still there when, in the summer of 1852, *A Sportsman's Sketches* appeared in book form. "The Singers" and "The Tryst," offered below, are taken from this collection. "Living Relics," written years later, was first published in 1874 in a miscellany sold for the benefit of the victims of the Samara famine and reprinted in an augmented edition of *A Sportsman's Sketches.*

The success of the *Sketches* encouraged him to go on writing. He produced a series of novels, the most notable of which are *Fathers and Children* and *Virgin Soil.* He also maintained his interest in shorter narratives, composing dozens of novellas and tales, some of which, like "A Lear of the Steppes" and "Old Portraits," are reminiscential in character. The year before his death—he died in France, with Mme. Viardot and her children about him—he published a sheaf of what he called "an old man's jottings," under the title, *Poems in Prose.*

# THE SINGERS

THE small village of Kolotovka once belonged to a lady known in the neighborhood by the nickname of Filly, in allusion to her pertness and mettlesomeness (her real name is lost in oblivion), but has of late years been the property of a German from Petersburg. The village lies on the slope of a barren hill, which is cut in half from top to bottom by a tremendous ravine. It is a yawning chasm, with shelving sides hollowed out by the action of rain and snow, and it winds along the very centre of the village street; it separates the two sides of the unlucky hamlet far more than a river would do, for a river could, at least, be crossed by a bridge. A few gaunt willows creep timorously down its sandy sides; at the very bottom, which is dry and yellow as copper, lie huge slabs of argillaceous rock. A cheerless position, there's no denying, yet all the surrounding inhabitants know the road to Kolotovka well; they go there often, and are always glad to go.

At the very summit of the ravine, a few paces from the point where it starts as a narrow fissure in the earth, there stands a small square hut. It stands alone, apart from all the others. It is thatched, and has a chimney; one window keeps watch like a sharp eye over the ravine, and on winter evenings when it is lighted from within, it is seen far away in the dim frosty fog, and its twinkling light is the guiding star of many a peasant on his road. A blue board is nailed up above the door; this hut is a tavern, called "The Cheerful Nook." Spirits are sold here probably no cheaper than the usual price, but it is far more frequented than any other establishment of the same sort in the neighborhood. The explanation of this is to be found in the tavern-keeper, Nikolay Ivanych.

Nikolay Ivanych—once a slender, curly-headed and rosy-cheeked young fellow, now an excessively stout, grizzled man with a fat face, sly and good-natured little eyes, and a shiny forehead, with wrinkles like lines drawn all over it—has lived for more than twenty years in Kolotovka. Nikolay Ivanych is a shrewd, acute fellow, like the majority of tavern-keepers. Though he makes no conspicuous effort to please or to talk to people, he has the art of attracting and keeping customers, who find it particularly pleasant to sit at his bar under the placid and genial, though alert, eye of the phlegmatic host. He has a great deal of common sense; he thoroughly understands the landowner's conditions of life, the peasant's, and the tradesman's. He could give sensible advice on difficult points, but, like a cautious man and an egoist, prefers to stand aloof, and at most—and that only in the case of his favorite customers—by remote hints, dropped, as it were, unintentionally, to lead them into the true way. He is an authority on everything that is of interest or importance to a Russian: on horses and cattle, on timber, bricks, and crockery, on woolen stuffs and on leather, on songs and dances. When he has no customers he is usually sitting like a sack on the ground before the door of his hut, his thin legs tucked under him, exchanging a friendly greeting with every passer-by. He has seen a great deal in his time; many a score of petty landowners, who used to come to him for spirits, he has seen pass away before him; he knows everything that is done for eighty miles round, and never gossips, never gives a sign of knowing what is unsuspected by the most keen-sighted police-officer. He keeps his own counsel, laughs, and makes his glasses ring. His neighbors respect him; the civilian general Shcherepetenko, the landowner highest in rank in the district, gives him a condescending nod whenever he drives past his little house. Nikolay Ivanych is a man of influence; he made a notorious horse-thief return a horse he had taken from the stable of one of his friends; he brought the peasants of a neighboring village to their senses when they refused to accept a new overseer, and so on. It must not be imagined, though, that he does this from love of justice, from devotion to his neighbor—no! he simply tries to prevent anything that might, in any way, interfere with his ease and comfort.

Nikolay Ivanych is married, and has children. His wife, a smart, sharp-nosed and keen-eyed woman of the tradesman class, has grown somewhat stout of late years, like her husband. He relies on her in everything, and she keeps the key of the cash-box. Drunken brawlers are afraid of her; she does not like them; they bring little profit and make a great deal of noise: those who are taciturn and surly in their cups are more to her taste. Nikolay Ivanych's children are still small; the first four all died, but those that are left take after their parents: it is a pleasure to look at their intelligent, healthy little faces.

It was an insufferably hot day in July when, slowly dragging my feet along, I went up alongside the Kolotovka ravine with my dog towards the Cheerful Nook. The sun blazed, as it were, fiercely in the sky, baking the parched earth relentlessly; the air was thick with stifling dust. Glossy crows and ravens with gaping beaks looked plaintively at the passers-by, as though asking for sympathy; only the sparrows did not droop, but, pluming their feathers, twittered more vigorously than ever as they quarreled among the hedges, or flew up all together from the dusty road, and hovered in gray clouds over the green hemp fields. I was tormented by thirst. There was no water near: in Kolotovka, as in many other villages of the steppes, the peasants, having no spring or well, drink a sort of thin mud out of the pond. . . . For no one could call that repulsive beverage water. I wanted to ask for a glass of beer or kvas at Nikolay Ivanych's.

It must be confessed that at no time of the year does Kolotovka present a very cheering spectacle; but it has a particularly depressing effect when the relentless rays of a dazzling July sun pour down full upon the brown, tumble-down roofs of the houses and the deep ravine, and the parched, dusty common over which the thin, long-legged hens are straying hopelessly, and the remains of the old manor-house, now a hollow, gray framework of aspenwood, with holes instead of windows, overgrown with nettles, wormwood, and rank grass, and the pond black, as though charred, and covered with goose feathers, with its edge of half-dried mud, and its broken-down dike, near which, on the finely trodden, ash-like earth, sheep, breathless and gasping with the heat, huddle dejectedly together, their heads drooping with weary patience, as though waiting for this insufferable heat to pass at last. With weary steps I drew near Nikolay Ivanych's dwelling, arousing in the village children the usual wonder manifested in a concentrated, meaningless stare, and in the dogs an indignation expressed in such hoarse and furious barking that it seemed as if it were tearing their very entrails and left them breathless and choking, when suddenly in the tavern doorway there appeared a tall peasant without a cap, in a frieze cloak, girt about below his waist with a blue handkerchief. He looked like a house-serf; thick gray hair stood up in disorder above his withered and wrinkled face. He was calling to someone hurriedly, waving his arms, which obviously were not quite under his control. It could be seen that he had been drinking already.

"Come, come along!" he stammered, raising his shaggy eyebrows with an effort. "Come, Blinkard, come along! Ah, brother, how you creep along, 'pon my word! It's too bad, brother. They're waiting for you within, and here you crawl along. . . . Come."

"Well, I'm coming, I'm coming!" called a jarring voice, and from behind a hut a little, short, fat, lame man came into sight. He wore a rather tidy cloth coat, pulled half on, and a high pointed cap right over his brows, which gave his round plump face a sly and comic expression. His little yellow eyes moved restlessly about, his thin lips wore a continual forced smile, while his sharp, long nose peered forward saucily in front like a rudder. "I'm coming, my dear fellow." He went hobbling towards the tavern. "What are you calling me for? . . . Who's waiting for me?"

"What am I calling you for?" repeated the man in the frieze coat reproachfully. "You're a queer fish, Blinkard: we call you to come to the tavern, and you ask what for? Here are honest folks all waiting for you: Yashka the Turk, and the Wild Master, and the contractor from Zhizdry. Yashka's got a bet on with the contractor: the stake's a pot of beer—for the one that does best, sings the best, I mean . . . do you see?"

"Is Yashka going to sing?" said the man addressed as Blinkard, with lively interest. "But isn't it your humbug, Gabbler?"

"I'm not humbugging," answered the Gabbler, with dignity, "it's you are crazy. I should think he would sing since he's got a bet on it, you precious innocent, you noodle, Blinkard!"

"Well, come in, simpleton!" retorted the Blinkard.

"Then give us a kiss at least, lovey," stammered the Gabbler, opening wide his arms.

"Get out, you great softy!" responded the Blinkard contemptuously, giving him a poke with his elbow, and both, stooping, entered the low doorway.

The conversation I had overheard roused my curiosity exceedingly. More than once rumors had reached me of Yashka the Turk as the best singer in the vicinity, and here was an opportunity all at once of hearing him in competition with another master of the art. I quickened my steps and went into the house.

Few of my readers have probably had an opportunity of getting a good view of any village taverns, but we sportsmen go everywhere. They are constructed on an exceedingly simple plan. They usually consist of a dark entry, and an inner room with a chimney, divided in two by a partition, behind which none of the customers have a right to go. In this partition there is a wide opening cut above a broad oak table. At this table or bar the spirits are served. Sealed up bottles of various sizes stand on the shelves, right opposite the opening. In the front part of the room, devoted to customers, there are benches, two or three empty barrels, and a corner table. Village taverns are for the most part rather dark, and you hardly ever see on their wainscoted walls any of the glaring cheap prints which few huts are without.

When I went into the Cheerful Nook, a fairly large party were already assembled there.

In his usual place behind the bar, almost filling up the entire opening in the partition, stood Nikolay Ivanych in a striped print shirt; with a lazy smile on his full face, he poured out with his plump white hand two glasses of spirits for the Blinkard and the Gabbler as they came in; behind him, in a corner near the window, could be seen his sharp-eyed wife. In the middle of the room was standing Yashka the Turk, a thin, graceful fellow of three-and-twenty, dressed in a long skirted coat of blue nankin. He looked a smart factory hand, and could not, to judge by his appearance, boast of very good health. His hollow cheeks, his large, restless gray eyes, his straight nose, with its delicate mobile nostrils, his pale brown curls brushed back over the sloping white brow, his full but beautiful, expressive lips, and his whole face betrayed a passionate and sensitive nature. He was in a state of great excitement; he blinked, his breathing was hurried, his hands shook, as though in fever, and he was really in a fever—that sudden fever of excitement which is so well-known to all who have to speak and sing before an audience. Near him stood a man of about forty, with broad shoulders and broad jaws, with a low forehead, narrow Tartar eyes, a short flat nose, a square chin, and shining black hair coarse as bristles. The expression of his face—a swarthy face, with a sort of leaden hue in it—and especially of his pale lips, might almost have been called savage, if it had not been so still and dreamy. He hardly stirred a muscle; he only looked slowly about him like a bull under the yoke. He was dressed in a sort of surtout, not overnew, with smooth brass buttons; an old black silk handkerchief was twisted round his immense neck. He was called the Wild Master. Right opposite him, on a bench under the holy pictures, was sitting Yashka's rival, the contractor from Zhizdry; he was a short, stoutly-built man about thirty, pockmarked, and curly-headed, with a blunt, turn-up nose, lively brown eyes, and a scanty beard. He looked keenly about him, and, sitting with his hands under him, he kept carelessly swinging his legs and tapping with his feet, which were encased in stylish top-boots with a colored edging. He wore a new thin coat of gray cloth, with a plush collar, in sharp contrast with the crimson shirt below, buttoned close across the chest. In the opposite corner, to the right of the door, a peasant sat at the table in a narrow, shabby coat, with a huge rent on the shoulder. The sunlight fell in a narrow, yellowish streak through the dusty panes of the two small windows, but it seemed as if it struggled in vain with the habitual darkness of the room; all the objects in it were dimly, as it were, patchily lighted up. On the other hand, it was almost cool in the room, and the sense of stifling heat dropped off me like a weary load directly I crossed the threshold.

My entrance, I could see, was at first somewhat disconcerting to Nikolay Ivanych's customers; but observing that he greeted me as a friend, they were reassured, and took no more notice of me. I asked for some beer and sat down in the corner, near the peasant in the ragged smock.

"Well, well," piped the Gabbler, suddenly draining a glass of spirits at one gulp, and accompanying his exclamation with the strange gesticulations, without which he seemed unable to utter a single word; "what are we waiting for? If we're going to begin, then begin. Hey, Yasha?"

"Begin, begin," chimed in Nikolay Ivanych approvingly.

"Let's begin, by all means," observed the contractor coolly, with a self-confident smile; "I'm ready."

"And I'm ready," Yakov pronounced in a voice thrilled with excitement.

"Well, begin, lads," whined the Blinkard. But, in spite of the unanimously expressed desire, neither began; the contractor did not even get up from the bench—they all seemed to be waiting for something.

"Begin!" said the Wild Master sharply and sullenly. Yashka started. The contractor pulled down his girdle and cleared his throat.

"But who's to begin?" he inquired in a slightly changed voice of the Wild Master, who still stood motionless in the middle of the room, his stalwart legs wide apart and his powerful arms thrust up to the elbow into his breeches pockets.

"You, you, contractor," stammered the Gabbler; "you, to be sure, brother."

The Wild Master looked at him from under his brows. The Gabbler gave a faint squeak, in confusion looked away at the ceiling, twitched his shoulder, and said no more.

"Cast lots," the Wild Master pronounced emphatically; "and the pot on the table."

Nikolay Ivanych bent down, and with a gasp picked up the pot of beer from the floor and set it on the table.

The Wild Master glanced at Yakov, and said "Come!"

Yakov fumbled in his pockets, took out a groat, and marked it with his teeth. The contractor pulled from under the skirts of his long coat a new leather purse, deliberately untied the string, and shaking out a quantity of small change into his hand, picked out a new groat. The Gabbler held out his dirty cap, with its broken peak hanging loose; Yakov dropped his groat in, and the contractor his.

"You must pick out one," said the Wild Master, turning to the Blinkard.

The Blinkard smiled complacently, took the cap in both hands, and began shaking it.

For an instant a profound silence reigned; the coins clinked faintly, jingling against each other. I looked round attentively; every face wore an expression of intense expectation; the Wild Master himself showed signs of uneasiness; my neighbor, even, the peasant in the tattered smock, craned his neck inquisitively. The Blinkard put his hand into the cap and took out the contractor's groat; everyone drew a long breath. Yakov flushed, and the contractor passed his hand over his hair.

"There, I said you'd begin," cried the Gabbler; "didn't I say so?"

"There, there, don't cluck," remarked the Wild Master contemptuously. "Begin," he went on, with a nod to the contractor.

"What song am I to sing?" asked the contractor, beginning to be nervous.

"What you choose," answered the Blinkard; "sing what you think best."

"What you choose, to be sure," Nikolay Ivanych chimed in, slowly smoothing his hand on his breast, "you're quite at liberty about that. Sing what you like; only sing well; and we'll give a fair decision afterwards."

"A fair decision, of course," put in the Gabbler, licking the edge of his empty glass.

"Let me clear my throat a bit, mates," said the contractor, fingering the collar of his coat.

"Come, come, no nonsense—begin!" protested the Wild Master, and he looked down.

The contractor thought a minute, shook his head, and stepped forward.

Yakov's eyes were riveted upon him.

But before I enter upon a description of the contest itself, I think it will not be amiss to say a few words about each of the personages taking part in my story. The lives of some of them were known to me already when I met them in the Cheerful Nook; I collected some facts about the others later on.

Let us begin with the Gabbler. This man's real name was Yevgraf Ivanovich; but no one in the whole neighborhood knew him as anything but the Gabbler, and he himself referred to himself by that nickname: so well did it fit him. Indeed, nothing could have been more appropriate to his insignificant, ever-restless features. He was a dissipated, unmarried house-serf, whose own masters had long ago got rid of him, and who, without any employment, without earning a groat, found means to get drunk every day at other people's expense. He had a great number of acquaintances who treated him to drinks of spirits and tea, though they could not have said why they did so themselves; for, far from being entertaining in company, he bored every one with his meaningless chatter, his insufferable familiarity, his spasmodic gestures and incessant, unnatural laugh. He could neither sing nor dance; he had never said a clever, or even a sensible thing in his life; he chattered away, telling lies about everything—a regular Gabbler! And yet not a single drinking party for thirty miles around took place without his lank figure turning up among the guests; so that they were used to him by now, and put up with his presence as a necessary evil. They all, it is true, treated him with contempt; but the Wild Master was the only one who knew how to keep his foolish sallies in check.

The Blinkard was not in the least like the Gabbler. His nickname, too, suited him, though he was no more given to blinking than other people; it is a well-known fact, that the Russian peasants have a talent for finding good nicknames. In spite of my endeavors to get more detailed information about this man's past, many passages in his life have remained spots of darkness to me, and probably to many other people, episodes buried, as the bookmen say, in the darkness of oblivion. I could only find out that he was once a coachman in the service of an old childless lady; that he had run away with three horses he was in charge of; had been lost for a whole year, and no doubt, convinced by experience of the drawbacks and hardships of a wandering life, he had gone back, a cripple, and flung himself at his mistress's feet. He succeeded in a few years in smoothing over his offense by his exemplary conduct, and, gradually getting higher in her favor, at last gained her complete confidence, was made a bailiff, and on his mistress's death, turned out—in what way was never known—to have received his freedom. He got admitted into the class of tradesmen; rented patches of market garden from the neighbors; grew rich, and now was living in ease and comfort. He was a man of experience, who knew on which side his bread was buttered; was more actuated by prudence than by either good or ill nature; had knocked about, understood men, and knew how to turn them to his own advantage. He was cautious, and at the same time enterprising, like a fox; though he was as fond of gossip as an old woman, he never let out his own affairs, while he made everyone else talk freely of theirs. He did not affect to be a simpleton though, as so many crafty men of his sort do; indeed it would have been difficult for him to take any one in, in that way; I have never seen a sharper, keener pair of eyes than his tiny cunning little "peepers," as they call them in Orel. They were never simply looking about; they were always looking one up and down and through and through. The Blinkard would sometimes ponder for weeks together over some apparently simple undertaking, and again he would suddenly decide on a desperately bold line of action, which one would fancy would bring him to ruin. . . . But it would be sure to turn out all right; everything would go smoothly. He was lucky, and believed in his own luck, and believed in omens. He was exceedingly superstitious in general. He was not liked, because he would have nothing much to do with anyone, but he was respected. His whole family consisted of one little son, whom he idolized, and who, brought up by such a father, is likely to get on in the world. "Little Blinkard'll be his father over again," is said of him already, in undertones by the old men, as they sit on their mud walls gossiping on summer evenings, and every one knows what that means; there is no need to say more.

As to Yashka the Turk and the contractor, there is no need to say much about them. Yakov, called the Turk because he actually was descended from a Turkish woman, a prisoner of war, was by nature an artist in every sense of the word, and by calling, a ladler in a paper factory belonging to a merchant. As for the contractor, his career, I must own, I know nothing of; he struck me as being a smart towns-man of the tradesman class, ready to turn his hand to anything. But the Wild Master calls for a more detailed account.

The first impression the sight of this man produced on you was a sense of coarse, heavy, irresistible power. He was clumsily built, "knocked together," as they say among us, but there was an air of triumphant vigor about him, and—strange to say—his bearlike figure was not without a certain grace of its own, proceeding, perhaps, from his absolutely placid confidence in his own strength. It was hard to decide at first to what class this Hercules belonged: he did not look like a house-serf, nor a tradesman, nor an impoverished clerk out of work, nor a small ruined landowner, such as takes to being a hunts-man or a fighting man; he was, in fact, quite individual. No one knew where he came from or what brought him into our district; it was said that he came of free peasant-proprietor stock, and had once been in the government service somewhere, but nothing positive was known about this; and indeed there was no one from whom one could learn—certainly not from him; he was the most silent and morose of men. So much so that no one knew for certain what he lived on; he followed no trade, visited no one, associated with scarcely anyone; yet he had money to spend; little enough, it is true, still he had some. In his behavior he was not exactly retiring—retiring was not a word that could be applied to him: he lived as though he noticed no one about him, and cared for no one. The Wild Master (that was the nickname they had given him; his real name was Perevlesov) enjoyed an immense influence in the whole district; he was obeyed with eager promptitude, though he had no kind of right to give orders to anyone, and did not himself evince the slightest pretension to authority over the people with whom he came into casual contact. He spoke—they obeyed: strength always has an influence of its own. He scarcely drank at all, had nothing to do with women, and was passionately fond of singing. There was much that was mysterious about this man; it seemed as though vast forces sullenly reposed within him, knowing, as it were, that once roused, once bursting free, they were bound to crush him and everything they came in contact with; and I am greatly mistaken if, in this man's life, there had not been some such outbreak; if it was not owing to the lessons of experience, to a narrow escape from ruin, that he now kept himself so tightly in hand. What especially struck me in him was the combination of a sort of inborn natural ferocity with an equally inborn generosity—a combination I have never met in any other man.

And so the contractor stepped forward, and, half shutting his eyes, began singing in high falsetto. He had a fairly sweet and pleasant voice, though rather hoarse: he played with his voice like a woodlark, twisting and turning it in incessant roulades and trills up and down the scale, continually returning to the highest notes, which he held and prolonged with special care. Then he would break off, and again suddenly take up the first motive with a sort of go-ahead daring. His modulations were at times rather bold, at times rather comical; they would have given a connoisseur great satisfaction, and have made a German furiously indignant. He was a Russian *tenore di grazia, ténor léger*. He sang a song to a lively dance-tune, the words of which, all that I could catch through the endless maze of variations, ejaculations and repetitions, were as follows:

> A tiny patch of land, young lass,
>     I'll plow for thee,
> And tiny crimson flowers, young lass,
>     I'll sow for thee.

He sang; all listened to him with great attention. He seemed to feel that he had to do with really musical people, and therefore was exerting himself to do his best. And they really are musical in our part of the country; the village of Sergievskoe on the Orel highroad is deservedly noted throughout Russia for its harmonious chorus-singing. The contractor sang for a long while without evoking much enthusiasm in his audience; he lacked the support of a chorus; but at last, after one particularly bold flourish, which set even the Wild Master smiling, the Gabbler could not refrain from a shout of delight. Every one was roused. The Gabbler and the Blinkard began joining in, in an undertone, and exclaiming: "Bravely done! . . . Take it, you rogue! . . . Sing it out, you serpent! Hold it! That shake again, you dog you! . . . May Herod confound your soul!" and so on. Nikolay Ivanych behind the bar was nodding his head from side to side approvingly. The Gabbler at last was swinging his legs, tapping with his feet and twitching his shoulder, while Yashka's eyes fairly glowed like coal, and he trembled all over like a leaf, and smiled nervously. The Wild Master alone did not change countenance, and stood motionless as before; but his eyes, fastened on the contractor, looked somewhat softened, though the expression of his lips was still scornful. Emboldened by the signs of general approbation, the contractor went off in a whirl of flourishes, and began to round off such trills, to turn such shakes off his tongue, and to make such furious play with his throat, that when at last, pale, exhausted, and bathed in hot perspiration, he uttered the last dying note, his whole body flung back, a general united shout greeted him in a violent outburst. The Gabbler threw himself on his neck and began strangling him in his long, bony arms; a flush came out on Nikolay Ivanych's oily face, and he seemed to have grown younger; Yashka shouted like mad: "Capital, capital!"—even my neighbor, the peasant in the torn smock, could not restrain himself, and with a blow of his fist on the table he cried: "Aha! well done, damn my soul, well done!" And he spat on one side with an air of decision.

"Well, brother, you've given us a treat!" bawled the Gabbler, not releasing the exhausted contractor from his embraces; "you've given us a treat, there's no denying! You've won, brother, you've won! I congratulate you—the quart's yours! Yashka's miles behind you . . . I tell you: miles . . . take my word for it." (And again he hugged the contractor to his breast.)

"There, let him alone, let him alone; there's no being rid of you" . . . said the Blinkard with vexation; "let him sit down on the bench; he's tired, see . . . You're a ninny, brother, a perfect ninny! What are you sticking to him like a wet leaf for . . ."

"Well, then, let him sit down, and I'll drink to his health," said the Gabbler, and he went up to the bar. "At your expense, brother," he added, addressing the contractor.

The latter nodded, sat down on the bench, pulled a piece of cloth out of his cap, and began wiping his face, while the Gabbler, with greedy haste, emptied his glass, and, with a grunt, assumed, after the manner of confirmed drinkers, an expression of careworn melancholy.

"You sing beautifully, brother, beautifully," Nikolay Ivanych observed caressingly. "And now it's your turn, Yasha; mind, now, don't be afraid. We shall see who's who; we shall see. The contractor sings beautifully, though, 'pon my soul, he does."

"Very beautifully," observed Nikolay Ivanych's wife, and she looked with a smile at Yakov.

"Beautifully, ha!" repeated my neighbor in an undertone.

"Ah, a wild man of the woods!" the Gabbler vociferated suddenly, and going up to the peasant with the rent on his shoulder, he pointed at him with his finger, while he pranced about and went off into an insulting guffaw. "Ha! ha! get along! wild man of the woods! Here's a ragamuffin from Woodland village! What brought you here?" he bawled amidst laughter.

The poor peasant was abashed, and was just about to get up and make off as fast as he could, when suddenly the Wild Master's iron voice was heard:

"What does the insufferable brute mean?" he articulated, grinding his teeth.

"I wasn't doing nothing," muttered the Gabbler. "I didn't . . . I only . . ."

"There, all right, shut up!" retorted the Wild Master. "Yakov, begin!"

Yakov took himself by his throat:

"Well, really, brothers, . . . something. . . . Hm, I don't know, on my word, what. . . ."

"Come, that's enough; don't be timid. For shame! . . . why go back? . . . Sing the best you can, by God's gift."

And the Wild Master looked down expectant. Yakov was silent for a minute; he glanced round, and covered his face with his hand. All had their eyes simply fastened upon him, especially the contractor, on whose face a faint, involuntary uneasiness could be seen through his habitual expression of self-confidence and the triumph of his success. He leant back against the wall, and again put both hands under him, but did not swing his legs as before. When at last Yakov uncovered his face it was pale as a dead man's; his eyes gleamed faintly under their drooping lashes. He gave a deep sigh, and began to sing. . . . The first sound of his voice was faint and unequal, and seemed not to come from his chest, but to be wafted from somewhere afar off, as though it had floated by chance into the room. A strange effect was produced on all of us by this trembling, resonant note; we glanced at one another, and Nikolay Ivanych's wife seemed to draw herself up. This first note was followed by another, bolder and prolonged, but still obviously quivering, like a harpstring when suddenly struck by a stray finger it throbs in a last, swiftly-dying quiver; the second was followed by a third, and, gradually gaining fire and breadth, the strains swelled into a pathetic melody. "Not one little path ran into the field," he sang, and sweet and mournful it was in our ears. I have seldom, I must confess, heard a voice like it; it was slightly hoarse, and not perfectly true; there was even something morbid about it at first; but it had genuine depth of passion, and youth and sweetness and a sort of fascinating, careless, pathetic melancholy. A spirit of truth and fire, a Russian spirit, was sounding and breathing in that voice, and it seemed to go straight to your heart, to go straight to all that was Russian in it. The song swelled and flowed. Yakov was clearly carried away by enthusiasm; he was not timid now; he surrendered himself wholly to the rapture of his art; his voice no longer trembled; it quivered, but with the scarce perceptible inward quiver of passion, which pierces like an arrow to the very soul of the listeners; and he steadily gained strength and firmness and breadth. I remember I once saw at sunset on a flat sandy shore, when the tide was low and the sea's roar came weighty and menacing from the distance, a great white sea-gull; it sat motionless, its silky bosom facing the crimson glow of the setting sun, and only now and then opening wide its great wings to greet the well-known sea, to greet the sinking lurid sun: I recalled it, as I heard Yakov. He sang, utterly forgetful of his rival and all of us; he seemed supported, as a bold swimmer by the waves, by our silent, passionate sympathy. He sang, and in every sound of his voice one seemed to feel something dear and akin to us, something of breadth and space, as though the familiar steppes were unfolding before our eyes and stretching away into endless distance. I felt the tears gathering in my bosom and rising to my eyes; suddenly I was struck by dull, smothered sobs. . . . I looked round—the innkeeper's wife was weeping, her bosom pressed close to the window. Yakov threw a quick glance at her, and he sang more sweetly, more melodiously than ever; Nikolay Ivanych looked down; the Blinkard turned away; the Gabbler, quite touched, stood, his gaping mouth stupidly open; the humble peasant was sobbing softly in the corner, and shaking his head with a plaintive murmur; and on the iron visage of the Wild Master, from under his overhanging brows there slowly rolled a heavy tear; the contractor raised his clenched fist to his brow, and did not stir. . . . I don't know how the general emotion would have ended, if Yakov had not suddenly come to a full stop on a high, exceptionally shrill note—as though his voice had broken. No one called out, or even stirred; every one seemed to be waiting to see whether he was not going to sing more; but he opened his eyes as though wondering at our silence, looked round at all of us with a face of inquiry, and saw that the victory was his. . . .

"Yasha," said the Wild Master, laying his hand on his shoulder, and he could say no more.

We all stood, as it were, petrified. The contractor softly rose and went up to Yakov.

"You . . . yours . . . you've won," he articulated at last with an effort, and rushed out of the room. His rapid, decided action, as it were, broke the spell; we all suddenly fell into noisy, delighted talk. The Gabbler bounded up and down, stammered and brandished his arms like mill-sails; the Blinkard limped up to Yakov and began kissing him; Nikolay Ivanych got up and solemnly announced that he would add a second pot of beer on his own account. The Wild Master laughed a sort of kind, simple laugh, which I should never have expected to see on his face; the humble peasant as he wiped his eyes, cheeks, nose, and beard on his sleeves, kept repeating in his corner, "Ah, beautiful it was, by God! blast me for the son of a dog, but it was fine!" while Nikolay Ivanych's wife, her face red with weeping, got up quickly and went away. Yakov was enjoying his triumph like a child; his whole face was transformed, his eyes especially fairly glowed with happiness. They dragged him to the bar; he beckoned the weeping peasant up to it, and sent the innkeeper's little son to look for the contractor, who was not found, however; and the festivities began. "You'll sing to us again; you're going to sing to us till evening," the Gabbler declared, flourishing his hands in the air.

I took one more look at Yakov and went out. I did not want to stay—I was afraid of spoiling the impression I had received. But the heat was as insupportable as before. It seemed hanging in a thick, heavy layer right over the earth; over the dark blue sky, tiny bright fires seemed whisking through the finest, almost black dust. Everything was still; and there was something hopeless and oppressive in this profound hush of exhausted nature. I made my way to a hayloft, and lay down on the fresh-cut, but already almost dry grass. For a long while I could not go to sleep; for a long while Yakov's irresistible voice was ringing in my ears. . . . At last the heat and fatigue regained their sway, however, and I fell into a dead sleep. When I waked up, everything was in darkness; the hay scattered around smelt strong and was slightly damp; through the slender rafters of the half-open roof pale stars were faintly twinkling. I went out. The glow of sunset had long died away, and its last trace showed in a faint light on the horizon; but above the freshness of the night there was still a feeling of heat in the atmosphere, lately baked through by the sun, and the breast still craved for a draught of cool air. There was no wind, nor were there any clouds; the sky all round was clear, and transparently dark, softly glimmering with innumerable, but scarcely visible stars. There were lights twinkling about the village; from the brightly lit tavern close by rose a confused, discordant din, amid which I fancied I recognized the voice of Yakov. Violent laughter came from there in an outburst at times. I went up to the little window and pressed my face against the pane. I saw a cheerless, though varied and animated scene; all were drunk—all from Yakov upwards. With breast bared, he sat on a bench, and singing in a thick voice a street song to a dance-tune, he lazily fingered and strummed on the strings of a guitar. His moist hair hung in tufts over his fearfully pale face. In the middle of the room, the Gabbler, completely "screwed" and without his coat, was hopping about in a dance before the peasant in the gray smock; the peasant, on his side, was with difficulty stamping and scraping with his feet, and grinning meaninglessly over his disheveled beard; he waved one hand from time to time, as much as to say, "Here goes!" Nothing could be more ludicrous than his face; however much he twitched up his eyebrows, his heavy lids would hardly rise, but seemed lying upon his scarcely visible, dim, and mawkish eyes. He was in that amiable frame of mind of a perfectly intoxicated man, when every passer-by, directly he looks him in the face, is sure to say, "Bless you, brother, bless you!" The Blinkard, as red as a lobster, and his nostrils dilated wide, was laughing malignantly in a corner; only Nikolay Ivanych, as befits a good tavern-keeper, preserved his composure unchanged. The room was thronged with many new faces; but the Wild Master I did not see in it.

I turned away with rapid steps and began descending the hill on which Kolotovka lies. At the foot of this hill stretches a wide plain; plunged in the misty waves of the evening haze, it seemed more immense, and was, as it were, merged in the darkening sky. I walked with long strides along the road by the ravine, when all at once from somewhere far away in the plain came a boy's clear voice: "Antropka! Antropka-a-a! . . ." He shouted in obstinate and tearful desperation, with long, long drawing out of the last syllable.

He was silent for a few instants, and started shouting again. His voice rang out clear in the still, lightly slumbering air. Thirty times at least he had called the name, Antropka. When suddenly, from the farthest end of the plain, as though from another world, there floated a scarcely audible reply:

"Wha-a-t?"

The boy's voice shouted back at once with gleeful exasperation: "Come here, devil! woo-od imp!"

"What fo-or?" replied the other, after a long interval.

"Because dad wants to thrash you!" the first voice shouted back hurriedly.

The second voice did not call back again, and the boy fell to shouting "Antropka!" once more. His cries, fainter and less and less frequent, still floated up to my ears, when it had grown completely dark, and I had turned the corner of the wood which skirts my village and lies over three miles from Kolotovka. . . . "Antropka-a-a!" was still audible in the air, filled with the shadows of night.

1850

# THE TRYST

I WAS sitting in a birchwood in autumn, about the middle of September. From early morning a fine rain had been falling, with intervals from time to time of warm sunshine; the weather was unsettled. The sky was at one time overcast with soft white clouds, at another it suddenly cleared in parts for an instant, and then behind the parting clouds could be seen a blue, bright and tender as a beautiful eye. I sat looking about and listening. The leaves faintly rustled over my head; from the sound of them alone one could tell what time of year it was. It was not the gay laughing tremor of the spring, nor the subdued whispering, the prolonged gossip of the summer, nor the chill and timid faltering of late autumn, but a scarcely audible, drowsy chatter. A slight breeze was faintly humming in the treetops. Wet with the rain, the copse in its inmost recesses was for ever changing as the sun shone or hid behind a cloud; at one moment it was all a radiance, as though suddenly everything were smiling in it; the slender stems of the thinly-growing birch-trees took all at once the soft luster of white silk, the tiny leaves lying on the earth were on a sudden flecked and flaring with purplish gold, and the graceful stalks of the high, curly bracken, decked already in their autumn color, the hue of an overripe grape, seemed interlacing in endless tangling crisscross before one's eyes; then suddenly again everything around was faintly bluish; the glaring tints died away instantaneously, the birch-trees stood all white and lusterless, white as fresh-fallen snow, before the cold rays of the winter sun have caressed it; and slily, stealthily there began drizzling and whispering through the wood the finest rain. The leaves on the birches were still almost all green, though perceptibly paler; only here and there stood one young tree, all red or golden, and it was a sight to see how it flamed in the sunshine when the sunbeams suddenly pierced with tangled flecks of light through the thick network of delicate twigs, freshly washed by the sparkling rain. Not one bird could be heard; all were in hiding and silent, except that at times there rang out the metallic, bell-like sound of the jeering tomtit. Before halting in this birch copse I had been through a wood of tall aspen-trees with my dog. I confess I have no great liking for that tree, the aspen, with its pale-lilac trunk and the grayish-green metallic leaves which it flings high as it can, and unfolds in a quivering fan in the air; I do not care for the eternal shaking of its round, slovenly leaves, awkwardly hooked on to long stalks. It is only fine on some summer evenings when, rising singly above low undergrowth, it faces the reddening beams of the setting sun, and shines and quivers, bathed from root to top in one unbroken yellow glow, or when, on a clear windy day, it is all rippling, rustling, and whispering to the blue sky, and every leaf is, as it were, taken by a longing to break away, to fly off and soar into the distance. But, as a rule, I don't care for the tree, and so, not stopping to rest in the aspen wood, I made my way to the birch-copse, nestled down under one tree whose branches started low down near the ground, and were consequently capable of shielding me from the rain, and after admiring the surrounding view a little, I fell into that sweet untroubled sleep only known to sportsmen.

I cannot say how long I was asleep, but when I opened my eyes, all the depths of the wood were filled with sunlight, and in all directions across the joyously rustling leaves there were glimpses and, as it were, flashes of intense blue sky; the clouds had vanished, driven away by the blustering wind; the weather had changed to fair, and there was that feeling of peculiar dry freshness in the air which fills the heart with a sense of boldness, and is almost always a sure sign of a still bright evening after a rainy day. I was just about to get up and try my luck again when suddenly my eyes fell on a motionless human figure. I looked attentively; it was a young peasant girl. She was sitting twenty paces off, her head bent in thought, and her hands lying in her lap; one of them, half-open, held a nosegay of wild flowers, which softly stirred on her checked petticoat with every breath. Her clean white smock, buttoned up at the throat and wrists, lay in short soft folds about her figure; two rows of big yellow beads fell from her neck to her bosom. She was very pretty. Her thick fair hair of a lovely, almost ashen hue was parted into two carefully combed semicircles, under the narrow crimson fillet, which was brought down almost on to her forehead, white as ivory; the rest of her face was faintly tanned that golden hue which is only taken by a delicate skin. I could not see her eyes—she did not raise them; but I saw her delicate high eyebrows, her long lashes; they were wet, and on one of her cheeks there shone in the sun the traces of quickly drying tears, reaching right down to her rather pale lips. Her little head was very charming altogether; even her rather thick and snub nose did not spoil it. I was especially taken with the expression of her face; it was so simple and gentle, so sad and so full of childish wonder at its own sadness. She was obviously waiting for some one; something made a faint crackling in the wood; she raised her head at once, and looked round; in the transparent shade I caught a rapid glimpse of her eyes, large, clear, and timorous, like a fawn's. For a few instants she listened, not moving her wide open eyes from the spot whence the faint sound had come; she sighed, turned her head slowly, bent still lower, and began sorting her flowers. Her eyelids turned red, her lips twitched faintly, and a fresh tear rolled from under her thick eyelashes, and stood brightly shining on her cheek. Rather a long while passed thus; the poor girl did not stir, except for a despairing movement of her hands now and then—and she kept listening, listening. . . . Again there was a crackling sound in the wood: she started. The sound did not cease, grew more distinct, and came closer; at last one could hear quick resolute footsteps. She drew herself up and seemed frightened; her intent gaze was all aquiver, all aglow with expectation. Through the thicket quickly appeared the figure of a man. She gazed at it, suddenly flushed, gave a radiant, blissful smile, tried to rise, and sank back again at once, turned white and confused, and only raised her quivering, almost supplicating eyes to the man approaching, when the latter stood still beside her.

I looked at him with curiosity from my ambush. I confess he did not make an agreeable impression on me. He was, to judge by external signs, the pampered valet of some rich young gentleman. His attire betrayed pretensions to style and fashionable carelessness; he wore a shortish coat of a bronze color, doubtless from his master's wardrobe, buttoned up to the top, a pink cravat with lilac ends, and a black velvet cap with a gold ribbon, pulled forward right on to his eyebrows. The round collar of his white shirt mercilessly propped up his ears and cut his cheeks, and his starched cuffs hid his whole hand to the red crooked fingers, adorned by gold and silver rings, with turquoise forget-me-nots. His red, fresh, impudent-looking face belonged to the order of faces which, as far as I have observed, are almost always repulsive to men, and unfortunately are very often attractive to women. He was obviously trying to give a scornful and bored expression to his coarse features; he was incessantly screwing up his milky gray eyes—small enough at all times; he scowled, dropped the corners of his mouth, affected to yawn, and with careless, though not perfectly natural nonchalance, pushed back his modishly curled red locks, or pinched the yellow hairs sprouting on his thick upper lip—in fact, he gave himself insufferable airs. He began his antics directly he caught sight of the young peasant girl waiting for him; slowly, with a swaggering step, he went up to her, stood a moment shrugging his shoulders, stuffed both hands in his coat pockets, and barely vouchsafing the poor girl a cursory and indifferent glance, he dropped on to the ground.

"Well," he began, still gazing away, swinging his leg and yawning, "have you been here long?"

The girl could not at once answer.

"Yes, a long while, Viktor Alexandrych," she said at last, in a voice hardly audible.

"Ah!" (He took off his cap, majestically passed his hand over his thick, stiffly curled hair, which grew almost down to his eyebrows, and looking round him with dignity, he carelessly covered his precious head again.) "And I quite forgot all about it. Besides, it rained!" (He yawned again.) "Lots to do; there's no looking after everything; and he's always scolding. We set off tomorrow. . . ."

"Tomorrow?" uttered the young girl. And she fastened her startled eyes upon him.

"Yes, tomorrow. . . . Come, come, come, please!" he added, in a tone of vexation, seeing she was shaking all over and softly bending her head; "please, Akulina, don't cry. You know, I can't stand that." (And he wrinkled up his snub nose.) "Else I'll go away at once. . . . What silliness—sniveling!"

"There, I won't, I won't!" cried Akulina, hurriedly gulping down her tears with an effort. "You are starting tomorrow?" she added, after a brief silence: "when will God grant that we see each other again, Viktor Alexandrych?"

"We shall see each other, we shall see each other. If not next year —then later. The master wants to enter the service in Petersburg, I fancy," he went on, pronouncing his words with careless condescension through his nose; "and perhaps we shall go abroad too."

"You will forget me, Viktor Alexandrych," said Akulina mournfully.

"No, why so? I won't forget you; only you be sensible, don't be a fool; obey your father. . . . And I won't forget you—no-o." (And he placidly stretched and yawned again.)

"Don't forget me, Viktor Alexandrych," she went on in a supplicating voice. "I think none could love you as I do. I have given you everything. . . . You tell me to obey my father, Viktor Alexandrych. . . . But how can I obey my father? . . ."

"Why not?" (He uttered these words, as it were, from his stomach, lying on his back with his hands behind his head.)

"But how can I, Viktor Alexandrych?—you know yourself . . ." She broke off. Viktor played with his steel watch-chain.

"You're not a fool, Akulina," he said at last, "so don't talk nonsense. I desire your good—do you understand me? To be sure, you're not a fool—not altogether a mere rustic, so to say; and your mother, too, wasn't always a peasant. Still you've no education—so you ought to do what you're told."

"But it's frightful, Viktor Alexandrych."

"O-oh! that's nonsense, my dear; a queer thing to be afraid of! What have you got there?" he added, moving closer to her; "flowers?"

"Yes," Akulina responded dejectedly. "That's some wild tansy I picked," she went on, brightening up a little; "it's good for calves. And this is bud-marigold—against the king's evil. Look, what an exquisite flower! I've never seen such a lovely flower before. These are forget-me-nots, and that's mother-darling. . . . And these I picked for you," she added, taking from under a yellow tansy a small bunch of blue cornflowers, tied up with a thin blade of grass. "Do you like them?"

Viktor languidly held out his hand, took the flowers, carelessly sniffed at them, and began twirling them in his fingers, looking upwards. Akulina watched him. . . . In her mournful eyes there was such tender devotion, adoring submission and love. She was afraid of him, and did not dare to cry, and was saying good-bye to him and admiring him for the last time; while he lay, lolling like a sultan, and with magnanimous patience and condescension put up with her adoration. I must own, I glared indignantly at his red face, on which, under the affectation of scornful indifference, one could discern vanity soothed and satisfied. Akulina was so sweet at that instant; her whole soul was confidingly and passionately laid bare before him, full of longing and caressing tenderness, while he . . . he dropped the cornflowers on the grass, pulled out of the side pocket of his coat a round eyeglass set in a brass rim, and began sticking it in his eye; but however much he tried to hold it with his frowning eyebrow, his pursed-up cheek and nose, the eyeglass kept tumbling out and falling into his hand.

"What is it?" Akulina asked at last in wonder.

"An eyeglass," he answered with dignity.

"What for?"

"Why, to see better."

"Show me."

Viktor scowled, but gave her the glass.

"Don't break it; look out."

"No fear, I won't break it." (She put it to her eye.) "I see nothing," she said innocently.

"But you must shut your eye," he retorted in the tones of a displeased teacher. (She shut the eye before which she held the glass.)

"Not that one, not that one, you fool! the other!" cried Viktor, and he took away his eyeglass, without allowing her to correct her mistake.

Akulina flushed a little, gave a faint laugh, and turned away.

"It's clear it's not for the likes of us," she said.

"I should think not, indeed!"

The poor girl was silent and gave a deep sigh.

"Ah, Viktor Alexandrych, what it will be like for me to be without you!" she said suddenly.

Viktor rubbed the glass on the lappet of his coat and put it back in his pocket.

"Yes, yes," he said at last, "at first it will be hard for you, certainly." (He patted her condescendingly on the shoulder; she softly took his hand from her shoulder and timidly kissed it.) "There, there, you're a good girl, certainly," he went on, with a complacent smile; "but what's to be done? You can see for yourself! me and the master could never stay on here; it will soon be winter now, and winter in the country—you know yourself—is simply disgusting. It's quite another thing in Petersburg! There there are simply such wonders as a silly girl like you could never fancy in your dreams! Such horses and streets, and society, and civilization—simply marvelous! . . ." (Akulina listened with devouring attention, her lips slightly parted, like a child.) "But what's the use," he added, turning over on the ground, "of my telling you all this? Of course, you can't understand it!"

"Why so, Viktor Alexandrych! I understand; I understood everything."

"My eye, what a girl it is!"

Akulina looked down.

"You used not to talk to me like that once, Viktor Alexandrych," she said, not lifting her eyes.

"Once? . . . once! . . . My goodness!" he remarked, as though in indignation.

They both were silent.

"It's time I was going," said Viktor, and he was already rising on to his elbow.

"Wait a little longer," Akulina besought him in a supplicating voice.

"What for? . . . Why, I've said good-bye to you."

"Wait a little," repeated Akulina.

Viktor lay down again and began whistling. Akulina never took her eyes off him. I could see that she was gradually being overcome by emotion; her lips twitched, her pale cheeks faintly glowed.

"Viktor Alexandrych," she began at last in a broken voice, "it's too bad of you . . . it is too bad of you, Viktor Alexandrych, indeed it is!"

"What's too bad?" he asked frowning, and he slightly raised his head and turned it towards her.

"It's too bad, Viktor Alexandrych. You might at least say one kind word to me at parting; you might have said one little word to me, a poor, luckless, forlorn." . . .

"But what am I to say to you?"

"I don't know; you know that best, Viktor Alexandrych. Here you are going away, and one little word. . . . What have I done to deserve it?"

"You're such a queer creature! What can I do?"

"One word at least."

"There, she keeps on at the same thing," he commented with annoyance, and he got up.

"Don't be angry, Viktor Alexandrych," she added hurriedly, with difficulty suppressing her tears.

"I'm not angry, only you're silly. . . . What do you want? You know I can't marry you, can I? I can't, can I? What is it you want then, eh?" (He thrust his face forward as though expecting an answer, and spread his fingers out.)

"I want nothing . . . nothing," she answered falteringly, and she ventured to hold out her trembling hands to him; "but only a word at parting."

And her tears fell in a torrent.

"There, that means she's gone off into crying," said Viktor coolly, pushing down his cap on to his eyes.

"I want nothing," she went on, sobbing and covering her face with her hands; "but what is there before me in my family? What is there before me? What will happen to me? What will become of me, poor wretch? They will marry me to a hateful . . . poor, forsaken . . . Poor me!"

"Sing away, sing away," muttered Viktor in an undertone, fidgeting with impatience as he stood.

"And he might say one word, one word. . . . He might say, 'Akulina . . . I . . .'"

Sudden heartbreaking sobs prevented her from finishing; she lay with her face in the grass and bitterly, bitterly she wept. . . . Her whole body shook convulsively, her neck fairly heaved. . . . Her long-suppressed grief broke out in a torrent at last. Viktor stood over her, stood a moment, shrugged her shoulders, turned away and strode off.

A few instants passed . . . she grew calmer, raised her head, jumped up, looked round and wrung her hands; she tried to run after him, but her legs gave way under her—she fell on her knees. . . . I could not refrain from rushing up to her; but, almost before she had time to look at me, making a superhuman effort she got up with a faint shriek and vanished behind the trees, leaving her flowers scattered on the ground.

I stood a minute, picked up the bunch of cornflowers, and went out of the wood into the open country. The sun had sunk low in the pale clear sky; its rays too seemed to have grown pale and chill; they did not shine; they were diffused in an unbroken, watery light. It was within half an hour of sunset, but there was scarcely any of the glow of evening. A gusty wind scurried to meet me across the yellow parched stubble; little curled-up leaves, scudding hurriedly before it, flew by across the road, along the edge of the copse; the side of the copse facing the fields like a wall, was all shaking and lighted up by tiny gleams, distinct, but not glowing; on the reddish plants, the blades of grass, the straws on all sides, were sparkling and stirring innumerable threads of autumn spiderwebs. I stopped . . . I felt sad at heart: under the bright but chill smile of fading nature, the dismal dread of coming winter seemed to steal upon me. High overhead flew a cautious crow, heavily and sharply cleaving the air with his wings; he turned his head, looked sideways at me, flapped his wings and, cawing abruptly, vanished behind the wood; a great flock of pigeons flew up playfully from a threshing floor, and suddenly eddying round in a column, scattered busily about the country. Sure sign of autumn! Some one came driving over the bare hillside, his empty cart rattling loudly. . . .

I turned homewards; but it was long before the figure of poor Akulina faded out of my mind, and her cornflowers, long since withered, are still in my keeping.

1850

# MOOMOO

IN ONE of the outlying streets of Moscow, in a gray house with white columns and a balcony, warped so that it was all askew, there once lived a lady, a widow, surrounded by a numerous household of serfs. Her sons were in the government service at Petersburg; her daughters were married; she went out very little, and in solitude lived through the last years of her miserly and dreary old age. Her day, a joyless and gloomy day, had long been over; but the evening of her life was blacker than night.

Of all her servants, the most remarkable personage was the porter, Gerasim, a man full twelve inches over the normal height, of heroic build, and deaf and dumb from his birth. The lady, his owner, had taken him from the village where he had lived alone in a little hut, apart from his brothers, and was reckoned about the most punctual of her peasants in the payment of the seigniorial dues. Endowed with extraordinary strength, he did the work of four men; work flew apace under his hands, and it was a pleasant sight to see him when he was plowing, while, with his huge palms pressing hard upon the plow, he seemed alone, unaided by his poor horse, to cleave the yielding bosom of the earth, or when, about St. Peter's Day, he plied his scythe with a furious energy that might have mown a young birch copse up by the roots, or swiftly and untiringly wielded a flail over two yards long, while the hard oblong muscles of his shoulders rose and fell like a lever. His perpetual silence lent a solemn dignity to his unwearying labor. He was a splendid peasant, and, except for his affliction, any girl would have been glad to marry him. . . . But now they had taken Gerasim to Moscow, bought him boots, had him made a full-skirted coat for summer, a sheepskin for winter, put into his hand a broom and a spade, and appointed him porter.

At first he intensely disliked his new mode of life. From his childhood he had been used to field labor, to village life. Shut off by his affliction from the society of men, he had grown up, dumb and mighty, as a tree grows on fruitful soil. When he was transported to the town, he could not understand what was being done with him; he was miserable and stupefied, with the stupefaction of some strong young bull, taken straight from the meadow, where the rich grass stood up to his belly, taken and put in the truck of a railway train, and there, while smoke and sparks and gusts of steam puff out upon the sturdy beast, whirled onwards, whirled along with loud roar and whistle, whither—God knows! Gerasim's new duties seemed a mere trifle to him after his hard toil as a peasant; in half an hour, all his work was done, and he would once more stand stockstill in the middle of the courtyard, staring open-mouthed at all the passers-by, as though trying to wrest from them the explanation of his perplexing position; or he would suddenly go off into some corner, and flinging the broom or the spade a long way off, throw himself on his face on the ground, and lie for hours together without stirring, like a caged beast. But man gets used to anything, and Gerasim got used at last to living in town.

He had little work to do; his whole duty consisted in keeping the courtyard clean, bringing in a barrel of water twice a day, splitting and dragging in wood for the kitchen and the house, keeping out strangers, and watching at night. And it must be said he did his duty zealously. In his courtyard there was never a shaving lying about, never a speck of dust; if sometimes, in the muddy season, the wretched nag, put in his charge for fetching water, got stuck in the road, he would simply give it a shove with his shoulder, and set not only the cart but the horse itself moving. If he set to chopping wood, the axe fairly rang like glass, and chips and chunks flew in all directions. And as for strangers, after he had one night caught two thieves and knocked their heads together—knocked them so that there was not the slightest need to take them to the police-station afterwards—everyone in the neighborhood began to feel a great respect for him; even those who came in the daytime, by no means robbers, but simply unknown persons, at the sight of the terrible porter, waved him away and shouted at him as though he could hear their shouts.

With all the rest of the servants Gerasim was on terms, hardly friendly—they were afraid of him—but familiar; he regarded them as his fellows. They explained themselves to him by signs, and he understood them, and exactly carried out all orders, but knew his own rights too, and soon no one dared to take his seat at the table.

Gerasim was altogether of a strict and serious temper, he liked order in everything; even the cocks did not dare to fight in his presence, or woe betide them! directly he caught sight of them, he would seize them by the legs, swing them ten times round in the air like a wheel, and throw them in different directions. There were geese, too, kept in the yard; but the goose, as is well known, is a dignified and reasonable bird; Gerasim felt a respect for them, looked after them, and fed them; he was himself not unlike a gander of the steppes. He was assigned a little garret over the kitchen; he arranged it himself to his own liking, made a bedstead in it of oak boards with four stumps of wood for legs—a truly Titanic bedstead; one might have put a ton or two on it—it would not have bent under the load; under the bed was a solid chest; in a corner stood a little table of the same strong kind, and near the table a three-legged stool, so solid and squat that Gerasim himself would sometimes pick it up and drop it again with a smile of delight. The garret was locked up by means of a padlock that looked like a loaf of bread, only black; the key of this padlock Gerasim always carried about him in his girdle. He did not like people to come to his garret.

So passed a year, at the end of which a little incident befell Gerasim.

The old lady, in whose service he lived as porter, adhered in everything to the ancient ways, and kept a large number of servants. In her house were not only laundresses, sempstresses, carpenters, tailors and tailoresses, there was even a harness-maker—he was reckoned as a veterinary surgeon, too—and a doctor for the servants; there was a household doctor for the mistress; there was, lastly a shoemaker, by name Kapiton Klimov, a hard drinker. Klimov regarded himself as an injured creature, whose merits were unappreciated, a cultivated man from Petersburg, who ought not to be living in Moscow without occupation—in the wilds, so to speak; and if he drank, as he himself expressed it emphatically, with a blow on his chest, it was sorrow drove him to it. So one day his mistress had a conversation about him with her head steward, Gavrila, a man whom, judging solely from his little yellow eyes and nose like a duck's beak, fate itself, it seemed, had marked out as a person in authority. The lady expressed her regret at the corruption of the morals of Kapiton, who had, only the evening before, been picked up in the street.

"Now, Gavrila," she observed, all of a sudden, "now, if we were to marry him, what do you think, perhaps he would be steadier?"

"Why not marry him, indeed, 'm? He could be married, 'm," answered Gavrila, "and it would be a very good thing, to be sure, 'm."

"Yes; only who is to marry him?"

"Ay, 'm. But that's at your pleasure, 'm. He may, any way, so to say, be wanted for something; he can't be turned adrift altogether."

"I fancy he likes Tatyana."

Gavrila was on the point of making some reply, but he shut his lips tightly.

"Yes! . . . let him marry Tatyana," the lady decided, taking a pinch of snuff complacently. "Do you hear?"

"Yes, 'm," Gavrila articulated, and he withdrew.

Returning to his own room (it was in a little lodge, and was almost filled up with metal-bound trunks), Gavrila first sent his wife away, and then sat down at the window and pondered. His mistress's unexpected arrangement had clearly put him in a difficulty. At last he got up and sent for Kapiton. Kapiton made his appearance. . . . But before reporting their conversation to the reader, we consider it not out of place to relate in few words who this Tatyana was, whom it was to be Kapiton's lot to marry, and why the great lady's order had disturbed the steward.

Tatyana, one of the laundresses referred to above (as a trained and skillful laundress she was in charge of the fine linen only), was a woman of twenty-eight, thin, fair-haired, with moles on her left cheek. Moles on the left cheek are regarded as of evil omen in Russia —a token of unhappy life. . . . Tatyana could not boast of her good luck. From her earliest youth she had been badly treated; she had done the work of two, and had never known affection; she had been poorly clothed and had received the smallest wages. Relations she had practically none; an uncle she had once had, a butler, left behind in the country as useless, and other uncles of hers were peasants—that was all. At one time she had passed for a beauty, but her good looks were soon gone. In disposition, she was very meek, or, rather, intimidated; towards herself, she felt perfect indifference; of others, she stood in mortal dread; she thought of nothing but how to get her work done in good time, never talked to anyone, and trembled at the very name of her mistress, though the latter scarcely knew her by sight.

When Gerasim was brought from the country, she was ready to die with fear on seeing his huge figure, tried all she could to avoid meeting him, even dropped her eyelids when sometimes she chanced to run past him, hurrying from the house to the laundry. Gerasim at first paid no special attention to her, then he used to smile when she came his way, then he began even to stare admiringly at her, and at last he never took his eyes off her. She took his fancy, whether by the mild expression of her face or the timidity of her movements, who can tell? So one day as she was stealing across the yard, with a starched dressing-jacket of her mistress's carefully poised on her outspread fingers . . . someone suddenly grasped her vigorously by the elbow; she turned round and fairly screamed; behind her stood Gerasim. With a foolish smile, making inarticulate caressing grunts, he held out to her a gingerbread cock with gold tinsel on his tail and wings. She was about to refuse it, but he thrust it forcibly into her hand, shook his head, walked away, and turning round, once more grunted something very affectionately to her. From that day forward he gave her no peace; wherever she went, he was on the spot at once, coming to meet her, smiling, grunting, waving his hands; all at once he would pull a ribbon out of the bosom of his smock and put it in her hand, or would sweep the dust out of her way. The poor girl simply did not know how to behave or what to do.

Soon the whole household knew of the dumb porter's wiles; jeers, jokes, sly hints were showered upon Tatyana. At Gerasim, however, it was not everyone who would dare to scoff; he did not like jokes; indeed, in his presence, she, too, was left in peace. Whether she liked it or not, the girl found herself under his protection. Like all deaf-mutes, he was very suspicious, and very readily perceived when they were laughing at him or at her. One day, at dinner, the wardrobe-keeper, Tatyana's superior, fell to nagging at her, and brought the poor thing to such a state that she did not know where to look, and was almost crying with vexation. Gerasim got up all of a sudden, stretched out his gigantic hand, laid it on the wardrobe-maid's head, and looked into her face with such grim ferocity that her head positively flopped upon the table. Everyone was still. Gerasim took up his spoon again and went on with his cabbage-soup. "Look at him, the dumb devil, the wood-demon!" they all muttered in undertones, while the wardrobe-maid got up and went out into the maids' room. Another time, noticing that Kapiton—the same Kapiton who was the subject of the conversation reported above—was gossiping somewhat too amiably with Tatyana, Gerasim beckoned to him, led him into the cart-shed, and taking up by one end a shaft that was standing in a corner, lightly, but most significantly, menaced him with it. Since then no one addressed a word to Tatyana. And all this cost him nothing. It is true the wardrobe-maid, as soon as she reached the maids' room, promptly fell into a fainting-fit, and behaved altogether so skillfully that Gerasim's rough action reached his mistress's knowledge the same day. But the capricious old lady only laughed, and several times, to the great offense of the wardrobe-maid, forced her to repeat how he had pushed her head down with his heavy hand, and next day she sent Gerasim a rouble. She looked on him with favor as a strong and faithful watchman. Gerasim stood in considerable awe of her, but, all the same, he had hopes of her favor, and was prepared to go to her with a petition for leave to marry Tatyana. He was only waiting for a new coat, promised him by the steward, to present a proper appearance before his mistress, when this same mistress suddenly took it into her head to marry Tatyana to Kapiton.

The reader will now readily understand the perturbation of mind that overtook the steward Gavrila after his conversation with his mistress. "My lady," he thought, as he sat at the window, "favors Gerasim, to be sure"—(Gavrila was well aware of this, and that was why he himself looked on him with an indulgent eye)—"still he is a speechless creature. I could not, indeed, put it before the mistress that Gerasim's courting Tatyana. And, after all, it's true enough; what sort of husband would he make? But on the other hand, that devil, God forgive me, has only got to find out they're marrying Tatyana to Kapiton, he'll smash up everything in the house, 'pon my soul! There's no reasoning with him; why, he's such a devil, God forgive my sins, there's no getting over him nohow . . . 'pon my soul!"

Kapiton's entrance broke the thread of Gavrila's reflections. The dissipated shoemaker came in, his hands behind him, and lounging carelessly against a projecting angle of the wall, near the door, crossed his right foot in front of his left, and tossed his head, as much as to say, "What do you want?"

Gavrila looked at Kapiton, and drummed with his fingers on the window-frame. Kapiton merely screwed up his leaden eyes a little, but he did not look down, he even grinned slightly, and passed his hand over his whitish locks which were sticking up in all directions. "Well, here I am. What is it?"

"You're a pretty fellow," said Gavrila, and paused. "A pretty fellow you are, there's no denying!"

Kapiton only twitched his little shoulders. "Are you any better, pray?" he thought to himself.

"Just look at yourself, now, look at yourself," Gavrila went on reproachfully. "Now, whatever do you look like?"

Kapiton serenely surveyed his shabby tattered coat, and his patched trousers, and with special attention stared at his burst boots, especially the one on the toe of which his right foot so gracefully rested, and he fixed his eyes again on the steward.

"Well?"

"Well?" repeated Gavrila. "Well? And then you say 'well'? You look like old Nick himself, God forgive my saying so, that's what you look like."

Kapiton blinked rapidly.

"Go on abusing me, go on, if you like, Gavrila Andreich," he thought to himself again.

"Here you've been drunk again," Gavrila began, "drunk again, haven't you? Eh? Come, answer me!"

"Owing to the weakness of my health, I have exposed myself to spiritous beverages, certainly," replied Kapiton.

"Owing to the weakness of your health! . . . They let you off too easy, that's what it is; and you've been apprenticed in Petersburg. . . . Much you learned in your apprenticeship! You simply eat your bread in idleness."

"In that matter, Gavrila Andreich, there is one to judge me, the Lord God Himself, and no one else. He also knows what manner of man I be in this world, and whether I eat my bread in idleness. And as for your contention regarding drunkenness, in that matter, too, I am not to blame, but rather a friend; he led me into temptation, but was diplomatic and got away, while I . . ."

"While you were left, like a goose, in the street. Ah, you're a dissolute fellow! But that's not the point," the steward went on, "I've something to tell you. Our lady . . ." here he paused a minute, "it's our lady's pleasure that you should be married. Do you hear? She imagines you may be steadier when you're married. Do you understand?"

"To be sure, I do."

"Well, then. For my part I think it would be better to give you a good hiding. But there—it's her business. Well? Are you agreeable?"

Kapiton grinned.

"Matrimony is an excellent thing for anyone, Gavrila Andreich; and, as far as I am concerned, I shall be quite agreeable."

"Very well, then," replied Gavrila, while he reflected to himself: there's no denying the man expresses himself very properly. "Only there's one thing," he pursued aloud: "the wife our lady's picked out for you is an unlucky choice."

"Why, who is she, permit me to inquire?"

"Tatyana."

"Tatyana?"

And Kapiton opened his eyes, and moved a little away from the wall.

"Well, what are you in such a taking for? . . . Isn't she to your taste, hey?"

"Not to my taste, do you say, Gavrila Andreich! She's right enough, a hardworking steady girl. . . . But you know very well yourself, Gavrila Andreich, why that fellow, that wild man of the woods, that monster of the steppes, he's after her, you know. . . ."

"I know, mate, I know all about it," the butler cut him short in a tone of annoyance: "but there, you see . . ."

"But upon my soul, Gavrila Andreich! why, he'll kill me, by God, he will, he'll crush me like some fly; why, he's got a fist—why, you kindly look yourself what a fist he's got; why, he's simply got a fist like Minin and Pozharsky's. You see he's deaf, he beats and don't hear how he's beating! He swings his great fists, as if he's asleep. And there's no possibility of pacifying him; and for why? Why, because, as you know yourself, Gavrila Andreich, he's deaf, and what's more, has no more wit than the heel of my foot. Why, he's a sort of beast, a heathen idol, Gavrila Andreich, and worse . . . a block of wood; what have I done that I should have to suffer from him now? Sure enough, I don't mind anything by now; I've knocked about, I've had enough to put up with, I've become as soiled as a kolomna pot, but still I'm a man, after all, and not a worthless pot."

"I know, I know, don't go talking away. . . ."

"Lord, my God!" the shoemaker continued warmly, "when is the end? when, O Lord! A poor wretch I am, a poor wretch whose sufferings are endless! What a life, what a life mine's been, come to think of it! In my young days, I was beaten by a German I was prentice to; in the prime of life beaten by my own countrymen, and last of all, in ripe years, see what I have been brought to. . . ."

"Ugh, you flabby soul!" said Gavrila Andreich. "Why do you make so many words about it?"

"Why, do you say, Gavrila Andreich? It's not a beating I'm afraid of, Gavrila Andreich. A gentleman may chastise me in private, but give me a civil word before folks, and I'm a man still; but see now, whom I've to do with. . . ."

"Come, get along," Gavrila interposed impatiently. Kapiton turned away and staggered off.

"But, if it were not for him," the steward shouted after him, "you would consent for your part?"

"I signify my acquiescence," retorted Kapiton as he disappeared. His fine language did not desert him, even in the most trying positions.

The steward walked several times up and down the room.

"Well, call Tatyana now," he said at last.

A few instants later, Tatyana had come up almost noiselessly, and was standing in the doorway.

"What are your orders, Gavrila Andreich?" she said in a soft voice.

The steward looked at her intently.

"Well, Tatyana," he said, "would you like to be married? Our lady has chosen a husband for you."

"Yes, Gavrila Andreich. And whom has she deigned to name as a husband for me?" she added falteringly.

"Kapiton, the shoemaker."

"Yes, sir."

"He's a featherbrained fellow, that's certain. But it's just for that the mistress reckons upon you."

"Yes, sir."

"There's one difficulty . . . you know the deaf man, Gerasim, he's courting you, you see. How did you come to bewitch such a bear? But you see, he'll kill you, very like, he's such a bear. . . ."

"He'll kill me, Gavrila Andreich, he'll kill me, and no mistake."

"Kill you. . . . Well, we shall see about that. What do you mean by saying he'll kill you? Has he any right to kill you? Tell me yourself."

"I don't know, Gavrila Andreich, about his having any right or not."

"What a woman! why, you've made him no promise, I suppose. . . ."

"What are you pleased to ask of me?"

The steward was silent for a little, thinking, "You're a meek soul! Well, that's right," he said aloud; "we'll have another talk with you later, now you can go, Tatyana; I see you're not unruly, certainly."

Tatyana turned, steadied herself a little against the doorpost, and went away.

"And perhaps, our lady will forget all about this wedding by tomorrow," thought the steward; "and here am I worrying myself for nothing! As for that insolent fellow, we must tie him down, if it comes to that, we must let the police know . . ." "Ustinya Fyedorovna!" he shouted in a loud voice to his wife, "heat the samovar, my good soul. . . ." All that day Tatyana hardly went out of the laundry. At first she had started crying, then she wiped away her tears, and set to work as before. Kapiton stayed till late at night at the gin-shop with a friend of his, a man of gloomy appearance, to whom he related in detail how he used to live in Petersburg with a gentleman, who would have been all right, except that he was a bit too strict, and he had a slight weakness besides, he was too fond of drink; and, as to the fair sex, he didn't stick at anything. His gloomy companion merely said yes; but when Kapiton announced at last that, in a certain event, he would have to lay hands on himself tomorrow, his gloomy companion remarked that it was bedtime. And they parted in surly silence.

Meanwhile, the steward's anticipations were not fulfilled. The old lady was so much taken up with the idea of Kapiton's wedding, that even in the night she talked of nothing else to one of her companions, who was kept in her house solely to entertain her in case of sleeplessness, and, like a night cabman, slept in the day. When Gavrila came to her after morning tea with his report, her first question was: "And how about our wedding—is it getting on all right?" He replied, of course, that it was getting on first rate, and that Kapiton would appear before her to pay his reverence to her that day. The old lady was not quite well; she did not give much time to business. The steward went back to his own room, and called a council. The matter certainly called for serious consideration. Tatyana would make no difficulty, of course; but Kapiton had declared in the hearing of all that he had but one head to lose, not two or three. . . . Gerasim turned rapid sullen looks on everyone, would not budge from the steps of the maids' quarters, and seemed to guess that some mischief was being hatched against him.

They met together. Among them was an old butler nicknamed Uncle Tail, to whom every one look respectfully for counsel, though all they got out of him was, "Here's a pretty pass! To be sure, to be sure, to be sure!" As a preliminary measure of security, to provide against contingencies, they locked Kapiton up in the storeroom where the filter was kept; then considered the question with the gravest deliberation. It would, to be sure, be easy to have recourse to force. But Heaven save us! there would be an uproar, the mistress would be put out—it would be awful! What should they do? They thought and thought, and at last thought out a solution. It had many a time been observed that Gerasim could not bear drunkards. . . . As he sat at the gates, he would always turn away with disgust when some one passed by intoxicated, with unsteady steps and his cap on one side of his ear. They resolved that Tatyana should be instructed to pretend to be tipsy, and should pass by Gerasim staggering and reeling about. The poor girl refused for a long while to agree to this, but they persuaded her at last; she saw, too, that it was the only possible way of getting rid of her adorer.

She went out. Kapiton was released from the storeroom; for, after all, he had an interest in the affair. Gerasim was sitting on the curbstone at the gate, scraping the ground with a spade. . . . From behind every corner, from behind every window-blind, the others were watching him. . . .

The trick succeeded beyond all expectations. On seeing Tatyana, at first, he nodded as usual, making caressing, inarticulate sounds; then he looked carefully at her, dropped his spade, jumped up, went to her, brought his face close to her face. . . . In her fright she staggered more than ever, and shut her eyes. . . . He took her by the arm, whirled her right across the yard, and going into the room where the council had been sitting, pushed her straight at Kapiton. Tatyana fairly swooned away. . . . Gerasim stood, looked at her, waved his hand, laughed, and went off, stepping heavily, to his garret.

. . . For the next twenty-four hours, he did not come out of it. The postilion Antipka said afterwards that he saw Gerasim through a crack in the wall, sitting on his bedstead, his cheek in his hand. From time to time he uttered soft regular sounds; he was wailing a dirge, that is, swaying backwards and forwards with his eyes shut, and shaking his head as drivers or bargemen do when they chant their melancholy songs. Antipka could not bear it, and he came away from the crack. When Gerasim came out of the garret next day, no particular change could be observed in him. He only seemed, as it were, more morose, and took not the slightest notice of Tatyana or Kapiton. The same evening, they both had to appear before their mistress with geese under their arms, and in a week's time they were married. Even on the day of the wedding Gerasim showed no change of any sort in his behavior. Only, he came back from the river without water, he had somehow broken the barrel on the road; and at night, in the stable, he washed and rubbed down his horse so vigorously, that it swayed like a blade of grass in the wind, and staggered from one leg to the other under his fists of iron.

All this had taken place in the spring. Another year passed by, during which Kapiton became a hopeless drunkard, and as being absolutely of no use for anything, was sent away to a distant village with his wife. On the day of his departure, he put a very good face on it at first, and declared that he would always be at home, send him where they would, even to the other end of the world; but later on he lost heart, began grumbling that he was being taken to uneducated people, and collapsed so completely at last that he could not even put his own hat on. Some charitable soul stuck it on his forehead, set the peak straight in front, and thrust it on with a slap from above. When everything was quite ready, and the peasants already held the reins in their hands, and were only waiting for the words "With God's blessing!" to start, Gerasim came out of his garrett, went up to Tatyana, and gave her as a parting present a red cotton handkerchief he had bought for her a year ago. Tatyana, who had up to that instant borne all the revolting details of her life with great indifference, could not control herself upon that; she burst into tears, and as she took her seat in the cart, she kissed Gerasim three times like a good Christian. He meant to accompany her as far as the town gate, and did walk beside her cart for a while, but he stopped suddenly at the Crimean Ford, waved his hand, and walked away along the riverside.

It was getting towards evening. He walked slowly, watching the water. All of a sudden he fancied something was floundering in the mud close to the bank. He stooped over, and saw a little white-and-black puppy, who, in spite of all its efforts, could not get out of the water; it was struggling, slipping back, and trembling all over its thin wet little body. Gerasim looked at the unlucky little dog, picked it up with one hand, put it into the bosom of his coat, and hurried with long steps homewards. He went into his garret, put the rescued puppy on his bed, covered it with his thick overcoat, ran first to the stable for straw, and then to the kitchen for a cup of milk. Carefully folding back the overcoat, and spreading out the straw, he set the milk on the bedstead. The poor little puppy was not more than three weeks old, its eyes were only just open—one eye still seemed rather larger than the other; it did not know how to lap out of a cup, and did nothing but shiver and blink. Gerasim took hold of its head softly with two fingers, and dipped its little nose into the milk. The pup suddenly began lapping greedily, sniffing, shaking itself, and choking. Gerasim watched and watched it, and all at once he laughed outright. . . . All night long he was waiting on it, keeping it covered, and rubbing it dry. He fell asleep himself at last, and slept quietly and happily by its side.

No mother could have looked after her baby as Gerasim looked after his little nursling. At first, she—for the pup turned out to be a bitch—was very weak, sickly, and ugly; but by degrees she grew stronger and improved in looks and, thanks to the unflagging care of her preserver, in eight months' time she was transformed into a very pretty dog of the spaniel breed, with long ears, a bushy spiral tail, and large expressive eyes. She was devotedly attached to Gerasim, and was never a yard from his side; she always followed him about wagging her tail. He had even given her a name—the dumb know that their inarticulate noises call the attention of others. He called her Moomoo. All the servants in the house liked her, and called her Moomoo, too. She was very intelligent, she was friendly with everyone, but was only fond of Gerasim. Gerasim, on his side, loved her passionately, and he did not like it when other people stroked her; whether he was afraid for her, or jealous—God knows! She used to wake him in the morning, pulling at his coat; she used to take the reins in her mouth, and bring up to him the old horse that carried the water, with whom she was on very friendly terms. With an expression of importance on her face she used to go with him to the river; she used to watch his brooms and spades, and never allowed any one to go into his garret. He cut a little hole in his door on purpose for her, and she seemed to feel that only in Gerasim's garret she was completely mistress and at home; and directly she went in, she used to jump with a satisfied air upon the bed. At night she did not sleep at all, but she never barked without sufficient cause, like some stupid house-dog, who, sitting on its hind-legs, blinking, with its nose in the air, barks simply from dullness, at the stars, usually three times in succession. No! Moomoo's delicate little voice was never raised without good reason; either some stranger was passing close to the fence, or there was some suspicious sound or rustle somewhere. . . . In fact, she was an excellent watchdog. It is true that there was another dog in the yard, a tawny old dog with brown spots, called Wolf, but he was never, even at night, let off the chain; and, indeed, he was so decrepit that he did not even wish for freedom. He used to lie curled up in his kennel, and only rarely uttered a sleepy, almost noiseless bark, which broke off at once, as though he were himself aware of its uselessness. Moomoo never went into the mistress's house; and when Gerasim carried wood into the rooms, she always stayed behind, impatiently waiting for him at the steps, pricking up her ears and turning her head to right and to left at the slightest creak of the door. . . .

So passed another year. Gerasim went on performing his duties as house-porter, and was very well content with his lot, when suddenly an unexpected incident occurred. . . . One fine summer day the old lady was walking up and down the drawing-room with her dependents. She was in high spirits; she laughed and made jokes. Her servile companions laughed and joked too, but they did not feel particularly mirthful; the household did not much like it, when their mistress was in a lively mood, for, to begin with, she expected from everyone prompt and complete participation in her merriment, and was furious if anyone showed a face that did not beam with delight, and secondly, these outbursts never lasted long with her, and were usually followed by a sour and gloomy mood. That day she had got up in a lucky hour; at cards she took the four knaves, which means the fulfillment of one's wishes (she used to try her fortune on the cards every morning), and her tea struck her as particularly delicious, for which her maid was rewarded by words of praise, and by two copecks in money. With a sweet smile on her wrinkled lips, the lady walked about the drawing-room and went up to the window. A flower-garden had been laid out before the window, and in the very middle bed, under a rosebush, lay Moomoo busily gnawing a bone. The lady caught sight of her.

"Mercy on us!" she cried suddenly; "what dog is that?"

The companion, addressed by the old lady, hesitated, poor thing, in that wretched state of uneasiness which is common in any person in a dependent position who doesn't know very well what significance to give to the exclamation of a superior.

"I d-d-don't know," she faltered: "I fancy it's the dumb man's dog."

"Mercy!" the lady cut her short: "but it's a charming little dog! Order it to be brought in. Has he had it long? How is it I've never seen it before? . . . Order it to be brought in."

The companion flew at once into the hall.

"Boy, boy!" she shouted: "bring Moomoo in at once! She's in the flower-garden."

"Her name's Moomoo then," observed the lady: "a very nice name."

"Oh, very, indeed!" chimed in the companion. "Make haste, Stepan!"

Stepan, a sturdily-built young fellow, whose duties were those of a footman, rushed headlong into the flower-garden, and tried to capture Moomoo; but she cleverly slipped from his fingers, and with her tail in the air, fled full speed to Gerasim, who was at that instant in the kitchen, knocking out and cleaning a barrel, turning it upside down in his hands like a child's drum. Stepan ran after her, and tried to catch her just at her master's feet; but the sensible dog would not let a stranger touch her, and with a bound, she got away. Gerasim looked on with a smile at all this ado; at last, Stepan got up, much amazed, and hurriedly explained to him by signs that the mistress wanted the dog brought in to her. Gerasim was a little astonished; he called Moomoo, however, picked her up, and handed her over to Stepan. Stepan carried her into the drawing-room, and put her down on the parquet floor. The old lady began calling the dog to her in a coaxing voice. Moomoo, who had never in her life been in such magnificent apartments, was very much frightened, and made a rush for the door, but, being driven back by the obsequious Stepan, she began trembling, and huddled close up against the wall.

"Moomoo, Moomoo, come to me, come to your mistress," said the lady; "come, silly thing . . . don't be afraid."

"Come, Moomoo, come to the mistress," repeated the companions. "Come along!"

But Moomoo looked round her uneasily, and did not stir.

"Bring her something to eat," said the old lady. "How stupid she is! she won't come to her mistress. What's she afraid of?"

"She's not used to your honor yet," ventured one of the companions in a timid and conciliatory voice.

Stepan brought in a saucer of milk, and set it down before Moomoo, but Moomoo would not even sniff at the milk, and still shivered, and looked round as before.

"Ah, what a silly you are!" said the lady, and going up to her, she stooped down, and was about to stroke her, but Moomoo turned her head abruptly, and showed her teeth. The lady hurriedly drew back her hand. . . .

A momentary silence followed. Moomoo gave a faint whine, as though she would complain and apologize. . . . The old lady moved back scowling. The dog's sudden movement had frightened her.

"Ah!" shrieked all the companions at once, "she's not bitten you, has she? Heaven forbid!" (Moomoo had never bitten anyone in her life.) "Ah! ah!"

"Take her away," said the old lady in a changed voice. "Wretched little dog! What a spiteful creature!"

And, turning round deliberately, she went towards her boudoir. Her companions looked timidly at one another, and were about to follow her but she stopped, stared coldly at them, and said, "What's that for, pray? I've not called you," and went out.

The companions waved their hands to Stepan in despair. He picked up Moomoo, and flung her promptly outside the door, just at Gerasim's feet, and half an hour later a profound stillness reigned in the house, and the old lady sat on her sofa looking blacker than a thundercloud.

What trifles, if you think of it, will sometimes disturb anyone!

Till evening the lady was out of humor; she did not talk to any one, did not play cards, and passed a bad night. She fancied the eau-de-Cologne they gave her was not the same as she usually had, and that her pillow smelt of soap, and she made the wardrobe-maid smell all the bed linen—in fact she was very upset and cross altogether. Next morning she ordered Gavrila to be summoned an hour earlier than usual.

"Tell me, please," she began, directly the latter, not without some inward trepidation, crossed the threshold of her boudoir, "what dog was that barking all night in our yard? It wouldn't let me sleep!"

"A dog, 'm . . . what dog, 'm . . . maybe, the dumb man's dog, 'm," he brought out in a rather unsteady voice.

"I don't know whether it was the dumb man's or whose, but it wouldn't let me sleep. And I wonder what we have such a lot of dogs for! I wish to know. We have a yard dog, haven't we?"

"Oh, yes'm, we have, 'm. Wolf, 'm."

"Well, why more, what do we want more dogs for? It's simply introducing disorder. There's no one in control in the house—that's what it is. And what does the dumb man want with a dog? Who gave him leave to keep dogs in my yard? Yesterday I went to the window, and there it was lying in the flower-garden; it had dragged in some nastiness it was gnawing, and my roses are planted there. . . ."

The lady ceased.

"Let her be gone this very day . . . do you hear?"

"Yes'm."

"Today. Now go. I will send for you later for the report."

Gavrila went away.

As he went through the drawing-room, the steward by way of maintaining order moved a bell from one table to another; he stealthily blew his ducklike nose in the hall, and went into the outer hall. In the outer hall, on a bench Stepan was asleep in the attitude of a slain warrior in a battle picture, his bare legs thrust out below the coat which served him for a blanket. The steward gave him a shove, and whispered some instructions to him, to which Stepan responded with something between a yawn and a laugh. The steward went away, and Stepan got up, put on his coat and his boots, and went out and stood on the steps. Five minutes had not passed before Gerasim made his appearance with a huge bundle of hewn logs on his back, accompanied by the inseparable Moomoo. (The lady had given orders that her bedroom and boudoir should be heated even in the summer.) Gerasim turned sideways before the door, shoved it open with his shoulder, and staggered into the house with his load. Moomoo, as usual, stayed behind to wait for him. Then Stepan, seizing his chance, suddenly pounced on her, like a kite on a chicken, held her down to the ground, gathered her up in his arms, and without even putting on his cap, ran out of the yard with her, got into the first fly he met, and galloped off to a market-place. There he soon found a purchaser, to whom he sold her for fifty copeks, on condition that he would keep her for at least a week tied up; then he returned at once. But before he got home, he got off the fly, and going right round the yard, jumped over the fence into the yard from a back street. He was afraid to go in at the gate for fear of meeting Gerasim.

His anxiety was unnecessary, however; Gerasim was no longer in the yard. On coming out of the house he had at once missed Moomoo. He never remembered her failing to wait for his return, and began running up and down, looking for her, and calling her in his own way. . . . He rushed up to his garret, up to the hayloft, ran out into the street, this way and that. . . . She was lost! He turned to the other serfs, with the most despairing signs, questioned them about her, pointing to her height from the ground, describing her with his hands. . . . Some of them really did not know what had become of Moomoo, and merely shook their heads, others did know, and smiled to him for all response, while the steward assumed an important air, and began scolding the coachmen. Then Gerasim ran right out of the yard.

It was dark by the time he came back. From his worn-out look, his unsteady walk, and his dusty clothes, it might be surmised that he had been running over half Moscow. He stood still opposite the windows of the mistress' house, took a searching look at the steps where a group of house-serfs were crowded together, turned away, and uttered once more his inarticulate "Moomoo." Moomoo did not answer. He went away. Everyone looked after him, but no one smiled or said a word, and the inquisitive postilion Antipka reported next morning in the kitchen that the dumb man had been groaning all night.

All the next day Gerasim did not show himself, so that they were obliged to send the coachman Potap for water instead of him, at which the coachman Potap was anything but pleased. The lady asked Gavrila if her orders had been carried out. Gavrila replied that they had. The next morning Gerasim came out of his garret, and went about his work. He came in to his dinner, ate it, and went out again, without a greeting to anyone. His face, which had always been lifeless, as with all deaf-mutes, seemed now to be turned to stone. After dinner he went out of the yard again, but not for long; he came back, and went straight up to the hayloft. Night came on, a clear moonlight night. Gerasim lay breathing heavily, and incessantly turning from side to side. Suddenly he felt something pull at the skirt of his coat. He started, but did not raise his head, and even shut his eyes tighter. But again there was a pull, stronger than before; he jumped up . . . Before him, with an end of rope round her neck, was Moomoo, twisting and turning. A prolonged cry of delight broke from his speechless breast; he caught up Moomoo, and hugged her tight in his arms, she licked his nose and eyes, and beard and mustache, all in one instant. . . . He stood a little, thought a minute, crept cautiously down from the hayloft, looked round, and having satisfied himself that no one could see him, made his way successfully to his garret.

Gerasim had guessed before that his dog had not got lost by her own doing, that she must have been taken away by the mistress' orders; the servants had explained to him by signs that his Moomoo had snapped at her, and he determined to take his own measures. First he fed Moomoo with a bit of bread, fondled her, and put her to bed, then he fell to meditating, and spent the whole night long in meditating how he could best conceal her. At last he decided to leave her all day in the garret, and only to come in now and then to see her, and to take her out at night. The hole in the door he stopped up effectually with his old overcoat, and almost before it was light he was already in the yard, as though nothing had happened, even—innocent guile!—the same expression of melancholy on his face. It did not even occur to the poor deaf man that Moomoo would betray herself by her whining; in reality, everyone in the house was soon aware that the dumb man's dog had come back, and was locked up in his garret, but from sympathy with him and with her, and partly, perhaps, from dread of him, they did not let him know that they had found out his secret. The steward scratched his head, and gave a despairing wave of his hand, as much as to say, "Well, well, God have mercy on him! If only it doesn't come to the mistress' ears!"

But the dumb man had never shown such energy as on that day; he cleaned and scraped the whole courtyard, pulled up every single weed with his own hand, tugged up every stake in the fence of the flower-garden, to satisfy himself that they were strong enough, and unaided drove them in again; in fact, he toiled and labored so that even the old lady noticed his zeal. Twice in the course of the day Gerasim went stealthily in to see his prisoner; when night came on, he lay down to sleep with her in the garret, not in the hayloft, and only at two o'clock in the night he went out to give her a turn in the fresh air. After walking about the courtyard a good while with her, he was just turning back, when suddenly a rustle was heard behind the fence on the side of the back street. Moomoo pricked up her ears, growled—went up to the fence, sniffed, and gave vent to a loud shrill bark. Some drunkard had thought fit to take refuge under the fence for the night. At that very time the old lady had just fallen asleep after a prolonged fit of "nervous agitation"; these fits of agitation always overtook her after too hearty a supper. The sudden bark waked her up: her heart palpitated, and she felt faint. "Girls, girls!" she moaned. "Girls!" The terrified maids ran into her bedroom. "Oh, oh, I am dying!" she said, flinging her arms about in her agitation. "Again, that dog again! . . . Oh, send for the doctor. They mean to be the death of me. . . . The dog, the dog again! Oh!" And she let her head fall back, which always signified a swoon. They rushed for the doctor, that is, for the household physician, Hariton. This doctor, whose whole qualification consisted in wearing soft-soled boots, knew how to feel the pulse delicately. He used to sleep fourteen hours out of the twenty-four, but the rest of the time he was always sighing, and continually dosing the old lady with cherry-bay drops. This doctor ran up at once, fumigated the room with burnt feathers, and when the old lady opened her eyes, promptly offered her a wineglass of the hallowed drops on a silver tray. The old lady took them, but began again at once in a tearful voice complaining of the dog, of Gavrila, and of her fate, declaring that she was a poor old woman, and that everyone had forsaken her, no one pitied her, everyone wished her dead. Meanwhile the luckless Moomoo had gone on barking, while Gerasim tried in vain to call her away from the fence. "There . . . there . . . again," groaned the old lady, and once more she turned up the whites of her eyes. The doctor whispered to a maid, she rushed into the outer hall, and shook Stepan, he ran to wake Gavrila, Gavrila in a fury ordered the whole household to get up.

Gerasim turned round, saw lights and shadows moving in the windows, and with a premonition of dire trouble in his heart, put Moomoo under his arm, ran into his garret, and locked himself in. A few minutes later five men were banging at his door, but feeling the resistance of the bolt, they stopped. Gavrila ran up in a fearful state of mind, and ordered them all to wait there and watch till morning. Then he flew off himself to the maids' quarter, and through an old companion, Lyubov Lyubimovna, with whose assistance he used to steal tea, sugar, and other groceries and to falsify the accounts, sent word to the mistress that the dog had unhappily run back from somewhere, but that tomorrow she should be killed, and would the mistress be so gracious as not to be angry and to overlook it. The old lady would probably not have been so soon appeased, but the doctor had in his haste given her fully forty drops instead of twelve. The strong dose of narcotic acted; in a quarter of an hour the old lady was in a sound and peaceful sleep; while Gerasim was lying with a white face on his bed, holding Moomoo's mouth tightly shut.

Next morning the lady woke up rather late. Gavrila was waiting till she should be awake, to give the order for a final assault on Gerasim's stronghold, while he prepared himself to face a fearful storm. But the storm did not come off. The old lady lay in bed and sent for the eldest of her dependent companions.

"Lyubov Lyubimovna," she began in a subdued weak voice— she was fond of playing the part of an oppressed and forsaken victim; needless to say, everyone in the house was made extremely uncomfortable at such times—"Lyubov Lyubimovna, you see my position; go, my love, to Gavrila Andreich, and talk to him a little. Can he really prize some wretched cur above the repose—the very life—of his mistress? I could not bear to think so," she added, with an expression of deep feeling. "Go, my love; be so good as to go to Gavrila Andreich for me."

Lyubov Lyubimovna went to Gavrila's room. What conversation passed between them is not known, but a short time after, a whole crowd of people was moving across the yard in the direction of Gerasim's garret. Gavrila walked in front, holding his cap on with his hand, though there was no wind. The footmen and cooks were close behind him; Uncle Tail was looking out of a window, giving instructions, that is to say, simply waving his hands. At the rear there was a crowd of small boys skipping and hopping along; half of them were outsiders who had run up. On the narrow staircase leading to the garret sat one guard; at the door were standing two more with sticks. They began to mount the stairs, which they entirely blocked up. Gavrila went up to the door, knocked with his fist, shouting, "Open the door!"

A stifled bark was audible, but there was no answer.

"Open the door, I tell you," he repeated.

"But, Gavrila Andreich," Stepan observed from below, "he's deaf, you know—he doesn't hear."

They all laughed.

"What are we to do?" Gavrila rejoined from above.

"Why, there's a hole there in the door," answered Stepan, "so you shake a stick in there."

Gavrila bent down.

"He's stuffed it up with a coat or something."

"Well, you just push the coat in."

At this moment a smothered bark was heard again.

"See, see—she speaks for herself," was remarked in the crowd, and again they laughed.

Gavrila scratched his ear.

"No, mate," he responded at last, "you can poke the coat in yourself, if you like."

"All right, let me."

And Stepan scrambled up, took the stick, pushed in the coat, and began waving the stick about in the opening, saying, "Come out, come out!" as he did so. He was still waving the stick, when suddenly the door of the garret was flung open; all the crowd flew pellmell down the stairs instantly, Gavrila first of all. Uncle Tail locked the window.

"Come, come, come," shouted Gavrila from the yard, "mind what you're about."

Gerasim stood without stirring in his doorway. The crowd gathered at the foot of the stairs. Gerasim, with his arms akimbo, looked down on all these poor creatures in German coats; in his red peasant's shirt he looked like a giant before them. Gavrila took a step forward.

"Mind, mate," he said, "don't be insolent."

And he began to explain to him by signs that the mistress insisted on having his dog; that he must hand it over at once, or it would be the worse for him.

Gerasim looked at him, pointed to the dog, made a motion with hand round his neck as though he were pulling a noose tight, and glanced with a face of inquiry at the steward.

"Yes, yes," the latter assented, nodding; "yes, just so."

Gerasim dropped his eyes, then all of a sudden roused himself and pointed to Moomoo, who was all the while standing beside him, innocently wagging her tail and pricking up her ears inquisitively. Then he repeated the strangling action round his neck and significantly struck himself on the breast, as though announcing he would take upon himself the task of killing Moomoo.

"But you'll deceive us," Gavrila waved back in response.

Gerasim looked at him, smiled scornfully, struck himself again on the breast, and slammed-to the door.

They all looked at one another in silence.

"What does that mean?" Gavrila began. "He's locked himself in."

"Let him be, Gavrila Andreich," Stepan advised; "he'll do it if he's promised. He's like that, you know. . . . If he makes a promise, it's a certain thing. He's not like us others in that. The truth's the truth with him. Yes, indeed."

"Yes," they all repeated, nodding their heads, "yes—that's so—yes."

Uncle Tail opened his window, and he too said, "Yes."

"Well, maybe, we shall see," responded Gavrila; "anyway, we won't take off the guard. Here you, Yeroshka!" he added, addressing a poor fellow in a yellow nankeen coat, who considered himself to be a gardener, "what have you to do? Take a stick and sit here, and if anything happens, run to me at once!"

Yeroshka took a stick, and sat down on the bottom stair. The crowd dispersed, all except a few inquisitive small boys, while Gavrila went home and sent word through Lyubov Lyubimovna to the mistress, that everything had been done, while he sent a postilion for a policeman in case of need. The old lady tied a knot in her handkerchief, sprinkled some eau-de-Cologne on it, sniffed at it, and rubbed her temples with it, drank some tea, and, being still under the influence of the cherry-bay drops, fell asleep again.

An hour after all this hubbub the garret door opened, and Gerasim showed himself. He had on his best coat; he was leading Moomoo by a string. Yeroshka moved aside and let him pass. Gerasim went to the gates. All the small boys in the yard stared at him in silence. He did not even turn round; he only put his cap on in the street. Gavrila sent the same Yeroshka to follow him and keep watch on him as a spy. Yeroshka, seeing from a distance that he had gone into a cookshop with his dog, waited for him to come out again.

Gerasim was well known at the cookshop, and his signs were understood. He asked for cabbage soup with meat in it, and sat down with his arms on the table. Moomoo stood beside his chair, looking calmly at him with her intelligent eyes. Her coat was glossy; one could see she had just been combed down. They brought Gerasim the soup. He crumbled some bread into it, cut the meat up small, and put the plate on the ground. Moomoo began eating in her usual refined way, her little muzzle daintily held so as scarcely to touch her food. Gerasim gazed a long while at her; two big tears suddenly rolled from his eyes; one fell on the dog's brow, the other into the soup. He shaded his face with his hand. Moomoo ate up half the plateful, and came away from it, licking her lips. Gerasim got up, paid for the soup, and went out, followed by the rather perplexed glances of the waiter. Yeroshka, seeing Gerasim, hid round a corner, and letting him get in front, followed him again.

Gerasim walked without haste, still holding Moomoo by a string. When he got to the corner of the street, he stood as though reflecting, and suddenly set off with rapid steps to the Crimean Ford. On the way he went into the yard of a house, where a lodge was being built, and carried away two bricks under his arm. At the Crimean Ford, he turned along the bank, went to a place where there were two little rowing-boats fastened to stakes (he had noticed them before), and jumped into one of them with Moomoo. A lame old man came out of a shed in the corner of a kitchen-garden and shouted after him; but Gerasim only nodded, and began rowing so vigorously, though against stream, that in an instant he had darted two hundred yards away. The old man stood for a while, scratched his back first with the left and then with the right hand, and went back hobbling to the shed.

Gerasim rowed on and on. Moscow was soon left behind. Meadows stretched along either bank, market gardens, fields, and copses; peasants' huts began to make their appearance. There was the fragrance of the country. He threw down his oars, bent his head down to Moomoo, who was sitting facing him on a dry cross seat— the bottom of the boat was full of water—and stayed motionless, his mighty hands clasped upon her back, while the boat was gradually carried back by the current towards the town. At last Gerasim drew himself up hurriedly, with a sort of sick anger in his face, he tied up the bricks he had taken with a string, made a running noose, put it round Moomoo's neck, lifted her up over the river, and for the last time looked at her. . . . she watched him confidingly and without any fear, wagging her tail. He turned away, frowned, and wrung his hands. . . . Gerasim heard nothing, neither the quick shrill whine of Moomoo as she fell, nor the heavy splash of the water; for him the noisiest day was soundless and silent as even the stillest night is not silent to us. When he opened his eyes again, little wavelets were hurrying over the river, chasing one another; as before they broke against the boat's side, and only far away behind wide circles moved widening to the bank.

Directly Gerasim had vanished from Yeroshka's sight, the latter returned home and reported what he had seen.

"Well, then," observed Stepan, "he'll drown her. Now we can feel easy about it. If he once promises a thing. . . ."

No one saw Gerasim during the day. He did not have dinner at home. Evening came on; they were all gathered together to supper, except him.

"What a strange creature that Gerasim is!" piped a fat laundrymaid; "fancy, upsetting himself like that over a dog. . . . Upon my word!"

"But Gerasim has been here," Stepan cried all at once, scraping up his porridge with a spoon.

"How? When?"

"Why, a couple of hours ago. Yes, indeed! I ran against him at the gate; he was going out again from here; he was coming out of the yard. I tried to ask him about his dog, but he wasn't in the best of humors, I could see. Well, he gave me a shove; I suppose he only meant to put me out of his way, as if he'd say, 'Let me go, do!' but he fetched me such a crack on my neck, so seriously, that—oh! oh!" And Stepan, who could not help laughing, shrugged up and rubbed the back of his head. "Yes," he added, "he has got a fist; it's something like a fist, there's no denying that!"

They all laughed at Stepan, and after supper they separated to go to bed.

Meanwhile, at that very time, a gigantic figure with a bag on his shoulders and a stick in his hand, was eagerly and persistently stepping out along the T—— highroad. It was Gerasim. He was hurrying on without looking round; hurrying homewards, to his own village, to his own country. After drowning poor Moomoo, he had run back to his garret, hurriedly packed a few things together in an old horsecloth, tied it up in a bundle, tossed it on his shoulder, and so was ready. He had noticed the road carefully when he was brought to Moscow; the village his mistress had taken him from lay only about twenty miles off the highroad. He walked along it with a sort of invincible purpose, a desperate and at the same time joyous determination. He walked, his shoulders thrown back and his chest expanded, his eyes fixed greedily straight before him. He hastened as though his old mother were waiting for him at home, as though she were calling him to her after long wanderings in strange parts, among strangers. The summer night, that was just drawing in, was still and warm; on one side, where the sun had set, the horizon was still light and faintly flushed with the last glow of the vanished day; on the other side a blue-gray twilight had already risen up. The night was coming up from that quarter. Quails were about in hundreds; corncrakes were calling to one another in the thickets. . . . Gerasim could not hear them; he could not hear the delicate night-whispering of the trees, by which his strong legs carried him, but he smelt the familiar scent of the ripening rye, which was wafted from the dark fields; he felt the wind, flying to meet him—the wind from home— beat caressingly upon his face, and play with his hair and his beard. He saw before him the whitening road homewards, straight as an arrow. He saw in the sky stars innumerable, lighting up his way, and stepped out, strong and bold as a lion, so that when the rising sun shed its moist rosy light upon the still fresh and unwearied traveler, already thirty miles lay between him and Moscow.

In a couple of days he was at home, in his little hut, to the great astonishment of the soldier's wife who had been settled there. After praying before the holy picture, he set off at once to the village elder. The village elder was at first surprised; but the hay-cutting had just begun; Gerasim was a first-rate mower, and they put a scythe into his hand on the spot, and he went to mow in his old way, mowing so that the peasants were fairly astounded as they watched his wide sweeping strokes and the heaps he raked together. . . .

In Moscow the day after Gerasim's flight they missed him. They went to his garret, rummaged about in it, and spoke to Gavrila. He came, looked, shrugged his shoulders, and decided that the dumb man had either run away or had drowned himself with his stupid dog. They gave information to the police, and informed the lady. The old lady was furious, burst into tears, gave orders that he was to be found whatever happened, declared she had never ordered the dog to be destroyed, and, in fact, gave Gavrila such a rating that he could do nothing all day but shake his head and murmur, "Well!" until Uncle Tail checked him at last, sympathetically echoing "We-ell!" At last the news came from the country of Gerasim's being there. The old lady was somewhat pacified; at first she issued a mandate for him to be brought back without delay to Moscow; afterwards, however, she declared that such an ungrateful creature was absolutely of no use to her. Soon after this she died herself; and her heirs had no thought to spare for Gerasim; they let their mother's other servants redeem their freedom on payment of an annual rent.

And Gerasim is living still, a lonely man in his lonely hut; he is strong and healthy as before, and does the work of four men as before, and as before is serious and steady. But his neighbors have observed that ever since his return from Moscow he has quite given up the society of women; he will not even look at them, and does not keep even a single dog. "It's his good luck, though," the peasants reason; "that he can get on without female folk; and as for a dog— what need has he of a dog? you wouldn't get a thief to go into his yard for any money!" Such is the fame of the dumb man's Titanic strength.

1854

# A LEAR OF THE STEPPES

WE WERE a party of six, gathered together one winter evening at the house of an old college friend. The conversation turned on Shakespeare, on his types, and how profoundly and truly they were taken from the very heart of humanity. We admitted particularly their truth to life, their actuality. Each of us spoke of the Hamlets, the Othellos, the Falstaffs, even the Richard the Thirds and Macbeths —the two last only potentially, it is true, resembling their proto-types—whom he had happened to come across.

"And I, gentlemen," cried our host, a man well past middle age, "used to know a King Lear!"

"How was that?" we questioned him.

"Oh, would you like me to tell you about him?"

"Please do."

And our friend promptly began his narrative.

## I

All my childhood [he began] and early youth, up to the age of fifteen, I spent in the country, on the estate of my mother, a wealthy landowner in X—— province. Almost the most vivid impression, that has remained in my memory of that far-off time, is the figure of our nearest neighbor, Martyn Petrovich Harlov. Indeed it would be diffi-cult for such an impression to be obliterated: I never in my life after-wards met anything in the least like Harlov. Picture to yourselves a man of gigantic stature. On his huge carcass was set, a little askew, and without the least trace of a neck, a prodigious head. A perfect haystack of tangled yellowish-gray hair stood up all over it, growing almost down to the bushy eyebrows. On the broad expanse of his purple face, that looked as though it had been peeled, there protruded a sturdy knobby nose; diminutive little blue eyes stared out haughtily, and a mouth gaped open that was diminutive too, but crooked, chapped, and of the same color as the rest of the face. The voice that proceeded from this mouth, though hoarse, was exceedingly strong and resonant. . . . Its sound recalled the clank of iron bars, carried in a cart over a badly paved road; and when Harlov spoke, it was as though some one were shouting in a high wind across a wide ravine. It was difficult to tell just what Harlov's face expressed, it was such an expanse. . . . One felt one could hardly take it all in at one glance. But it was not disagreeable—a certain grandeur indeed could be discerned in it, only it was exceedingly astounding and unusual. And what hands he had—positive cushions! What fingers, what feet! I remember I could never gaze without a certain respectful awe at the four-foot span of Martyn Petrovich's back, at his shoulders, like millstones. But what especially struck me was his ears! They were just like great twists of bread, full of bends and curves; his cheeks seemed to support them on both sides. Martyn Petrovich used to wear—winter and summer alike—a Cossack dress of green cloth, girt about with a small Circassian strap, and tarred boots. I never saw a cravat on him; and indeed what could he have tied a cravat round? He breathed slowly and heavily, like a bull, but walked without a sound. One might have imagined that having got into a room, he was in constant fear of upsetting and overturning everything, and so moved cautiously from place to place, sideways for the most part, as though slinking by. He was possessed of a strength truly Herculean, and in consequence enjoyed great renown in the neighborhood. Our common people retain to this day their reverence for Titanic heroes. Legends were invented about him. They used to recount that he had one day met a bear in the forest and had almost vanquished him; that having once caught a thief in his beehouse, he had flung him, horse and cart and all, over the hedge, and so on. Harlov himself never boasted of his strength. "If my right hand is blessed," he used to say, "so it is God's will it should be!" He was proud, only he did not take pride in his strength, but in his rank, his descent, his intelligence.

"Our family descended from the Swede Harlus," he used to maintain. "In the reign of Ivan Vasilyevich the Blind (fancy how

long ago!) he came to Russia, and that Swede Harlus did not wish
to be a Finnish count—but he wished to be a Russian nobleman, and
he was inscribed in the Golden Book. It's from him we Harlovs are
sprung! . . . And by the same token, all of us Harlovs are born
flaxen-haired, with light eyes and clean faces, because we're children
of the snow!"

"But, Martyn Petrovich," I once tried to object, "there never was
an Ivan Vasilyevich the Blind. There was an Ivan Vasilyevich the
Terrible. 'The Blind' was the name given to the Great Prince Vasily
Vasilyevich."

"What nonsense will you talk next!" Harlov answered serenely;
"since I say so, so it was!"

One day my mother took it into her head to commend him to
his face for his really remarkable incorruptibility.

"Ah, Natalya Nikolayevna!" he protested almost angrily; "what
a thing to praise me for, really! We gentlefolk can't be otherwise; so
that no churl, no low-born, servile creature dare even imagine evil
of us! I am a Harlov, my family has come down from"—here he
pointed up somewhere very high aloft in the ceiling—"and me not
be honest! How is it possible?"

Another time a high official, who had come into the neighborhood
and was staying with my mother, fancied he could make fun of
Martyn Petrovich. The latter had again referred to the Swede Harlus,
who came to Russia . . .

"In the days of King Solomon?" the official interrupted.

"No, not of King Solomon, but of the Great Prince Ivan Vasilyevich the Blind."

"But I imagine," the official pursued, "that your family is much
more ancient, and goes back to antediluvian days, when there were
still mastodons and megatheriums about."

These scientific names were absolutely meaningless to Martyn
Petrovich; but he realized that the dignitary was laughing at him.

"May be so," he boomed, "our family is, no doubt, very ancient;
in those days when my ancestor was in Moscow, they do say there
was as great a fool as your excellency living there, and such fools are
not seen twice in a thousand years."

The high official was in a furious rage, while Harlov threw his
head back, stuck out his chin, snorted and disappeared. Two days
later, he came in again. My mother began reproaching him. "It's a

lesson for him, ma'am," interposed Harlov, "not to fly off without knowing what he's about, to find out whom he has to deal with first." The dignitary was almost of the same age as Harlov; but this Titan was in the habit of regarding every one as not fully grown up. He had the greatest confidence in himself and was afraid of absolutely no one. "Can they do anything to me? Where on earth is the man that can?" he would ask, and suddenly he would go off into a short but deafening guffaw.

## II

My mother was exceedingly particular in her choice of acquaintances, but she made Harlov welcome with special cordiality and allowed him many privileges. Twenty-five years before, he had saved her life by holding up her carriage on the edge of a deep precipice, down which the horses had already fallen. The traces and straps of the harness broke, but Martyn Petrovich did not let go his hold of the wheel he had grasped, though the blood spurted out under his nails. My mother had arranged his marriage. She chose for his wife an orphan girl of seventeen, who had been brought up in her house; he was over forty at the time. Martyn Petrovich's wife was a frail creature—they said he carried her into his house in the palms of his hands—and she did not live long with him. She bore him two daughters, however. After her death, my mother continued her good offices to Martyn Petrovich. She placed his elder daughter in the district school, and afterwards found her a husband, and already had another in her eye for the second. Harlov was a fairly good manager. He had a little estate of nearly eight hundred acres, and had built on to his place a little, and the way the peasants obeyed him is indescribable. Owing to his stoutness, Harlov scarcely ever went anywhere on foot: the earth did not bear him. He used to go everywhere in a low racing droshky, himself driving a rawboned mare, thirty years old, with a scar on her shoulder, from a wound which she had received in the battle of Borodino, under the quartermaster of a cavalry regiment. This mare was always somehow lame in all four legs; she could not go at a walking pace, but could only change from a trot to a canter. She used to eat mugwort and wormwood along the hedges, which I have never noticed any other horse do. I remember I always used to wonder how such a broken-down nag could draw such a fearful weight. I won't venture to repeat how many hundred-weight were attributed to our neighbor. In the droshky behind Martyn Petrovich's back perched his swarthy page, Maximka. With his face and whole person squeezed close up to his master, and his bare feet propped on the hind axle bar of the droshky, he looked like a little leaf or worm which had clung by chance to the gigantic carcass before him. This same page boy used once a week to shave Martyn Petrovich. He used, so they said, to stand on a table to perform this operation. Some jocose persons averred that he had to run round his master's chin. Harlov did not like staying long at home, and so one might often see him driving about in his invariable equipage, with the reins in one hand (the other he held smartly on his knee with the elbow crooked upwards), with a diminutive old cap on the very top of his head. He looked boldly about him with his little bearlike eyes, shouted in a voice of thunder to all the peasants, artisans, and tradespeople he met. Priests he greatly disliked, and he would send vigorous abjurations after them when he met them. One day on overtaking me (I was out for a stroll with my gun), he hallooed at a hare that lay near the road in such a way that I could not get the roar and ring of it out of my ears all day.

## III

My mother, as I have already stated, made Martyn Petrovich very welcome. She knew what a profound respect he entertained for her person. "She is a real gentlewoman, one of our sort," was the way he used to refer to her. He used to style her his benefactress, while she saw in him a devoted giant, who would not have hesitated to face a whole mob of peasants in defence of her; and although no one foresaw the barest possibility of such a contingency, still, to my mother's notions, in the absence of a husband—she had early been left a widow—such a champion as Martyn Petrovich was not to be despised. And besides, he was a man of upright character, who curried favor with no one, never borrowed money or drank spirits; and no fool either, though he had received no sort of education. My mother trusted Martyn Petrovich: when she took it into her head to make her will, she asked him to witness it, and he drove home expressly to fetch his round iron-rimmed spectacles, without which he could not write. And with spectacles on nose, he succeeded, in a quarter of an hour, with many gasps and groans and great effort, in inscribing his Christian name, patronymic, and surname and his rank and designation, tracing enormous quadrangular letters, with tails and flourishes. Having completed this task, he declared he was tired out, and that writing for him was as hard work as catching fleas. Yes, my mother had a respect for him . . . He was not, however, admitted beyond the dining-room in our house. He carried a very strong odor about with him; there was a smell of the earth, of decaying forest, of marsh mud about him. "He's a forest-demon!" my old nurse would declare. At dinner a special table used to be laid apart in a corner for Martyn Petrovich, and he was not offended at that, he knew other people were ill at ease sitting beside him, and he too had greater freedom in eating. And he did eat too, as no one, I imagine, has eaten since the days of Polyphemus. At the very beginning of dinner, by way of a precautionary measure, they always served him a pot of some four pounds of porridge, "else you'd eat me out of house and home," my mother used to say. "That I should, ma'am," Martyn Petrovich would respond, grinning.

My mother liked to hear his reflections on any topic connected with the land. But she could not support the sound of his voice for long together. "What's the meaning of it, my good sir!" she would exclaim; "you might take something to cure yourself of it, really! You simply deafen me. Such a trumpet-blast!"

"Natalya Nikolayevna! benefactress!" Martyn Petrovich would rejoin, as a rule, "I'm not responsible for my throat. And what medicine would have any effect on me—kindly tell me that? I'd better hold my tongue for a bit."

In reality, I imagine, no medicine could have affected Martyn Petrovich. He was never ill.

He was not good at telling stories, and did not care for it. "Much talking gives me asthma," he used to remark reproachfully. It was only when one got him on to the year 1812—he had served in the militia, and had received a bronze medal, which he used to wear on festive occasions attached to a Vladimir ribbon—when one questioned him about the French, that he would relate some few anecdotes. He used, however, to maintain stoutly all the while that there never had been any Frenchmen, real ones, in Russia, only some poor marauders, who had straggled over from hunger, and that he had given many a good drubbing to such rabble in the forests.

## IV

And yet even this self-confident, unflinching giant had his moments of melancholy and depression. Without any visible cause he would suddenly begin to be sad; he would lock himself up alone in his room, and hum—positively hum—like a whole hive of bees; or he would call his page Maximka, and tell him to read aloud to him out of the solitary book which had somehow found its way into his house, an odd volume of Novikov's *The Toiler at Rest*, or else to sing to him. And Maximka, who by some strange freak of chance, could spell out print, syllable by syllable, would set to work with the usual chopping up of the words and shifting of the accent, bawling out phrases of the following description: "but man in his willfulness draws from this vacant space that he discovers in the creatures utterly opposite conclusions. Each creature separately, he says, is not capable of making me happy!" and so on.* Or he would chant in a shrill little voice a mournful song, of which nothing could be distinguished but some barely intelligible syllables. Meanwhile Martyn Petrovich would shake his head, make allusions to the transience of the affairs of this life, to the fact that all things will turn to ashes, fade away like grass, pass—and be no more! A picture had somehow come into his hands, representing a burning candle, which the winds, with puffed-out cheeks, were blowing upon from all sides; below was the inscription: "Such is the life of man." He was very fond of this picture; he had hung it up in his own room, but at ordinary, not melancholy, times he used to keep it turned face to the wall, so that it might not depress him. Harlov, that colossus, was afraid of death! To the consolations of religion, to prayer, however, he rarely had recourse in his fits of melancholy. Even then he chiefly relied on his own intelligence. He had no particular religious feeling; he was not often seen in church; he used to say, it is true, that he did not go on the ground that, owing to his corporeal dimensions, he was afraid of squeezing other people out. The fit of depression commonly ended in Martyn Petrovich's beginning to whistle, and suddenly, in a voice of thunder, ordering out his droshky, and dashing off about the neighborhood, vigorously brandishing his disengaged hand over the peak of his cap, as

* The Toiler at Rest, Moscow, 1785, part 3, p. 23.

though he would say, "For all that, I don't care a straw!" He was a regular Russian.

## V

Strong men, like Martyn Petrovich, are for the most part of a phlegmatic disposition; but he, on the contrary, was rather easily irritated. He was specially short-tempered with a certain Bychkov, who had found a refuge in our house, where he occupied a position between that of a buffoon and a dependent. He was the brother of Harlov's deceased wife, had been nicknamed Souvenir as a little boy, and Souvenir he had remained for every one, even the servants, who addressed him, it is true, as Souvenir Timofeich. His real name he seemed hardly to know himself. He was a pitiful creature, looked down upon by everyone; a toady, in fact. He had no teeth on one side of his mouth, which gave his little wrinkled face a crooked appearance. He was in a perpetual fuss and fidget; he used to poke himself into the maids' room, or into the countinghouse, or into the priest's quarters, or else into the bailiff's hut. He was expelled from everywhere, but he only shrugged himself up, and screwed up his little eyes, and laughed a pitiful mawkish laugh, like the sound of rinsing a bottle. It always seemed to me that had Souvenir had money, he would have turned into the basest person, unprincipled, spiteful, even cruel. Poverty kept him within bounds. He was only allowed drink on holidays. He was decently dressed, by my mother's orders, since in the evenings he took a hand in her game of picquet or boston. Souvenir was constantly repeating, "Certainly, d'rectly, d'rectly." "D'rectly what?" my mother would ask, with annoyance. He instantly drew back his hands, in a scare, and lisped, "At your service, ma'am!" Listening at doors, backbiting, and, above all, quizzing, teasing, were his sole interest, and he used to quiz as though he had a right to, as though he were avenging himself for something. He used to call Martyn Petrovich brother, and tormented him beyond endurance. "What made you kill my sister, Margarita Timofeyevna?" he used to persist, wrigging about before him and sniggering. One day Martyn Petrovich was sitting in the billiard-room, a cool apartment, in which no one had ever seen a single fly, and which our neighbor, disliking heat and sunshine, greatly favored on this account. He was sitting between the

wall and the billiard-table. Souvenir was fidgeting before his bulky
person, mocking him, grimacing. . . . Martyn Petrovich wanted to
get rid of him, and thrust both hands out in front of him. Luckily
for Souvenir he managed to get away, his brother-in-law's open
hands came into collision with the edge of the billiard-table, and
the billiard-board went flying off all its six screws. . . . What a
mass of batter Souvenir would have been turned into under those
mighty hands!

## VI

I had long been curious to see how Martyn Petrovich arranged
his household, what sort of a home he had. One day I invited myself
to accompany him on horseback as far as Yeskovo (that was the
name of his estate). "Upon my word, you want to have a look at
my dominion," was Martyn Petrovich's comment. "By all means!
I'll show you the garden, and the house, and the threshing-floor, and
everything. I have plenty of everything." We set off. It was reckoned hardly more than a couple of miles from our place to Yeskovo.
"Here it is—my dominion!" Martyn Petrovich roared suddenly, trying to turn his immovable neck, and waving his arm to right and
left. "It's all mine!" Harlov's homestead lay on the top of a sloping
hill. At the bottom, a few wretched-looking peasants' huts clus-
tered close to a small pond. At the pond, on a washing platform, an
old peasant woman in a check petticoat was beating some soaked
linen with a bat.

"Axinya!" boomed Martyn Petrovich, but in such a note that the
rooks flew up in a flock from an oat-field near. . . . "Washing
your husband's breeches?"

The peasant woman turned at once and bowed very low.

"Yes, sir," sounded her weak voice.

"Ay, ay! Yonder, look," Martyn Petrovich continued, proceeding at a trot alongside a half-rotting wattle fence, "that is my hemp-
patch; and that yonder's the peasants'; see the difference? And this
here is my garden; the apple-trees I planted, and the willows I
planted too. Else there was no timber of any sort here. Look at
that, and learn a lesson!"

We turned into the courtyard, shut in by a fence; right opposite
the gate, rose an old tumbledown lodge, with a thatch roof, and

steps up to it, raised on posts. On one side stood another, rather newer, and with a tiny attic; but it too was a ramshackle affair. "Here you may learn a lesson again," observed Harlov; "see what a little manor-house our fathers lived in; but now see what a mansion I have built myself." This "mansion" was like a house of cards. Five or six dogs, one more ragged and hideous than another, welcomed us with barking. "Sheep-dogs!" observed Martyn Petrovich. "Pure-bred Crimeans! Sh, damned brutes! I'll come and strangle you one after another!" On the steps of the new building, there came out a young man, in a long full nankeen overall, the husband of Martyn Petrovich's elder daughter. Skipping quickly up to the droshky, he respectfully supported his father-in-law under the elbow as he got up, and even made as though he would hold the gigantic feet, which the latter, bending his bulky person forward, lifted with a sweeping movement across the seat; then he assisted me to dismount from my horse.

"Anna!" cried Harlov, "Natalya Nikolayevna's son has come to pay us a visit; you must find some good cheer for him. But where's Yevlampia?" (Anna was the name of the elder daughter, Yevlampia of the younger.)

"She's not at home; she's gone into the fields to get cornflowers," responded Anna, appearing at a little window near the door.

"Is there any junket?" queried Harlov.

"Yes."

"And cream too?"

"Yes."

"Well, set them on the table, and I'll show the young gentleman my own room meanwhile. This way, please, this way," he added, addressing me, and beckoning with his forefinger. In his own house he treated me less familiarly; as a host he felt obliged to be more formally respectful. He led me along a corridor. "Here is where I abide," he observed, stepping sideways over the threshold of a wide doorway, "this is my room. Pray walk in!"

His room turned out to be a big unplastered apartment, almost empty; on the walls, on nails driven in askew, hung two riding-whips, a three-cornered hat, reddish with wear, a single-barreled gun, a saber, a sort of curious horse-collar inlaid with metal plates, and the picture representing a burning candle blown on by the winds. In one corner stood a wooden settle covered with a parti-colored rug. Hundreds of flies swarmed thickly about the ceiling; yet the room was cool. But .it reeked of that peculiar odor of the forest which always accompanied Martyn Petrovich.

"Well, is it a nice room?" Harlov questioned me.

"Very nice."

"Look-ye, there hangs my Dutch horse-collar," Harlov went on, dropping into his familiar tone again. "A splendid horse-collar! Got it by barter off a Jew. Just you look at it!"

"It's a good horse-collar."

"It's most practical. And just sniff it . . . what leather!" I smelt the horse-collar. It smelt of rancid oil and nothing else.

"Now, be seated,—there on the stool; make yourself at home," observed Harlov, while he himself sank on to the settle, and seemed to fall into a doze, shutting his eyes and even beginning to snore. I gazed at him without speaking with ever fresh wonder; he was a perfect mountain—there was no other word! Suddenly he started.

"Anna!" he shouted, while his huge stomach rose and fell like a wave on the sea. "What are you about? Look sharp! Didn't you hear me?"

"Everything's ready, father; come in," I heard his daughter's voice.

I inwardly marveled at the rapidity with which Martyn Petrovich's behests had been carried out; and followed him into the drawing-room, where, on a table covered with a red cloth with white flowers on it, lunch was already prepared: junket, cream, wheaten bread, even powdered sugar and ginger. While I set to work on the junket, Martyn Petrovich growled affectionately, "Eat, my friend, eat, my dear boy; don't despise our country cheer," and sitting down again in a corner, again seemed to fall into a doze. Before me, perfectly motionless, with downcast eyes, stood Anna Martynovna, while I saw through the window her husband walking my cob up and down the yard, and rubbing the chain of the snaffle with his own hands.

## VII

My mother did not like Harlov's elder daughter; she called her a stuck-up thing. Anna Martynovna scarcely ever came to pay us her respects, and behaved with chilly decorum in my mother's presence, though it was by her good offices she had been well educated at a boarding-school, and had been married, and on her wedding-day had received a thousand roubles and a yellow Turkish shawl, the latter, it is true, a trifle the worse for wear. She was a woman of medium height, thin, very brisk and rapid in her movements, with thick fair hair and a handsome dark face, on which the pale-blue narrow eyes showed up in a rather strange but pleasing way. She had a straight thin nose, her lips were thin too, and her chin was like the loop-end of a hairpin. No one looking at her could fail to think: "Well, you are a clever creature—and a spiteful one, too!" And for all that, there was something attractive about her too. Even the dark moles, scattered "like buckwheat" over her face, suited her and increased the feeling she inspired. Her hands thrust into her kerchief, she was slily watching me, looking downwards (I was seated, while she was standing). A wicked little smile strayed about her lips and her cheeks and in the shadow of her long eyelashes. "Ugh, you pampered little fine gentleman!" this smile seemed to express. Every time she drew a breath, her nostrils slightly distended—this, too, was rather strange. But all the same, it seemed to me that were Anna Martynovna to love me, or even to care to kiss me with her thin cruel lips, I should simply bound up to the ceiling with delight. I knew she was very severe and exacting, that the peasant women and girls went in terror of her—but what of that? Anna Martynova secretly excited my imagination . . . though after all, I was only fifteen then,—and at that age! . . .

Martyn Petrovich roused himself again. "Anna!" he shouted, "you ought to strum something on the pianoforte . . . young gentlemen are fond of that."

I looked round; there was a pitiful semblance of a piano in the room.

"Yes, father," responded Anna Martynovna. "Only what am I to play for the young gentleman? He won't find it interesting."

"Why, what did they teach you at your young ladies' seminary?"

"I've forgotten everything—besides, the strings are broken."

Anna Martynovna's voice was very pleasant, resonant and rather plaintive—like the note of some birds of prey.

"Very well," said Martyn Petrovich, and he lapsed into dreaminess again. "Well," he began once more, "wouldn't you like, then, to see the threshing-floor, and have a look round? Volodka will escort you.—Hi, Volodka!" he shouted to his son-in-law, who was still pacing up and down the yard with my horse, "take the young gentleman to the threshing-floor . . . and show him my farming generally. But I must have a nap! So! good-bye!"

He went out and I after him. Anna Martynovna at once set to work rapidly, and, as it were, angrily, clearing the table. In the doorway, I turned and bowed to her. But she seemed not to notice my bow, and only smiled again, more maliciously than before.

I took my horse from Harlov's son-in-law and led him by the bridle. We went together to the threshing-floor, but as we discovered nothing very remarkable about it, and as he could not suppose any great interest in farming in a young lad like me, we returned through the garden to the main road.

## VIII

I was well acquainted with Harlov's son-in-law. His name was Vladimir Vasilyevich Sletkin. He was an orphan, brought up by my mother, and the son of a petty official, to whom she had entrusted some business. He had first been placed in the district school, then he had entered the "seignioral countinghouse," then he had been put into the service in the government stores, and, finally, married to the daughter of Martyn Petrovich. My mother used to call him a little Jew, and certainly, with his curly hair, his black eyes always moist, like damson jam, his hook nose, and wide red mouth, he did suggest the Jewish type. But the color of his skin was white and he was altogether very good-looking. He was of a most obliging temper, so long as his personal advantage was not involved. Then he promptly lost all self-control from greediness, and was moved even to tears. He was ready to whine the whole day long to gain the paltriest trifle; he would remind one a hundred times over of a promise, and be hurt and complain if it were not carried out at once. He liked sauntering about the fields with a gun; and when he happened to get a hare or a wild duck, he would thrust his booty into his game-bag with peculiar zest, saying, "Now, you may be as tricky as you like, you won't escape me! Now you're *mine!*"

"You've a good horse," he began in his lisping voice, as he helped me to get into the saddle; "I ought to have a horse like that! But where can I get one? I've no such luck. If you'd ask your mamma, now—remind her."

"Why, has she promised you one?"

"Promised? No; but I thought that in her great kindness—"

"You should apply to Martyn Petrovich."

"To Martyn Petrovich?" Sletkin repeated, dwelling on each syllable. "To him I'm no better than a worthless page, like Maximka. He keeps a tight hand on us, that he does, and you get nothing from him for all your toil."

"Really?"

"Yes, by God. He'll say, 'My word's sacred!'—and there, it's as though he's chopped it off with an axe. You may beg or not, it's all one. Besides, Anna Martynovna, my wife, is not in such favour with him as Yevlampia Martynovna. O merciful God, bless us and save us!" he suddenly interrupted himself, flinging up his hands in despair. "Look! what's that? A whole half-rood of oats, our oats, some wretch has gone and cut. The villain! Just see! Thieves! thieves! It's a true saying, to be sure, don't trust Yeskovo, Beskovo, Yerino, and Belino! (these were the names of four neighboring villages). Ah, ah, what a thing! A rouble and a half's worth, or, maybe, two roubles' loss!"

In Sletkin's voice, one could almost hear sobs. I gave my horse a poke in the ribs and rode away from him.

Sletkin's ejaculations still reached my hearing, when suddenly at a turn in the road, I came upon the second daughter of Harlov, Yevlampia, who had, in the words of Anna Martynovna, gone into the fields to get cornflowers. A thick wreath of those flowers was twined about her head. We exchanged bows in silence. Yevlampia, too, was very good-looking, as much so as her sister, though in a different style. She was tall and stoutly built; everything about her was on a large scale: her head, and her feet and hands, and her snow-white teeth, and especially her eyes, prominent, languishing eyes, of the dark blue of glass beads. Everything about her, while still beautiful, had positively a monumental character (she was a true daughter of Martyn Petrovich). She did not, it seemed, know what to do with her massive fair mane, and she had twisted it in three plaits round her head. Her mouth was charming, crimson and fresh as a rose, and as she talked her upper lip was lifted in the middle in a very fascinating way. But there was something wild and almost fierce in the glance of her huge eyes. "A free bird, wild Cossack breed," so Martyn Petrovich used to say of her. I was in awe of her . . . This stately beauty reminded one of her father.

I rode on a little farther and heard her singing in a strong, even, rather harsh voice, a regular peasant voice; suddenly she ceased. I looked round and from the crest of the hill saw her standing beside Harlov's son-in-law, facing the rood of oats. The latter was gesticulating and pointing, but she stood without stirring. The sun lighted up her tall figure, and the wreath of cornflowers shone brilliantly blue on her head.

## IX

I believe I have already mentioned that, for this second daughter of Harlov's too, my mother had already prepared a match. This was one of the poorest of our neighbors, a retired army major, Gavrila Fedulych Zhitkov, a man no longer young, and, as he himself expressed it, not without a certain complacency, however, as though recommending himself, "battered and broken down." He could barely read and write, and was exceedingly stupid, but secretly aspired to become my mother's steward, as he felt himself to be a "man of action." "I can tan the peasants' hides for them, if I can do anything," he used to say, almost gnashing his own teeth, "because I was used to it," he used to explain, "in my former duties, I mean." Had Zhitkov been less of a fool, he would have realized that he had not the slightest chance of being steward to my mother, seeing that, for that, it would have been necessary to get rid of the present steward, one Kwieciński, a very capable Pole of great character, in whom my mother had the fullest confidence. Zhitkov had a long face, like a horse's; it was all overgrown with hair of a dusty whitish color; his cheeks were covered with it right up to the eyes; and even in the severest frosts, it was sprinkled with an abundant sweat, like drops of dew. At the sight of my mother, he drew himself upright as a post, his head positively quivered with zeal, his huge hands slapped a little against his thighs, and his whole person seemed to express: "Command! . . . and I will strive my utmost!" My mother was under no illusion on the score of his abilities, which did not, however, hinder her from taking steps to marry him to Yevlampia.

"Only, will you be able to manage her, my good sir?" she asked him one day.

Zhitkov smiled complacently.

"Upon my word, Natalya Nikolayevna! I used to keep a whole

regiment in order; they were tame enough in my hands; and what's this? A trumpery business!"

"A regiment's one thing, sir, but a well-bred girl, a wife, is a very different matter," my mother observed with displeasure.

"Upon my word, ma'am! Natalya Nikolayevna!" Zhitkov cried again, "that we're quite able to understand. In one word: a young lady, a delicate person!"

"Well!" my mother decided at length, "Yevlampia won't let herself be trampled upon."

## X

One day—it was the month of June, and evening was coming on— a servant announced the arrival of Martyn Petrovich. My mother was surprised: we had not seen him for over a week, but he had never visited us so late before. "Something has happened!" she exclaimed in an undertone. The face of Martyn Petrovich, when he rolled into the room and at once sank into a chair near the door, wore such an unusual expression, it was so preoccupied and positively pale, that my mother involuntarily repeated her exclamation aloud. Martyn Petrovich fixed his little eyes upon her, was silent for a space, sighed heavily, was silent again, and articulated at last that he had come about something . . . which . . . was of a kind, that on account of . . .

Muttering these disconnected words, he suddenly got up and went out.

My mother rang, ordered the footman, who appeared, to overtake Martyn Petrovich at once and bring him back without fail, but the latter had already had time to get into his droshky and drive away.

Next morning my mother, who was astonished and even alarmed, as much by Martyn Petrovich's strange behavior as by the extraordinary expression of his face, was on the point of sending a special messenger to him, when he made his appearance. This time he seemed more composed.

"Tell me, my good friend, tell me," cried my mother, directly she saw him, "whatever has happened to you? I thought yesterday, upon my word I did. . . . 'Mercy on us!' I thought, 'Hasn't our old friend gone right off his head?'"

"I've not gone off my head, madam," answered Martyn Petrovich; "I am not that sort of man. But I want to consult with you."

"What about?"

"I'm only in doubt, whether it will be agreeable to you in this same contingency—"

"Speak away, speak away, my good sir, but more simply. Don't alarm me! What's this same contingency? Speak more plainly. Or is it your melancholy come upon you again?"

Harlov scowled. "No, it's not melancholy—that comes upon me in the new moon; but allow me to ask you, madam, what do you think about death?"

My mother was taken aback. "About what?"

"About death. Can death spare anyone whatever in this world?"

"What have you got in your head, my good friend? Who of us is immortal? For all you're born a giant, even to you there'll be an end in time."

"There will! Oh, there will!" Harlov assented and he looked downcast. "I've had a vision come to me in my dreams," he brought out at last.

"What are you saying?" my mother interrupted him.

"A vision in my dreams," he repeated—"I'm a seer of visions, you know!"

"You!"

"I. Didn't you know it?" Harlov sighed. "Well, so. . . . Over a week ago, madam, I lay down, on the very last day of eating meat before St. Peter's fast-day; I lay down after dinner to rest a bit, well, and so I fell asleep, and dreamed that a raven colt ran into my room. And this colt began sporting about and grinning. Black as a beetle was the raven colt." Harlov ceased.

"Well?" said my mother.

"And all of a sudden this same colt turns round, and gives me a kick in the left elbow, right in the funny bone. . . . I waked up; my arm would not move nor my leg either. Well, thinks I, it's paralysis; however, I worked them up and down, and got them to move again; only there were shooting pains in the joints for a long time, and there are still. When I open my hand, the pains shoot through the joints."

"Why, Martyn Petrovich, you must have lain upon your arm somehow and crushed it."

"No, madam; pray, don't talk like that! It was an intimation . . . referring to my death, I mean."

"Well, upon my word," my mother was beginning.

"An intimation. Prepare thyself, man, as 'twere to say. And therefore, madam, here is what I have to announce to you, without a moment's delay. Not wishing," Harlov suddenly began shouting, "that the same death should come upon me, the servant of God, unawares, I have planned in my own mind this: to divide—now during my lifetime—my estate between my two daughters, Anna and Yevlampia, according as God Almighty directs me—" Martyn Petrovich stopped, groaned, and added, "without a moment's delay."

"Well, that would be a good idea," observed my mother; "though I think you have no need to be in a hurry."

"And seeing that herein I desire," Harlov continued, raising his voice still higher, "to be observant of all due order and legality, so I humbly beg your young son, Dmitry Semyonovich—I would not venture, madam, to trouble you—I beg the said Dmitry Semyonovich, your son, and I claim of my kinsman, Bychkov, as a plain duty, to assist at the ratification of the formal act and transference of possession to my two daughters—Anna, married, and Yevlampia, spinster. Which act will be drawn up in readiness the day after to-morrow at twelve o'clock, at my own place, Yeskovo, also called Kozulkino, in the presence of the constituted authorities and functionaries, who are thereto invited."

Martyn Petrovich with difficulty reached the end of this speech, which he had obviously learnt by heart, and which was interspersed with frequent sighs. . . . He seemed to have no breath left in his chest; his pale face was crimson again, and he several times wiped the sweat off it.

"So you've already composed the deed dividing your property?" my mother queried. "When did you manage that?"

"I managed it . . . oh! neither eating, nor drinking—"

"Did you write it yourself?"

"Volodka . . . oh! helped."

"And have you forwarded a petition?"

"I have, and the Chamber has sanctioned it, and notice has been given to the district court, and the temporary division of the local court has . . . oh! . . . been notified to be present."

My mother laughed. "I see, Martyn Petrovich, you've made every arrangement already—and how quickly. You've not spared money, I should say?"

"No, indeed, madam."

"Well, well! And you say you want to consult with me. Well, my little Dmitry can go; and I'll send Souvenir with him, and speak to Kwieciński. . . . But you haven't invited Gavrila Fedulych?"

"Gavrila Fedulych—Mr. Zhitkov—has had notice . . . from me also. As a betrothed, it was only fitting."

Martyn Petrovich had obviously exhausted all the resources of his eloquence. Besides, it always seemed to me that he did not look altogether favourably on the match my mother had made for his daughter; possibly, he had expected a more advantageous marriage for his darling Yevlampia.

He got up from his chair, and made a scrape with his foot. "Thank you for your consent."

"Where are you off to?" asked my mother. "Stay a bit; I'll order some lunch to be served you."

"Much obliged," responded Harlov. "But I cannot. . . . Oh! I must get home."

He backed and was about to move sideways, as his habit was, through the door.

"Stop, stop a minute," my mother went on, "can you possibly mean to make over the whole of your property without reserve to your daughters?"

"Certainly, without reserve."

"Well, but how about yourself—where are you going to live?"

Harlov positively flung up his hands in amazement. "You ask where? In my house, at home, as I've lived hitherto . . . so henceforward. Whatever difference could there be?"

"You have such confidence in your daughters and your son-in-law, then?"

"Were you pleased to speak of Volodka? A poor stick like him? Why, I can do as I like with him, whatever it is . . . what authority has he? As for them, my daughters, that is, to care for me till I'm in the grave, to give me meat and drink, and clothe me. . . . Merciful heavens! it's their first duty. I shall not long be an eyesore to them. Death's not over the hills—it's upon my shoulders."

"Death is in God's hands," observed my mother; "though that is their duty, to be sure. Only pardon me, Martyn Petrovich; your elder girl, Anna, is well known to be proud and imperious, and—well—the second has a fierce look. . . ."

"Natalya Nikolayevna!" Harlov broke in, "why do you say that? . . . Why, as though they . . . My daughters . . . Why, as though I . . . Forget their duty? Never in their wildest dreams . . . Offer opposition? To whom? Their parent . . . Dare to do such a thing? Have they not my curse to fear? They've passed their life long in fear and in submission—and all of a sudden . . . Good Lord!"

Harlov choked, there was a rattle in his throat.

"Very well, very well," my mother made haste to soothe him; "only I don't understand all the same what has put it into your head to divide the property up now. It would have come to them afterwards, in any case. I imagine it's your melancholy that's at the bottom of it all."

"Eh, ma'am," Harlov rejoined, not without vexation, "you will keep coming back to that. There is, maybe, a higher power at work in this, and you talk of melancholy. I thought to do this, madam, because myself, personally, while still alive, I wish to decide in my presence, who is to possess what, and with what I will reward each, so that they may possess, and feel thankfulness, and carry out my wishes, and what their father and benefactor has resolved upon, they may accept as a bountiful gift."

Harlov's voice broke again.

"Come, that's enough, that's enough, my good friend," my mother cut him short; "or your raven colt will be putting in an appearance in earnest."

"O Natalya Nikolayevna, don't talk to me of it," groaned Harlov. "That's my death come after me. Forgive my intrusion. And you, my little sir, I shall have the honor of expecting you the day after tomorrow."

Martyn Petrovich went out; my mother looked after him, and shook her head significantly. "This is a bad business," she murmured, "a bad business. You noticed"—she addressed herself to me—"he talked, and all the while seemed blinking, as though the sun were in his eyes; that's a bad sign. When a man's like that, his heart's sure to be heavy, and misfortune threatens him. You must go over the day after tomorrow with Vikenty Osipovich and Souvenir."

## XI

On the day appointed, our big family coach, with seats for four, harnessed with six bay horses, and with the head coachman, the gray-bearded and portly Alexeich, on the box, rolled smoothly up to the steps of our house. The importance of the act upon which Harlov was about to enter, and the solemnity with which he had invited us, had had their effect on my mother. She had herself given orders for this extraordinary state equipage to be brought out, and had directed Souvenir and me to put on our best clothes. She obviously wished to show respect to her protégé. As for Kwieciński, he always wore a frock coat and white tie. Souvenir chattered like a magpie all the way, giggled, wondered whether his brother would apportion him anything, and thereupon called him a dummy and an old fogy. Kwieciński, a man of severe and bilious temperament, could not put up with it at last. "What can induce you," he observed, in his distinct Polish accent, "to keep up such a continual unseemly chatter? Can you really be incapable of sitting quiet without these 'wholly superfluous' (his favorite phrase) inanities?" "All right, d'rectly," Souvenir muttered discontentedly, and he fixed his squinting eyes on the carriage window. A quarter of an hour had not passed, the smoothly trotting horses had scarcely begun to get warm under the straps of their new harness, when Harlov's homestead came into sight. Through the wide open gate, our carriage rolled into the yard. The diminutive postilion, whose legs hardly reached halfway down his horses' body, for the last time leaped up with a babyish shriek in the soft saddle, old Alexeich at once spread out and raised his elbows, a slight "wo-o" was heard, and we stopped. The dogs did not bark to greet us, and the serf boys, in long smocks that gaped open over their big stomachs, had all hidden themselves. Harlov's son-in-law was awaiting us in the doorway. I remember I was particularly struck by the birch boughs stuck in on both sides of the steps, as though it were Trinity Sunday. "Grandeur upon grandeur," Souvenir, who was the first to alight, squeaked through his nose. And certainly there was a solemn air about everything. Harlov's son-in-law was wearing a plush cravat with a satin bow, and an extraordinarily tight tail-coat; while Maximka, who popped out behind his back, had his hair so saturated with kvas, that it positively dripped.

We went into the parlor, and saw Martyn Petrovich towering— yes, positively towering—motionless, in the middle of the room. I don't know what Souvenir's and Kwieciński's feelings were at the sight of his colossal figure, but I felt something akin to awe. Martyn

Petrovich was attired in a gray Cossack coat—his militia uniform of 1812 it must have been—with a black stand-up collar. A bronze medal was to be seen on his breast, a saber hung at his side; he laid his left hand on the hilt, with his right he was leaning on the table, which was covered with a red cloth. Two sheets of paper, full of writing, lay on the table. Harlov stood motionless, not even gasping; and what dignity was expressed in his attitude, what confidence in himself, in his unlimited and unquestionable power! He barely greeted us with a motion of the head, and barely articulating "Be seated!" pointed the forefinger of his left hand in the direction of some chairs set in a row. Against the right-hand wall of the parlor were standing Harlov's daughters wearing their Sunday clothes: Anna, in a shot lilac-green dress, with a yellow silk sash; Yevlampia, in pink, with crimson ribbons. Near them stood Zhitkov, in a new uniform, with the habitual expression of dull and greedy expectation in his eyes, and with a greater profusion of sweat than usual over his hirsute countenance. On the left side of the room sat the priest, in a threadbare snuff-colored cassock, an old man, with rough brown hair. This head of hair, and the dejected lackluster eyes, and the big wrinkled hands, which seemed a burden even to himself, and lay like two rocks on his knees, and the tarred boots which peeped out beneath his cassock, all seemed to tell of a joyless laborious life. His parish was a very poor one. Beside him was the local police captain, a fattish, palish, dirty-looking little gentleman, with soft puffy little hands and feet, black eyes, black short-clipped mustaches, a continual cheerful but yet sickly little smile on his face. He had the reputation of being a great taker of bribes, and even a tyrant, as the expression was in those days. But not only the gentry, even the peasants were used to him, and liked him. He bent very free and easy and rather ironical looks around him; it was clear that all this "procedure" amused him. In reality, the only part that had any interest for him was the light lunch and spirits in store for us. But the attorney sitting near him, a lean man with a long face, narrow whiskers from his ears to his nose, as they were worn in the days of Alexander the First, was absorbed with his whole soul in Martyn Petrovich's proceedings, and never took his big serious eyes off him. In his concentrated attention and sympathy, he kept moving and twisting his lips, though without opening his mouth. Souvenir stationed himself next him, and began talking to him in a whisper, after first informing me that he was the chief freemason in the province The temporary division of the local court consists, as every one knows, of the police captain, the attorney, and the rural police commissioner; but the latter was either absent or kept himself in the background, so that I did not notice him. He bore, however, the nickname "the nonexistent" among us in the district, just as there are tramps called "the non-identified." I sat next Souvenir, Kwieciński next me. The face of the practical Pole showed unmistakable annoyance at our "wholly superfluous" expedition, and unnecessary waste of time. . . . "A grand lady's caprices! these Russian grandees' fancies!" he seemed to be murmuring to himself. . . . "Ugh, these Russians!"

## XII

When we were all seated, Martyn Petrovich hunched his shoulders, cleared his throat, scanned us all with his bearlike little eyes, and with a noisy sigh began as follows:

"Gentlemen, I have called you together for the following purpose. I am grown old, gentlemen, and overcome by infirmities. . . . Already I have had an intimation, the hour of death steals on, like a thief in the night. . . . Isn't that so, father?" he addressed the priest.

The priest started. "Quite so, quite so," he mumbled, his beard shaking.

"And therefore," continued Martyn Petrovich, suddenly raising his voice, "not wishing the said death to come upon me unawares, I purposed" . . . Martyn Petrovich proceeded to repeat, word for word, the speech he had made to my mother two days before. "In accordance with this my determination," he shouted louder than ever, "this deed" (he struck his hand on the papers lying on the table) "has been drawn up by me, and the constituted authorities have been invited by me, and wherein my will consists the following points will treat. I have ruled, my day is over!"

Martyn Petrovich put his round iron spectacles on his nose, took one of the written sheets from the table, and began:

"Deed of partition of the estate of the retired noncommissioned officer and nobleman, Martyn Harlov, drawn up by himself in his full and right understanding, and by his own good judgment, and wherein is precisely defined what benefits are assigned to his two daughters, Anna and Yevlampia—bow!"—(they bowed), "and in what way the serfs and other property, and livestock, be apportioned between the said daughters! Under my hand!"

"This is his document!" the police captain whispered to Kwieciński, with his invariable smile, "he wants to read it for the beauty of the style, but the legal deed is made out formally, without all these flourishes."

Souvenir was beginning to snigger. . . .

"In accordance with my will," put in Harlov, who had caught the police captain's remark.

"In accordance in every point," the latter hastened to respond cheerfully; "only, as you're aware, Martyn Petrovich, there's no dispensing with formality. And unnecessary details have been removed. For the chamber can't enter into the question of spotted cows and fancy drakes."

"Come here!" boomed Harlov to his son-in-law, who had come into the room behind us, and remained standing with an obsequious air near the door. He skipped up to his father-in-law at once.

"There, take it and read! It's hard for me. Only mind and don't mumble it! Let all the gentlemen present be able to understand it."

Sletkin took the paper in both hands, and began timidly, but distinctly, and with taste and feeling, to read the deed of partition. There was set forth in it with the greatest accuracy just what was assigned to Anna and what to Yevlampia, and how the division was to be made. Harlov from time to time interspersed the reading with phrases. "Do you hear, that's for you, Anna, for your zeal!" or, "That I give you, Yevlampia!" and both the sisters bowed, Anna from the waist, Yevlampia simply with a motion of the head. Harlov looked at them with stern dignity. "The farmhouse" (the little new building) was assigned by him to Yevlampia, as the younger daughter, "by the well-known custom." The reader's voice quivered and resounded at these words, unfavorable for himself; while Zhitkov licked his lips. Yevlampia gave him a sidelong glance; had I been in Zhitkov's shoes, I should not have liked that glance. The scornful expression, characteristic of Yevlampia, as of every genuine Russian beauty, had a peculiar shade at that moment. For himself, Martyn Petrovich reserved the right to go on living in the rooms he occupied, and assigned to himself, under the name of "rations," a full allowance "of normal provisions," and ten roubles a month for clothes. The last phrase of the deed Harlov wished to read himself. "And this my parental will," it ran, "to carry out and observe is a sacred and binding duty on my daughters, indeed a commandment; seeing that I am, after God, their father and head, and am not bounden to render an account to any, nor have so rendered. And do they carry out my will, so will my fatherly blessing be with them, but should they not so do, which God forbid, then will they be overtaken by my paternal curse that cannot be averted, now and forever, amen!" Harlov raised the deed high above his head. Anna at once dropped on her knees and touched the ground with her forehead; her husband, too, doubled up after her. "Well, and you?" Harlov turned to Yevlampia. She crimsoned all over, and she too bowed to the earth; Zhitkov bent his whole carcase forward.

"Sign!" cried Harlov, pointing his forefinger to the bottom of the deed. "Here: 'I thank and accept, Anna. I thank and accept, Yevlampia!'"

Both daughters rose, and signed one after the other. Sletkin rose too, and was feeling after the pen, but Harlov moved him aside, sticking his middle finger into his cravat, so that he gasped. The silence lasted a moment. Suddenly Martyn Petrovich gave a sort of sob, and muttering, "Well, now it's all yours!" moved away. His daughters and son-in-law looked at one another, went up to him and began kissing him just above his elbow. His shoulder they could not reach.

## XIII

The police captain read the real formal document, the deed of gift, drawn up by Martyn Petrovich. Then he went out on to the steps with the attorney and explained what had taken place to the crowd assembled at the gates, consisting of the witnesses required by law and other people from the neighborhood, Harlov's peasants, and a few house-serfs. Then began the ceremony of the new owners entering into possession. They came out, too, upon the steps, and the police captain pointed to them when, slightly scowling with one eyebrow, while his careless face assumed for an instant a threatening air, he exhorted the crowd to "subordination." He might well have dispensed with these exhortations: a less unruly set of countenances than those of the Harlov peasants, I imagine, have never existed in creation. Clothed in thin smocks and torn sheepskins, but very tightly girt round their waists, as is always the peasants' way on solemn occasions, they stood motionless as though cut out of stone, and whenever the police captain uttered any exclamation such as, "D'ye hear, you brutes? d'ye understand, you devils?" they suddenly bowed all at once, as though at the word of command. Each of these "brutes and devils" held his cap tight in both hands, and never took his eyes off the window, where Martyn Petrovich's figure was visible. The witnesses themselves were hardly less awed. "Is any impediment known to you," the police captain roared at them, "against the entrance into possession of these sole and legitimate heirs and daughters of Martyn Petrovich Harlov?"

All the witnesses seemed to huddle together at once.

"Do you know any, you devils?" the police captain shouted again.

"We know nothing, your excellency," responded sturdily a little old man, marked with smallpox, with a clipped beard and whiskers, a former soldier.

"I say! Yeremeich's a bold fellow!" the witnesses said of him as they dispersed.

In spite of the police captain's entreaties, Harlov would not come out with his daughters on to the steps. "My subjects will obey my will without that!" he answered. Something like sadness had come over him on the completion of the conveyance. His face had grown pale. This new unprecedented expression of sadness looked so out of place on Martyn Petrovich's broad and kindly features that I positively was at a loss what to think. Was an attack of melancholy coming over him? The peasants, on their side, too, were obviously puzzled. And no wonder! "The master's alive—there he stands, and such a master, too; Martyn Petrovich! And all of a sudden he won't be their owner. . . . A queer thing!" I don't know whether Harlov had an inkling of the notions that were straying through his "subjects'" heads, or whether he wanted to display his power for the last time, but he suddenly opened the little window, stuck his head out, and shouted in a voice of thunder, "obedience!" Then he slammed-to the window. The peasants' bewilderment was certainly not dispelled nor decreased by this proceeding. They became stonier than ever, and even seemed to cease looking at anything. The group of house-serfs (among them were two sturdy wenches, in short print dresses, with muscles such as one might perhaps match in Michael Angelo's "Last Judgment," and one utterly decrepit old man, hoary with age and half blind, in a rough frieze cloak, rumored to have been "cornet-player" in the days of Potemkin—the page Maximka, Harlov had reserved for himself), this group showed more life than the peasants; at least, it moved restlessly about.

The new mistresses themselves were very dignified in their attitude, especially Anna. Her thin lips tightly compressed, she looked obstinately down . . . her stern figure augured little good to the house-serfs. Yevlampia, too, did not raise her eyes; only once she turned round and deliberately, as it were with surprise, scanned her betrothed, Zhitkov, who had thought fit, following Sletkin, to come out, too, on to the steps. "What business have you here?" those handsome prominent eyes seemed to demand. Sletkin was the most changed of all. A bustling cheeriness showed itself in his whole bearing, as though he were overtaken by hunger; the movements of his head and his legs were as obsequious as ever but how gleefully he kept working his arms, how fussily he twitched his shoulder-blades. "Arrived at last!" he seemed to say.

Having finished the ceremony of the entrance into possession, the police captain, whose mouth was literally watering at the prospect of lunch, rubbed his hands in that peculiar manner which usually precedes the tossing-off of the first glass of spirits. But it appeared that Martyn Petrovich wished first to have a service performed with sprinkling of holy water. The priest put on an ancient and decrepit chasuble; a decrepit deacon came out of the kitchen, with difficulty kindling the incense in an old brazen church-vessel. The service began. Harlov sighed continually; he was unable, owing to his corpulence, to bow to the ground, but crossing himself with his right hand and bending his head, he pointed with the forefinger of his left hand to the floor. Sletkin positively beamed and even shed tears. Zhitkov, with dignity, in martial fashion, flourished his fingers only slightly between the third and fourth button of his uniform. Kwieciński, as a Catholic, remained in the next room. But the attorney prayed so fervently, sighed so sympathetically after Martyn Petrovich, and so persistently muttered and chewed his lips, turning his eyes upwards, that I felt moved, as I looked at him, and began to pray fervently too. At the conclusion of the service and the sprinkling with holy water, during which every one present, even the blind cornet-player, the contemporary of Potemkin, even Kwieciński, moistened their eyes with holy water, Anna and Yevlampia once more, at Martyn Petrovich's bidding, prostrated themselves to the ground to thank him.

Then at last came the moment of lunch. There were a great many dishes and all very nice; we all ate terribly much. The inevitable bottle of Don wine made its appearance. The police captain, who was of all of us the most familiar with the usages of the world, and besides, as a representative of the State, was the first to propose the toast to the health "of the fair proprietresses!" Then he proposed we should drink to the health of our most honored and most generous-hearted friend, Martyn Petrovich. At the words "most generous-hearted," Sletkin uttered a shrill little cry and ran to kiss his benefactor. . . . "There, that'll do, that'll do," muttered Harlov, as it were with annoyance, keeping him off with his elbow . . . But at this point a not quite pleasant, as they say, incident took place.

## XIV

Souvenir, who had been drinking continuously ever since the beginning of luncheon, suddenly got up from his chair as red as a beetroot, and pointing his finger at Martyn Petrovich, went off into his mawkish, paltry laugh.

"Generous-hearted! Generous-hearted!" he began croaking; "but we shall see whether this generosity will be much to his taste when he's stripped naked, the servant of God . . . and out in the snow, too!"

"What rot are you talking, fool?" said Harlov contemptuously.

"Fool! fool!" repeated Souvenir. "God Almighty alone knows which of us is the real fool. But you, brother, did my sister, your wife, to her death, and now you've done for yourself . . . ha-ha-ha!"

"How dare you insult our honored benefactor?" Sletkin began shrilly, and, tearing himself away from Martyn Petrovich, whose shoulder he had clutched, he flew at Souvenir. "But let me tell you, if our benefactor desires it, we can cancel the deed this very minute!"

"And yet, you'll strip him naked, and turn him out into the snow . . ." returned Souvenir, retreating behind Kwieciński.

"Silence!" thundered Harlov. "I'll pound you into a jelly! And you hold your tongue too, puppy!" he turned to Sletkin; "don't put in your word where you're not wanted! If I, Martyn Petrovich Harlov, have decided to make a deed of partition, who can cancel the same act against my will? Why, in the whole world there is no power." . . .

"Martyn Petrovich!" the attorney began in a mellow bass—he too had drunk a good deal, but his dignity was only increased thereby—"but how if the gentleman has spoken the truth? You have done a generous deed, to be sure; but what if—God forbid—in reality in place of fitting gratitude, some affront come of it?"

I stole a glance at both Martyn Petrovich's daughters. Anna's eyes were simply pinned upon the speaker, and a face more spiteful, more snakelike, and more beautiful in its very spite I had certainly never seen! Yevlampia sat turned away, with her arms folded. A smile more scornful than ever curved her full, rosy lips.

Harlov got up from his chair, opened his mouth, but apparently his tongue failed him. . . . He suddenly brought his fist down on the table, so that everything in the room danced and rang.

"Father," Anna said hurriedly, "they do not know us, and that is why they judge of us so. But don't, please, make yourself ill. You are angered for nothing, indeed; see, your face is, as it were, twisted awry."

Harlov looked towards Yevlampia; she did not stir, though Zhitkov, sitting beside her, gave her a poke in the side.

"Thank you, my daughter Anna," said Harlov huskily; "you are a sensible girl; I rely upon you and on your husband too." Sletkin once more gave vent to a shrill little sound; Zhitkov expanded his chest and gave a little scrape with his foot; but Harlov did not observe his efforts. "This dolt," he went on, with a motion of his chin in the direction of Souvenir, "is pleased to get a chance to tease me; but you, my dear sir," he addressed himself to the attorney, "it is not for you to pass judgment on Martyn Harlov; that is something beyond you. Though you are a man in official position, your words are most foolish. Besides, the deed is done, there will be no going back on my resolve. . . . Now, I will wish you good-day, I am going away. I am no longer the master of this house, but a guest in it. Anna, do you do your best; but I will go to my own room. Enough!"

Martyn Petrovich turned his back on us, and, without adding another word, walked deliberately out of the room.

This sudden withdrawal on the part of our host could not but break up the party, especially as the two hostesses also vanished not long after. Sletkin vainly tried to keep us. The police captain did not fail to blame the attorney for his uncalled-for candor. "Couldn't help it" the latter responded. . . . "My conscience spoke."

"There, you see that he's a mason," Souvenir whispered to me.

"Conscience!" retorted the police captain. "We know all about your conscience! I suppose it's in your pocket, just the same as it is with us sinners!"

The priest, meanwhile, even though already on his feet, foreseeing the speedy termination of the repast, lifted mouthful after mouthful to his mouth without a pause.

"You've got a fine appetite, I see," Sletkin observed to him sharply.

"Storing up for the future," the priest responded with a meek grimace; years of hunger were expressed in that reply.

The carriages rattled up . . . and we separated. On the way home, no one hindered Souvenir's chatter and silly tricks, as Kwieciński had announced that he was sick of all this "wholly superfluous" unpleasantness, and had set off home before us on foot. In his place, Zhitkov took a seat in our coach. The retired major wore a most dissatisfied expression, and kept twitching his mustaches like a spider.

"Well, your noble Excellency," lisped Souvenir, "is subordination exploded, eh? Wait a bit and see what will happen! They'll give you the sack too. Ah, a poor bridegroom you are, a poor bridegroom, an unlucky bridegroom!"

Souvenir was positively beside himself; while poor Zhitkov could do nothing but twitch his mustaches.

When I got home I told my mother all I had seen. She heard me to the end, and shook her head several times. "It's a bad business," was her comment. "I don't like all these innovations!"

## XV

Next day Martyn Petrovich came to dinner. My mother congratulated him on the successful conclusion of his project. "You are now a free man," she said, "and ought to feel more at ease."

"More at ease, to be sure, madam," answered Martyn Petrovich, by no means, however, showing in the expression of his face that he really was more at ease. "Now I can meditate upon my soul, and make ready for my last hour, as I ought."

"Well," queried my mother, "and do the shooting pains still tingle in your arms?"

Harlov twice clenched and unclenched his left arm. "They do, madam; and I've something else to tell you. As I begin to drop asleep, someone cries in my head, 'Take care!' 'Take care!'"

"That's nerves," observed my mother, and she began speaking of the previous day, and referred to certain circumstances which had attended the completion of the deed of partition. . . .

"To be sure, to be sure," Harlov interrupted her, "there was something of the sort . . . of no consequence. Only there's something I would tell you," he added, hesitating. "I was not disturbed yesterday by Souvenir's silly words—even Mr. Attorney, though he's no fool—even he did not trouble me; no, it was quite another person disturbed me—" Here Harlov faltered.

"Who?" asked my mother.

Harlov fastened his eyes upon her: "Yevlampia!"

"Yevlampia? Your daughter? How was that?"

"Upon my word, madam, she was like a stone! nothing but a statue! Can it be she has no feeling? Her sister, Anna—well, she was all she should be. She's a keen-witted creature! But Yevlampia—why, I'd shown her—I must own—so much partiality! Can it be she's no feeling for me! It's clear I'm in a bad way; it's clear I've a feeling that I'm not long for this world, since I make over everything to them; and yet she's like a stone! She might at least utter a sound! Bows—yes, she bows, but there's no thankfulness to be seen."

"There, give over," observed my mother, "we'll marry her to Gavrila Fedulych . . . she'll soon get softer in his hands."

Martyn Petrovich once more looked from under his brows at my mother. "Well, there's Gavrila Fedulych, to be sure! You have confidence in him, then, madam?"

"I've confidence in him."

"Very well; you should know best, to be sure. But Yevlampia, let me tell you, is like me. The character is just the same. She has the wild Cossack blood, and her heart's like a burning coal!"

"Why, do you mean to tell me you've a heart like that, my dear sir?"

Harlov made no answer. A brief silence followed.

"What are you going to do, Martyn Petrovich," my mother began, "in what way do you mean to set about saving your soul now? Will you set off to Mitrofany or to Kiev, or may be you'll go to the Optin hermitage, as it's in the neighborhood? There, they do say, there's a holy monk appeared . . . Father Makary they call him, no one remembers any one like him! He sees right through all sins."

"If she really turns out an ungrateful daughter," Harlov enunciated in a husky voice, "then it would be better for me, I believe, to kill her with my own hands!"

"What are you saying! Lord have mercy on you!" cried my mother. "Think what you're saying! There, see, what a pretty pass it's come to. You should have listened to me the other day when you came to consult me! Now, here, you'll go tormenting yourself, instead of thinking of your soul! You'll be tormenting yourself, and all to no purpose! Yes! Here you're complaining now, and fainthearted . . ."

This reproach seemed to stab Harlov to the heart. All his old pride came back to him with a rush. He shook himself, and thrust out his chin. "I am not a man, madam, Natalya Nikolayevna, to complain or be faint-hearted," he began sullenly. "I simply wished to reveal my feelings to you as my benefactress and a person I respect. But the Lord God knows (here he raised his hand high above his head) that this globe of earth will crumble to pieces before I will go back on my word, or . . . (here he positively snorted) show a faint heart, or regret what I have done! I had good reasons, be sure! My daughters will never fail in their obedience to me, forever and ever, amen!"

My mother stopped her ears. "What's this for, my good sir, like a trumpet-blast! If you really have such faith in your family, well, praise the Lord for it! You've quite put my brains in a whirl!"

Martyn Petrovich begged pardon, sighed twice, and was silent. My mother once more referred to Kiev, the Optin hermitage, and Father Makary. . . . Harlov assented, said that "he must . . . he must . . . he would have to . . . his soul" . . . and that was all. He did not regain his cheerfulness before he went away. From time to time he clenched and unclenched his fist, looked at his open hand, said that what he feared above everything was dying unshriven, from a stroke, and that he had made a vow to himself not to get angry, as anger vitiated his blood and drove it to his head. . . . Besides, he had now withdrawn from everything. What grounds could he have for getting angry? Let other people trouble themselves now and vitiate their blood!

As he took leave of my mother he looked at her in a strange way, mournfully and questioningly . . . and suddenly, with a rapid movement, drew out of his pocket the volume of *The Toiler at Rest*, and thrust it into my mother's hand.

"What's that?" she inquired.

"Read . . . here," he said hurriedly, "where the corner's turned down, about death. It seems to me, it's terribly well said, but I can't make it out at all. Can't you explain it to me, my benefactress? I'll come back again and you explain it me."

With these words Martyn Petrovich went away.

"He's in a bad way, he's in a bad way," observed my mother, directly he had disappeared through the doorway, and she set to work upon the *Toiler*. On the page turned down by Harlov were the following words:

"Death is a grand and solemn work of nature. It is nothing else than that the spirit, inasmuch as it is lighter, finer, and infinitely more penetrating than those elements to whose sway it has been subject, nay, even than the force of electricity itself, is chemically purified and striveth upward till what time it attaineth an equally spiritual abiding-place for itself . . . " and so on.

My mother read this passage through twice, and exclaiming, "Pooh!" she flung the book away.

Three days later, she received the news that her sister's husband was dead, and set off to her sister's country-seat, taking me with her. My mother proposed to spend a month with her, but she stayed on till late in the autumn, and it was only at the end of September that we returned to our own estate.

## XVI

The first news with which my valet, Prokofy, greeted me (he regarded himself as the seigniorial huntsman) was that there was an immense number of wild snipe on the wing, and that in the birch-copse near Yeskovo (Harlov's property), especially, they were simply swarming. I had three hours before me till dinnertime. I promptly seized my gun and my game-bag, and with Prokofy and a setter-dog, hastened to the Yeskovo copse. We certainly did find a great many wild snipe there, and, firing about thirty charges, killed five. As I hurried homewards with my booty, I saw a peasant plowing near the roadside. His horse had stopped, and with tearful and angry abuse he was mercilessly tugging with the cord reins at the animal's head, which was bent on one side. I looked attentively at the luckless beast, whose ribs were all but through its skin, and, bathed in sweat, heaved up and down with convulsive, irregular movements like a black-smith's bellows. I recognized it at once as the decrepit old mare, with the scar on her shoulder, who had served Martyn Petrovich so many years.

"Is Mr. Harlov living?" I asked Prokofy. The chase had so completely absorbed us, that up to that instant we had not talked of anything.

"Yes, he's alive. Why?"

"But that's his mare, isn't it? Do you mean to say that he's sold her?"

"His mare it is, to be sure; but as to selling, he never sold her. But they took her away from him, and handed her over to that peasant."

"How, took it? And he consented?"

"They never asked his consent. Things have changed here in your absence," Prokofy observed, with a faint smile in response to my look of amazement; "worse luck! My goodness, yes! Now Slet-kin's master, and orders every one about."

"But Martyn Petrovich?"

"Why, Martyn Petrovich has become the very last person here, you may say. He's on bread and water—what more can one say? They've crushed him altogether. Mark my words; they'll drive him out of the house."

The idea that it was possible to *drive* such a giant had never entered my head. "And what does Zhitkov say to it?" I asked at last. "I suppose he's married to the second daughter?"

"Married?" repeated Prokofy, and this time he grinned all over his face. "They won't let him into the house. 'We don't want you,' they say; 'get along home with you.' It's as I said; Sletkin directs everyone."

"But what does the young lady say?"

"Yevlampia Martynovna? Ah, master, I could tell you . . . but you're young—one must think of that. Things are going on here that are . . . oh! . . . oh! . . . oh! Hey! why, Dianka's setting, I do believe!"

My dog actually had stopped short, before a thick oak bush which bordered a narrow ravine by the roadside. Prokofy and I ran up to the dog; a snipe flew up out of the bush, we both fired at it and missed; the snipe settled in another place; we followed it.

The soup was already on the table when I got back. My mother scolded me. "What's the meaning of it?" she said with displeasure; "the very first day, and you keep us waiting for dinner." I brought her the wild snipe I had killed; she did not even look at them. There were also in the room Souvenir, Kwieciński and Zhitkov. The retired major was huddled in a corner, for all the world like a schoolboy in disgrace. His face wore an expression of mingled confusion and annoyance, his eyes were red. . . . One might positively have imagined he had recently been in tears. My mother remained in an ill humor. I was at no great pains to surmise that my late arrival did not count for much in it. During dinnertime she hardly talked at all. The major turned beseeching glances upon her from time to time, but ate a good dinner nevertheless. Souvenir was all of a shake. Kwieciński preserved his habitual self-confidence of demeanor.

"Vikenty Osipych," my mother addressed him, "I beg you to send a carriage tomorrow for Martyn Petrovich, since it has come to my knowledge that he has none of his own. And bid them tell him to come without fail, that I desire to see him."

Kwieciński was about to make some rejoinder, but he restrained himself.

"And let Sletkin know," continued my mother, "that I command him to present himself before me. . . . Do you hear? I command!"

"Yes, just so . . . that scoundrel ought—" Zhitkov was beginning in a subdued voice; but my mother gave him such a contemptuous look, that he promptly turned away and was silent.

"Do you hear? I command!" repeated my mother.

"Certainly, madam," Kwieciński replied submissively but with dignity.

"Martyn Petrovich won't come!" Souvenir whispered to me, as he came out of the dining-room with me after dinner. "You should

just see what's happened to him! It's past comprehension! It's come
to this, that whatever they say to him, he doesn't understand a word!
Yes! They've got the snake under the pitchfork!"

And Souvenir went off into his revolting laugh.


## XVII

Souvenir's prediction turned out correct. Martyn Petrovich
would not come to my mother. She was not at all pleased with this,
and despatched a letter to him. He sent her a square bit of paper,
on which the following words were written in big letters: "Indeed
I can't. I should die of shame. Let me go to my ruin. Thanks. Don't
torture me. Martyn Harlov." Sletkin did come, but not on the day
on which my mother had "commanded" his attendance, but twenty-
four hours later. My mother gave orders that he should be shown
into her boudoir. . . . God knows what their interview was about,
but it did not last long; a quarter of an hour, not more. Sletkin came
out of my mother's room, crimson all over, and with such a viciously
spiteful and insolent expression of face, that, meeting him in the
drawing-room, I was simply petrified, while Souvenir, who was
hanging about there, stopped short in the middle of a snigger. My
mother came out of her boudoir, also very red in the face, and announced, in the hearing of all, that Mr. Sletkin was never, upon any
pretext, to be admitted to her presence again, and that if Martyn
Petrovich's daughters were to make bold—they've impudence enough,
said she—to present themselves, they, too, were to be refused ad-
mittance. At dinnertime she suddenly exclaimed, "The vile little
Jew! I picked him out of the gutter, I made him a career, he owes
everything, everything to me—and he dares to tell me I've no business to meddle in their affairs! that Martyn Petrovich is full of whims
and fancies, and it's impossible to humor him! Humor him, indeed!
What a thing to say! Ah, he's an ungrateful wretch! An insolent
little Jew!"

Major Zhitkov, who happened to be one of the company at
dinner, imagined that now it was no less than the will of the Almighty for him to seize the opportunity and put in his word . . .
but my mother promptly settled him. "Well, and you're a fine one,
too, my man!" she commented. "Couldn't get the upper hand of a
girl, and he an officer! In command of a squadron! I can fancy

how it obeyed you! He take a steward's place indeed! A fine steward, he'd make!"

Kwieciński, who was sitting at the end of the table, smiled to himself a little malignantly, while poor Zhitkov could do nothing but twitch his mustaches, lift his eyebrows, and bury the whole of his hirsute countenance in his napkin.

After dinner, he went out on to the steps to smoke his pipe as usual, and he struck me as so miserable and forlorn, that, although I had never liked him, I joined him.

"How was it, Gavrila Fedulych," I began without further beating about the bush, "that your affair with Yevlampia Martynovna was broken off? I'd expected you to be married long ago."

The retired major looked at me dejectedly.

"A snake in the grass," he began, uttering each letter of each syllable with bitter distinctness, "has poisoned me with his fang, and turned all my hopes in life to ashes. And I could tell you, Dmitry Semyonovich, all his hellish wiles, but I'm afraid of angering your mamma. ("You're young yet"—Prokofy's expression flashed across my mind.) "Even as it is—" Zhitkov groaned.

"Patience . . . patience . . . nothing else is left me. (He struck his fist upon his chest.) Patience, old soldier, patience. I served the Czar faithfully . . . honorably . . . yes. I spared neither blood nor sweat, and now see what I am brought to. Had it been in the regiment—and the matter depending upon me," he continued after a short silence, spent in convulsively sucking at his cherrywood pipe, "I'd have . . . I'd have given it him with the flat side of my sword . . . three times over . . . till he'd had enough . . ."

Zhitkov took the pipe out of his mouth, and fixed his eyes on vacancy, as though admiring the picture he had conjured up.

Souvenir ran up, and began quizzing the major. I turned away from them, and determined, come what may, I would see Martyn Petrovich with my own eyes. . . . My boyish curiosity was greatly stirred.

## XVIII

Next day I set out with my gun and dog, but without Prokofy, to the Yeskovo copse. It was an exquisite day; I fancy there are no days like that in September anywhere but in Russia. The stillness was such that one could hear, a hundred paces off, the squirrel hopping over the dry leaves, and the broken twig feebly catching at the other branches, and falling, at last, on the soft grass—to lie there for ever, not to stir again till it rotted away. The air, neither warm nor chill, but only fragrant, and as it were keen, was faintly, deliciously stinging my eyes and my cheeks. A long spiderweb, delicate as a silken thread, with a white ball in the middle, floated smoothly in the air, and sticking to the butt-end of my gun, stretched straight out in the air—a sign of settled and warm weather. The sun shone with a brightness as soft as moonlight. Wild snipe were to be met with pretty often; but I did not pay special attention to them. I knew that the copse went on almost to Harlov's homestead, right up to the hedge of his garden, and I turned my steps in that direction, though I could not even imagine how I should get into the place itself, and was even doubtful whether I ought to try to do so, as my mother was so angry with its new owners. Sounds of life and humanity reached me from no great distance. I listened. . . . Someone was coming through the copse . . . straight towards me.

"You should have said so," I heard a woman's voice.

"Be reasonable," another voice broke in, the voice of a man. "Can one do it all at once?"

I knew the voices. There was the gleam of a woman's blue gown through the reddening nut bushes. Beside it showed a dark coat. Another instant—and there stepped out into the glade, five paces from me, Sletkin and Yevlampia.

They were disconcerted at once. Yevlampia promptly stepped back, away into the bushes. Sletkin thought a little, and came up to me. There was not a trace to be seen in his face of the obsequious meekness, with which he had paced up and down Harlov's courtyard, four months before, rubbing up my horse's snaffle. But neither could I perceive in it the insolent defiance which had so struck me on the previous day, on the threshold of my mother's boudoir. It was still as white and pretty as ever, but seemed broader and more solid.

"Well, have you shot many snipe?" he asked me, raising his cap, smiling, and passing his hand over his black curls; "you are shooting in our copse. . . . You are very welcome. We would not hinder you. . . . Quite the contrary."

"I have killed nothing today," I rejoined, answering his first question; "and I will go out of your copse this instant."

Sletkin hurriedly put on his cap. "Indeed, why so? We would

not drive you out—indeed, we're delighted. . . . Here's Yevlampia Martynovna will say the same. Yevlampia Martynovna, come here. Where have you hidden yourself?" Yevlampia's head appeared behind the bushes. But she did not come up to us. She had grown prettier, and seemed taller and bigger than ever.

"I'm very glad, to tell the truth," Sletkin went on, "that I have met you. Though you are still young in years, you have plenty of good sense already. Your mother was pleased to be very angry with me yesterday—she would not listen to reason of any sort from me, but I declare, as before God, so before you now, I am not to blame in any way. We can't treat Martyn Petrovich otherwise than we do; he's fallen into complete dotage. One can't humor all his whims, really. But we show him all due respect. Only ask Yevlampia Martynovna."

Yevlampia did not stir; her habitual scornful smile flickered about her lips, and her large eyes watched us with no friendly expression.

"But why, Vladimir Vasilyevich, have you sold Martyn Petrovich's mare?" (I was particularly impressed by that mare being in the possession of a peasant.)

"His mare, why did we sell it? Why, Lord have mercy on us— what use was she? She was simply eating her head off. But with the peasant she can work at the plow anyway. As for Martyn Petrovich, if he takes a fancy to drive out anywhere, he's only to ask us. We wouldn't refuse him a conveyance. On a holiday, we should be pleased."

"Vladimir Vasilyevich," said Yevlampia huskily, as though calling him away, and she still did not stir from her place. She was twisting some stalks of ripple grass round her fingers and snapping off their heads, slapping them against each other.

"About the page Maximka again," Sletkin went on, "Martyn Petrovich complains because we've taken him away and apprenticed him. But kindly consider the matter for yourself. Why, what had he to do waiting on Martyn Petrovich? Kick up his heels; nothing more. And he couldn't even wait on him properly; on account of his stupidity and his youth. Now we have sent him away to a harness-maker's. He'll be turned into a first-rate handicraftsman—and make a good thing of it for himself—and pay us quitrent too. And, living in a small way as we do, that's a matter of importance. On a little farm like ours, one can't afford to let anything slip."

"And this is the man Martyn Petrovich called a 'poor stick,' "
I thought. "But who reads to Martyn Petrovich now?" I asked.

"Why, what is there to read? He had one book—but, luckily,
that's been mislaid somewhere. . . . And what use is reading at his
age?"

"And who shaves him?" I asked again.

Sletkin gave an approving laugh, as though in response to an
amusing joke. "Why, nobody. At first he used to singe his beard
with a candle—but now he lets it be altogether. And it's all right!"

"Vladimir Vasilyevich!" Yevlampia repeated insistently: "Vladimir Vasilyevich!"

Sletkin made her a sign with his hand.

"Martyn Petrovich is clothed and cared for, and eats what we
do. What more does he want? He declared himself that he wanted
nothing more in this world but to think of his soul. If only he would
realize that everything now, however you look at it, is ours. He says
too that we don't pay him his allowance. But we've not always got
money ourselves; and what does he want with it, when he has everything provided for him? And we treat him as one of the family too.
I'm telling you the truth. The rooms, for instance, which he oc-
cupies—how we need them! There's simply not room to turn round
without them; but we don't say a word—we put up with it. We even
try to provide amusement for him. There, on St. Peter's Day, I
bought him some excellent hooks in the town—real English ones,
expensive hooks, to catch fish. There are lots of carp in our pond.
Let him sit and fish; in an hour or two, there'd be a nice little fish
soup provided. The most suitable occupation for old men."

"Vladimir Vasilyevich!" Yevlampia called for the third time in an
incisive tone, and she flung far away from her the grass she had
been twisting in her fingers, "I am going!" Her eyes met mine. "I
am going, Vladimir Vasilyevich!" she repeated, and vanished behind
a bush.

"I'm coming, Yevlampia Martynovna, directly!" shouted Sletkin.
"Martyn Petrovich himself agrees with us now," he went on, turning
again to me. "As first he was offended, certainly, and even grumbled, until, you know, he realized; he was, you remember, a hot-
tempered violent man—more's the pity! but there, he's grown quite
meek now. Because he sees his own interest. Your mamma—mercy on
us!—how she pitched into me! . . . To be sure: she's a lady that sets

as much store by her own authority as Martyn Petrovich used to do. But you come in and see for yourself. And you might put in a word when there's an opportunity. I feel Natalya Nikolayevna's bounty to me deeply. But we've got to live too."

"And how was it Zhitkov was refused?" I asked.

"Fedulych? That dolt?" Sletkin shrugged his shoulders. "Why, upon my word, what use could he have been? His whole life spent among soldiers—and now he has a fancy to take up farming. He can keep the peasants up to the mark, says he, because he's been used to punching men's faces. He can do nothing; even punching faces wants some sense. Yevlampia Martynovna refused him herself. He was a quite unsuitable person. Our whole estate would have gone to ruin with him!"

"Cooee!" sounded Yevlampia's musical voice.

"Coming! coming!" Sletkin called back. He held out his hand to me. Though unwillingly, I took it.

"I beg to take leave, Dmitry Semyonovich," said Sletkin, showing all his white teeth. "Shoot wild snipe as much as you like. It's wild game, belonging to no one. But if you come across a hare—you spare it; that game is ours. Oh, and something else! Won't you be having pups from your bitch? I should be obliged for one!"

"Cooee!" Yevlampia's voice rang out again.

"Cooee!" Sletkin responded, and rushed into the bushes.

## XIX

I remember, when I was left alone, I was absorbed in wondering how it was Harlov had not pounded Sletkin "into a jelly," as he said, and how it was Sletkin had not been afraid of such a fate. It was clear Martyn Petrovich really had grown "meek," I thought, and I had a still stronger desire to make my way into Yeskovo, and get at least a glance at that colossus, whom I could never picture to myself subdued and tractable.

I had reached the edge of the copse, when suddenly a big snipe, with a great rush of wings, darted up at my very feet, and flew off into the depths of the wood. I took aim; my gun missed fire. I was greatly annoyed; it had been such a fine bird, and I made up my mind to try if I couldn't make it rise a second time. I set off in the direction of its flight, and going some two hundred paces off into the wood I caught sight—in a little glade, under an overhanging birch-tree—not of the snipe, but of the same Sletkin once more. He was lying on his back, with both hands under his head, and with a smile of contentment gazing upwards at the sky, swinging his left leg, which was crossed over his right knee. He did not notice my approach. A few paces from him, Yevlampia was walking slowly up and down the little glade, with downcast eyes. It seemed as though she were looking for something in the grass—mushrooms or something; now and then, she stooped and stretched out her hand. She was singing in a low voice. I stopped at once, and fell to listening. At first I could not make out what it was she was singing, but afterwards I recognized clearly the following well-known lines of the old ballad:

> "Hither, hither, threatening storm-cloud,
> Slay for me my father-in-law,
> Strike for me my mother-in-law,
> The young wife I will kill myself!"

Yevlampia sang louder and louder; the last words she delivered with peculiar energy. Sletkin still lay on his back and laughed to himself, while she seemed all the time to be moving round and round him.

"Oh, indeed!" he commented at last. "The things that come into some people's heads!"

"What?" queried Yevlampia.

Sletkin raised his head a little. "What? Why, what words were those you were uttering?"

"Why, you know, Volodya, one can't leave the words out of a song," answered Yevlampia, and she turned and saw me. We both cried out aloud at once, and both rushed away in opposite directions.

I made my way hurriedly out of the copse, and crossing a narrow clearing, found myself facing Harlov's garden.

## XX

I had no time, nor would it have been of any use, to deliberate over what I had seen. Only a phrase kept recurring to my mind, "love spell," which I had lately heard, and over the meaning of which I had pondered a good deal. I walked alongside the garden fence and in a few moments, behind the silver poplars (they had not yet

lost a single leaf, and the foliage was luxuriantly thick and glistening),
I saw the yard and the houses that made up Martyn Petrovich's
homestead. The whole place struck me as having been tidied up and
pulled into shape. On every side one could perceive traces of unflagging and severe supervision. Anna Martynovna came out on to
the steps, and screwing up her blue-gray eyes, gazed for a long
while in the direction of the copse.

"Have you seen the master?" she asked a peasant, who was walking across the yard.

"Vladimir Vasilyevich?" responded the latter, taking his cap off.
"He went into the copse, surely."

"I know, he went to the copse. Hasn't he come back? Haven't
you seen him?"

"I've not seen him . . . nay."

The peasant continued standing bareheaded before Anna Martynovna.

"Well, you can go," she said. "Or no—wait a bit. Where's Martyn
Petrovich? Do you know?"

"Oh, Martyn Petrovich," answered the peasant, in a singsong
voice, alternately lifting his right and then his left hand, as though
pointing away somewhere, "is sitting yonder, at the pond, with a
fishing-rod. He's sitting in the reeds, with a rod. Catching fish,
maybe, God knows."

"Very well . . . you can go," repeated Anna Martynovna; "and
put away that wheel, it's lying about."

The peasant ran to carry out her command, while she remained
standing a few minutes longer on the steps, still gazing in the direction of the copse. Then she clenched one fist menacingly, and went
slowly back into the house. "Aksyutka!" I heard her imperious voice
calling within.

Anna Martynovna looked angry, and tightened her lips, thin
enough at all times, more than usual. She was carelessly dressed, and
a coil of loose hair had fallen down on to her shoulder. But in spite
of the negligence of her attire, and her irritable humor, she struck me,
just as before, as attractive, and I should have been delighted to kiss
the narrow hand which looked vicious too, as she twice irritably
pushed back the loose tress.

## XXI

"Can Martyn Petrovich have really taken to fishing?" I asked myself, as I turned towards the pond, which was on one side of the garden. I got onto the dam, looked in all directions. . . . Martyn Petrovich was nowhere to be seen. I bent my steps along one of the banks of the pond, and at last, at the very top of it, in a little creek, in the midst of flat broken-down stalks of reddish reed, I caught sight of a huge grayish mass. . . . I looked intently: it was Harlov. Bareheaded, unkempt, in a cotton smock torn at the seams, with his legs crossed under him, he was sitting motionless on the bare earth. So motionless was he that a sandpiper, at my approach, darted up from the dry mud a couple of paces from him, and flew with a whistle and a flash of its little wings over the surface of the water, showing that no one had moved to frighten him for a long while. Harlov's whole appearance was so extraordinary that my dog stopped short directly it saw him, lifted its tail, and growled. He turned his head a very little, and fixed his wild-looking eyes on me and my dog. He was greatly changed by his beard, though it was short, but thick and curly, like Persian lamb, with tufts of white. In his right hand lay the end of a rod, while the other end hovered feebly over the water. I felt an involuntary pang at my heart. I plucked up my spirits, however, went up to him, and wished him good morning. He slowly blinked as though just awake.

"What are you doing, Martyn Petrovich," I began, "catching fish here?"

"Yes . . . fish," he answered huskily, and pulled up the rod, on which there fluttered a piece of line, a fathom length, with no hook on it.

"Your tackle is broken off," I observed, and noticed the same moment that there was no sign of bait-tin nor worms near Martyn Petrovich. . . . And what sort of fishing could there be in September?

"Broken off?" he said, and he passed his hand over his face. "But it's all the same!"

He dropped the rod in again.

"Natalya Nikolayevna's son?" he asked me, after the lapse of two minutes, during which I had been gazing at him with secret bewilderment. Though he had grown terribly thinner, still he seemed a giant. But what rags he was dressed in, and how utterly he had gone to pieces!

"Yes," I answered, "I'm the son of Natalya Nikolayevna B."

"Is she well?"

"My mother is quite well. She was very much hurt at your refusal," I added; "she did not at all expect you would not wish to come and see her."

Martyn Petrovich's head sank on his breast. "Have you been there?" he asked, with a motion of his head.

"Where?"

"There, at the house. Haven't you? Go! What is there for you to do here? Go! It's useless talking to me. I don't like it."

He was silent for a while.

"You'd like to be always idling about with a gun! In my young days I used to be inclined the same way too. Only my father was strict and made me respect him too. Mind you, very different from fathers nowadays. My father flogged me with a horsewhip, and that was the end of it! I'd to give up idling about! And so I respected him. . . . Oo! . . . Yes! . . ."

Harlov paused again.

"Don't you stop here," he began again. "You go along to the house. Things are managed there now—it's first-rate. Volodka" . . . Here he faltered for a second. "Our Volodka's a good hand at everything. He's a fine fellow! yes, indeed, and a fine scoundrel too!"

I did not know what to say; Martyn Petrovich spoke very tranquilly.

"And you go and see my daughters. You remember, I daresay, I had daughters. They're managers too . . . clever ones. But I'm growing old, my lad; I'm on the shelf. Time to repose, you know. . . ."

"Nice sort of repose!" I thought, glancing round. "Martyn Petrovich!" I uttered aloud, "you really must come and see us."

Harlov looked at me. "Go along, my lad, I tell you."

"Don't hurt mamma's feelings; come and see us."

"Go away, my lad, go away," persisted Harlov. "What do you want to talk to me for?"

"If you have no carriage, mamma will send you hers."

"Go along!"

"But, really and truly, Martyn Petrovich!"

Harlov looked down again, and I fancied that his cheeks, dingy as though covered with earth, faintly flushed.

"Really, do come," I went on. "What's the use of your sitting here, of your making yourself miserable?"

"Making myself miserable?" he commented hesitatingly.

"Yes, to be sure—making yourself miserable!" I repeated.

Harlov said nothing, and seemed lost in thought. Emboldened by his silence, I determined to be open, to act straightforwardly, bluntly. (Do not forget, I was only fifteen then.)

"Martyn Petrovich!" I began, seating myself beside him. "I know everything, you see, positively everything. I know how your son-in-law is treating you—doubtless with the consent of your daughters. And now you are in such a position . . . But why lose heart?"

Harlov still remained silent, and simply dropped in his line; while I—what a clever fellow, what a philosopher I felt myself to be!

"Doubtless," I began again, "you acted imprudently in giving up everything to your daughters. It was most generous on your part, and I am not going to blame you. In our days it is a quality only too rare! But since your daughters are so ungrateful, you ought to show a contempt—yes, a contempt—for them . . . and not fret—"

"Stop!" muttered Harlov suddenly, gnashing his teeth, and his eyes, staring at the pond, glittered wrathfully . . . "Go away!"

"But, Martyn Petrovich—"

"Go away, I tell you . . . or I'll kill you!"

I had come quite close to him; but at the last words I instinctively jumped up. "What did you say, Martyn Petrovich?"

"I'll kill you, I tell you; go away!" With a wild moan, a roar, the voice broke from Harlov's breast, but he did not turn his head, and still stared wrathfully straight in front of him. "I'll take you and fling you and your fool's counsel into the water. You'll learn what it means to pester the old, you milksop!"

"He's gone mad!" flashed through my mind.

I looked at him more attentively, and was completely petrified; Martyn Petrovich was weeping! Tear after tear rolled from his eyelashes down his cheeks . . . while his face had assumed an expression utterly savage. . . .

"Go away!" he roared once more, "or I'll kill you, by God! as an example to others!"

He shook all over with a sidewise movement, and showed his teeth like a wild boar. I snatched up my gun and took to my heels. My dog flew after me, barking. He, too, was frightened.

When I got home, I naturally did not, by so much as a word to my mother, hint at what I had seen; but coming across Souvenir, I told him—the devil knows why—all about it. That loathsome person was so delighted at my story, so shrieked with laughter, and even danced with pleasure, that I could hardly forbear striking him.

"Ah! I should like," he kept repeating breathless with laughter, "to have seen that stone image, the Swede, Harlov, crawling into the mud and sitting in it. . . ."

"Go over to the pond if you're so curious."

"Yes; but what if he kills me?"

I felt horribly fed up with Souvenir, and regretted my ill-timed confidence. . . . Zhitkov, to whom he repeated my tale, looked at the matter somewhat differently.

"We shall have to call in the police," he concluded, "or, maybe, we shall have to send for a battalion of soldiers."

His forebodings with regard to the battalion did not come true; but something extraordinary really did happen.


## XXII

In the middle of October, three weeks after my interview with Martyn Petrovich, I was standing at the window of my own room on the second storey of our house, and thinking of nothing at all, I looked disconsolately at the yard and the road that lay beyond it. The weather had been disgusting for the last five days. Shooting was not even to be thought of. All things living had hidden themselves; even the sparrows made no sound, and the rooks had long ago disappeared from sight. The wind howled drearily, then whistled spasmodically. The low-hanging sky, unbroken by one streak of light, had changed from an unpleasant whitish to a leaden and still more sinister hue; and the rain, which had been pouring and pouring, mercilessly and unceasingly, suddenly fell in larger drops and at a sharper angle, and streamed with a rushing sound over the panes. The trees had been stripped utterly bare, and turned a sort of gray. It seemed there was nothing left on them to plunder; yet the wind would not be denied, but set to harassing them once more. Puddles, clogged with dead leaves, stood everywhere. Big bubbles, continually bursting and rising up again, leaped and glided over them. Along the roads, the mud lay thick and impassable. The cold penetrated the rooms, one's clothes, one's very bones. An involutary shiver passed over the body, and how sick one felt at heart! Sick, precisely, not sad. It seemed there would never again be sunshine, or brightness, or color in the world, but this rain and mire and gray damp and raw fog would last forever, and for ever would the wind whine and moan!

Well, I was standing moodily at my window, and I remember a sudden darkness came on—a bluish darkness—though the clock only pointed to twelve. Suddenly I fancied I saw a bear dash across our yard from the gates to the steps. Not on all-fours, certainly, but as he is depicted when he gets up on his hind-paws. I could not believe my eyes. If it were not a bear I had seen, it was, anyway, something enormous, black, shaggy. . . . I was still lost in wonder as to what it could be, when suddenly I heard below a furious knocking. It seemed something utterly unlooked for, something terrible was stumbling headlong into our house. Then began a commotion, a hurrying to and fro. . . .

I quickly went down the stairs, ran into the dining-room. . . .

At the drawing-room door facing me stood my mother, as though rooted to the spot. Behind her, peered several scared female faces. The butler, two footmen, and a page, his mouth wide open with astonishment, were packed together in the doorway of the hall. In the middle of the dining-room, covered with mire, disheveled, tattered, and soaking wet—so wet that steam rose all round and water was running in little streams over the floor—knelt, shaking ponderously, as it were, at the last gasp . . . the very monster I had seen dashing across the yard! And who was this monster? Harlov! I came up beside him and saw, not his face, but his head, which he was clutching, with both hands in the hair that was matted with mud. He was breathing heavily, fitfully; something positively rattled in his throat—and in all the bespattered dark mass, the only thing that could be clearly distinguished was the tiny whites of the eyes, which were straying wildly about. He was awful! The dignitary came into my mind whom he had once upbraided for comparing him to a mastodon. Truly, so might have looked some antediluvian creature that had just escaped another more powerful monster, which had attacked it in the eternal slime of the primeval swamps.

"Martyn Petrovich!" my mother cried at last, and she clasped her hands. "Is that you? Good God! Merciful heavens!"

"I—I—" we heard a broken voice, which seemed with effort and painfully to dwell on each sound. "Alas! It is I!"

"But what has happened to you? Mercy upon us!"

"Natalya Nikolayev-na—I have—run straight—to you—from home —on foot—"

"Through such mud! But you don't look like a man. Get up; sit down, anyway. . . . And you," she turned to the maidservants, "run quick for towels. And have you some dry clothes?" she asked the butler.

The butler gesticulated as though to say, Is it likely for such a size? . . . "But we could get a blanket," he replied, "or, there's a new horse-rug."

"But get up, get up, Martyn Petrovich, sit down," repeated my mother.

"They've turned me out, madam," Harlov moaned suddenly, and he flung his head back and stretched his hands out before him. "They've turned me out, Natalya Nikolayevna! My own daughters, out of my own home."

My mother sighed and groaned.

"What are you saying? Turned you out! What wickedness! What wickedness!" (She crossed herself.) "But do get up, Martyn Petrovich, I beg you!"

Two maidservants came in with towels and stood still before Harlov. It was clear they did not know how to attack this mountain of filth. "They have turned me out, madam, they have turned me out!" Harlov kept repeating meanwhile. The butler returned with a large woolen blanket, and he, too, stood still in perplexity. Souvenir's little head was thrust in at a door and vanished again.

"Martyn Petrovich! Get up! Sit down! And tell me everything properly," my mother commanded in a tone of determination.

Harlov rose. . . . The butler tried to assist him but only dirtied his hand, and, shaking his fingers, retreated to the door. Shifting from foot to foot and staggering, faltering, Harlov got to a chair and sat down. The maids again approached him with their towels, but he waved them off with his hand, and refused the blanket. Indeed, my mother herself did not insist; to dry Harlov was obviously out of the question; they contented themselves with hastily wiping up his traces on the floor.

## XXIII

"How have they turned you out?" my mother asked, as soon as he had a little time to recover himself.

"Madam! Natalya Nikolayevna!" he began, in a strained voice,— and again I was struck by the uneasy straying of his eyes; "I will tell you the truth; I am myself most of all to blame."

"Ay, to be sure; you would not listen to me at the time," assented my mother, sinking into an armchair and slightly moving a scented handkerchief before her nose; very strong was the smell that came from Harlov . . . the odor in a forest bog is not so strong.

"Alas! that's not where I erred, madam, but through pride. Pride has been my ruin, as it ruined King Nebuchadnezzar. I fancied God had given me my full share of sense, and if I resolved on anything, it followed it was right; so . . . And then the fear of death came . . . I was utterly confounded! 'I'll show them,' said I, to myself, 'at the last, my power and my strength! I'll bestow all on them— and they must feel it all their lives. . . .'" (Harlov suddenly shook all over. . . .) "Like a mangy dog they have driven me out of the house! This is their gratitude!"

"But in what way—" my mother began again.

"They took my page, Maximka, from me," Harlov interrupted her (his eyes were still wandering, he held both hands—the fingers interlaced—under his chin), "my carriage they took away, my monthly allowance they cut down, did not pay me the sum specified, cut me short all round, in fact; still I said nothing, bore it all! And I bore it by reason . . . alas! of my pride again. That my cruel enemies might not say, 'See, the old fool's sorry for it now'; and you too, do you remember, madam, had warned me; 'mind you, it's all to no purpose,' you said! and so I bore it. . . . Only, today I came into my room, and it was occupied already, and my bed they'd thrown out into the lumber-room! 'You can sleep there; even there we put up with you only out of charity; we've need of your room for the household.' And this was said to me by whom? Volodka Sletkin! the knave, the rat!"

Harlov's voice broke.

"But your daughters? What did they do?" asked my mother.

"But I bore it all," Harlov went on again; "bitterness, bitterness was in my heart, let me tell you, and shame. . . . I could not bear to look upon the light of day! That was why I was unwilling to come and see you, ma'am, from this same feeling, from shame for my disgrace! I have tried everything, my good friend; kindness, affection, and threats, and I reasoned with them, and more besides! I bowed down before them . . . like this." (Harlov showed how he had bowed down.) "And all in vain. And all of it I bore! At the beginning, at first, I'd very different thoughts; I'll up, I thought, and kill them. I'll crush them all, so that not a trace remains of them! . . . I'll let them know! Well, but after, I submitted! It's a cross, I thought, laid upon me; it's to bid me make ready for death. And all at once, today, driven out, like a cur! And by whom? Volodka! And you asked about my daughters; they've no will of their own at all. They're Volodka's slaves! Yes!"

My mother wondered. "In Anna's case I can understand that; she's a wife. . . . But how comes it your second . . ."

"Yevlampia? She's worse than Anna! She's completely surrendered herself to Volodka. That's the reason she refused your soldier, too. At his, at Volodka's bidding. Anna, to be sure, ought to resent it, and she can't bear her sister, but she submits! He's bewitched them, the cursed scoundrel! Though she, Anna, I daresay, is pleased to think that Yevlampia, who was always so proud—and now see what she's come to! . . . Oh . . . alas . . . alas! God, my God!"

My mother looked uneasily towards me. I moved a little away as a precautionary measure, for fear I should be sent away altogether. . . .

"I am very sorry indeed, Martyn Petrovich," she began, "that my former protégé has caused you so much sorrow, and has turned out so badly. But I, too, was mistaken in him. . . . Who could have expected this of him?"

"Madam," Harlov moaned out, and he struck himself a blow on the chest, "I cannot bear the ingratitude of my daughters! I cannot, madam! You know I gave them everything, everything! And besides, my conscience has been tormenting me. Many things . . . alas! many things I have thought over, sitting by the pond, fishing. 'If you'd only done good to anyone in your life!' was what I pondered upon, 'succored the poor, set the peasants free, to atone for having eaten up their lives. You must answer for them before God! Now their tears are revenged.' And what sort of life have they now? It was a deep pit even in my time—why disguise my sins?—but now there's no seeing the bottom! All these sins I have taken upon my soul; I have sacrificed my conscience for my children, and for this here's what I get! Kicked out of the house, like a cur!"

"Don't think about that, Martyn Petrovich," observed my mother.

"And when he told me, your Volodka," Harlov went on with fresh force, "when he told me I was not to live in my room any more—I laid every plank in that room with my own hands—when he said that to me—God only knows what passed within me! It was all confusion in my head, and like a knife in my heart. . . . Either to cut his throat or get out of the house! . . . So, I have run to you, my benefactress, Natalya Nikolayevna . . . where could I lay my head? And then the rain, the filth . . . I fell down twenty times, maybe! And now . . . in such unseemly . . ."

Harlov scanned himself and moved restlessly in his chair, as though intending to get up.

"Say no more, Martyn Petrovich," my mother interposed hurriedly; "what's there to make a fuss about? That you've made the floor dirty? That's no great matter! Come, I want to make you a proposition. Listen! They shall take you now to a special room, and make you up a clean bed—you undress, wash, and lie down and sleep a little. . . ."

"Natalya Nikolayevna! There's no sleeping for me!" Harlov responded drearily. "It's as though there were hammers beating in my brain! Me! like some good-for-nothing beast! . . ."

"Lie down and sleep," my mother repeated insistently. "And then we'll give you some tea—yes, and we'll have a talk. Don't lose heart, old friend! If they've driven you out of *your* house, in *my* house you will always find a home. . . . I have not forgotten, you know, that you saved my life."

"Benefactress!" moaned Harlov, and he covered his face with his hands. "*You* must save me now!"

This appeal touched my mother almost to tears. "I am ready and eager to help you, Martyn Petrovich, in every way I am able. But you must promise me that you will listen to me in future and dismiss every evil thought from you."

Harlov took his hands from his face. "If need be," he said, "I can forgive them, even!"

My mother nodded her head approvingly. "I am very glad to see you in such a truly Christian frame of mind, Martyn Petrovich; but we will talk of that later. Meanwhile, you put yourself to rights, and, most of all, sleep. Take Martyn Petrovich to the late master's room, the green room," said my mother, addressing the butler, "and whatever he asks for, let him have it on the spot! Give orders for his clothes to be dried and washed, and ask the housekeeper for what linen is needed. Do you hear?"

"Yes, madam," responded the butler.

"And as soon as he's awake tell the tailor to take his measure. And his beard will have to be shaved—not at once, but afterwards."

"Yes, madam," repeated the butler. "Martyn Petrovich, kindly come." Harlov got up, looked at my mother, was about to go up to her, but stopped, bowed to her from the waist, crossed himself three times to the image, and followed the butler. Behind him, I, too, slipped out of the room.

## XXIV

The butler conducted Harlov to the green room, and at once ran off for the wardroom maid, as it turned out there were no sheets on the bed. Souvenir, who met us in the passage and popped into the green room with us, promptly proceeded to dance, grinning and chuckling, round Harlov, who stood, his arms held a little away from him, and his legs apart, in the middle of the room, seeming lost in thought. The water was still dripping from him.

"The Swede! The Swede Harlus!" piped Souvenir, doubling up and holding his sides. "Mighty founder of the illustrious race of Harlovs, behold thy descendant! What does he look like? Dost thou recognize him? Ha, ha, ha! Your excellency, your hand, I beg; why, have you got on black gloves?"

I tried to restrain Souvenir, to put him to shame . . . but it was too late for that now.

"He called me parasite, toady! 'You've no roof,' said he, 'to call your own.' But now, no doubt about it, he's become as dependent as poor little me. Martyn Petrovich and Souvenir, the poor toady, are equal now. He'll have to live on charity too. They'll toss him the stale and dirty crust that the dog has sniffed at and refused. . . . And they'll tell him to eat it, too. Ha, ha, ha!"

Harlov still stood motionless, his head drawn in, his legs and arms held a little apart.

"Martyn Harlov, a nobleman born!" Souvenir went on shrieking. "What airs he used to give himself. 'Just look at me! Don't come near, or I'll knock you down!' . . . And when he was so clever as to give away and divide his property, didn't he crow! 'Gratitude! . . .' he cackled, 'gratitude!' But why were you so mean to me? Why didn't you make me a present? Maybe, I should have appreciated it more. And you see I was right when I said they'd strip you bare, and . . ."

"Souvenir!" I screamed; but Souvenir was not to be stopped. Harlov still did not stir. It seemed as though he were only now beginning to be aware how soaking-wet everything was that he had on, and was waiting to be helped off with his clothes. But the butler had not come back.

"And a military man too!" Souvenir began again. "In the year twelve, he saved his country! He showed proofs of his valor! I see how it is. Stripping the frozen marauders of their breeches is work he's quite equal to, but when a hussy stamps her foot at him he's frightened out of his skin."

"Souvenir!" I screamed a second time.

Harlov looked askance at Souvenir. Till that instant he seemed not to have noticed his presence, and only my exclamation aroused his attention.

"Look out, brother," he growled huskily, "don't dance yourself into trouble."

Souvenir fairly rolled about with laughter. "Ah, how you frighten me, most honored brother. You're a formidable person, to be sure. You must comb your hair, at any rate, or, God forbid, it'll get dry, and you'll never wash it clean again; you'll have to mow it with a sickle." Souvenir all of a sudden got into a fury. "And you give yourself airs still. A poor outcast, and he gives himself airs. Where's your home now? You'd better tell me that, you were always boasting of it. 'I have a home of my own,' he used to say, 'but you're homeless. My ancestral roof,' he would say." Souvenir clung to the word.

"Mr. Bychkov," I protested. "What are you about? you forget yourself."

But he persisted in chattering, and still danced and pranced up and down quite close to Harlov. And still the butler and the wardroom maid did not come.

I felt alarmed. I began to notice that Harlov, who, during his conversation with my mother, had gradually grown quieter, and even towards the end apparently resigned himself to his fate, was beginning to get worked up again. He breathed more hurriedly, the flesh under his ears suddenly seemed to swell, his fingers twitched, his eyes again began moving restlessly in the dark mask of his grim face. . . .

"Souvenir, Souvenir!" I cried. "Stop it, I'll tell mamma."

But Souvenir seemed possessed by the devil. "Yes, yes, most honored brother," he began again, "here we find ourselves, you and I, in a most delicate position. Your daughters, with your son-in-law, Vladimir Vasilyevich, are having a fine laugh at you under your roof. And you should at least curse them, as you promised. Even that you're not equal to. To be sure, how could you hold your own with Vladimir Vasilyevich? Why, you used to call him Volodka, too. He's no Volodka to you. *He* is Vladimir Vasilyevich, Mr. Sletkin, a landowner, a gentleman, while—what are you, pray?"

A furious roar drowned Souvenir's words. . . . Harlov exploded. He clenched his fists and raised them, his face turned purple, foam showed on his chapped lips, he shook with rage. "Roof, you say!" he thundered in his iron voice, "curse, you say. . . . No! I will not curse them. . . . They don't mind that . . . But the roof . . . I will tear the roof off them, and they shall have no roof over their heads, like me. They shall learn to know Martyn Harlov. My strength is not all gone yet; they shall find out what it means to laugh at me! . . . They shall have no roof over their heads!"

I was stupefied; never in my life had I witnessed such boundless anger. Not a man—a wild beast—dashed to and fro before me. I was dumfounded . . . As for Souvenir, he hid under the table in his fright.

"They shall not!" Harlov shouted for the last time, and almost knocking over the butler and the wardroom maid, he rushed out of the house. . . . He dashed headlong across the yard, and vanished beyond the gates.

## XXV

My mother was terribly angry when the butler came with an abashed countenance to report Martyn Petrovich's sudden and unexpected departure. He did not dare to conceal the cause of this retreat; I was obliged to confirm his story. "Then it was all your doing!" my mother cried, at the sight of Souvenir, who had run in like a hare, and was even approaching to kiss her hand: "Your vile tongue is to blame for it all!" "Excuse me, d'rectly, d'rectly . . ." faltered Souvenir, stuttering and drawing back his elbows behind him. "D'rectly, . . . d'rectly . . . I know your 'd'rectly,'" my mother repeated reprovingly, and she sent him out of the room. Then she rang the bell, sent for Kwieciński, and gave him orders to set off on the spot to Yeskovo, with a carriage, to find Martyn Petrovich at all costs, and to bring him back. "Do not let me see you without him," she concluded. The gloomy Pole bowed his head without a word, and went away.

I went back to my own room, sat down again at the window, and I pondered a long while, I remember, on what had taken place before my eyes. I was puzzled; I could not understand how it was that Harlov, who had endured the insults of his own family almost without a murmur, had lost all self-control and been unable to put up with the jeers and pinpricks of such an abject creature as Souvenir. I did not understand in those days what insufferable bitterness there may sometimes be in a foolish taunt, even when it comes from lips one scorns. . . . The hated name of Sletkin, uttered by Souvenir, had been like a spark thrown into powder. The sore spot could not endure this final prick.

About an hour passed by. Our coach drove into the yard; but our steward sat in it alone. And my mother had said to him, "Don't let me see you without him." Kwieciński jumped hurriedly out of the carriage, and ran up the steps. His face had a perturbed look—something very unusual with him. I promptly rushed downstairs, and followed at his heels into the drawing-room. "Well? have you brought him?" asked my mother.

"I have not brought him," answered Kwieciński, "and I could not bring him."

"How's that? Have you seen him?"

"Yes."

"What has happened to him? A fit?"

"No; nothing has happened."

"How is it you didn't bring him?"

"He's pulling his house to pieces."

"What?"

"He's standing on the roof of the new building, and pulling it to pieces. Forty boards or more, I should guess, must have come down by now, and some five of the rafters too." ("They shall not have a roof over their heads." Harlov's words came back to me.)

My mother stared at Kwieciński. "Alone . . . he's standing on the roof, and pulling the roof down?"

"Exactly so. He is walking about on the flooring of the garret and smashing everything to right and left of him. His strength, you are aware, madam, is superhuman. And the roof too, one must say, is a poor affair; half-inch deal shingles, laid wide apart, one-inch nails."

My mother looked at me, as though wishing to make sure whether she had heard aright. "Laid wide apart," she repeated, obviously not understanding the meaning of one word. "Well, what then?" she said at last.

"I have come for instructions. There's no doing anything without men to help. The peasants there are gone into hiding in fright."

"And his daughters—what of them?"

"His daughters are doing nothing. They're running to and fro, shouting . . . this and that . . . all to no purpose."

"And is Sletkin there?"

"He's there too. He's making more outcry than all of them—but he can't do anything."

"And Martyn Petrovich is standing on the roof?"

"On the roof . . . that is, in the garret—and pulling the roof to pieces."

"Yes, yes," said my mother, "laid wide apart."

The situation was obviously a serious one. What steps were to be taken? Send to the town for the police captain? Get together the peasants? My mother was quite at her wits' end. Zhitkov, who had come in to dinner, was nonplused too. It is true he made another reference to a battalion of soldiers; he offered no advice, however, but confined himself to looking submissive and devoted. Kwieciński, seeing he would not get any instructions, suggested to my mother—

with the contemptuous respectfulness peculiar to him—that if she would authorize him to take a few of the stableboys, gardeners, and other house-serfs, he would make an effort . . .

"Yes, yes," my mother cut him short, "do make an effort, dear Vikenty Osipych! Only make haste, please, and I will take all responsibility on myself!"

Kwieciński smiled coldly. "One thing let me make clear, madam, beforehand; it's impossible to reckon on any result, seeing that Mr. Harlov's strength is so great, and he is so desperate too; he feels himself to have been very cruelly wronged!"

"Yes, yes," my mother assented; "and it's all that vile Souvenir's fault! Never will I forgive him for it. Go and take the servants and set off, Vikenty Osipych!"

"You'd better take plenty of cord, Mr. Steward, and some firemen's hooks," Zhitkov brought out in his bass—"and if there is such a thing as a net, it would be as well to take that along too. We once had in our regiment . . ."

"Kindly refrain from instructing me, sir," Kwieciński cut him short, with an air of vexation; "I know what is needed without your advice."

Zhitkov was offended, and protested that as he imagined he, too, was called upon . . .

"No, no!" interposed my mother; "you'd better stay where you are . . . Let Vikenty Osipych act alone . . . Make haste, Vikenty Osipych!"

Zhitkov was still more offended, while Kwieciński bowed and went out.

I rushed off to the stable, hurriedly saddled my horse myself, and set off at a gallop along the road to Yeskovo.

## XXVI

The rain had ceased, but the wind was blowing with redoubled force—straight into my face. Halfway there, the saddle almost slipped round under me; the girth had got loose; I got off and tried to tighten the straps with my teeth. . . . All at once I heard someone calling me by name . . . Souvenir was running towards me across the green fields. "What!" he shouted to me from some way off. "Was your curiosity too much for you? How could you help it? . . . I'm on my way there, too, straight after Harlov. . . . You might live your life out and not see a thing like this!"

"You want to enjoy what you have done," I said indignantly, and, jumping on my horse, I set off again at a gallop. But the indefatigable Souvenir kept at my heels, and guffawed and grimaced even as he ran. At last, Yeskovo was reached—there was the dam, and there was the long hedge and the willows of the homestead . . . I rode up to the gate, dismounted, tied up my horse, and stood still in amazement.

Of one third of the roof of the newer house nothing was left but the skeleton; boards and shingles lay in disorderly heaps on the ground on both sides of the building. Even supposing the roof to be, as Kwieciński had said, a poor affair, even so, it was something incredible! On the floor of the garret, in a whirl of dust and rubbish, a blackish gray mass was moving to and fro with awkward agility. Now it shook the remaining chimney, built of brick, (the other had fallen already), then tore up the boarding and flung it down, then clutched at the very rafters. It was Harlov. He struck me as being exactly like a bear at this moment too; the head, and back, and shoulders were a bear's, and he put his feet down wide apart without bending them—also like a bear. The bitter wind was blowing upon him from every side, lifting his matted locks. It was horrible to see, here and there, red patches of bare flesh through the rents in his tattered clothes; it was horrible to hear his wild husky muttering.

There were a lot of people in the yard; peasant-women, boys, and servant-girls hugged the fence. A few peasants huddled together in a separate group a little way off. The old village priest, whom I knew, was standing, bareheaded, on the steps of the other house, and holding a brass cross in both hands, from time to time, silently and hopelessly, raised it, and, as it were, showed it to Harlov. Beside the priest stood Yevlampia with her back against the wall, gazing fixedly at her father. Anna, at one moment, pushed her head out of the window, then vanished, then hurried into the yard, then went back into the house. Sletkin—pale, livid—in an old dressing-gown and smoking-cap, with a single-barreled rifle in his hands, kept running to and fro with little steps. He was hysterical. He was gasping, threatening, shaking, pointing the gun at Harlov, then letting it drop back on his shoulder—pointing it again, shrieking, weeping. . . . On seeing Souvenir and me he flew to us.

"Look, look, what is going on here!" he wailed. "Look! He's gone out of his mind, he's raving mad . . . and see what he's doing! I've sent for the police already—but no one comes! No one comes! If I do fire at him, the law couldn't touch me, for every man has a right to defend his own property! And I will fire! . . . By God, I'll fire!"

He ran off toward the house.

"Martyn Petrovich, look out! If you don't get down, I'll fire!"

"Fire away!" came a husky voice from the roof. "Fire away! And meanwhile here's a little present for you!"

A long plank, turning over twice in the air, fell violently to the earth, just at Sletkin's feet. He positively jumped into the air, while Harlov chuckled.

"Merciful Jesus!" faltered someone behind me.

I looked round: Souvenir. "Ah!" I thought, "he's left off laughing now!"

Sletkin clutched a peasant, who was standing near, by the collar.

"Climb up now, climb up, climb up, all of you, you devils," he wailed, shaking the man with all his force, "save my property!"

The peasant took a couple of steps forward, threw his head back, waved his arms, shouted: "Hi! Master!", shifted from one foot to the other uneasily, and then turned back.

"A ladder! Bring a ladder!" Sletkin addressed the other peasants.

"Where are we to get it?" was heard in answer.

"And if we had a ladder," one voice pronounced deliberately, "who'd care to climb up? We're not such fools! He'd wring your neck for you—in a twinkling!"

"He'd kill one in no time," said one young lad with flaxen hair and a half-idiotic face.

"To be sure he would," the others agreed. It struck me that, even if there had been no obvious danger, the peasants would yet have been loath to carry out their new owner's orders. They almost approved of Harlov, though they were amazed at him.

"Ugh, you robbers!" moaned Sletkin; "you shall all catch it . . ."

But at this moment, with a heavy rumble, the last chimney came crashing down, and, in the midst of the cloud of yellow dust that flew up instantly, Harlov—uttering a piercing shriek and lifting his bleeding hands high in the air—turned facing us. Sletkin pointed the gun at him again.

Yevlampia pulled him back by the elbow.

"Don't interfere!" he snarled savagely at her.

"And you—don't you dare!" she answered; and her blue eyes flashed menacingly under her scowling brows. "Father's pulling his house down. It's his own."

"You lie: it's ours!"

"You say ours; but I say it's his."

Sletkin hissed with fury; Yevlampia stared hard at him.

"Ah, how d'ye do! my delightful daughter!" Harlov thundered from above. "How d'ye do! Yevlampia Martynovna! How are you getting on with your sweetheart? Are your kisses sweet, and your fondling?"

"Father!" rang out Yevlampia's musical voice.

"Eh, daughter?" answered Harlov; and he came down to the very edge of the wall. His face, as far as I could make it out, wore a strange smile, a bright, mirthful—and for that very reason peculiarly strange and evil—smile. . . . Many years later I saw just the same smile on the face of a man condemned to death.

"Stop, father; come down. We are at fault; we will give everything back to you. Come down."

"What do you mean by disposing of what's ours?" put in Sletkin. Yevlampia merely scowled more angrily.

"I will give you back my share. I will give up everything. Stop, come down, father! Forgive us; forgive me."

Harlov still went on smiling. "It's too late, my darling," he said, and each of his words rang out like brass. "Too late your stony heart is touched! The rock's started rolling downhill—there's no holding it back now! And don't look at me now; I'm a doomed man! You'd do better to look at your Volodka; see what a pretty fellow you've picked out! And look at your venomous sister; there's her foxy nose yonder thrust out of the window; she's egging on that husband of hers! No, my good friends; you would rob me of a roof over my head, so I will leave you not one beam upon another! With my own hands I built it, with my own hands I destroy it—yes, with my hands alone! See, I've taken no axe to help me!"

He spat on his palms, and clutched at the rafter again.

"Enough, father," Yevlampia was saying meanwhile, and her voice had grown marvelously caressing, "let bygones be bygones. Come, trust me; you always trusted me. Come, get down; come to

me, to my little room, to my soft bed. I will dry you and warm you;
I will bind up your wounds; see, you have torn your hands. You
shall live with me as in Christ's bosom; food shall be sweet to you—
and sleep sweeter yet. Come, we have done wrong! yes, we were
puffed up, we have sinned; come, forgive!"

Harlov shook his head. "Talk away! Me believe you! Never
again! You've murdered all trust in my heart! You've murdered
everything! I was an eagle, and became a worm for you . . . and
you—you would even crush the worm? Have done! I loved you, you
know very well—but now you are no daughter to me, and I'm no
father to you . . . I'm a doomed man! Don't meddle! As for you,
fire away, coward, mighty man of valor!" Harlov bellowed suddenly
at Sletkin. "Why is it you keep aiming and don't shoot? Are you
mindful of the law: if the recipient of a gift commits an attempt upon
the life of the giver," Harlov enunciated distinctly, "then the giver
is empowered to claim everything back again? Ha, ha! don't be
afraid, law-abiding man! I'd make no claims. I'll make an end of
everything myself. . . . Here goes!"

"Father!" for the last time Yevlampia besought him.

"Silence!"

"Martyn Petrovich! brother, be generous and forgive!" babbled
Souvenir.

"Father! dear father!"

"Silence, bitch!" shouted Harlov. At Souvenir he did not even
glance—he merely spat in his direction.


## XXVII

At that instant, Kwieciński, with all his retinue—in three carts—
appeared at the gates. The tired horses panted, the men jumped out,
one after another, into the mud.

"Aha!" Harlov shouted at the top of his voice. "An army . . .
here it comes, an army! A whole army they're sending against me!
Capital! Only I give warning—if anyone comes up here to me on the
roof, I'll send him flying down, head over heels! I'm an inhospitable
master; I don't like visitors at wrong times! No indeed!"

He was hanging with both hands onto the front rafters of the
roof, the so-called supports of the pediment, and shaking them violently. Balancing on the edge of the garret flooring, he dragged

them, as it were, after him, chanting rhythmically like a bargeman, "One more pull! One more! O-oh!"

Sletkin ran up to Kwieciński and was beginning to whimper and pour out complaints. . . . The latter begged him "not to interfere," and proceeded to carry out the plan he had evolved. He took up his position in front of the house, and began, by way of diversion, to explain to Harlov that what he was about was unworthy of his rank. . . .

"One more pull! one more!" chanted Harlov.

. . . "That Natalya Nikolayevna was greatly displeased at his proceedings, and had not expected it of him." . . .

"One more pull! One more! O-oh!" Harlov chanted . . . while, meantime, Kwieciński had despatched the four sturdiest and boldest of the stableboys to the other side of the house to clamber up the roof from behind. Harlov, however, detected the plan of attack; he suddenly left the supports and ran quickly to the back part of the roof. His appearance was so alarming that the two stableboys who had already got up to the garret, slid instantly back again to the ground down the water-pipe, to the great glee of the serf boys, who positively roared with laughter. Harlov shook his fist after them and, going back to the front part of the house, again clutched at the supports and began once more loosening them, singing again like a bargeman.

Suddenly he stopped and stared. . . .

"Maximushka, my dear! my friend!" he cried. "Is it you?"

I looked round. . . . There, actually, was Maximka, stepping out from the crowd of peasants. Grinning and showing his teeth, he walked forward. His master, the harness-maker, had probably let him come home for a holiday.

"Climb up to me, Maximushka, my faithful servant," Harlov went on; "together let us rid ourselves of evil Tartar folk, of Lithuanian thieves!"

Maximka, still grinning, promptly began climbing up the roof. . . . But they seized him and pulled him back—goodness knows why; possibly as an example to the rest; he could hardly have been much aid to Martyn Petrovich.

"Oh, all right! Good!" Harlov pronounced, in a voice of menace, and again he took hold of the supports.

"Vikenty Osipovich! with your permission, I'll shoot," Sletkin turned to Kwieciński; "more to frighten him, see, than anything; my gun's only charged with snipe-shot." But Kwieciński had not time to answer him, when the front couple of beams, viciously shaken in Harlov's iron hands, heeled over with a loud crack and crashed into the yard; and with it, not able to stop himself, came Harlov too, and fell with a heavy thud on the earth. Everyone shuddered and drew a deep breath. . . . Harlov lay without stirring on his breast, and on his back lay the top central beam of the roof, which had come down with the falling gable's timbers.

## XXVIII

They ran up to Harlov, rolled the beam off him, turned him over on his back. His face was lifeless, there was blood about his mouth; he did not seem to breathe. "The breath is gone out of him,' muttered the peasants, standing about him. They ran to the well for water, brought a whole bucketful, and drenched Harlov's head. The mud and dust ran off his face, but he looked as lifeless as ever. They dragged up a bench, set it against the house itself, and with difficulty raising the huge body of Martyn Petrovich, laid it there with the head leaning against the wall. The page Maximka approached, fell on one knee, and, his other leg stretched out behind him, in a theatrical way, supported his former master's arm. Yevlampia, pale as death, stood directly facing her father, her great eyes fastened immovably upon him. Anna and Sletkin did not come near him. All were silent, all, as it were, waited for something.

At last we heard broken, bubbling noises in Harlov's throat, as though he were choking.

. . . Then he feebly moved one, his right, hand (Maximka supported the left), opened one, the right eye, and slowly gazing about him, as though overcome by some fearful kind of drunkenness, groaned, articulated gutturally, "I'm sma-ashed," and as though after a moment's thought, added, "Here it is, the ra-ven co-olt!" The blood suddenly gushed thickly from his mouth . . . his whole body began to quiver. . . .

"The end!" I thought. . . . But once more Harlov opened the same eye (the left eyelid lay as motionless as on a dead man's face), and fixing it on Yevlampia, he articulated, hardly above a breath, "Well, daugh-ter—you—I do not . . ."

Kwieciński, with a sharp motion of his hand, beckoned to the priest, who was still standing on the steps. . . . The old man came up, his narrow cassock clinging about his feeble knees. But suddenly there was a sort of horrible twitching in Harlov's legs and in his abdomen too; an irregular convulsion passed upwards over his face. Yevlampia's face seemed quivering and working in the same way. Maximka began crossing himself. . . . I was seized with horror; I ran out to the gates, squeezed myself close to them, not looking round. A minute later a soft murmur ran through the crowd, behind my back, and I understood that Martyn Petrovich was no more.

His skull had been fractured by the beam and his ribs crushed, as it appeared at the post-mortem examination.

## XXIX

What had he wanted to say to her as he lay dying? I asked myself as I went home on my cob: "I do not . . . curse," or "do not . . . pardon." The rain had come on again, but I rode at a walking pace. I wanted to be alone as long as possible; I wanted to give myself up to my reflections, unchecked. Souvenir had gone back in one of the carts that had come with Kwieciński. Young and frivolous as I was at that time, the sudden sweeping change (not in mere details only) that is invariably called forth in all hearts by the coming of death—expected or unexpected, it makes no difference!—its majesty, its gravity, and its candour could not fail to impress me. I was indeed impressed, . . . but for all that, my troubled, childish eyes noted many things at once; they noted how Sletkin, hurriedly and furtively, as though it were something stolen, popped the gun out of sight; how he and his wife became, both of them, instantly the object of a sort of unspoken but universal ostracism. To Yevlampia, though her fault was probably no less than her sister's, this ostracism did not extend. She even aroused a certain sympathy, when she fell at her dead father's feet. But that she too was guilty, that was none the less felt by all. "The old man was wronged," said a gray-haired peasant with a big head, leaning, like some ancient judge, with both hands and his beard on a long staff; "on your soul lies the sin! You wronged him!" That saying was at once accepted by every one as the final judgment. The peasants' sense of justice found expression in it, I felt that at once. I noticed too that, at the first, Sletkin did not *dare* to give orders. Without him, they lifted up the body and carried it into the house. Without asking him, the priest went for everything needful to the church, while the village elder ran to the village to send off a cart and horse to the town. Even Anna Martynovna did not venture to use her ordinary imperious tone in ordering the samovar to be heated, "for hot water, to wash the deceased." Her orders were more like an entreaty, and she was answered rudely. . . .

I was absorbed all the while by the question, What was it exactly he wanted to say to his daughter? Did he want to forgive her or to curse her? Finally I decided that it was—forgiveness.

Three days later, the funeral of Martyn Petrovich took place. The cost of the ceremony was undertaken by my mother, who was deeply grieved at his death, and gave orders that no expense was to be spared. She did not herself go to the church, because she was unwilling, as she said, to set eyes on those two vile hussies and that "nasty little Jew." But she sent Kwieciński, me, and Zhitkov, though from that time forward she always spoke of the latter as a regular old woman. Souvenir she did not admit to her presence, and was furious with him for long after, saying that he was the murderer of her friend. He felt his disgrace acutely; he was continually running, on tiptoe, up and down the room, next to the one where my mother was; he gave himself up to a sort of scared and abject melancholy, shuddering and muttering, "d'rectly!"

In church, and during the procession, Sletkin struck me as having recovered his self-possession. He gave orders and bustled about in his old way, and kept a greedy lookout that not a superfluous farthing should be spent, though his own pocket was not in question. Maximka, in a new Cossack dress, also a present from my mother, gave vent to such tenor notes in the choir, that certainly no one could have any doubts as to the sincerity of his devotion to the deceased. Both the sisters were duly attired in mourning, but they seemed more stupefied than grieved, especially Yevlampia. Anna wore a meek, Lenten air, but made no attempt to weep, and was continually passing her handsome, thin hand over her hair and cheek. Yevlampia seemed deep in thought all the time. The universal, unbending alienation, condemnation, which I had noticed on the day of Harlov's death, I detected now too on the faces of all the people in the church, in their actions and their glances, but still more grave and, as it were, impersonal. It seemed as though all those people felt that the sin into which the Harlov family had fallen—this great sin—had gone now before the presence of the one righteous Judge, and that for that reason, there was no need now for them to trouble themselves and be indignant. They prayed devoutly for the soul of the dead man, whom in life they had not specially liked, whom they had feared indeed. Very abruptly had death overtaken him.

"And it's not as though he had been drinking heavily, brother," said one peasant to another, in the porch.

"You can get drunk without drinking—if things fall out that way," responded the other.

"He was wronged," the first peasant repeated the phrase that summed it up.

"Wronged," the others murmured after him.

"The deceased was a hard master to you, wasn't he?" I asked a peasant, whom I recognized as one of Harlov's serfs.

"He was a master, certainly," answered the peasant, "but still . . . he was wronged!"

"Wronged," . . . I heard again in the crowd.

At the grave, too, Yevlampia stood, as it were, lost. Thoughts were torturing her . . . painful thoughts. I noticed that Sletkin, who several times addressed some remark to her, she treated as she had once treated Zhitkov, and worse still.

Some days later, there was a rumor all over our neighborhood, that Yevlampia Martynovna had left the home of her father forever, leaving all the property that came to her to her sister and brother-in-law, and only taking some hundreds of roubles. . . . "So Anna's bought her out, it seems!" remarked my mother; "but you and I, certainly," she added, addressing Zhitkov, with whom she was playing picquet—he took Souvenir's place, "are not skillful hands!" Zhitkov looked dejectedly at his mighty palms. . . . "Hands like that! Not skillful!" he seemed to be saying to himself. . . .

Soon after, my mother and I went to live in Moscow, and many years passed before it was my lot to behold Martyn Petrovich's daughters again.

## XXX

But I did see them again. Anna Martynovna I came across in the most ordinary way.

After my mother's death I paid a visit to our village, where I had

not been for over fifteen years, and there I received an invitation
from the mediator (at that time the process of settling the boundaries
between the land of the peasants and that of their former owners was
taking place over the whole of Russia with a slowness not yet forgotten) to a meeting of the other landowners of our neighborhood,
to be held on the estate of the widow Anna Sletkin. The news that
my mother's "nasty little Jew," with the prune-colored eyes, no
longer existed in this world, caused me, I confess, no regret whatever. But it was interesting to get a glimpse of his widow. She had
the reputation in the neighborhood of a first-rate manager. And so it
proved; her estate and homestead and the house itself (I could not
help glancing at the roof; it was an iron one) all turned out to be
in excellent order; everything was neat, clean, tidied-up, where needful—painted, as though its mistress were a German. Anna Martynovna herself, of course, looked older. But the peculiar, cold, and,
as it were, wicked charm which had once so fascinated me had not
altogether left her. She was dressed in rustic fashion, but elegantly.
She received us, not cordially—that word was not applicable to her
—but courteously, and on seeing me, a witness of that fearful scene,
not an eyelash quivered. She made not the slightest reference to my
mother, nor her father, nor her sister, nor her husband.

She had two daughters, both very pretty, slim young things, with
charming little faces and a bright and friendly expression in their
black eyes. There was a son, too, a little like his father, but still a
boy to be proud of! During the discussions among the landowners,
Anna Martynovna's attitude was composed and dignified, she showed
no sign of being specially obstinate, nor specially grasping. But none
had a truer perception of their own interests than she of hers; none
could more convincingly expound and defend their rights. All the
laws "pertinent to the case," even the ministerial circulars, she had
thoroughly mastered. She spoke little, and in a quiet voice, but every
word she uttered was to the point. It ended in our all signifying our
agreement to all her demands, and making concessions, which we
could only marvel at ourselves. On our way home, some of the
worthy landowners even used harsh words of themselves; they all
groaned and shook their heads.

"Ah, she's got brains, that woman!" said one.

"A tricky baggage!" put in another less delicate proprietor.
"Smooth in word, but cruel in deed!"

"And a screw into the bargain!" added a third; "not a glass of vodka nor a morsel of caviare for us—what do you think of that?"

"What can one expect of her?" suddenly croaked a gentleman who had been silent till then, "everyone knows she poisoned her husband!"

To my astonishment, nobody thought fit to controvert this awful and certainly unfounded charge! I was the more surprised at this, as, in spite of the slighting expressions I have reported, all of them felt respect for Anna Martynova, not excluding the indelicate landowner. As for the mediator, he waxed positively eloquent.

"Put her on a throne," he exclaimed, "she'd be another Semiramis or Catherine the Second! The discipline among her peasants is a perfect model. . . . The education of her children is model! What a head! What brains!"

Without going into the question of Semiramis and Catherine, there was no doubt Anna Martynovna was living a very happy life. Ease, inward and external, the pleasant serenity of spiritual health, seemed the very atmosphere about herself, her family, all her surroundings. How far she had deserved such happiness . . . that is another question. Such questions, though, are only propounded in youth. Everything in the world, good and bad, comes to man, not through his deserts, but in consequence of some as yet unknown but logical laws which I will not take upon myself to indicate, though I sometimes fancy I have a dim perception of them.

## XXXI

I questioned the mediator about Yevlampia Martynovna, and learnt that she had been lost sight of completely ever since she left home, and probably "had departed this life long ago."

So our worthy mediator expressed himself . . . but I am convinced that I *have seen* Yevlampia, that I have come across her. This is how it was.

Four years after my meeting with Anna Martynovna, I was spending the summer at Murino, a little hamlet near Petersburg, a well-known resort of summer visitors of the middle class. The shooting was pretty decent about Murino at that time, and I used to go out with my gun almost every day. I had a companion on my expeditions, a man of the tradesman class, called Vikulov, a very sensible and good-natured fellow; but, as he said of himself, of no position whatever. This man had been simply everywhere, and everything! Nothing could astonish him, he knew everything—but he cared for nothing but shooting and wine. Well, one day we were on our way home to Murino, and we chanced to pass a solitary house, standing at the crossroads, and enclosed by a high, close paling. It was not the first time I had seen the house, and every time it excited my curiosity. There was something mysterious, locked-up, grimly dumb, something suggestive of a prison or a hospital about it. Nothing of it could be seen from the road but its steep, dark, red-painted roof. There was only one gate in the whole fence, and this was locked and looked as if it had never been opened. No sound came from the other side of it. For all that, we felt that some one was certainly living in the house; it had not at all the air of a deserted dwelling. On the contrary, everything about it was stout and tight, and strong, as if it could stand a siege!

"What is that fortress?" I asked my companion. "Don't you know?"

Vikulov gave a sly wink. "A fine building, eh? The police captain of these parts gets a nice little income out of it!"

"How's that?"

"I'll tell you. You've heard, I daresay, of the Flagellant dissenters —that do without priests, you know?"

"Yes."

"Well, it's there that their mother superior lives."

"A woman?"

"Yes—the mother; mother of God, as they put it."

"Nonsense!"

"I tell you, it is so. She is a strict one, they say. . . . A regular commander-in-chief! She deals in thousands! I'd take her, and all these mothers of God . . . But what's the use of talking?"

He called his Pegashka, a marvelous dog, with an excellent scent, but with no notion of setting. Vikulov was obliged to tie her hind paws to keep her from running so furiously.

His words sank into my memory. I sometimes went out of my way to pass by the mysterious house. One day I had just got up to it, when suddenly—wonderful to relate!—a bolt grated in the gates, a key creaked in the lock, then the gates themselves slowly opened, there appeared a large horse's head, with a plaited forelock under a decorated yoke, and slowly there rolled into the road a small cart, like those driven by horse-dealers and hagglers. On the leather cushion of the cart, near to me, sat a peasant of about thirty, of a remarkably handsome and attractive appearance, in a neat black smock, and a black cap, pulled down low on his forehead. He was carefully driving the well-fed horse, whose sides were as broad as a stove. Beside the peasant, on the far side of the cart, sat a tall woman, as straight as an arrow. Her head was covered with a costly-looking black shawl. She was dressed in a short jerkin of dove-colored velvet, and a dark blue merino skirt; her white hands she held discreetly clasped on her bosom.

The cart turned on the road to the left, and brought the woman within two paces of me; she turned her head a little, and I recognized Yevlampia Harlov. I knew her at once, I did not doubt for one instant, and indeed no doubt was possible; eyes like hers, and above all that cut of the lips—haughty and sensual—I had never seen in anyone else. Her face had grown longer and thinner, the skin was darker, here and there lines could be discerned; but, above all, the expression of the face was changed! It is difficult to do justice in words to the self-confidence, the sternness, the pride it had gained! Not simply the serenity of power—the fullness of power was visible in every feature. The careless glance she cast at me told of long years of habitually meeting nothing but reverent, unquestioning obedience. That woman clearly lived surrounded, not by worshipers, but by slaves. She had clearly forgotten even the time when any command, any desire of hers, was not carried out on the instant!

I called her loudly by her name and patronymic; she gave a faint start, looked at me a second time, not with alarm, but with contemptuous wrath, as though asking, "Who dares to disturb me?" and barely parting her lips, uttered a word of command. The peasant sitting beside her started forward, with a wave of his arm struck the horse with the reins—the horse set off at a strong rapid trot, and the cart disappeared.

Since then I have not seen Yevlampia again. In what way Martyn Petrovich's daughter came to be a Holy Virgin in the Flagellant sect I cannot imagine. But, who knows, very likely she has founded a sect which will be called—or even now is called—after her name, the Yevlampian sect?

Anything may be, anything may come to pass.

And so this is what I had to tell you of my Lear of the steppes, of his family and his doings.

The story-teller ceased, and we talked a little longer, and then parted, each to his home.

1870

# LIVING RELICS

O my long-suffering native land,
Land of the Russian people.
F. TYUTCHEV.

A FRENCH proverb says that "a dry fisherman and a wet hunter
are a sorry sight." Never having had any taste for fishing, I cannot
decide what are the fisherman's feelings in fine bright weather, and
how far in bad weather the pleasure derived from the abundance of
fish compensates for the unpleasantness of being wet. But for the
sportsman rain is a real calamity. It was to just this calamity that
Yermolay and I were exposed on one of our expeditions after grouse
in the Belevsky district. The rain never ceased from early morning.
What didn't we do to escape it? We put mackintosh capes almost
right over our heads, and stood under the trees to avoid the raindrops.
. . . The waterproof capes, to say nothing of their hindering our
shooting, let the water through in the most shameless fashion; and
under the trees, though at first, certainly, the rain did not reach us,
afterwards the water collected on the leaves suddenly rushed through,
every branch dripped on us like a waterspout, a chill stream made its
way under the necktie, and trickled down our spines. . . . This was
"quite unpleasant," as Yermolay expressed it. "No, Pyotr Petrovich,"
he cried at last; "we can't go on like this. . . . There's no shooting
today. The dogs' scent is drowned. The guns miss fire. . . . Pugh!
What a mess!"

"What's to be done?" I queried.

"Well, let's go to Alekseyevka. You don't know it, perhaps—
there's a farmstead of that name belonging to your mother; it's seven
miles from here. We'll stay the night there, and tomorrow. . . ."

"Come back here?"

"No, not here. . . . I know of some places beyond Alekseyevka
. . . ever so much better than here for grouse!"

I did not proceed to question my faithful companion why he had not taken me to those parts before, and the same day we made our way to my mother's farmstead, the existence of which, I must confess, I had not even suspected up till then. At this farmstead, it turned out, there was a little lodge. It was very old, but, as it had not been inhabited, it was clean; I passed a fairly tranquil night in it.

The next day I woke up very early. The sun had only just risen; there was not a single cloud in the sky; everything around shone with a double brilliance—the brightness of the fresh morning rays and of yesterday's downpour. While they were harnessing me a cart, I went for a stroll about a small orchard, now neglected and run wild, which enclosed the little lodge on all sides with its fragrant, sappy growth. Ah, how sweet it was in the open air, under the bright sky, where the larks were trilling, whence their bell-like notes rained down like silvery beads! On their wings, doubtless, they had carried off drops of dew, and their songs seemed steeped in dew. I took my cap off my head and drew a glad deep breath. . . . On the slope of a shallow ravine, close to the hedge, could be seen a beehive; a narrow path led to it, winding like a snake between dense walls of high grass and nettles, above which struggled up, God knows whence brought, the pointed stalks of dark-green hemp.

I turned along this path; I reached the beehive. Beside it stood a little wattled shanty, where they put the beehives for the winter. I peeped into the half-open door; it was dark, still, dry within; there was a scent of mint and balm. In the corner were some trestles fitted together, and on them, covered with a quilt, a little figure of some sort. . . . I was walking away. . . .

"Master, master! Pyotr Petrovich!" I heard a voice, faint, slow, and hoarse, like the whispering of marsh rushes.

I stopped.

"Pyotr Petrovich! Come in, please!" the voice repeated. It came from the corner where were the trestles I had noticed.

I drew near, and was struck dumb with amazement. Before me lay a living human being; but what sort of a creature was it?

A head utterly withered, of a uniform coppery hue—like some very ancient holy picture, yellow with age; a sharp nose like a keen-edged knife; the lips could barely be seen—only the teeth flashed white and the eyes; and from under the kerchief some thin wisps of yellow hair straggled on to the forehead. At the chin, where the quilt was folded, two tiny hands of the same coppery hue were moving, the fingers slowly twitching like little sticks. I looked more intently; the face, far from being ugly, was positively beautiful, but strange and dreadful; and the face seemed the more dreadful to me that on it—on its metallic cheeks—I saw, struggling . . . struggling, and unable to form itself—a smile.

"You don't recognize me, master?" whispered the voice again: it seemed to be breathed from the almost unmoving lips. "And, indeed, how should you? I'm Lukerya. . . . Do you remember, who used to lead the dance at your mother's, at Spasskoe? . . . Do you remember, I used to be leader of the choir too?"

"Lukerya!" I cried. "Is it you? Can it be?"

"Yes, it's I, master—I, Lukerya."

I did not know what to say, and gazed in stupefaction at the dark motionless face with the clear, death-like eyes fastened upon me. Was it possible? This mummy Lukerya—the greatest beauty in all our household—that tall, plump, pink-and-white, singing, laughing, dancing creature! Lukerya, our smart Lukerya, whom all our lads were courting, for whom I heaved some secret sighs—I, a boy of sixteen!

"Mercy, Lukerya!" I said at last. "What is it has happened to you?"

"Oh, such a misfortune befell me! But don't be squeamish, sir; don't draw away from my trouble; sit there on that little tub—a little nearer, or you won't be able to hear me. . . . I've not much of a voice nowadays! . . . Well, I am glad to see you! What brought you to Alekseyevka?"

Lukerya spoke very softly and feebly, but without pausing.

"Yermolay, the huntsman, brought me here. But you tell me. . . ."

"Tell you about my trouble? Certainly, sir. It happened to me a long while ago now—six or seven years. I had only just been betrothed then to Vasily Polyakov—do you remember, such a fine-looking fellow he was, with curly hair?—he waited at table at your mother's. But you weren't in the country then; you had gone away to Moscow to study. We were very much in love, Vasily and me; I could never get him out of my head; and it was in the spring it all happened. Well, one night . . . not long before sunrise, it was . . . I couldn't sleep; a nightingale in the garden was singing so wonderfully sweet! . . . I could not help getting up and going out on to the steps to listen. It trilled and trilled . . . and all at once I fancied someone called me; it seemed like Vasya's voice, so softly, 'Lusha!' . . . I looked round, and being half asleep, I suppose, I missed my footing and fell straight down from the top step, and flop on to the ground! And I thought I wasn't much hurt, for I got up directly and went back to my room. Only it seems something inside me—in my body—was broken. . . . Let me get my breath . . . half a minute . . . sir."

Lukerya ceased, and I looked at her with surprise. What surprised me particularly was that she told her story almost cheerfully, without sighs and groans, not complaining nor asking for sympathy.

"Ever since that happened," Lukerya went on, "I began to pine away and get thin; my skin got dark; walking was difficult for me; and then—I lost the use of my legs altogether; I couldn't stand or sit; I had to lie down all the time. And I didn't care to eat or drink; I got worse and worse. Your mother, in the kindness of her heart, made me see doctors, and sent me to a hospital. But there was no curing me. And not one doctor could even say what my illness was. What didn't they do to me?—they burnt my spine with hot irons, they put me in lumps of ice, and it was all no good. I got quite numb in the end. . . . So the gentlemen decided it was no use doctoring me any more, and there was no sense in keeping cripples up at the great house . . . well, and so they sent me here—because I've relations here. So here I live, as you see."

Lukerya was silent again, and again she tried to smile.

"But this is awful—your position!" I cried. And not knowing how to go on, I asked: "And what of Vasily Polyakov?" A most stupid question it was.

Lukerya turned her eyes a little away.

"What of Polyakov? He grieved—he grieved for a bit—and he is married to another, a girl from Glinnoe. Do you know Glinnoe? It's not far from us. Her name's Agrafena. He loved me dearly—but, you see, he's a young man; he couldn't stay a bachelor. And what sort of a helpmeet could I be? The wife he found for himself is a good, sweet woman—and they have children. He lives here; he's a clerk at a neighbor's; your mamma let him go off with a passport, and he's doing very well, praise God."

"And so you go on lying here all the time?" I asked again.

"Yes, sir, I've been lying here seven years. In the summertime I lie here in this shanty, and when it gets cold they move me out into the bathhouse: I lie there."

"Who waits on you? Does anyone look after you?"

"Oh, there are kind folks here as everywhere; they don't desert me. Yes, they see to me a little. As to food, I eat nothing to speak of; but water is here, in the pitcher; it's always kept full of pure spring water. I can reach to the pitcher myself: I can still use one arm. There's a little girl here, an orphan; now and then she comes to see me, the kind child. She was here just now. . . . You didn't meet her? Such a pretty, fair little thing. She brings me flowers. I'm very fond of them. We've none in the garden now—there were some—but they've all disappeared. But, you know, wild flowers too are nice; they smell even sweeter than garden flowers. Lilies of the valley, now . . . what could be sweeter?"

"And aren't you dull and miserable, my poor Lukerya?"

"Why, what is one to do? I wouldn't tell a lie about it. At first it was very wearisome; but later on I got used to it, I got more patient—it was nothing; there are others worse off still."

"How do you mean?"

"Why, some haven't a roof to shelter them, and there are some blind or deaf; while I, thank God, have splendid sight, and hear everything—everything. If a mole burrows in the ground—I hear even that. And I can smell every scent, even the faintest! When the buckwheat comes into flower in the meadow, or the lime-tree in the garden—I don't need to be told of it, even; I'm the first to know directly. Anyway, if there's the least bit of a wind blowing from that quarter. No, why should I anger God? Many people are far worse off than me. Look at this, again: anyone in health may easily fall into sin; but I'm cut off even from sin. The other day, Father Aleksey, the priest, came to give me the sacrament, and he says: 'There's no need,' says he, 'to confess you; you can't fall into sin in your condition, can you?' But I said to him, 'How about sinning in thought, father?' 'Ah, well,' says he, and he laughed himself, 'that's no great sin.'

"But I fancy I'm no great sinner even in that way, in thought," Lukerya went on, "for I've trained myself not to think, and above all, not to remember. The time goes faster."

I must own I was astonished. "You're always alone, Lukerya: how can you prevent the thoughts from coming into your head? Or are you constantly asleep?"

"Oh, no, sir! I can't always sleep. Though I've no great pain, still I've an ache, there, right inside, and in my bones too; it won't let me sleep as I ought. No . . . but there, I lie by myself; I lie here and lie here, and don't think: I feel that I'm alive, I breathe; and I put myself all into that. I look and listen. The bees buzz and hum in the hive; a dove sits on the roof and coos; a hen comes along with her chickens to peck up crumbs; or a sparrow flies in, or a butterfly—that's a great treat for me. Last year some swallows even built a nest over there in the corner, and brought up their little ones. Oh, how interesting it was! One would fly to the nest, press close, feed a young one, and be off again. Before you know it, another would take her place. Sometimes it wouldn't fly in, but only dart past the open door; and the little ones would begin to squeak, and open their beaks directly. . . . I was hoping they would come back the next year, but they say a sportsman here shot them with his gun. And what could he gain by it? It's hardly bigger, the swallow, than a beetle. . . . What wicked men you are, you sportsmen!"

"I don't shoot swallows," I hastened to remark.

"And once," Lukerya began again, "it was comical, really. A hare ran in, it did really! The hounds, I suppose, were after it; anyway, it seemed to tumble straight in at the door! . . . It squatted quite near me, and sat so a long while; it kept sniffing with its nose, and twitching its whiskers—like a regular officer! and it looked at me. It understood, to be sure, that I was no danger to it. At last it got up, went hop-hop to the door, looked round in the doorway; and off it went! Such a funny fellow it was!"

Lukerya glanced at me, as much as to say, "Wasn't it funny?" To satisfy her, I laughed. She moistened her parched lips.

"Well, in the winter, of course, I'm worse off, because it's dark: to burn a candle would be a pity, and what would be the use? I can read, to be sure, and was always fond of reading, but what could I read? There are no books of any kind, and even if there were, how could I hold a book? Father Aleksey brought me a calendar to entertain me, but he saw it was no good, so he took and carried it away again. But even though it's dark, there's always something to listen to: a cricket chirps, or a mouse begins scratching somewhere. That's when it's a good thing—not to think!

"And I repeat the prayers too," Lukerya went on, after taking breath a little; "only I don't know many of them—the prayers, I mean. And besides, why should I weary the Lord God? What can I ask Him for? He knows better than I what I need. He has laid a cross upon me: that means that He loves me. So we are commanded to understand. I repeat the Lord's Prayer, the Hymn to the Virgin, the Supplication of all the Afflicted, and I lie still again, without any thought at all, and am all right!"

Two minutes passed by. I did not break the silence, and did not stir on the narrow tub which served me as a seat. The cruel stony stillness of the living, unlucky creature lying before me communicated itself to me; I too turned, as it were, numb.

"Listen, Lukerya," I began at last; "listen to the suggestion I'm going to make to you. Would you like me to arrange for them to take you to a hospital—a good hospital in the town? Who knows, perhaps you might yet be cured; anyway, you would not be alone—"

Lukerya's eyebrows fluttered faintly. "Oh, no, sir," she answered in a troubled whisper; "don't move me into a hospital; don't touch me. I shall only have more agony to bear there! How could they cure me now? . . . Why, there was a doctor came here once; he wanted to examine me. I begged him, for Christ's sake, not to disturb me. It was no use. He began turning me over, pounding my hands and legs, and pulling me about. He said, 'I'm doing this for Science; I'm a servant of Science—a scientific man! And you,' he said, 'really oughtn't to oppose me, because I've a medal given me for my labors, and it's for you simpletons I'm toiling.' He mauled me about, told me the name of my disease—some wonderful long name—and with that he went away; and all my poor bones ached for a week after. You say I'm all alone; always alone. Oh, no, not always; they come to see me—I'm quiet—I don't bother them. The peasant girls come in and chat a bit; a pilgrim woman will wander in, and tell me tales of Jerusalem, of Kiev, of the holy towns. And I'm not afraid of being alone. Indeed, it's better—ay, ay! Master, don't touch me, don't take me to the hospital. . . . Thank you, you are kind; only don't touch me, there's a dear!"

"Well, as you like, as you like, Lukerya. You know, I only suggested it for your good."

"I know, master, that it was for my good. But, master dear, who can help another? Who can enter into his soul? Every man must help himself! You won't believe me, perhaps. I lie here sometimes so alone . . . and it's as though there were no one else in the world but me. As if I alone were living! And it seems to me as though something were blessing me. . . . I'm carried away by dreams that are really marvellous!"

"What do you dream of, then, Lukerya?"

"That, too, master, I couldn't say; one can't explain. Besides, one forgets afterwards. It's like a cloud coming over and bursting, then it grows so fresh and sweet; but just what it was, there's no knowing! Only my idea is, if folks were near me, I should have nothing of that, and should feel nothing except my misfortune."

Lukerya heaved a painful sigh. Her breathing, like her limbs, was not under her control.

"When I come to think, master, of you," she began again, "you are very sorry for me. But you mustn't be too sorry, really! I'll tell you one thing; for instance, I sometimes, even now. . . . Do you remember how merry I used to be in my time? A regular madcap! . . . So do you know what? I sing songs even now."

"Sing? . . . You?"

"Yes; I sing the old songs, songs for dances, for feasts, Christmas songs, all sorts! I know such a lot of them, you see, and I've not forgotten them. Only dance songs I don't sing. In my state now, it wouldn't suit me."

"How do you sing them? To yourself?"

"To myself, yes; and aloud too. I can't sing loud, but still one can understand it. I told you a little girl waits on me. A clever little orphan she is. So I have taught her; four songs she has learnt from me already. Don't you believe me? Wait a minute, I'll show you directly. . . ."

Lukerya took breath. . . . The thought that this half-dead creature was making ready to begin singing raised an involuntary feeling of dread in me. But before I could utter a word a long-drawn-out, hardly audible, but pure and true note, was quivering in my ears . . . it was followed by a second and a third. "In the meadows," sang Lukerya. She sang, the expression of her stony face unchanged, even her eyes riveted on one spot. But how touchingly tinkled out that poor struggling little voice, that wavered like a thread of smoke: how she longed to pour out all her soul in it! . . . I felt no dread now; my heart throbbed with unutterable pity.

"Ah, I can't!" she said suddenly. "I've not the strength. I'm so upset with joy at seeing you."

She closed her eyes.

I laid my hand on her tiny, chill fingers. . . . She glanced at me, and her dark lids, fringed with golden eyelashes, closed again, and were still as an ancient statue's. An instant later they glistened in the half-darkness. . . . They were moistened by a tear.

As before, I did not stir.

"How silly I am!" said Lukerya suddenly, with unexpected force, and opened her eyes wide: she tried to wink the tears out of them. "I ought to be ashamed! What am I doing? It's a long time since I have been like this . . . not since that day when Vasya Polyakov was here last spring. While he sat with me and talked I was all right; but when he had gone away how I did cry in my loneliness! Where did I get the tears from? But, there! we girls get our tears for nothing. Master," added Lukerya, "perhaps you have a handkerchief. . . . If you won't mind, wipe my eyes."

I made haste to carry out her desire, and left her the handkerchief. She refused it at first. . . . "What good's such a gift to me?" she said. The handkerchief was plain enough, but clean and white. Afterwards she clutched it in her weak fingers, and did not loosen them again. As I got used to the darkness in which we both were, I could clearly make out her features, could even perceive the delicate flush that peeped out under the coppery hue of her face, could discover in the face, so at least it seemed to me, traces of its former beauty.

"You asked me, master," Lukerya began again, "whether I sleep. I sleep very little, but every time I fall asleep I've dreams—such splendid dreams! I'm never ill in my dreams; I'm always so well, and young. . . . There's one thing's sad: I wake up and long for a good stretch, and I'm all as if I were in chains. I once had such an exquisite dream! Shall I tell it you? Well, listen. I dreamt I was standing in a meadow, and all round me was rye, so tall, and ripe as gold! . . . and I had a reddish dog with me—such a wicked dog; it kept trying to bite me. And I had a sickle in my hands; not a simple sickle; it seemed to be the moon itself—the moon as it is when it's the shape of a sickle. And with this same moon I had to cut the rye clean. Only I was very weary with the heat, and the moon blinded me, and I felt lazy; and cornflowers were growing all about, and such big ones! And they all turned their heads to me. And I thought in my dream I would pick them; Vasya had promised to come, so I'd pick myself a wreath first; I'd still time to plait it. I began picking cornflowers, but they kept melting away from between my fingers, do what I would. And I couldn't make myself a wreath. And meanwhile I heard someone coming up to me, so close, and calling, 'Lusha! Lusha!' . . . 'Ah,' I thought, 'what a pity I hadn't time!' No matter, I put that moon on my head instead of cornflowers. I put it on like a tiara, and I was all brightness directly; I made the whole field light around me. And, behold! over the very top of the ears there came gliding very quickly towards me, not Vasya, but Christ Himself! And how I knew it was Christ I can't say; they don't paint Him like that—only it was He! No beard, tall, young, all in white, only His belt was golden; and He held out His hand to me. 'Fear not,' said He. 'My bride adorned, follow Me; you shall lead the choral dance in the heavenly kingdom, and sing the songs of Paradise.' And how I clung to His hand! My dog at once followed at my heels . . . but then we began to float upwards! He in front. . . . His wings spread wide over all the sky, long like a sea-gull's—and I after Him! And my dog had to stay behind. Then only I understood that that dog was my illness, and that in the heavenly kingdom there was no place for it."

Lukerya paused a minute.

"And I had another dream, too," she began again; "but maybe it was a vision. I really don't know. It seemed to me I was lying in this very shanty, and my dead parents, father and mother, come to me and bow low to me, but say nothing. And I asked them, 'Why do you bow down to me, father and mother?' 'Because,' they said, 'you suffer much in this world, so that you have not only set free your own soul, but have taken a great burden from off us too. And for us in the other world it is much easier. You have made an end of your own sins; now you are expiating our sins.' And having said this, my parents bowed down to me again, and I could not see them; there was nothing but the walls to be seen. I was in great doubt afterwards what had happened with me. I even told the priest of it at confession. Only he thinks it was not a vision, because visions come only to people of ecclesiastical rank.

"And I'll tell you another dream," Lukerya went on. "I dreamt I was sitting on the high-road, under a willow; I had a stick, had a wallet on my shoulders, and my head tied up in a kerchief, just like a pilgrim woman! And I had to go somewhere, a long, long way off, on a pilgrimage. And pilgrims kept coming past me; they came along slowly, all going one way; their faces were weary, and all very much like one another. And I dreamt that moving about among them was a woman, a head taller than the rest, and wearing a peculiar dress, not like ours—not Russian. And her face too was peculiar—a worn face and severe. And all the others moved away from her; but she suddenly turns, and comes straight to me. She stood still, and looked at me; and her eyes were yellow, large, and clear as a falcon's. And I ask her, 'Who are you?' And she says to me, 'I'm your death.' Instead of being frightened, it was quite the other way. I was as pleased as could be; I crossed myself! And the woman, my death, says to me: 'I'm sorry for you, Lukerya, but I can't take you with me. Farewell!' Good God! how sad I was then! . . . 'Take me,' said I, 'good mother, take me, darling!' And my death turned to me, and began speaking to me. . . . I knew that she was appointing me my hour, but indistinctly, incomprehensibly. 'After St. Peter's day,' said she. . . . With that I awoke. . . . Yes, I have such wonderful dreams!"

Lukerya turned her eyes upwards . . . and sank into thought. . . .

"Only the sad thing is, sometimes a whole week will go by without my getting to sleep once. Last year a lady came to see me, and she gave me a little bottle of medicine against sleeplessness; she told me to take ten drops at a time. It did me so much good, and I used to sleep; only the bottle was all finished long ago. Do you know what medicine that was, and how to get it?"

The lady had obviously given Lukerya opium. I promised to get her another bottle like it, and could not refrain from again wondering aloud at her patience.

"Ah, master!" she answered, "why do you say so? What do you mean by patience? There, Simeon Stylites now had patience certainly, great patience; for thirty years he stood on a pillar! And another saint had himself buried in the earth, right up to his breast, and the ants ate his face. . . . And I'll tell you what I was told by a good scholar: there was once a country, and the Ishmaelites made war on it, and they tortured and killed all the inhabitants; and do what they would, the people could not get rid of them. And there appeared among these people a holy virgin; she took a great sword, put on armor weighing eighty pounds, went out against the Ishmaelites and drove them all beyond the sea. Only when she had driven them out, she said to them: 'Now burn me, for that was my vow, that I would die a death by fire for my people.' And the Ishmaelites took her and burnt her, and the people have been free ever since then! That was a noble deed, now! But what am I!"

I wondered whence and in what shape the legend of Joan of Arc had reached her, and after a brief silence, I asked Lukerya how old she was.

"Twenty-eight . . . or nine. . . . It won't be thirty. But why count the years! I've something else to tell you. . . ."

Lukerya suddenly gave a sort of choked cough, and groaned. . . .

"You are talking a great deal," I observed to her; "it may be bad for you."

"It's true," she whispered, hardly audibly; "it's time to end our talk; but what does it matter! Now, when you leave me, I can be silent as long as I like. Anyway, I've opened my heart. . . ."

I began bidding her good-bye. I repeated my promise to send her the medicine, and asked her once more to think well and tell me—if there wasn't anything she wanted.

"I want nothing; I am content with all, thank God!" she articulated with very great effort, but with emotion; "God give good health to all! But there, master, you might speak a word to your mamma—the peasants here are poor—if she could take the least bit off their rent! They've not land enough, and no advantages. . . . They would pray to God for you. . . . But I want nothing; I'm quite contented with all."

I gave Lukerya my word that I would carry out her request, and had already walked to the door. . . . She called me back again.

"Do you remember, master," she said, and there was a gleam of something wonderful in her eyes and on her lips, "what hair I used to have? Do you remember, right down to my knees! It was long before I could make up my mind to it. . . . Such hair as it was! But how could it be kept combed? In my state! . . . So I had it cut off. . . . Yes. . . . Well, good-bye, master! I can't talk any more." . . .

That day, before setting off to shoot, I had a conversation with the village constable about Lukerya. I learnt from him that in the village they called Lukerya "Living Relics"; that she gave them no trouble, however; they never heard complaint or repining from her. "She asks nothing, but, on the contrary, she's grateful for every-

thing; a gentle soul, one must say, if any there be. Stricken of God,"
so the constable concluded, "for her sins, one must suppose; but we
do not go into that. And as for judging her, no—no, we do not judge
her. Let her be!"

.        .        .        .        .        .

A few weeks later I heard that Lukerya was dead. So her death
had come for her . . . and "after St. Peter's day." They told me
that on the day of her death she kept hearing the sound of bells,
though it was reckoned over five miles from Alekseyevka to the
church, and it was a weekday. Lukerya, however, had said that the
sounds came not from the church, but from above! Probably she
did not dare to say—from heaven.

1874

# OLD PORTRAITS

ABOUT thirty miles from our village there lived, many years ago, a distant cousin of my mother's, a retired officer of the Guards, and rather wealthy landowner, Alexey Sergeich Telegin. He lived on his estate and birthplace, Suhodol, did not go out anywhere, and so did not visit us; but I used to be sent, twice a year, to pay him my respects—at first with my tutor, but later on alone. Alexey Sergeich always gave me a very cordial reception, and I used to stay three or four days at a time with him. He was an old man even when I first made his acquaintance; I was twelve, I remember, on my first visit, and he was then over seventy. He was born in the days of the Empress Elisabeth—in the last year of her reign. He lived alone with his wife, Malanya Pavlovna; she was ten years younger than he. They had two daughters; but their daughters had been long married, and rarely visited Suhodol; they were not on the best of terms with their parents, and Alexey Sergeich hardly ever mentioned their names.

I see, even now, the old-fashioned house, a typical manor-house of the steppes. One story in height, with immense attics, it was built at the beginning of this century, of amazingly thick beams of pine—such beams came in plenty in those days from the Zhizdra pine-forests; they have passed out of memory now! It was very spacious, and contained a great number of rooms, rather low-pitched and dark, it is true; the windows in the walls had been made small for the sake of greater warmth. In the usual fashion (I ought rather to say, in what was then the usual fashion), the offices and house-serfs' huts surrounded the manorial house on all sides, and the garden was close to it—a small garden, but containing fine fruit-trees, juicy apples, and pipless pears. The flat steppe of rich, black earth stretched for ten miles round. No lofty object for the eye; not a tree, nor even a belfry; somewhere, maybe, jutting up, a windmill, with rents in its sails; truly, wellnamed Suhodol (Dry Plain)! Inside the house the rooms were filled with ordinary, simple furniture; somewhat unusual was the little milepost that stood in the window of the drawing-room, with the following inscription: "If you walk sixty-eight times around this drawing-room you will have gone a mile; if you walk eighty-seven times from the furthest corner of the parlor to the right-hand corner of the billiard-room, you will have gone a mile," and so on. But what most of all impressed a guest at the house for the first time was the immense collection of pictures hanging on the walls, for the most part works of the so-called Italian masters: all old-fashioned landscapes of a sort, or mythological and religious subjects. But all these pictures were very dark, and even cracked with age; in one, all that met the eye was some patches of flesh-color; in another, undulating red draperies on an unseen body; or an arch which seemed to be suspended in the air; or a dishevelled tree with blue foliage; or the bosom of a nymph with an immense breast, like the lid of a soup-tureen; a cut watermelon, with black seeds; a turban, with a feather in it, above a horse's head; or the gigantic brown leg of an apostle, suddenly thrust out, with a muscular calf, and toes turned upwards. In the drawing-room in the place of honor hung a portrait of the Empress Catherine II, full length; a copy of the famous portrait by Lampi—an object of the special reverence, one might say the adoration, of the master of the house. From the ceiling hung glass lusters in bronze settings, very small and very dusty.

Alexey Sergeich himself was a stumpy, paunchy little old man, with a chubby face of one uniform tint, yet pleasant, with drawn-in lips, and very lively little eyes under high eyebrows. He wore his scanty locks combed to the back of his head; it was only since 1812 that he had given up wearing powder. Alexey Sergeich invariably wore a gray "redingote," with three capes falling over his shoulders, a striped waistcoat, chamois-leather breeches, and high boots of dark red morocco, with heart-shaped scallops and tassels at the tops; he wore a white muslin cravat, a jabot, lace cuffs, and two gold English "turnip watches," one in each pocket of his waistcoat. In his right hand he usually carried an enameled snuffbox full of "Spanish" snuff, and his left hand leaned on a cane with a silver-chased knob, worn smooth by long use. Alexey Sergeich had a little nasal, piping voice, and an invariable smile—kindly, but, as it were, condescending, and not without a certain self-complacent dignity. His laugh, too, was kindly—a shrill little laugh that tinkled like glass beads. Courteous and affable he was to the last degree—in the old-fashioned manner of the days of Catherine—and he moved his hands with slow, rounded gestures, also in the old style. His legs were so weak that he could not walk, but ran with hurried little steps from one armchair to another, in which he would suddenly sit down, or rather fall softly, like a cushion.

As I have said already, Alexey Sergeich went out nowhere, and saw very little of his neighbors, though he liked society, for he was very fond of talking! It is true that he had society in plenty in his own house; various Nikanor Nikanoryches, Sevastey Sevasteiches, Feudilches, Miheiches, all poor gentlemen in shabby Cossack coats and camisoles, often from the master's wardrobe, lived under his roof, to say nothing of the poor gentlewomen in chintz gowns, black kerchiefs thrown over their shoulders, and worsted reticules in their tightly clenched fingers—all sorts of Avdotya Savishnas, Pelageya Mironovnas, and plain Feklushkas and Arinkas, who found a home in the women's quarters. Never less than fifteen persons sat down to Alexey Sergeich's table. . . . He was such a hospitable man!

Among all those dependents two were particularly conspicuous: a dwarf, nicknamed Janus, or the Double-faced, of Danish—or, as some maintained, Jewish—extraction, and the mad Prince L. Contrary to what was customary in those days, the dwarf did nothing to amuse the master or mistress, and was not a jester—quite the opposite; he was always silent, had an ill-tempered and sullen appearance, and scowled and gnashed his teeth directly a question was addressed to him. Alexey Sergeich called him a philosopher, and positively respected him; at table the dishes were handed to him first, after the guests and master and mistress. "God has afflicted him," Alexey Sergeich used to say; "such is His Divine will; but it's not for me to afflict him further." "How is he a philosopher?" I asked him once. (Janus didn't take to me; if I went near him he would fly into a rage, and mutter thickly, "Stranger! Keep off!") "Eh, God bless me! isn't he a philospher?" answered Alexey Sergeich. "Look ye, little sir, how wisely he holds his tongue!" "But why is he double-faced?"

"Because, little sir, he has one face on the outside—and so you, surface-gazers, judge him. . . . But the other, the real face he hides. And that face I know, and no one else—and I love him for it . . . because that face is good. You, for instance, look and see nothing . . . but I see without a word: he is blaming me for something; for he's a severe critic! And it's always with good reason. That, little sir, you can't understand; but you may believe an old man like me!"

The real history of the two-faced Janus—where he came from, and how he came into Alexey Sergeich's hands—no one knew; but the story of Prince L. was well known to everyone. A lad of twenty, of a wealthy and distinguished family, he went to Petersburg, to serve in a regiment of the Guards. At the first levee the Empress Catherine noticed him, stood still before him, and, pointing at him with her fan, she said aloud, addressing one of her courtiers, who happened to be near, "Look, Adam Vasilyevich, what a pretty fellow! a perfect doll!" The poor boy's head was completely turned; when he got home he ordered his coach out, and, putting on a ribbon of St. Anne, proceeded to drive all over the town, as though he had reached the pinnacle of fortune. "Drive over everyone," he shouted to his coachman, "who does not move out of the way!" All this was promptly reported to the Empress: the decree went forth that he should be declared insane, and put under the guardianship of two of his brothers; and they, without a moment's delay, carried him off to the country, and flung him into a stone cell in chains. As they wanted to get the benefit of his property, they did not let the poor wretch out, even when he had completely recovered his balance, and positively kept him locked up till he really did go out of his mind. But their misdeeds did not profit them; Prince L. outlived his brothers, and, after long years of adversity, he came into the charge of Alexey Sergeich, whose kinsman he was. He was a stout, completely bald man, with a long, thin nose and prominent blue eyes. He had quite forgotten how to talk—he simply uttered a sort of inarticulate grumbling; but he sang old-fashioned Russian ballads beautifully, preserving the silvery freshness of his voice to extreme old age; and, while he was singing, he pronounced each word clearly and distinctly. He had attacks at times of a sort of fury, and then he became terrible: he would stand in the corner, with his face to the wall, and all perspiring and red—red all down his bald head and down his neck—he used to go off into vicious chuckles, and, stamp-

ing with his feet, order someone—his brothers probably—to be punished. "Beat 'em!" he growled hoarsely, coughing and choking with
laughter; "flog 'em, don't spare 'em! beat, beat, beat the monsters,
my oppressors! That's it! That's it!" On the day before his death
he greatly alarmed and astonished Alexey Sergeich. He came, pale
and subdued, into his room, and, making him a low obeisance, first
thanked him for his care and kindness, and then asked him to send
for a priest, for death had come to him—he had seen death, and he
must forgive everyone and purify his soul. "How did you see death?"
muttered Alexey Sergeich in bewilderment at hearing connected
speech from him for the first time. "In what shape? with a scythe?"
"No," answered Prince L.; "a simple old woman in a jacket, but
with only one eye in her forehead, and that eye without an eyelid."
And the next day Prince L. actually did die, after having discharged
all his duties and taken leave of everyone in a rational and affecting
manner. "That's just how I shall die," Alexey Sergeich would sometimes observe. And, as a fact, something of the same sort did happen
with him—but of that later.

But now let us go back to our story. Of the neighbors, as I have
stated already, Alexey Sergeich saw little; and they did not care
much for him, called him a queer fish, stuck up, and a scoffer, and
even a *Martinist* who recognized no authorities, though they had
no clear idea of the meaning of this term. To a certain extent the
neighbors were right: Alexey Sergeich had lived in his Suhodol for
almost seventy years on end, and had had hardly anything whatever
to do with the existing authorities, with the police or the law-courts.
"Police-courts are for robbers, and discipline for the soldier," he
used to say; "but I, thank God, am neither robber nor soldier!"
Rather queer Alexey Sergeich certainly was, but the soul within him
was by no means a petty one. I will tell you something about him.

To tell the truth, I never knew what were his political opinions,
if an expression so modern can be used in reference to him; but, in
his own way, he was an aristocrat—more an aristocrat than a typical
Russian country gentleman. More than once he expressed his regret
that God had not given him a son and heir, "for the honor of our
name, to keep up the family." In his own room there hung on the
wall the family tree of the Telegins, with many branches, and a
multitude of little circles like apples, in a golden frame. "We Telegins," he used to say, "are an ancient line, from long, long ago:

however many there've been of us Telegins, we have never hung about great men's anterooms; we've never bent our backs, or stood about in waiting, nor picked up a living in the courts, nor run after decorations; we've never gone trailing off to Moscow, nor intriguing in Petersburg; we've sat at home, each in his hole, his own man on his own land . . . homekeeping birds, sir!—I myself, though, I did serve in the Guards—but not for long, thank you." Alexey Sergeich preferred the old days. "There was more freedom in those days, more decorum; on my honor, I assure you! but since the year 1800" (why from that year, precisely, he did not explain), "militarism, the soldiery, have got the upper hand. Our military gentlemen stuck some sort of turbans of cocks' feathers on their heads then, and turned into cocks themselves; began binding their necks up as stiff as could be . . . they croaked, their eyes bulged—how could they help it, indeed? The other day a police corporal came to me; 'I've come to you,' says he, 'honorable sir,' . . . (fancy his thinking to surprise me with that! . . . I know I'm honorable without his telling me!) 'I have business with you.' And I said to him, 'My good sir, you'd better first unfasten the hooks on your collar, or else, God have mercy on us—you'll sneeze, and what will happen to you! What would happen to you! You'll burst open like a puff-ball, and I shall have to answer for it!' And they do drink, these military gentlemen—oh, oh, oh! I generally order homemade champagne to be given them, because to them, good wine or poor, it's all the same; it runs so smoothly, so quickly, down their throats—how can they distinguish it? And, another thing, they've started sucking at a pap-bottle, smoking a tobacco pipe. Your military gentleman thrusts his pap-bottle under his mustaches, between his lips, and puffs the smoke out of his nose, his mouth, and even his ears—and fancies himself a hero! There are my sons-in-law—though one of them's a senator, and the other is some sort of an administrator over there—they suck the pap-bottles, and they reckon themselves clever fellows too!"

Alexey Sergeich could not endure smoking; and moreover, he could not endure dogs, especially little dogs. "If you're a Frenchman, to be sure, you may well keep a lapdog: you run and you skip about here and there, and it runs after you with its tail up . . . but what's the use of it to people like us?" He was exceedingly neat and particular. Of the Empress Catherine he never spoke but with enthusiasm, and in exalted, rather bookish phraseology: "Half divine she was, not human! Only look, little sir, at that smile," he would add, pointing reverentially to Lampi's portrait, "and you will agree: half divine! I was so fortunate as to be deemed worthy to behold that smile close in my lifetime, and never will it be effaced from my heart!" And thereupon he would relate anecdotes of the life of Catherine, such as I have never happened to read or hear elsewhere. Here is one of them. Alexey Sergeich did not permit the slightest allusion to the weaknesses of the great Czaritsa. "And, besides," he exclaimed, "can you judge of her as of other people?"

One day while she was sitting in her peignoir during her morning toilette, she commanded her hair to be combed. . . . And what do you think? The lady-in-waiting passed the comb through, and sparks of electricity simply showered out! Then she summoned to her presence the court physician Rogerson, who happened to be in waiting at the court, and said to him: "I am, I know, censured for certain actions; but do you see this electricity? Consequently, as such is my nature and constitution, you can judge for yourself, as you are a doctor, that it is unjust for them to censure me, and they ought to understand me!"

The following incident remained indelible in Alexey Sergeich's memory. He was standing one day on guard indoors, in the palace— he was only sixteen at the time—and behold the Empress comes walking past him; he salutes . . . "and she," Alexey Sergeich would exclaim at this point with much feeling, "smiling at my youth and my zeal, deigned to give me her hand to kiss and patted my cheek, and asked me who I was, where I came from, of what family,' and then" . . . here the old man's voice usually broke . . . "then she bade me greet my mother in her name and thank her for having brought up her children so well. And whether I was on earth or in heaven, and how and where she deigned to vanish, whether she floated away into the heights or went her way into the other apartments . . . to this day I do not know!"

More than once I tried to question Alexey Sergeich about those far-away times, about the people who made up the Empress's circle. . . . But for the most part he edged off the subject. "What's the use of talking about old times?" he used to say . . . "it's only making one's self miserable, remembering that then one was a fine young fellow, and now one hasn't a tooth left in one's head. And what is there to say? Those were good old times . . . but there, let's be done with them! And as for those folks—you were asking, you troublesome boy, about the favorites!—haven't you seen how a bubble comes up on the water? As long as it lasts and is whole, what colors play upon it! Red, and blue, and yellow—a perfect rainbow or diamond you'd say it was! Only it soon bursts, and there's no trace of it left. And so it was with those folks."

"But how about Potiomkin?" I once inquired.

Alexey Sergeich looked grave. "Potiomkin, Grigory Alexandrovich, was a statesman, a theologian, a pupil of Catherine's, her cherished child, one must say. . . . But enough of that, little sir!"

Alexey Sergeich was a very devout man, and, though it was a great effort, he attended church regularly. Superstition was not noticeable in him; he laughed at omens, the evil eye, and such "nonsense," but he did not like a hare to run across his path, and to meet a priest was not altogether agreeable to him. For all that, he was very respectful to clerical persons, and went up to receive their blessing, and even kissed the priest's hand every time, but he was not willing to enter into conversation with them. "Such an extremely strong odor comes from them," he explained: "and I, poor sinner, am fastidious beyond reason; they've such long hair, and all oily, and they comb it out on all sides—they think they show me respect by so doing, and they clear their throats so loudly when they talk—from shyness, may be, or I dare say they want to show respect in that way too. And besides, they make one think of one's last hour. And, I don't know how it is, but I still want to go on living. Only, my little sir, don't you repeat my words; we must respect the clergy—it's only fools that don't respect them; and I'm to blame for babbling nonsense in my old age."

Alexey Sergeich, like most of the noblemen of his day, had received very little education; but he had, to some extent, made good the deficiency himself by reading. He read none but Russian books of the end of last century; the more modern authors he thought insipid and deficient in style. . . . While he read, he had placed at his side on a round, one-legged table, a silver tankard of frothing spiced kvass of a special sort, which sent an agreeable fragrance all over the house. He used to put on the end of his nose a pair of big, round spectacles, but in latter years he did not so much read as gaze dreamily over the rims of his spectacles, lifting his eyebrows, chewing his lips, and sighing. Once I caught him weeping with a book on his knees, greatly, I own, to my surprise.

He had recalled these lines:

> O pitiful race of man!
> Peace is unknown to thee!
> Thou canst not find it save
> In the dust of the grave. . . .
> Bitter, bitter is that sleep!
> Rest, rest in death . . . but living weep!

These lines were the composition of a certain Gormich-Gormitsky, a wandering poet, to whom Alexey Sergeich had given a home in his house, as he struck him as a man of delicate feeling and even of subtlety; he wore slippers adorned with bows, spoke with a broad accent, and frequently sighed, turning his eyes to heaven; in addition to all these qualifications, Gormich-Gormitsky spoke French decently, having been educated in a Jesuit college, while Alexey Sergeich only "followed conversation." But having once got terribly drunk at the tavern, that same subtle Gormitsky showed a turbulence beyond all bounds; he gave a fearful thrashing to Alexey Sergeich's valet, the male cook, two laundry-maids who chanced to get in his way, and a carpenter from another village, and he broke several panes in the windows, screaming furiously all the while: "There, I'll show them, these Russian loafers, roughhewn *katsaps!*" *

And the strength the frail-looking creature put forth! It was hard work for eight men to master him! For this violent proceeding Alexey Sergeich ordered the poet to be turned out of the house, after being put, as a precautionary measure, in the snow—it was winter-time—to sober him.

"Yes," Alexey Sergeich used to say, "my day is over; I was a spirited steed, but I've run my last race now. Then, I used to keep poets at my expense, and I used to buy pictures and books of the Jews, geese of the best breeds, and pouter-pigeons of pure blood. . . . I used to go in for everything! Though dogs I never did care for, because keeping them goes with drinking, foulness, and buffoonery! I was a young man of spirit, not to be outdone. That there should be anything of Telegin's and not first-rate . . . why, it was

* South-Russian term of opprobrium applied to Great Russians.—Ed.

not to be thought of! And I had a splendid stud of horses. And my horses came—from what stock do you think, young sir? Why, from none other than the celebrated stables of the Czar Ivan Alexeich, brother of Peter the Great . . . it's the truth I'm telling you! All fawn-colored stallions, sleek—their manes to their knees, their tails to their hoofs. . . . Lions! And all that was—and is buried in the past. Vanity of vanities—all is vanity! But still—why regret it? Every man has his limits set him. There's no flying above the sky, no living in the water, no getting away from the earth. . . . We'll live a bit longer, anyway!"

And the old man would smile again and sniff his Spanish snuff.

The peasants liked him; he was, in their words, a kind master, not easily angered. Only they, too, repeated that he was a worn-out steed. In former days Alexey Sergeich used to go into everything himself—he used to drive out to the fields, and to the mill, and to the dairy, and peep into the granaries and the peasants' huts; everyone knew his racing droshky, upholstered in crimson plush, and drawn by a tall mare, with a broad white stripe on her forehead, called "Beacon," from the same famous stables. Alexey Sergeich used to drive her himself, the ends of the reins wound around his fists. But when his seventieth year came, the old man let everything go, and handed over the management of the estate to the bailiff Antip, of whom he was secretly afraid, and whom he called Micromégas (a reminiscence of Voltaire!), or simply, plunderer. "Well, plunderer, what have you to say? Have you stacked a great deal in your barn?" he would ask with a smile, looking straight into the plunderer's eyes. "All, by your good favor, please your honor," Antip would respond cheerfully. "Favor's all very well, only you mind what I say, Micromégas! don't you dare lay hands on the peasants, my subjects! If they come to complain . . . I've a cane, you see, not far off!" "Your cane, your honor, Alexey Sergeich, I always keep well in mind," Antip Micromégas would respond, stroking his beard. "All right, don't forget it." And the master and the bailiff would laugh in each other's faces.

With the servants, and with the serfs in general, his "subjects" (Alexey Sergeich liked that word) he was gentle in his behavior. "Because, think a little, nephew; nothing of their own, but the cross on their neck—and that copper—and daren't hanker after other people's goods . . . how can one expect sense of them?" It is needless to state that of the so-called "serf question" no one ever dreamed in those days; it could not disturb the peace of mind of Alexey Sergeich: he was quite happy in the possession of his "subjects"; but he was severe in his censure of bad masters, and used to call them the enemies of their class. He divided the nobles generally into three groups: the prudent, "of whom there are too few"; the prodigal, "of whom there are quite enough"; and the senseless, "of whom there are shoals and shoals."

"And if any one of them is harsh and oppressive with his subjects"—he would say—"then he sins against God, and is guilty before men!"

Yes, the house-serfs had an easy life of it with the old man; his other "subjects" no doubt fared worse, in spite of the cane with which he threatened Micromégas. And what a lot there were of them, those house-serfs, in his house! And for the most part sinewy, hairy, grumbling old fellows, with stooping shoulders, in long-skirted nankeen coats, belted round the waist, with a strong, sour smell always clinging to them. And in the women's quarters you heard nothing but the patter of bare feet, the swish of petticoats. The chief valet was called Irinarkh, and Alexey Sergeich always called him in a long-drawn-out call: "I-ri-na-a-arkh!" The others he called: "Boy! Lad! Whoever's there of my subjects!" Bells he could not endure: "It's not an eating-house, God forbid!" And what used to surrpise me was that whatever time Alexey Sergeich called his valet, he always promptly made his appearance, as though he had sprung out of the earth, and with a scrape of his heels, his hands behind his back, would stand before his master, a surly, as it were angry, but devoted servant!

Alexey Sergeich was liberal beyond his means; but he did not like to be called "benefactor." "Benefactor to you, indeed, sir! . . . I'm doing myself a benefit, and not you, sir!" (when he was angry or indignant, he always addressed people with greater formality.) "Give to a beggar once," he used to say, "and give him twice, and three times. . . . And—if he should come a fourth time, give to him still—only then you might say too: It's time, my good man, you found work for something else, not only for your mouth." "But, uncle," one asked, sometimes, "suppose even after that the beggar came again, a fifth time?" "Oh, well, give again the fifth time." He used to have the sick, who came to him for aid, treated at his expense, though he had no faith in doctors himself, and never sent for them. "My mother," he declared, "used to cure illnesses of all sorts with olive oil and salt—she gave it internally, and rubbed it on too—it always answered splendidly. And who was my mother? She was born in the days of Peter the Great—only fancy that!"

Alexey Sergeich was a Russian in everything; he liked none but Russian dishes, he was fond of Russian songs, but the accordion—a "manufactured contrivance"—he hated; he liked looking at the serf-girls' dances and the peasant-women's jigs; in his youth, I was told, he had been an enthusiastic singer and a dashing dancer; he liked steaming himself in the bath, and steamed himself so vigorously that Irinarkh, who, serving him as bathman, used to beat him with a bundle of birch-twigs steeped in beer, to rub him with a handful of tow, and then with a woolen cloth—the truly devoted Irinarkh used to say every time, as he crept off the shelf red as a "new copper statue": "Well, this time I, the servant of God, Irinarkh Tolobeyev, have come out alive. How will it be next time?"

And Alexey Sergeich spoke excellent Russian, a little old-fashioned, but choice and pure as spring water, continually interspersing his remarks with favorite expressions: " 'Pon my honor, please God, howsoever that may be, sir, and young sir. . . ."

But enough of him. Let us talk a little about Alexey Sergeich's wife, Malanya Pavlovna.

Malanya Pavlovna was born in Moscow. She had been famous as the greatest beauty in Moscow—*la Vénus de Moscou*. I knew her as a thin old woman with delicate but insignificant features, with crooked teeth, like a hare's, in a tiny little mouth, with a multitude of finely crimped little yellow curls on her forehead, and painted eyebrows. She invariably wore a pyramidal cap with pink ribbons, a high ruff round her neck, a short white dress, and prunella slippers with red heels; and over her dress she wore a jacket of blue satin, with a sleeve hanging loose from her right shoulder. This was precisely the costume in which she was arrayed on St. Peter's Day in the year 1789! As a young girl, she went with her relations on that day to the Hodynka field to see the famous boxing-match arranged by Count Orlov. "And Count Alexey Grigorevich" (oh, how often I used to hear this story!) "noticing me, approached, bowed very low, taking his hat in both hands, and said: 'Peerless beauty,' said he, 'why have you hung that sleeve from your shoulder? Do you, too, wish to try a tussle with me? ... I'm at your service; only I will tell you before-hand you have vanquished me—I give in! And I am your captive.' And everyone was looking at us and wondering." And that very costume she had worn continually ever since. "Only I didn't wear a cap, but a hat *à la bergère de Trianon;* and though I was powdered, yet my hair shone through it, positively shone through it like gold!"

Malanya Pavlovna was foolish to the point of "holy innocence," as it is called; she chattered quite at random, as though she were hardly aware herself of what dropped from her lips—and mostly about Orlov. Orlov had become, one might say, the principal interest of her life. She usually walked ... or rather swam, into the room with a rhythmic movement of the head, like a peacock, stood still in the middle, with one foot strangely turned out, and two fingers holding the tip of the loose sleeve (I suppose this pose, too, must once have charmed Orlov); she would glance about her with haughty nonchalance, as befits a beauty—and with a positive sniff, and a murmur of "What next!" as though some importunate gallant were besieging her with compliments, she would go out again, tapping her heels and shrugging her shoulders. She used, too, to take Spanish snuff out of a tiny bonbonnière, picking it up with a tiny golden spoon; and from time to time, especially when anyone unknown to her appeared, she would hold up—not to her eyes (she had splendid sight) but to her nose—a double eyeglass in the shape of a half-moon, with a coquettish turn of her little white hand, one finger held out separate from the rest.

How often has Malanya Pavlovna described to me her wedding in the church of the Ascension, in Arbat—such a fine church!—and how all Moscow was there ... "and the crush there was!—awful! Carriages with teams, golden coaches, outriders ... one outrider of Count Zavadovsky got run over! and we were married by the archbishop himself—and what a sermon he gave us! everyone was crying—wherever I looked I saw tears ... and the governor-general's horses were tawny, like tigers. And the flowers, the flowers that were brought! ... Simply loads of flowers!" And how on that day a foreigner, a wealthy, tremendously wealthy person, had shot him-self for love—and how Orlov too had been there. ... And going up to Alexey Sergeich, he had congratulated him and called him a lucky man ... "A lucky man you are, you silly fellow!" said he. And how in answer to these words Alexey Sergeich had made a wonderful bow, and had swept the floor from left to right with the plumes of his hat, as if he would say: "Your Excellency, there is a line now between you and my spouse, which you will not overstep!" And Orlov, Alexey Grigorevich understood at once, and commended him. "Oh! that was a man! such a man!" And how, "One day, Alexis and I were at his house at a ball—I was married then—and he had the most marvelous diamond buttons! And I could not resist it, I admired them. 'What marvelous diamonds you have, Count!' said I. And he, taking up a knife from the table, at once cut off a button and presented it to me and said: 'In your eyes, my charmer, the diamonds are a hundred times brighter; stand before the looking-glass and compare them.' And I stood so, and he stood beside me. 'Well, who's right?' said he, while he simply rolled his eyes, looking me up and down. And Alexey Sergeich was very much put out about it, but I said to him: 'Alexis,' said I, 'please don't you be put out; you ought to know me better!' And he answered me: 'Don't disturb yourself, Mélanie!' And these very diamonds are now round my medallion of Alexey Grigorevich—you've seen it, I dare say, my dear;—I wear it on feastdays on a St. George ribbon, because he was a brave hero, a knight of St. George: he burned the Turks."

For all that, Malanya Pavlovna was a very kind-hearted woman; she was easily pleased. "She's not one to snarl, nor to sneer," the maids used to say of her. Malanya Pavlovna was passionately fond of sweet things—and a special old woman who looked after nothing but the jam, and so was called the jam-maid, would bring her, ten times a day, a china dish with rose-leaves crystallized in sugar, or barberries in honey, or sherbet of bananas. Malanya Pavlovna was afraid of solitude—dreadful thoughts are apt to come over one, she would say—and was almost always surrounded by companions, whom she would urgently implore: "Talk, talk! why do you sit like that, simply keeping your seats warm!" and they would begin twittering like canaries. She was no less devout than Alexey Sergeich, and was very fond of praying; but as, in her own words, she had never learned to repeat prayers well, she kept for the purpose a poor deacon's widow who prayed with such relish! Never stumbled over a word in her life! And this deacon's widow certainly could utter the words of prayer in a sort of unbroken flow, not interrupting the stream to breathe out or breathe in, while Malanya Pavlovna listened and was much moved. She had another widow in attendance on her—it was her duty to tell her stories in the night. "But only the old ones," Malanya Pavlovna would beg—"those I know already; the new ones are all so farfetched."

Malanya Pavlovna was flighty in the extreme, and at times she was fanciful too; some ridiculous notion would suddenly come into her head. She did not like the dwarf, Janus, for instance; she was always fancying he would suddenly get up and shout, "Don't you know who I am? The prince of the Buriats. Mind, you are to obey me!" Or else that he would set fire to the house in a fit of spleen. Malanya Pavlovna was as liberal as Alexey Sergeich; but she never gave money—she did not like to soil her hands—but kerchiefs, bracelets, dresses, ribbons; or she would send pies from the table, or a piece of roast meat, or a bottle of wine. She liked feasting the peasant-women, too, on holidays; they would dance, and she would tap with her heels and throw herself into attitudes.

Alexey Sergeich was well aware that his wife was a fool; but almost from the first year of his marriage he had schooled himself to keep up the fiction that she was very witty and fond of saying cutting things. Sometimes when her chatter began to get beyond all bounds, he would threaten her with his finger, and say as he did so: "Ah, the tongue, the tongue! what it will have to answer for in the other world! It will be pierced with a red-hot pin!"

Malanya Pavlovna was not offended, however, at this; on the contrary, she seemed to feel flattered at hearing a reproof of that sort, as though she would say, "Well! is it my fault, if I'm naturally witty?"

Malanya Pavlovna adored her husband, and had been all her life the pattern of a faithful wife; but there had been a romance even in her life—a young cousin, an hussar, killed, as she supposed, in a duel on her account; but, according to more trustworthy reports, killed by a blow on the head from a billiard-cue in a tavern brawl. A water-color portrait of this object of her affections was kept by her in a secret drawer. Malanya Pavlovna always blushed up to her ears when she mentioned Kapiton—such was the name of the young hero—and Alexey Sergeich would designedly scowl, shake his finger at his wife again, and say: "No trusting a horse in the field nor a woman in the house. Don't talk to me of Kapiton, he's Cupidon!" Then Malanya Pavlovna would be all of a flutter and say: "Alexis, Alexis, it's too bad of you! In your young days you flirted, I've no

doubt, with all sorts of misses and madams—and so now you imagine
. . ." "Come, that's enough, that's enough, my dear Malanya," Alexey
Sergeich would interrupt with a smile. "Your gown is white—but
whiter still your soul!" "Yes, Alexis, it is whiter!" "Ah, what a
tongue, what a tongue!" Alexis would repeat, patting her hand.

To speak of "views" in the case of Malanya Pavlovna would be
even more inappropriate than in the case of Alexey Sergeich; yet I
once chanced to witness a strange manifestation of my aunt's secret
feelings. In the course of conversation I once somehow mentioned the
famous chief of police, Sheshkovsky; Malanya Pavlovna turned suddenly livid—positively livid, green, in spite of her rouge and paint—
and in a thick and perfectly unaffected voice (a very rare thing
with her—she usually minced a little, intoned, and lisped) she said:
"Oh, what a name to utter! And towards nightfall, too! Don't utter
that name!" I was astonished; what kind of significance could his
name have for such a harmless and inoffensive creature, incapable—
not merely of doing—even of thinking of anything not permissible?
Anything but cheerful reflections were aroused in me by this terror,
manifesting itself after almost half a century.

Alexey Sergeich died in his eighty-eighth year—in the year 1848,
which apparently disturbed even him. His death, too, was rather
strange. He had felt well the same morning, though by that time he
never left his easy-chair. And all of a sudden he called his wife:
"Malanya, my dear, come here."

"What is it, Alexis?"

"It's time for me to die, my dear, that's what it is."

"Mercy on you, Alexey Sergeich! Why so?"

"Because, first of all, one must know when to take leave; and,
besides, I was looking the other day at my feet. . . . Look at my
feet . . . they are not mine . . . say what you like . . . look at my
hands, look at my stomach . . . that stomach's not mine—so really
I'm using up another man's life. Send for the priest; and meanwhile,
put me to bed—I shall not get up again."

Malanya Pavlovna was terribly upset; however, she put the old
man to bed and sent for the priest. Alexey Sergeich confessed, took
the sacrament, said good-bye to his household, and fell asleep.
Malanya Pavlovna was sitting by his bedside.

"Alexis!" she cried suddenly, "don't frighten me, don't shut your
eyes! Are you in pain?"

The old man looked at his wife: "No, no pain . . . but it's difficult . . . difficult to breathe." Then after a brief silence: "Malanya," he said, "so life has•slipped by—and do you remember when we were married . . . what a couple we were?"

"Yes, we were, my handsome, charming Alexis!"

The old man was silent again. "Malanya, my dear, shall we meet again in the next world?"

"I will pray God for it, Alexis," and the old woman burst into tears.

"Come, don't cry, silly; maybe the Lord God will make us young again then—and again we shall be a fine pair!"

"He will make us young, Alexis!"

"With the Lord all things are possible," observed Alexey Sergeich. "He worketh great marvels!—maybe He will make you sensible. . . . There, my love, I was joking; come, let me kiss your hand."

"And I yours."

And the two old people kissed each other's hands simultaneously.

Alexey Sergeich began to grow quieter and to sink into forgetfulness. Malanya Pavlovna watched him tenderly, brushing the tears off her eyelashes with her finger-tips. For two hours she continued sitting there.

"Is he asleep?" the old woman with the talent for praying inquired in a whisper, peeping in behind Irinarkh, who, immovable as a post, stood in the doorway, gazing intently at his expiring master.

"He is asleep," answered Malanya Pavlovna also in a whisper. And suddenly Alexey Sergeich opened his eyes.

"My faithful companion," he faltered, "my honored wife, I would bow down at your little feet for all your love and faithfulness—but how to get up? Let me sign you with the cross."

Malanya Pavlovna moved closer, bent down. . . . But the hand he had raised fell back powerless on the quilt, and a few moments later Alexey Sergeich was no more.

His daughters arrived only on the day of the funeral with their husbands; they had no children, either of them. Alexey Sergeich showed them no animosity in his will, though he never even mentioned them on his deathbed. "My heart has grown hard to them," he once said to me. Knowing his kindly nature, I was surprised at his words. It is hard to judge between parents and children. "A great ravine starts from a little rift," Alexey Sergeich said to me once in this connection: "a wound a yard wide may heal; but once cut off even a finger nail, it will not grow again."

I fancy the daughters were ashamed of their accentric old parents.

A month later and Malanya Pavlovna too passed away. From the very day of Alexey Sergeich's death she had hardly risen from her bed, and had not put on her usual attire; but they buried her in the blue jacket, and with Orlov's medallion on her shoulder, only without the diamonds. Those her daughters divided, on the pretext that the diamonds should be used in the setting of some holy pictures; in reality, they used them to adorn their own persons.

And so I can see my old friends as though they were alive and before my eyes, and pleasant is the memory I preserve of them. And yet on my very last visit to them (I was a student by then) an incident occurred which jarred upon the impression of patriarchal harmony always produced in me by the Telegin household.

Among the house-serfs there was one called Suhoys' Ivan, a coachman or coachboy, as they referred to him on account of his small size, in spite of his being no longer young. He was a tiny little man, brisk, snub-nosed, surly-headed, with an everlastingly smiling, childish face, and little eyes, like a mouse's. He was a great joker, a most comical fellow; he was great at all sorts of tricks—he used to fly kites, let off fireworks and rockets, play all sorts of games, gallop standing on the horse's back, fly higher than all the rest in the swing, and could even make Chinese shadows. No one could amuse children better; and he would gladly spend the whole day looking after them. When he started laughing, the whole house would seem to liven up; they would answer him—one would say one thing, one another, but he always made them all merry. . . . And even if they abused him, they could not but laugh. Ivan danced marvelously, especially the so-called "fish dance." When the chorus struck up a dance tune, the fellow would come into the middle of the ring, and then there would begin such a turning and skipping and stamping, and then he would fall flat on the ground, and imitate the movement of a fish brought out of the water onto dry land; such turning and wriggling, he could positively kick the back of his head with his heels; and then he would get up and shriek—the earth seemed simply quivering under him. At times Alexey Sergeich, who, as I have said already, exceedingly liked to watch dancing, could not resist shouting, "Little Vanya, here! coachboy! Dance us the fish, smartly now"; and a minute later he would whisper enthusiastically: "Ah, what a fellow it is!"

Well, on my last visit, this Ivan came into my room, and, without saying a word, fell on his knees.

"Ivan, what's the matter?"

"Save me, sir."

"Why, what is it?"

And thereupon Ivan told me his trouble.

He had been exchanged, twenty years ago, by the Suhoy family for a serf of the Telegins'—simply exchanged without any kind of formality or written deed: the man given in exchange for him had died, but the Suhoys had forgotten about Ivan, and he had stayed on in Alexey Sergeich's house as his own serf; only his nickname had served to recall his origin. But now his former masters were dead; the estate had passed into other hands; and the new owner, who was reported to be a cruel and oppressive man, having learned that one of his serfs was detained without cause or reason at Alexey Sergeich's, began to demand him back; in case of refusal he threatened legal proceedings, and the threat was not an empty one, as he was of the rank of privy councilor, and had great weight in the province. Ivan had rushed in terror to Alexey Sergeich. The old man was sorry for his dancer, and he offered to buy Ivan from the privy councilor for a considerable sum. But the privy councilor would not hear of it; he was a Little Russian, and obstinate as the devil. The poor fellow would have to be given up.

"I have spent my life here, and I'm at home here; I have served here, here I have eaten my bread, and here I want to die," Ivan said to me—and there was no smile on his face now; on the contrary, it looked turned to stone. . . . "And now I am to go to this wretch. . . . Am I a dog to be flung from one kennel to another with a noose round my neck? . . . to be told: 'There, get along with you!' Save me, master; beg your uncle, remember how I always amused you. . . . Or else there'll be harm come of it; it won't end without sin."

"What sort of sin, Ivan?"

"I shall kill that gentleman. I shall simply go and say to him, 'Master, let me go back; or else, mind, be careful of yourself. . . . I shall kill you.'"

If a siskin or a chaffinch could have spoken, and had begun

declaring that it would peck another bird to death, it would not have
reduced me to greater amazement than did Ivan at that moment.
What! Suhoys' Vanya, that dancing, jesting, comical fellow, the
favorite playfellow of children, and a child himself, that kindest-
hearted of creatures, a murderer! What ridiculous nonsense! Not for
an instant did I believe him; what astonished me to such a degree
was that he was capable of saying such a thing. Anyway I appealed
to Alexey Sergeich. I did not repeat what Ivan had said to me, but
began asking him whether something couldn't be done.

"My young sir," the old man answered, "I should be only too
happy—but what's to be done? I offered this Little Russian an immense compensation—I offered him three hundred roubles, 'pon my
honor, I tell you! But he—there's no moving him! What's one to do?
The transaction was not legal, it was done on trust, in the old-fashioned way . . . and now see what mischief's come of it! This Little
Russian fellow, you see, will take Ivan by force, do what we will:
his arm is powerful, the governor eats cabbage-soup at his table;
he'll be sending along soldiers. And I'm afraid of those soldiers! In
former days, to be sure, I would have stood up for Ivan, come what
might; but now, look at me, what a feeble creature I have grown!
How can I make a fight for it?" It was true; on my last visit I found
Alexey Sergeich greatly aged; even the centers of his eyes had that
milky color that babies' eyes have, and his lips wore not his old conscious smile, but that unnatural, mawkish, unconscious grin, which
never, even in sleep, leaves the faces of very decrepit old people.

I told Ivan of Alexey Sergeich's decision. He stood still, was silent
for a little, shook his head.

"Well," said he at last, "what is to be there's no escaping. Only
my mind's made up. There's nothing left, then, but to play the fool
to the end. Something for drink, please!"

I gave him something; he drank himself drunk, and that day
danced the "fish dance" so that the serf-girls and peasant-women
positively shrieked with delight—he surpassed himself in his antics
so wonderfully.

Next day I went home, and three months later, in Petersburg, I
heard that Ivan had kept his word. He had been sent to his new
master; his master had called him into his room, and explained to him
that he would be made coachman, that a team of three ponies would
be put in his charge, and that he would be severely dealt with if he

did not look after them well, and were not punctual in discharging his duties generally. "I'm not fond of joking," he said. Ivan heard the master out, first bowed down to his feet, and then announced it was as his honor pleased, but he could not be his servant.

"Let me off for a yearly quitrent, your honor," said he, "or send me for a soldier; or else mischief'll come of it!"

The master flew into a rage. "Ah, what a fellow you are! How dare you speak to me like that? In the first place, I'm to be called 'your excellency,' and not 'your honor'; and, secondly, you're beyond the age, and not of a size to be sent for a soldier; and, lastly, what mischief do you threaten me with? Do you mean to set the house on fire, eh?"

"No, your Excellency, not set the house on fire."

"Murder me, then, eh?"

Ivan was silent. "I'm not your servant," he said at last.

"Oh well, I'll show you," roared the master, "whether you're my servant or not." And he had Ivan cruelly punished, but yet had the three ponies put into his charge, and made him coachman in the stables.

Ivan apparently submitted; he began driving about as coachman. As he drove well, he soon gained favor with the master, especially as Ivan was very quiet and steady in his behavior, and the ponies improved so much in his hands; he turned them out as sound and sleek as cucumbers—it was quite a sight to see. The master took to driving out with him oftener than with the other coachmen. Sometimes he would ask him, "I say, Ivan, do you remember how badly we got on when we met? You've got over all that nonsense, eh?" But Ivan never made any response to such remarks.

So one day the master was driving with Ivan to the town in his three-horse sledge with bells and a high back covered with carpet. The horses began to walk up the hill, and Ivan got off the box-seat and went behind the back of the sledge as though he had dropped something. It was a sharp frost; the master sat wrapped up, with a beaver cap pulled down on to his ears. Then Ivan took an axe from under his skirt, came up to the master from behind, knocked off his cap, and saying, "I warned you, Pyotr Petrovich—you've yourself to blame now!" he split his head at one blow. Then he stopped the ponies, put the cap on his dead master, and, getting on the box-seat again, drove him to the town, straight to the courts of justice.

"Here's the Suhoy general for you, dead; I have killed him. As I warned him, so I did. Tie me up."

They took Ivan, tried him, sentenced him to the knout, and then to hard labor. The lighthearted, birdlike dancer was sent to the mines, and there passed out of sight for ever. . . .

Yes; one can but repeat, in another sense, Alexey Sergeich's words: "They were good old times . . . but let's be done with them!"

1881

# Fyodor Dostoevsky . . . 1821–1881

THE SON of a doctor attached to a Moscow charity hospital, Fyodor Dostoevsky had an unhappy childhood and youth. He was at an engineering school in Petersburg (Leningrad) when his father, then retired, was murdered by his own serfs. Upon graduation, young Dostoevsky entered the government service, only to resign his post a year later, at the age of twenty-three, in order to devote himself to writing. He was busy with *Poor Folk*, his first novel, when there appeared unmistakable symptoms of the malady which, together with penury, was to torment him all his life: he was an epileptic.

With the publication of *Poor Folk* in 1846 he leapt into fame. Several short stories followed. In the spring of 1849—he was then working on his second novel—the rising young author was arrested as a member of a group of intellectuals who met secretly to discuss radical reforms. He was condemned to death, but at the last moment the sentence was commuted to four years of hard labor in Siberia. Shortly after his release, while he was serving as a private there, he married the widow of a petty official.

On his return to the capital, after a lapse of ten years, he resumed his literary activity, which now included the editorship of a magazine, *Vremya* (Time). It was to this periodical that he contributed "An Unpleasant Predicament" as well as his prison memoirs, *The Dead House*. The magazine was suppressed in 1863 and succeeded by another in which he published "Notes from the Underground." Meanwhile he had managed to make a brief sojourn in western Europe, where he contracted another disease: the gambling fever.

Shortly after his return from abroad his wife died, and in 1867 he married a second time. His bride was the stenographer to whom he had been dictating *The Gambler*, a short novel, and part of *Crime and Punishment*. This was the first of the series of major novels upon which his fame chiefly rests. At the same time he continued his journalistic activities, producing a one-man periodical entitled *The Writer's Diary*. Here appeared his last short stories, notably "The Dream of a Ridiculous Man," as well as the autobiographic sketch, "The Peasant Marey." The publication of his last novel, *The Brothers Karamazov*, further enhanced his immense reputation at home. He died in the midst of plans for what he felt was to be a greater work than he had yet achieved.

# AN HONEST THIEF

ONE morning, just as I was about to set off to my office, Agrafena, my cook, washerwoman and housekeeper, came in to me and, to my surprise, entered into conversation.

She had always been such a silent, simple creature that, except her daily inquiry about dinner, she had not uttered a word for the last six years. I, at least, had heard nothing else from her.

"Here I have come in to have a word with you, sir," she began abruptly; "you really ought to let the little room."

"Which little room?"

"Why, the one next the kitchen, to be sure."

"What for?"

"What for? Why because folks do take in lodgers, to be sure."

"But who would take it?"

"Who would take it? Why, a lodger would take it, to be sure."

"But, my good woman, one could not put a bedstead in it; there wouldn't be room to move! Who could live in it?"

"Who wants to live there! As long as he has a place to sleep in. Why, he would live in the window."

"In what window?"

"In what window! As though you didn't know! The one in the passage, to be sure. He would sit there, sewing or doing anything else. Maybe he would sit on a chair, too. He's got a chair; and he has a table, too; he's got everything."

"Who is 'he' then?"

"Oh, a good man, a man of experience. I will cook for him. And I'll ask him three roubles a month for his board and lodging."

After prolonged efforts I succeeded at last in learning from Agrafena that an elderly man had somehow managed to persuade her to admit him into the kitchen as a lodger and boarder. Any notion Agrafena took into her head had to be carried out; if not, I knew she would give me no peace. When anything was not to her liking, she at once began to brood, and sank into a deep dejection that would last for a fortnight or three weeks. During that period my dinners were spoiled, my linen was mislaid, my floors went unscrubbed; in short, I had a great deal to put up with. I had observed long ago that this inarticulate woman was incapable of conceiving a project, of originating an idea of her own. But if anything like a notion or a project was by some means put into her feeble brain, to prevent its being carried out meant, for a time, her moral assassination. And so, as I cared more for my peace of mind than for anything else, I consented forthwith.

"Has he a passport anyway, or something of the sort?"

"To be sure, he has. He is a good man, a man of experience; three roubles he's promised to pay."

The very next day the new lodger made his appearance in my modest bachelor quarters; but I was not put out by this, indeed I was inwardly pleased. I lead as a rule a very lonely, hermit's existence. I have scarcely any friends; I hardly ever go anywhere. As I had spent ten years never coming out of my shell, I had, of course, grown used to solitude. But another ten or fifteen years or more of the same solitary existence, with the same Agrafena, in the same bachelor quarters, was in truth a somewhat cheerless prospect. And therefore a new inmate, if well-behaved, was a Heaven-sent blessing.

Agrafena had spoken truly: my lodger was certainly a man of experience. From his passport it appeared that he was a veteran, a fact which I should have known indeed from his face. A veteran is easily recognized. Astafy Ivanovich was an admirable specimen of his class. We got on very well together. What was best of all, Astafy Ivanovich would sometimes tell a story, describing some incident in his own life. In the perpetual boredom of my existence such a story-teller was a veritable treasure. One day he told me one of these stories. It made an impression on me. The following event was what led to it.

I was left alone in the flat; both Astafy and Agrafena were out on business of their own. All of a sudden from the inner room I heard somebody—I fancied a stranger—come in; I went out; there actually was a stranger in the passage, a short fellow wearing no overcoat in spite of the cold autumn weather.

"What do you want?"

"Does a clerk called Alexandrov live here?"

"Nobody of that name here, brother. Good-bye."

"Why, the porter told me it was here," said my visitor, cautiously retiring towards the door.

"Be off, be off, brother, get along."

Next day after dinner, while Astafy Ivanovich was fitting on a coat which he was altering for me, again someone came into the passage. I half opened the door.

Before my very eyes my yesterday's visitor, with perfect composure, took my wadded greatcoat from the peg and, stuffing it under his arm, darted out of the flat. Agrafena stood all the time staring at him, agape with astonishment and doing nothing for the protection of my property. Astafy Ivanovich flew in pursuit of the thief and ten minutes later came back out of breath and empty-handed. He had vanished completely.

"Well, there's a piece of ill luck, Astafy Ivanovich!"

"It's a good job your cloak remains! Or he would have left you on the rocks, the thief!"

But the whole incident had so impressed Astafy Ivanovich that I forgot the theft as I looked at him. He could not get over it. Every minute or two he would drop the work upon which he was engaged, and would describe over again how it had all happened, how he had been standing, how the greatcoat had been taken down before his very eyes, not a yard away, and how it had come to pass that he could not catch the thief. Then he would sit down to his work again, then leave it once more, and at last I saw him go down to the porter to tell him all about it, and to upbraid him for letting such a thing happen in his domain. Then he came back and began scolding Agrafena. Then he sat down to his work again, and long afterwards he was still muttering to himself how it had all happened, how he stood there and I here, how before our eyes, not a yard away, the thief took the coat off the peg, and so on. In short, though Astafy Ivanovich understood his business, he was a terrible slow-coach and busy-body.

"He's made fools of us, Astafy Ivanovich," I said to him in the evening, as I gave him a glass of tea. I wanted to while away the time by recalling the story of the lost greatcoat, the frequent repetition of which, together with the great earnestness of the speaker, was beginning to become very amusing.

"Fools, indeed, sir! Even though it is no business of mine, I am put out. It makes me angry though it is not my coat that was lost. To my thinking there is no vermin in the world worse than a thief. A robber shows some daring at least, but a sneak-thief steals the work of your hands, the sweat of your brow, your time . . . Ugh, it's nasty! One can't speak of it! it's too vexing. How is it you don't feel the loss of your property, sir?"

"Yes, you are right, Astafy Ivanovich, better if the thing had been burnt; it's annoying to let the thief have it, it's disagreeable."

"Disagreeable! I should think so! Yet, to be sure, there are thieves and thieves. And I have happened, sir, to come across an honest thief."

"An honest thief? But how can a thief be honest, Astafy Ivanovich?"

"There you are right indeed, sir. How can a thief be honest? There are none such. I only meant to say that he was an honest man, sure enough, and yet he stole. I was simply sorry for him."

"Why, how was that, Astafy Ivanovich?"

"It was about two years ago, sir. I had been nearly a year out of a place, and just before I lost my place I made the acquaintance of a poor lost creature. We got acquainted in a public-house. He was a drunkard, a vagrant, a beggar, he had been in a situation of some sort, but from his drinking habits he had lost his work. Such a ne'er-do-well! God only knows what he had on! Often you wouldn't be sure if he'd a shirt under his coat; everything he could lay his hands upon he would drink away. But he was not one to quarrel; he was a quiet fellow. A soft, good-natured chap. And he'd never ask, he was ashamed; but you could see for yourself the poor fellow wanted a drink, and you would stand it him. And so we got friendly, that's to say, he stuck to me. . . . It was all one to me. And what a man he was, to be sure! Like a little dog he would follow me; wherever I went there he would be; and all that after our first meeting, and he as thin as a thread-paper! At first it was 'let me stay the night'; well, I let him stay.

"I looked at his passport, too; the man was all right.

"Well, the next day it was the same story, and then the third day he came again and sat all day in the window and stayed the night. Well, thinks I, he is sticking to me; give him food and drink and shelter at night, too—here am I, a poor man, and a hanger-on to keep as well! And before he came to me, he used to go in the same way to a government clerk's; he attached himself to him; they were always drinking together; but he, through trouble of some sort, drank himself into the grave. My man was called Yemelyan Ilyich. I pondered and pondered what I was to do with him. To drive him away I was ashamed. I was sorry for him; such a pitiful, God-forsaken creature I never did set eyes on. And not a word said either; he does not ask, but just sits there and looks into your eyes like a dog. To think what drinking will bring a man down to!

"I kept asking myself how am I to say to him: 'You must be moving, Yemelyanushka, there's nothing for you here, you've come to the wrong place; I shall soon not have a bite for myself, how am I to keep you too?'

"I sat and wondered what he'd do when I said that to him. And I seemed to see how he'd stare at me, if he were to hear me say that, how long he would sit and not understand a word of it. And when it did come home to him at last, how he would get up from the window, would take up his bundle—I can see it now, the red-check kerchief full of holes, with God knows what wrapped up in it, which he had always with him, and then how he would set his shabby old coat to rights, so that it would look decent and keep him warm, so that no holes would be seen—he was a man of delicate feelings! And how he'd open the door and go out with tears in his eyes. Well, there's no letting a man go to ruin like that. . . . One's sorry for him.

"And then again, I think, how am I off myself? Wait a bit, Yemelyanushka, says I to myself, you've not long to feast with me: I shall soon be going away and then you will not find me.

"Well, sir, our family made a move; and Alexander Filimonovich, my master (now deceased, God rest his soul), said, 'I am thoroughly satisfied with you, Astafy Ivanovich; when we come back from the country we will take you on again.' I had been butler with them; a nice gentleman he was, but he died that same year. Well, after seeing him off, I took my belongings, what little money I had, and I thought I'd have a rest for a time, so I went to an old woman I knew, and I took a corner in her room. There was only one corner free in it. She had been a nurse, so now she had a pension and a room of her own. Well, now good-bye, Yemelyanushka, thinks I, you won't find me now, my boy.

"And what do you think, sir? I had gone out to see a man I knew, and when I came back in the evening, the first thing I saw was Yemelyanushka! There he was, sitting on my box and his check bundle beside him; he was sitting in his ragged old coat, waiting for me. And to while away the time he had borrowed a church book from the old lady, and was holding it wrong side upwards. He'd scented me out! My heart sank. Well, thinks I, there's no help for it —why didn't I turn him out at first? So I asked him straight off: 'Have you brought your passport, Yemelyanushka?'

"I sat down on the spot, sir, and began to ponder: will a vagabond like that be very much trouble to me? And on thinking it over it seemed he would not be much trouble. He must be fed, I thought. Well, a bit of bread in the morning, and to make it go down better I'll buy him an onion. At midday I should have to give him another bit of bread and an onion; and in the evening, onion again with kyass, with some more bread if he wanted it. And if some cabbage soup were to come our way, then we should both have our fill. I am no great eater myself, and a drinking man, as we all know, never eats; all he wants is herb-brandy or green vodka. He'll ruin me with his drinking, I thought, but then another idea came into my head, sir, and took great hold on me. So much so that if Yemelyanushka had gone away I should have felt that I had nothing to live for, I do believe. . . . I determined on the spot to be a father and guardian to him. I'll keep him from ruin, I thought, I'll wean him from the glass! You wait a bit, thought I; very well, Yemelyanushka, you may stay, only you must behave yourself; you must obey orders.

"Well, thinks I to myself, I'll begin by training him to work of some sort, but not all at once; let him enjoy himself a little first, and I'll look round and find something you are fit for, Yemelyanushka. For every sort of work a man needs a special ability, you know, sir. And I began to watch him on the quiet; I soon saw Yemelyanushka was a desperate character. I began, sir, with a word of advice: I said this and that to him. 'Yemelyanushka,' said I, 'you ought to take thought and mend your ways. Have done with drinking! Just look what rags you go about in: that old coat of yours, if I may make bold to say so, is fit for nothing but a sieve. A pretty state of things!

It's time to draw the line, sure enough.' Yemelyanushka sat and listened to me with his head hanging down. Would you believe it, sir? It had come to such a pass with him, he'd lost his tongue through drink and could not speak a word of sense. Talk to him of cucumbers and he'd answer back about beans! He would listen and listen to me and then heave such a sigh. 'What are you sighing for, Yemelyan Ilyich?' I asked him.

" 'Oh, nothing; don't you mind me. Astafy Ivanovich. Do you know there were two women fighting in the street today, Astafy Ivanovich? One upset the other woman's basket of cranberries by accident.'

" 'Well, what of that?'

" 'And the second one upset the other's cranberries on purpose and trampled them under foot, too.'

" 'Well, and what of it, Yemelyan Ilyich?'

" 'Why, nothing, Astafy Ivanovich, I just mentioned it.'

" ' "Nothing, I just mentioned it!" Yemelyanushka, my boy, I thought, you've squandered and drunk away your brains!

" 'And do you know, a gentleman dropped a bill on the pavement in Gorohovy Street, no, it was Sadovy Street. And a peasant saw it and said, "That's my luck"; and at the same time another man saw it and said, "No, it's my bit of luck. I saw it before you did." '

" 'Well, Yemelyan Ilyich?'

" 'And the fellows had a fight over it, Astafy Ivanovich. But a policeman came up, took away the note, gave it back to the gentleman and threatened to take up both men.'

" 'Well, but what of that? What is there edifying about it, Yemelyanushka?'

" 'Why, nothing, to be sure. Folks laughed, Astafy Ivanovich.'

"Ach, Yemelyanushka! What do folks matter? You've sold your soul for a brass farthing! But do you know what I have to tell you, Yemelyan Ilyich?'

" 'What, Astafy Ivanovich?'

" 'Take a job of some sort, that's what you must do. For the hundredth time I say to you, set to work, have some mercy on yourself!'

" 'What could I set to, Astafy Ivanovich? I don't know what job I could set to, and there is no one who will take me on, Astafy Ivanovich.'

" 'That's how you came to be turned off, Yemelyanushka, you drinking man!'

" 'And do you know Vlas, the waiter, was called to the police-station today, Astafy Ivanovich?'

" 'Why did they send for him, Yemelyanushka?' I asked.

" 'I could not say why, Astafy Ivanovich. I suppose they wanted him there, and that's why they sent for him.'

"A-ach, thought I, we are in a bad way, poor Yemelyanushka! The Lord is chastising us for our sins. Well, sir, what is one to do with such a man?

"But a cunning fellow he was, and no mistake. He'd listen and listen to me, but at last I suppose he got sick of it. As soon as he saw I was beginning to get angry, he'd pick up his old coat and out he'd slip and leave no trace. He'd wander about all day and come back at night drunk. Where he got the money from, the Lord only knows; I had no hand in that.

" 'No,' said I, 'Yemelyan Ilyich, you'll come to a bad end. Give over drinking, mind what I say now, give it up! Next time you come home in liquor, you can spend the night on the stairs. I won't let you in!'

"After hearing that threat, Yemelyanushka sat at home that day and the next; but on the third he slipped off again. I waited and waited; he didn't come back. Well, at last I don't mind owning, I was in a fright, and I felt for the man too. What have I done to him? I thought. I've scared him away. Where's the poor fellow gone to now? He'll get lost maybe. Lord have mercy upon us!

"Night came on, he did not come. In the morning I went out into the entry; I looked, and if he hadn't gone to sleep in the entry! There he was with his head on the step, and chilled to the marrow of his bones.

" 'What next, Yemelyanushka, God have mercy on you! Where will you get to next!'

" 'Why, you were—sort of—angry with me, Astafy Ivanovich, the other day, you were vexed and promised to make me sleep in the entry, so I didn't—sort of —venture to come in, Astafy Ivanovich, and so I lay down here. . . .'

"I did feel angry and sorry too.

" 'Surely you might undertake some other duty, Yemelyan-ushka, instead of lying here guarding the steps,' I said.

" 'Why, what other duty, Astafy Ivanovich?'

" 'You lost soul'—I was in such a rage, I called him that—'if you could but learn tailoring work! Look at your old rag of a coat! It's not enough to have it in tatters, here you are sweeping the steps with it! You might take a needle and patch up your rags, as decency demands. Ah, you drunken man!'

"What do you think, sir? He actually did take a needle. Of course I said it in jest, but he was so scared he set to work. He took off his coat and began threading the needle. I watched him; as you may well guess, his eyes were all red and bleary, and his hands were all of a shake. He kept shoving and shoving the thread and could not get it through the eye of the needle; he kept screwing his eyes up and wetting the thread and twisting it in his fingers—it was no good! He gave it up and looked at me.

" 'Well,' said I, 'this is a nice way to treat me! If there had been folks by to see, I don't know what I should have done! Why, you simple fellow, I said it you in joke, as a reproach. Give over your nonsense, God bless you! Sit quiet and don't put me to shame, don't sleep on my stairs and make a laughingstock of me.'

" 'Why, what am I to do, Astafy Ivanovich? I know very well I am a drunkard and good-for-nothing! I can do nothing but vex you, my bene—bene—factor. . . .'

"And at that his blue lips began to quiver all of a sudden, and a tear ran down his white cheek and trembled on his stubbly chin, and then poor Yemelyanushka burst into a regular flood of tears. Mercy on us! I felt as though a knife were thrust into my heart! The sensitive creature! I'd never have expected it. Who could have guessed it? No, Yemelyanushka, thought I, I shall give you up altogether. You can go your way like the rubbish you are.

"Well, sir, why make a long story of it? And the whole affair is so trifling; it's not worth wasting words upon. Why, you, sir, for instance, would not have given a thought to it, but I would have given a great deal—if I had a great deal to give—that it never should have happened at all.

"I had a pair of riding-breeches by me, sir, deuce take them, fine, first-rate riding-breeches they were too, blue with a check in it. They'd been ordered by a gentleman from the country, but he would not have them after all; said they were not full enough, so they were left on my hands. It struck me they were worth something. At the secondhand dealer's I ought to get five silver roubles for them, or if not I could turn them into two pairs of trousers for Petersburg gentlemen and have a piece over for a waistcoat for myself. Of course for poor people like us everything comes in handy. And it happened just then that Yemelyanushka was having a sad time of it. There he sat day after day: he did not drink, not a drop passed his lips, but he sat and moped like an owl. It was sad to see him —he just sat and brooded. Well, thought I, either you've not got a copper to spend, my lad, or else you're turning over a new leaf of yourself, you've given it up, you've listened to reason. Well, sir, that's how it was with us; and just then came a holiday. I went to vespers; when I came home I found Yemelyanushka sitting in the window, drunk and rocking to and fro.

"Ah! so that's what you've been up to, my lad! And I went to get something out of my chest. And when I looked in, the breeches were not there. . . . I rummaged here and there; they'd vanished. When I'd ransacked everywhere and saw they were not there, something seemed to stab me to the heart. I ran first to the old woman and began accusing her; of Yemelyanushka I'd not the faintest suspicion, though there was cause for it in his sitting there drunk.

" 'No,' said the old body, 'God be with you, my fine gentleman, what good are riding-breeches to me? Am I going to wear such things? Why, a skirt I had I lost the other day through a fellow of your sort . . . I know nothing; I can tell you nothing about it,' she said.

" 'Who has been here, who has been in?' I asked.

" 'Why, nobody has been, my good sir,' says she; 'I've been here all the while; Yemelyan Ilyich went out and came back again; there he sits, ask him.'

" 'Yemelyanushka,' said I, 'have you taken those new riding-breeches for anything—you remember the pair I made for that gentleman from the country?'

" 'No, Astafy Ivanovich,' said he; 'I've not—sort of—touched them.'

"I was in a state! I hunted high and low for them—they were nowhere to be found. And Yemelyanushka sits there rocking himself to and fro. I was squatting on my heels facing him and bending over the chest, and all at once I stole a glance at him. . . .

"Alack, I thought; my heart suddenly grew hot within me and

I felt myself flushing up too. And suddenly Yemelyanushka looked at me.

" 'No, Astafy Ivanovich,' said he, 'those riding-breeches of yours, maybe, you are thinking, maybe, I took them, but I never touched them.'

" 'But what can have become of them, Yemelyan Ilyich?'

" 'No, Astafy Ivanovich,' said he, 'I've never seen them.'

" 'Why, Yemelyan Ilyich, I suppose they've run off of themselves, eh?'

" 'Maybe they have, Astafy Ivanovich.'

"When I heard him say that, I got up at once, went up to the window, lighted the lamp and sat down to work at my sewing. I was altering a waistcoat for a clerk who lived below us. And wasn't there a burning pain and ache in my breast! I shouldn't have minded so much if I had put all the clothes I had in the fire. Yemelyanushka seemed to have an inkling of what a rage I was in. When a man is guilty, you know, sir, he scents trouble far off, like the birds of the air before a storm.

" 'Do you know what, Astafy Ivanovich,' Yemelyanushka began, and his poor old voice was shaking as he said the words, 'Antip Prohorych, the doctor's assistant, married the coachman's wife this morning, who died the other day—'

"I did give him a look, sir, a nasty look it was; Yemelyanushka understood it too. I saw him get up, go to the bed, and begin to rummage there for something. I waited—he was busy there a long time and kept muttering all the while, 'No, not here, where can the blessed things have got to!'

"I waited to see what he'd do; I saw him creep under the bed on all fours. I couldn't bear it any longer. 'What are you crawling about under the bed for, Yemelyan Ilyich?' said I.

" 'Looking for the breeches, Astafy Ivanovich. Maybe they've dropped down there somewhere.'

" 'Why should you try to help a poor simple man like me,' said I, 'crawling on your knees for nothing, sir?'—I called him that in my vexation.

" 'Oh, never mind, Astafy Ivanovich, I'll just look. They'll turn up, maybe, somewhere.'

" 'H'm,' said I, 'look here, Yemelyan Ilyich!'

" 'What is it, Astafy Ivanovich?' said he.

" 'Haven't you simply stolen them from me like a thief and a robber, in return for the bread and salt you've eaten here?' said I.

"I felt so angry, sir, at seeing him fooling about on his knees before me.

" 'No, Astafy Ivanovich.'

"And he stayed lying as he was on his face under the bed. A long time he lay there and then at last crept out. I looked at him and the man was as white as a sheet. He stood up, and sat down near me in the window and sat so for some ten minutes.

" 'No, Astafy Ivanovich,' he said, and all at once he stood up and came towards me, and I can see him now; he looked dreadful as sin. 'No, Astafy Ivanovich,' said he, 'I never—sort of—touched your breeches.'

"He was all of a shake, poking himself in the chest with a trembling finger, and his poor old voice shook so that I was frightened, sir, and sat as though I was rooted to the window-seat.

" 'Well, Yemelyan Ilyich,' said I, 'as you will, forgive me if I, in my foolishness, have accused you unjustly. As for the breeches, let them go hang; we can live without them. We've still our hands, thank God; we need not go thieving or begging from some other poor man; we'll earn our bread.'

"Yemelyanushka heard me out and went on standing there before me. I looked up, and he had sat down. And there he sat all the evening without stirring. At last I lay down to sleep. Yemelyanushka went on sitting in the same place. When I looked out in the morning, he was lying curled up in his old coat on the bare floor; he felt too crushed even to come to bed. Well, sir, I felt no more liking for the fellow from that day, in fact for the first few days I hated him. I felt as one may say as though my own son had robbed me, and done me a deadly hurt. Ach, thought I, Yemelyanushka, Yemelyanushka! And Yemelyanushka, sir, went on drinking for a whole fortnight without stopping. He was drunk all the time, and regularly besotted. He went out in the morning and came back late at night, and for a whole fortnight I didn't get a word out of him. It was as though grief was gnawing at his heart, or as though he wanted to do for himself completely. At last he stopped; he must have come to the end of all he'd got, and then he sat in the window again. I remember he sat there without speaking for three days and three nights; all of a sudden I saw that he was crying. He was just sitting there, sir, and crying like anything; a perfect stream, as though he didn't know how his tears were flowing. And it's a sad thing, sir, to see a grown-up man and an old man, too, crying from woe and grief.

" 'What's the matter, Yemelyanushka?' said I.

"He began to tremble so that he shook all over. I spoke to him for the first time since that evening.

" 'Nothing, Astafy Ivanovich.'

" 'God be with you, Yemelyanushka, what's lost is lost. Why are you moping about like this?' I felt sorry for him.

" 'Oh, nothing, Astafy Ivanovich, it's no matter. I want to find some work to do, Astafy Ivanovich.'

" 'And what sort of work, pray, Yemelyanushka?'

" 'Why, any sort; perhaps I could find a situation such as I used to have. I've been already to ask Fedosey Ivanych. I don't like to be a burden on you, Astafy Ivanovich. If I can find a situation, Astafy Ivanovich, then I'll pay it you all back, and make you a return for all your hospitality.'

" 'Enough, Yemelyanushka, enough; let bygones be bygones—and no more to be said about it. Let us go on as we used to do before.'

" 'No, Astafy Ivanovich, you, maybe, think—but I never touched your riding-breeches.'

" 'Well, have it your own way; God be with you, Yemely-anushka.'

" 'No, Astafy Ivanovich, I can't go on living with you, that's clear. You must excuse me, Astafy Ivanovich.'

" 'Why, God bless you, Yemelyan Ilyich, who's offending you and driving you out of the place—am I doing it?'

" 'No, it's not the proper thing for me to live with you like this, Astafy Ivanovich. I'd better be going.'

"He was so hurt, it seemed, he stuck to his point. I looked at him, and sure enough, up he got and pulled his old coat over his shoulders.

" 'But where are you going, Yemelyan Ilyich? Listen to reason: what are you about? Where are you off to?'

" 'No, good-bye, Astafy Ivanovich, don't keep me now'—and he was blubbering again—'I'd better be going. You're not the same now.'

" 'Not the same as what? I am the same. But you'll be lost by yourself like a poor helpless babe, Yemelyan Ilyich.'

" 'No, Astafy Ivanovich, when you go out now, you lock up your chest and it makes me cry to see it, Astafy Ivanovich. You'd better let me go, Astafy Ivanovich, and forgive me all the trouble I've given you while I've been living with you.'

"Well, sir, the man went away. I waited for a day; I expected he'd be back in the evening—no. Next day no sign of him, nor the third day either. I began to get frightened, I was so worried, I couldn't drink, I couldn't eat, I couldn't sleep. The fellow had quite disarmed me. On the fourth day I went out to look for him; I peeped into all the taverns, to inquire for him—but no, Yemelyanushka was lost. 'Have you managed to keep yourself alive, Yemelyanushka?' I wondered. 'Perhaps he is lying dead under some hedge, poor drunkard, like a sodden log.' I went home more dead than alive. Next day I went out to look for him again. And I kept cursing myself that I'd been such a fool as to let the man go off by himself. On the fifth day it was a holiday—in the early morning I heard the door creak. I looked up and there was my Yemelyanushka coming in. His face was blue and his hair was covered with dirt as though he'd been sleeping in the street; he was as thin as a match. He took off his old coat, sat down on the chest and looked at me. I was delighted to see him, but I felt more upset about him than ever. For you see, sir, if I'd been overtaken in some sin, as true as I am here, sir, I'd have died like a dog before I'd have come back. But Yemelyanushka did come back. And a sad thing it was, sure enough, to see a man sunk so low. I began to look after him, to talk kindly to him, to comfort him.

" 'Well, Yemelyanushka,' said I, 'I am glad you've come back. Had you been away much longer I should have gone to look for you in the taverns again today. Are you hungry?'

" 'No, Astafy Ivanovich.'

" 'Come, now, aren't you really? Here, brother, is some cabbage soup left over from yesterday; there was meat in it; it is good stuff. And here is some bread and onion. Come, eat it, it'll do you no harm.'

"I made him eat it, and I saw at once that the man had not tasted food for maybe three days—he was as hungry as a wolf. So it was hunger that had driven him to me. My heart was melted looking at the poor fellow. 'Let me run to the tavern,' thought I, 'I'll get something to ease his heart, and then we'll make an end of it. I've no more anger in my heart against you, Yemelyanushka!' I brought him some vodka. 'Here, Yemelyan Ilyich, let us have a drink for the holiday. Like a drink? And it will do you good.' He held out his hand, held it out greedily; he was just taking it, and then he stopped himself. But a minute after I saw him take it, and lift it to his mouth, spilling it on his sleeve. But though he got it to his lips he set it down on the table again.

" 'What is it, Yemelyanushka?'

" 'Nothing, Astafy Ivanovich, I—sort of——'

" 'Won't you drink it?'

" 'Well, Astafy Ivanovich, I'm not—sort of—going to drink any more, Astafy Ivanovich.'

" 'Do you mean you've given it up altogether, Yemelyanushka, or are you only not going to drink today?'

"He did not answer. A minute later I saw him rest his head on his hand.

" 'What's the matter, Yemelyanushka, are you ill?'

" 'Why, yes, Astafy Ivanovich, I don't feel well.'

"I took him and laid him down on the bed. I saw that he really was ill: his head was burning hot and he was shivering with fever. I sat by him all day; towards night he was worse. I mixed him some oil and onion and kvas and bread broken up.

" 'Come, eat some of this,' said I, 'and perhaps you'll be better.' He shook his head. 'No,' said he, 'I won't have any dinner today, Astafy Ivanovich.'

"I made some tea for him, I quite flustered our old woman—he was no better. Well, thinks I, it's a bad lookout! The third morning I went for a medical gentleman. There was one I knew living close by, Kostopravov by name. I'd made his acquaintance when I was in service with the Bosomyagins; he'd attended me. The doctor came and looked at him. 'He's in a bad way,' said he, 'it was no use sending for me. But if you like I can give him a powder.' Well, I didn't give him a powder, I thought that's just the doctor's little game; and then the fifth day came.

"He lay, sir, dying before my eyes. I sat in the window with my work in my hands. The old woman was heating the stove. We were all silent. My heart was simply breaking over him, the good-for-nothing fellow; I felt as if it were a son of my own I was losing. I knew that Yemelyanushka was looking at me. I'd seen the man all the day long making up his mind to say something and not daring to.

"At last I looked up at him; I saw such misery in the poor fellow's eyes. He had kept them fixed on me, but when he saw that I was looking at him, he looked down at once.

" 'Astafy Ivanovich.'

" 'What is it, Yemelyanushka?'

" 'If you were to take my old coat to a secondhand dealer's, how much do you think they'd give you for it, Astafy Ivanovich?'

" 'There's no knowing how much they'd give. Maybe they would give a rouble for it, Yemelyan Ilyich.'

"But if I had taken it they wouldn't have given anything for it, but would have laughed in my face for bringing such a trumpery thing. I simply said that to comfort the poor fellow, knowing the simpleton he was.

" 'But I was thinking, Astafy Ivanovich, they might give you three roubles for it; it's made of cloth, Astafy Ivanovich. How could they only give one rouble for a cloth coat?'

" 'I don't know, Yemelyan Ilyich,' said I, 'if you are thinking of taking it you should certainly ask three roubles to begin with.'

"Yemelyanushka was silent for a time, and then he addressed me again:

" 'Astafy Ivanovich.'

" 'What is it, Yemelyanushka?' I asked.

" 'Sell my coat when I die, and don't bury me in it. I can lie as well without it; and it's a thing of some value—it might come in useful.'

"I can't tell you how it made my heart ache to hear him. I saw that the death agony was coming on him. We were silent again for a bit. So an hour passed by. I looked at him again: he was still staring at me, and when he met my eyes he looked down again.

" 'Do you want some water to drink, Yemelyan Ilyich?' I asked.

" 'Give me some, God bless you, Astafy Ivanovich.'

"I gave him a drink.

" 'Thank you, Astafy Ivanovich,' said he.

" 'Is there anything else you would like, Yemelyanushka?'

" 'No, Astafy Ivanovich, there's nothing I want, but I—sort of—

" 'What?'

" 'I only—'

" 'What is it, Yemelyanushka?'

" 'Those riding-breeches—it was—sort of—I who took them—Astafy Ivanovich.'

" 'Well, God forgive you, Yemelyanushka,' said I, 'you poor, sorrowful creature. Depart in peace.'

"And I was choking myself, sir, and the tears were in my eyes. I turned aside for a moment.

" 'Astafy Ivanovich—'

"I saw Yemelyanushka wanted to tell me something; he was trying to sit up, trying to speak, and mumbling something. He flushed red all over suddenly, looked at me . . . then I saw him turn white again, whiter and whiter, and he seemed to sink away all in a minute. His head fell back, he drew one breath and gave up his soul to God."

1848

# AN UNPLEASANT PREDICAMENT

THIS unpleasant business occurred at the epoch when the regeneration of our beloved fatherland and the struggle of her valiant sons towards new hopes and destinies were beginning with irresistible force and with a touchingly naïve impetuosity. One winter evening in that period, between eleven and twelve o'clock, three highly respectable gentlemen were sitting in a comfortable and even luxuriously furnished room in a handsome house of two storeys on the Petersburg Side, and were engaged in a staid and edifying conversation on a very interesting subject. These three gentlemen were all of general's rank. They were sitting round a little table, each in a soft and handsome armchair, and as they talked, they quietly and luxuriously sipped champagne. The bottle stood on the table on a silver stand with ice around it. The fact was that the host, a privy councilor called Stepan Nikiforovich Nikiforov, an old bachelor of sixty-five, was celebrating his removal to a house he had just bought, and as it happened, also his birthday, which he had never kept before. The festivity, however, was not on a very grand scale; as we have seen already, there were only two guests, both of them former colleagues and former subordinates of Mr. Nikiforov; that is, an actual civil councilor called Semyon Ivanovich Shipulenko, and another actual civil councilor, Ivan Ilyich Pralinsky. They had arrived for tea at nine o'clock, then had begun upon the wine, and knew that at exactly half-past eleven they would have to set off home. Their host had all his life been fond of regularity. A few words about him.

He had begun his career as a petty clerk with nothing to back him, had quietly plodded on for forty-five years, knew very well what to work towards, had no ambition to draw the stars down from heaven, though he had two stars already, and particularly disliked expressing his own opinion on any subject. He was honest, too, that is, he had not happened to do anything particularly dishonest; he was a bachelor because he was an egoist; he had plenty of brains, but he could not bear showing his intelligence; he particularly disliked slovenliness and enthusiasm, regarding it as moral slovenliness; and towards the end of his life had become completely absorbed in a voluptuous, indolent comfort and systematic solitude. Though he sometimes visited people of a rather higher rank than his own, yet from his youth up he could never endure entertaining visitors himself; and of late, if he did not play a game of patience, he had been satisfied with the society of his dining-room clock, and would spend the whole evening dozing in his armchair, listening placidly to its ticking under its glass case on the chimneypiece. In appearance he was closely shaven and extremely proper-looking, he was well-preserved, looking younger than his age; he promised to go on living many years longer, and closely followed the rules of the highest good breeding. His post was a fairly comfortable one: he had to preside somewhere and to sign something. In short, he was regarded as a first-rate man. He had only one passion, or more accurately, one keen desire: that was, to have his own house, and a house built like a gentleman's residence, not a commercial investment. His desire was at last realized: he looked out and bought a house on the Petersburg Side, a good way off, it is true, but it had a garden and was an elegant house. The new owner decided that it was better for being a good way off: he did not like entertaining at home, and for driving to see anyone or to the office he had a handsome carriage of a chocolate hue, a coachman, Mihey, and two little but strong and handsome horses. All this was honorably acquired by the careful frugality of forty years, so that his heart rejoiced over it.

This was how it was that Stepan Nikiforovich felt such pleasure in his placid heart that he actually invited two friends to see him on his birthday, which he had hitherto carefully concealed from his most intimate acquaintances. He had special designs on one of these visitors. He lived in the upper storey of his new house, and he wanted a tenant for the lower half, which was built and arranged in exactly the same way. Stepan Nikiforovich was reckoning upon Semyon

Ivanovich Shipulenko, and had twice that evening broached the subject in the course of conversation. But Semyon Ivanovich made no response. The latter, too, was a man who had doggedly made a way for himself in the course of long years. He had black hair and whiskers, and a face that always had a shade of jaundice. He was a married man of morose disposition who liked to stay at home; he ruled his household with a rod of iron; he performed his official duties with the greatest self-confidence. He, too, knew perfectly well what goal he was making for, and better still, what he never would reach. He was in a good position, and he was sitting tight there. Though he looked upon the new reforms with a certain distaste, he was not particularly agitated about them: he was extremely self-confident, and listened with a shade of ironical malice to Ivan Ilyich Pralinsky expatiating on new themes. All of them had been drinking rather freely, however, so that Stepan Nikiforovich himself condescended to take part in a slight discussion with Mr. Pralinsky concerning the latest reforms. But we must say a few words about his Excellency, Mr. Pralinsky, especially as he is the chief hero of the present story.

The actual civil councilor Ivan Ilyich Pralinsky had only been "his Excellency" for four months; in short, he was a young general. He was young in years, too—only forty-three, no more—and he looked and liked to look even younger. He was a tall, handsome man, he was smart in his dress, and prided himself on its solid, dignified character; with great aplomb he displayed an order of some consequence on his breast. From his earliest childhood he had known how to acquire the airs and graces of aristocratic society, and being a bachelor, dreamed of a wealthy and even aristocratic bride. He dreamed of many other things, though he was far from being stupid. At times he was a great talker, and even liked to assume a parliamentary pose. He came of a good family. He was the son of a general, and brought up in the lap of luxury; in his tender childhood he had been dressed in velvet and fine linen, had been educated at an aristocratic school, and though he acquired very little learning there he was successful in the service, and had worked his way up to being a general. The authorities looked upon him as a capable man, and even expected great things from him in the future. Stepan Nikiforovich, under whom Ivan Ilyich had begun his career in the service, and under whom he had remained until he was made a general, had never considered him an able man and he expected of him nothing whatever. What he liked in him was that he belonged to a good family, had property—that is, a big block of buildings, let out in flats, in charge of an overseer—was connected with persons of consequence, and what was more, had a majestic bearing. Stepan Nikiforovich blamed him inwardly for excess of imagination and instability. Ivan Ilyich himself felt at times that he had too much *amour-propre* and even sensitiveness. Strange to say, he had attacks from time to time of morbid tenderness of conscience and even a kind of faint remorse. With bitterness and a secret soreness of heart he recognized now and again that he did not fly so high as he imagined. At such moments he sank into despondency, especially when he was suffering from hemorrhoids, called his life *une existence manquée,* and ceased—privately, of course—to believe even in his parliamentary capacities, calling himself a talker, a maker of phrases; and though all that, of course, did him great credit, it did not in the least prevent him from raising his head again half an hour later, and growing even more obstinately, even more conceitedly self-confident, and assuring himself that he would yet succeed in making his mark, and that he would be not only a great official, but a statesman whom Russia would long remember. He actually dreamed at times of monuments. From this it will be seen that Ivan Ilyich aimed high, though he hid his vague hopes and dreams deep in his heart, even with a certain trepidation. In short, he was a good-natured man and a poet at heart.

Of late years these morbid moments of disillusionment had begun to be more frequent. He had become peculiarly irritable, ready to take offense, and was apt to take any contradiction as an affront. But reformed Russia gave him great hopes. His promotion to the rank of general was the finishing touch. He was roused; he held his head up. He suddenly began talking freely and eloquently. He talked about the new ideas, which he very quickly and unexpectedly made his own and professed with vehemence. He sought opportunities for speaking, drove about the town, and in many places succeeded in gaining the reputation of a desperate Liberal, which flattered him greatly.

That evening, after drinking four glasses, he was particularly exuberant. He wanted on every point to confute Stepan Nikiforovich, whom he had not seen for some time past, and whom he had hitherto always respected and even obeyed. He considered him for some reason reactionary, and fell upon him with exceptional heat. Stepan Nikiforovich hardly answered him, but only listened slyly, though the subject interested him. Ivan Ilyich got hot, and in the heat of the discussion sipped his glass more often than he ought to have done. Then Stepan Nikiforovich took the bottle and at once filled his glass again, which for some reason seemed to offend Ivan Ilyich, especially as Semyon Ivanovich Shipulenko, whom he particularly despised and indeed feared on account of his cynicism and ill-nature, preserved a treacherous silence and smiled more frequently than was necessary. "They seem to take me for a schoolboy," flashed across Ivan Ilyich's mind.

"No, it was time, high time," he went on hotly. "We have put it off too long, and to my thinking humanity is the first consideration, humanity toward our inferiors, remembering that they, too, are men. Humanity will save everything and bring out all that is . . ."

"He-he-he-he!" was heard from the direction of Semyon Ivanovich.

"But why are you giving us such a talking to?" Stepan Nikiforovich protested at last, with an affable smile. "I must own, Ivan Ilyich, I have not been able to make out, so far, what you are maintaining. You advocate humanity. That is love of your fellow-creatures, isn't it?"

"Yes, if you like. I . . ."

"Allow me! As far as I can see, that's not the only ·thing. Love of one's fellow-creatures has always been fitting. The reform movement is not confined to that. All sorts of questions have arisen relating to the peasantry, the law courts, economics, government contracts, morals and . . . and . . . and there is no end to those questions, and all of them together may give rise to great upheavals, so to say. That is what we have been anxious about, and not simply humanity. . . ."

"Yes, the thing is a bit deeper than that," observed Semyon Ivanovich.

"I quite understand, and allow me to observe, Semyon Ivanovich, that I can't agree to being inferior to you in depth of understanding," Ivan Ilyich observed sarcastically and with excessive sharpness. "However, I will make so bold as to assert, Stepan Nikiforovich, that you have not understood me either. . . ."

"No, I haven't."

"And yet I maintain and everywhere advance the idea that humanity and nothing else towards one's subordinates, from the official in one's department down to the copying clerk, from the copying clerk down to the house-serf, from the servant down to the peasant ——humanity, I say, may serve, so to speak, as the cornerstone of the coming reforms and the reformation of things in general. Why? Because. Take a syllogism: I am humane, consequently I am loved. I am loved, so confidence is felt in me. There is a feeling of confidence, and so there is trust. There is trust, and so there is love . . . that is, no, I mean to say that if they trust me they will believe in the reforms, they will understand, so to speak, the essential nature of them, will, so to speak, embrace each other in a moral sense, and will settle the whole business in a friendly way, fundamentally. What are you laughing at, Semyon Ivanovich? Can't you understand?"

Stepan Nikiforovich raised his eyebrows without speaking; he was surprised.

"I fancy I have drunk a little too much," said Semyon Ivanovich sarcastically, "and so I am a little slow of comprehension. Not quite all my wits about me."

Ivan Ilyich winced.

"We should break down," Stepan Nikiforovich pronounced suddenly, after a slight pause of hesitation.

"How do you mean we should break down?" asked Ivan Ilyich, surprised at Stepan Nikiforovich's abrupt remark.

"Why, we should break under the strain." Stepan Nikiforovich evidently did not care to explain further.

"I suppose you are thinking of new wine in old bottles?" Ivan Ilyich replied, not without irony. "Well, I can answer for myself, anyway."

At that moment the clock struck half-past eleven.

"One sits on and on, but one must go at last," said Semyon Ivanovich, getting up.

But Ivan Ilyich was ahead of him; he got up from the table and took his sable cap from the chimney-piece. He looked as though he had been insulted.

"So how is it to be, Semyon Ivanovich? Will you think it over?" said Stepan Nikiforovich, as he saw the visitors out.

"About the flat, you mean? I'll think it over, I'll think it over."

"Well, when you have made up your mind, let me know as soon as possible."

"Still on business?" Mr. Pralinsky observed affably, in a slightly ingratiating tone, playing with his hat. It seemed to him as though they were forgetting him.

Stepan Nikiforovich raised his eyebrows and remained mute, as a sign that he would not detain his visitors. Semyon Ivanovich made haste to bow himself out.

"Well . . . after that what is one to expect . . . if you don't understand the simple rules of good manners . . ." Mr. Pralinsky reflected to himself, and held out his hand to Stepan Nikiforovich in a particularly offhand way.

In the hall Ivan Ilyich wrapped himself up in his light, expensive fur coat; he tried for some reason not to notice Semyon Ivanovich's shabby raccoon, and they both began descending the stairs.

"The old man seemed offended," said Ivan Ilyich to the silent Semyon Ivanovich.

"No, why?" answered the latter with cool composure.

"Servile flunky," Ivan Ilyich thought to himself.

They went out at the front door. Semyon Ivanovich's sledge with a grey ugly horse drove up.

"What the devil! What has Trifon done with my carriage?" cried Ivan Ilyich, not seeing his carriage.

The carriage was nowhere to be seen. Stepan Nikiforovich's servant knew nothing about it. They appealed to Varlam, Semyon Ivanovich's coachman, and received the answer that he had been standing there all the time and that the carriage had been there, but now there was no sign of it.

"An unpleasant predicament," Mr. Shipulenko pronounced. "Shall I take you home?"

"Scoundrelly people!" Mr. Pralinsky cried with fury. "He asked me, the rascal, to let him go to a wedding close here in the Petersburg Side; some crony of his was getting married, deuce take her! I sternly forbade him to absent himself, and now I'll bet he has gone off there."

"He certainly has gone there, sir," observed Varlam; "but he promised to be back in a minute, to be here in time, that is."

"Well, there it is! I had a presentiment that this would happen! I'll give it to him!"

"You'd better give him a good flogging once or twice at the police-station, then he will do what you tell him," said Semyon Ivanovich, as he wrapped the rug round him.

"Please don't you trouble, Semyon Ivanovich!"

"Well, won't you let me take you along?"

"*Merci, bon voyage.*"

Semyon Ivanovich drove off, while Ivan Ilyich set off on foot along the wooden sidewalk, conscious of a rather acute irritation.

"Yes, indeed I'll give it to you now, you rogue! I am going on foot on purpose to make you feel it, to frighten you! He will come back and hear that his master has gone off on foot . . . the black-guard!"

Ivan Ilyich had never abused anyone like this, but he was greatly angered, and besides, there was a buzzing in his head. He was not given to drink, so five or six glasses soon affected him. But the night was enchanting. There was a frost, but it was remarkably still and there was no wind. There was a clear, starry sky. The full moon was bathing the earth in soft silver light. It was so lovely that after walking some fifty paces Ivan Ilyich almost forgot his troubles. He felt particularly pleased. People quickly change from one mood to another when they are a little drunk. He was even pleased with the ugly little wooden houses of the deserted street.

"It's really a capital thing that I am walking," he thought; "it's a lesson to Trifon and a pleasure to me. I really ought to walk oftener. And I shall soon pick up a sledge on the Great Prospect. It's a glorious night. What little houses they all are! I suppose small fry live here, clerks, tradesmen, perhaps. . . . That Stepan Nikiforovich! What reactionaries they all are, those old fogies! Fogies, yes, *c'est le mot.* He is a sensible man, though; he has that *bon sense,* sober, practical understanding of things. But they are old, old. There is a lack of . . . what is it? There is a lack of something. . . . 'We shall break down.' What did he mean by that? He actually pondered when he said it. He didn't understand me a bit. And yet how could he help understanding? It was more difficult not to understand it than to understand it. The chief thing is that I am convinced, convinced in my soul. Humanity . . . the love of one's kind. Restore a man to himself, revive his personal dignity, and then . . . when the ground is prepared, get to work. I believe that's clear? Yes! Allow me, your Excellency; take a syllogism, for instance: we meet, for instance, a clerk, a poor, downtrodden clerk. 'Well . . . who are you?' Answer: 'A clerk.' Very good, a clerk; further: 'What sort of clerk are you?' Answer: 'I am such and such a clerk,' he says. 'Are you in the service?' 'I am.' 'Do you want to be happy?' 'I do.' 'What do you need for happiness?' 'This and that.' 'Why?' 'Because . . .' and there the man understands me with a couple of words, the man's mine, the man is caught, so to speak, in a net, and I can do what I like with him, that is, for his good. Horrid man that Semyon Ivanovich! And what a nasty phiz he has! . . . 'Flog him at the police-station,' he said that on purpose. No, you are talking rubbish; you can flog, but I'm not going to; I shall punish Trifon with words, I shall punish him with reproaches, he will feel it. As for flogging, h'm! . . . it is an open question, h'm! . . . What about going to Emérance? Oh, damnation take it, the cursed sidewalk!" he cried out, suddenly trip-ping up. "And this is the capital. Enlightenment! One might break one's leg. H'm! I detest that Semyon Ivanovich; a most revolting phiz. He was chuckling at me just now when I said they would em-brace each other in a moral sense. Well, and they will embrace each other, and what's that to do with you? I am not going to embrace you; I'd rather embrace a peasant. . . . If I meet a peasant, I shall talk to him. I was drunk, though, and perhaps did not express myself properly. Possibly I am not expressing myself rightly now. . . . H'm! I shall never touch wine again. In the evening you babble, and next morning you are sorry for it. After all, I am walking quite steadily. . . . But they are all scoundrels, anyhow!"

So Ivan Ilyich meditated incoherently and by snatches, as he went on striding along the sidewalk. The fresh air began to affect him, set his mind working. Five minutes later he would have felt soothed and sleepy. But all at once, scarcely two paces from the Great Pros-pect, he heard music. He looked round. On the other side of the street, in a very tumbledown-looking long wooden house of one storey, there was a great fête, there was the scraping of violins, and the droning of a double bass, and the squeaky tooting of a flute play-ing a very gay quadrille tune. Under the windows stood an audience, mainly of women in wadded pelisses with kerchiefs on their heads; they were making every effort to see something through a crack in the shutters. Evidently there was a gay party within. The sound of the thud of dancing feet reached the other side of the street. Ivan Ilyich saw a policeman standing not far off, and went up to him.

"Whose house is that, brother?" he asked, flinging his expensive

fur coat open, just far enough to allow the policeman to see the imposing decoration on his breast.

"It belongs to the registration clerk Pseldonimov," answered the
policeman, drawing himself up instantly, discerning the decoration.

"Pseldonimov? Bah! Pseldonimov! What is he up to? Getting
married?"

"Yes, your Honor, to a daughter of a titular councilor, Mlekopitayev, a titular councilor . . . used to serve in the municipal department. That house goes with the bride."

"So that now the house is Pseldonimov's and not Mlekopitayev's?"

"Yes, Pseldonimov's, your Honor. It was Mlekopitayev's, but
now it is Pseldonimov's."

"H'm! I am asking you, my man, because I am his chief. I am a
general in the same office in which Pseldonimov serves."

"Just so, your Excellency."

The policeman drew himself up more stiffly than ever, while Ivan
Ilyich seemed to ponder. He stood still and meditated. . . .

Yes, Pseldonimov really was in his department and in his own
office; he remembered that. He was a little clerk with a salary of ten
roubles a month. As Mr. Pralinsky had received his department very
lately he might not have remembered precisely all his subordinates,
but Pseldonimov he remembered just because of his surname. It had
caught his eye from the very first, so that at the time he had had the
curiosity to look with special attention at the possessor of such a
surname. He remembered now a very young man with a long hooked
nose, with tufts of flaxen hair, lean and ill-nourished, in an impossible
uniform, and with unmentionables so impossible as to be actually
unseemly; he remembered how the thought had flashed through his
mind at the time: shouldn't he give the poor fellow ten roubles for
Christmas, to spend on his wardrobe? But as the poor fellow's face
was too austere, and his expression extremely unprepossessing, even
exciting repulsion, the good-natured idea somehow faded away of
itself, so Pseldonimov did not get his bonus. He had been the more
surprised when this same Pseldonimov had not more than a week
before asked for leave to be married. Ivan Ilyich remembered that
he had somehow not had time to go into the matter, so that the matter of the marriage had been settled offhand, in haste. But yet he did
remember exactly that Pseldonimov was receiving a wooden house
and four hundred roubles in cash as dowry with his bride. The cir-

cumstance had surprised him at the time; he remembered that he had
made a slight jest over the juxtaposition of the names Pseldonimov
and Mlekopitayev. He remembered all that clearly.

He recalled it, and grew more and more pensive. It is well known
that whole trains of thought sometimes pass through our brains instantaneously as though they were sensations, without being translated into human speech, still less into literary language. But we
will try to translate these sensations of our hero's, and present to the
reader at least the kernel of them, so to say, what was most essential
and nearest to reality in them. For many of our sensations when
translated into ordinary language seem absolutely unreal. That is why
they never find expression, though every one has them. Of course
Ivan Ilyich's sensations and thoughts were a little incoherent. But
you know the reason.

"Why," flashed through his mind, "here we all talk and talk, but
when it comes to action—it all ends in nothing. Here, for instance,
take this Pseldonimov: he has just come from his wedding full of
hope and excitement, looking forward to his wedding feast. . . .
This is one of the most blissful days of his life. . . . Now he is busy
with his guests, is giving a banquet, a modest one, poor, but gay and
full of genuine gladness. . . . What if he knew that at this very moment I, I, his superior, his chief, was standing by his house listening
to the music? Yes, really how would he feel? No, what would he
feel if I suddenly walked in? H'm! . . . Of course at first he would
be frightened, he would be dumb with embarrassment. . . . I should
be in his way, and perhaps should upset everything. Yes, that would
be so if any other general went in, but not I. . . . That's a fact, anyone else, but not I. . . .

"Yes, Stepan Nikiforovich! You did not understand me just now,
but here is an example ready for you.

"Yes, we·all make an outcry about acting humanely, but we are
not capable of heroism, of fine actions.

"What sort of heroism? This sort. Consider: in the existing relations of the various members of society, for me, for me, after midnight to go in to the wedding of my subordinate, a registration clerk,
at ten roubles the month—why, it would mean embarrassment, a revolution, the last days of Pompeii, a nonsensical folly. No one would
understand it. Stepan Nikiforovich would die before he understood
it. Why, he said we should break down. Yes, but that's you old peo-

ple, inert, paralytic people; but I shan't break down, I will transform the last day of Pompeii into a day of the utmost sweetness for my subordinate, and a wild action into an action normal, patriarchal, lofty and moral. How? Like this. Kindly listen. . . .

"Here . . . I go in, suppose; they are amazed, leave off dancing, look wildly at me, draw back. Quite so, but at once I speak out: I go straight up to the frightened Pseldonimov, and with a most cordial, affable smile, in the simplest words, I say: 'This is how it is, I have been at his Excellency Stepan Nikiforovich's. I expect you know, close here in the neighborhood. . . .' Well, then, lightly, in a laughing way, I shall tell him of my adventure with Trifon. From Trifon I shall pass on to saying how I walked here on foot. . . . 'Well, I heard music, I inquired of a policeman, and learned, brother, that it was your wedding. Let me go in, I thought, to my subordinate's; let me see how my clerks enjoy themselves and . . . celebrate their wedding. I suppose you won't turn me out?' Turn me out! What a word for a subordinate! How the devil could he dream of turning me out! I fancy that he would be half crazy, that he would rush headlong to seat me in an armchair, would be trembling with delight, would hardly know what he was doing for the first minute!

"Why, what can be simpler, more elegant than such an action? Why did I go in? That's another question! That is, so to say, the moral aspect of the question. That's the pith

"H'm, what was I thinking about, yes!

"Well, of course they will make me sit down with the most important guest, some titular councilor or a relation who's a retired captain with a red nose. Gogol describes these eccentrics so capitally. Well, I shall make acquaintance, of course, with the bride, I shall compliment her, I shall encourage the guests. I shall beg them not to stand on ceremony. To enjoy themselves, to go on dancing. I shall make jokes, I shall laugh; in fact, I shall be affable and charming. I am always affable and charming when I am pleased with myself. . . . H'm . . . the point is that I believe I am still a little, well, not drunk exactly, but . . .

"Of course, as a gentleman I shall be quite on an equality with them, and shall not expect any especial marks of. . . . But morally, morally, it is a different matter; they will understand and appreciate it. . . . My actions will evoke their nobler feelings. . . . Well, I shall stay for half an hour . . . even for an hour; I shall leave, of course, before supper; but they will be bustling about, baking and roasting, they will be making low bows, but I will only drink a glass, congratulate them and refuse supper. I shall say—'business.' And as soon as I pronounce the word 'business,' all of them will at once have sternly respectful faces. By that I shall delicately remind them that there is a difference between them and me. The earth and the sky. It is not that I want to impress that on them, but it must be done . . . it's even essential in a moral sense, when all is said and done. I shall smile at once, however, I shall even laugh, and then they will all pluck up courage again. . . . I shall jest a little again with the bride; h'm! . . . I may even hint that I shall come again in just nine months to stand godfather, he-he! And she will be sure to be brought to bed by then. They multiply, you know, like rabbits. And they will all roar with laughter and the bride will blush; I shall kiss her feelingly on the forehead, even give her my blessing . . . and next day my exploit will be known at the office. Next day I shall be stern again, next day I shall be exacting again, even implacable, but they will all know what I am like. They will know my heart, they will know my essential nature: 'He is stern as a chief, but as a man he is an angel!' And I shall have conquered them; I shall have captured them by one little act which would never have entered your head; they would be mine; I should be their father, they would be my children. . . . Come now, your Excellency Stepan Nikiforovich, go and do likewise. . . .

"But do you know, do you understand, that Pseldonimov will tell his children how the General himself feasted and even drank at his wedding! Why, you know those children would tell their children, and those would tell their grandchildren as a most sacred story that a grand gentleman, a statesman (and I shall be all that by then) did them the honor, and so on, and so on. Why, I am morally elevating the humiliated, I restore him to himself. . . . Why, he gets a salary of ten roubles a month! . . . If I repeat this five or ten times, or something of the sort, I shall gain popularity all over the place. . . . My name will be printed on the hearts of all, and the devil only knows what will come of that popularity! . . ."

These, or something like these, were Ivan Ilyich's reflections, (a man says all sorts of things sometimes to himself, gentlemen, especially when he is in a rather eccentric condition). All these meditations passed through his mind in something like half a minute, and of course he might have confined himself to these dreams and, after mentally putting Stepan Nikiforovich to shame, have gone very peacefully home and to bed. And he would have done well. But the trouble of it was that the moment was an eccentric one.

As ill-luck would have it, at that very instant the self-satisfied faces of Stepan Nikiforovich and Semyon Ivanovich suddenly rose before his heated imagination.

"We shall break down!" repeated Stepan Nikiforovich, smiling disdainfully.

"He-he-he," Semyon Ivanovich seconded him with his nastiest smile.

"Well, we'll see whether we do break down!" Ivan Ilyich said resolutely, with a rush of heat to his face.

He stepped down from the sidewalk and with resolute steps went straight across the street towards the house of his registration clerk Pseldonimov.

His star drew him onward. He walked confidently in at the open gate and contemptuously thrust aside with his foot the shaggy, husky little sheep-dog who flew at his legs with a hoarse bark, more as a matter of form than with any real intention. Along a wooden plank he went to the covered porch which gave like a booth on the yard, and by three decaying wooden steps he went up to the tiny entry. Here, though a tallow candle or something in the way of a night light was burning somewhere in a corner, it did not prevent Ivan Ilyich from putting his left foot just as it was, in its galosh, into a galantine which had been stood out there to cool. Ivan Ilyich bent down, and looking with curiosity, saw that there were two other dishes of some sort of jelly and also two shapes apparently of blanc-mange. The squashed galantine embarrassed him, and for one brief instant the question flashed through his mind, whether he should not slink away at once. But he considered this too low. Reflecting that no one would have seen him, and that they would never think he had done it, he hurriedly wiped his galosh to conceal all traces, fumbled for the felt-covered door, opened it and found himself in a very little anteroom. Half of it was literally piled up with greatcoats, wadded jackets, cloaks, capes, scarves and galoshes. In the other half the musicians had been installed; two violins, a flute, and a double bass, a band of four, picked up, of course, in the street. They were sitting at an unpainted wooden table, lighted by a single tallow candle, and with the utmost vigor were sawing out the last figure of the quadrille. From the open door into the drawing-room one could see the dancers in the midst of dust, tobacco smoke and fumes. There was a frenzy of gayety. There were sounds of laughter, shouts and shrieks from the ladies. The gentlemen stamped like a squadron of horses. Above all the bedlam there rang out words of command from the leader of the dance, probably an extremely free-and-easy, and even unbuttoned gentleman: "Gentlemen, advance, ladies' chain, set to partners!" and so on, and so on. Ivan Ilyich in some excitement cast off his coat and galoshes, and with his cap in his hand went into the room. He was no longer reflecting, however.

For the first minute nobody noticed him; all were absorbed in dancing the quadrille to the end. Ivan Ilyich stood as though entranced, and could make out nothing definite in the chaos. He caught glimpses of ladies' dresses, of gentlemen with cigarettes between their teeth. He caught a glimpse of a lady's pale blue scarf which flicked him on the nose. After the wearer, a medical student, with his hair blown in all directions, pranced by in wild delight and jostled violently against him on the way. He caught a glimpse, too, of an officer of some description, who looked half a mile high. Someone in an unnaturally shrill voice shouted, "O-o-oh, Pseldonimov!" as the speaker flew by stamping. It was sticky under Ivan Ilyich's feet; evidently the floor had been waxed. In the room, which was a very small one, there were about thirty people.

But a minute later the quadrille was over, and almost at once the very thing Ivan Ilyich had pictured when he was dreaming on the sidewalk took place.

A stifled murmur, a strange whisper passed over the whole company, including the dancers, who had not yet had time to take breath and wipe their perspiring faces. All eyes, all faces began quickly turning towards the newly arrived guest. Then they all seemed to draw back a little and beat a retreat. Those who had not noticed him were pulled by their coats or dresses and informed. They looked round and at once beat a retreat with the others. Ivan Ilyich was still standing at the door without moving a step forward, and between him and the company there stretched an ever widening empty space of floor strewn with countless sweetmeat wrappings, bits of paper and cigarette ends. All at once a young man in a uniform, with a shock of flaxen hair and a hooked nose, stepped timidly out into that empty space. He moved forward, hunched up, and looked at the unexpected visitor exactly with the expression with which a dog looks at its master when the latter has called him up and is going to kick him.

"Good evening, Pseldonimov, do you know me?" said Ivan Ilyich, and felt at the same minute that he had said this very awkwardly; he felt, too, that he was perhaps doing something horribly stupid at that moment.

"You-our Ex-cel-len-cy!" muttered Pseldonimov.

"To be sure. . . . I have called in to see you quite by chance, my friend, as you can probably imagine. . . ."

But evidently Pseldonimov could imagine nothing. He stood with staring eyes in the utmost preplexity.

"You won't turn me out, I suppose. . . . Pleased or not, you must make a visitor welcome. . . ." Ivan Ilyich went on, feeling that he was confused to a point of unseemly feebleness; that he was trying to smile and was utterly unable; that the humorous reference to Stepan Nikiforovich and Trifon was becoming more and more impossible. But as ill luck would have it, Pseldonimov did not recover from his stupefaction, and still gazed at him with a perfectly idiotic air. Ivan Ilyich winced, he felt that in another minute something incredibly foolish would happen.

"I am not in the way, am I? . . . I'll go away," he faintly articulated, and there was a tremor at the right corner of his mouth.

But Pseldonimov had recovered himself.

"Good heavens, your Excellency . . . the honor . . ." he muttered, bowing hurriedly. "Graciously sit down, your Excellency. . . ." And recovering himself still further, he motioned him with both hands to a sofa before which a table had been moved away to make room for the dancing.

Ivan Ilyich felt relieved and sank on the sofa; at once someone flew to move the table up to him. He took a cursory look round and saw that he was the only person sitting down, all the others were standing, even the ladies. A bad sign. But it was not yet time to reassure and encourage them. The company still held back, while before him, bending double, stood Pseldonimov, utterly alone, still completely at a loss and very far from smiling. It was horrid; in short, our hero endured such misery at that moment that his Harun-al-

Rashid-like descent upon his subordinates for the sake of principle might well have been reckoned an heroic action. But suddenly a little figure made its appearance beside Pseldonimov, and began bowing. To his inexpressible pleasure and even happiness, Ivan Ilyich at once recognized him as the head clerk of his office, Akim Petrovich Zubikov, and though, of course, he was not acquainted with him, he knew him to be a businesslike and exemplary clerk. He got up at once and held out his hand to Akim Petrovich—his whole hand, not two fingers. The latter took it in both of his with the deepest respect. The general was triumphant, the situation was saved.

And now indeed Pseldonimov was no longer, so to say, the second person, but the third. It was possible to address his remarks to the head clerk in his necessity, taking him for an acquaintance and even an intimate one, and Pseldonimov meanwhile could only be silent and in a tremor of reverence. So that the proprieties were observed. And some explanation was essential, Ivan Ilyich felt that; he saw that all the guests were expecting something, that the whole household was gathered together in the doorway, almost creeping, climbing over one another in their anxiety to see and hear him. What was horrid was that the head clerk in his foolishness remained standing.

"Why are you standing?" said Ivan Ilyich, awkwardly motioning him to a seat on the sofa beside him.

"Oh, don't trouble. . . . I'll sit here." And Akim Petrovich hurriedly sat down on a chair, almost as it was being placed for him by Pseldonimov, who remained obstinately standing.

"Can you imagine what happened," addressing himself exclusively to Akim Petrovich in a rather quavering, though free and easy voice. He even drawled out his words, with special emphasis on some syllables, pronounced the vowel *ah* like *eh;* in short, felt and was conscious that he was being affected but could not control himself: some external force was at work. He was painfully conscious of many things at that moment.

"Can you imagine, I have only just come from Stepan Nikiforovich Nikiforov's, you have heard of him perhaps, the privy councilor. You know . . . on that special committee. . . ."

Akim Petrovich bent his whole person forward respectfully: as much as to say, "Of course we have heard of him."

"He is your neighbor now," Ivan Ilyich went on, for one instant for the sake of ease and good manners addressing Pseldonimov, but he quickly turned away again, on seeing from the latter's eyes that it made absolutely no difference to him.

"The old fellow, as you know, has been dreaming all his life of buying himself a house. . . . Well, and he has bought it. And a very pretty house too. Yes. . . . And today was his birthday and he had never celebrated it before, he used even to keep it secret from us, he was too stingy to admit it, he-he. But now he is so delighted over his new house, that he invited Semyon Ivanovich Shipulenko and me, you know."

Akim Petrovich bent forward again. He bent forward zealously. Ivan Ilyich felt somewhat comforted. It had struck him, indeed, that the head clerk possibly was guessing that he was an indispensable support for his Excellency at that moment. That would have been more horrid than anything.

"So we sat together, the three of us, he gave us champagne, we talked about problems . . . even dis-pu-ted. . . . He-he!"

Akim Petrovich raised his eyebrows respectfully.

"Only that is not the point. When I take leave of him at last—he is a punctual old fellow, goes to bed early, you know, in his old age —I go out. . . . My Trifon is nowhere to be seen! I am anxious, I make inquiries. 'What has Trifon done with the carriage?' It comes out that hoping I should stay on, he had gone off to the wedding of some friend of his, or sister maybe. . . . Goodness only knows. Somewhere here on the Petersburg Side. And took the carriage with him while he was about it."

Again for the sake of good manners the general glanced in the direction of Pseldonimov. The latter promptly gave a wriggle, but not at all the sort of wriggle the general would have liked. "He has no sympathy, no heart," flashed through his brain.

"You don't say so!" said Akim Petrovich, greatly impressed. A faint murmur of surprise ran through all the crowd.

"Can you fancy my position. . . ." (Ivan Ilyich glanced at them all). "There was nothing for it, I set off on foot, I thought I would trudge to the Great Prospect, and there find some cabby . . . he-he!"

"He-he-he!" Akim Petrovich echoed. Again a murmur, but this time on a more cheerful note, passed through the crowd. At that moment the chimney of a lamp on the wall broke with a crash. Some-one rushed zealously to see to it. Pseldonimov started and looked sternly at the lamp, but the general took no notice of it, and all was serene again.

"I walked . . . and the night was so lovely, so still. All at once I heard a band, stamping, dancing. I inquired of a policeman; it is Pseldonimov's wedding. Why, you are giving a ball to all Petersburg Side, my friend. Ha-ha." He turned to Pseldonimov again.

"He-he-he! To be sure," Akim Petrovich responded. There was a stir among the guests again, but what was most foolish was that Pseldonimov, though he bowed, did not smile even now, but seemed as though he were made of wood. "Is he a fool or what?" thought Ivan Ilyich. "He ought to have smiled at that point, the ass, and everything would have run easily." There was a fury of impatience in his heart.

"I thought I would go in to see my clerk. He won't turn me out I expect . . . pleased or not, one must welcome a guest. You must please excuse me, my dear fellow. If I am in the way, I will go . . . I only came in to have a look. . . ."

But little by little a general stir was beginning.

Akim Petrovich looked at him with a mawkishly sweet expression as though to say, "How could your Excellency be in the way?" All the guests stirred and began to display the first symptoms of being at their ease. Almost all the ladies sat down. A good sign and a reassuring one. The boldest spirits among them fanned themselves with their handkerchiefs. One of them in a shabby velvet dress said something with intentional loudness. The officer addressed by her would have liked to answer her as loudly, but seeing that they were the only ones speaking aloud, he subsided. The men, for the most part government clerks, with two or three students among them, looked at one another as though egging each other on to unbend, cleared their throats, and began to move a few steps in different directions. No one, however, was particularly timid, but they were all restive, and almost all of them looked with a hostile expression at the personage who had burst in upon them, to destroy their gayety. The officer, ashamed of his cowardice, began to edge up to the table.

"But I say, my friend, allow me to ask you your name," Ivan Ilyich asked Pseldonimov.

"Porfiry Petrovich, your Excellency," answered the latter, with staring eyes as though on parade.

"Introduce me, Porfiry Petrovich, to your bride. . . . Take me to her . . . I . . ."

And he showed signs of a desire to get up. But Pseldonimov ran full speed to the drawing-room. The bride, however, was standing close by at the door, but as soon as she heard herself mentioned, she hid. A minute later Pseldonimov led her up by the hand. The guests all moved aside to make way for them. Ivan Ilyich got up solemnly and addressed himself to her with a most affable smile.

"Very, very much pleased to make your acquaintance," he pronounced with a most aristocratic half-bow, "and especially on such a day. . . ."

He gave a meaning smile. There was an agreeable flutter among the ladies.

"*Charmée*," the lady in the velvet dress pronounced, almost aloud.

The bride was a match for Pseldonimov. She was a thin little lady not more than seventeen, pale, with a very small face and a sharp little nose. Her quick, active little eyes were not at all embarrassed; on the contrary, they looked at him steadily and even with a shade of resentment. Evidently Pseldonimov was marrying her for her beauty. She was dressed in a white muslin dress over a pink slip. Her neck was thin, and she had a figure like a chicken's with the bones all sticking out. She was not equal to making any response to the general's affability.

"But she is very pretty," he went on, in an undertone, as though addressing Pseldonimov only, though intentionally speaking so that the bride could hear.

But on this occasion, too, Pseldonimov again answered absolutely nothing, and did not even wriggle. Ivan Ilyich fancied that there was something cold, suppressed in his eyes, as though he had something peculiarly malignant in his mind. And yet he had at all costs to wring some sensibility out of him. Why, that was the object of his coming.

"They are a couple, though!" he thought.

And he turned again to the bride, who had seated herself beside him on the sofa, but in answer to his two or three questions he got nothing but "Yes" or "No," and hardly that.

"If only she had been overcome with confusion," he thought to himself, "then I should have begun to banter her. But as it is, my position is impossible."

And as ill-luck would have it, Akim Petrovich, too, was mute; though this was only due to his foolishness, it was still unpardonable.

"My friends! Haven't I perhaps interfered with your enjoyment?" he said, addressing the whole company.

He felt that the very palms of his hands were perspiring.

"No . . . don't trouble, your Excellency; we are beginning directly, but now . . . we are getting cool," answered the officer.

The bride looked at him with pleasure; the officer was not old, and wore the uniform of some branch of the service. Pseldonimov was still standing in the same place, bending forward, and it seemed as though his hooked nose stood out further than ever. He looked and listened like a footman standing with the greatcoat on his arm, waiting for the end of his master's farewell conversation. Ivan Ilyich made this comparison himself. He was losing his head; he felt that he was in an awkward position, that the ground was giving way under his feet, that he had got in somewhere and could not find his way out, as though he were in the dark.

Suddenly the guests all moved aside, and a short, thick-set, middle-aged woman made her appearance, dressed plainly though she was in her best, with a big shawl on her shoulders, pinned at her throat, and on her head a cap to which she was evidently unaccustomed. In her hands she carried a small round tray on which stood a full but uncorked bottle of champagne and two glasses, neither more nor less. Evidently the bottle was intended for only two guests.

The middle-aged lady approached the general.

"Don't look down on us, your Excellency," she said, bowing. "Since you have deigned to do my son the honor of coming to his wedding, we beg you graciously to drink to the health of the young people. Do not disdain us; do us the honor."

Ivan Ilyich clutched at her as though she were his salvation. She was by no means an old woman—forty-five or forty-six, not more; but she had such a good-natured, rosy-cheeked, such a round and candid Russian face, she smiled so good-humoredly, bowed so simply, that Ivan Ilyich was almost comforted and began to hope again.

"So you are the mo-other of your so-on?" he said, getting up from the sofa.

"Yes, my mother, your Excellency," mumbled Pseldonimov, craning his long neck and thrusting forward his long nose again.

"Ah! I am delighted—de-light-ed to make your acquaintance."

"Do not refuse us, your Excellency."

"With the greatest pleasure."

The tray was put down. Pseldonimov dashed forward to pour out the wine. Ivan Ilyich, still standing, took the glass.

"I am particularly, particularly glad on this occasion, that I can," he began, "—that I can . . . testify before all of you . . . In short, as your chief . . . I wish you, madam" (he turned to the bride), "and you, friend Porfiry, I wish you the fullest, completest happiness for many long years."

And he positively drained the glass with feeling, the seventh he had drunk that evening. Pseldonimov looked at him gravely and even sullenly. The general was beginning to feel an agonizing hatred of him.

"And that scarecrow" (he looked at the officer) "keeps obtruding himself. He might at least have shouted 'Hurrah!' and it would have gone off, it would have gone off . . ."

"And you too, Akim Petrovich, drink a glass to their health," added the mother, addressing the head clerk. "You are his superior, he is under you. Look after my boy, I beg you as a mother. And don't forget us in the future, our good, kind friend, Akim Petrovich."

"How nice these old Russian women are!" thought Ivan Ilyich. "She has livened us all up. I have always loved the people—"

At that moment another tray was brought to the table; it was brought in by a maid wearing a crackling cotton dress that had never been washed, and a crinoline. She could hardly grasp the tray in both hands, it was so big. On it there were numbers of plates of apples, sweets, fruit meringues and fruit cheeses, walnuts and so on, and so on. The tray had been till then in the drawing-room for the delectation of all the guests, and especially the ladies. But now it was brought to the general alone.

"Do not disdain our humble fare, your Excellency. What we have we are pleased to offer," the old lady repeated, bowing.

"Delighted!" said Ivan Ilyich, and with real pleasure took a walnut and cracked it between his fingers. He had made up his mind to win popularity at all costs.

Meantime the bride suddenly giggled.

"What is it?" asked Ivan Ilyich with a smile, encouraged by this sign of life.

"Ivan Kostenkinych, here, makes me laugh," she answered, looking down.

The general distinguished, indeed, a flaxen-headed young man, exceedingly good-looking, who was sitting on a chair at the other end of the sofa, whispering something to Madame Pseldonimov. The young man stood up. He was apparently very young and very shy.

"I was telling the lady about a 'dream book,' your Excellency," he muttered as though apologizing.

"About what sort of 'dream book'?" asked Ivan Ilyich condescendingly.

"There is a new 'dream book,' a literary one. I was telling the lady that to dream of Mr. Panayev means spilling coffee on one's shirt front."

"What innocence!" thought Ivan Ilyich, with positive annoyance.

Though the young man flushed very red as he said it, he was incredibly delighted that he had said this about Mr. Panayev.

"To be sure, I have heard of it . . ." responded his Excellency.

"No, there is something better than that," said a voice quite close to Ivan Ilyich. "There is a new encyclopedia being published, and they say Mr. Krayevsky will write articles . . . and satirical literature."

This was said by a young man who was by no means embarrassed, but rather free and easy. He was wearing gloves and a white waistcoat, and carried a hat in his hand. He did not dance, and looked condescending, for he was on the staff of a satirical paper called *The Firebrand*, and gave himself airs accordingly. He had come casually to the wedding, invited as an honored guest of the Pseldonimovs, with whom he was on intimate terms and with whom only a year before he had lived in very poor lodgings, kept by a German woman. He drank vodka, however, and for that purpose had more than once withdrawn to a snug little back room to which all the guests knew their way. The general disliked him extremely.

"And the reason that's funny," broke in joyfully the flaxen-headed young man, who had talked of the shirt front and at whom the young man on the comic paper looked with hatred in consequence, "it's funny, your Excellency, because it is supposed by the writer that Mr. Krayevsky does not know how to spell, and thinks that 'satirical' ought to be written with a *y* instead of an *i*."

But the poor young man scarcely finished his sentence; he could see from his eyes that the general knew all this long ago, for the general himself looked embarrassed, and evidently because he knew it. The young man seemed inconceivably ashamed. He succeeded in effacing himself completely, and remained very melancholy all the rest of the evening. But to make up for that the young man on the staff of the *Firebrand* came up nearer, and seemed to be intending to sit down somewhere close by. Such free and easy manners struck Ivan Ilyich as rather shocking.

"Tell me, please, Porfiry," he began, in order to say something, "why—I have always wanted to ask you about it in person—why you are called Pseldonimov instead of Pseudonimov? Your name surely must be Pseudonimov."

"I cannot inform you exactly, your Excellency," said Pseldonimov.

"It must have been that when his father went into the service they made a mistake in his papers, so that he has remained now Pseldonimov," put in Akim Petrovich. "That does happen."

"Un-doubted-ly," the general said with warmth, "un-doubted-ly; for only think, Pseudonimov comes from the literary word pseudonym, while Pseldonimov means nothing."

"Due to foolishness," added Akim Petrovich.

"You mean what is due to foolishness?"

"The Russian common people in their foolishness often alter letters, and sometimes pronounce them in their own way. For instance, they say *nevalid* instead of *invalid*."

"Oh, yes, *nevalid*, he-he-he . . ."

"Mumber, too, they say, your Excellency," boomed out the tall officer, who had long been itching to distinguish himself in some way.

"What do you mean by mumber?"

"Mumber instead of number, your Excellency."

"Oh, yes, mumber . . . instead of number. . . . To be sure, to be sure . . . He-he-he!" Ivan Ilyich had to do a chuckle for the benefit of the officer too.

The officer straightened his tie.

"Another thing they say is nigh by," the young man on the comic paper put in. But his Excellency tried not to hear this. His chuckles were not at everybody's disposal.

"Nigh by, instead of nearby," the young man on the comic paper persisted, in evident irritation.

Ivan Ilyich looked at him sternly.

"Come, why persist?" Pseldonimov whispered to him.

"Why, I was talking. Mayn't one speak?" the latter protested in a whisper; but he said no more and with secret fury walked out of the room.

He made his way straight to the attractive little back room where, for the benefit of the dancing gentlemen, vodka of two sorts, salt fish, caviar cut into slices and a bottle of very strong sherry of Russian make had been set early in the evening on a little table, covered with a Yaroslav cloth. With anger in his heart he was pouring himself out a glass of vodka, when suddenly the medical student with the dishevelled locks, the foremost dancer and cutter of capers at Pseldonimov's ball, rushed in. He fell on the decanter with greedy haste.

"They are just going to begin!" he said rapidly, helping himself. "Come and look, I am going to dance a solo on my head; after supper I shall risk the fish dance. It is just the thing for the wedding. So to speak, a friendly hint to Pseldonimov. She's a jolly creature that Kleopatra Semyonovna, you can venture on anything you like with her."

"He's a reactionary," said the young man on the comic paper gloomily, as he tossed off his vodka.

"Who is a reactionary?"

"Why, the personage before whom they set those sweetmeats. He's a reactionary, I tell you."

"What nonsense!" muttered the student, and he rushed out of the room, hearing the opening bars of the quadrille.

Left alone, the young man on the comic paper poured himself out another glass to give himself more assurance and independence; he drank and ate a snack of something, and never had the actual civil councilor Ivan Ilyich made for himself a bitterer foe more implacably bent on revenge than was the young man on the staff of the *Firebrand* whom he had so slighted, especially after the latter had drunk two glasses of vodka. Alas! Ivan Ilyich suspected nothing of the sort. He did not suspect another circumstance of prime importance either, which had an influence on the mutual relations of the guests and his Excellency. The fact was that though he had given a proper and even detailed explanation of his presence at his clerk's wedding, this explanation did not really satisfy anyone, and the visitors were still embarrassed. But suddenly everything was transformed as though by magic, all were reassured and ready to enjoy themselves, to laugh, to shriek, to dance, exactly as though the unexpected visitor were not in the room. The cause of it was a rumor, a whisper, a report which spread in some unknown way that the visitor was not quite . . . it seemed—was, in fact, "a little top-heavy." And though this seemed at first a horrible calumny, it began by degrees to appear to be justified; suddenly everything became clear. What was more, they felt all at once extraordinarily free. And it was just at this moment that the quadrille for which the medical student was in such haste, the last before supper, began.

And just as Ivan Ilyich meant to address the bride again, intending to provoke her with some innuendo, the tall officer suddenly dashed up to her and with a flourish dropped on one knee before her. She immediately jumped up from the sofa, and whisked off with him to take her place in the quadrille. The officer did not even apologize, and she did not even glance at the general as she went away; she seemed, in fact, relieved to escape.

'After all she has a right to be,' thought Ivan Ilyich, 'and of course they don't know how to behave.' "Hm! Don't you stand on ceremony, friend Porfiry," he said, addressing Pseldonimov. "Perhaps you have . . . arrangements to make . . . or something . . . please don't put yourself out." 'Why does he keep guard over me?' he thought to himself.

Pseldonimov, with his long neck and his eyes fixed intently upon him, began to be insufferable. In fact, all this was not the thing, not the thing at all, but Ivan Ilyich was still far from admitting this.

The quadrille began.

"Will you allow me, your Excellency?" asked Akim Petrovich, holding the bottle respectfully in his hands and preparing to pour from it into his Excellency's glass.

"I . . . I really don't know, whether . . ."

But Akim Petrovich, with reverent and radiant face, was already filling the glass. After filling the glass, he proceeded, writhing and wriggling, as it were stealthily, as it were furtively, to pour himself out some, with this difference, that he did not fill his own glass to within a finger length of the top, and this seemed somehow more respectful. He was like a woman in travail as he sat beside his chief. What could he talk about, indeed? Yet to entertain his Excellency was an absolute duty since he had the honor of keeping him company. The champagne served as a resource, and his Excellency, too, was pleased that he had filled his glass—not for the sake of the champagne, for it was warm and perfectly abominable, but just morally pleased.

"The old chap would like to have a drink himself," thought Ivan Ilyich, "but he doesn't venture till I do. I mustn't prevent him. And indeed it would be absurd for the bottle to stand between us untouched."

He took a sip, anyway it seemed better than sitting doing nothing.

"I am here," he said, with pauses and emphasis, "I am here, you know, so to speak, accidentally, and, of course, it may be . . . that some people would consider . . . it unseemly for me to be at such . . . a gathering."

Akim Petrovich said nothing, but listened with timid curiosity.

"But I hope you will understand, with what object I have come. . . . I haven't really come simply to drink wine . . . he-he!"

Akim Petrovich tried to chuckle, following the example of his Excellency, but again he could not get it out, and again he made absolutely no consolatory answer.

"I am here . . . in order, so to speak, to encourage . . . to show, so to speak, a moral aim," Ivan Ilyich continued, feeling vexed at Akim Petrovich's stupidity, but he suddenly subsided into silence himself. He saw that poor Akim Petrovich had dropped his eyes as though he were in fault. The general in some confusion made haste to take another sip from his glass, and Akim Petrovich clutched at the bottle as though it were his only hope of salvation and filled the glass again.

"You haven't many resources," thought Ivan Ilyich, looking sternly at poor Akim Petrovich. The latter, feeling that stern general-like eye upon him, made up his mind to remain silent for good and not to raise his eyes. So they sat beside each other for a couple of minutes—two sickening minutes for Akim Petrovich.

A couple of words about Akim Petrovich. He was a man of the old school, as meek as a hen, reared from infancy to obsequious servility, and at the same time a good-natured and even honorable man. He was a Petersburg Russian; that is, his father and his father's father were born, grew up and served in Petersburg and had never once left Petersburg. That is quite a special type of Russian. They have hardly any idea of Russia, though that does not trouble them at all. Their whole interest is confined to Petersburg and chiefly the place in which they serve. All their thoughts are concentrated on preference for farthing points, on the grocery, and their month's salary. They don't know a single Russian custom, a single Russian song except "Luchinushka," and that only because it is played on the barrel organs. However, there are two fundamental and invariable signs by which you can at once distinguish a Petersburg Russian from a real Russian. The first sign is the fact that Petersburg Russians, all without exception, speak of the newspaper as the *Academic News* and never call it the *Petersburg News*. The second and equally trustworthy sign is that Petersburg Russians never make use of the word "breakfast," but always call it "Frühstück" with especial emphasis on the first syllable. By these radical and distinguishing signs you can tell them apart; in short, this is a humble type which has been formed during the last thirty-five years. Akim Petrovich, however, was by no means a fool. If the general had asked him a question about anything in his own province he would have answered and kept up a conversation; as it was, it was unseemly for a subordinate even to answer such questions as these, though Akim Petrovich was dying from curiosity to know something more detailed about his Excellency's real intentions.

Meanwhile Ivan Ilyich sank more and more into meditation and a sort of whirl of ideas; in his absorption he sipped his glass every half-minute. Akim Petrovich at once zealously filled it up. Both were silent. Ivan Ilyich began looking at the dances, and immediately something attracted his attention. One circumstance even surprised him. . . .

The dances were certainly lively. Here people danced in the simplicity of their hearts to amuse themselves and even to romp wildly. Among the dancers few were really skilful, but the unskilled stamped so vigorously that they might have been taken for agile ones. The officer was among the foremost; he particularly liked the figures in which he was left alone, to perform a solo. Then he performed the most marvelous capers. For instance, standing upright as a post, he would suddenly bend over to one side, so that one expected him to fall over; but with the next step he would suddenly bend over in the opposite direction at the same acute angle to the floor. He kept the most serious face and danced in the full conviction that everyone was watching him. Another gentleman, who had had rather more than he could carry before the quadrille, dropped asleep beside his partner so that his partner had to dance alone. The young registration clerk, who had danced with the lady in the blue scarf through all the figures and through all the five quadrilles which they had danced that evening, played the same prank the whole time: that is, he dropped a little behind his partner, seized the end of her scarf, and as they crossed over succeeded in imprinting some twenty kisses on the scarf. His partner sailed along in front of him, as though she noticed nothing. The medical student really did dance on his head, and excited frantic enthusiasm, stamping, and shrieks of delight. In short, the absence of constraint was very marked. Ivan Ilyich, whom the wine was beginning to affect, began by smiling, but by degrees a bitter doubt began to steal into his heart; of course he liked free-and-easy manners and unconventionality. He desired, he had even inwardly prayed for free-and-easy manners, when they had all held back, but now that unconventionality had gone beyond all limits. One lady, for instance, the one in the shabby dark blue velvet dress, bought fourth-hand, in the sixth figure pinned her dress so as to turn it into —something like trousers. This was the Kleopatra Semyonovna with whom one could venture to do anything, as her partner, the medical student, had expressed it. The medical student defied description: he was simply a Fokin. How was it? They had held back and now they were so quickly emancipated! One might think it nothing, but this transformation was somehow strange; it indicated something. It was as though they had forgotten Ivan Ilyich's existence. Of course he was the first to laugh, and even ventured to applaud. Akim Petrovich chuckled respectfully in unison, though, indeed, with evident pleasure and no suspicion that his Excellency was beginning to nourish in his heart a new gnawing anxiety.

"You dance capitally, young man," Ivan Ilyich was obliged to say to the medical student as he walked past him.

The student turned sharply towards him, made a grimace, and bringing his face close into unseemly proximity to the face of his Excellency, crowed like a cock at the top of his voice. This was too much. Ivan Ilyich got up from the table. In spite of that, a roar of inexpressible laughter followed, for the crow was an extraordinarily good imitation, and the whole performance was utterly unexpected. Ivan Ilyich was still standing in bewilderment, when suddenly Pseldonimov himself made his appearance, and with a bow, began begging him to come to supper. His mother followed him.

"Your Excellency," she said, bowing, "do us the honor, do not disdain our humble fare."

"I . . . I really don't know," Ivan Ilyich was beginning. "I did not come with that idea . . . I . . . meant to be going . . ."

He was, in fact, holding his hat in his hands. What is more, he had at that very moment taken an inward vow at all costs to depart at once and on no account whatever to consent to remain, and . . . he remained. A minute later he led the procession to the table. Pseldonimov and his mother walked in front, clearing the way for him. They made him sit down in the seat of honor, and again a bottle of champagne, opened but not begun, was set beside his plate. By way of *hors d'œuvres* there were salt herrings and vodka. He put out his hand, poured out a large glass of vodka and drank it off. He had never drunk vodka before. He felt as though he were rolling down a hill, were flying, flying, flying, that he must stop himself, catch at something, but there was no possibility of it.

His position was certainly becoming more and more eccentric. What is more, it seemed as though fate were mocking at him. God knows what had happened to him in the course of an hour or so. When he went in he had, so to say, opened his arms to embrace all humanity, all his subordinates; and here not more than an hour had passed and in all his aching heart he felt and knew that he hated Pseldonimov and was cursing him, his wife and his wedding. What was more, he saw from his face, from his eyes alone, that Pseldonimov himself hated him, that he was looking at him with eyes that almost said: "If only you would take yourself off, curse you! Foisting yourself on us!" All this he had read for some time in his eyes.

Of course as he sat down to table, Ivan Ilyich would sooner have had his hand cut off than have owned, not only aloud, but even to himself, that this was really so. The moment had not fully arrived yet. There was still a moral vacillation. But his heart, his heart . . . it ached! It was clamoring for freedom, for air, for rest. Ivan Ilyich was really too good-natured.

He knew, of course, that he ought long before to have gone away, not merely to have gone away but to have made his escape. That all this was not the same, but had turned out utterly different from what he had dreamed of on the sidewalk.

"Why did I come? Did I come here to eat and drink?" he asked himself as he tasted the salt herring. He even had attacks of skepticism. There was at moments a faint stir of irony in regard to his own fine action at the bottom of his heart. He actually wondered at times why he had come in.

But how could he go away? To go away like this without having finished the business properly was impossible. What would people say? They would say that he was frequenting low company. Indeed it really would amount to that if he did not end it properly. What would Stepan Nikiforovich, Semyon Ivanovich say (for of course it would be all over the place by tomorrow)? What would be said in the offices, at the Shembels', at the Shubins'? No, he must take his departure in such a way that all should understand why he had come, he must make clear his moral aim. . . . And meantime the dramatic moment would not present itself. "They don't even respect me," he went on, thinking. "What are they laughing at? They are as free and easy as though they had no feeling. . . . But I have long suspected that all the younger generation are without feeling! I must remain at all costs! They have just been dancing, but now at table they will all be gathered together. . . . I will talk about questions, about reforms, about the greatness of Russia. . . . I can still win their enthusiasm! Yes! Perhaps nothing is yet lost. . . . Perhaps it is always like this in reality. What should I begin upon with them to attract them? What plan can I hit upon? I am lost, simply lost. . . . And what is it they want, what is it they require? . . . I see they are laughing together there. Can it be at me, merciful heavens! But what is it I want . . . why is it I am here, why don't I go away, why do I go on persisting?" . . . He thought this, and a sort of shame, a deep unbearable shame, rent his heart more and more intensely.

But everything went on in the same way, one thing after another.

Just two minutes after he had sat down to the table one terrible thought overwhelmed him completely. He suddenly felt that he was horribly drunk, that is, not as he was before, but hopelessly drunk. The cause of this was the glass of vodka which he had drunk after the champagne, and which had immediately produced an effect. He was conscious, he felt in every fiber of his being that he was growing hopelessly feeble. Of course his assurance was greatly increased, but consciousness had not deserted him, and it kept crying out: "It is bad, very bad and, in fact, utterly unseemly!" Of course his unstable drunken reflections could not rest long on one subject; there began to be apparent and unmistakably so, even to himself, two opposite sides. On one side there was swaggering assurance, a desire to con-quer, a disdain of obstacles and a desperate confidence that he would attain his object. The other side showed itself in the aching of his heart, and a sort of gnawing in his soul. "What would they say? How would it all end? What would happen tomorrow, to-morrow, tomorrow?" . . .

He had felt vaguely before that he had enemies in the company. "No doubt that was because I was drunk," he thought with agoniz-ing doubt. What was his horror when he actually, by unmistakable signs, convinced himself now that he really had enemies at the table, and that it was impossible to doubt of it.

"And why—why?" he wondered.

At the table there were all the thirty guests, of whom several were quite tipsy. Others were behaving with a careless and sinister independence, shouting and talking at the top of their voices, bawling out the toasts before the time, and pelting the ladies with pellets of bread. One unprepossessing personage in a greasy coat had fallen off his chair as soon as he sat down, and remained so till the end of supper. Another one made desperate efforts to stand on the table, to propose a toast, and only the officer, who seized him by the tails of his coat, moderated his premature ardor. The supper was a pellmell affair, although they had hired a cook who had been in the service of a general; there was the galantine, there was tongue and potatoes, there were rissoles with green peas, there was, finally, a goose, and last of all blancmange. Among the drinks were beer, vodka and sherry. The only bottle of champagne was standing beside the gen-eral, which obliged him to pour it out for himself and also for Akim Petrovich, who did not venture at supper to officiate on his own initiative. The other guests had to drink the toasts in Caucasian wine or anything else they could get. The table was made up of several tables put together, among them even a card-table. It was covered with many tablecloths, amongst them one colored Yaroslav cloth;

the gentlemen sat alternately with the ladies. Pseldonimov's mother
would not sit down to the table; she bustled about and supervised.
But another sinister female figure, who had not shown herself till
then, appeared on the scene, wearing a reddish silk dress, with a
very high cap on her head and a bandage round her face for toothache. It appeared that this was the bride's mother, who had at last
consented to emerge from a back room for supper. She had refused
to appear till then owing to her implacable hostility to Pseldonimov's
mother, but to that we will refer later. This lady looked spitefully,
even sarcastically, at the general, and evidently did not wish to be
presented to him. To Ivan Ilyich this figure appeared suspicious in
the extreme. But apart from her, several other persons were suspicious and inspired involuntary apprehension and uneasiness. It even
seemed that they were in some sort of plot together against Ivan
Ilyich. At any rate it seemed so to him, and throughout the whole
supper he became more and more convinced of it. A gentleman with
a beard, some sort of free artist, was particularly sinister; he even
looked at Ivan Ilyich several times, and then turning to his neighbor,
whispered something. Another person present was unmistakably
drunk, but yet, from certain signs, was to be regarded with suspicion.
The medical student, too, gave rise to unpleasant expectations. Even
the officer himself was not quite to be depended on. But the young
man on the comic paper was blazing with hatred, he lolled in his
chair, he looked so haughty and conceited, he snorted so aggres-
sively! And though the rest of the guests took absolutely no notice
of the young journalist, who had contributed only four wretched
poems to the *Firebrand*, and had consequently become a Liberal and
evidently, indeed, disliked him, yet when a pellet of bread aimed in
his direction fell near Ivan Ilyich, he was ready to stake his head that
it had been thrown by no other than the young man in question.

All this, of course, had a pitiable effect on him.

Another observation was particularly unpleasant. Ivan Ilyich became aware that he was beginning to articulate indistinctly and with
difficulty, that he was longing to say a great deal, but that his tongue
refused to obey him. And then he suddenly seemed to forget himself, and worst of all he would suddenly go off into a loud burst of
laughter, apropos of nothing. This inclination quickly passed off after
a glass of champagne which Ivan Ilyich had not meant to drink,
though he had poured it out and suddenly drunk it quite by acci-

dent. After that glass he felt at once almost inclined to cry. He felt that he was sinking into a most peculiar state of sentimentality; he began to be again filled with love, he loved everyone, even Pseldonimov, even the young man on the comic paper. He suddenly longed to embrace all of them, to forget everything and to be reconciled. What is more, to tell them everything openly, all, all; that is, to tell them what a good, nice man he was, with what wonderful talents. What services he would do for his country, how good he was at entertaining the fair sex, and above all, how progressive he was, how humanely ready he was to be indulgent to all, to the very lowest; and finally in conclusion to tell them frankly all the motives that had impelled him to turn up at Pseldonimov's uninvited, to drink two bottles of champagne and to make him happy with his presence.

"The truth, the holy truth and candor before all things! I will capture them by candor. They will believe me, I see it clearly; they actually look at me with hostility, but when I tell them all I shall conquer them completely. They will fill their glasses and drink my health with shouts. The officer will break his glass on his spur. Perhaps they will even shout hurrah! Even if they want to toss me after the Hussar fashion I will not oppose them, and indeed it would be very jolly! I will kiss the bride on her forehead; she is charming. Akim Petrovich is a very nice man, too. Pseldonimov will improve, of course, later on. He will acquire, so to speak, a society polish. . . . And although, of course, the younger generation has not that delicacy of feeling, yet . . . yet I will talk to them about the contemporary significance of Russia among the European States. I will refer to the peasant question, too; yes, and . . . and they will all like me and I shall leave with glory! . . ."

These dreams were, of course, extremely agreeable, but what was unpleasant was that in the midst of these roseate anticipations, Ivan Ilyich suddenly discovered in himself another unexpected propensity, that was to spit. Anyway saliva began running from his mouth apart from any will of his own. He observed this on Akim Petrovich, whose cheek he spluttered upon and who sat not daring to wipe it off from respectfulness. Ivan Ilyich took his dinner napkin and wiped it himself, but this immediately struck him himself as so incongruous, so opposed to all common sense, that he sank into silence and began wondering. Though Akim Petrovich emptied his glass, yet he sat as though he were scalded. Ivan Ilyich reflected now that he had for almost a quarter of an hour been talking to him about some most interesting subject, but that Akim Petrovich had not only seemed embarrassed as he listened, but positively frightened. Pseldonimov, who was sitting one chair away from him, also craned his neck towards him, and bending his head sideways, listened to him with the most unpleasant air. He actually seemed to be keeping a watch on him. Turning his eyes upon the rest of the company, he saw that many were looking straight at him and laughing. But what was strangest of all, was, that he was not in the least embarrassed by it; on the contrary, he sipped his glass again and suddenly began speaking so that all could hear:

"I was saying just now," he began as loudly as possible, "I was saying just now, ladies and gentlemen, to Akim Petrovich, that Russia . . . yes, Russia . . . in short, you understand, that I mean to s-s-say . . . Russia is living, it is my profound conviction, through a period of hu-hu-manity . . ."

"Hu-hu-manity . . ." was heard at the other end of the table.

"Hu-hu . . ."

"Tu-tu!"

Ivan Ilyich stopped. Pseldonimov got up from his chair and began trying to see who had shouted. Akim Petrovich stealthily shook his head, as though admonishing the guests. Ivan Ilyich saw this distinctly, but in his confusion said nothing.

"Humanity!" he continued obstinately; "and this evening . . . and only this evening I said to Stepan Niki-ki-forovich . . . yes . . . that . . . that the regeneration, so to speak, of things . . ."

"Your Excellency!" was heard a loud exclamation at the other end of the table.

"What is your pleasure?" answered Ivan Ilyich, pulled up short and trying to distinguish who had called to him.

"Nothing at all, your Excellency. I was carried away, continue! Con-ti-nue!" the voice was heard again.

Ivan Ilyich felt upset.

"The regeneration, so to speak, of those same things."

"Your Excellency!" the voice shouted again.

"What do you want?"

"How do you do!"

This time Ivan Ilyich could not restrain himself. He broke off his speech and turned to the assailant who had disturbed the general harmony. He was a very young lad, still at school, who had taken more than a drop too much, and was an object of great suspicion to the general. He had been shouting for a long time past, and had even broken a glass and two plates, maintaining that this was the proper thing to do at a wedding. At the moment when Ivan Ilyich turned towards him, the officer was beginning to pitch into the noisy youngster.

"What are you about? Why are you yelling? We shall turn you out, that's what we shall do."

"I don't mean you, your Excellency, I don't mean you. Continue!" cried the hilarious schoolboy, lolling back in his chair. "Continue, I am listening, and am very, ve-ry, ve-ry much pleased with you! Praisewor-thy, praisewor-thy!"

"The wretched boy is drunk," said Pseldonimov in a whisper.

"I see that he is drunk, but . . ."

"I was just telling a very amusing anecdote, your Excellency!" began the officer, "about a lieutenant in our company who was talking just like that to his superior officers; so this young man is imitating him now. To every word of his superior officers he said 'praiseworthy, praiseworthy!' He was turned out of the army ten years ago on account of it."

"What-at lieutenant was that?"

"In our company, your Excellency, he went out of his mind over the word 'praiseworthy.' At first they tried gentle methods, then they put him under arrest. . . . His commanding officer admonished him in the most fatherly way, and he answered, 'praiseworthy, praiseworthy!' And strange to say, the officer was a fine-looking man, over six feet. They meant to courtmartial him, but then they perceived that he was mad."

"So . . . a schoolboy. A schoolboy's prank need not be taken seriously. For my part, I am ready to overlook it. . . ."

"They held a medical inquiry, your Excellency."

"What! Did they dissect him?"

"Upon my word, but he was alive, wasn't he?"

A loud and almost universal roar of laughter resounded among the guests, who had till then behaved with decorum. Ivan Ilyich was furious.

"Ladies and gentlemen!" he shouted, at first scarcely stammering.

"I am fully capable of apprehending that a man is not dissected alive. I imagined that in his derangement he had ceased to be alive—that is, that he had died—that is, I mean to say—that you don't like me—and yet I like you all. . . . Yes, I like Por-Porfiry . . . . I am lowering myself by speaking like this. . . ."

At that moment Ivan Ilyich spluttered so that a great dab of saliva flew on to the tablecloth in a most conspicuous place. Pseldonimov flew to wipe it off with a table-napkin. This last disaster crushed Ivan Ilyich completely.

"My friends, this is too much," he cried in despair.

"The man is drunk, your Excellency," Pseldonimov prompted him again.

"Porfiry, I see that you . . . all . . . yes! I say that I hope . . . yes, I call upon you all to tell me in what way have I lowered myself?"

Ivan Ilyich was almost crying.

"Your Excellency, good heavens!"

"Porfiry, I appeal to you. . . . Tell me, when I came—yes—, to your wedding, I had an object. I was aiming at moral elevation. . . . I wanted it to be felt. . . . I appeal to all: am I greatly lowered in your eyes or not?"

A deathlike silence. That was just it, a deathlike silence, and to such a downright question. "They might at least shout now!" flashed through his Excellency's head. But the guests only looked at one another. Akim Petrovich sat more dead than alive, while Pseldonimov, numb with terror, was repeating to himself the awful question which had occurred to him more than once already: "What shall I have to pay for all this tomorrow?"

At this point the young man on the comic paper, who was very drunk but who had hitherto sat in morose silence, addressed Ivan Ilyich directly, and with flashing eyes began answering in the name of the whole company.

"Yes," he said in a loud voice, "yes, you have lowered yourself. Yes, you are a reactionary—re-ac-tion-ary!"

"Young man, you are forgetting yourself! To whom are you speaking, so to say?" Ivan Ilyich cried furiously, jumping up from his seat again.

"To you; and secondly, I am not a young man. . . . You've come to give yourself airs and try to win popularity."

"Pseldonimov, what does this mean?" cried Ivan Ilyich.

But Pseldonimov was reduced to such horror that he stood still like a post and was utterly at a loss what to do. The guests, too, sat mute in their seats. All but the artist and the schoolboy, who applauded and shouted, "Bravo, bravo!"

The young man on the comic paper went on shouting with unrestrained violence:

"Yes, you came to show off your humanity! You've hindered the enjoyment of everyone. You've been drinking champagne without thinking that it is beyond the means of a clerk at ten roubles a month. And I suspect that you are one of those high officials who are a little too fond of the young wives of their clerks! What is more, I am convinced that you support the farming of taxes. . . . Yes, yes, yes!"

"Pseldonimov, Pseldonimov," shouted Ivan Ilyich, holding out his hands to him. He felt that every word uttered by the comic young man was a fresh dagger at his heart.

"Directly, your Excellency; please do not disturb yourself!" Pseldonimov cried energetically, rushing up to the comic young man, seizing him by the collar and dragging him away from the table. Such physical strength could indeed not have been expected from the weakly-looking Pseldonimov. But the comic young man was very drunk, while Pseldonimov was perfectly sober. Then he gave him two or three cuffs in the back, and thrust him out of the door.

"You are all scoundrels!" roared the young man of the comic paper. "I will caricature you all tomorrow in the *Firebrand*."

They all leapt up from their seats.

"Your Excellency, your Excellency!" cried Pseldonimov, his mother and several others, crowding round the general. "Your Excellency, do not be disturbed!"

"No, no," cried the general, "I am annihilated. . . . I came—I meant to bless you, so to speak. And this is how I am paid, for everything, everything! . . ."

He sank on to a chair as though unconscious, laid both his arms on the table, and bowed his head over them, straight into a plate of blancmange. There is no need to describe the general horror. A minute later he got up, evidently meaning to go out, gave a lurch, stumbled against the leg of a chair, fell full length on the floor and snored. . . .

This is what is apt to happen to men who don't drink when they accidentally take a glass too much. They preserve their consciousness to the last point, to the last minute, and then fall to the ground as though struck down. Ivan Ilyich lay on the floor absolutely unconscious. Pseldonimov clutched at his hair and sat as though petrified in that position. The guests made haste to depart, commenting each in his own way on the incident. It was about three o'clock in the morning.

The worst of it was that Pseldonimov's circumstances were far worse than could have been imagined, in spite of the unattractiveness of his present surroundings. And while Ivan Ilyich is lying on the floor and Pseldonimov is standing over him tearing his hair in despair, we will break off the thread of our story and say a few explanatory words about Porfiry Petrovich Pseldonimov.

Not more than a month before his wedding he was in a state of hopeless destitution. He came from a province where his father had served in some department and where he had died while awaiting his trial on some charge. When five months before his wedding, Pseldonimov, who had been in hopeless misery in Petersburg for a whole year before, got his berth at ten roubles a month, he revived both physically and mentally, but he was soon crushed by circumstances again. Only two Pseldonimovs remained in the world, himself and his mother, who had left the province after her husband's death. The mother and son barely existed in the freezing cold, and sustained life on the most dubious substances. There were days when Pseldonimov himself went with a jug to the Fontanka for water to drink. When he got his place he succeeded in settling with his mother in a "corner." She took in washing, while for four months he scraped together every farthing to get himself boots and an overcoat. And what troubles he had to endure at his office; his superiors approached him with the question: "How long is it since you've had a bath?" There was a rumor about him that under the collar of his uniform there were nests of bugs. But Pseldonimov was a man of strong character. On the surface he was mild and meek; he had the merest smattering of education, he was practically never heard to talk of anything. I do not know for certain whether he thought, made plans, theorized, had dreams. But on the other hand there was being formed within him an instinctive, furtive, unconscious determination to fight his way out of his wretched circumstances. He had the persistence of an ant. Destroy an ants' nest, and they will begin at once re-erecting it; destroy it again, and they will begin again without wearying. He was a constructive house-building animal. One could see from his brow that he would make his way, would build his nest, and perhaps even save for a rainy day. His mother was the only creature in the world who loved him, and she loved him beyond everything. She was a woman of resolute character, hard-working and indefatigable, and at the same time good-natured.

So perhaps they might have lived in their corner for five or six years till their circumstances changed, if they had not come across the retired titular councilor Mlekopitayev, who had been a clerk in the treasury and had served at one time in the provinces, but had latterly settled in Petersburg and had established himself there with his family. He knew Pseldonimov, and had at one time been under some obligation to his father. He had some money, not a large sum, of course, but there it was; how much it was no one knew, not his wife, nor his elder daughter, nor his relations. He had two daughters, and as he was an awful bully, a drunkard, a domestic tyrant, and in addition to that an invalid, he took it into his head one day to marry one of his daughters to Pseldonimov: "I knew his father," he would say, "he was a good fellow and his son will be a good fellow." Mlekopitayev did exactly as he liked, his word was law. He was very queer and wilful. For the most part he spent his time sitting in an armchair, having lost the use of his legs from some disease which did not, however, prevent him from drinking vodka. For days together he would be drinking and swearing. He was an ill-natured man. He always wanted to have someone whom he could be continually tormenting. And for that purpose he kept several distant relations: his sister, a sickly and peevish woman; two of his wife's sisters, also ill-natured and very free with their tongues, and his old aunt, who had through some accident a broken rib; he kept another dependent also, a Russianized German, for the sake of her talent for entertaining him with stories from the *Arabian Nights*. His sole gratification consisted in jeering at all these unfortunate women and abusing them every minute with all his energies; though they, not excepting his wife, who had been born with toothache, dared not utter a word in his presence. He continually set them at loggerheads, inventing and fostering spiteful backbiting and dissensions among them, and then laughed and rejoiced seeing how they were ready to tear one another to pieces. He was very much delighted when his elder daughter, who had lived in great poverty for ten years with her husband, an officer of some sort, and was at last left a widow, came to live with him with three little sickly children. He could not endure her children, but as her arrival had increased the material upon which he could work his daily experiments, the old man was very much pleased. All these ill-natured women and sickly children, together with their tormenter, were crowded together in a wooden house on Petersburg Side, and did not get enough to eat because the old man was stingy and gave out to them money a copeck at a time, though he did not grudge himself vodka; they did not get enough sleep because the old man suffered from sleeplessness and insisted on being amused. In short, they all were in misery and cursed their fate.

It was at that time that Mlekopitayev's eye fell upon Pseldonimov. He was struck by his long nose and submissive air. His weakly and unprepossessing younger daughter had just reached the age of seventeen. Though she had at one time attended a German school, she had acquired scarcely anything but the alphabet. Then she grew up rickety and anemic in fear of her crippled drunken father's crutch, in a bedlam of domestic backbiting, eavesdropping and scolding. She had never had any friends or any brains. She had for a long time been eager to be married. In company she sat mute, but at home with her mother and the women of the household she was spiteful and cantankerous. She was particularly fond of pinching and smacking her sister's children, telling tales of their pilfering bread and sugar, and this led to endless and implacable strife with her elder sister. Her old father himself offered her to Pseldonimov. Miserable as the latter's position was, he yet asked for a little time to consider. His mother and he hesitated for a long time. But with the young lady there was to come as dowry a house, and though it was a nasty little wooden house of one storey, yet it was property of a kind. Moreover, they would give four hundred roubles with her and how long it would take him to save it up himself! "What am I taking the man into my house for?" shouted the drunken bully. "In the first place, because you are all females, and I am sick of female society. I want Pseldonimov, too, to dance to my piping. For I am his benefactor. And in the second place, I am doing it because you are all cross and don't want it, so I'll do it to spite you. What I have said, I have said! And you beat her, Porfiry, when she is your wife; she has been possessed of seven devils ever since she was born. You beat them out of her, and I'll get the stick ready."

Pseldonimov made no answer, but he had already decided. Even before the wedding his mother and he were taken into the house, washed, clothed, provided with boots and money for the wedding. The old man took them under his protection possibly just because the whole family was prejudiced against them. He positively liked Pseldonimov's mother, so that he actually restrained himself and did not jeer at her. On the other hand, he made Pseldonimov dance the Cossack dance a week before the wedding.

"Well, that's enough. I only wanted to see whether you remembered your position before me or not," he said at the end of the dance. He allowed just enough money for the wedding, with nothing to spare, and invited all his relations and acquaintances. On Pseldonimov's side there was no one but the young man who wrote for the *Firebrand*, and Akim Petrovich, the guest of honor. Pseldonimov was perfectly aware that his bride cherished an aversion for him, and that she was set upon marrying the officer intsead of him. But he put up with everything, he had made a compact with his mother to do so. The old father had been drunk and abusive and foul-tongued the whole of the wedding day and during the party in the evening. The whole family took refuge in the back rooms and were crowded there to suffocation. The front rooms were devoted to the dance and the supper. At last when the old man fell asleep dead drunk at eleven o'clock, the bride's mother, who had been particularly displeased with Pseldonimov's mother that day, made up her mind to lay aside her wrath, become gracious and join the company. Ivan Ilyich's arrival had turned everything upside down. Madame Mlekopitayev was overcome with embarrassment, and began grumbling that she had not been told that the general had been invited. She was assured that he had come uninvited, but was so stupid as to refuse to believe it. Champagne had to be got. Pseldonimov's mother had only one rouble, while Pseldonimov himself had not one copeck. He had to grovel before his ill-natured mother-in-law, to beg for the money for one bottle and then for another. They pleaded for the sake of his future position in the service, for his career, they tried to persuade her. She did at last give from her own purse, but she forced Pseldonimov to swallow such a cupful of gall and bitterness that more than once he ran into the room where the nuptial couch had been prepared, and madly clutching at his hair and trembling all over with impotent rage, he buried his head in the bed destined for the joys of paradise. No, indeed, Ivan Ilyich had no notion of the price paid for the two bottles of Jackson he had drunk that evening. What was the horror, the misery and even the despair of Pseldonimov when Ivan Ilyich's visit ended in this unexpected way. He had a prospect again of no end of misery, and perhaps a night of tears and outcries from his peevish bride, and upbraidings from her unreasonable relations. Even apart from this his head ached already, and there was dizziness and mist before his eyes. And here Ivan Ilyich needed looking after, at three o'clock at night he had to hunt for a doctor or a carriage to take him home, and a carriage it must be, for it would be impossible to let an ordinary cabby take him home in that condition. And where could he get the money even for a carriage? Madame Mlekopitayev, furious that the general had not addressed two words to her, and had not even looked at her at supper, declared that she had not a copeck. Possibly she really had not a copeck. Where could he get it? What was he to do? Yes, indeed, he had good cause to tear his hair.

Meanwhile Ivan Ilyich was moved to a little leather sofa that stood in the dining-room. While they were clearing the tables and putting them away, Pseldonimov was rushing all over the place to borrow money, he even tried to get it from the servants, but it appeared that nobody had any. He even ventured to trouble Akim Petrovich who had stayed after the other guests. But good-natured as he was, the latter was reduced to such bewilderment and even alarm at the mention of money that he uttered the most unexpected and foolish phrases:

"Another time, with pleasure," he muttered, "but now—you really must excuse me. . . ."

And taking his cap, he ran as fast as he could out of the house. Only the good-natured youth who had talked about the dream book was any use at all; and even that came to nothing. He, too, stayed after the others, showing genuine sympathy with Pseldonimov's misfortunes. At last Pseldonimov, together with his mother and the young man, decided in consultation not to send for a doctor, but rather to fetch a carriage and take the invalid home, and meantime to try certain domestic remedies till the carriage arrived, such as moistening his temples and his head with cold water, putting ice on his head, and so on. Pseldonimov's mother undertook this task. The friendly youth flew off in search of a carriage. As there were not even ordinary cabs to be found on the Petersburg Side at that hour, he went off to some livery stables at a distance to wake up the coachmen. They began bargaining, and declared that five roubles would be little to ask for a carriage at that time of night. They agreed to come, however, for three. When at last, just before five o'clock, the young man arrived at Pseldonimov's with the carriage, they had changed their minds. It appeared that Ivan Ilyich, who was still unconscious, had become so seriously unwell, was moaning and tossing so terribly, that to move him and take him home in such a condition was impossible and actually unsafe. "What will it lead to next?" said Pseldonimov, utterly disheartened. What was to be done? A new problem arose: if the invalid remained in the house, where should he be moved and where could they put him? There were only two bedsteads in the house: one large double bed in which old Mlekopitayev and his wife slept, and another double bed of imitation walnut which had just been purchased and was destined for the newly married couple. All the other inhabitants of the house slept on the floor side by side on feather beds, for the most part in bad condition and stuffy, anything but presentable in fact, and even of these the supply was insufficient; there was not one to spare. Where could the invalid be put? A feather bed might perhaps have been found—it might in the last resort have been pulled from under some one, but where and on what could a bed have been made up? It seemed that the bed must be made up in the drawing-room, for that room was the furthest from the bosom of the family and had a door into the passage. But on what could the bed be made? Surely not upon chairs. We all know that beds can only be made up on chairs for schoolboys when they come home for the week end, and it would be terribly lacking in respect to make up a bed in that way for a personage like Ivan Ilyich. What would be said next morning when he found himself lying on chairs? Pseldonimov would not hear of that.

The only alternative was to put him on the bridal couch. This bridal couch, as we have mentioned already, was in a little room that opened out of the dining-room, on the bedstead was a double mattress actually newly bought first-hand, clean sheets, four pillows in pink calico covered with frilled muslin cases. The quilt was of pink satin, and it was quilted in patterns. Muslin curtains hung down from a golden ring overhead, in fact it was all just as it should be, and the guests who had all visited the bridal chamber had admired the decoration of it; though the bride could not endure Pseldonimov, she had several times in the course of the evening run in to have a look at it on the sly. What was her indignation, her wrath, when she learned that they meant to move an invalid, suffering from something not unlike a mild attack of cholera, to her bridal couch! The bride's mother took her part, broke into abuse and vowed she would complain to her husband next day, but Pseldonimov asserted himself and insisted: Ivan Ilyich was moved into the bridal chamber, and a bed was made up on chairs for the young people. The bride whimpered, would have liked to pinch him, but dared not disobey; her papa had a crutch with which she was very familiar, and she knew that her papa would call her to account next day. To console her they carried the pink satin quilt and the pillows in muslin cases into the drawing-room. At that moment the youth arrived with the carriage, and was in a panic finding that the carriage was not wanted. He was left to pay for it himself, and he never had as much as a ten-copeck piece. Pseldonimov explained that he was utterly bankrupt. They tried to parley with the driver. But he began to be noisy and even to batter on the shutters. How it ended I don't know exactly. I believe the youth was carried off by way of a hostage to Fourth Rozhdestvensky Street, where he hoped to rouse a student who was spending the night at a friend's, and to ask whether he had any money.

It was going on for five o'clock in the morning when the young people were left alone and shut up in the drawing-room. Pseldonimov's mother spent the whole night by the bedside of the sufferer. She installed herself on a rug on the floor and covered herself with on old coat, but could not sleep because she had to get up every minute; Ivan Ilyich had a terrible attack of colic. Madame Pseldonimov, a woman of courage and greatness of soul, undressed him with her own hands, took off all his things, looked after him as if he were her own son, and spent the whole night carrying basins, etc., from the bedroom across the passage and bringing them back again empty. And yet the misfortunes of that night were not yet over.

Not more than ten minutes after the young people had been shut up alone in the drawing-room, a piercing shriek was suddenly heard, not a cry of joy, but a shriek of the most sinister kind. The screams were followed by a noise, a crash, as though of the falling of chairs, and instantly there burst into the still dark room a perfect crowd of exclaiming and frightened women, attired in every kind of dishabille. These women were the bride's mother, her elder sister, abandoning for the moment the sick children, and her three aunts, even the one with a broken rib dragged herself in. Even the cook was there, and the German lady who told stories, whose own feather bed, the best in the house, and her only property, had been forcibly dragged from under her for the young couple, trailed in together with the others. All these respectable and sharp-eyed ladies had, a quarter of an hour before, made their way on tiptoe from the kitchen across the passage, and were listening in the anteroom, devoured by unaccountable curiosity. Meanwhile some one lighted a candle, and a surprising spectacle met the eyes of all. The chairs supporting the broad feather bed only at the sides had parted under the weight, and the feather bed had fallen between them on the floor. The bride was sobbing with anger, this time she was mortally offended. Pseldonimov, morally shattered, stood like a criminal caught in a crime. He did not even attempt to defend himself. Shrieks and exclamations sounded on all sides. Pseldonimov's mother ran up at the noise, but the bride's mamma on this occasion got the upper hand. She began by showering strange and for the most part quite undeserved reproaches, such as: "A nice husband you are, after this. What are you good for after such a disgrace?" and so on; and at last carried her daughter away from her husband, undertaking to bear the full responsibility for doing so with her ferocious husband, who would demand an explanation. All the others followed her out exclaiming and shaking their heads. No one remained with Pseldonimov except his mother, who tried to comfort him. But he sent her away at once.

He was beyond consolation. He made his way to the sofa and sat down in the most gloomy confusion of mind just as he was, barefooted and in nothing but his night attire. His thoughts whirled in a tangled crisscross in his mind. At times he mechanically looked about the room where only a little while ago the dancers had been whirling madly, and in which the cigarette smoke still lingered. Cigarette ends and sweetmeat papers still littered the slopped and dirty floor. The wreck of the nuptial couch and the overturned chairs bore witness to the transitoriness of the fondest and surest earthly hopes and dreams. He sat like this almost an hour. The most oppressive thoughts kept coming into his mind, such as: What was in store for him in the office now? He recognized with painful clearness that he would have, at all costs, to transfer to another department; that he could not possibly remain where he was after all that had happened that evening. He thought, too, of Mlekopitayev, who would probably make him dance the Cossack dance next day to test his meekness. He reflected, too, that though Mlekopitayev had given fifty roubles for the wedding festivities, every copeck of which had been spent, he had not thought of giving him the four hundred roubles yet, no mention had been made of it, in fact. And, indeed, even the house had not been formally made over to him. He thought, too, of his wife who had left him at the most critical moment of his life, of the tall officer who had dropped on one knee before her. He had noticed that already; he thought of the seven devils which according to the testimony of her own father were in possession of his wife, and of the crutch in readiness to drive them out. . . . Of course, he felt equal to bearing a great deal, but destiny had let loose such surprises upon him that he might well have doubts of his fortitude. So Pseldonimov mused dolefully.

Meanwhile the candle end was going out, its fading light, falling straight upon Pseldonimov's profile, threw a colossal shadow of it on the wall, with a drawn-out neck, a hooked nose, and with two tufts of hair sticking out on his forehead and the back of his head. At last, when the air was growing cool with the chill of early morning, he got up, frozen and spiritually numb, crawled to the feather bed that was lying between the chairs, and without rearranging anything, without putting out the candle end, without even laying the pillow under his head, fell into a leaden, deathlike sleep, such as the sleep of men condemned to flogging on the morrow must be.

On the other hand, what could be compared with the agonizing night spent by Ivan Ilyich Pralinsky on the bridal couch of the unlucky Pseldonimov! For some time, headache, vomiting and other most unpleasant symptoms did not leave him for one second. He was in the torments of hell. The faint glimpses of consciousness that visited his brain, lighted up such an abyss of horrors, such gloomy and revolting pictures, that it would have been better for him not to have returned to consciousness. Everything was still in a turmoil in his mind, however. He recognized Pseldonimov's mother, for instance, heard her gentle admonitions, such as: "Be patient, my dear; be patient, good sir, it won't be so bad presently." He recognized her, but could give no logical explanation of her presence beside him. Revolting phantoms haunted him, most frequently of all he was haunted by Semyon Ivanych; but looking more intently, he saw that it was not Semyon Ivanych but Pseldonimov's nose. He had visions, too, of the free-and-easy artist, and the officer and the old lady with her face tied up. What interested him most of all was the gilt ring which hung over his head, through which the curtains hung. He could distinguish it plainly in the dim light of the candle end which lighted up the room, and he kept wondering inwardly: What was the object of that ring, why was it there, what did it mean? He questioned the old lady several times about it, but apparently did not say what he meant; and she evidently did not understand it, however much he struggled to explain. At last by morning the symptoms had ceased and he fell into a sleep, a sound sleep without dreams. He slept about an hour, and when he woke he was almost completely conscious, with an insufferable headache, and disgusting taste in his mouth and on his tongue, which seemed turned into a piece of cloth. He sat up in the bed, looked about him, and pondered. The pale light of morning peeping through the cracks of the shutters in a narrow streak, quivered on the wall. It was about seven o'clock in the morning. But when Ivan Ilyich suddenly grasped the position and recalled all that had happened to him since the evening; when he remembered all his adventures at supper, the failure of his magnanimous action, his speech at table; when he realized all at once with horrifying clearness all that might come of this now, all that people would say and think of him; when he looked round and saw to what a mournful and hideous condition he had reduced the peaceful bridal couch of his clerk—oh, then such deadly shame, such agony overwhelmed him, that he uttered a shriek, hid his face in his hands and fell back on the pillow in despair. A minute later he jumped out of bed, saw his clothes carefully folded and brushed on a chair beside him, and seizing them, and as quickly as he could, in desperate haste began putting them on, looking round and seeming terribly frightened at something. On another chair close by lay his greatcoat and fur cap, and his yellow gloves were in his cap. He meant to steal away secretly. But suddenly the door opened and the elder Madame Pseldonimov walked in with an earthware jug and basin. A towel was hanging over her shoulder. She set down the jug, and without further conversation told him that he must wash.

"Come, my good sir, wash; you can't go without washing. . . ."

And at that instant Ivan Ilyich recognized that if there was one being in the whole world whom he need not fear, and before whom he need not feel ashamed, it was that old lady. He washed. And long afterwards, at painful moments of his life, he recalled among other pangs of remorse all the circumstances of that waking, and that earthenware basin, and the china jug filled with cold water in which there were still floating icicles, and the oval cake of soap at fifteen copecks, in pink paper with letters embossed on it, evidently bought for the bridal pair though it fell to Ivan Ilyich to use it, and the old lady with the linen towel over her left shoulder. The cold water refreshed him, he dried his face, and without even thanking this sister of mercy, he snatched up his hat, flung over his shoulders the coat handed to him by Pseldonimov, and crossing the passage and the kitchen where the cat was already mewing, and the cook sitting up in her bed staring after him with greedy curiosity, ran out into the yard, into the street, and threw himself into the first sledge he came across. It was a frosty morning. A chilly yellow fog still hid the house and everything. Ivan Ilyich turned up his collar. He thought that everyone was looking at him, that they were all recognizing him, all. . . .

For eight days he did not leave the house or show himself at the office. He was ill, wretchedly ill, but more morally than physically. He lived through a perfect hell in those days, and they must have been reckoned to his account in the other world. There were moments when he thought of becoming a monk and entering a monastery. There really were. His imagination, indeed, took special excursions during that period. He pictured subdued subterranean singing, an open coffin, living in a solitary cell, forests and caves; but when he came to himself he recognized almost at once that all this was dreadful nonsense and exaggeration, and was ashamed of this nonsense. Then began attacks of moral agony on the theme of his *existence manquée*. Then shame flamed up again in his soul, took complete possession of him at once, consumed him like fire and reopened his wounds. He shuddered as pictures of all sorts rose before his mind. What would people say about him, what would they think when he walked into his office? What a whisper would dog his steps for a whole year, ten years, his whole life! His story would go down to posterity. He sometimes fell into such dejection that he was ready to go straight off to Semyon Ivanovich and ask for his forgiveness and friendship. He did not even justify himself, there was no limit to his blame of himself. He could find no extenuating circumstances, and was ashamed of trying to.

He had thoughts, too, of resigning his post at once and devoting himself to human happiness as a simple citizen, in solitude. In any case he would have to change his whole circle of acquaintances completely, and so thoroughly as to eradicate all memory of himself. Then the thought occurred to him that this, too, was nonsense, and that if he adopted greater severity with his subordinates it might all be set right. Then he began to feel hope and courage again. At last, at the expiration of eight days of hesitation and agonies, he felt that he could not endure to be in uncertainty any longer, and *un beau matin* he made up his mind to go to the office.

He had pictured a thousand times over his return to the office as he sat at home in misery. With horror and conviction he told himself that he would certainly hear behind him an ambiguous whisper, would see ambiguous faces, would intercept ominous smiles. What was his surprise when nothing of the sort happened. He was greeted with respect; he was met with bows; everyone was grave; everyone was busy. His heart was filled with joy as he made his way to his own room.

He set to work at once with the utmost gravity, he listened to some reports and explanations, settled doubtful points. He felt as though he had never explained knotty points and given his decisions so intelligently, so judiciously as that morning. He saw that they were satisfied with him, that they respected him, that he was treated with respect. The most thin-skinned sensitiveness could not have discovered anything.

At last Akim Petrovich made his appearance with some document. The sight of him sent a stab to Ivan Ilyich's heart, but only for an instant. He went into the business with Akim Petrovich, talked with dignity, explained things, and showed him what was to be done. The only thing he noticed was that he avoided looking at Akim Petrovich for any length of time, or rather Akim Petrovich seemed afraid of catching his eye, but at last Akim Petrovich had finished and began to collect his papers.

"And there is one other matter," he began as dryly as he could, "the clerk Pseldonimov's petition to be transferred to another department. His Excellency Semyon Ivanovich Shipulenko has promised him a post. He begs your gracious assent, your Excellency."

"Oh, so he is being transferred," said Ivan Ilyich, and he felt as though a heavy weight had rolled off his heart. He glanced at Akim Petrovich, and at that instant their eyes met. "Certainly, I for my part . . . I will use . . ." answered Ivan Ilyich; "I am ready."

Akim Petrovich evidently wanted to slip away as quickly as he could. But in a rush of generous feeling Ivan Ilyich determined to speak out. Apparently some inspiration had come to him again.

"Tell him," he began, bending a candid glance full of profound meaning upon Akim Petrovich, "tell Pseldonimov that I feel no ill-will, no, I do not! . . . That on the contrary I am ready to forget all that is past, to forget it all. . . ."

But all at once Ivan Ilyich broke off, looking with wonder at the strange behavior of Akim Petrovich, who suddenly seemed transformed from a sensible person into a fearful fool. Instead of listening and hearing Ivan Ilyich to the end, he suddenly flushed crimson in the silliest way, began with positively unseemly haste making strange little bows, and at the same time edging towards the door. His whole appearance betrayed a desire to sink through the floor, or more accurately, to get back to his table as quickly as possible. Ivan Ilyich, left alone, got up from his chair in confusion; he looked in the looking-glass without noticing his face.

"No, severity, severity and nothing but severity," he whispered almost unconsciously, and suddenly a vivid flush overspread his face. He felt suddenly more ashamed, more weighed down than he had been in the most insufferable moments of his eight days of tribulation. "I did break down!" he said to himself, and sank helplessly into his chair.

1862

# NOTES FROM THE UNDERGROUND

## A TALE

### PART I

#### The Underground *

I

I AM A sick man. . . . I am a spiteful man. I am an unattractive man. I believe my liver is diseased. However, I know nothing at all about my disease, and do not know for certain what ails me. I don't consult a doctor for it, and never have, though I have a respect for medicine and doctors. Besides, I am extremely superstitious, sufficiently so to respect medicine, anyway (I am well-educated enough not to be superstitious, but I am superstitious). No, I refuse to consult a doctor from spite. That you probably will not understand. Well, I understand it, though. Of course, I can't explain who it is precisely that I am mortifying in this case by my spite: I am perfectly well aware that I cannot "pay out" the doctors by not consulting them; I know better than any one that by all this I am only injuring myself and no one else. But still, if I don't consult a doctor it is from spite. My liver is bad, well—let it get worse!

* The author of the Notes and the Notes themselves are, of course, imaginary. Nevertheless it is clear that such persons as the writer of these notes not only may, but positively must, exist in our society, when we consider the circumstances under which our society was formed. I have tried to expose to the view of the public more distinctly than is commonly done one of the characters of the recent past. He is one of the representatives of a generation still living. In this fragment, entitled "The Underground," this person introduces himself and his views, and, as it were, tries to explain the causes owing to which he has made his appearance and was bound to make his appearance in our midst. In the second fragment there will appear the actual notes of this person concerning certain events in his life.—AUTHOR'S NOTE.

I have been going on like that for a long time—twenty years. Now I am forty. I used to be in the government service, but am no longer. I was a spiteful official. I was rude and took pleasure in being so. I did not take bribes, you see, so I was bound to find a recompense in that, at least. (A poor jest, but I will not scratch it out. I wrote it thinking it would sound very witty; but now that I have seen myself that I only wanted to show off in a despicable way, I will not scratch it out on purpose!)

When petitioners used to come for information to the table at which I sat, I used to grind my teeth at them, and felt intense enjoyment when I succeeded in making anybody unhappy. I almost always did succeed. For the most part they were all timid people—of course, they were petitioners. But of the uppish ones there was one officer in particular I could not endure. He simply would not be humble, and clanged his sword in a disgusting way. I carried on a feud with him for eighteen months over that sword. At last I got the better of him. He left off clanking it. That happened in my youth, though.

But do you know, gentlemen, what was the chief point about my spite? Why, the whole point, the real sting of it lay in the fact that continually, even in the moment of the acutest spleen, I was inwardly conscious with shame that I was not only not a spiteful but not even an embittered man, that I was simply scaring sparrows at random and amusing myself by it. I might foam at the mouth, but bring me a doll to play with, give me a cup of tea with sugar in it, and maybe I might be appeased. I might even be genuinely touched, though probably I should grind my teeth at myself afterwards and lie awake at night with shame for months after. That was my way.

I was lying when I said just now that I was a spiteful official. I was lying from spite. I was simply amusing myself with the petitioners and with the officer, and in reality I never could become spiteful. I was conscious every moment in myself of many, very many elements absolutely opposite to that. I felt them positively swarming in me, these opposite elements. I knew that they had been swarming in me all my life and craving some outlet, but I would not let them, would not let them, purposely would not let them come out. They tormented me till I was ashamed: they drove me to convulsions and—sickened me, at last, how they sickened me! Now, are not you fancying, gentlemen, that I am expressing remorse for something now, that I am asking your forgiveness for something? I am sure you are fancying that . . . However, I assure you I do not care if you are. . . .

It was not only that I could not become spiteful, I did not know how to become anything: neither spiteful nor kind, neither a rascal nor an honest man, neither a hero nor an insect. Now, I am living out my life in my corner, taunting myself with the spiteful and useless consolation that an intelligent man cannot become anything seriously, and it is only the fool who becomes anything. Yes, a man in the nineteenth century must and morally ought to be pre-eminently a characterless creature; a man of character, an active man is pre-eminently a limited creature. That has been my conviction these forty years. I am forty years old now, and you know forty years is a whole lifetime; you know it is extreme old age. To live longer than forty years is bad manners, is vulgar, immoral. Who does live beyond forty? Answer that, sincerely and honestly. I will tell you who do: fools and worthless fellows. I tell all old men that to their face, all these venerable old men, all these silver-haired and reverend seniors! I tell the whole world that to its face! I have a right to say so, for I shall go on living to sixty myself. To seventy! To eighty! . . . Stay, let me take breath. . . .

You imagine no doubt, gentlemen, that I want to amuse you. You are mistaken in that, too. I am by no means such a mirthful person as you imagine, or as you may imagine; however, irritated by all this babble (and I feel that you are irritated) you think fit to ask me who I am—then my answer is, I am a collegiate assessor. I was in the service that I might have something to eat (and solely for that reason), and when last year a distant relation left me six thousand roubles in his will I immediately retired from the service and settled down in my corner. I used to live in this corner before, but now I have settled down in it. My room is a wretched, horrid one on the outskirts of the town. My servant is an old countrywoman, ill-natured from stupidity, and, moreover, there is always a nasty smell about her. I am told that the Petersburg climate is bad for me, and that with my small means it is very expensive to live in Petersburg. I know all that better than all these sage and experienced counselors and monitors. . . . But I am remaining in Petersburg; I am not going away from Petersburg! I am not going away because . . . ech! Why, it is absolutely no matter whether I am going away or not going away.

But what can a decent man speak of with most pleasure?
Answer: Of himself.
Well, so I will talk about myself.

## II

I want now to tell you, gentlemen, whether you care to hear it
or not, why I could not even become an insect. I tell you solemnly,
that I have many times tried to become an insect. But I was not equal
even to that. I swear, gentlemen, that to be too conscious is an illness
—a real thoroughgoing illness. For man's everyday needs, it would
have been quite enough to have the ordinary human consciousness,
that is, half or a quarter of the amount which falls to the lot of a cultivated man of our unhappy nineteenth century, especially one who
has the fatal ill-luck to inhabit Petersburg, the most abstract and pre-
meditated town on the whole terrestial globe. (There are premedi-
tated and unpremeditated towns.) It would have been quite enough,
for instance, to have the consciousness by which all so-called direct
persons and men of action live. I bet you think I am writing all this
from affectation, to be witty at the expense of men of action; and
what is more, that from ill-bred affectation, I am clanking a sword
like my officer. But, gentlemen, whoever can pride himself on his
diseases and even swagger over them?

Though, after all, every one does do that; people do pride themselves on their diseases, and I do, maybe, more than any one. We will
not dispute it; my contention was absurd. But yet I am firmly persuaded that a great deal of consciousness, every sort of consciousness, in fact, is a disease. I stick to that. Let us leave that, too, for a
minute. Tell me this: why does it happen that at the very, yes, at
the very moments when I am most capable of feeling every refinement of all that is "good and beautiful," as they used to say at one
time, it would, as though of design, happen that I not only felt but
did such ugly things, such that. . . . Well, in short, actions that all,
perhaps, commit; but which, as though purposely, occurred to me at
the very time when I was most conscious that they ought not to be
committed. The more conscious I was of goodness and of all that
was "good and beautiful," the more deeply I sank into my mire and
the more ready I was to sink in it altogether. But the chief point was
that all this was, as it were, not accidental in me, but as though it

were bound to be so. It was as though it were my most normal condition, and not in the least disease or depravity, so that at last all desire in me to struggle against this depravity passed. It ended by my almost believing (perhaps actually believing) that this was perhaps my normal condition. But at first, in the beginning, what agonies I endured in that struggle! I did not believe it was the same with other people, and all my life I hid this fact about myself as a secret. I was ashamed (even now, perhaps, I am ashamed): I got to the point of feeling a sort of secret, abnormal, despicable enjoyment in returning home to my corner on some disgusting Petersburg night, acutely conscious that that day I had committed a loathsome action again, that what was done could never be undone, and secretly, inwardly gnawing, gnawing at myself for it, tearing and consuming myself till at last the bitterness turned into a sort of shameful accursed sweetness, and at last—into positive real enjoyment! Yes, into enjoyment, into enjoyment! I insist upon that. I have spoken of this because I keep wanting to know for a fact whether other people feel such enjoyment? I will explain; the enjoyment was just from the too intense consciousness of your own degradation; it was that you yourself felt that you had reached the last barrier; that it was horrible, but it could not be otherwise; that there was no escape for you; that you never could become a different man; that even if time and faith were still left you to change into something different, you would most likely not wish to change; or if you did wish to, even then you would do nothing; because perhaps in reality there was nothing for you to change into.

And the worst of it was, and the root of it all, that it was all in accord with the normal fundamental laws of over-acute consciousness, and with the inertia that was the direct result of those laws, and that consequently one was not only unable to change but could do absolutely nothing. Thus it follows, as the result of acute consciousness, that one is not to blame for being a scoundrel; as though that were any consolation to the scoundrel once he has come to realize that he actually is a scoundrel. But enough. . . . Ech, I have talked a lot of nonsense, but what have I explained? How is enjoyment of this to be explained? But I will explain it. I will get to the bottom of it! That is why I have taken up my pen. . . .

I, for instance, have a great deal of *amour propre*. I am as suspicious and prone to take offence as a humpback or a dwarf. But upon my word I sometimes have had moments when if I had happened to be slapped in the face I should, perhaps, have been positively glad of it. I say, in earnest, that I should probably have been able to discover even in that a peculiar sort of enjoyment—the enjoyment, of course, of despair; but in despair there are the most intense enjoyments, especially when one is very acutely conscious of the hopelessness of one's position. And when one is slapped in the face—why then the consciousness of being rubbed into a pulp would positively overwhelm one. The worst of it is, look at it which way one will, it still turns out that I was always the most to blame in everything. And what is most humiliating, to blame through no fault of my own but, so to say, through the laws of nature. In the first place, to blame because I am cleverer than any of the people surrounding me. (I have always considered myself cleverer than any of the people surrounding me, and sometimes, would you believe it, have been positively ashamed of it. At any rate, I have all my life, as it were, turned my eyes away and never could look people straight in the face.) To blame, finally, because even if I had had magnanimity, I should only have suffered more from the sense of its uselessness. I should certainly never have been able to do anything from being magnanimous—neither to forgive, for my assailant would perhaps have slapped me due to the laws of nature, and one cannot forgive the laws of nature; nor to forget, for even if it were owing to the laws of nature, it is insulting all the same. Finally, even if I had wanted to be anything but magnanimous, had desired on the contrary to revenge myself on my assailant, I could not have revenged myself on any one for anything because I should certainly never have made up my mind to do anything, even if I had been able to. Why should I not have made up my mind? About that in particular I want to say a few words.

### III

There are people who know how to revenge themselves and to stand up for themselves in general; how do they do it? Why, when they are possessed, let us suppose, by the feeling of revenge, then for the time there is nothing else but that feeling left in their whole being. Such a gentleman simply dashes straight for his object like an infuriated bull with its horns down, and nothing but a wall will stop him. (By the way: facing the wall, such gentlemen—that is, the "direct" persons and men of action—are genuinely nonplused. For them a wall is not an evasion, as for us people who think and consequently do nothing; it is not an excuse for turning aside, an excuse for which we are always very glad, though we scarcely believe in it ourselves, as a rule. No, they are nonplused in all sincerity. The wall has for them something tranquillizing, morally soothing, final— maybe even something mysterious . . . but of the wall later.)

Well, such a direct person I regard as the real normal man, as his tender mother nature wished to see him when she graciously brought him into being on the earth. I envy such a man till I am green in the face. He is stupid. I am not disputing that, but perhaps the normal man should be stupid, how do you know? Perhaps it is very beautiful, in fact. And I am the more persuaded of that suspicion, if one can call it so, by the fact that if you take, for instance, the antithesis of the normal man, that is, the man of acute consciousness, who has come, of course, not out of the lap of nature but out of a retort (this is almost mysticism, gentlemen, but I suspect this, too), this retort-made man is sometimes so nonplused in the presence of his antithesis that with all his exaggerated consciousness he genuinely thinks of himself as a mouse and not a man. It may be an acutely conscious mouse, yet it is a mouse, while the other is a man, and therefore, et cetera, et cetera. And the worst of it is, he himself, his very own self, looks on himself as a mouse; no one asks him to do so; and that is an important point.

Now let us look at this mouse in action. Let us suppose, for instance, that it feels insulted, too (and it almost always does feel insulted), and wants to revenge itself, too. There may even be a greater accumulation of spite in it than in *l'homme de la nature et de la vérité*. The base and nasty desire to vent that spite on its assailant rankles perhaps even more nastily in it than in *l'homme de la nature et de la vérité*. For through his innate stupidity the latter looks upon his revenge as justice pure and simple; while in consequence of his acute consciousness the mouse does not believe in the justice of it. To come at last to the deed itself, to the very act of revenge. Apart from the one fundamental nastiness, the luckless mouse succeeds in creating around it so many other nastinesses in the form of doubts and questions, adds to the one question so many unsettled questions, that there inevitably works up around it a sort of fatal brew, a stinking mess, made up of its doubts, emotions, and of the contempt spat upon it by the direct men of action who stand solemnly about it as judges and arbitrators, laughing at it till their healthy sides ache. Of course the only thing left for it is to dismiss all that with a wave of its paw, and, with a smile of assumed contempt in which it does not even itself believe, creep ignominiously into its mousehole. There in its nasty, stinking, underground home our insulted, crushed and ridiculed mouse promptly becomes absorbed in cold, malignant and, above all, everlasting spite. For forty years together it will remember its injury down to the smallest, most ignominious details, and every time will add, of itself, details still more ignominious, spitefully teasing and tormenting itself with its own imagination. It will itself be ashamed of its imaginings, but yet it will recall it all, it will go over and over every detail, it will invent unheard of things against itself, pretending that those things might happen, and will forgive nothing. Maybe it will begin to revenge itself, too, but, as it were, piecemeal, in trivial ways, from behind the stove, incognito, without believing either in its own right to vengeance, or in the success of its revenge, knowing that from all its efforts at revenge it will suffer a hundred times more than he on whom it revenges itself, while he, I daresay, will not even scratch himself. On its deathbed it will recall it all over again, with interest accumulated over all the years and. . . .

But it is just in that cold, abominable half despair, half belief, in that conscious burying oneself alive for grief in the underground for forty years, in that acutely recognized and yet partly doubtful hopelessness of one's position, in that hell of unsatisfied desires turned inward, in that fever of oscillations, of resolutions determined for ever and repented of again a minute later—that the savor of that strange enjoyment of which I have spoken lies. It is so subtle, so difficult of analysis, that persons who are a little limited, or even simply persons of strong nerves, will not understand a single atom of it. "Possibly," you will add on your own account with a grin, "people will not understand it either who have never received a slap in the face," and in that way you will politely hint to me that I, too, perhaps, have had the experience of a slap in the face in my life, and so I speak as one who knows. I bet that you are thinking that. But set your minds at rest, gentlemen, I have not received a slap in the face, though it is absolutely a matter of indifference to me what you may think about it. Possibly, I even regret, myself, that I have given so few slaps in the face during my life. But enough . . . not another word on that subject of such extreme interest to you.

I will continue calmly concerning persons with strong nerves who do not understand a certain refinement of enjoyment. Though in certain circumstances these gentlemen bellow their loudest like bulls, though this, let us suppose, does them the greatest credit, yet, as I have said already, confronted with the impossible they subside at once. The impossible means the stone wall! What stone wall? Why, of course, the laws of nature, the deductions of natural science, mathematics. As soon as they prove to you, for instance, that you are descended from a monkey, then it is no use scowling, accept it for a fact. When they prove to you that in reality one drop of your own fat must be dearer to you than a hundred thousand of your fellow creatures, and that this conclusion is the final solution of all so-called virtues and duties and all such prejudices and fancies, then you have just to accept it, there is no help for it, for twice two is a law of mathematics. Just try refuting it.

"Upon my word," they will shout at you, "it is no use protesting: it is a case of twice two makes four! Nature does not ask your permission, she has nothing to do with your wishes, and whether you like her laws or dislike them, you are bound to accept her as she is, and consequently all her conclusions. A wall, you see, is a wall . . . and so on, and so on."

Merciful Heavens! but what do I care for the laws of nature and arithmetic, when, for some reason I dislike those laws and the fact that twice two makes four? Of course I cannot break through the wall by battering my head against it if I really have not the strength to knock it down, but I am not going to be reconciled to it simply because it is a stone wall and I have not the strength.

As though such a stone wall really were a consolation, and really did contain some word of conciliation, simply because it is as true as twice two makes four. Oh, absurdity of absurdities! How much better it is to understand it all, to recognize it all, all the impossibilities and stone walls; not to be reconciled to one of those impossibilities and stone walls if it disgusts you to be reconciled; by the way of the most inevitable logical combinations to reach the most revolting conclusions on the everlasting theme that even for the stone wall you are yourself somehow to blame, though again it is as clear as day you are not to blame in the least, and therefore grinding your teeth in silent impotence to sink voluptuously into inertia, brooding on the fact that there is no one even for you to feel vindictive against, that you have not, and perhaps never will have, an object for your spite, that it is a sleight of hand, a bit of juggling, a card-sharper's trick, that it is simply a mess, no knowing what and no knowing who, but in spite of all these uncertainties and jugglings, still there is an ache in you, and the more you do not know, the worse the ache.

## IV

"Ha, ha, ha! You will be finding enjoyment in toothache next," you cry, with a laugh.

"Well? Even in toothache there is enjoyment," I answer. I had toothache for a whole month and I know there is. In that case, of course, people are not spiteful in silence, but moan; but they are not candid moans, they are malignant moans, and the malignancy is the whole point. The enjoyment of the sufferer finds expression in those moans; if he did not feel enjoyment in them he would not moan. It is a good example, gentlemen, and I will develop it. Those moans express in the first place all the aimlessness of your pain, which is so humiliating to your consciousness; the whole legal system of nature on which you spit disdainfully, of course, but from which you suffer all the same, while she does not. They express the consciousness that you have no enemy to punish, but that you have pain; the consciousness that in spite of all possible Vagenheims you are in complete slavery to your teeth; that if someone wishes it, your teeth will leave off aching, and if he does not, they will go on aching another three months; and that finally if you are still contumacious and still protest, all that is left you for your own gratification is to thrash yourself or beat your wall with your fist as hard as you can, and absolutely nothing more. Well, these mortal insults, these jeers on the part of someone unknown, end at last in an enjoyment which sometimes reaches the highest degree of voluptuousness. I ask you, gentlemen, listen sometimes to the moans of an educated man of the nineteenth century suffering from toothache, on the second or third day of the attack, when he is beginning to moan, not as he moaned on the first day, that is, not simply because he has toothache, not just as any coarse peasant, but as a man affected by progress and European civilization, a man who is "divorced from the soil and the national elements," as they express it nowadays. His moans become nasty, disgustingly malignant, and go on for whole days and nights. And of course he knows that he is doing himself no sort of good with his moans; he knows better than anyone that he is only lacerating and harassing himself and others for nothing; he knows that even the audience before whom he is making his efforts, and his whole family, listen to him with loathing, do not put a groat's worth of faith in him, and inwardly understand that he might moan differently, more simply, without trills and flourishes, and that he is only amusing himself like that from ill-humor, from malignancy. Well, it is in all these recognitions and disgraces that there lies a voluptuous pleasure. As though he would say: "I am worrying you, I am lacerating your hearts, I am keeping everyone in the house awake. Well, stay awake then, you, too, feel every minute that I have toothache. I am not a hero to you now, as I tried to seem before, but simply a nasty person, an impostor. Well, so be it, then! I am very glad that you see through me. It is nasty for you to hear my despicable moans: well, let it be nasty; here I will let you have a nastier flourish in a minute. . . ." You do not understand even now, gentlemen? No, it seems our development and our consciousness must go further to understand all the intricacies of this pleasure. You laugh? Delighted. My jests, gentlemen, are of course in bad taste, jerky, involved, lacking self-confidence. But of course that is because I do not respect myself. Can a man of perception respect himself at all?

V

Come, can a man who attempts to find enjoyment in the very feeling of his own degradation possibly have a spark of respect for himself? I am not saying this now from any mawkish kind of remorse. And, indeed, I could never endure saying, "Forgive me, Papa, I won't do it again," not because I am incapable of saying that—on the contrary, perhaps just because I have been too capable of it, and in what a way, too! As though of design I used to get into trouble in cases when I was not to blame in any way. That was the nastiest part of it. At the same time I was genuinely touched and penitent, I used to shed tears and, of course, deceived myself, though I was not acting in the least and there was a sick feeling in my heart at the time. . . . For that one could not blame even the laws of nature, though the laws of nature have continually and all my life offended me more than anything. It is loathsome to remember it all, but it was loathsome even then. Of course, a minute or so later I would realize wrathfully that it was all a lie, a revolting lie, an affected lie, that is, all this penitence, this emotion, these vows of reform. You will ask why did I worry myself with such antics. Answer: because it was very dull to sit with one's hands folded, and so one began cutting capers. That is really it. Observe yourselves more carefully, gentlemen, then you will understand that it is so. I invented adventures for myself and made up a life, so as at least to live in some way. How many times it has happened to me—well, for instance, to take offense simply on purpose, for nothing; and one knows oneself, of course, that one is offended at nothing, that one is putting it on, but yet one brings oneself, at last, to the point of being really offended. All my life I have had an impulse to play such pranks, so that in the end I could not control it in myself. Another time, twice, in fact, I tried hard to fall in love. I suffered, too, gentlemen, I assure you. In the depth of my heart there was no faith in my suffering, only a faint stir of mockery, but yet I did suffer, and in the real, orthodox way; I was jealous, beside myself . . . and it was all from ennui, gentlemen, all from ennui; inertia overcame me.

You know the direct, legitimate fruit of consciousness is inertia, that is, conscious sitting-with-the-hands-folded. I have referred to this already. I repeat, I repeat with emphasis: all "direct" persons and men of action are active just because they are stupid and limited. How explain that? I will tell you: in consequence of their limitation they take immediate and secondary causes for primary ones, and in that way persuade themselves more quickly and easily than other people do that they have found an infallible foundation for their activity, and their minds are at ease and you know that is the chief thing. To begin to act, you know, you must first have your mind completely at ease and no trace of doubt left in it. Why, how am I, for example to set my mind at rest? Where are the primary causes on which I am to build? Where are my foundations? Where am I to get them from? I exercise myself in reflection, and consequently with me every primary cause at once draws after itself another still more primary, and so on to infinity. That is just the essence of every sort of consciousness and reflection. It must be a case of the laws of nature again. What is the result of it in the end? Why, just the same.

Remember I spoke just now of vengeance. (I am sure you did not take it in.) I said that a man revenges himself because he sees justice in it. Therefore he has found a primary cause, that is, justice. And so he is at rest on all sides, and consequently he carries out his revenge calmly and successfully, being persuaded that he is doing a just and honest thing. But I see no justice in it, I find no sort of virtue in it either, and consequently if I attempt to revenge myself, it is only out of spite. Spite, of course, might overcome everything, all my doubts, and so might serve quite successfully in place of a primary cause, precisely because it is not a cause. But what is to be done if I have not even spite (I began with that just now, you know). In consequence again of those accursed laws of consciousness, anger in me is subject to chemical disintegration. You look into it, the object flies off into air, your reasons evaporate, the criminal is not to be found, the wrong becomes not a wrong but a phantom, something like the toothache, for which no one is to blame, and consequently there is only the same outlet left again—that is, to beat the wall as hard as you can. So you give it up with a wave of the hand because you have not found a fundamental cause. And try letting yourself be carried away by your feelings, blindly, without reflection, without a primary cause, repelling consciousness at least for a time; hate or love, if only not to sit with your hands folded. The day after tomorrow, at the latest, you will begin despising yourself for having knowingly deceived yourself. Result: a soap-bubble and inertia. Oh, gentlemen, do you know, perhaps I consider myself an intelligent man, only because all my life I have been able neither to begin nor to finish anything. Granted I am a babbler, a harmless vexatious babbler, like all of us. But what is to be done if the direct and sole vocation of every intelligent man is babble, that is, the intentional pouring of water through a sieve?

## VI

Oh, if I had done nothing simply from laziness! Heavens, how I should have respected myself, then. I should have respected myself because I should at least have been capable of being lazy; there would at least have been one quality, as it were, positive in me, in which I could have believed myself. Question: What is he? Answer: A sluggard; how very pleasant it would have been to hear that of oneself! It would mean that I was positively defined, it would mean that there was something to say about me. "Sluggard"—why, it is a calling and vocation, it is a career. Do not jest, it is so. I should then be a member of the best club by right, and should find my occupation in continually respecting myself. I knew a gentlemen who prided himself all his life on being a connoisseur of Lafite. He considered this as his positive virtue, and never doubted himself. He died, not simply with a tranquil, but with a triumphant, conscience, and he was quite right, too. Then I should have chosen a career for myself, I should have been a sluggard and a glutton, not a simple one, but, for instance, one with sympathies for everything good and beautiful. How do you like that? I have long had visions of it. That "good and beautiful" weighs heavily on my mind at forty. But that is at forty; then—oh, then it would have been different! I should have found for myself a form of activity in keeping with it, to be precise, drinking to the health of everything "good and beautiful." I should have snatched at every opportunity to drop a tear into my glass and then to drain it to all that is "good and beautiful." I should then have turned everything into the good and the beautiful; in the nastiest, unquestionable trash, I should have sought out the good and the beautiful. I should have exuded tears like a wet sponge. An artist, for instance, paints a picture worthy of Gué. At once I drink to the health of the artist who painted the picture worthy of Gué, because I love all that is "good and beautiful." An author has written *As You Like It*: at once I drink to his health because I love all that is "good and beautiful."

I should claim respect for doing so. I should persecute anyone who would not show me respect. I should live at ease, I should die with dignity, why, it is charming, perfectly charming! And what a good round belly I should have grown, what a treble chin I should have established, what a ruby nose I should have colored for myself, so that everyone would have said, looking at me: "Here is an asset! Here is something real and solid!" And, say what you like, it is very agreeable to hear such remarks about oneself in this negative age.

### VII

But these are all golden dreams. Oh, tell me, who was it first announced, who was it first proclaimed, that man only does nasty things because he does not know his own interests; and that if he were enlightened, if his eyes were opened to his real normal interests, man would at once cease to do nasty things, would at once become good and noble because, being enlightened and understanding his real advantage, he would see his own advantage in the good and nothing else, and we all know that not one man can, consciously, act against his own interests, consequently, so to say, through necessity, he would begin doing good? Oh, the babe! Oh, the pure, innocent child! Why, in the first place, when in all these thousands of years has there been a time when man has acted only from his own interest? What is to be done with the millions of facts that bear witness that men, *consciously*, that is fully understanding their real interests, have left them in the background and have rushed headlong on another path, to meet peril and danger, compelled to this course by nobody and by nothing, but, as it were, simply disliking the beaten track, and have obstinately, wilfully, struck out another difficult, absurd way, seeking it almost in the darkness. So, I suppose, this obstinacy and perversity were pleasanter to them than any advantage. . . . Advantage! What is advantage? And will you take it upon yourself to define with perfect accuracy in what the advantage of man consists? And what if it so happens that a man's advantage, *sometimes*, not only may, but even must, consist in his desiring in certain cases what is harmful to himself and not advantageous? And if so, if there can be such a case, the whole principle falls into dust. What do you think—are there such cases? You laugh; laugh away, gentlemen, but only answer me: have man's advantages been reckoned up with perfect certainty? Are there not some which not only have not been included but cannot possibly be included under any classification? You see, you gentlemen have, to the best of my knowledge, taken your whole register of human advantages from the averages of statistical figures and politico-economic formulas. Your advantages are prosperity, wealth, freedom, peace—and so on, and so on. So that the man who should, for instance, go openly and knowingly in opposition to all that list would, to your thinking, and indeed mine, too, of course, be an obscurantist or an absolute madman: wouldn't he? But, you know, this is what is surprising: why does it so happen that all these statisticians, sages and lovers of humanity, when they reckon up human advantages, invariably leave out one? They don't even take it into their reckoning in the form in which it should be taken, and the whole reckoning depends upon that. It would be no great matter, they would simply have to take it, this advantage, and add it to the list. But the trouble is, that this strange advantage does not fall under any classification and is not in place in any list. I have a friend for instance . . . Ech! gentlemen, but of course he is your friend, too; and indeed there is no one, no one, to whom he is not a friend! When he prepares for any undertaking this gentleman immediately explains to you, elegantly and clearly, exactly how he must act in accordance with the laws of reason and truth. What is more, he will talk to you with excitement and passion of the true normal interests of man; with irony he will upbraid the shortsighted fools who do not understand their own interests, nor the true significance of virtue; and, within a quarter of an hour, without any sudden outside provocation, but simply through something inside him which is stronger than all his interests, he will go off on quite a different tack—that is, act in direct opposition to what he has just been saying about himself, in opposition to the laws of reason, in opposition to his own advantage, in fact in opposition to everything . . . I warn you that my friend is a compound personality, and therefore it is difficult to blame him as an individual. The fact is, gentlemen, it seems there must really exist something that is dearer to almost every man than his greatest advantages, or (not to be illogical) there is a most advantageous advantage (the very one omitted of which we spoke just now) which is more important and more advantageous than all other advantages, for the sake of which a man if necessary is ready to act in opposition to all laws; that is, in opposition to reason, honor, peace, prosperity—in fact, in opposition to all those excellent and useful things, if only he can attain that fundamental, most advantageous advantage which is dearer to him than all.

"Yes, but it's advantage all the same," you will retort. But excuse me, I'll make the point clear, and it is not a case of playing upon words. What matters is, that this advantage is remarkable from the very fact that it breaks down all our classifications, and continually shatters every system constructed by lovers of mankind for the benefit of mankind. In fact, it upsets everything. But before I mention this advantage to you, I want to compromise myself personally, and therefore I boldly declare that all these fine systems, all these theories for explaining to mankind their real normal interests, in order that inevitably striving to pursue these interests they may at once become good and noble—are, in my opinion, so far, mere logical exercises! Yes, logical exercises. Why, to maintain this theory of the regeneration of mankind by means of the pursuit of his own advantage is to my mind almost the same thing as . . . as to affirm, for instance, following Buckle, that through civilization mankind becomes softer, and consequently less bloodthirsty and less fitted for warfare. Logically it does seem to follow from his arguments. But man has such a predilection for systems and abstract deductions that he is ready to distort the truth intentionally, he is ready to deny the evidence of his senses only to justify his logic. I take this example because it is the most glaring instance of it. Only look about you: blood is being spilt in streams, and in the merriest way, as though it were champagne. Take the whole of the nineteenth century in which Buckle lived. Take Napoleon—the Great and also the present one. Take North America—the eternal union. Take the farce of Schleswig-Holstein. . . . And what is it that civilization softens in us? The only gain of civilization for mankind is the greater capacity for variety of sensations—and absolutely nothing more. And through the development of this many-sidedness man may come to finding enjoyment in bloodshed. In fact, this has already happened to him. Have you noticed that it is the most civilized gentlemen who have been the subtlest slaughterers, to whom the Attilas and Stenka Razins could not hold a candle, and if they are not so conspicuous as the Attilas and Stenka Razins it is simply because they are so often met with, are so ordinary and have become so familiar to us. In any case civilization has made mankind if not more bloodthirsty, certainly more vilely, more loathsomely bloodthirsty. In former days he saw justice in bloodshed and with his conscience at peace exterminated those he thought proper to kill. Now we do think bloodshed abominable and yet we engage in this abomination, and with more energy than ever. Which is worse? Decide that for yourselves. They say that Cleopatra (excuse an instance from Roman history) was fond of sticking gold pins into her slave-girls' breasts and derived gratification from their screams and writhings. You will say that that was in comparatively barbarous times; that these are barbarous times too, because, also comparatively speaking, pins are stuck in even now; that though man has now learned to see more clearly than in barbarous ages, he is still far from having learnt to act as reason and science would dictate. But yet you are fully convinced that he will be sure to learn when he gets rid of certain old bad habits, and when common sense and science have completely re-educated human nature and turned it in a normal direction. You are confident that then man will cease from *intentional* error and will, so to say, be compelled not to want to set his will against his normal interests. That is not all; then, you say, science itself will teach man (though to my mind it's a superfluous luxury) that he never has really had any caprice or will of his own, and that he himself is something in the nature of a piano-key or the stop of an organ, and that there are, besides, things called the laws of nature; so that everything he does is not done by his willing it, but is done of itself, by the laws of nature. Consequently we have only to discover these laws of nature, and man will no longer have to answer for his actions and life will become exceedingly easy for him. All human actions will then, of course, be tabulated according to these laws, mathematically, like tables of logarithms up to 108,000, and entered in an index; or, better still, there will be published certain well-intentioned works in the nature of encyclopedic dictionaries, in which everything will be so clearly calculated and noted that there will be no more deeds or adventures in the world.

Then—this is all what you say—new economic relations will be established, all ready-made and worked out with mathematical exactitude, so that every possible question will vanish in the twinkling of an eye, simply because every possible answer to it will be provided. Then the "Palace of Crystal" will be built. Then . . . In fact, those will be halcyon days. Of course there is no guaranteeing (this is my comment) that it will not be, for instance, frightfully dull then (for what will one have to do when everything will be calculated according to tables), but on the other hand, everything will be extraordinary rational. Of course boredom may lead you to anything. It is boredom sets one sticking gold pins into people, but all that does not matter. What is bad (this is my comment again) is that I dare say people will be thankful for the gold pins then. Man is stupid, you know, phenomenally stupid; or rather he is not at all stupid, but he is so ungrateful that you could not find another like him in all creation. I, for instance, would not be in the least surprised if all of a sudden, apropos of nothing, in the midst of general prosperity a gentleman with an ignoble, or rather with a reactionary and ironical, countenance were to arise and, putting his arms akimbo, say to us all: "I say, gentlemen, hadn't we better kick over the whole show here and scatter rationalism to the winds, simply to send these logarithms to the devil, and to enable us to live once more at our own sweet foolish will!" That again would not matter; but what is annoying is that he would be sure to find followers—such is the nature of man. And all that for the most foolish reason, which, one would think, was hardly worth mentioning; that is, that man everywhere and at all times, whoever he may be, has preferred to act as he chose and not in the least as his reason and advantage dictated. And one may choose what is contrary to one's own interests, and sometimes one *positively ought* (that is my idea). One's own free unfettered choice, one's own caprice, however wild it may be, one's own fancy worked up at times to frenzy—is that very "most advantageous advantage" which we have overlooked, which comes under no classification and against which all systems and theories are continually being shattered to atoms. And how do these wiseacres know that man wants a normal, a virtuous choice? What has made them conceive that man must want a rationally advantageous choice? What man wants is simply *independent* choice, whatever that independence may cost and wherever it may lead. And choice, of course, the devil only knows what choice. . . .

VIII

"Ha! ha! ha! But you know there is no such thing as choice in reality, say what you like," you interpose with a chuckle. "Science has succeeded in so far analyzing man that we know already that choice and what is called freedom of will is nothing else than—"

Stay, gentlemen, I meant to begin with that myself. I confess, I was rather frightened. I was just going to say that the devil only knows what choice depends on, and that perhaps that was a very good thing, but I remembered the teaching of science . . . and pulled myself up. And here you have begun upon it. Indeed, if there really is some day discovered a formula for all our desires and caprices—that is, an explanation of what they depend upon, by what laws they arise, how they develop, what they are aiming at in one case and in another and so on, that is, a real mathematical formula—then, most likely, man will at once cease to feel desire, indeed, he will be certain to. For who would want to choose by rule? Besides, he will at once be transformed from a human being into an organ-stop or something of the sort; for what is a man without desire, without free will and without choice, if not a stop in an organ? What do you think? Let us reckon the chances—can such a thing happen or not?

"H'm!" you decide. "Our choice is usually mistaken from a false view of our advantage. We sometimes choose absolute nonsense, because in our foolishness we see in that nonsense the easiest means for attaining a supposed advantage. But when all that is explained and worked out on paper (which is perfectly possible, for it is contemptible and senseless to suppose that some laws of nature man will never understand), then certainly so-called desires will no longer exist. For if a desire should come into conflict with reason, we shall then reason and not desire, because it will be impossible retaining our reason to be *senseless* in our desires, and in that way knowingly act against reason and desire to injure ourselves. And as all choice and reasoning can be really calculated—because there will some day be discovered the laws of our so-called free will—so, joking apart, there may one day be something like a table constructed of them, so that we really shall choose in accordance with it. If, for instance, some day they calculate and prove to me that I made a long nose at someone because I could not help making a long nose at him and that I had to do it in that particular way, what *freedom* is left me, especially if I am a learned man and have taken my degree somewhere? Then I should be able to calculate my whole life for thirty years beforehand. In short, if this could be arranged, there would be nothing left for us to do; anyway, we should have to understand that. And, in fact, we ought unwearyingly to repeat to ourselves that at such and such a time and in such and such circumstances nature does not ask our leave; that we have got to take her as she is and not fashion her to suit our fancy, and if we really aspire to formulas and tables of rules, and well, even . . . to the chemical retort, there's no help for it, we must accept the retort too, or else it will be accepted without our consent. . . ."

Yes, but here I come to a stop! Gentlemen, you must excuse me for being overphilosophical; it's the result of forty years underground! Allow me to indulge my fancy. You see, gentlemen, reason is an excellent thing, there's no disputing that, but reason is nothing but reason and satisfies only the rational side of man's nature, while will is a manifestation of the whole life, that is, of the whole of human life including reason and all the impulses. And although our life, in this manifestation of it, is often worthless, yet it is life and not simply extracting square roots. Here I, for instance, quite naturally want to live, in order to satisfy all my capacities for life, and not simply my capacity for reasoning, that is, not simply one twentieth of my capacity for life. What does reason know? Reason only knows what it has succeeded in learning (some things, perhaps, it will never learn; this is a poor comfort, but why not say so frankly?) and human nature acts as a whole, with everything that is in it, consciously or unconsciously, and, even if it goes wrong, it lives. I suspect, gentlemen, that you are looking at me with compassion; you tell me again that an enlightened and developed man, such, in short, as the future man will be, cannot consciously desire anything disadvantageous to himself, that that can be proved mathematically. I thoroughly agree, it can—by mathematics. But I repeat for the hundredth time, there is one case, one only, when man may consciously, purposely, desire what is injurious to himself, what is stupid, very stupid—simply in order to have the right to desire for himself even what is very stupid and not to be bound by an obligation to desire only what is sensible. Of course, this very stupid thing, this caprice of ours, may be in reality, gentlemen, more advantageous for us than anything else on earth, especially in certain cases. And in particular it may be more advantageous than any advantage even when it does us obvious harm, and contradicts the soundest conclusions of our reason concerning our advantage—for in any circumstances it preserves for us what is most precious and most important—that is, our personality, our individuality. Some, you see, maintain that this really is the most precious thing for mankind; choice can, of course, if it chooses, be in agreement with reason; and especially if this be not abused but kept within bounds. It is profitable and sometimes even praiseworthy. But very often, and even most often, choice is utterly and stubbornly opposed to reason . . . and . . . and . . . do you know that that, too, is profitable, sometimes even praiseworthy?

Gentlemen, let us suppose that man is not stupid. (Indeed one cannot refuse to suppose that, if only from the one consideration, that, if man is stupid, then who is wise?) But if he is not stupid, he is monstrously ungrateful! Phenomenally ungrateful. In fact, I believe that the best definition of man is the ungrateful biped. But that is not all, that is not his worst defect; his worst defect is his perpetual moral obliquity, perpetual—from the days of the Flood to the

Schleswig-Holstein period. Moral obliquity and consequently lack of good sense; for it has long been accepted that lack of good sense is due to no other cause than moral obliquity. Put it to the test and cast your eyes upon the history of mankind. What will you see? Is it a grand spectacle? Grand, if you like. Take the Colossus of Rhodes, for instance, that's worth something. With good reason Mr. Anayevsky testifies of it that some say that it is the work of man's hands, while others maintain that it has been created by nature herself. Is it many-colored? Maybe it is many-colored, too: if one takes the dress uniforms, military and civilian, of all peoples in all ages—that alone is worth something, and if you take the undress uniforms you will never get to the end of it; no historian would be equal to the job. Is it monotonous? Maybe it's monotonous too; it's fighting and fighting; they are fighting now, they fought before and they fought after—you will admit, that it is almost too monotonous. In short, one may say anything about the history of the world—anything that might enter the most disordered imagination. The only thing one can't say is that it's rational. The very word sticks in one's throat. And, indeed, this is the odd thing that is continually happening: there are continually turning up in life moral and rational persons, sages and lovers of humanity who make it their object to live all their lives as morally and rationally as possible, to be, so to speak, a light to their neighbors simply in order to show them that it is possible to live morally and rationally in this world. And yet we all know that those very people sooner or later have been false to themselves, playing some queer trick, often a most unseemly one. Now I ask you: what can be expected of man since he is a being endowed with such strange qualities? Shower upon him every earthly blessing, drown him in a sea of happiness, so that nothing but bubbles of bliss can be seen on the surface; give him economic prosperity, such that he should have nothing else to do but sleep, eat cakes and busy himself with the continuation of his species, and even then, out of sheer ingratitude, sheer spite, man would play you some nasty trick. He would even risk his cakes and would deliberately desire the most fatal rubbish, the most uneconomic absurdity, simply to introduce into all this positive good sense his pernicious fantastic element. It is just his fantastic dreams, his vulgar folly that he will desire to retain, simply in order to prove to himself—as though that were necessary—that men still are men and not the keys of a piano, which the laws of nature threaten to control so completely that soon one will be able to desire nothing but by the calendar. And that is not all: even if man really were nothing but a piano-key, even if this were proved to him by natural science and mathematics, even then he would not become reasonable, but would purposely do something perverse out of simple ingratitude, simply to gain his point. And if he does not find means, he will contrive destruction and chaos, will contrive sufferings of all sorts, only to gain his point! He will launch a curse upon the world, and as only man can curse (it is his privilege, the primary distinction between him and other animals), maybe by his curse alone he will attain his object—that is, convince himself that he is a man and not a piano-key! If you say that all this, too, can be calculated and tabulated—chaos and darkness and curses, so that the mere possibility of calculating it all beforehand would stop it all, and reason would reassert itself, then man would purposely go mad in order to be rid of reason and gain his point! I believe in it, I answer for it, for the whole work of man really seems to consist in nothing but proving to himself every minute that he is a man and not a piano-key! It may be at the cost of his skin, it may be by cannibalism! And this being so, can one help being tempted to rejoice that it has not yet come off, and that desire still depends on something we don't know?

You will scream at me (that is, if you condescend to do so) that no one is touching my free will, that all they are concerned with is that my will should of itself, of its own free will, coincide with my own normal interests, with the laws of nature and arithmetic.

Good heavens, gentlemen, what sort of free will is left when we come to tabulation and arithmetic, when it will all be a case of twice two make four? Twice two makes four without my will. As if free will meant that!

## IX

Gentlemen, I am joking, and I know myself that my jokes are not brilliant, but you know one can't take everything as a joke. I am, perhaps jesting while I gnash my teeth. Gentlemen, I am tormented by questions: answer them for me. You, for instance, want to cure men of their old habits and reform their will in accordance with science and good sense. But how do you know, not only that it is possible, but also that it is *desirable*, to reform man in that way? And what leads you to the conclusion that man's inclinations *need* reforming? In short, how do you know that such a reformation will be a benefit to man? And to go to the root of the matter, why are you so positively convinced that not to act against his real normal interests guaranteed by the conclusions of reason and arithmetic is certainly always advantageous for man and must always be a law for mankind? So far, you know, this is only your supposition. It may be the law of logic, but not the law of humanity. Perhaps you think, gentlemen, that I am mad? Allow me to defend myself. I agree that man is pre-eminently a creative animal, predestined to strive consciously for an object and to engage in engineering—that is, incessantly and eternally to make new roads, *wherever they may lead*. But the reason why he wants sometimes to go off at a tangent may just be that he is *predestined* to make the road, and perhaps, too, that however stupid the "direct" practical man may be, the thought sometimes will occur to him that the road almost always does lead *somewhere*, and that the destination it leads to is less important than the process of making it, and that the chief thing is to save the well-conducted child from despising engineering, and so giving way to the fatal idleness, which, as we all know, is the mother of all the vices. Man likes to make roads and to create, that is a fact beyond dispute. But why has he such a passionate love for destruction and chaos also? Tell me that! But on that point I want to say a couple of words myself. May it not be that he loves chaos and destruction (there can be no disputing that he does sometimes love it) because he is instinctively afraid of attaining his object and completing the edifice he is constructing? Who knows, perhaps he only loves that edifice from a distance, and is by no means in love with it at close quarters; perhaps he only loves building it and does not want to live in it, but will leave it, when completed, for the use of *les animaux domestiques*—such as the ants, the sheep, and so on. Now the taste of the ants is quite different. They have a marvellous edifice of that pattern which endures forever —the ant-heap.

With the ant-heap the respectable race of ants began and with the ant-heap they will probably end, which does the greatest credit to their perseverance and good sense. But man is a frivolous and incongruous creature, and perhaps, like a chess player, loves the process of the game, not the end of it. And who knows (there is no saying with certainty), perhaps the only goal on earth to which mankind is striving lies in this incessant process of attaining, in other words, in life itself, and not in the thing to be attained, which must always be expressed as a formula, as positive as twice two makes four, and such positiveness is not life, gentlemen, but is the beginning of death. Anyway, man has always been afraid of this mathematical certainty, and I am afraid of it now. Granted that man does nothing but seek that mathematical certainty, he traverses oceans, sacrifices his life in the quest, but to succeed, really to find it, he dreads, I assure you. He feels that when he has found it there will be nothing for him to look for. When workmen have finished their work they do at least receive their pay, they go to the tavern, then they are taken to the police-station—and there is occupation for a week. But where can man go? Anyway, one can observe a certain awkwardness about him when he has attained such objects. He loves the process of attaining, but does not quite like to have attained, and that, of course, is very absurd. In fact, man is a comical creature; there seems to be a kind of jest in it all. But yet mathematical certainty is, after all, something insufferable. Twice two makes four seems to me simply a piece of insolence. Twice two makes four is a pert coxcomb who stands with arms akimbo barring your path and spitting. I admit that twice two makes four is an excellent thing, but if we are to give everything its due, twice two makes five is sometimes a very charming thing too.

And why are you so firmly, so triumphantly, convinced that only the normal and the positive—in other words, only what is conducive to welfare—is for the advantage of man? Is not reason in error as regards advantage? Does not man, perhaps, love something besides well-being? Perhaps he is just as fond of suffering? Perhaps suffering is just as great a benefit to him as well-being? Man is sometimes extraordinarily, passionately, in love with suffering, and that is a fact. There is no need to appeal to universal history to prove that; only ask yourself, if you are a man and have lived at all. As far as my personal opinion is concerned, to care only for well-being seems to me positively ill-bred. Whether it's good or bad, it is sometimes very pleasant, too, to smash things. I hold no brief for suffering nor for well-being either. I am standing for . . . my caprice, and for its being guaranteed to me when necessary. Suffering would be out of place in vaudevilles, for instance; I know that. In the "Palace of Crystal" it is unthinkable; suffering means doubt, negation, and what would be the good of a "palace of crystal" if there could be any doubt about it? And yet I think man will never renounce real suffering, that is, destruction and chaos. Why, suffering is the sole origin of consciousness. Though I did lay it down at the beginning that consciousness is the greatest misfortune for man, yet I know man prizes it and would not give it up for any satisfaction. Consciousness, for instance, is infinitely superior to twice two makes four. Once you have mathematical certainty there is nothing left to do or to understand. There will be nothing left but to bottle up your five senses and plunge into contemplation. While if you stick to consciousness, even though the same result is attained, that is, there is nothing left to do, you can at least flog yourself at times, and that will, at any rate, liven you up. Reactionary as it is, it is better than nothing.

X

You believe in a crystal palace that can never be destroyed—a palace at which one will not be able to put out one's tongue or make a long nose on the sly. And perhaps that is just why I am afraid of this edifice, that it is of crystal and can never be destroyed and that one cannot put one's tongue out at it even on the sly.

You see, if it were not a palace, but a henhouse, I might creep into it to avoid getting wet, and yet I would not call the henhouse a palace out of gratitude to it for keeping me dry. You laugh and say that in such circumstances a henhouse is as good as a mansion. Yes, I answer, if one had to live simply to keep out of the rain.

But what is to be done if I have taken it into my head that that is not the only object in life, and that if one must live one had better live in a mansion. That is my choice, my desire. You will only eradicate it when you have changed my preference. Well, do change it, allure me with something else, give me another ideal. But meanwhile I will not take a henhouse for a mansion. The palace of crystal may be an idle dream, it may be that it is inconsistent with the laws of nature and that I have invented it only through my own stupidity, through the old-fashioned irrational habits of my generation. But what does it matter to me that it is inconsistent? That makes no difference since it exists in my desires, or rather exists as long as my desires exist. Perhaps you are laughing again? Laugh away; I will put up with any mockery rather than pretend that I am satisfied when I am hungry. I know, anyway, that I will not be put off with a compromise, with a recurring zero, simply because it is consistent with the laws of nature and actually exists. I will not accept as the crown of my desires a block of buildings with tenements for the poor on a lease of a thousand years, and perhaps with the signboard of a dentist hanging out. Destroy my desires, eradicate my ideals, show me something better, and I will follow you. You will say, perhaps, that it is not worth your trouble; but in that case I can give you the answer. We are discussing things seriously; but if you won't deign to give me your attention, I will drop your acquaintance. I can retreat into my underground hole.

But while I am alive and have desires I would rather my hand were withered away than bring one brick to such a building! Don't remind me that I have just rejected the crystal palace for the sole reason that one cannot put out one's tongue at it. I did not say that, because I am so fond of putting my tongue out. Perhaps the only thing I resented was that of all your edifices there has not been one at which one could not put out one's tongue. On the contrary, I would let my tongue be cut off out of gratitude if things could be so arranged that I should lose all desire to put it out. It is not my fault that things cannot be so arranged, and that one must be satisfied with model flats. Then why am I made with such desires? Can I have been constructed simply in order to come to the conclusion that my whole mechanism is a cheat? Can this be the whole purpose? I do not believe it.

But do you know what: I am convinced that we underground folk ought to be kept on a curb. Though we may sit forty years underground without speaking, when we do come out into the light of day and break out, we talk and talk and talk. . . .

## XI

The long and the short of it is, gentlemen, that it is better to do nothing! Better conscious inertia! And so hurrah for the underground! Though I have said that I envy the normal man to the last drop of my bile, yet I should not care to be in his place such as he is now (though I shall not cease envying him). No, no; anyway the underground life is more advantageous. There, at any rate, one can. . . . Oh, but even now I am lying! I am lying because I know myself that it is not the underground that is better, but something different, quite different, for which I am thirsting, but which I cannot find! Damn the underground!

I will tell you another thing that would be better, and that is, if I myself believed in any part of what I have just written. I swear to you, gentlemen, there is not one thing, not one word of what I have written that I really believe. That is, I believe it, perhaps, but at the same time I feel and suspect that I am lying like a cobbler.

"Then why have you written all this?" you will say to me.

"I ought to put you underground for forty years without anything to do and then come to you in your cellar, to find out what stage you have reached! How can a man be left with nothing to do for forty years?"

"Isn't·that shameful, isn't that humiliating?" you will say, perhaps, wagging your heads contemptuously. "You thirst for life and try to settle the problems of life by a logical tangle. And how persistent, how insolent are your sallies, and at the same time what a funk you are in! You talk nonsense and are pleased with it; you say impudent things and are in continual alarm and apologizing for them. You declare that you are afraid of nothing and at the same time try to ingratiate yourself with us. You declare that you are gnashing your teeth and at the same time you try to be witty so as to amuse us. You know that your witticisms are not witty, but you are evidently well satisfied ·with their literary value. You may, perhaps, have really suffered, but you have no respect for your own suffering. You may have sincerity, but you have no modesty; out of the pettiest vanity you expose your sincerity to publicity and ignominy. You doubtlessly mean to say something, but hide your last word through fear, because you have not the resolution to utter it, and only have a cowardly impudence. You boast of consciousness, but you are not sure of your ground, for though your mind works, yet your heart is darkened and corrupt, and you cannot have a full, genuine consciousness without a pure heart. And how intrusive you are, how you insist and grimace! Lies, lies, lies!"

Of course I have myself made up all the things you say. That, too, is from underground. I have been for forty years listening to you through a crack in the wall. I have invented them myself, there was nothing else I could invent. It is no wonder that I have learned this by heart and it has taken a literary form. . . .

But can you really be so credulous as to think that I will print all this and give it to you to read too? And another problem: why do I call you "gentlemen," why do I address you as though you really were my readers? Such confessions as I intend to make are never printed nor given to other people to read. Anyway, I am not strong-minded enough for that, and I don't see why I should be. But you see a fancy has occurred to me and I want to realize it at all costs. Let me explain.

Every man has reminiscences which he would not tell to everyone, but only to his friends. He has other matters in his mind which he would not reveal even to his friends, but only to himself, and that in secret. But there are other things which a man is afraid to tell even to himself, and every decent man has a number of such things stored away in his mind. The more decent he is, the greater the number of such things in his mind. Anyway, I have only lately determined to remember some of my early adventures. Till now I have always avoided •them, even with a certain uneasiness. Now, when I am not only recalling them, but have actually decided to write an account of them, I want to try the experiment whether one can, even with oneself, be perfectly open and not take fright at the whole truth. I will observe, in parenthesis, that Heine says that a true autobiography is almost an impossibility, and that man is bound to lie about himself. He considers that Rousseau certainly told lies about himself in his confessions, and even intentionally lied, out of vanity. I am convinced that Heine is right; I quite understand how sometimes one may, out of sheer vanity, attribute regular crimes to oneself, and indeed I can very well conceive that kind of vanity. But Heine judged of people who made their confessions to the public. I write only for myself, and I wish to declare once and for all that if I write as though I were addressing readers, that is simply because it is easier for me to write in that form. It is a form, an empty form—I shall never have readers. I have made this plain already. . . .

I don't wish to be hampered by any restrictions in the compilation of my notes. I shall not attempt any system or method. I shall jot things down as I remember them.

But here, perhaps, someone will catch at the word and ask me: if you really don't reckon on readers, why do you make such compacts with yourself—and on paper too—that is, that you won't attempt any system or method, that you jot things down as you remember them, and so on, and so on? Why are you explaining? Why do you apologize?

Well there it is, I answer.

There is a whole psychology in all this, though. Perhaps it is simply that I am a coward. And perhaps I purposely imagine an audience before me in order to be more dignified while I write. There may be thousands of reasons. Again, what precisely is my object in writing? If it is not for the benefit of the public, why should I not simply recall these incidents in my own mind without putting them on paper?

Quite so; but yet it is more imposing on paper. There is something more impressive in it; I shall be better able to criticize myself and improve my style. Besides, I shall perhaps obtain actual relief from writing. Today, for instance, I am particularly oppressed by one memory of a distant past. It came back vividly to my mind a few days ago, and has remained haunting me like an annoying tune that one cannot get rid of. And yet I must get rid of it somehow. I have hundreds of such reminiscences; but at times some one stands out from the hundreds and oppresses me. For some reason I believe that if I write it down I shall get rid of it. Why not try?

Besides, I am bored, and I never have anything to do. Writing will be a sort of work. They say work makes man kind-hearted and honest. Well here is a chance for me, anyway.

Snow is falling today, yellow and dingy. It fell yesterday, too, and a few days ago. I fancy it is the wet snow that has reminded me of that incident which I cannot shake off now. And so, let it be a story apropos of the the wet snow.


# PART II

## Apropos of the Wet Snow

When from dark error's subjugation
My words of passionate exhortation
   Had wrenched thy fainting spirit free;
And writhing prone in thine affliction
Thou didst recall with malediction
   The vice that had encompassed thee:
And when thy slumbering conscience, fretting

By recollection's torturing flame,
Thou didst reveal the hideous setting
    Of thy life's current ere I came:
When suddenly I saw thee sicken,
    And weeping, hide thine anguished face,
Revolted, maddened, horror-stricken,
    At memories of foul disgrace.
                —NEKRASOV (*translated by Juliet Soskice*).

I

At that time I was only twenty-four. My life was even then
gloomy, ill-regulated, and as solitary as that of a savage. I made
friends with no one and positively avoided talking, and buried myself
more and more in my hole. At work in the office I never looked at
any one, and I was perfectly well aware that my companions not
only regarded me as a queer fellow, but even looked upon me—I
always fancied this—with a sort of loathing. I sometimes wondered
why it was that nobody except me fancied that he was looked upon
with aversion? One of the clerks had a most repulsive, pockmarked
face, which was positively villainous. I believe I should not have
dared to look at any one if I had such an unsightly countenance.
Another wore such a very dirty old uniform that there was an unpleasant odor in his proximity. Yet not one of these gentlemen
showed the slightest self-consciousness—either about their clothes or
their countenance or their character in any way. Neither of them
ever imagined that they were regarded with repulsion; if they had
imagined it, they would not have minded—so long as their superiors
did not look at them in that way. It is clear to me now that, owing
to my unbounded vanity and to the high standard I set for myself,
I often looked at myself with furious discontent, which verged on
loathing, and so I inwardly attributed the same feeling to everyone.
I hated my face, for instance: I thought it disgusting, and even suspected that there was something base in my expression, and so every
day when I turned up at the office I tried to behave as independently
as possible, and to assume a lofty expression, so that I might not be
suspected of being abject. "My face may be ugly," I thought, "but
let it be lofty, expressive, and, above all, *extremely* intelligent." But
I was positively and painfully certain that it was impossible for my

countenance ever to express those qualities. And what was worst of all, I thought it actually stupid looking, and I would have been quite satisfied if I could have looked intelligent. In fact, I would even have put up with looking base if, at the same time, my face could have been thought strikingly intelligent.

Of course, I hated my fellow clerks one and all, and I despised them all, yet at the same time I was, as it were, afraid of them. In fact, it happened at times that I thought more highly of them than of myself. It somehow happened quite suddenly that I alternated between despising them and thinking them superior to myself. A cultivated and decent man cannot be vain without setting a fearfully high standard for himself, and without despising and almost hating himself at certain moments. But whether I despised them or thought them superior I dropped my eyes almost every time I met anyone. I even made experiments whether I could face So-and-so's looking at me, and I was always the first to drop my eyes. This worried me to distraction. I had a sickly dread, too, of being ridiculous, and so had a slavish passion for the conventional in everything external. I loved to fall into the common rut, and had a whole-hearted terror of any kind of eccentricity in myself. But how could I live up to it? I was morbidly sensitive, as a man of our age should be. They were all stupid, and as like one another as so many sheep. Perhaps I was the only one in the office who fancied that I was a coward and a slave, and I fancied it just because I was more highly developed. But it was not only that I fancied it, it really was so. I was a coward and a slave. I say this without the slightest embarrassment. Every decent man of our age must be a coward and a slave. That is his normal condition. Of that I am firmly persuaded. He is made and constructed to that very end. And not only at the present time owing to some casual circumstances, but always, at all times, a decent man is bound to be a coward and a slave. It is the law of nature for all decent people all over the earth. If any one of them happens to be valiant about something, he need not be comforted nor carried away by that; he would show the white feather just the same before something else. That is how it invariably and inevitably ends. Only donkeys and mules are valiant, and they only till they are pushed up to the wall. It is not worth while to pay attention to them for they really are of no consequence.

Another circumstance, too, worried me in those days: that there was no one like me and I was unlike anyone else. "I am alone and they are *all*," I thought—and pondered.

From that it is evident that I was still a youngster.

The very opposite sometimes happened. It was loathsome sometimes to go to the office; things reached such a point that I often came home ill. But all at once, apropos of nothing, there would come a phase of skepticism and indifference (everything happened to me in phases), and I myself would laugh at my intolerance and fastidiousness, I would reproach myself with being *romantic*. At one time I was unwilling to speak to anyone, while at other times I would not only talk, but go to the length of contemplating making friends with them. All my fastidiousness would suddenly, without rhyme or reason, vanish. Who knows, perhaps I never had really had it, and it had simply been affected, and got out of books. I have not decided that question even now. Once I quite made friends with them, visited their homes, played preference, drank vodka, talked of promotions. . . . But here let me make a digression.

We Russians, speaking generally, have never had those foolish transcendental "romantics"—German, and still more French—on whom nothing produces any effect; if there were an earthquake, if all France perished at the barricades, they would still be the same, they would not even have the decency to affect a change, but would still go on singing their transcendental songs to the hour of their death, because they are fools. We, in Russia, have no fools; that is well known. That is what distinguishes us from foreign lands. Consequently these transcendental natures are not found amongst us in their pure form. The idea that they are is due to our "realistic" journalists and critics of that day, always on the look-out for Kostanzhoglos and Uncle Pyotr Ivanychs and foolishly accepting them as our ideal; they have slandered our romantics, taking them for the same transcendental sort as in Germany or France. On the contrary, the characteristics of our romantics are absolutely and directly opposed to the transcendental European type, and no European standard can be applied to them. (Allow me to make use of this word "romantic" —an old-fashioned and much respected word which has done good service and is familiar to all). The characteristics of our romantics are to understand everything, to *see everything and to see it often incomparably more clearly than our most realistic minds see it*; to refuse to accept anyone or anything, but at the same time not to despise anything; to give way, to yield, from policy; never to lose sight of a useful practical object (such as rent-free quarters at the government expense, pensions, decorations), to keep their eye on that object through all the enthusiasms and volumes of lyrical poems, and at the same time to preserve "the good and the beautiful" inviolate within them to the hour of their death, and to preserve themselves also, incidently, like some precious jewel wrapped in cotton wool if only for the benefit of "the good and the beautiful." Our romantic is a man of great breadth and the greatest rogue of all our rogues, I assure you. . . . I can assure you from experience, indeed. Of course, that is, if he is intelligent. But what am I saying! The romantic is always intelligent, and I only meant to observe that although we have had foolish romantics they don't count, and they were only so because in the flower of their youth they degenerated into Germans, and to preserve their precious jewel more comfortably, settled somewhere out there—by preference in Weimar or the Black Forest.

I, for instance, genuinely despised my official work and did not openly abuse it simply because I was in it myself and got a salary for it. Anyway, take note, I did not openly abuse it. Our romantic would rather go out of his mind—a thing, however, which very rarely happens—than take to open abuse, unless he had some other career in view; and he is never kicked out. At most, they would take him to the lunatic asylum as "the King of Spain" if he should go very mad. But it is only the thin, fair people who go out of their minds in Russia. Innumerable romantics attain later in life to considerable rank in the service. Their many-sidedness is remarkable! And what a faculty they have for the most contradictory sensations! I was comforted by this thought even in those days, and I am of the same opinion now. That is why there are so many "broad natures" among us who never lose their ideal even in the depths of degradation; and though they never stir a finger for their ideal, though they are arrant thieves and knaves, yet they tearfully cherish their first ideal and are extraordinarily honest at heart. Yes, it is only among us that the most incorrigible rogue can be absolutely and loftily honest at heart without in the least ceasing to be a rogue. I repeat, our romantics, frequently, become such accomplished rascals (I use the term "rascals" affectionately), suddenly display such a sense of reality and practical knowledge, that their bewildered superiors and the public generally can only ejaculate in amazement.

Their many-sidedness is really amazing, and goodness knows what it may develop into later on, and what the future has in store for us. It is not poor material! I do not say this from any foolish or boastful patriotism. But I feel sure that you are again imagining that I am joking. Or perhaps it's just the contrary, and you are convinced that I really think so. Anyway, gentlemen, I shall welcome both views as an honor and a special favor. And do forgive my digression.

I did not, of course, maintain friendly relations with my comrades and soon was at loggerheads with them, and in my youth and inexperience I even gave up bowing to them, abruptly. That, however, only happened to me once. As a rule, I was always alone.

In the first place, I spent most of my time at home, reading. I tried to stifle all that was continually seething within me by means of external impressions. And the only external means I had was reading. Reading, of course, was a great help—exciting me, giving me pleasure and pain. But at times it bored me fearfully. One longed for movement in spite of everything, and I plunged all at once into dark, underground, loathsome vice of the pettiest kind. My wretched passions were acute, smarting, from my continual, sickly irritability. I had hysterical impulses, with tears and convulsions. I had no resource except reading, that is, there was nothing in my surroundings which I could respect and which attracted me. I was overwhelmed with depression, too; I had an hysterical craving for incongruity and for contrast, and so I took to vice. I have not said all this to justify myself. . . . But, no! I am lying. I did want to justify myself. I make that little observation for my own benefit, gentlemen. I don't want to lie. I vowed to myself I would not.

And so, furtively, timidly, in solitude, at night, I indulged in filthy vice, with a feeling of shame which never deserted me, even at the most loathsome moments, and which at such moments nearly made me curse. Already even then I had my underground world in my soul. I was fearfully afraid of being seen, of being met, of being recognized. I visited various obscure haunts.

One night as I was passing a tavern I saw through a lighted window some gentlemen fighting with billiard cues, and saw one of them thrown out of window. At other times I should have felt very much disgusted, but I was in such a mood at the time that I actually envied the gentleman thrown out of window—and I envied him so much that I even went into the tavern and into the billiard room. "Perhaps," I thought, "I'll have a fight, too, and they'll throw me out of window."

I was not drunk—but what is one to do—the blues will drive a man to such a pitch of hysteria. But nothing happened. It seemed that I was not even equal to being thrown out of the window and I went away without having my fight.

An officer put me in my place from the first moment.

I was standing by the billiard table and in my ignorance blocking up the way, and he wanted to pass; he took me by the shoulders and without a word—without a warning or explanation—moved me from where I was standing to another spot and passed by as though he had not noticed me. I could have forgiven blows, but I could not forgive his having moved me without noticing me.

Devil knows what I would have given for a real regular quarrel —a more decent, a more *literary* one, so to speak. I had been treated like a fly. This officer was over six foot, while I was a spindly little fellow. But the quarrel was in my hands. I had only to protest and I certainly would have been thrown out of the window. But I changed my mind and preferred to beat an embittered retreat.

From the tavern I went straight home, confused and troubled, and the next night I went on with my petty debauch, still more furtively, abjectly and miserably than before, as it were, with tears in my eyes —but still I did go out again. Don't imagine, though, it was cowardice made me slink away from the officer: I never have been a coward at heart, though I have always been a coward in action. Don't be in a hurry to laugh—I assure you I can explain it all.

Oh, if only that officer had been one of the sort who would consent to fight a duel! But no, he was one of those gentlemen (alas, long extinct!) who preferred fighting with cues or, like Gogol's Lieutenant Pirogov, appealing to the police. They did not fight duels and would have thought a duel with a civilian like me an utterly unseemly procedure in any case—and they looked upon the duel altogether as something impossible, something free-thinking and French. But they were quite ready to bully, especially when they were over six foot.

I did not slink away through cowardice, but through an unbounded vanity. I was afraid not of his six foot, nor of getting a sound thrashing and being thrown out of the window; I should have had physical courage enough, I assure you; but I had not the moral courage. What I was afraid of was that everyone present, from the insolent marker down to the lowest little stinking, pimply clerk in a greasy collar, would jeer at me and fail to understand when I began to protest and to address them in literary language. For of the point of honor—not of honor, but of the point of honor (*point d'honneur*) —one cannot speak among us except in literary language. You can't allude to the "point of honor" in ordinary language. I was fully convinced (the sense of reality, in spite of all my romanticism!) that they would all simply split their sides with laughter, and that the officer would not simply beat me, that is, without insulting me, but would certainly prod me in the back with his knees, kick me round the billiard table, and only then perhaps have pity and drop me out of the window.

Of course, this trivial incident could not end for me in that alone. I often met that officer afterwards in the street and noticed him very carefully. I am not quite sure whether he recognized me, I imagine not; I judge from certain signs. But I—I stared at him with spite and hatred and so it went on . . . for several years! My resentment grew even deeper with years. At first I began making stealthy inquiries about this officer. It was difficult for me to do so, for I knew no one. But one day I heard someone shout his surname in the street as I was following him at a distance, as though I were tied to him— and so I learnt his surname. Another time I followed him to his flat, and for ten copecks learned from the porter where he lived, on which storey, whether he lived alone or with others, and so on— in fact, everything one could learn from a porter. One morning, though I had never tried my hand with the pen, it suddenly occurred to me to write a satire on this officer in the form of a novel which would unmask his villainy. I wrote the novel with relish. I did unmask his villainy, I even exaggerated it; at first I so altered his surname that it could easily be recognized, but on second thoughts I changed it, and sent the story to *Otechestvennye zapiski*. But at that time such attacks were not the fashion and my story was not printed. That was a great vexation to me.

Sometimes I was positively choked with resentment. At last I determined to challenge my enemy to a duel. I composed a splendid, charming letter to him, imploring him to apologize to me, and hinting rather plainly at a duel in case of refusal. The letter was so composed that if the officer had had the least understanding of the good and the beautiful he would certainly have flung himself on my neck and have offered me his friendship. And how fine that would have been! How we should have got on together! "He could have shielded me with his higher rank, while I could have improved his mind with my culture, and, well . . . my ideas, and all sorts of things might have happened." Only fancy, this was two years after his insult to me, and my challenge would have been a ridiculous anachronism, in spite of all the ingenuity of my letter in disguising and explaining away the anachronism. But, thank God (to this day I thank the Almighty with tears in my eyes) I did not send the letter to him. Cold shivers run down my back when I think of what might have happened if I had sent it.

And all at once I revenged myself in the simplest way, by a stroke of genius! A brilliant thought suddenly dawned upon me. Sometimes on holidays I used to stroll along the sunny side of the Nevsky about four o'clock in the afternoon. Though it was hardly a stroll so much as a series of innumerable miseries, humiliations and resentments; but no doubt that was just what I wanted. I used to wriggle along in a most unseemly fashion, like an eel, continually moving aside to make way for generals, for officers of the guards and the hussars, or for ladies. At such minutes there used to be a convulsive twinge at my heart, and I used to feel hot all down my back at the mere thought of the wretchedness of my attire, of the wretchedness and abjectness of my little scurrying figure. This was a regular martyrdom, a continual, intolerable humiliation at the thought, which passed into an incessant and direct sensation, that I was a mere fly in the eyes of all this world, a nasty, disgusting fly—more intelligent, more highly developed, more refined in feeling than any of them, of course—but a fly that was continually making way for everyone, insulted and injured by everyone. Why I inflicted this torture upon myself, why I went to the Nevsky, I don't know. I felt simply drawn there at every possible opportunity.

Already then I began to experience a rush of the enjoyment of which I spoke in the first chapter. After my affair with the officer I felt even more drawn there than before: it was on the Nevsky that I met him most frequently, there I could admire him. He, too, went there chiefly on holidays. He, too, turned out of his path for generals and persons of high rank, and he, too, wriggled between them like an eel; but people like me, or even the better dressed ones, he simply walked over; he made straight for them as though there was nothing but empty space before him, and never, under any circumstances, turned aside. I gloated over my resentment watching him and . . . always resentfully made way for him. It exasperated me that even in the street I could not be on an even footing with him.

"Why must you invariably be the first to move aside?" I kept asking myself in hysterical rage, waking up sometimes at three o'clock in the morning. "Why it is you and not he? There's no regulation about it; there's no written law. Let the making way be equal as it usually is when refined people meet: he moves halfway and you move halfway; you pass with mutual respect."

But that never happened, and I always moved aside, while he did not even notice my making way for him. And lo and behold a bright idea dawned upon me! "What," I thought, "if I meet him and don't move to one side? What if I don't move aside on purpose, if I even knock up against him? How would that be?" This audacious idea took such a hold on me that it gave me no peace. I was dreaming of it continually, horribly, and I purposely went more frequently to the Nevsky in order to picture more vividly how I should do it when I did do it. I was delighted. This intention seemed to me more and more practical and possible.

"Of course I shall not really push him," I thought, already more good-natured in my joy. "I will simply not turn aside, will run up against him, not very violently, but just so that we shoulder each other—just as much as decency permits. I will push against him just as much as he pushes against me." At last I made up my mind completely. But my preparations took a great deal of time. To begin with, when I carried out my plan I should need to be looking rather more decent, and so I had to think of my get-up. "In case of emergency, if, for instance, there were any sort of public scandal (and the public there is of the most *recherché:* the Countess walks there; Prince D. walks there; all the literary world is there), I must be well dressed; that inspires respect and of itself puts us on an equal footing in the eyes of society."

With this object I asked for some of my salary in advance, and bought at Churkin's a pair of black gloves and a decent hat. Black gloves seemed to me both more dignified and *bon ton* than the lemon-colored ones which I had contemplated at first. "The color is too gaudy, it looks as though one were trying to be conspicuous," and

I did not take the lemon-colored ones. I had got ready long before-hand a good shirt, with white bone studs; my overcoat was the only thing that held me back. The coat in itself was a very good one, it kept me warm; but it was wadded and it had a raccoon collar which was the height of vulgarity. I had to change the collar at any sacrifice, and to have a beaver one like an officer's. For this purpose I began visiting the shops and after several attempts I pitched upon a piece of cheap German beaver. Though these German beavers soon grow shabby and look wretched, yet at first they look exceedingly well, and I only needed it for one occasion. I asked the price; even so, it was too expensive. After thinking it over thoroughly I decided to sell my raccoon collar. The rest of the money—a considerable sum for me, I decided to borrow from Anton Antonych Setochkin, my immediate superior, an unassuming person, though grave and judicious. He never lent money to anyone, but I had, on entering the service, been specially recommended to him by an important personage who had got me my berth. I was horribly worried. To borrow from Anton Antonych seemed to me monstrous and shameful. I did not sleep for two or three nights. Indeed, I did not sleep well at that time, I was in a fever; I had a vague sinking at my heart or else a sudden throbbing, throbbing, throbbing! Anton Antonych was surprised at first, then he frowned, then he reflected, and did after all lend me the money, receiving from me a written authorization to take from my salary a fortnight later the sum that he had lent me.

In this way everything was at last ready. The handsome beaver replaced the mean-looking raccoon, and I began by degrees to get to work. It would never have done to act offhand, at random; the plan had to be carried out skillfully, by degrees. But I must confess that after many efforts I began to despair: we simply could not run into each other. I made every preparation, I was quite determined—it seemed as though we should run into one another directly—and before I knew what I was doing I had stepped aside for him again and he had passed without noticing me. I even prayed as I approached him that God would grant me determination. One time I had made up my mind thoroughly, but it ended in my stumbling and falling at his feet because at the very last instant when I was six inches from him my courage failed me. He very calmly stepped over me, while I flew to one side like a ball. That night I was ill again, feverish and delirious.

And suddenly it ended most happily. The night before I had made up my mind not to carry out my fatal plan and to abandon it all, and with that object I went to the Nevsky for the last time, just to see how I would abandon it all. Suddenly, three paces from my enemy, I unexpectedly made up my mind—I closed my eyes, and we ran full tilt, shoulder to shoulder, against one another! I did not budge an inch and passed him on a perfectly equal footing! He did not even look round and pretended not to notice it; but he was only pretending, I am convinced of that. I am convinced of that to this day! Of course, I got the worst of it—he was stronger, but that was not the point. The point was that I had attained my object, I had kept up my dignity, I had not yielded a step, and had put myself publicly on an equal social footing with him. I returned home feeling that I was fully avenged for everything. I was delighted. I was triumphant and sang Italian arias. Of course, I will not describe to you what happened to me three days later; if you have read my first chapter you can guess that for yourself. The officer was afterwards transferred; I have not seen him now for fourteen years. What is the dear fellow doing now? Whom is he walking over?

## II

But the period of my dissipation would end and I always felt very sick afterwards. It was followed by remorse—I tried to drive it away: I felt too disgusted. By degrees, however, I grew used to that too. I grew used to everything, or rather I voluntarily resigned my-self to enduring it. But I had a means of escape that reconciled every-thing—that was to find refuge in "the good and the beautiful," in dreams, of course. I was a terrible dreamer, I would dream for three months on end, tucked away in my corner, and you may believe me that at those moments I had no resemblance to the gentleman who, in the perturbation of his chicken heart, put a collar of German beaver on his overcoat. I suddenly became a hero. I would not have admitted my six-foot lieutenant even if he had called on me. I could not even picture him before me then. What my dreams were and how I could satisfy myself with them—it is hard to say now, but at the time I was satisfied with them. Though, indeed, even now, I am to some extent satisfied with them. Dreams were particularly sweet and vivid after a spell of dissipation; they came with remorse and with tears, with curses and transports. There were moments of such positive intoxication, of such happiness, that there was not the faintest trace of irony within me, on my honor. I had faith, hope, love. I believed blindly at such times that by some miracle, by some external circumstance, all this would suddenly open out, expand; that suddenly a vista of suitable activity—beneficent, good, and, above all, *ready-made* (what sort of activity I had no idea, but the great thing was that it should be all ready for me)—would rise up before me—and I should come out into the light of day, almost riding a white horse and crowned with laurel. Anything but the foremost place I could not conceive for myself, and for that very reason I quite contentedly occupied the lowest in reality. Either to be a hero or to grovel in the mud—there was nothing between. That was my ruin, for when I was in the mud I comforted myself with the thought that at other times I was a hero, and the hero was a cloak for the mud: for an ordinary man it was shameful to defile himself, but a hero was too lofty to be utterly defiled, and so he might defile himself. It is worth noting that these attacks of the "good and the beautiful" visited me even during the period of dissipation and just at the times when I was touching bottom. They came in separate spurts, as though reminding me of themselves, but did not banish the dissipation by their appearance. On the contrary, they seemed to add a zest to it by contrast, and were only sufficiently present to serve as an appetizing sauce. That sauce was made up of contradictions and sufferings, of agonizing inward analysis, and all these pangs and pin-pricks gave a certain piquancy, even a significance to my dissipation—in fact, completely answered the purpose of an appetizing sauce. There was a certain depth of meaning in it. And I could hardly have resigned myself to the simple, vulgar, direct debauchery of a clerk and have endured all the filthiness of it. What could have allured me about it then and have drawn me at night into the street? No, I had a lofty way of getting out of it all.

And what loving-kindness, oh Lord, what loving-kindness I felt at times in those dreams of mine! in those "escapes into the good and the beautiful"; though it was fantastic love, though it was never applied to anything human in reality, yet there was so much of this love that one did not feel afterwards even the impulse to apply it in reality; that would have been superfluous. Everything, however, passed satisfactorily by a lazy and fascinating transition into the sphere of art, that is, into the beautiful forms of life, lying ready, largely stolen from the poets and novelists and adapted to all sorts of needs and uses. I, for instance, was triumphant over everyone; everyone, of course, was in dust and ashes, and was forced spontaneously to recognize my superiority, and I forgave them all. I was a poet and a grand gentleman, I fell in love; I came in for countless millions and immediately devoted them to humanity, and at the same time I confessed before all the people my shameful deeds, which, of course, were not merely shameful, but had in them much that was "good and beautiful," something in the Manfred style. Everyone would kiss me and weep (what idiots they would be if they did not), while I should go barefoot and hungry preaching new ideas and fighting a victorious Austerlitz against the obscurantists. Then the band would play a march, an amnesty would be declared, the Pope would agree to retire from Rome to Brazil; then there would be a ball for the whole of Italy at the Villa Borghese on the shores of Lake Como, Lake Como being for that purpose transferred to the neighborhood of Rome; then would come a scene in the bushes, and so on, and so on—as though you did not know all about it! You will say that it is vulgar and contemptible to drag all this into the marketplace after all the tears and transports which I have myself confessed. But why is it contemptible? Can you imagine that I am ashamed of it all, and that it was stupider than anything in your life, gentlemen? And I can assure you that some of these fancies were by no means badly composed. . . . It did not all happen on the shores of Lake Como. And yet you are right—it really is vulgar and contemptible. And most contemptible of all is that now I am attempting to justify myself to you. And even more contemptible than that is my making this remark now. But that's enough, or there will be no end to it: each step will be more contemptible than the last. . . .

I could never stand more than three months of dreaming at a time without feeling an irresistible desire to plunge into society. To plunge into society meant to visit my superior at the office, Anton Antonych Setochkin. He was the only steady acquaintance I have had in my life, and I wonder at the fact myself now. But I only went to see him when that phase came over me, and when my dreams had reached such a point of bliss that it became essential at once to embrace my fellows and all mankind; and for that purpose I needed, at least, one human being, actually existing. I had to call on Anton

Antonych, however, on Tuesday—his day at home; so I had always to time my passionate desire to embrace humanity so that it might fall on a Tuesday.

This Anton Antonych lived on the fourth storey in a house at Five Corners, in four low-pitched rooms, one smaller than the other, of a particularly mean and sallow appearance. His two daughters and their aunt used to pour out the tea. Of the daughters one was thirteen and the other fourteen, they both had snub noses, and I was awfully shy of them because they were always whispering and giggling together. The master of the house usually sat in his study on a leather couch in front of the table with some gray-headed gentleman, usually a colleague from our office or some other department. I never saw more than two or three visitors there, always the same. They talked about the excise duty, about business in the senate, about salaries, about promotions, about his Excellency, and the best means of pleasing him, and so on. I had the patience to sit like a fool beside these people for four hours at a stretch, listening to them without knowing what to say to them or venturing to say a word. I became stupefied, several times I felt myself perspiring, I was overcome by a sort of paralysis; but this was pleasant and good for me. On returning home I deferred for a time my desire to embrace all mankind.

I had however one other acquaintance of a sort, Simonov, who was an old schoolfellow. Indeed I had a number of schoolfellows in Petersburg, but I did not associate with them and had even given up nodding to them in the street. I believe I had transferred to the department I was in simply to avoid their company and to cut off all connection with my hateful childhood. Curses on that school and all those terrible years of penal servitude! In short, I parted from my schoolfellows as soon as I got out into the world. There were two or three left to whom I nodded in the street. One of them, Simonov, who had been in no way distinguished at school, was of a quiet and equable disposition; but I discovered in him a certain independence of character and even honesty. I don't even suppose that he was particularly stupid. I had at one time spent some rather soulful moments with him, but these had not lasted long and had somehow been suddenly clouded over. He was evidently uncomfortable at these reminiscences, and was, I fancy, always afraid that I might take up the same tone again. I suspected that he had an aversion for me, but still I went on going to see him, not being quite certain of it.

And so on one occasion, unable to endure my solitude and knowing that as it was Thursday Anton Antonych's door would be closed, I thought of Simonov. Climbing up to his fourth storey I was thinking that the man disliked me and that it was a mistake to go and see him. But as it always happened that such reflections impelled me, as though purposely, to put myself into a false position, I went in. It was almost a year since I had last seen Simonov.

III

I found two of my old schoolfellows with him. They seemed to be discussing an important matter. All of them took scarcely any notice of my entrance, which was strange, for I had not met them for years. Evidently they looked upon me as something on the level of a common fly. I had not been treated like that even at school, though they all hated me. I knew, of course, that they must despise me now for my lack of success in the service, and for having let myself sink so low, going about badly dressed and so on—which seemed to them a sign of my incapacity and insignificance. But I had not expected such contempt. Simonov was positively surprised at my turning up. Even in former days he had always seemed surprised at my coming. All this disconcerted me: I sat down, feeling rather miserable, and began listening to what they were saying.

They were engaged in warm and earnest conversation about a farewell dinner which they wanted to arrange for the next day to a comrade of theirs called Zverkov, an officer in the army, who was going away to a distant province. This Zverkov had been at school with me too. I had begun to hate him, particularly in the upper forms. In the lower forms he had simply been a pretty, playful boy whom everybody liked. I had hated him, however, even in the lower forms, just because he was a pretty and playful boy. He was always bad at his lessons and got worse and worse as he went on; however, he left with a good certificate, as he had powerful friends. During his last year at school he came in for an estate of two hundred serfs, and as almost all of us were poor, he took up a swaggering tone among us. He was vulgar in the extreme, but at the same time he was a good-natured fellow, even in his swaggering. In spite of superficial, fantastic and sham notions of honor and dignity, all but very few of us positively groveled before Zverkov, and the more so the more he swaggered. And it was not from any interested motive that they groveled, but simply because he had been favored by the gifts of nature. Moreover, it was, as it were, an accepted idea among us that Zverkov was a specialist in regard to tact and the social graces. This last fact particularly infuriated me. I hated the abrupt self-confident tone of his voice, his admiration of his own witticisms, which were often frightfully stupid, though he was bold in his language; I hated his handsome, but stupid face (for which I would, however, have gladly exchanged my intelligent one), and the free-and-easy military manners in fashion in the forties. I hated the way in which he used to talk of his future conquests of women (he did not venture to begin his attack upon women until he had the epaulettes of an officer, and was looking forward to them with impatience), and boasted of the duels he would constantly be fighting. I remember how I, invariably so taciturn, suddenly fastened upon Zverkov, when one day talking at a moment of leisure with his schoolfellows of his future relations with the fair sex, and growing as sportive as a puppy in the sun, he all at once declared that he would not leave a single village girl on his estate unnoticed, that that was his *droit de seigneur,* and that if the peasants dared to protest he would have them all flogged and double the tax on them, the bearded rascals. Our servile rabble applauded, but I attacked him, not from compassion for the girls and their fathers, but simply because they were applauding such an insect.

I got the better of him on that occasion, but though Zverkov was stupid, he was lively and impudent, and so laughed it off, and in such a way that my victory was not really complete: the laugh was on his side. He got the better of me on several occasions afterwards, but without malice, jestingly, casually. I remained angrily and contemptuously silent and would not answer him. When we left school he made advances to me; I did not rebuff them, for I was flattered, but we soon parted and quite naturally. Afterwards I heard of his barrack-room success as a lieutenant, and of the fast life he was leading. Then there came other rumors—of his successes in the service. By then he had taken to cutting me in the street, and I suspected that he was afraid of compromising himself by greeting a personage as insignificant as me. I saw him once in the theater, in the third tier of boxes. By then he was wearing shoulder-straps. He was twisting and twirling about, ingratiating himself with the daughters of an ancient General. In three years he had gone off considerably, though he was still rather handsome and adroit. One could see that by the time he was thirty he would be corpulent. So it was for this Zverkov that my schoolfellows were going to give a dinner on his departure. They had kept up with him for those three years, though privately they did not consider themselves on an equal footing with him, I am convinced of that.

Of Simonov's two visitors, one was Ferfichkin, a Russianized German—a little fellow with the face of a monkey, a blockhead who was always deriding everyone, a very bitter enemy of mine from our days in the lower forms—a vulgar, impudent, swaggering fellow, who affected a most sensitive feeling of personal honor, though, of course, he was a wretched little coward at heart. He was one of those worshipers of Zverkov who made up to the latter from interested motives, and often borrowed money from him. Simonov's other visitor, Trudolyubov, was a person in no way remarkable—a tall young fellow, in the army, with a cold face, fairly honest, though he worshiped success of every sort, and was only capable of thinking of promotion. He was some sort of distant relation of Zverkov's, and this, foolish as it seems, gave him a certain importance among us. He always thought me of no consequence whatever; his behaviour to me, though not quite courteous, was tolerable.

"Well, with seven roubles each," said Trudolyubov, "twenty-one roubles between the three of us, we ought to be able to get a good dinner. Zverkov, of course, won't pay."

"Of course not, since we are inviting him," Simonov decided.

"Can you imagine," Ferfichkin interrupted hotly and conceitedly, like some insolent flunky boasting of his master the General's decorations, "can you imagine that Zverkov will let us pay alone? He will accept from delicacy, but he will order half a dozen bottles of champagne."

"Do we want half a dozen for the four of us?" observed Trudolyubov, taking notice only of the half-dozen.

"So the three of us, with Zverkov for the fourth, twenty-one roubles, at the Hôtel de Paris at five o'clock tomorrow," Simonov, who had been asked to make the arrangements, concluded finally.

"How twenty-one roubles?" I asked in some agitation, with a show of being offended; "if you count me, it will not be twenty-one, but twenty-eight roubles."

It seemed to me that to invite myself so suddenly and unexpectedly would be positively graceful, and that they would all be conquered at once and would look at me with respect.

"Do you want to join, too?" Simonov observed, with no appearance of pleasure, seeming to avoid looking at me. He knew me through and through.

It infuriated me that he knew me so thoroughly.

"Why not? I am an old schoolfellow of his, too, I believe, and I must own I feel hurt that you have left me out," I said, boiling over again.

"And where were we to find you?" Ferfichkin put in roughly.

"You never were on good terms with Zverkov," Trudolyubov added, frowning.

But I had already clutched at the idea and would not give it up.

"It seems to me that no one has a right to form an opinion upon that," I retorted in a shaking voice, as though something tremendous had happened. "Perhaps that is just my reason for wishing it now, that I have not always been on good terms with him."

"Oh, there's no making you out . . . with these refinements," Trudolyubov jeered.

"We'll put your name down," Simonov decided, addressing me. "Tomorrow at five o'clock at the Hôtel de Paris."

"What about the money?" Ferfichkin began in an undertone, indicating me to Simonov, but he broke off, for even Simonov was embarrassed.

"That will do," said Trudolyubov, getting up. "If he wants to come so much, let him."

"But it's a private thing, among us friends," Ferfichkin said crossly, as he, too, picked up his hat. "It's not an official gathering."

"We do not want at all, perhaps . . ."

They went away. Ferfichkin did not greet me in any way as he went out, Trudolyubov barely nodded. Simonov, with whom I was left tête-à-tête, was in a state of vexation and perplexity, and looked at me queerly. He did not sit down and did not ask me to.

"H'm . . . yes . . . tomorrow, then. Will you pay your share now? I just ask so as to know," he muttered in embarrassment.

I flushed crimson, and as I did so I remembered that I had owed Simonov fifteen roubles for ages—which I had, indeed, never forgotten, though I had not paid it.

"You will understand, Simonov, that I could have no idea when I came here. . . . I am very much vexed that I have forgotten. . . ."

"All right, all right, that doesn't matter. You can pay tomorrow after the dinner. I simply wanted to know. . . . Please don't . . ."

He broke off and began pacing the room still more vexed. As he walked he began to stamp with his heels.

"Am I keeping you?" I asked, after two minutes of silence.

"Oh!" he said, starting, "that is—to be truthful—yes. I have to go and see someone . . . not far from here," he added in an apologetic voice, somewhat abashed.

"My goodness, why didn't you say so?" I cried, seizing my cap, with an astonishingly free-and-easy air, which was the last thing I should have expected of myself.

"It's close by . . . not two paces away," Simonov repeated, accompanying me to the front door with a fussy air which did not suit him at all. "So five o'clock, punctually, tomorrow," he called down the stairs after me. He was very glad to get rid of me. I was in a fury.

"What possessed me, what possessed me to force myself upon them?" I wondered, grinding my teeth as I strode along the street, "for a scoundrel, a pig like that Zverkov! Of course, I had better not go; of course, I must just snap my fingers at them. I am not bound in any way. I'll send Simonov a note by tomorrow's post. . . ."

But what made me furious was that I knew for certain that I should go, that I should make a point of going; and the more tactless, the more unseemly my going would be, the more certainly I would go.

And there was a positive obstacle to my going: I had no money. All I had was nine roubles, I had to give seven of that to my servant, Apollon, for his monthly wages. That was all I paid him—he had to keep himself.

Not to pay him was impossible, considering his character. But I will talk about that fellow, about that plague of mine, another time.

However, I knew I should go and should not pay him his wages.

That night I had the most hideous dreams. No wonder; all the evening I had been oppressed by memories of my miserable days at school, and I could not shake them off. I was sent to the school by distant relations, upon whom I was dependent and of whom I have heard nothing since—they sent me there, a forlorn, silent boy, already crushed by their reproaches, already troubled by doubt, and looking with savage distrust at everyone. My schoolfellows met me with spiteful and merciless gibes because I was not like any of them. But I could not endure their taunts; I could not give in to them with the ignoble readiness with which they gave in to one another. I hated them from the first, and shut myself away from everyone in timid, wounded and disproportionate pride. Their coarseness revolted me. They laughed cynically at my face, at my clumsy figure; and yet what stupid faces they had themselves. In our school the boys' faces seemed in a special way to degenerate and grow stupider. How many fine-looking boys came to us! In a few years they became repulsive. Even at sixteen I wondered at them morosely; even then I was struck by the pettiness of their thoughts, the stupidity of their pursuits, their games, their conversations. They had no understanding of such essential things, they took no interest in such striking, impressive subjects, that I could not help considering them inferior to myself. It was not wounded vanity that drove me to it, and for God's sake do not thrust upon me your hackneyed remarks, repeated to nausea, that "I was only a dreamer," while they even then had an understanding of life. They understood nothing, they had no idea of real life, and I swear that that was what made me most indignant with them. On the contrary, the most obvious, striking reality they accepted with fantastic stupidity and even at that time were accustomed to respect success. Everything that was just, but despised and looked down upon, they laughed at heartlessly and shamefully. They took rank for intelligence; even at sixteen they were already talking about a snug berth. Of course, a great deal of it was due to their stupidity, to the bad examples with which they had always been surrounded in their childhood and boyhood. They were monstrously depraved. Of course, a great deal of that, too, was superficial and an assumption of cynicism; of course, there were glimpses of youth and freshness even in their depravity; but even that freshness was not attractive, and showed itself in a certain rakishness.

I hated them horribly, though perhaps I was worse than any of them. They repaid me in the same way, and did not conceal their aversion for me. But by then I did not desire their affection: on the contrary I continually longed for their humiliation. To escape from their derision I purposely began to make all the progress I could with my studies and forced my way to the very top. This impressed them. Moreover, they all began by degrees to grasp that I had already read books none of them could read, and understood things (not forming part of our school curriculum) of which they had not even heard. They took a savage and sarcastic view of it, but were morally impressed, especially as the teachers began to notice me on those grounds. The mockery ceased, but the hostility remained, and cold and strained relations became permanent between us.

In the end I could not put up with it: with the years a craving for society, for friends, developed in me. I attempted to get on friendly terms with some of my schoolfellows; but somehow or other my intimacy with them was always strained and soon ended of itself. Once, indeed, I did have a friend. But I was already a tyrant at heart; I wanted to exercise unbounded sway over him; I tried to instill into him a contempt for his surroundings; I required of him a disdainful and complete break with those surroundings. I frightened him with my passionate affection; I reduced him to tears, to hysterics. He was a simple and devoted soul; but when he devoted himself to me entirely I began to hate him immediately and repulsed him—as though all I needed him for was to win a victory over him, to subjugate him and nothing else. But I could not subjugate all of them; my friend was not at all like them either, he was, in fact, a rare exception. The first thing I did on leaving school was to give up the special job for which I had been destined so as to break all ties, to curse my past and shake the dust from off my feet. . . . And goodness knows why, after all that, I should go trudging off to Simonov's!

Early next morning I roused myself and jumped out of bed with excitement, as though it were all about to happen at once. But I believed that some radical change in my life was coming, and would inevitably come that day. Owing to its rarity, perhaps, any external event, however trivial, always made me feel as though some radical change in my life were at hand. I went to the office, however, as usual, but sneaked away home two hours earlier to get ready. The great thing, I thought, is not to be the first to arrive, or they will think I am overjoyed at coming. But there were thousands of such great points to consider, and they all agitated and overwhelmed me. I polished my boots a second time with my own hands; nothing in the world would have induced Apollon to clean them twice a day, as he considered that it was more than his duties required of him. I stole the brushes to clean them from the passage, being careful he should not detect it, for fear of his contempt. Then I minutely examined my clothes and thought that everything looked old, worn and threadbare. I had let myself get too slovenly. My uniform, perhaps, was tidy, but I could not go out to dinner in my uniform. The worst of it was that on the knee of my trousers was a big yellow stain. I had a foreboding that that stain would deprive me of nine-tenths of my personal dignity. I knew, too, that it was very abject to think so. "But this is no time for thinking: now I am in for the real thing," I thought, and my heart sank. I knew, too, perfectly well even then, that I was monstrously exaggerating the facts. But how could I help it? I could not control myself and was already shaking with fever. With despair I pictured to myself how coldly and disdainfully that "scoundrel" Zverkov would meet me; with what dull-witted, invincible contempt the blockhead Trudolyubov would look at me; with what impudent rudeness the insect Ferfichkin would snigger at me in order to curry favour with Zverkov; how completely Simonov would take it all in, and how he would despise me for the abjectness of my vanity and lack of spirit—and, worse of all, how paltry, *unliterary*, commonplace it would all be.

Of course, the best thing would be not to go at all. But that was altogether impossible; if I feel impelled to do anything, I seem to be pitchforked into it. I should have jeered at myself ever afterwards: "So you funked it, you funked it, you funked the *real thing!*" On the contrary, I passionately longed to show all that "rabble" that I was by no means such a spiritless creature as I seemed to myself. What is more, even in the acutest paroxysm of this cowardly fever, I dreamed of getting the upper hand, of dominating them, carrying them away, making them like me—if only for my "elevation of thought and unmistakable wit." They would abandon Zverkov, he would sit on one side, silent and ashamed, while I should crush him. Then, perhaps, we would be reconciled and drink to our everlasting friendship; but what was most bitter and most humiliating for me was that I knew even then, knew fully and for certain, that I needed nothing of all this really, that I did not really want to crush, to subdue, to attract them, and that I did not care a straw really for the result, even if I did achieve it. Oh, how I prayed for the day to pass quickly! In unutterable anguish I went to the window, opened the movable pane and looked out into the troubled darkness of the thickly falling wet snow.

At last my wretched little clock hissed out five. I seized my hat and trying not to look at Apollon, who had been all day expecting his month's wages, but in his foolishness was unwilling to be the first to speak about it, I slipped between him and the door and jumping into a high-class sledge, on which I spent my last half rouble, I drove up in grand style to the Hôtel de Paris.

## IV

I had been certain the day before that I should be the first to arrive. But it was not a question of being the first to arrive. Not only were they not there, but I had difficulty in finding our room. The table was not even laid. What did it mean? After a good many questions I elicited from the waiters that the dinner had been ordered not for five, but for six o'clock. This was confirmed at the buffet too. I felt really ashamed to go on questioning them. It was only twenty-five minutes past five. If they changed the dinner hour they ought at least to have let me know—that is what the post is for, and not to have put me in an absurd position in my own eyes and . . . and even before the waiters. I sat down; the servant began laying the table; I felt even more humiliated when he was present. Towards six o'clock they brought in candles, though there were lamps burning in the room. It had not occurred to the waiter, however, to bring them in at once when I arrived. In the next room two gloomy, angry-looking persons were eating their dinners in silence at two different tables. There was a great deal of noise, even shouting, in a room further away; one could hear the laughter of a crowd of people, and nasty little shrieks in French: there were ladies at the dinner. It was sickening, in fact. I have rarely passed more wretched moments, so much so that when they did arrive all together punctually at six I was overjoyed to see them, as though they were my deliverers, and even forgot that it was incumbent upon me to show resentment.

Zverkov walked in at the head of them; evidently he was the leading spirit. He and all of them were laughing; but, seeing me, Zverkov drew himself up a little, and walked up to me slowly with a slight, rather jaunty bend from the waist. He shook hands with me in a friendly, but not overfriendly, fashion, with a sort of circumspect courtesy like that of a general, as though in giving me his hand he were warding off something. I had imagined, on the contrary, that on coming in he would at once break into his habitual thin, shrill laugh and fall to making his insipid jokes and witticisms. I had been preparing for them ever since the previous day, but I had not expected such condescension, such high-official courtesy. So, then, he felt himself ineffably superior to me in every respect! If he only meant to insult me by that high-official tone, it would not matter, I thought—I could pay him back for it one way or another. But what if, in reality, without the least desire to be offensive, that sheepshead had a notion in earnest that he was superior to me and could only look at me in a patronizing way? The very supposition made me gasp.

"I was surprised to hear of your desire to join us," he began, lisping and drawling, which was something new. "You and I seem to have seen nothing of one another. You fight shy of us. You shouldn't. We are not such terrible people as you think. Well, anyway, I am glad to renew our acquaintance."

And he turned carelessly to put his hat down on the window-sill.

"Have you been waiting long?" Trudolyubov inquired.

"I arrived at five o'clock as you told me yesterday," I answered aloud, with an irritability that threatened an explosion.

"Didn't you let him know that we had changed the hour?" said Trudolyubov to Simonov.

"No, I didn't. I forgot," the latter replied, with no sign of regret, and without even apologizing to me he went off to order the *hors d'œuvres*.

"So you've been here a whole hour? Oh, poor fellow!" Zverkov cried ironically, for to his notions this was bound to be extremely funny. That rascal Ferfichkin followed with his nasty little snigger like a puppy yapping. My position struck him, too, as exquisitely ludicrous and embarrassing.

"It isn't funny at all!" I cried to Ferfichkin, more and more irritated. "It wasn't my fault, but other people's. They neglected to let me know. It was . . . it was . . . it was simply absurd."

"It's not only absurd, but something else as well," muttered Trudolyubov, naïvely taking my part. "You are not hard enough upon it. It was simply rudeness—unintentional, of course. And how could Simonov . . . h'm!"

"If a trick like that had been played on me," observed Ferfichkin, "I should . . ."

"But you should have ordered something for yourself," Zverkov interrupted, "or simply asked for dinner without waiting for us."

"You will allow that I might have done that without your permission," I rapped out. "If I waited, it was . . ."

"Let us sit down, gentlemen," cried Simonov, coming in. "Everything is ready; I can answer for the champagne; it is capitally frozen. . . . You see, I did not know your address, where was I to look for you?" he suddenly turned to me, but again he seemed to avoid looking at me. Evidently he had something against me. It must have been what happened yesterday.

All sat down; I did the same. It was a round table. Trudolyubov was on my left, Simonov on my right. Zverkov was sitting opposite, Ferfichkin next to him, between him and Trudolyubov.

"Tell me, are you . . . in a government office?" Zverkov went on making a show of an interest in me. Seeing that I was embarrassed, he seriously thought that he ought to be friendly to me, and, so to speak, cheer me up.

"Does he want me to throw a bottle at his head?" I thought, in a fury. In my novel surroundings I was unnaturally ready to be irritated.

"In the N—— office," I answered jerkily, with my eyes on my plate.

"And ha-ave you a go-od berth? I say, what ma-ade you leave your original job?"

"What ma-ade me was that I wanted to leave my original job," I drawled more than he, hardly able to control myself. Ferfichkin went off into a guffaw. Simonov looked at me ironically. Trudolyubov left off eating and began looking at me with curiosity.

Zverkov winced, but he tried not to notice it.

"And the remuneration?"

"What remuneration?"

"I mean, your sa-alary?"

"Why are you cross-examining me?" However, I told him at once what my salary was. I turned horribly red.

"It is not very handsome," Zverkov observed majestically.

"Yes, you can't afford to dine at cafés on that," Ferfichkin added insolently.

"To my thinking it's very poor," Trudolyubov observed gravely.

"And how thin you have grown! How you have changed!" added

Zverkov, with a shade of venom in his voice, scanning me and my attire with a sort of insolent compassion.

"Oh, spare his blushes," cried Ferfichkin, sniggering.

"My dear sir, allow me to tell you I am not blushing," I broke out at last; "do you hear? I am dining here, at this café, at my own expense, not at other people's—note that, Mr. Ferfichkin."

"Wha-at? Isn't everyone here dining at his own expense? You would seem to be . . ." Ferfichkin flew out at me, turning as red as a lobster, and looking me in the eye with fury.

"Yes," I answered, feeling I had gone too far, "and I imagine it would be better to talk of something more intelligent."

"You intend to show off your intelligence, I suppose?"

"Don't disturb yourself, that would be quite out of place here."

"Why are you clacking away like that, my good sir, eh? Have you gone out of your wits in your government office?"

"Enough, gentlemen, enough!" Zverkov cried, authoritatively.

"How stupid it is!" muttered Simonov.

"It really is stupid. We have met here, a company of friends, for a farewell dinner to a comrade and you carry on an altercation," said Trudolyubov, rudely addressing himself to me alone. "You invited yourself to join us, so don't disturb the general harmony."

"Enough, enough!" cried Zverkov. "Give over, gentlemen, it's out of place. Better let me tell you how I nearly got married the day before yesterday. . . ."

And then followed a burlesque narrative of how this gentleman had almost been married two days before. There was not a word about the marriage, however, but the story was adorned with generals, colonels and kammer-junkers, while Zverkov almost took the lead among them. It was greeted with approving laughter; Ferfichkin positively squealed.

No one paid any attention to me, and I sat crushed and humiliated.

"Good Heavens, these are not the people for me!" I thought. "And what a fool I have made of myself before them! I let Ferfichkin go too far, though. The brutes imagine they are doing me an honor in letting me sit down with them. They don't understand that it's an honor to them and not to me! I've grown thinner! My clothes! Oh, damn my trousers! Zverkov noticed the yellow stain on the knee as soon as he came in. . . . But what's the use! I must get up at once,

this very minute, take my hat and simply go without a word . . .
with contempt! And tomorrow I can send a challenge. The scoundrels! As though I cared about the seven roubles. They may think.
. . . Damn it! I don't care about the seven roubles. I'll go this
minute!"

Of course I remained.

I drank sherry and Lafite by the glassful in my discomfiture. Being unaccustomed to it, I was quickly affected. My annoyance increased as the wine went to my head. I longed all at once to insult
them all in a most flagrant manner and then go away. To seize the
moment and show what I could do, so that they would say, "He's
clever, though he is absurd," and . . . and . . . in fact, damn them
all!

I scanned them all insolently with my drowsy eyes. But they
seemed to have forgotten me altogether. They were noisy, vocifer-
ous, cheerful. Zverkov was talking all the time. I began listening.
Zverkov was talking of some sumptuous lady whom he had at last
led on to declaring her love (of course, he was lying like a horse),
and how he had been helped in this affair by an intimate friend of
his, a Prince Kolya, an officer in the hussars, who had three thousand
serfs.

"And yet this Kolya, who has three thousand serfs, has not put
in an appearance here tonight to see you off," I cut in suddenly.

For a minute everyone was silent. "You are drunk already." Trudolyubov deigned to notice me at last, glancing contemptuously in
my direction. Zverkov, without a word, examined me as though I
were an insect. I dropped my eyes. Simonov made haste to fill up the
glasses with champagne.

Trudolyubov raised his glass, as did everyone else but me.

"Your health and good luck on the journey!" he cried to Zverkov. "To old times, to our future, hurrah!"

They all tossed off their glasses, and crowded round Zverkov to
kiss him. I did not move; my full glass stood untouched before me.

"Why, aren't you going to drink it?" roared Trudolyubov, losing
patience and turning menacingly to me.

"I want to make a speech separately, on my own account . . .
and then I'll drink it, Mr. Trudolyubov."

"Spiteful brute!" muttered Simonov. I drew myself up in my
chair and feverishly seized my glass, prepared for something extraor-

dinary, though I did not know myself precisely what I was going to say.

"*Silence!*" cried Ferfichkin. "Now for a display of wit!"

Zverkov waited very gravely, knowing what was coming.

"Mr. Lieutenant Zverkov," I began, "let me tell you that I hate phrases, phrasemongers and men in corsets . . . that's the first point, and there is a second one to follow it."

There was a general stir.

"The second point is: I hate ribaldry and ribald talkers. Especially ribald talkers! The third point: I love justice, truth and honesty." I went on almost mechanically, for I was beginning to shiver with horror myself and had no idea how I came to be talking like this. "I love thought, Monsieur Zverkov; I love true comradeship, on an equal footing and not . . . H'm . . . I love. . . . But, however, why not? I will drink your health, too, Mr. Zverkov. Seduce the Circassian girls, shoot the enemies of the fatherland and . . . and . . . to your health, Monsieur Zverkov!"

Zverkov got up from his seat, bowed to me and said:

"I am very much obliged to you." He was frightfully offended and turned pale.

"Damn the fellow!" roared Trudolyubov, bringing his fist down on the table.

"Well, he wants a punch in the face for that," squealed Ferfichkin.

"We ought to turn him out," muttered Simonov.

"Not a word, gentlemen, not a movement!" cried Zverkov solemnly, checking the general indignation. "I thank you all, but I can show him for myself how much value I attach to his words."

"Mr. Ferfichkin, you will give me satisfaction tomorrow for your words just now!" I said aloud, turning with dignity to Ferfichkin.

"A duel, you mean? Certainly," he answered. But probably I was so ridiculous as I challenged him and it was so out of keeping with my appearance that everyone, including Ferfichkin, was prostrate with laughter.

"Yes, let him alone, of course! He is quite drunk," Trudolyubov said with disgust.

"I shall never forgive myself for letting him join us," Simonov muttered again.

"Now is the time to throw a bottle at their heads," I thought to myself. I picked up the bottle . . . and filled my glass. . . . "No, I'd better sit on to the end," I went on thinking; "you would be pleased, my friends if I went away. Nothing will induce me to go. I'll go on sitting here and drinking to the end, on purpose, as a sign that I don't think you of the slightest consequence. I will go on sitting and drinking, because this is a public-house and I paid my entrance money. I'll sit here and drink, for I look upon you as so many pawns, as inanimate pawns. I'll sit here and drink and sing if I want to, yes, sing, for I have the right to . . . to sing . . . H'm!"

But I did not sing. I simply tried not to look at any of them. I assumed most unconcerned attitudes and waited with impatience for them to speak *first*. But alas, they did not address me! And oh, how I wished, how I wished at that moment to be reconciled to them! It struck eight, at last nine. They moved from the table to the sofa. Zverkov stretched himself on a lounge and put one foot on a round table. Wine was brought there. He did, as a fact, order three bottles on his own account. I, of course, was not invited to join them. They all sat round him on the sofa. They listened to him, almost with reverence. It was evident that they were fond of him. "What for? What for?" I wondered. From time to time they were moved to drunken enthusiasm and kissed each other. They talked of the Caucasus, of the nature of true passion, of snug berths in the service, of the income of an hussar called Podharzhevsky, whom none of them knew personally, and rejoiced in the largeness of it, of the extraordinary grace and beauty of a Princess D., whom none of them had ever seen; then it came to Shakespeare's being immortal.

I smiled contemptuously and walked up and down the other side of the room, opposite the sofa, from the table to the stove and back again. I tried my very utmost to show them that I could do without them, and yet I purposely made a noise with my boots, thumping with my heels. But it was all in vain. They paid no attention. I had the patience to walk up and down in front of them from eight o'clock till eleven, in the same place, from the table to the stove and back again. "I walk up and down to please myself and no one can prevent me." The waiter who came into the room stopped, from time to time, to look at me. I was somewhat giddy from turning round so often; at moments it seemed to me that I was in delirium. During those three hours I was three times soaked with sweat and dry again. At times, with an intense, acute pang I was stabbed to the heart by the thought that ten years, twenty years, forty years would pass, and that even in forty years I would remember with loathing and humiliation those filthiest, most ludicrous, and most awful moments of my life. No one could have gone out of his way to degrade himself more shamelessly, and I fully realized it, fully, and yet I went on pacing up and down from the table to the stove. "Oh, if you only knew what thoughts and feelings I am capable of, how cultured I am!" I thought at moments, mentally addressing the sofa on which my enemies were sitting. But my enemies behaved as though I were not in the room. Once—only once—they turned towards me, just when Zverkov was talking about Shakespeare, and I suddenly gave a contemptuous laugh. I laughed in such an affected and disgusting way that they all at once broke off their conversation, and silently and gravely for two minutes watched me walking up and down from the table to the stove, *taking no notice of them*. But nothing came of it: they said nothing, and two minutes later they ceased to notice me again. It struck eleven.

"Friends," cried Zverkov getting up from the sofa, "let us all be off now, *there!*"

"Of course, of course," the others assented. I turned sharply to Zverkov. I was so harassed, so exhausted, that I would have cut my throat to put an end to it. I was in a fever; my hair, soaked with perspiration, stuck to my forehead and temples.

"Zverkov, I beg your pardon," I said abruptly and resolutely. "Ferfichkin, yours too, and everyone's, everyone's: I have insulted you all!"

"Aha! A duel is not in your line, old man," Ferfichkin hissed venomously.

It sent a sharp pang to my heart.

"No, it's not the duel I am afraid of, Ferfichkin! I am ready to fight you tomorrow, after we are reconciled. I insist upon it, in fact, and you cannot refuse. I want to show you that I am not afraid of a duel. You shall fire first and I shall fire into the air."

"He is comforting himself," said Simonov.

"He's simply raving," said Trudolyubov.

"But let us pass. Why are you barring our way? What do you want?" Zverkov answered disdainfully.

They were all flushed; their eyes were bright: they had been drinking heavily.

"I ask for your friendship, Zverkov; I insulted you, but—"

"Insulted? *You* insulted *me?* Understand, sir, that you never, under any circumstances, could possibly insult *me.*"

"And that's enough for you. Out of the way!" concluded Trudolyubov.

"Olympia is mine, friends, that's agreed!" cried Zverkov.

"We won't dispute your right, we won't dispute your right," the others answered, laughing.

I stood as though spat upon. The party went noisily out of the room. Trudolyubov struck up some stupid song. Simonov remained behind for a moment to tip the waiters. I suddenly went up to him.

"Simonov! give me six roubles!" I said, with desperate resolution.

He looked at me in extreme amazement, with vacant eyes. He, too, was drunk.

"You don't mean you are coming with us?"

"Yes."

"I've no money," he snapped out, and with a scornful laugh he went out of the room.

I clutched at his overcoat. It was a nightmare.

"Simonov, I saw you had money. Why do you refuse me? Am I a scoundrel? Beware of refusing me: if you knew, if you knew why I am asking! My whole future, my whole plans depend upon it!"

Simonov pulled out the money and almost flung it at me.

"Take it, if you have no sense of shame!" he pronounced pitilessly, and ran to overtake them.

I was left for a moment alone. Disorder, the remains of dinner, a broken wineglass on the floor, spilt wine, cigarette ends, fumes of drink and delirium in my brain, an agonizing misery in my heart and finally the waiter, who had seen and heard all and was looking inquisitively into my face.

"I am going there!" I cried. "Either they shall all go down on their knees to beg for my friendship, or I will give Zverkov a slap in the face!"

### v

"So this is it, this is it at last—contact with real life," I muttered as I ran headlong downstairs. "This is very different from the Pope's

leaving Rome and going to Brazil, very different from the ball on
Lake Como!"

"You are a scoundrel," a thought flashed through my mind, "if
you laugh at this now."

"No matter!" I cried, answering myself. "Now everything is
lost!"

There was no trace of them to be seen, but that made no difference—I knew where they had gone.

At the steps was standing a solitary night sledgedriver in a rough
peasant coat, powdered over with the still falling, wet, and as it were
warm, snow. It was hot and steamy. The little shaggy piebald horse
was also covered with snow and coughing, I remember that very
well. I made a rush for the roughly made sledge; but as soon as I
raised my foot to get into it, the recollection of how Simonov had
just given me six roubles seemed to double me up and I tumbled into
the sledge like a sack.

"No, I must do a great deal to make up for all that," I cried.
"But I will make up for it or perish on the spot this very night.
Start!"

We set off. There was a perfect whirl in my head.

"They won't go down on their knees to beg for my friendship.
That is a mirage, a cheap mirage, revolting, romantic and fantastical
—that's another ball on Lake Como. And so I am bound to slap
Zverkov's face! It is my duty to. And so it is settled; I am flying to
give him a slap in the face. Hurry up!"

The driver tugged at the reins.

"As soon as I go in I'll give it him. Ought I before giving him
the slap to say a few words by way of preface? No. I'll simply go in
and give it him. They will all be sitting in the drawing-room, and
he with Olympia on the sofa. That damned Olympia! She laughed
at my looks on one occasion and refused me. I'll pull Olympia's hair,
pull Zverkov's ears! No, better one ear, and pull him by it round the
room. Maybe they will all begin beating me and will kick me out.
That's most likely, indeed. No matter! Anyway, I shall first slap him;
the initiative will be mine; and by the laws of honor that is everything: he will be branded and cannot wipe off the slap by any blows,
by nothing but a duel. He will be forced to fight. And let them beat
me now. Let them, the ungrateful wretches! Trudolyubov will beat
me hardest, he is so strong; Ferfichkin will be sure to catch hold side-

ways and tug at my hair. But no matter, no matter! That's what I am going for. The blockheads will be forced at last to see the tragedy of it all! When they drag me to the door I shall call out to them that in reality they are not worth my little finger. Get on, driver, get on!" I cried to the driver. He started and flicked his whip, I shouted so savagely.

"We shall fight at daybreak, that's a settled thing. I've done with the office. Ferfichkin made a joke about it just now. But where can I get pistols? Nonsense! I'll get my salary in advance and buy them. And powder, and bullets? That's the second's business. And how can it all be done by daybreak? And where am I to get a second? I have no friends. Nonsense!" I cried, lashing myself up more and more. "It's of no consequence! the first person I meet in the street is bound to be my second, just as he would be bound to pull a drowning man out of water. The most eccentric things may happen. Even if I were to ask the director himself to be my second tomorrow, he would be bound to consent, if only from a feeling of chivalry, and to keep the secret! Anton Antonych. . . ."

The fact is, that at that very minute the disgusting absurdity of my plan and the other side of the question was clearer and more vivid to my imagination than it could be to anyone on earth. But. . . .

"Get on, driver, get on, you rascal, get on!"

"Ugh, sir!" said the son of toil.

Cold shivers suddenly ran down me. Wouldn't it be better . . . to go straight home? My God, my God! Why had I invited myself to this dinner yesterday? But no, it's impossible. And my walking up and down for three hours from the table to the stove? No, they, they and no one else must pay for my walking up and down! They must wipe out this dishonor! Drive on!

And what if they give me into custody? They won't dare! They'll be afraid of the scandal. And what if Zverkov is so contemptuous that he refuses to fight a duel? He is sure to; but in that case I'll show them . . . I will turn up at the posting station when he is setting off tomorrow, I'll catch him by the leg, I'll pull off his coat when he gets into the carriage. I'll get my teeth into his hand, I'll bite him. "See what lengths you can drive a desperate man to!" He may hit me on the head and they may belabor me from behind. I will shout to the assembled multitude: "Look at this young puppy who is driving off to captivate Circassian girls after letting me spit in his face!"

Of course, after that everything will be over! The office will have vanished off the face of the earth. I shall be arrested, I shall be tried, I shall be dismissed from the service, thrown into jail, sent to Siberia. Never mind! In fifteen years when they let me out of prison I will trudge off to him, a beggar, in rags. I shall find him in some provincial town. He will be married and happy. He will have a grown-up daughter. . . . I shall say to him: "Look, monster, at my hollow cheeks and my rags! I've lost everything—my career, my happiness, art, science, *the woman I loved*, and all through you. Here are pistols. I have come to discharge my pistol and . . . and I . . . forgive you." Then I shall fire into the air and he will hear nothing more of me. . . .

I was actually on the point of tears, though I knew perfectly well at that moment that all this was out of *Sylvio* and Lermontov's *Masquerade*. And all at once I felt horribly ashamed, so ashamed that I stopped the horse, got out of the sledge, and stood still in the snow in the middle of the street. The driver gazed at me, sighing and astonished.

What was I to do? I could not go on there—it was evidently stupid, and I could not leave things as they were, because that would seem as though . . . Heavens, how could I leave things! And after such insults! "No!" I cried, throwing myself into the sledge again. "It is ordained! It is fate! Drive on, drive on!"

And in my impatience I punched the sledge-driver on the back of the neck.

"What are you up to? What are you hitting me for?" the peasant shouted, but he whipped up his nag so that it began kicking.

The wet snow was falling in big flakes; regardless of it, I unbuttoned my coat. I forgot everything else, for I had finally decided on the slap, and felt with horror that it was going to happen *now, at once*, and that *no force could stop it*. The deserted street lamps gleamed sullenly in the snowy darkness like torches at a funeral. The snow drifted under my greatcoat, under my coat, under my cravat, and melted there. I did not wrap myself up—all was lost, anyway.

At last we arrived. I jumped out, almost unconscious, ran up the steps and began knocking and kicking at the door. I felt fearfully weak, particularly in my legs and my knees. The door was opened quickly as though they knew I was coming. As a fact, Simonov had warned them that perhaps another gentleman would arrive, and this was a place in which one had to give notice and to observe certain precautions. It was one of those "millinery establishments" which were abolished by the police a good time ago. By day it really was a shop; but at night, if one had an introduction, one might visit it for other purposes.

I walked rapidly through the dark shop into the familiar drawing-room, where there was only one candle burning, and stood still in amazement: there was no one there. "Where are they?" I asked somebody. But by now, of course, they had separated. Before me was standing a person with a stupid smile, the "madam" herself, who had seen me before. A minute later a door opened and another person came in.

Taking no notice of anything I strode about the room, and, I believe, I talked to myself. I felt as though I had been saved from death and was conscious of this, joyfully, all over: I should have given that slap, I should certainly, certainly have given it! But now they were not here and . . . everything had vanished and changed! I looked round. I could not realize my condition yet. I looked mechanically at the girl who had come in: and had a glimpse of a fresh, young, rather pale face, with straight, dark eyebrows, and with grave, as it were wondering, eyes that attracted me at once; I should have hated her if she had been smiling. I began looking at her more intently and, as it were, with effort. I had not fully collected my thoughts. There was something simple and good-natured in her face, but something strangely grave. I am sure that this stood in her way here, and no one of those fools had noticed her. She could not, however, have been called a beauty, though she was tall, strong-looking, and well built. She was very simply dressed. Something loathsome stirred within me. I went straight up to her.

I chanced to look into the glass. My harassed face struck me as revolting in the extreme, pale, angry, abject, with disheveled hair. "No matter, I am glad of it," I thought; "I am glad that I shall seem repulsive to her; I like that."

## VI

. . . Somewhere behind a partition a clock began gasping, as though squeezed hard, as though some one were strangling it. After an unnaturally prolonged wheezing there followed a shrill, nasty, and as it were unexpectedly rapid, chime—as though someone were suddenly jumping forward. It struck two. I woke up, though I had indeed not been asleep but lying half dozing.

It was almost completely dark in the narrow, cramped, low-pitched room, cumbered up with an enormous wardrobe and piles of cardboard boxes and all sorts of frippery and litter. The candle end that had been burning on the table was going out and gave a faint flicker from time to time. In a few minutes there would be complete darkness.

I was not long in coming to myself; everything came back to my mind at once, without an effort, as though it had been in ambush to pounce upon me again. And, indeed, even while I was unconscious a point seemed continually to remain in my memory unforgotten, and round it my dreams moved drearily. But strange to say, everything that had happened to me on that day seemed to me now, on waking, to be in the far, far away past, as though I had long, long ago lived all that down.

My head was full of fumes. Something seemed to be hovering over me, rousing me, exciting me, and making me restless. Misery and spite seemed surging up in me again and seeking an outlet. Suddenly I saw beside me two wide open eyes scrutinizing me curiously and persistently. The look in those eyes was coldly detached, sullen, as it were utterly remote; it weighed upon me.

A grim idea came into my brain and passed all over my body, as a horrible sensation, such as one feels when one goes into a damp and mouldy cellar. There was something unnatural in those two eyes, beginning to look at me only now. I recalled, too, that during those two hours I had not said a single word to this creature, and had, in fact, considered it utterly superfluous; in fact, the silence had for some reason gratified me. Now I suddenly realized vividly the hideous idea—revolting as a spider—of vice, which, without love, grossly and shamelessly begins with that in which true love finds its consummation. For a long time we gazed at each other like that, but she did not drop her eyes before mine and her expression did not change, so that at last I felt uncomfortable.

"What is your name?" I asked abruptly, to put an end to it.

"Liza," she answered almost in a whisper, but somehow far from graciously, and she turned her eyes away.

I was silent.

"What weather! The snow . . . it's disgusting!" I said, almost to myself, putting my arm under my head despondently, and gazing at the ceiling.

She made no answer. This was horrible.

"Have you always lived in Petersburg?" I asked a minute later, almost angrily, turning my head slightly towards her.

"No."

"Where do you come from?"

"From Riga," she answered reluctantly.

"Are you a German?"

"No, Russian."

"Have you been here long?"

"Where?"

"In this house?"

"A fortnight."

She spoke more and more jerkily. The candle went out; I could no longer distinguish her face.

"Have you a father and mother?"

"Yes . . . no . . . I have."

"Where are they?"

"There . . . in Riga."

"Who are they?"

"Oh, nobody."

"How's that? Who are they? What kind of people?"

"Tradespeople."

"Have you always lived with them?"

"Yes."

"How old are you?"

"Twenty."

"Why did you leave them?"

"Oh, for no reason."

That answer meant: "Let me alone; I feel sick, sad."

We were silent.

God knows why I did not go away. I felt myself more and more sick and dreary. The images of the previous day began of themselves, apart from my will, flitting through my memory in confusion. I suddenly recalled something I had seen that morning when, full of anxious thoughts, I was hurrying to the office.

"I saw them carrying a coffin out yesterday and they nearly

dropped it," I suddenly said aloud, not that I desired to open the conversation, but as it were by accident.

"A coffin?"

"Yes, in the Haymarket; they were bringing it up out of a cellar."

"From a cellar?"

"Not from a cellar, but from a basement. Oh, you know—down below—from a house of ill-fame. It was filthy all round . . . Egg-shells, litter—a stench. It was loathsome."

Silence.

"A nasty day to be buried," I began, simply to avoid being silent.

"Nasty, in what way?"

"The snow, the wet." (I yawned.)

"It makes no difference," she said suddenly, after a brief silence.

"No, it's horrid." (I yawned again.) "The gravediggers must have sworn at getting drenched by the snow. And there must have been water in the grave."

"Why water in the grave?" she asked, with a sort of curiosity, but speaking even more harshly and abruptly than before.

I suddenly began to feel provoked.

"Why, there must have been water at the bottom a foot deep. You can't dig a dry grave in Volkovo Cemetery."

"Why?"

"Why? Why, the place is waterlogged. It's a regular marsh. So they bury them in water. I've seen it myself—many times."

(I had never seen it once, indeed I had never been in Volkovo, and had only heard stories of it.)

"Do you mean to say, you don't mind how you die?"

"But why should I die?" she answered, as though defending herself.

"Why, some day you will die, and you will die just the same as that dead woman. She was—a girl like you. She died of consumption."

"A wench would have died in hospital . . ." (She knows all about it already: she said "wench," not "girl.")

"She was in debt to her madam," I retorted, more and more provoked by the discussion; "and went on earning money for her up to the end, though she was in consumption. Some sledgedrivers standing by were talking about her to some soldiers and telling them so. No doubt they knew her. They were laughing. They were going to meet in a pothouse to drink to her memory."

A great deal of this was my invention. Silence followed, profound silence. She did not stir.

"And is it better to die in a hospital?"

"Isn't it just the same? Besides, why should I die?" she added irritably.

"If not now, a little later."

"Well, then, later."

"Soon enough! Now you are young, pretty, fresh, you fetch a high price. But after another year of this life you will be very different—you will go off."

"In a year?"

"Anyway, in a year you will be worth less," I continued malignantly. "You will go from here to something lower, another house; a year later—to a third, lower and lower, and in seven years you will come to a basement in the Haymarket. That is, if you are lucky. But it would be much worse if you got some disease, consumption, say . . . and caught a chill, or something or other. It's not easy to get over an illness in your way of life. If you catch anything you may not get rid of it. And so you will die."

"Oh, well, then I shall die," she answered, quite viciously, and she made a quick movement.

"Aren't you sorry?"

"Sorry for what?"

"Sorry that life's over."

Silence.

"Have you been engaged to be married? Eh?"

"What's that to you?"

"Oh, I am not cross-examining you. It's nothing to me. Why are you so cross? Of course you may have had your own troubles. What is it to me? It's simply that I felt sorry."

"Sorry for whom?"

"Sorry for you."

"No need," she whispered hardly audibly, and again made a faint movement.

That incensed me at once. What! I was so gentle with her, and she. . . .

"Why, do you think that you are on the right path?"

"I don't think anything."

"That's what's wrong, that you don't think. Realize it while there is still time. There still is time. You are still young, good-looking; you might love, be married, be happy. . . ."

"Not all married women are happy," she snapped out in the rude abrupt tone she had used at first.

"Not all, of course, but anyway it is much better than the life here. Infinitely better. Besides, with love one can live even without happiness. Even in sorrow life is sweet; life is sweet, however one lives. But here what is there but . . . foulness. Phew!"

I turned away with disgust; I was no longer reasoning coldly. I began myself to feel what I was saying and warmed to the subject. I was already longing to expound the cherished ideas I had brooded over in my corner. Something suddenly flared up in me. An object had appeared before me.

"Never mind my being here, I am not an example for you. I am, perhaps, worse than you are. I was drunk when I came here, though," I hastened, however, to say in self-defence. "Besides, a man is no example for a woman. It's a different thing. I may degrade and defile myself, but I am not anyone's slave. I come and go, and that's an end of it. I shake it off, and I am a different man. But you are a slave from the start. Yes, a slave! You give up everything, your whole freedom. If you want to break your chains afterwards, you won't be able to: you will be more and more tightly ensnared. It is an accursed bondage. I know it. I won't speak of anything else, maybe you won't understand, but tell me: no doubt you are in debt to your madam? There, you see," I added, though she made no answer, but only listened in silence, entirely absorbed, "that's a bondage for you! You will never buy your freedom. They will see to that. It's like selling your soul to the devil. . . . And besides . . . perhaps I, too, am just as unlucky—how do you know—and wallow in the mud on purpose, out of misery? You know, men take to drink from grief; well, maybe I am here from grief. Come, tell me, what is there good here? Here you and I—came together—just now and did not say one word to one another all the time, and it was only afterwards you began staring at me like a wild creature, and I at you. Is that loving? Is that how one human being should meet another? It's hideous, that's what it is!"

"Yes!" she assented sharply and hurriedly.

I was positively astounded by the promptitude of this "Yes." So the same thought may have been straying through her mind when she was staring at me just before. So she, too, was capable of certain thoughts? "Damn it all, this is interesting, this is kinship!" I thought, almost rubbing my hands. And indeed it's easy to master a young soul like that!

It was the game that attracted me most.

She turned her head nearer to me, and it seemed to me in the darkness that she propped herself on her arm. Perhaps she was scrutinizing me. How I regretted that I could not see her eyes. I heard her deep breathing.

"Why have you come here?" I asked her, with a note of authority already in my voice.

"Oh, I don't know."

"But how nice it would be to be living in your father's house! It's warm and free; you have a home of your own."

"But what if it's worse than this?"

"I must take the right tone," flashed through my mind. "I may not get far with sentimentality." But it was only a momentary thought. I swear she really did interest me. Besides, I was exhausted and moody. And cunning so easily goes hand in hand with feeling.

"Who denies it!" I hastened to answer. "Anything may happen. I am convinced that someone has wronged you, and that you are more sinned against than sinning. Of course, I know nothing of your story, but it's not likely a girl like you has come here of her own inclination. . . ."

"A girl like me?" she whispered, hardly audibly; but I heard it.

Damn it all, I was flattering her. That was horrid. But perhaps it was a good thing. . . . She was silent.

"See, Liza, I will tell you about myself. If I had had a home from childhood, I shouldn't be what I am now. I often think that. However bad it may be at home, anyway they are your father and mother, and not enemies, strangers. Once a year at least, they'll show their love of you. Anyway, you know you are at home. I grew up without a home; and perhaps that's why I've turned so—unfeeling."

I waited again. "Perhaps she doesn't understand," I thought, "and, indeed, it is absurd—it's moralizing."

"If I were a father and had a daughter, I believe I should love my daughter more than my sons, really," I began indirectly, as though talking of something else, to distract her attention. I must confess I blushed.

"Why so?" she asked.

Ah! so she was listening!

"I don't know, Liza. I knew a father who was a stern, austere man, but used to go down on his knees to his daughter, used to kiss her hands, her feet, he couldn't make enough of her, really. When she danced at parties he used to stand for five hours at a stretch, gazing at her. He was mad over her: I understand that! She would fall asleep tired at night, and he would wake to kiss her in her sleep and make the sign of the cross over her. He would go about in a dirty old coat, he was stingy to everyone else, but would spend his last groat for her, giving her expensive presents, and it was his greatest delight when she was pleased with what he gave her. Fathers always love their daughters more than the mothers do. Some girls live happily at home! And I believe I should never let my daughters marry."

"What next?" she said, with a faint smile.

"I should be jealous, I really should. To think that she should kiss anyone else! That she should love a stranger more than her father! It's painful to imagine it. Of course, that's all nonsense, of course every father would be reasonable at last. But I believe before I should let her marry, I should worry myself to death; I should find fault with all her suitors. But I should end by letting her marry whom she herself loved. The one whom the daughter loves always seems the worst to the father, you know. That is always so. So many family troubles come from that."

"Some are glad to sell their daughters, rather than marrying them honorably."

Ah, so that was it!

"Such a thing, Liza, happens in those accursed families in which there is neither love nor God," I retorted warmly, "and where there is no love, there is no sense either. There are such families, it's true, but I am not speaking of them. You must have seen wickedness in your own family, if you talk like that. Truly, you must have been unlucky. M'h! . . . that sort of thing mostly comes about through poverty."

"And is it any better with the gentry? Even among the poor, honest people live happily."

"H'm . . . yes. Perhaps. Another thing, Liza, man is fond of reckoning up his troubles, but does not count his joys. If he counted them up as he ought, he would see that every lot has enough happiness provided for it. And what if all goes well with the family, if the blessing of God is upon it, if the husband is a good one, loves you, cherishes you, never leaves you! There is happiness in such a family! Sometimes there is even happiness in the midst of sorrow; and indeed sorrow is everywhere. If you marry *you will find out for yourself.* But think of the first years of married life with one you love: what happiness, what happiness there sometimes is in it! And indeed it's the ordinary thing. In those early days even quarrels with one's husband end happily. Some women get up quarrels with their husbands just because they love them. Indeed, I knew a woman like that: she seemed to say that because she loved him, she would torment him and make him feel it. You know that you may torment a man on purpose through love. Women are particularly given to that, thinking to themselves 'I will love him so, I will make so much of him afterwards, that it's no sin to torment him a little now.' And all in the house rejoice in the sight of you, and you are happy and gay and peaceful and honorable. . . . Then there are some women who are jealous. If he went off anywhere—I knew one such woman, she couldn't restrain herself, but would jump up at night and run off on the sly to find out where he was, whether he was with some other woman. That's a pity. And the woman herself knows it's wrong, and her heart fails her and she suffers, but she loves—it's all through love. And how sweet it is to make it up after quarrels, to own herself in the wrong or to forgive him! And they are both so happy all at once—as though they had met anew, been married over again; as though their love had begun afresh. And no one, no one should know what passes between husband and wife if they love one another. And whatever quarrels there may be between them they ought not to call in their own mother to judge between them and tell tales of one another. They are their own judges. Love is a holy mystery and ought to be hidden from all other eyes, whatever happens. That makes it holier and better. They respect one another more, and much is built on respect. And if once there has been love, if they have married for love, why should love pass away? Surely one can keep it! It is rare that one cannot keep it. And if the husband is kind and straightforward, why should not love last? The first phase of married love will pass, it is true, but then there will come a love that is better still. Then there will be the union of souls, they will have everything in common, there will be no secrets between them. And once they have children, the most difficult times will seem happy to them, so long as there is love and courage. Even toil will be a joy, you may deny yourself bread for your children and even that will be a joy. They will love you for it afterwards; so you are laying by for your future. As the children grow up you feel that you are an example, a support for them; that even after you die your children will always keep your thoughts and feelings, because they have received them from you, they will take on your semblance and likeness. So you see this is a great duty. How can it fail to draw the father and mother nearer? People say it's a trial to have children. Who says that? It is heavenly happiness! Are you fond of little children, Liza? I am awfully fond of them. You know—a little rosy baby boy at your bosom, and what husband's heart is not touched, seeing his wife nursing his child! A plump little rosy baby, sprawling and snuggling, chubby little hands and feet, clean tiny little nails, so tiny that it makes one laugh to look at them; eyes that look as if they understand everything. And while it sucks, it clutches at your bosom with its little hand, plays. When its father comes up, the child tears itself away from the bosom, flings itself back, looks at its father, laughs, as though it were fearfully funny, and falls to sucking again. Or it will bite its mother's breast when its little teeth are coming, while it looks sideways at her with its little eyes as though to say, 'Look, I am biting!' Is not all that happiness when the three are together, husband, wife and child? One can forgive a great deal for the sake of such moments. Yes, Liza, one must first learn to live oneself before one blames others!"

"It's with pictures, pictures like that one must get at you," I thought to myself, though I did speak with real feeling, and all at once I flushed crimson. "What if she were suddenly to burst out laughing, what should I do then?" That idea drove me to fury. Towards the end of my speech I really was excited, and now my vanity was somehow wounded. The silence continued. I almost nudged her.

"Why are you—" she began and stopped.

But I understood: there was a quiver of something different in her voice, not abrupt, harsh and unyielding as before, but something soft and shamefaced, so shamefaced that I suddenly felt ashamed and guilty.

"What?" I asked, with tender curiosity.

"Why, you . . ."

"What?"

"Why, you—speak somehow like a book," she said, and again there was a note of irony in her voice.

That remark sent a pang to my heart. It was not what I was expecting.

I did not understand that she was hiding her feelings under irony, that this is usually the last refuge of modest and chaste-souled people when the privacy of their souls is coarsely and intrusively invaded, and that their pride makes them refuse to surrender till the last moment and shrink from giving expression to their feelings before you. I ought to have guessed the truth from the timidity with which she had repeatedly approached her sarcasm, only bringing herself to utter it at last with an effort. But I did not guess, and an evil feeling took possession of me.

"Wait a bit!" I thought.

VII

"Oh, hush, Liza! How can you talk about being like a book, when it makes even me, an outsider, feel sick? Though I don't look at it as an outsider, for, indeed, it touches me to the heart. . . . Is it possible, is it possible that you do not feel sick at being here yourself? Evidently habit does wonders! God knows what habit can do to one. Can you seriously think that you will never grow old, that you will always be good-looking, and that they will keep you here forever and ever? I say nothing of the loathsomeness of the life here. . . . Though let me tell you this about it—about your present life, I mean; though you are young now, attractive, nice, with soul and feeling, yet you know as soon as I came to myself just now I felt at once sick at being here with you! One can only come here when one is drunk. But if you were anywhere else, living as good people live, I should perhaps be more than attracted by you, should fall in love with you, should be glad of a look from you, let alone a word; I should hang about your door, should go down on my knees to you, should look upon you as my betrothed and think it an honor to be allowed to. I should not dare to have an impure thought about you.

But here, you see, I know that I have only to whistle and you have to come with me whether you like it or not. I don't consult your wishes, but you mine. The lowest laborer hires himself as a workman but he doesn't make a slave of himself altogether; besides, he knows that he will be free again presently. But when are you free? Only think what you are giving up here! What is it you are making a slave of? It is your soul, together with your body; you are selling your soul, which you have no right to dispose of! You give your love to be outraged by every drunkard! Love! But that's everything, you know, it's a priceless diamond, it's a maiden's treasure, love—why, a man would be ready to give his soul, to face death to gain that love. But how much is your love worth now? You are sold, all of you, body and soul, and there is no need to strive for love when you can have everything without love. And you know there is no greater insult to a girl than that, do you understand? To be sure, I have heard that they comfort you, poor fools, they let you have lovers of your own here. But you know that's simply a farce, that's simply a sham, it's just laughing at you, and you are taken in by it! Why, do you suppose he really loves you, that lover of yours? I don't believe it. How can he love you when he knows you may be called away from him any minute? He would be a low fellow if he did! Will he have a grain of respect for you? What have you in common with him? He laughs at you and robs you—that is all his love amounts to! You are lucky if he does not beat you. Very likely he does beat you, too. Ask him, if you have got one, whether he will marry you. He will laugh in your face, if he doesn't spit in it or give you a blow—though maybe all he is worth himself is two bad groats. And for what have you ruined your life, if you come to think of it? For the coffee they give you to drink and the plentiful meals? But with what object are they feeding you up? An honest girl couldn't swallow the food, for she would know what she was being fed for. You are in debt here, and, of course, you will always be in debt, and you will go on in debt to the end, till the visitors here begin to scorn you. And that will soon happen, don't rely upon your youth—all that flies by express train here, you know. You will be kicked out. And not simply kicked out; long before that she'll begin nagging at you, scolding you, abusing you, as though you had not sacrificed your health for her, had not thrown away your youth and your soul for her benefit, but as though you had ruined her, beggared her, robbed her. And don't expect anyone to take your part: the others, your companions, will attack you, too, to win her favor, for all are in slavery here, and have lost all conscience and pity here long ago. They have become utterly vile, and nothing on earth is viler, more loathsome, and more insulting than their abuse. And you are laying down everything here, unconditionally, youth and health and beauty and hope, and at twenty-two you will look like a woman of five-and-thirty, and you will be lucky if you are not diseased, pray to God to keep you from it! No doubt you are thinking now that you have a gay time and no work to do! Yet there is no work harder or more dreadful in the world or ever has been. One would think that the heart alone would be worn out with tears. And you won't dare to say a word, not half a word when they drive you away from here; you will go away as though you were to blame. You will change to another house, then to a third, then somewhere else, till you come down at last to the Haymarket. There you will be beaten at every turn; that is good manners there, the visitors don't know how to be friendly without beating you. You don't believe that it is so hateful there? Go and look for yourself some time, you can see with your own eyes. Once, one New Year's Day, I saw a woman at a door. They had turned her out as a joke, to give her a taste of the frost because she had been crying so much, and they shut the door behind her. At nine o'clock in the morning she was already quite drunk, disheveled, half-naked, covered with bruises, her face was powdered, but she had a black eye, blood was trickling from her nose and her teeth; some cabman had just given her a drubbing. She was sitting on the stone steps, a salt fish of some sort was in her hand; she was crying, wailing something about her luck and beating with the fish on the steps, and cabmen and drunken soldiers were crowding in the doorway taunting her. You don't believe that you will ever be like that? I should be sorry to believe it, too, but how do you know? Maybe ten years, eight years ago that very woman with the salt fish came here fresh as a cherub, innocent, pure, knowing no evil, blushing at every word. Perhaps she was like you, proud, ready to take offence, not like the others; perhaps she looked like a queen, and knew what happiness was in store for the man who would love her and whom she would love. Do you see how it ended? And what if at that very minute when she was beating on the filthy steps with that fish, drunken and disheveled— what if at that very minute she recalled the pure early days in her father's house, when she used to go to school and the neighbor's son watched for her on the way, declaring that he would love her as long as he lived, that he would devote his life to her, and when they vowed to love one another forever and be married as soon as they were grown up! No, Liza, it would be happy for you if you were to die soon of consumption in some corner, in some cellar like that woman just now. In the hospital, do you say? You will be lucky if they take you, but what if you are still of use to the madam here? Consumption is a queer disease, it is not like fever. The patient goes on hoping till the last minute and says he is all right. He deludes himself. And that just suits your madam. Don't doubt it, that's how it is; you have sold your soul, and what is more you owe money, so you daren't say a word. But when you are dying, all will abandon you, all will turn away from you, for then there will be nothing to get from you. What's more, they will reproach you for cumbering the place, for being so long over dying. However you beg, you won't get a drink of water without abuse: 'Whenever are you going off, you nasty hussy, you won't let us sleep with your moaning, you make the gentlemen sick.' That's true, I have heard such things said myself. They will thrust you dying into the filthiest corner in the cellar—in the damp and darkness; what will your thoughts be, lying there alone? When you die, strange hands will lay you out, with grumbling and impatience; no one will bless you, no one will sigh for you, they will only want to get rid of you as soon as may be; they will buy a coffin, take you to the grave as they did that poor woman today, and celebrate your memory at the tavern. In the grave, sleet, filth, wet snow—no need to put themselves out for you— 'Let her down, Vanyuha; it's just like her luck—even here, she is head-foremost, the hussy. Shorten the cord, you rascal.' 'It's all right as it is.' 'All right, is it? Why, she's on her side! She was a fellow-creature, after all! But, never mind, throw the earth on her.' And they won't care to waste much time quarreling over you. They will scatter the wet blue clay as quick as they can and go off to the tavern . . . and there your memory on earth will end; other women have children to go to their graves, fathers, husbands. While for you neither tear, nor sigh, nor remembrance; no one in the whole world will ever come to you, your name will vanish from the face of the earth—as though you had never existed, never been born at all! Nothing but filth and mud, however you knock at your coffin lid at night, when the dead arise, however you cry: 'Let me out, kind people, to live in the light of day! My life was no life at all; my life has been thrown away like a dishclout; it was drunk away in the tavern at the Haymarket; let me out, kind people, to live in the world again.' "

And I worked myself up to such a pitch that I began to have a lump in my throat myself, and—and all at once I stopped, sat up in dismay, and bending over apprehensively, began to listen with a beating heart. I had reason to be troubled.

I had felt for some time that I was turning her soul upside down and rending her heart, and—and the more I was convinced of it, the more eagerly I desired to gain my object as quickly and as effectually as possible. It was the exercise of my skill that carried me away; yet it was not merely sport. . . .

I knew I was speaking stiffly, artificially, even bookishly, in fact, I could not speak except "like a book." But that did not trouble me: I knew, I felt that I should be understood and that this very bookishness might be an assistance. But now, having attained my effect, I was suddenly panic-stricken. Never before had I witnessed such despair! She was lying on her face, thrusting her face into the pillow and clutching it in both hands. Her heart was being torn. Her youthful body was shuddering all over as though in convulsions. Suppressed sobs rent her bosom and suddenly burst out in weeping and wailing, then she pressed closer into the pillow: she did not want anyone here, not a living soul, to know of her anguish and her tears. She bit the pillow, bit her hand till it bled (I saw that afterwards), or, thrusting her fingers into her disheveled hair, seemed rigid with the effort of restraint, holding her breath and clenching her teeth. I began saying something, begging her to calm herself, but felt that I did not dare; and all at once, in a sort of cold shiver, almost in terror, began fumbling in the dark, trying hurriedly to get dressed to go. It was dark: though I tried my best I could not finish dressing quickly. Suddenly I felt a box of matches and a candlestick with a whole candle in it. As soon as the room was lighted up, Liza sprang up, sat up in bed, and with a contorted face, with a half insane smile, looked at me almost senselessly. I sat down beside her and took her hands; she came to herself, made an impulsive movement towards me, would have caught hold of me, but did not dare, and slowly bowed her head before me.

"Liza, my dear, I was wrong . . . Forgive me, my dear," I began, but she squeezed my hand in her fingers so tightly that I felt I was saying the wrong thing and stopped.

"This is my address, Liza, come to me."

"I will come," she answered resolutely, her head still bowed.

"But now I am going, good-bye . . . till we meet again."

I got up; she, too, stood up and suddenly flushed all over, gave a shudder, snatched up a shawl that was lying on a chair and muffled herself in it to her chin. As she did this she gave another sickly smile, blushed and looked at me strangely. I felt wretched; I was in haste to get away—to disappear.

"Wait a minute," she said suddenly, in the passage just at the doorway, stopping me with her hand on my overcoat. She put down the candle in hot haste and ran off; evidently she had thought of something or wanted to show me something. As she ran away she flushed, her eyes shone, and there was a smile on her lips—what was the meaning of it? Against my will I waited: she came back a minute later with an expression that seemed to ask forgiveness for something. In fact, it was not the same face, not the same look as the evening before: sullen, mistrustful and obstinate. Her eyes now were imploring, soft, and at the same time trustful, caressing, timid. The expression with which children look at people they are very fond of, of whom they are asking a favor. Her eyes were a light hazel, they were lovely eyes, full of life, and capable of expressing love as well as sullen hatred.

Making no explanation, as though I, as a sort of higher being, must understand everything without explanations, she held out a piece of paper to me. Her whole face was positively beaming at that instant with naïve, almost childish, triumph. I unfolded it. It was a letter to her from a medical student or some one of that sort—a very high-flown and flowery, but extremely respectful, love-letter. I don't recall the words now, but I remember well that through the high-flown phrases there was apparent a genuine feeling, which cannot be feigned. When I had finished reading it I met her glowing, questioning, and childishly impatient eyes fixed upon me. She fastened her eyes upon my face and waited impatiently for what I should say. In a few words, hurriedly, but with a sort of joy and pride, she explained to me that she had been to a dance somewhere in a private house, a family of "very nice people, *who knew nothing*, absolutely nothing, for she had only come here so lately and it had all happened . . . and she hadn't made up her mind to stay and was certainly going away as soon as she had paid her debt . . ." and at that party there had been the student who had danced with her all the evening. He had talked to her, and it turned out that he had known her in former days in Riga when he was a child, they had played together, but a very long time ago—and he knew her parents, but *about this* he knew nothing, nothing whatever, and had no suspicion! And the day after the dance (three days ago) he had sent her that letter through the friend with whom she had gone to the party . . . and . . . well, that was all.

She dropped her shining eyes with a sort of bashfulness as she finished.

The poor girl was keeping that student's letter as a precious treasure, and had run to fetch it, her only treasure, because she did not want me to go away without knowing that she, too, was honestly and genuinely loved; that she, too, was addressed respectfully. No doubt that letter was destined to lie in her box and lead to nothing. But none the less, I am certain that she would keep it all her life as a precious treasure, as her pride and justification, and now at such a minute she had thought of that letter and brought it with naïve pride to raise herself in my eyes that I might see, that I, too, might think well of her. I said nothing, pressed her hand and went out. I so longed to get away. . . . I walked all the way home, in spite of the fact that the melting snow was still falling in heavy flakes. I was exhausted, shattered, in bewilderment. But behind the bewilderment the truth was already gleaming. The loathsome truth!

VIII

It was some time, however, before I consented to recognize that truth. Waking up in the morning after some hours of heavy, leaden sleep, and immediately realizing all that had happened on the previous day, I was positively amazed at my last night's *sentimentality* with Liza, at all those "outcries of horror and pity . . . To think of having such an attack of womanish hysteria, pah!" I concluded. And what did I thrust my address upon her for? What if she comes? Let her come, though; it doesn't matter. . . . But *obviously*, that was not now the chief and the most important matter: I had to make haste and at all costs save my reputation in the eyes of Zverkov and

Simonov as quickly as possible; that was the chief business. And I was so taken up that morning that I actually forgot all about Liza.

First of all I had at once to repay what I had borrowed the day before from Siminov. I resolved on a desperate measure: to borrow fifteen roubles straight off from Anton Antonych. As luck would have it he was in the best of humors that morning, and gave it to me at once, on the first asking. I was so delighted at this that, as I signed the I O U with a swaggering air, I told him casually that the night before "I had been keeping it up with some friends at the Hôtel de Paris; we were giving a farewell party to a comrade, in fact, I might say a friend of my childhood, and you know—a desperate rake, fearfully spoilt—of course, he belongs to a good family, and has considerable means, a brilliant career; he is witty, charming, a regular Lovelace, you understand; we drank an extra 'half-dozen' and . . ."

And it went off all right; all this was uttered very easily, unconstrainedly and complacently.

On reaching home I promptly wrote to Simonov.

To this hour I am lost in admiration when I recall the truly gentlemanly, good-humored, candid tone of my letter. With tact and good-breeding, and, above all, entirely without superfluous words, I blamed myself for all that had happened. I defended myself, "if I really may be allowed to defend myself," by alleging that being utterly unaccustomed to wine, I had been intoxicated with the first glass, which I said, I had drunk before they arrived, while I was waiting for them at the Hôtel de Paris between five and six o'clock. I begged Simonov's pardon especially; I asked him to convey my explanations to all the others, especially to Zverkov, whom "I seemed to remember as though in a dream" I had insulted. I added that I would have called upon all of them myself, but my head ached, and besides I had not the face to. I was particularly pleased with a certain lightness, almost carelessness (strictly within the bounds of politeness, however), which was apparent in my style, and better than any possible arguments, gave them at once to understand that I took rather an independent view of "all that unpleasantness last night"; that I was by no means so utterly crushed as you, my friends, probably imagine; but on the contrary, looked upon it as a gentleman serenely respecting himself should look upon it. "On a young hero's past no censure is cast!"

"There is actually an aristocratic playfulness about it!" I thought admiringly, as I read over the letter. And it's all because I am an intellectual and cultivated man! Another man in my place would not have known how to extricate himself, but here I have got out of it and am as jolly as ever again, and all because I am "a cultivated and educated man of our day." And, indeed, perhaps, everything was due to the wine yesterday. H'm! . . . no, it was not the wine. I did not drink anything at all between five and six when I was waiting for them. I had lied to Simonov; I had lied shamelessly; and indeed I wasn't ashamed now. . . . Hang it all though, the great thing was that I was rid of it.

I put six roubles in the letter, sealed it up, and asked Apollon to take it to Simonov. When he learned that there was money in the letter, Apollon became more respectful and agreed to take it. Towards evening I went out for a walk. My head was still aching and giddy after yesterday. But as evening came on and the twilight grew denser, my impressions and, following them, my thoughts, grew more and more different and confused. Something was not dead within me, in the depths of my heart and conscience it would not die, and it showed itself in acute depression. For the most part I jostled my way through the most crowded business streets, along Meshchansky Street, along Sadovy Street and in Yusupov Garden. I always particularly liked sauntering along these streets in the dusk, just when there were crowds of working-people of all sorts going home from their daily work, with faces looking cross with anxiety. What I liked was just that cheap bustle, that bare prose. On this occasion the jostling of the streets irritated me more than ever. I could not make out what was wrong with me, I could not find the clue, something seemed rising up continually in my soul, painfully, and refusing to be appeased. I returned home completely upset, it was just as though some crime were lying on my conscience.

The thought that Liza was coming worried me continually. It seemed queer to me that of all my recollections of yesterday this tormented me, as it were, especially, as it were, quite separately. Everything else I had quite succeeded in forgetting by the evening; I dismissed it all and was still perfectly satisfied with my letter to Simonov. But on this point I was not satisfied at all. It was as though I were worried only by Liza. "What if she comes," I thought incessantly, "well, it doesn't matter, let her come! H'm! it's horrid that she should see, for instance, how I live. Yesterday I seemed such a hero to her, while now, h'm! It's horrid, though, that I have let myself go so, the room looks like a beggar's. And I brought myself to go out to dinner in such a suit! And my American leather sofa with the stuffing sticking out. And my dressing-gown, which will not cover me, such tatters, and she will see all this and she will see Apollon. That beast is certain to insult her. He will fasten upon her in order to be rude to me. And I, of course, shall be panic-stricken as usual, I shall begin bowing and scraping before her and pulling my dressing-gown round me, I shall begin smiling, telling lies. Oh, the beastliness! And it isn't the beastliness of it that matters most! There is something more important, more loathsome, viler! Yes, viler! And to put on that dishonest lying mask again!" . . .

When I reached that thought I fired up all at once.

"Why dishonest? How dishonest? I was speaking sincerely last night. I remember there was real feeling in me, too. What I wanted was to excite an honorable feeling in her. . . . Her crying was a good thing, it will have a good effect."

Yet I could not feel at ease. All that evening, even when I had come back home, even after nine o'clock, when I calculated that Liza could not possibly come, she still haunted me, and what was worse, she came back to my mind always in the same position. One moment out off all that had happened last night stood vividly before my imagination; the moment when I struck a match and saw her pale, distorted face, with its look of torture. And what a pitiful, what an unnatural, what a distorted smile she had at that moment! But I did not know then, that fifteen years later I should still in my imagination see Liza, always with the pitiful, distorted, inappropriate smile which was on her face at that minute.

Next day I was ready again to look upon it all as nonsense, due to over-excited nerves, and, above all, as *exaggerated*. I was always conscious of that weak point of mine, and sometimes very much afraid of it. "I exaggerate everything, that is where I go wrong," I repeated to myself every hour. But, however, "Liza will very likely come all the same," was the refrain with which all my reflections ended. I was so uneasy that I sometimes flew into a fury: "She'll come, she is certain to come!" I cried, running about the room, "if not today, she will come tomorrow; she'll find me out! The damnable romanticism of these pure hearts! Oh, the vileness—oh, the silliness

—oh, the stupidity of these 'wretched sentimental souls!' Why, how fail to understand? How could one fail to understand? . . ."

But at this point I stopped short, and in great confusion, indeed.

And how few, how few words, I thought, in passing, were needed; how little of the idyllic (and affectedly, bookishly, artifically idyllic too) had sufficed to turn a whole human life at once according to my will. That's virginity, to be sure! Freshness of soil!

At times a thought occurred to me, to go to her, "to tell her all," and beg her not to come to me. But this thought stirred such wrath in me that I believed I should have crushed that "damned" Liza if she had chanced to be near me at the time. I should have insulted her, have spat at her, have turned her out, have struck her!

One day passed, however, another and another; she did not come and I began to grow calmer. I felt particularly bold and cheerful after nine o'clock, I even sometimes began dreaming, and rather sweetly; I, for instance, become the salvation of Liza, simply through her coming to me and my talking to her. . . . I develop her, educate her. Finally, I notice that she loves me, loves me passionately. I pretend not to understand (I don't know, however, why I pretend, just for effect, perhaps). At last all confusion, transfigured, trembling and sobbing, she flings herself at my feet and says that I am her savior, and that she loves me better than anything in the world. I am amazed, but . . . "Liza," I say, "can you imagine that I have not noticed your love, I saw it all, I divined it, but I did not dare to approach you first, because I had an influence over you and was afraid that you would force yourself, from gratitude, to respond to my love, would try to rouse in your heart a feeling which was perhaps absent, and I did not wish that . . . because it would be tyranny . . . it would be indelicate (in short, I launch off at that point into European, inexplicably lofty subtleties à la George Sand), but now, now you are mine, you are my creation, you are pure, you are good, you are my noble wife.

> Into my house come bold and free,
> Its rightful mistress there to be."

Then we begin living together, go abroad and so on, and so on. In fact, in the end it seemed vulgar to me myself, and I began putting out my tongue at myself.

Besides, they won't let her out, "the strumpet!" I thought. They

don't let them go out very readily, especially in the evening (for
some reason I fancied she would come in the evening, and at seven
o'clock precisely). Though she did say she was not altogether a
slave there yet, and had certain rights; so, h'm! Damn it all, she will
come, she is sure to come!

It was a good thing, in fact, that Apollon distracted my attention
at that time by his rudeness. He drove me beyond all patience! He
was the bane of my life, the curse laid upon me by Providence. We
had been squabbling continually for years, and I hated him. My
God, how I hated him! I believe I had never hated anyone in my
life as I hated him, especially at some moments. He was an elderly,
dignified man, who worked part of his time as a tailor. But for some
unknown reason he despised me beyond all measure, and looked
down upon me insufferably. Though, indeed, he looked down
upon everyone. Simply to glance at that flaxen, smoothly brushed
head, at the tuft of hair he combed up on his forehead and oiled with
sunflower oil, at that dignified mouth, compressed into the shape of
the letter V, made one feel one was confronting a man who never
doubted himself. He was a pedant, to the most extreme point, the
greatest pedant I had met on earth, and with that had a vanity only
befitting Alexander of Macedon. He was in love with every button
on his coat, every nail on his fingers—absolutely in love with them,
and he looked it! In his behavior to me he was a perfect tyrant, he
spoke very little to me, and if he chanced to glance at me he gave me
a firm, majestically self-confident and invariably ironical look that
drove me sometimes to fury. He did his work with the air of doing
me the greatest favor. Though he did scarcely anything for me, and
did not, indeed, consider himself bound to do anything. There could
be no doubt that he looked upon me as the greatest fool on earth,
and that if he "did not get rid of me" it was because he could get
wages from me every month. He consented to do nothing for me
for seven roubles a month. Many sins should be forgiven me for
what I suffered from him. My hatred reached such a point that sometimes his very step almost threw me into convulsions. What I loathed
particularly was his lisp. His tongue must have been a little too long
or something of that sort, for he continually lisped, and seemed to be
very proud of it, imagining that it greatly added to his dignity. He
spoke in a slow, measured tone, with his hands behind his back and
his eyes fixed on the ground. He maddened me particularly when

he read aloud the psalms to himself behind his partition. Many a battle I waged over that reading! But he was awfully fond of reading aloud in the evening, in a slow, even singsong voice, as though over the dead. It is interesting that that is how he has ended: he hires himself out to read the psalms over the dead, and at the same time he kills rats and makes blacking. But at that time I could not get rid of him, it was as though he were chemically combined with my existence. Besides, nothing would have induced him to consent to leave me. I could not live in furnished lodgings: my lodging was my private solitude, my shell, my cave, in which I concealed myself from all mankind, and Apollon seemed to me, for some reason, an integral part of that flat, and for seven years I could not turn him away.

To be two or three days behind with his wages, for instance, was impossible. He would have made such a fuss, I should not have known where to hide my head. But I was so exasperated with everyone during those days, that I made up my mind for some reason and with some object to *punish* Apollon and not to pay him for a fortnight the wages that were owing him. I had for a long time— for the last two years—been intending to do this, simply in order to teach him not to give himself airs with me, and to show him that if I liked I could withhold his wages. I purposed to say nothing to him about it, and was purposely silent indeed, in order to score off his pride and force him to be the first to speak of his wages. Then I would take the seven roubles out of a drawer, show him I had the money put aside on purpose, but that I wouldn't, I wouldn't, I simply wouldn't pay him his wages, I wouldn't just because that is "what I wish," because "I am master, and it is for me to decide," because he had been disrespectful, because he had been rude; but if he were to ask respectfully I might be softened and give it to him, otherwise he might wait another fortnight, another three weeks, a whole month. . . .

But angry as I was, yet he got the better of me. I could not hold out for four days. He began as he always did begin in such cases, for there had been such cases already, there had been attempts (and it may be observed I knew all this beforehand, I knew his nasty tactics by heart). He would begin by fixing upon me an exceedingly severe stare, keeping it up for several minutes at a time, particularly on meeting me or seeing me out of the house. If I held out and pretended not to notice these stares, he would, still in silence. proceed to further tortures. All at once, apropos of nothing, he would walk softly and smoothly into my room, when I was pacing up and down or reading, stand at the door, one hand behind his back and one foot behind the other, and fix upon me a stare more than severe, utterly contemptuous. If I suddenly asked him what he wanted, he would make me no answer, but continue staring at me persistently for some seconds, then, with a peculiar compression of his lips and a most significant air, deliberately turn round and deliberately go back to his room. Two hours later he would come out again and again present himself before me in the same way. It had happened that in my fury I did not even ask him what he wanted, but simply raised my head sharply and imperiously and began staring back at him. So we stared at one another for two minutes; at last he turned with deliberation and dignity and went back again for two hours.

If I were still not brought to reason by all this, but persisted in my revolt, he would suddenly begin sighing while he looked at me, long, deep sighs as though measuring by them the depths of my moral degradation, and, of course, it ended at last by his triumphing completely: I raged and shouted, but still was forced to do what he wanted.

This time the usual staring maneuvers had scarcely begun when I lost my temper and flew at him in a fury. I was irritated beyond endurance apart from him.

"Stay," I cried, in a frenzy, as he was slowly and silently turning, with one hand behind his back, to go to his room, "stay! Come back, come back, I tell you!" and I must have bawled so unnaturally, that he turned round and even looked at me with some wonder. However, he persisted in saying nothing, and that infuriated me.

"How dare you come and look at me like that without being sent for? Answer!"

After looking at me calmly for half a minute, he began turning round again.

"Stay!" I roared, running up to him, "don't stir! There. Answer, now: what did you come in to look at?"

"If you have any order to give me it's my duty to carry it out," he answered, after another silent pause, with a slow, measured lisp, raising his eyebrows and calmly twisting his head from one side to another, all this with exasperating composure.

"That's not what I am asking you about, you executioner!" I cried, turning crimson with anger. "I'll tell you why you came here myself; you see, I don't give you your wages, you are so proud you don't want to bow down and ask for them, and so you come to punish me with your stupid stares, to worry me and you have no sus-pi-cion how stupid it is—stupid, stupid, stupid, stupid!" . . .

He would have turned round again without a word, but I seized him.

"Listen," I shouted to him. "Here's the money, do you see, here it is" (I took it out of the table drawer); "here's the seven roubles complete, but you are not going to have it, you—are—not—going—to—have it until you come respectfully with bowed head to beg my pardon. Do you hear?"

"That cannot be," he answered, with the most unnatural self-confidence.

"It shall be so," I said, "I give you my word of honor, it shall be!"

"And there's nothing for me to beg your pardon for," he went on, as though he had not noticed my exclamations at all. "Why, besides, you called me 'executioner,' for which I can summon you to the police-station at any time for insulting behavior."

"Go, summon me," I roared, "go at once, this very minute, this very second! You are an executioner all the same! an executioner!"

But he merely looked at me, then turned, and regardless of my loud calls to him, he walked to his room with an even step and without looking round.

"If it had not been for Liza nothing of this would have happened," I decided inwardly. Then, after waiting a minute, I myself went behind his screen with a dignified and solemn air, though my heart was beating slowly and violently.

"Apollon," I said quietly and emphatically, though I was breathless, "go at once without a minute's delay and fetch the police officer."

He had meanwhile settled himself at his table, put on his spectacles and taken up some sewing. But, hearing my order, he burst into a guffaw.

"At once, go this minute! Go on, or else you can't imagine what will happen."

"You are certainly out of your mind," he observed, without even raising his head, lisping as deliberately as ever and threading his needle. "Whoever heard of a man sending for the police against himself? And as for being frightened—you are upsetting yourself about nothing, for nothing will come of it."

"Go!" I shrieked, clutching him by the shoulder. I felt I should strike him in a minute.

But I did not notice the door from the passage softly and slowly open at that instant and a figure come in, stop short, and begin staring at us in perplexity. I glanced, nearly swooned with shame, and rushed back to my room. There, clutching at my hair with both hands, I leaned my head against the wall and stood motionless in that position.

Two minutes later I heard Apollon's deliberate footsteps. "There is some woman asking for you," he said, looking at me with peculiar severity. Then he stood aside and let in Liza. He would not go away, but stared at us sarcastically.

"Go away, go away," I commanded in desperation. At that moment my clock began whirring and wheezing and struck seven.

## IX

Into my house come bold and free,
Its rightful mistress there to be.
—*From the same poem.*

I stood before her crushed, crestfallen, revoltingly confused, and I believe I smiled as I did my utmost to wrap myself in the skirts of my ragged wadded dressing-gown—exactly as I had imagined the scene not long before in a fit of depression. After standing over us for a couple of minutes Apollon went away, but that did not make me more at ease. What made it worse was that she, too, was overwhelmed with confusion, more so, in fact, than I should have expected. At the sight of me, of course.

"Sit down," I said mechanically, moving a chair up to the table, and I sat down on the sofa. She obediently sat down at once and gazed at me open-eyed, evidently expecting something from me at once. This naïveté of expectation drove me to fury, but I restrained myself.

She ought to have tried not to notice, as though everything had been as usual, while instead of that, she . . . and I dimly felt that I should make her pay dearly for *all this*.

"You have found me in a strange position, Liza," I began, stammering and knowing that this was the wrong way to begin. "No, no, don't imagine anything," I cried, seeing that she had suddenly flushed. "I am not ashamed of my poverty. . . . On the contrary, I look with pride on my poverty. I am poor but honorable. . . . One can be poor and honorable," I muttered. "However—would you like tea?"

"No," she was beginning.

"Wait a minute."

I leapt up and ran to Apollon. I had to get out of the room somehow.

"Apollon," I whispered in feverish haste, flinging down before him the seven roubles which had remained all the time in my clenched fist, "here are your wages, you see I give them to you; but for that you must come to my rescue: bring me tea and a dozen rusks from the restaurant. If you won't go, you'll make me a miserable man! You don't know what this woman is. . . . This is—everything! You may be imagining something. . . . But you don't know what this woman is!" . . .

Apollon, who had already sat down to his work and put on his spectacles again, at first glanced askance at the money without speaking or putting down his needle; then, without paying the slightest attention to me or making any answer he went on busying himself with his needle, which he had not yet threaded. I waited, standing before him for three minutes with my arms crossed *à la Napoléon*. My temples were moist with sweat. I was pale, I felt it. But, thank God, he must have been moved to pity, looking at me. Having threaded his needle he deliberately got up from his seat, deliberately moved back his chair, deliberately took off his spectacles, deliberately counted the money, and finally asking me over his shoulder, "Shall I get a whole portion?" deliberately walked out of the room. As I was going back to Liza, the thought occurred to me on the way: shouldn't I run away just as I was in my dressing-gown, no matter where, and then let happen what would.

I sat down again. She looked at me uneasily. For some minutes we were silent.

"I will kill him," I shouted suddenly, striking the table with my fist so that the ink spurted out of the inkstand.

"What are you saying!" she cried, starting.

"I will kill him! kill him!" I shrieked, suddenly striking the table in absolute frenzy, and at the same time fully understanding how stupid it was to be in such a frenzy. "You don't know, Liza, what that torturer is to me. He is my torturer. . . . He has gone now to fetch some rusks; he—"

And suddenly I burst into tears. It was an hysterical attack. How ashamed I felt in the midst of my sobs; but still I could not restrain them.

She was frightened.

"What is the matter? What is wrong?" she cried, fussing about me.

"Water, give me water, over there!" I muttered in a faint voice, though I was inwardly conscious that I could have got on very well without water and without muttering in a faint voice. But I was, what is called, *putting it on*, to save appearances, though the attack was a genuine one.

She gave me water, looking at me in bewilderment. At that moment Apollon brought in the tea. It suddenly seemed to me that this commonplace, prosaic tea was horribly undignified and paltry after all that had happened, and I blushed crimson. Liza looked at Apollon with positive alarm. He went out without a glance at either of us.

"Liza, do you despise me?" I asked, looking at her fixedly, trembling with impatience to know what she was thinking.

She was confused, and did not know what to answer.

"Drink your tea," I said to her angrily. I was angry with myself, but, of course, it was she who would have to pay for it. A horrible spite against her suddenly surged up in my heart; I believe I could have killed her. To revenge myself on her I swore inwardly not to say a word to her all the time. "She is the cause of it all," I thought.

Our silence lasted for five minutes. The tea stood on the table; we did not touch it. I had got to the point of purposely refraining from beginning in order to embarrass her further; it was awkward for her to begin alone. Several times she glanced at me with mournful perplexity. I was obstinately silent. I was, of course, myself the chief sufferer, because I was fully conscious of the disgusting meanness of my spiteful stupidity, and yet at the same time I could not restrain myself.

"I want to . . . get away . . . from there altogether," she began, to break the silence in some way, but, poor girl, that was just what she ought not to have spoken about at such a stupid moment to a man so stupid as I was. My heart positively ached with pity for her tactless and unnecessary straightforwardness. But something hideous at once stifled all compassion in me; it even provoked me to greater venom. I did not care what happened. Another five minutes passed.

"Perhaps I am in your way," she began timidly, hardly audibly, and was getting up.

But as soon as I saw this first impulse of wounded dignity I positively trembled with spite, and at once burst out.

"Why have you come to me, tell me that, please?" I began, gasping for breath and regardless of logical connection in my words. I longed to have it all out at once, at one burst; I did not even trouble how to begin. "Why have you come? Answer, answer," I cried, hardly knowing what I was doing. "I'll tell you, my good girl, why you have come. You've come because I talked sentimental stuff to you then. So now you are soft as butter and longing for fine sentiments again. So you may as well know that I was laughing at you then. And I am laughing at you now. Why are you shuddering? Yes, I was laughing at you! I had been insulted just before, at dinner, by the fellows who came that evening before me. I came to you, meaning to thrash one of them, an officer; but I didn't succeed, I didn't find him; I had to avenge the insult on someone to get back my own again; you turned up, I vented my spleen on you and laughed at you. I had been humiliated, so I wanted to humiliate; I had been treated like a rag, so I wanted to show my power. . . . That's what it was, and you imagined I had come there on purpose to save you. Yes? You imagined that? You imagined that?"

I knew that she would perhaps be muddled and not take it all in exactly, but I knew, too, that she would grasp the gist of it very well indeed. And so, indeed, she did. She turned white as a handkerchief, tried to say something, and her lips worked painfully; but she sank on a chair as though she had been felled by an axe. And all the time afterwards she listened to me with her lips parted and her eyes wide open, shuddering with awful terror. The cynicism, the cynicism of my words overwhelmed her. . . .

"Save you!" I went on, jumping up from my chair and running up and down the room before her. "Save you from what? But perhaps I am worse than you myself. Why didn't you throw it in my teeth when I was giving you that sermon: 'But what did you come here yourself for? was it to read us a sermon?' Power, power was what I wanted then, sport was what I wanted, I wanted to wring out your tears, your humiliation, your hysteria—that was what I wanted then! Of course, I couldn't keep it up then, because I am a wretched creature, I was frightened, and, the devil knows why, gave you my address in my folly. Afterwards, before I got home, I was cursing and swearing at you because of that address, I hated you already because of the lies I had told you. Because I only like playing with words, only dreaming, but, do you know, what I really want is that you should all go to hell. That is what I want. I want peace; yes, I'd sell the whole world for a copeck, straight off, so long as I was left in peace. Is the world to go to pot, or am I to go without my tea? I say that the world may go to pot for me so long as I always get my tea. Did you know that, or not? Well, anyway, I know that I am a blackguard, a scoundrel, an egoist, a sluggard. Here I have been shuddering for the last three days at the thought of your coming. And do you know what has worried me particularly for these three days? That I posed as such a hero to you, and now you would see me in a wretched torn dressing-gown, beggarly, loathsome. I told you just now that I was not ashamed of my poverty; so you may as well know that I am ashamed of it; I am more ashamed of it than of anything, more afraid of it than of being found out if I were a thief, because I am as vain as though I had been skinned and the very air blowing on me hurt. Surely by now you must realize that I shall never forgive you for having found me in this wretched dressing-gown, just as I was flying at Apollon like a spiteful cur. The savior, the former hero, was flying like a mangy, unkempt sheep-dog at his lackey, and the lackey was jeering at him! And I shall never forgive you for the tears I could not help shedding before you just now, like some silly woman put to shame! And for what I am confessing to you now, I shall never forgive *you* either! Yes—you must answer for it all because you turned up like this, because I am a blackguard, because I am the nastiest, stupidest, absurdest and most envious of all the worms on earth, who are not a bit better than I am, but, the devil knows why, are never put to confusion; while I shall always be insulted by every louse, that is my doom! And what is it to me that you don't understand a word of this! And what do I care, what do I care about you, and whether you go to ruin there or not? Do you understand? How I shall hate you now after saying this, for having been here and listening. Why, it's not once in a lifetime a man speaks out like this, and then it is in hysterics! . . . What more do you want? Why do you still stand confronting me, after all this? Why are you worrying me? Why don't you go?"

But at this point a strange thing happened. I was so accustomed to think and imagine everything from books, and to picture everything in the world to myself just as I had made it up in my dreams beforehand, that I could not all at once take in this strange circumstance. What happened was this: Liza, insulted and crushed by me, understood a great deal more than I imagined. She understood from all this what a woman understands first of all, if she feels genuine love, that is, that I was myself unhappy.

The frightened and wounded expression on her face was followed first by a look of sorrowful perplexity. When I began calling myself a scoundrel and a blackguard and my tears flowed (the tirade was accompanied throughout by tears) her whole face worked convulsively. She was on the point of getting up and stopping me; when I finished she took no notice of my shouting: "Why are you here, why don't you go away?" but realized only that it must have been very bitter to me to say all this. Besides, she was so crushed, poor girl; she considered herself infinitely beneath me; how could she feel anger or resentment? She suddenly leapt up from her chair with an irresistible impulse and held out her hands, yearning towards me, though still timid and not daring to stir. . . . At this point there was a revulsion in my heart, too. Then she suddenly rushed to me, threw her arms round me and burst into tears. I, too, could not restrain myself, and sobbed as I never had before.

"They won't let me . . . I can't be good!" I managed to articulate; then I went to the sofa, fell on it face downwards, and sobbed on it for a quarter of an hour in genuine hysterics. She came close to me, put her arms round me and stayed motionless in that position.

But the trouble was that the hysterics could not go on forever, and (I am writing the loathsome truth) lying face downwards on the sofa with my face thrust into my nasty leather pillow, I began by degrees to be aware of a far-away, involuntary but irresistible feeling that it would be awkward now for me to raise my head and look Liza straight in the face. Why was I ashamed? I don't know, but I was ashamed. The thought, too, came into my overwrought brain that our parts now were completely changed, that she was now the heroine, while I was just such a crushed and humiliated creature as she had been before me that night—four days ago. . . . And all this came into my mind during the minutes I was lying on my face on the sofa.

My God! can it be that I was envious of her then?

I don't know, to this day I cannot decide, and at the time, of course, I was still less able to understand what I was feeling than now. I cannot get on without domineering and tyrannizing over someone, but . . . there is no explaining anything by reasoning and so it is useless to reason.

I conquered myself, however, and raised my head; I had to do so sooner or later . . . and I am convinced to this day that it was just because I was ashamed to look at her that another feeling was suddenly kindled and flamed up in my heart . . . a feeling of mastery and possession. My eyes gleamed with passion, and I gripped her hands tightly. How I hated her and how I was drawn to her at that minute! The one feeling intensified the other. It was almost like an act of vengeance. At first there was a look of amazement, even of terror on her face, but only for one instant. She warmly and rapturously embraced me.

x

A quarter of an hour later I was rushing up and down the room in frenzied impatience, from minute to minute I went up to the screen and peeped through the crack at Liza. She was sitting on the ground with her head leaning against the bed, and must have been crying. But she did not go away, and that irritated me. This time she understood it all. I had insulted her finally, but . . . there's no need to describe it. She realized that my outburst of passion had been simply revenge, a fresh humiliation, and that to my earlier, almost causeless hatred was added now a *personal hatred*, born of envy. . . . Though I do not maintain positively that she understood all this distinctly; but she certainly did fully understand that I was a despicable man, and what was worse, incapable of loving her.

I know I shall be told that this is incredible—but it is incredible to be as spiteful and stupid as I was; it may be added that it was strange I should not love her, or at any rate, appreciate her love. Why is it strange? In the first place, by then I was incapable of love, for I repeat, with me loving meant tyrannizing and showing my moral superiority. I have never in my life been able to imagine any other sort of love, and have nowadays come to the point of sometimes thinking that love really consists in the right—freely given by the beloved object—to tyrannize over her.

Even in my underground dreams I did not imagine love except as a struggle. I began it always with hatred and ended it with moral subjugation, and afterwards I never knew what to do with the subjugated object. And what is there to wonder at in that, since I had succeeded in so corrupting myself, since I was so out of touch with "real life," as to have actually thought of reproaching her, and putting her to shame for having come to me to hear "fine sentiments"; and did not even guess that she had come not to hear fine sentiments, but to love me, because to a woman all reformation, all salvation from any sort of ruin, and all moral renewal is included in love and can only show itself in that form.

I did not hate her so much, however, when I was running about the room and peeping through the crack in the screen. I was only insufferably oppressed by her being here. I wanted her to disappear. I wanted "peace," to be left alone in my underground world. Real life oppressed me with its novelty so much that I could hardly breathe.

But several minutes passed and she still remained, without stirring, as though she were unconscious. I had the shamelessness to tap softly at the screen as though to remind her. . . . She started, sprang up, and flew to seek her kerchief, her hat, her coat, as though making her escape from me. . . . Two minutes later she came from behind the screen and looked with heavy eyes at me. I gave a spiteful grin, which was forced, however, to *keep up appearances,* and I turned away from her eyes.

"Good-bye," she said, going toward the door.

I ran up to her, seized her hand, opened it, thrust something in it and closed it again. Then I turned at once and dashed away in haste to the other corner of the room to avoid seeing, anyway. . . .

I did mean a moment since to tell a lie—to write that I did this accidentally, not knowing what I was doing, through foolishness, through losing my head. But I don't want to lie, and so I will say straight out that I opened her hand and put the money in it . . . from spite. It came into my head to do this while I was running up and down the room and she was sitting behind the screen. But this I can say for certain: though I did that cruel thing purposely, it was not an impulse from the heart, but came from my evil brain. This cruelty was so affected, so purposely made up, so completely a product of the brain, of books, that I could not even keep it up a minute—first I dashed away to avoid seeing her, and then in shame and despair rushed after Liza. I opened the door in the passage and began listening.

"Liza! Liza!" I cried on the stairs, but in a low voice, not boldly.

There was no answer, but I fancied I heard her footsteps, lower down on the stairs.

"Liza!" I cried, more loudly.

No answer. But at that minute I heard the stiff outer glass door open heavily with a creak and slam violently, the sound echoed up the stairs.

She had gone. I went back to my room in hesitation. I felt horribly oppressed.

I stood still at the table, beside the chair on which she had sat and looked aimlessly before me. A minute passed, suddenly I started; straight before me on the table I saw. . . . In short, I saw a crumpled blue five-rouble note, the one I had thrust into her hand a minute before. It was the same note; it could be no other, there was no other in the flat. So she had managed to fling it from her hand on the table at the moment when I had dashed into the further corner.

Well! I might have expected that she would do that. Might I have expected it? No, I was such an egoist, I was so lacking in respect for my fellow-creatures that I could not even imagine she would do so. I could not endure it. A minute later I flew like a madman to dress, flinging on what I could at random, and ran headlong after her. She could not have got two hundred paces away when I ran out into the street.

It was still night and the snow was coming down in masses and falling almost perpendicularly, covering the pavement and the empty street as though with a pillow. There was no one in the street, no sound was to be heard. The street lamps shed a disconsolate and useless glimmer. I ran two hundred paces to the cross-roads and stopped short.

Where had she gone? And why was I running after her?

Why? To fall down before her, to sob with remorse, to kiss her feet, to entreat her forgiveness! I longed for that, my whole breast was being rent to pieces, and never, never shall I recall that minute with indifference. But—what for? I thought. Should I not begin to hate her, perhaps, even tomorrow, just because I had kissed her feet today? Should I give her happiness? Had I not recognized that day, for the hundredth time, what I was worth? Should I not torture her?

I stood in the snow, gazing into the troubled darkness and pondered this.

"And will it not be better?" I mused fantastically, afterwards, at home, stifling the living pang of my heart with fantastic dreams. "Will it not be better that she should keep the resentment of the insult forever? Resentment—why, it is purification; it is a most stinging and painful consciousness! Tomorrow I should have defiled her soul and have exhausted her heart, while now the feeling of insult will never die in her heart, and however loathsome the filth awaiting her—the feeling of insult will elevate and purify her . . . by hatred . . . h'm! . . . perhaps, too, by forgiveness. . . . Will all that make things easier for her though?" . . .

And, indeed, I will ask on my own account here an idle question: which is better—cheap happiness or exalted suffering? Well, which is better?

So I dreamed as I sat at home that evening, almost dead with the pain in my soul. Never have I endured such suffering and remorse, yet could there have been the faintest doubt when I ran out from my lodging that I should turn back halfway? I never met Liza again and I have heard nothing of her. I will add, too, that I remained for a long time afterwards pleased with the phrase about the benefit from resentment and hatred in spite of the fact that I almost fell ill from misery.

Even now, so many years later, all this is somehow a very evil memory. I have many evil memories now, but . . . hadn't I better end my "Notes" here? I believe I made a mistake in beginning to write them, anyway I have felt ashamed all the time I've been writing this story; so it's not so much literature as a corrective punishment. Why, to tell long stories, showing how I have spoiled my life through morally rotting in my corner, through lack of fitting environment, through divorce from real life, and rankling spite in my underground world, would certainly not be interesting; a novel needs a hero, and all the traits for an anti-hero are *expressly* gathered together here, and what matters most, it all produces a most unpleasant impression, for we are all divorced from life, we are all cripples, every one of us, more or less. We are so divorced from it that we feel at times a sort of loathing for real "living life," and so cannot bear to be reminded of it. Why, we have come almost to looking upon real "living life" as an effort, almost as hard work, and we are all privately agreed that it is better in books. And why do we fuss and fume sometimes? Why are we perverse, and why do we ask for something else? We don't know what ourselves. It would be the worse for us if our petulant prayers were answered. Come, try, give any one of us, for instance, a little more independence, untie our hands, widen the spheres of our activity, relax the control and we . . . yes, I assure you . . . we should be begging to be under control again at once. I know that you will very likely be angry with me for that, and will begin shouting and stamping. "Speak for yourself," you say, "and for your miseries in your underground hole, and don't dare to say: 'all of us.' " Excuse me, gentlemen, I am not justifying myself with that "all of us." As for what concerns me in particular I have only carried to an extreme in my life what you have not dared to carry halfway, and what's more, you have taken your cowardice for good sense, and have found comfort in deceiving yourselves. So that perhaps, after all, there is more life in me than in you. Look into it more carefully! Why, we don't even know what living means now, what it is, and what it is called! Leave us alone without books and we shall be lost and in confusion at once. We shall not know what to join on to, what to cling to, what to love and what to hate, what to respect and what to despise. It's a burden to us even to be human beings—men with our own real body and blood; we are ashamed of it, we think it a disgrace and try to contrive to be some sort of impossible generalized man. We are stillborn, and for generations past have not been begotten by living fathers, and that suits us better and better. We are developing a taste for it. Soon we shall contrive to be born somehow of an idea. But enough; I don't want to write more "from the Underground."

[*The "notes" of this paradoxalist do not end here, however. He could not refrain from going on with them, but it seems to us that we may as well stop here.*]

1864

# THE PEASANT MAREY

IT WAS the second day in Easter week. The air was warm, the sky was blue, the sun was high, warm, bright, but my soul was very gloomy. I sauntered behind the prison barracks. I stared at the palings of the stout prison fence, counting them; but I had no inclination to count them, though it was my habit to do so. This was the second day of the "holidays" in the prison; the convicts were not taken out to work, there were numbers of men drunk, loud abuse and quarrelling was springing up continually in every corner. There were hideous, disgusting songs and card-parties installed beside the platform-beds. Several of the convicts who had been sentenced by their comrades, for special violence, to be beaten till they were half dead, were lying on the platform-bed, covered with sheepskins till they should recover and come to themselves again; knives had already been drawn several times. For these two days of holiday all this had been torturing me till it made me ill. And indeed I could never endure without repulsion the noise and disorder of drunken people, and especially in this place. On these days even the prison officials did not look into the prison, made no searches, did not look for vodka, understanding that they must allow even these outcasts to enjoy themselves once a year, and that things would be even worse if they did not. At last a sudden fury flamed up in my heart. A political prisoner called M. met me; he looked at me gloomily, his eyes flashed and his lips quivered. "*Je hais ces brigands!*" he hissed at me through his teeth, and walked on. I returned to the prison ward, though only a quarter of an hour before I had rushed out of it as though I were crazy, when six stalwart fellows had all together flung themselves upon the drunken Tatar Gazin to suppress him and had begun beating him; they beat him stupidly, a camel might have been killed by such blows, but they knew that this Hercules was not easy to kill, and so they beat him without uneasiness. Now on returning I noticed on the bed in the furthest corner of the room Gazin lying unconscious, almost without sign of life. He lay covered with a sheepskin, and everyone walked round him, without speaking; though they confidently hoped that he would come to himself next morning, yet if luck was against him, maybe from a beating like that, the man would die. I made my way to my own place opposite the window with the iron grating, and lay on my back with my hands behind my head and my eyes shut. I liked to lie like that; a sleeping man is not molested, and meanwhile one can dream and think. But I could not dream, my heart was beating uneasily, and M.'s words, *"Je hais ces brigands!"* were echoing in my ears. But why describe my impressions? I sometimes dream even now of those times at night, and I have no dreams more agonizing. Perhaps it will be noticed that even to this day I have scarcely once spoken in print of my life in prison. *The House of the Dead* I wrote fifteen years ago in the character of an imaginary person, a criminal who had killed his wife. I may add by the way that since then, very many persons have supposed, and even now maintain, that I was sent to penal servitude for the murder of my wife.

Gradually I sank into forgetfulness and by degrees was lost in memories. During the whole course of my four years in prison I was continually recalling all my past, and seemed to live over again the whole of my life in recollection. These memories rose up of themselves, it was not often that I summoned them of my own will. Each would begin from some point, some little thing, at times unnoticed, and then by degrees there would rise up a complete picture, some vivid and complete impression. I used to analyze these impressions, give new features to what had happened long ago, and best of all, I used to correct it, correct it continually, that was my great amusement. On this occasion, I suddenly for some reason remembered an unnoticed moment in my early childhood when I was only nine years old—a moment which I should have thought I had utterly forgotten; but at that time I was particularly fond of memories of my early childhood. I remembered the month of August in our country house: a dry bright day but rather cold and windy; summer was waning and soon we should have to go to Moscow to be bored all winter with French lessons, and I was so sorry to leave the country. I walked past the threshing-floor and, going down the ravine, I went up to the dense thicket of bushes that covered the further side of the ravine as far as the copse. And I plunged right into the midst of the bushes, and heard a peasant plowing alone on the clearing about thirty paces away. I knew that he was plowing up the steep hill and the horse was moving with effort, and from time to time the peasant's call "Come up!" floated upwards to me. I knew almost all our peasants, but I did not know who it was plowing now, and, indeed, I did not care, I was absorbed in my own affairs. I was busy, too; I was breaking off switches from the nut trees to whip the frogs with. Nut sticks make such fine whips, but they do not last; while birch twigs are just the opposite. I was interested, too, in beetles and other insects; I used to collect them, some were very ornamental. I was very fond, too, of the little nimble red and yellow lizards with black spots on them, but I was afraid of snakes. Snakes, however, were much more rare than lizards. There were not many mushrooms there. To get mushrooms one had to go to the birch wood, and I was about to set off there. And there was nothing in the world that I loved so much as the wood with its mushrooms and wild berries, with its beetles and its birds, its hedgehogs and squirrels, with its damp smell of dead leaves which I loved so much, and even as I write I smell the fragrance of our birch wood: these impressions will remain for my whole life. Suddenly in the midst of the profound stillness I heard a clear and distinct shout, "Wolf!" I shrieked and, beside myself with terror, calling out at the top of my voice, ran out into the clearing and straight to the peasant who was plowing.

It was our peasant Marey. I don't know if there is such a name, but every one called him Marey—a thick-set, rather well-grown peasant of fifty, with a good many gray hairs in his dark brown, spreading beard. I knew him, but had scarcely ever happened to speak to him till then. He stopped his horse on hearing my cry, and when, breathless, I caught with one hand at his plow and with the other at his sleeve, he saw how frightened I was.

"There is a wolf!" I cried, panting.

He flung up his head, and could not help looking round for an instant, almost believing me.

"Where is the wolf?"

"A shout . . . someone shouted: 'wolf' . . ." I faltered out.

"Nonsense, nonsense! A wolf? Why, it was your fancy! How could there be a wolf?" he muttered, reassuring me. But I was trembling all over, and still kept tight hold of his smock frock, and I must have been quite pale. He looked at me with an uneasy smile, evidently anxious and troubled over me.

"Why, you have had a fright, aïe, aïe!" He shook his head. "There, dear. . . . Come, little one, aïe!"

He stretched out his hand, and all at once stroked my cheek.

"Come, come, there; Christ be with you! Cross yourself!"

But I did not cross myself. The corners of my mouth were twitching, and I think that struck him particularly. He put out his thick, black-nailed, earth-stained finger and softly touched my twitching lips.

"Aïe, there, there," he said to me with a slow, almost motherly smile. "Dear, dear, what is the matter? There; come, come!"

I grasped at last that there was no wolf, and that the shout that I had heard was my fancy. Yet that shout had been so clear and distinct, but such shouts (not only about wolves) I had imagined once or twice before, and I was aware of that. (These hallucinations passed away later as I grew older.)

"Well, I will go then," I said, looking at him timidly and inquiringly.

"Well, do, and I'll keep watch on you as you go. I won't let the wolf get you," he added, still smiling at me with the same motherly expression. "Well, Christ be with you! Come, run along then." And he made the sign of the cross over me and then over himself. I walked away, looking back almost at every tenth step. Marey stood still with his mare as I walked away, and looked after me and nodded to me every time I looked round. I must own I felt a little ashamed at having let him see me so frightened, but I was still very much afraid of the wolf as I walked away, until I reached the first barn half-way up the slope of the ravine; there my fright vanished completely, and all at once our yard-dog Volchok flew to meet me. With Volchok I felt quite safe, and I turned round to Marey for the last time; I could not see his face distinctly, but I felt that he was still nodding and smiling affectionately at me. I waved to him; he waved back at me and started his little mare. "Come up!" I heard his call in the distance again, and the little mare pulled at the plow again.

All this I recalled all at once, I don't know why, but with extraordinary minuteness of detail. I suddenly roused myself and sat up on the sleeping-platform, and, I remember, found myself still smiling quietly at my memories. I brooded over them for another minute.

When I got home that day I told no one of my "adventure" with Marey. And indeed it was hardly an adventure. And in fact I soon forgot Marey. When I met him now and then afterwards, I never even spoke to him about the wolf or anything else; and all at once now, twenty years afterwards in Siberia, I remembered this meeting with such distinctness to the smallest detail. So it must have lain hidden in my soul, though I knew nothing of it, and rose suddenly to my memory when it was wanted; I remembered the soft motherly smile of the poor serf, the way he signed me with the cross and shook his head. "There, there, you have had a fright, little one!" And I remembered particularly the thick earth-stained finger with which he softly and with timid tenderness touched my quivering lips. Of course anyone would have reassured a child, but something quite different seemed to have happened in that solitary meeting; and if I had been his own son, he could not have looked at me with eyes shining with greater love. And what made him like that? He was our serf and I was his little master, after all. No one would know that he had been kind to me and reward him for it. Was he, perhaps, very fond of little children? Some people are. It was a solitary meeting in the deserted fields, and only God, perhaps, may have seen from above with what deep and humane civilized feeling, and with what a delicate, almost feminine tenderness, the heart of a coarse, brutally ignorant Russian serf, who had as yet no expectation, no idea even of his freedom, may be filled. Was not this, perhaps, what Konstantin Aksakov meant when he spoke of the high degree of culture of our peasantry?

And when I got down off the bed and looked around me, I remember I suddenly felt that I could look at these unhappy creatures with quite different eyes, and that suddenly by some miracle all hatred and anger had vanished utterly from my heart. I walked about, looking into the faces that I met. That shaven peasant, branded on his face as a criminal, bawling his hoarse, drunken song, may be that very Marey; I cannot look into his heart.

I met M. again that evening. Poor fellow! he could have no memories of Russian peasants, and no other view of these people but: "*Je hais ces brigands!*" Yes, the Polish prisoners had more to bear than I.

# Nikolay Leskov . . . 1831–1895

LESKOV was thirty before he began writing. He had then a wide knowledge of Russian life, gained through traffic with all manner of people in connection with his duties first as a government employee, like his father before him, and then as an assistant to a manager of large estates, a Scotsman related to the Leskovs by marriage. Orphaned at sixteen, the future writer had to quit school to earn a living, so that he was largely a self-taught man. It was as a journalist writing on matters of practical import that he broke into print. By 1869 he had published two volumes of short stories, as well as a novel, which earned him the reputation of a reactionary, a reputation confirmed by a second novel which appeared in 1870. He ceased his attacks on the radicals in his later work and some of it, indeed, antagonized the conservatives.

He wrote several other novels, including *Cathedral Folk*, a remarkable story of the clergy. The ecclesiastical life is the subject of other tales which he wrote in the seventies and in which he championed Orthodoxy. Later he wrote a series of stories which go by the general title: *The Righteous*. Here he sought to show that Russia did not lack those righteous men for whose sake Sodom was spared. "The Sentry" is one of these stories. Meanwhile, his attitude toward the Church bureaucracy became increasingly critical, and this brought about the loss of the government sinecures that had been granted him. Toward the end of his life he gave partial adherence to the Tolstoyan philosophy, with its scorn of official Christianity.

Leskov left behind a large body of writing: the edition of his works which appeared in 1902–3, though not complete, comprised thirty-six volumes. The major part of it consists of shorter narratives, extremely varied in style as well as content. Only posthumously has he received general recognition.

# CHERTOGON

## I

THIS rite of *chertogon* is something one can see only in Moscow, and Moscow alone, and then only if one has especial luck and connections.

I witnessed it from start to finish, thanks to a singularly lucky concatenation of circumstances, and want to write it down for the true cognoscenti and lovers of the serious and majestic in the national vein.

Although on the one side I am of the nobility, I am, on the other, near to the *people:* my mother came from the mercantile class. She left an exceedingly wealthy house to marry—but the marriage was an elopement, out of love for my father. My late father was a devil of a fellow as far as the fair sex was concerned, and whatever goal he set himself he attained. And that's how he had scored with my dear mother; the only thing was, because of that very savoir-faire my mother's parents gave her no dowry—except, of course, a trousseau, a couple of beds, and God's own mercy, all of which she received together with forgiveness and an everlasting parental blessing. My old folks were living in Orel—living in need yet proudly, never asking my mother's rich kin for anything; not only that, but they had nothing to do with them. However, when the time came for me to go to the university, my mother began saying:

"Please drop in on your uncle, Ilya Fedoseyevich, and give him my regards. That wouldn't be lowering yourself at all, for we should respect our elder kinsmen; after all, he's my brother, a religious man, and has great weight in Moscow. He's prominent on all reception committees—always out in front with the salver of bread and salt, or with a holy image. And the Governor receives him, and so does the Metropolitan. His counsel ought to be of benefit to you."

And, although, having made a thorough study of Philaret's *Catechism*, I did not believe in God, I nevertheless did love my mother, and so it occurred to me one day: "There, I've been in Moscow nearly a year now, yet I still haven't carried out my mother's wish; guess I'll go and call on Uncle Ilya without any further delay, give him my mother's regards, and really see what he can teach me."

Respect for my elders had been a habit with me since childhood —especially for such elders as numbered both Metropolitans and Governors among their friends.

I got up right then and there, brushed my clothes, and started out for Uncle Ilya's.

## II

It was about six in the evening, I'd say. The day was warm, mild, shot with gray—a very fine day, in short. Uncle's house was well known, one of the best in Moscow—everybody knew it. Only I'd never been there, and had never seen my uncle, even from a distance.

However, I went there boldly enough, reasoning that if he received me it would be all right, and if he didn't it would be no great loss either.

I came to his house; there was a carriage and pair standing at the entrance; leonine, that's what those horses were, raven-black, their manes flowing free, their hides sleek and glossy as the best satin.

I went up the steps and announced myself: "I'm Ilya Fedoseyevich's nephew—the student; please inform him."

"He's coming down right away," his servants told me; "he's going for a ride."

A very simple figure appeared, a Russian figure, but quite majestic; there was a likeness to my mother about the eyes, but his expression was different: he was what they call a substantial figure of a man.

I introduced myself. He heard me out in silence, offered me his hand quietly, and, "Get in; we'll go for a ride," he said.

I wanted to decline, but somehow lost my assurance and took a seat in the carriage.

"To the Park!" he commanded.

The leonine steeds got into their stride at once and soared away; all you could feel was the rear of the carriage bouncing a little, and when we got outside the city they raced at a still livelier rate.

We sat there without uttering a word; but I did notice that Uncle had shoved his silk opera hat on his head so hard that its edge was cutting into his forehead, and that his face had a certain expression—of what they call the blues, and that of the kind you get from tedium.

He was looking this way and that, and once he darted a look at me and, for no reason whatsoever, let drop:

"There's no living any more."

I didn't know what answer to make and let the remark pass in silence.

Again we rode on and on, and I thought to myself: "Wherever is he taking me?" And it began to look to me as if I'd gotten into a mess.

But Uncle suddenly seemed to have made up his mind about something and began issuing directions to the driver in rapid succession:

"Turn right! Now left! When you come to the Yar, stop!"

I saw a great many of the help come pouring out of the restaurant to meet us, and all of them almost scraped the ground with their foreheads, they bowed that low to my uncle; but he didn't even as much as budge out of the carriage but ordered them to call the proprietor out to him. They dashed off. A Frenchman appeared; he, too, evinced the utmost deference, but Uncle still didn't budge; he just kept tapping his teeth with the ivory knob of his cane, and said:

"How many outsiders have you got in there?"

"There'll be up to thirty in the common rooms," answered the Frenchman, "and three of the private rooms are taken."

"Chase 'em all out!"

"Very good!"

"It's seven now," said my uncle, after glancing at his watch. "I'll get here at eight. Will everything be ready?"

"No," the other answered, "it'll be hard to manage it by eight; many of the guests have reservations. But if you'll be kind enough to come here at nine there won't be a single stranger in the place by then."

"Very well!"

"And what arrangements do you wish us to make?"

"Get the gypsies, of course."

"And—"

"An orchestra."

"One?"

"No, better make it two."

"Should we send for Ryabyka?"

"Of course."

"Any French ladies?"

"Don't need 'em."

"And the wine cellar?"

"All of it."

"What about the menu?"

"Let's have your bill of fare."

They handed him a menu.

Uncle glanced at it, and apparently failed to make head or tail of it—it was even possible that he didn't care to; he flipped the card with his cane and said:

"All of it—for a hundred people."

And with that he rolled the card into a tube and shoved it into a pocket of his caftan.

The Frenchman was tickled, but at the same time he was in a tight spot:

"I'm unable," he said, "to serve enough of everything for a hundred guests. There are some very expensive items on that bill of fare—we can only serve five or six people with some of those things."

"Well, what am I supposed to do—sort out my guests? See that everyone gets whatever he asks for. Understand?"

"I understand."

"Otherwise, brother, even Ryabyka won't help you." He turned to the driver. "Get going!"

We left the restaurateur and his waiters bowing and scraping at the entrance and rolled away.

At that point I became utterly convinced that I was out of my depth and made an attempt to tell Uncle goodbye, but he didn't hear me. He was very much preoccupied. We rode on, and did nothing but stop this man and that.

"Be at the Yar at nine," my uncle said briefly to each one.

As for the men whom he said this to, they were all venerable oldsters, and every man of them doffed his hat and accepted the invitation just as briefly:

"I'm your guest, Fedoseich—I'm your guest!"

I don't remember how many we stopped in this manner, but I think there must have been a score; and just as it was striking nine we again rolled up to the Yar. A whole horde of servants came pouring out of the place to meet us, and supported my uncle under the arms, while the Frenchman himself flicked the dust off Uncle's trousers with his napkin at the front entrance.

"Place cleaned out?" asked Uncle.

"There's just one General that overstayed," said the Frenchman. "He begged ever so hard to be allowed to wind up his dinner in a private room—"

"Chase him out this minute!"

"He'll be through very soon."

"I won't have it; I've given him time enough—now let him get out and finish his dinner out on the lawn."

I don't know what the outcome of this would have been, but at that moment the General came out with his two ladies, got into a carriage and drove off, while the guests my uncle had invited during his drive through the Park began arriving in quick succession.


### III

The restaurant was spick and span, and entirely free of guests. Only in one of the halls there sat a giant of a man; he met my uncle in silence and, still without saying a word to him, took the cane out of his hands and put it away somewhere. Uncle yielded the stick to him without the least argument, and right then and there also handed over his purse and billfold to the giant.

This grizzled, massive giant was that same Ryabyka concerning whom the order, incomprehensible to me, had been issued to the restaurateur in my presence. He was some sort of schoolteacher, but evidently he had some sort of specific duty here as well. He was just as indispensable a feature as the gypsies, the musicians, and the whole retinue which immediately put in an appearance in full force. The only thing I could not grasp was what role the teacher was to play; but insight into that could not be granted one as inexperienced as I.

The brightly illuminated restaurant was going full blast; the music thundered away, while the gypsies strolled about and helped themselves to snacks at the buffet, and Uncle made a tour of inspection through the rooms, the garden, the grotto, and the balconies. He was looking everywhere to see "if there weren't any that didn't belong," while the teacher walked beside him, an inseparable companion; but when they returned to the main hall, where all the guests were assembled, one could notice a great difference between them: the tour of inspection had not had the same effect upon them—the teacher was just as sober as when they had begun it, while my uncle was thoroughly fuddled.

How this could have occurred in so short a space of time I don't know, but he was in an excellent mood; he took his place at the head of the table—and the lid was off.

The doors were locked, and an ultimatum was issued to all the world outside: "None of them can come over to us, and none of us can go over to them." There was an abyss separating our world and the world of the outsiders: an abyss of all that wine, of all those viands and, above all, an abyss of utterly unbridled debauch—I won't say a hideous one, but wild, frenzied, such a one as I could not even convey an idea of. Nor ought that to be demanded of me, inasmuch as, perceiving myself immured here and cut off from the world, I lost confidence and hastened to get drunk as speedily as possible. And for that reason I shall not give an account of how this night passed, inasmuch as it is not given to my pen to describe all of it; I recall only two battle scenes and the finale; but it was precisely in them that the element of the *dreadful* lay.

## IV

They announced some Ivan Stepanovich or other; as it turned out later, he was the most important manufacturer and businessman in all Moscow.

This brought about a lull.

"Why, you were told nobody's to be admitted," Uncle answered.

"He's begging ever so hard to be let in . . ."

"Just let him go back where he came from."

The waiter went off, but returned hesitantly:

"Ivan Stepanych," said the fellow, "ordered me to say that he asks most humbly to be let in."

"No, I won't have it!"

"Let him pay a fine," suggested some of the others.

"N-n-no! Give him the bounce—and I won't have any fines."

But the waiter reappeared and announced still more timidly:

"He's willing to pay any penalty, he says; the only thing is, he says, he feels no end sad to be left out at his age—"

Uncle got up, and his eyes flashed; but at that moment Ryabyka sprang up to his full height between them. With his left hand, just as though he were picking up a chick between thumb and forefinger, he flung the waiter off to one side, while with his right he made my uncle sit down again.

Some of the guests spoke up for Ivan Stepanovich; they begged that he be let in—take a hundred roubles from him for the benefit of the musicians, and let him in.

"He's one of us; an old man, a churchgoer—where's he to go at this hour? Cut him adrift, and, like as not, he may even raise a rumpus before the small fry. You ought to take pity on him."

Uncle listened to reason.

"If things aren't going to be run my way, they won't be run your way either; I'm granting admission to Ivan Stepanovich; the only thing is, he'll have to pound the kettledrums."

The emissary went out and then came back.

"He begs to be allowed to pay a penalty instead," he said.

"The hell with him! If he doesn't want to beat the drums, he doesn't have to; let him go where he likes."

In a short while Ivan Stepanovich couldn't hold out and sent in somebody to say that he *consented* to pound the kettledrums.

"Let him come."

The man who came in was of exceedingly great stature and staid appearance; he was austere of mien, the fire in his eyes greatly dimmed, his back no longer erect, while his beard was matted and so gray that it was of a greenish hue. He made an attempt to be jocose and to greet my uncle, but was put in his place.

"Later on, later—all that can come later on," my uncle shouted at him. "You go and pound the drums now."

"Pound the drums!" the others joined in.

"Hey, there, musicians! Something with a lot of kettledrums in it!"

The orchestra struck up a loud piece; the substantial citizen took the wooden sticks and began thumping the kettledrums, in time and out.

The din and uproar were hellish; they were all tickled and kept shouting: "Louder!"

Ivan Stepanovich tried harder.

"Louder! Louder! Still louder!"

The ancient pounded away with all his might, like Freiligrath's Black King, and, at last, the goal was attained: the kettledrums emitted a horrible crash, the skin split, everyone guffawed, the general din surpassing all imagination, and Ivan Stepanovich's sentence was commuted to a fine of five hundred roubles for ruining the kettledrums, the money to go to the musicians.

He paid up, mopped the sweat off his face, took a seat at the table and, just as everybody was drinking his health, noticed with not a little horror that his son-in-law was one of the guests.

Again laughter, again bedlam, and so on, until my mind went blank. During the rare intervals of lucidity I saw the gypsy women dancing, and my uncle, in a squatting position, throwing out now one leg, now the other; later on I saw him leap to his feet and confront somebody, but right then and there Ryabyka sprang up out of the ground between them, and the somebody went flying off to one side, while my uncle resumed his seat. And, plunged deep into the table before him, were two forks. Whereupon I understood Ryabyka's role.

But now the freshness of a Moscow morning was wafted through a window; I came to myself again, but somehow as if only to doubt my own reason. A battle was in progress, and forests were being chopped down; one could hear crashes, thunder; the trees were swaying—virginal, exotic trees; behind them swarthy faces were huddled together, while in the foreground frightful-looking axes were being laid to the roots; and it was Uncle who was doing the chopping, and Ivan Stepanovich was hacking away as well. A picture out of the Middle Ages, no less.

This was the Capture of the Gypsy Women—they were seeking shelter behind the trees in the grotto; the male gypsies were not defending them, leaving everything to the energy of the women themselves. There was no separating the jocose from the serious in the situation: plates, chairs, and rocks from the grotto were hurtling through the air, but the besiegers kept hacking deeper and deeper into the forest, and the doughtiest in the attack were Ivan Stepanych and my uncle.

At last the stronghold was taken, the gypsy women seized, embraced, thoroughly kissed; each captor shoved a hundred-rouble note down the corsage of his captive, and the affair was over. . . .

Yes, everything quieted down at once. Everything was over. No one had intervened, but this was enough. There was a feeling in the air that, even as there had been "no living" without this, so now, on the other hand, it was enough.

Everybody had had his fill, and all were satisfied. Perhaps there was additional significance in the fact that the teacher said it was "time for him to go to his classes," but, outside of that, nothing really mattered: the Walpurgis Night had passed, and "living" had begun again.

The gathering did not disperse, there was no exchange of good-byes—the crowd simply evaporated; neither the gypsies nor the musicians were to be seen. The restaurant was a scene of utter havoc: there wasn't a single drape untorn, not a single mirror unbroken; even the great luster in the center of the ceiling—even that was lying all in shards on the floor, and its crystal prisms were crunching under the feet of the help, exhausted and barely able to crawl about. Uncle was sitting all by himself in the middle of a divan and drinking cider; from time to time he would recall something, and then his legs jerked. Ryabyka, who was in a hurry to get to his classes, was standing by his side.

A bill was handed to the two—a short bill, "in round figures."

Ryabyka looked it over carefully and demanded a rebate of fifteen hundred. He met with little opposition and a total was arrived at: it came to seventeen thousand, and the prudent Ryabyka, after looking the bill over once more, announced that this was fair enough.

My uncle let drop but one syllable: "Pay." After which he clapped on his high hat and nodded to me to follow him out.

I perceived to my horror that he had not forgotten anything, and that it was impossible for me to give him the slip. He terrified me beyond measure, and I could not imagine how I could remain face to face with him when he was in this humor. He had taken me along with him, without exchanging as much as two sensible words with me, and there he was, dragging me along; and there was no getting away from him. What would become of me? All my tipsiness actually left me. I was simply afraid of this frightful, wild beast, with his incredible fancies and horrible frenzy.

But now we were already leaving. In the vestibule a throng of waiters surrounded us. Uncle was issuing the orders. "A fiver to each," while Ryabyka was paying off; lesser sums were paid to the caretakers, watchmen, policemen, gendarmes, all of whom had rendered us services of some sort of other. These demands were met, satisfactorily. But all this ran into money, while in addition, as far as the eye could see through the park, there were cab drivers waiting. There was no end of them, and they too were waiting for us—waiting for Father Ilya Fedoseich, "in case his honor might want to send for something."

Their number was ascertained and three roubles issued to each, and Uncle and I got into our carriage, whereupon Ryabyka handed Uncle his purse and billfold.

Ilya Fedoseich took a hundred-rouble note out of the billfold and passed it over to Ryabyka.

The latter turned the note over in his hand:

"Too little," said he, rudely.

Uncle added two twenty-five-rouble notes.

"But that's not enough, either—why, there wasn't a single row."

Uncle added another twenty-five-rouble note, after which the teacher handed Uncle his cane and said goodbye to him with a bow.

## V

The two of us were left face to face, racing back to Moscow, while behind us, with many urgent cries and much rattling of wheels, careered all the tatterdemalion cabbies. I couldn't understand what they were after, but my uncle understood. This was really an outrage; they wanted to extract additional blackmail from him, and so, under the pretext of showing special attention to Ilya Fedoseich, they were subjecting "his honor" and his respectability to universal disgrace.

Moscow was right ahead of us, and all of it in full view, all of it bathed in the morning light, wreathed with wisps of smoke from chimneys, and echoing with the pealing of peaceful church-bells summoning to worship.

To the right and left of us were rows of produce-stalls, stretching away to the city gate. When we had come up to the first stall on our right, Uncle got out of the carriage and walked up to a tub of linden-wood standing near the threshold of the shop and asked the owner:

"Is that honey?"

"Honey it is."

"How much for the tub?"

"We sell it at retail, by the pound."

"Sell it wholesale; figure out what it comes to."

I don't remember the exact sum; I think the dealer figured it came to either seventy or eighty roubles.

Uncle tossed him the money.

By that time the cortege had caught up with us.

"Do you love me, my fine fellows, my Moscow cabbies?"

"Nacherly—always ready to serve your Honor—"

"You feel attached to me, don't you?"

"No end—"

"Take your wheels off."

The others looked puzzled.

"Be quick about it—be quick!" Uncle commanded.

Those who were spryer and smarter than the others, a score or so of them, dug down under their boxes, got out their bolt-keys and began loosening the bolts.

"Fine!" said Uncle. "Now grease the axles with honey."

"Little Father!"

"Come on, grease 'em!"

"Such fine stuff. . . . It'd be more interestin' to put it in the mouth—"

"Grease 'em!"

And, without insisting further, Uncle got into his carriage again and we flew off, while the others, as many as there were of them, were left there with their wheels off, standing over the tub of honey, which they probably did not use as axle grease, but either poured right into their pockets, as best they could, or else sold back to the dealer. At any rate, they had to let us go—and then we found ourselves at the baths.

Here I expected the end of the world to come upon me as, neither dead nor alive, I wallowed in a marble tub, while Uncle stretched himself out on the floor—in no simple, ordinary way, however, but somehow apocalyptically. The entire enormous mass of his obese body lay on the floor, supported only by the very tips of his fingers and toes, and upon these points of support his lobster-red body quivered under the spray of the cold shower beating upon him, while he roared with the restrained roar of a bear pulling out a splinter. This lasted for half an hour or so, and all that time he kept on quivering all over that very same way, like a dish of jelly on a rickety table, until at last he jumped up suddenly, asked for cider, and we dressed and drove to the Frenchman's.

Here we had our hair trimmed, curled a little and slicked down, and went on foot into the city proper to my uncle's shop.

There was still nothing like a talk with me, nor any sign of a dismissal.

Only once did he address me:

"Bide your time; nothing comes all at once; that which you don't understand now, you will, with the years."

In his shop he said a prayer, after casting a proprietary look over everything, and took his place behind the counter. The outside of the vessel had been cleansed, but there was still a vile mess brewing deep within it and seeking purification.

I perceived this and had by now ceased to fear him. I found this engrossing; I wanted to see how he would absolve himself: by abstinence, or through an act of grace?

About ten he began to be very fidgety; he was expecting his neighbor and kept watching out for him, so that the three of us might go out for our morning tea; together it would be cheaper for us by as much as a five-copeck piece. The neighbor did not emerge: he had died a sudden death.

Uncle crossed himself on hearing the news:

"We'll all die some day," said he.

This death did not faze him in the least, even though he and the late departed had been having tea together at the same tavern for all of forty years.

We called in the owner of the shop on the other side of us, and we went out more than once and had this and that to eat, but all this without a drop of strong drink. I passed the whole day sitting about with Uncle and going about with him, and toward evening he sent for a carriage to take him to the Convent of the All-Glorified Virgin.

Here, too, they knew him and met him with the same deference as at the Yar.

"I would prostrate myself before the All-Glorified and repent me of my sins. And this—allow me to introduce him—this is my nephew, my sister's son."

"If you please," said the nuns, "if you please! Whom else should the All-Glorified receive repentance from if not from you, who have always been a benefactor of Her cloister? Now is the best time to come before Her—there's an evening mass going on."

"I'll wait till it's over—I like to worship without any other people around, and to have a blessed light arranged for me, a dim one."

A dim light was duly arranged for him: all the image-lamps save one or two were extinguished, and a large, deep one in a tumbler of green glass placed before the All-Glorified One Herself.

Uncle did not fall on his knees but rather slumped, then struck his forehead on the floor and lay flat, face down, let out a nasal sob, and seemed to go off into a coma.

Two of the nuns and I seated ourselves in a dark nook, behind a door. There was a prolonged pause. Uncle was still lying there, no sound escaping him nor any sign of his having been moved by the spirit. It seemed to me that he had fallen asleep, and I even suggested this to the nuns. One of the sisters, who had had great experience, pondered awhile, shook her head and, having lit the tiniest of tapers, cupped it in her hand and crept, ever so softly, toward the penitent. Having tiptoed around him softly, she came back and whispered:

"It's working—and working all around, at that."

"What signs do you see?"

She bent down and motioned to me to do the same:

"Look right against the light, where his feet are," she said.

"I see them."

"Look what a struggle is going on there!"

I looked more closely, and actually did notice some sort of struggle going on: Uncle was sprawling there, ever so reverently, in a supplicating position, yet it seemed for all the world as if two tomcats were fighting at his feet; now one cat, now the other was giving battle, and all this ever so rapidly: they were fairly hopping.

"Where did those cats ever come from, Mother?" I asked.

"You only think those are cats there," she answered, "but those aren't cats—it's a temptation he's fighting; you see, his spirit is rising to heaven as a flame, but his poor feet are still tripping it in hell."

I saw that this was actually so; Uncle was finishing his dance of yesterday, the *trepak;* but as for his spirit—was it actually rising to heaven as a flame at that same moment?

But he, as if in answer to this, suddenly drew a deep sigh, and let such a cry escape him!

"I shan't rise up until Thou forgive me! For Thou alone art holy, whereas all of us are but fiends accursed!" And with that he broke into sobs.

And, truly, his sobs were such that all three of us began to sob with him, imploring: "Lord, grant him his supplication!"

And, before we noticed it, he was already standing beside us, and was saying to me in a soft, unctuous voice:

"Come—we will celebrate now."

"Were you found worthy, little Father, of seeing a reflection of the Glory?"

"No," he answered, "I wasn't found worthy of a reflection, but . . . Well, this was the way of it—"

He made a fist and raised it—as you might raise an ·urchin ·by his hair.

"You were raised up?"

"Yes."

The nuns fell to crossing themselves, and so did I, while Uncle made things clearer:

"Now," he said, "I am forgiven! Right from the very top, from under the cupola, an open hand came down and clutched my hair, and pulled me right up on my feet—"

And now he was no longer of the rejected, and was happy; he bestowed a generous gift on the convent, where he had attained this miracle through prayer, and again felt "living," and sent my mother all that had been coming to her as a dowry, and led me into the goodly faith of the Russian folk.

From that time forth I fathomed the spirit of the folk in degradation and in exaltation. . . . And that is what they call *chertogon,* "that is to say, the casting out of the devil of alien imaginations." But it is only in Moscow, I repeat, that one may be found worthy of witnessing this rite, and then only if one has especial luck, or through the great influence of most dignified ancients.

1881

# THE SENTRY

## I

THE event an account of which is here brought to the reader's notice is touching and terrible in its effect upon the protagonist of the piece, and its outcome is so singular that a thing of this sort could hardly have occurred in any other country but Russia.

It is partly a court anecdote, partly a bit of history that characterizes rather well the manners and spirit of a very curious, yet little known period: the eighteen thirties.

There is not a shred of invention in the following tale.

## II

In the winter of 1839, just before Epiphany, there was a great thaw in Petersburg. It was so slushy that it seemed almost as if spring were on the way: the snow was melting, during the day water dripped from the roofs, and the ice in the rivers grew blue and swollen. On the Neva, just in front of the Winter Palace, there was open water in several places. A warm but very strong wind was blowing from the west, the water was driven in from the bay and the signal guns boomed.

The guard at the Palace was made up of a company of the Izmailovski regiment, commanded by a brilliantly educated and socially prominent young officer, Nikolay Ivanovich Miller, who subsequently became a full general and a lyceum director. He was a man of so-called "humane" propensities, a trait which had early been noted in him and which, in the eyes of the highest authorities, somewhat impaired his prospects in the service.

In reality Miller was an efficient and reliable officer; and in those days mounting guard at the Palace involved no danger. It was a time of perfect peace and tranquillity. Nothing was required of the Palace guards except the scrupulous discharge of sentry duty. Nevertheless, it was precisely while Captain Miller was on guard that an extraordinary and alarming occurrence took place, doubtless scarcely remembered now by the few then living who are still in our midst.

## III

At first all went well with the guard: the posts were distributed, the men took their places, and all was in perfect order. Emperor Nicholas Pavlovich was in good health, he had gone for a drive in the evening, had returned home and retired. The whole Palace was wrapped in slumber. A night of utter tranquillity descended. Silence reigned in the guardroom. Captain Miller had pinned his white handkerchief over the traditional grease-spot on the high, morocco-upholstered back of the officers' chair and settled down with a book to while away the time.

Captain Miller had always been a passionate reader, and so was never bored. He read on and did not notice that the night was passing. Suddenly, just before two o'clock, he was aroused by a most alarming occurrence: before him stood the sergeant on duty, pale, shaking with terror, and jabbering rapidly:

"There's trouble, your honor, trouble!"

"What's wrong?"

"A terrible disaster has occurred!"

Captain Miller jumped to his feet in indescribable alarm and only with difficulty ascertained the exact nature of the "terrible disaster."

## IV

This is what had happened: a sentry, a private of the Izmailovski regiment, named Postnikov, standing at what is now known as the "Jordan" entrance to the Palace, became aware that a man was drowning in the patch of open water in the ice of the Neva just in front of the Palace, and was desperately calling for help.

Private Postnikov, formerly a domestic serf, was a very high-strung and sensitive fellow. For a long time he listened to the distant

cries and moans of the drowning man, and they turned him numb
with horror. In anguish he scanned the visible expanse of the quay,
but by the malice of Fate neither there nor on the Neva was a living
soul to be seen.

There was no one to help the drowning man, and he was sure to
go under . . .

Meanwhile he continued to struggle stubbornly.

There seemed but one thing left to him: to go to the bottom without further expenditure of energy. But no! His feeble cries and calls
for help now broke off and ceased, and then were heard again, always
closer and closer to the Palace quay. Evidently the man had not lost
his bearings and was making straight for the light of the quay lan-
terns. But he hadn't the ghost of a chance, for he was heading for the
"Jordan": the hole cut in the ice for the blessing of the waters on
Epiphany. There he would be drawn under the ice and that would
be the end of him . . . Again he was quiet, but a minute later he
was splashing and moaning: "Save me, save me!" He was now so
close that the swishing of the water was heard distinctly . . .

Private Postnikov reflected that it would be extremely easy to save
the man. If he were to run out onto the ice, the man was sure to be
within reach. One had merely to throw him a rope or pass him a pole
or the gun, and he would be saved. He was so close that he could
seize it with his hands and climb out. But Postnikov remembered the
service regulations and his oath; he knew that he was a sentry, and
that a sentry dare not leave his sentry-box on any pretext or for
any reason whatsoever.

On the other hand, Postnikov's heart was a rebellious one: it
ached, it throbbed, it failed him. If only he could tear it out and
trample on it: the groans and cries were so painful to hear. It was
horrible to watch another man agonize and not come to his aid, when
really it was quite possible to do so, for the sentry-box would not
run away, and no harm would be done to anybody.

"Shall I run down, eh? No one will see . . . Oh, Lord, to get it
over with! There he's groaning again."

By the end of the half-hour that this went on, Private Postnikov
was completely worn out and began to experience "mental doubts."
He was an intelligent and conscientious soldier with a good head on
his shoulders, and he knew perfectly well that for a sentry to leave
his post was a crime that meant court-martial, then a flogging and

forced labor or possibly even a firing squad. But from the swollen
river came moans, sounding closer and closer, and he could hear
gurgling and desperate floundering.

"I'm drow-owning! Help, I'm drowning!"

Now he was reaching the hole in the ice—and that would be the
end!

Once more and then again Postnikov glanced round. Not a soul
to be seen, only the lamps shook and flickered in the gale, and on
the wind was borne a faltering, broken cry, perhaps the last cry . . .

There was another splash, a single outcry, and a gurgle.

The sentry could bear it no longer and deserted his post.

## V

Postnikov rushed to the stairs, ran out onto the ice, his heart beating violently, then waded through the water that had overflowed the
ice-hole and, quickly locating the drowning man, held out to him
the stock of his gun. The man clutched the butt-end, and Postnikov,
holding on to the bayonet, pulled him out of the water.

Both rescued and rescuer were dripping-wet, and as the former,
in a state of exhaustion, was shaking and unable to keep on his feet,
Private Postnikov had not the heart to leave him on the ice, but led
him onto the quay and began looking about for someone to whom he
could turn him over. While all this was going on, a sleigh had made
its appearance on the embankment. It was carrying an officer of the
now disbanded Palace Company of Invalids.

This gentleman, who arrived on the scene at a moment so in-
opportune for Postnikov, was apparently of a very frivolous disposition, and a rather scatter-brained, impudent fellow, to boot. He
jumped out of the sleigh and demanded:

"Who is this? Who are all these people?"

"He was sinking, drowning—" Postnikov began.

"What do you mean—drowning? Who was drowning? Was it
you? Why at this spot?"

The man who had been pulled out of the water was merely gasping, and as for Postnikov, he had vanished: he had shouldered his
musket and gone back to his sentry-box.

Whether or not the officer guessed what had happened, he
dropped his inquiries abruptly. He immediately bundled the rescued

man into his sleigh and took him to the station-house of the Admiralty District on Morskaya Street.

There the officer informed the police sergeant that the dripping man he had brought with him had been drowning in an ice-hole opposite the Palace, and that he had rescued him at the peril of his own life.

The man was still sopping-wet, chilled, and spent. What with his fright and exhaustion, he was practically unconscious, and it was a matter of indifference to him who had rescued him.

A sleepy medical assistant on the police force was working on him, while in the office a report was being drawn up on the basis of the officer's oral deposition. The police, naturally given to suspicion, were wondering how he had managed to emerge from the water as dry as pepper. The officer, eager to get the medal "for the rescue of those in mortal danger," explained it by a happy concurrence of circumstances, but did so lamely and unconvincingly. Someone was dispatched to rouse the inspector, and others were sent to make further inquiries.

Meanwhile the incident had rapidly started another series of events in the Palace.

## VI

The developments that occurred after the officer of the Invalids had departed with the rescued man in his sleigh, remained unknown in the Palace guardroom. There the soldiers and their officer knew only that Postnikov, a private of their regiment, had deserted his sentry-box in order to save a man's life, that, this being a grave breach of military duty, Postnikov was certain to be court-martialed and flogged, and that all his superiors from the company commander up would have to face grave consequences, which they could neither avert nor mitigate.

The wet and shivering Postnikov was of course immediately relieved of his post, and when he was brought to the guardroom he candidly told Captain Miller all that we already know, mentioning every detail down to the point when the officer of the Invalids put the rescued man into his sleigh and ordered the driver to hurry to the Admiralty police station.

This last circumstance added to the danger of the situation. The officer was bound to give a full account to the police inspector, and the inspector would instantly lay the matter before the Chief of Police, Kokoshkin, who would report it to the Emperor in the morning, and then there would be the devil to pay!

There was no time for deliberation; the superior officer had to be called in.

Captain Miller at once dispatched a troubled note to his battalion commander, Lieutenant-Colonel Svinin, asking him to come to the Palace guardroom as soon as he could and to give him all possible assistance in his terrible predicament.

It was already about three A.M., and Kokoshkin was accustomed to present his report to the Emperor rather early, so that there was little time left for thought and action.

## VII

Lieutenant-Colonel Svinin did not have the compassionate and kindly heart for which Captain Miller had always been distinguished. Svinin was not a heartless man, but first and foremost he was a careerist, a type which in our time is again remembered with regret. Svinin had a reputation for severity, and in fact he flaunted the strictness with which he disciplined his men. He was not cruel by nature, and never sought to cause anyone useless suffering, but if a man broke any of the rules of the service, he was inexorable. He considered it out of place to enter into a discussion of the motives of the culprit, but held to the rule that in the service a fault was a fault. And so everyone in the company knew that Private Postnikov was not going to escape the penalty for deserting his post, and that Svinin was not going to break his heart over it.

Such was the character of this staff officer, as his comrades and superiors knew it. Among them there were some who did not sympathize with Svinin, for at that time "humaneness" and similar erroneous notions had not quite vanished. Svinin was quite indifferent as to whether "the humanitarians" blamed or praised him. To beg and entreat Svinin or to try to move him to pity was entirely useless. He had the thick skin that was usual with the careerists of the period.

Yet, like Achilles, he had a weak spot. His official career had begun well, and of course he zealously watched over it, careful that, as on a full-dress uniform, not a particle of dust should settle on it. And now this unfortunate step on the part of a member of the battalion entrusted to him was bound to cast a shadow on the reputation of the entire unit. Those on whom Svinin's well launched and tenderly nurtured official career depended would not stop to inquire whether or not the battalion commander was to blame for what one of his men had done at the prompting of noble compassion. Indeed, many would be glad to place a log across his path to clear the way for a relative or to push forward some young protégé of highly stationed personages, especially if the Czar should be annoyed and remark to the regimental commander, as was sure to happen, that he had "poor officers" and that the men were "undisciplined." And who was to blame for it? Svinin, of course. And the word would go round that Svinin was "lax," and the reproach would remain a permanent blot on his reputation. Then he would never distinguish himself among his contemporaries, nor add his portrait to the gallery of notables of the Russian Empire.

Few studied history at the time, but people believed in history and were particularly eager to take part in the making thereof.

## VIII

It was about eight in the morning when Svinin received Captain Miller's alarmed note, and he at once leapt out of bed and put on his uniform, arriving at the .guardroom of the Winter Palace frightened and angry. Here he.forthwith questioned Private Postnikov and satisfied himself that the incredible incident had actually taken place. Private Postnikov again frankly recounted to his battalion commander all that had happened during his watch, just as he had previously related it to his company commander. The soldier stated that he "was guilty before God and the Czar, and deserved no mercy." While on guard, he said, he had heard the groans of a man drowning in an ice-hole; torn between duty and compassion, he had been tormented for a long time, and in the end, yielding to temptation, had given up the struggle: he had deserted the sentry-box, jumped onto the ice, and pulled the drowning man out of the water, and then, as ill luck would have it, he had fallen under the eye of an officer of the Company of Invalids.

Lieutenant-Colonel Svinin was in despair. He gave himself the only satisfaction possible under the circumstances: he wreaked his anger on Postnikov by immediately placing him under arrest and confining him to the regimental lockup. Then he made a few sharp remarks to Captain Miller, throwing up to him his "humanitarianism," which, he observed, was of no earthly use in the army. But all this could not mend matters. It was quite impossible to find an excuse, let alone a justification for such a transgression as a sentry's desertion of his post. And so there remained only one way out: to conceal the whole matter from the Emperor.

But was it possible to conceal such an occurrence?

Apparently not, since the man's rescue was known not only to all the soldiers on guard duty, but also to that abominable officer of the Invalids who must have already reported the matter to General Kokoshkin.

Where was Svinin to rush now? To whom could he turn? Where was he to seek help and protection?

Svinin was on the point of dashing off to Grand Duke Michael Pavlovich and disclosing everything without reserve. Such a move was in those days not unusual. Let the hot-tempered Grand Duke fly into a rage about it and shout himself hoarse. This was of no consequence, for the more rudely he handled one at first, the more insulting he was, the sooner he relented and himself took up the cudgels·in the culprit's defense. Such flare-ups were not infrequent, and they were indeed sometimes solicited. *Names will never hurt you,* and Svinin was anxious to bring the business to such a favorable conclusion. But was it possible to gain admission to the Palace in the dead of night and to disturb the Grand Duke? On the other hand, to wait till morning and appear before Michael Pavlovich after Kokoshkin had made his report to·the Czar would be useless. And while Svinin was thus floundering amidst all these perplexities, he suddenly perceived another way out, which till then had been hidden from him as by a fog.

## IX

One of the well known rules of tactics is this: at the moment when the greatest danger threatens from a beleaguered fortress, it is advisable not to retreat from the walls, but to come closer to them. Svinin resolved not to do any of the things that had at first occurred to him, but to go straight to Kokoshkin.

Many frightful stories, as well as absurd ones, were always being repeated at that time in Petersburg about the Chief of Police, General Kokoshkin. Among other things, it was stated that he was exceedingly tactful, and that, thanks to this trait, he was able to make a mountain out of a molehill and, with equal ease, a molehill out of a mountain.

Kokoshkin was indeed very stern and terrible, and inspired great fear in all who encountered him. But he sometimes winked at the pranks of the gay young blades among the military, and as there were not a few such scamps in those days they found in him a powerful and zealous champion. Generally speaking, he knew the ropes and was able to do a great deal, if only he chose to. This side of his character was known to both Svinin and Miller. In fact, Miller encouraged his battalion commander to take the risk of seeing Kokoshkin at once and to entrust himself to the man's magnanimity and tactfulness. The General would, no doubt, find a way of extricating all concerned from their difficulties, without arousing the Czar's anger, which Kokoshkin, to his honor be it said, always carefully avoided doing.

Svinin donned his overcoat, raised his eyes to heaven, and exclaiming several times, "Lord, Lord!" drove off to Kokoshkin.

It was already past four o'clock in the morning.

## X

Chief of Police Kokoshkin was roused from his sleep and informed ·that Lieutenant-Colonel Svinin had arrived on business of great importance and urgency.

The General immediately got up and came out to receive Svinin in a dressing-gown, rubbing his forehead, yawning, and stretching. He listened with keen attention, but quite calmly, to all Svinin had to relate. He·broke in on the explanations and pleas for mercy only once.

"The soldier," he said, "deserted his sentry-box and rescued a man?"

"Yes, sir," replied Svinin.

"And ·the sentry-box?"

"It remained vacant in the meantime."

"H'm-m. . . . I know that it remained vacant. I am glad it wasn't stolen."

Svinin was confirmed in his conviction that the General had

been apprised of everything, that he had already decided how he was to present the case to the Emperor at the morning audience, and that nothing would make him change his mind. Otherwise an incident such as the desertion of his post by a Palace sentry would no doubt have disturbed the energetic Chief of Police to a much greater degree.

As a matter of fact, Kokoshkin knew nothing about it. The police inspector to whom the officer had brought the rescued man did not think the incident of great importance. In his opinion, it was not a matter of sufficient gravity to warrant rousing the weary Chief of Police in the middle of the night. Besides, the whole affair appeared to the inspector to be rather suspicious, because the officer's clothes were entirely dry, which could not have been the case if he had really rescued the drowning man at the peril of his own life. The inspector thought that he was dealing with a vain, mendacious fellow who wanted another medal to wear on his chest, and for that reason, while his assistant was drawing up a report, he detained the officer and tried to get at the truth by dwelling on small details.

He was also rather annoyed that the incident had occurred in his district, and that the drowning man had been rescued not by a policeman but by an army officer.

As for Kokoshkin's lack of excitement, it had a simple explanation: first, he was terribly tired after a grueling day and after having attended two fires during the night; and, second, Private Postnikov's breach of discipline did not directly concern him as Chief of Police.

Nevertheless, Kokoshkin instantly went into action. He sent for the inspector of the Admiralty District, ordering him to appear at once, together with the officer and the rescued man, and he asked Svinin to wait in the small reception room adjacent to his study. Then he retired to the study and, without closing the door, sat down at the desk and began to sign papers; but a moment later his head sank onto his arms, and he fell fast asleep right there at the desk.

## XI

In those days there were neither telegraphs nor telephones in the city, and in order to convey official orders speedily the "forty thousand couriers" who have been immortalized in Gogol's comedy darted in every direction. They were not as fast as the telegraph or the telephone, of course, but they lent considerable animation to the city and testified to the ceaseless vigilance of the authorities.

By the time the inspector of the Admiralty police district had arrived, quite out of breath, and with him the rescuer and the rescued, the worn-out General had had a nap which thoroughly refreshed him. This was apparent both from the expression of his face and from the improvement in the functioning of his mental faculties.

Kokoshkin ordered the newcomers to enter his study and invited Svinin to step in, too.

"The report?" he demanded of the inspector in a voice that sounded refreshed.

The inspector silently handed him a folded sheet and then said in a whisper:

"I must beg permission to say a word to Your Excellency in private . . ."

"Very well."

Kokoshkin stepped into a window recess, followed by the inspector.

"What is it?"

The inspector's indistinct buzz was heard and the loud grunts of the General: "H'm-m. . . . So! Well, what of it? It is possible. . . . They manage to come out dry. . . . Nothing else?"

"Nothing, sir."

The General left the recess, sat down at his desk, and began to read. He read the report in silence, betraying neither anxiety nor suspicion, and then, turning to the rescued man, spoke in a loud, firm voice:

"How is it, brother, that you found yourself in the water opposite the Palace?"

"My fault," replied the man.

"That's it. Were you drunk?"

"My fault; I wasn't drunk, but I'd had a drop."

"How did you get into the water?"

"I wanted to take a short-cut across the ice, lost my way, and got into an ice-hole."

"You couldn't see where you were going?"

"It was pitch-dark all round, Your Excellency."

"So you didn't see who pulled you out?"

"Begging your pardon, I couldn't. It was this gentleman, I think."
He pointed to the officer and added: "I couldn't see. I was scared."

"That's it. You were prowling about, when you ought to have
been asleep! Now take a good look at this man and remember who
it was that rescued you. A noble-hearted man risked his life to
save you!"

"I shall remember it as long as I live."

And turning to the officer, he said: "What is your name, sir?"
The officer gave his Christian name.

"Do you hear that?" Kokoshkin asked the rescued.

"I do, Your Excellency."

"Are you Orthodox?"

"Orthodox, Your Excellency."

"Have a prayer said for his health."

"I will, Your Excellency."

"Pray to God for him, and now clear out: you are no longer
wanted."

The man bowed to the ground and tumbled out, hugely pleased
that he had been allowed to go.

Svinin stood there, amazed at the turn things had taken by the
grace of God.

## XII

Then Kokoshkin turned to the officer of the Company of Invalids.

"You rescued this man at the risk of your own life?"

"Yes, Your Excellency."

"There were no witnesses of the occurrence, and, I suppose, there
couldn't have been any, because of the lateness of the hour?"

"Yes, Your Excellency, it was dark, and there was no one on
the quay except the sentries."

"The sentries needn't be mentioned: a sentry guards his post and
must not let anything distract him. I credit this report completely. It
is based on what you told them, isn't it?"

These words Kokoshkin spoke with particular emphasis, as though
threatening or reprimanding someone. But the officer was not
abashed. With bulging eyes and chest thrown out, he answered:

"Yes, it is perfectly true, Your Excellency."

"Your action merits a reward."

The officer started to bow gratefully.

"There's nothing to thank me for," continued Kokoshkin. "I shall report your valiant deed to our gracious Emperor, and perhaps this very day a medal will decorate your breast. And now you may go home, take a hot drink, and do not leave the house, as I may need you."

The officer beamed, bowed, and left.

Kokoshkin looked after him and remarked:

"It is possible that the Emperor himself will wish to see him."

"Yes, sir," the inspector said brightly.

"You are free to go."

The police inspector withdrew and, having closed the door behind him, crossed himself out of pious habit.

The officer of the Company of Invalids was waiting for the inspector downstairs, and they went off together better friends than when they had arrived.

Svinin alone remained in the study of the Chief of Police. Kokoshkin first stared hard at him for a considerable length of time and then said:

"You haven't been to see the Grand Duke?"

In those days when "the Grand Duke" was mentioned, everyone knew that Grand Duke Michael Pavlovich was meant.

"I came straight to you," was Svinin's reply.

"Who was the officer on duty?"

"Captain Miller."

Kokoshkin again scrutinized Svinin and then said:

"I think you told me something different before."

Svinin failed to grasp the meaning of this and said nothing, while Kokoshkin added:

"Well, it doesn't matter. Have a good sleep."

The audience was over.

## XIII

At one o'clock in the afternoon the officer of the Company of Invalids was indeed again summoned by Kokoshkin, who very amiably informed him that the Emperor was highly gratified to know that among the officers of the Company of Invalids attached to his Palace there were such vigilant and valiant men, and that he bestowed upon him the medal "for the rescue of those in mortal danger." And with these words Kokoshkin handed the medal to the hero, and the officer departed to show it off.

The incident might therefore have been considered closed, but Lieutenant-Colonel Svinin felt that the business was somehow unfinished and thought himself called upon to dot the *i*.

The affair upset him to such an extent that he was ill for three days. On the fourth day he quit his bed, drove out to the House of Peter the Great, had a thanksgiving mass said before the icon of our Savior; and, returning home with his spirit calmed, he sent for Captain Miller.

"Well, Nikolay Ivanovich," he said to Miller, "the storm that was threatening us has blown over, thank God, and the unfortunate affair with the sentry has been satisfactorily settled. Now, I think, we can breathe quietly again. Doubtless we owe this, first, to God's mercy, and second, to General Kokoshkin. People may say that he is harsh and heartless, but I am filled with gratitude for his magnanimity and with respect for his tact and resourcefulness. It was wonderful the way he masterfully took advantage of the vanity of that fraud from the Invalids, who, truth to tell, deserved a good flogging in the stable for his impudence instead of a medal. But there was no alternative: he had to be made use of for the salvation of the others, and Kokoshkin handled the affair so cleverly that there wasn't the slightest unpleasantness; on the contrary, everybody is content and very well pleased. Between you and me, I have learned from an unimpeachable source that Kokoshkin himself is *very pleased* with me. He was flattered that I went directly to him and that I refrained from arguing with the rascal who got the medal. In a word, no one has suffered and everything was done with so much tact that there is nothing to fear in the future; but yet there is a trifle that we still have to settle. We must tactfully follow Kokoshkin's example and conclude the business on our part in such a way as to insure ourselves against any future charges. There is still one person whose position remains unregulated. I mean Private Postnikov. He is still behind bars, and he is no doubt racked by the thought of what is in store for him. We must put an end to his misery."

"Yes, it's high time," Miller urged, delighted.

"Yes, indeed. And you are the best man to do it. Please go to the barracks at once, assemble your company, and release Postnikov from jail, and see that he receives two hundred strokes before the ranks."

## XIV

Miller was dumfounded and made an attempt to persuade Svinin, in view of the happy conclusion of the affair, to extend a complete pardon to Private Postnikov, especially since he had already endured so much suffering while in prison, awaiting his fate. But Svinin lost his temper and did not even allow Miller to proceed.

"No," he interrupted, "none of that: just now I spoke of tact, and you are at once ready to commit a tactless act. Quit it."

Then he shifted to a drier and more official tone and added firmly:

"And since you personally are not without blame in this matter and indeed are much at fault, for there is a softness in your character which does not befit an army man and which results in a lack of discipline on the part of the men under you, I hereby order you to be present at the flogging and to see to it that it is carried out seriously, indeed with the utmost severity. To that end, please issue orders that the punishment be carried out by young soldiers newly arrived from the ranks of the regular army, because the old-timers are all infected in this respect with the liberalism of the Guard: they don't flog a comrade properly, but only scare the fleas on his back. I will look into see for myself whether the culprit is properly tanned."

It was out of the question, of course, to evade an official order issued by a superior officer, and tender-hearted Captain Miller was obliged to carry out with the utmost precision the instructions given him by his battalion commander.

The company was drawn up in the courtyard of the regiment's barracks, the rods were fetched in sufficient quantity from the stores, and Private Postnikov, brought from the lockup, was "properly tanned" with the zealous aid of young comrades recently arrived from the army ranks. These men, uninfected by the liberalism of the Guard, thoroughly dressed their comrade's hide, as ordered by the battalion commander. Thereupon, Postnikov, having received his punishment, was lifted up on the very overcoat on which he had been flogged and carried to the regimental hospital.

## XV

Battalion Commander Svinin, having been informed that the punishment had been carried out, with fatherly solicitude at once visited Postnikov in the hospital and, to his satisfaction, convinced himself by direct examination that his orders had been carried out to the letter. The high-strung and tender-hearted man had been "properly tanned." Svinin was pleased and issued an order that the patient be given, as a present from him, a pound of sugar and a quarter of a pound of tea, with which he might regale himself while he convalesced. Postnikov, on his cot, heard the instruction concerning tea and sugar, and said:

"I am much pleased, Your Honor, and thank you for your fatherly kindness."

And "pleased" he really was, for, in the three days which he had spent in the lockup he had prepared himself for a much worse eventuality. Two hundred strokes with the rods in those stern days was nothing compared to the punishments that men endured by order of the military courts; and such a punishment would indeed have been meted out to Postnikov, were it not that, by good luck, the bold and strategic moves, described above, had been made.

But the number of those pleased by the incident related above was not confined to the persons mentioned thus far.

## XVI

Private Postnikov's exploit was quietly bruited about in various circles of the capital, which in those days, when the press was mute, lived in an atmosphere of endless gossip. As the story was transmitted orally, the name of the hero, Private Postnikov, was lost, but on the other hand the tale grew in size and assumed an intriguing, romantic character.

It was rumored that some mysterious swimmer was making for the Palace from the direction of the Fortress of Saints Peter and Paul, that one of the sentries posted at the Palace fired a shot and wounded the swimmer, that an officer of the Company of Invalids who was passing by jumped into the water and rescued him, for which the officer received a just reward, while the sentry got the punishment he deserved. This absurd rumor even reached the abbey inhabited at the time by an ecclesiastical dignitary, who was discreet, yet not indifferent to mundane matters and who was furthermore favorably disposed toward the devout Svinin family of Moscow of which the battalion commander was a member.

The story of the shot seemed dubious to the astute ecclesiastic. Who was this nocturnal swimmer? If he was an escaped prisoner, why then punish the sentry who had only done his duty in firing at him when he was swimming across the Neva from the fortress? And if he was not a prisoner, but some important personage who had to be saved, how could the sentry know about it? In that case, too, things could not have happened as was frivolously rumored. The laity is very careless and given to idle talk, but those who dwell in monasteries and abbeys take a more prudent attitude and get at the gist of worldly matters.

## XVII

One day when Svinin happened to be visiting His Eminence to receive a blessing from him, his distinguished host broached the subject of "the shot." Svinin told him the whole truth, which, as we know, had nothing in common with the rumor.

His Eminence heard the true story in silence, gently fingering his white rosary and without taking his eyes off the narrator. And when Svinin had finished, His Eminence spoke in a voice that was like the rippling of gentle waters:

"Hence one may conclude that in this matter not everything has been set forth *everywhere* in accordance with the whole truth?"

Svinin became confused and answered evasively that the report had been made not by him, but by General Kokoshkin.

His Eminence again passed the beads through his waxen fingers several times and dropped the remark:

"A distinction must be made between what is false and what is not wholly true."

Again the fingering of the rosary, again silence, and at last words sounding like the rippling of gentle waters:

"A half-truth is not falsehood. But concerning this let the least be said."

"It is really so," said Svinin, encouraged. "What disturbs me most, of course, is that I was obliged to punish this soldier, who, though he failed in his duty—"

Again the fingering of the rosary, and the ecclesiastic's mild voice broke in:

"One must never fail to perform one's official duty."

"Yes, but he did it out of magnanimity, out of compassion, and besides, after such an inner struggle and at such a risk: he knew that, while saving another man's life, he was endangering his own. . . . It was a sublime, sacred sentiment."

"What is sacred is known to God alone, and bodily punishment administered to a man of the people is not pernicious, nor is it in conflict either with the customs of nations or with the spirit of Holy Writ. It is easier for the coarse body to bear the rod than for the soul to endure more subtle chastisement. In this matter, you have in no wise violated justice."

"But he is even deprived of the reward for the rescue of those in mortal danger."

"To rescue those in danger is no merit, but indeed a duty. He who could save a life and does not is subject to punishment by law; he who does has but performed his duty."

A pause, the rosary, and rippling words:

"It perhaps profiteth a warrior more to suffer humiliation and wounds for his noble exploit than to be distinguished by a decoration. But the most important thing in this matter is that it be treated with the utmost discretion, and that what actually happened should never be mentioned anywhere."

Obviously His Eminence, too, was pleased.

## XVIII

Had I the boldness of Heaven's fortunate favorites, to whom, because of their great faith, it is given to penetrate the mysteries of God's designs, I should perhaps dare allow myself the conjecture that God Himself was probably pleased with the conduct of Postnikov, this meek soul that He had created. But my faith is small; it does not enable me to comprehend things supernal: I am of the earth, earthy. I think of those mortals who love goodness for its own sake and expect no rewards for it whatsoever. These upright, steadfast men, too, should be, I think, sincerely pleased with the holy aspiration toward selfless love and the no less holy patience of the humble hero of my accurate and artless tale.

1887

# Leo Tolstoy . . . 1828–1910

TOLSTOY's childhood and youth were those of any titled aristocrat in the empire of Nicholas I. Born on the family estate of Yasnaya Polyana, in central Russia, the young count spent his most impressionable years in the atmosphere of the manor and of the Moscow mansion. He took some courses at the University of Kazan, made a weak attempt at improving the lot of his peasants, sowed his wild oats, and enlisted in the army, joining a unit that was engaged in border warfare in the Caucasus.

It was here, at the age of twenty-four, that he completed the first part of his autobiographic story, "Childhood, Boyhood and Youth," and this was promptly printed by the leading Petersburg review. In 1854 he was transferred to the garrison at Sevastopol, then under siege. He snatched time from the fighting to write his *Sevastopol Tales*, the first of which appears below. With the close of the Crimean War he returned to civilian life. He did some traveling abroad, and when at home devoted himself seriously to the education of the peasant children at Yasnaya, editing a pedagogical review; and he also acted as a magistrate arbitrating local disputes arising out of the Emancipation Act. Meanwhile he was writing steadily, chiefly shorter narratives, producing, among other stories, "Three Deaths," and drafting "Polikushka."

He was thirty-four when he married the daughter of a Moscow physician, a girl half his age, who was to give him thirteen children and to prove a faithful helpmate until toward the end of his life they found themselves tragically at odds. For many years after his marriage he led the life of a public-minded gentleman farmer and contented paterfamilias who happened to be a great novelist. During this period he wrote *War and Peace* and *Anna Karenina*. In the interval between these two books he compiled a reader for children. His satisfaction in mere living had always been crossed by an uneasy search for a moral justification of life, and when he turned fifty he underwent a spiritual crisis which resulted in his conversion to an unorthodox kind of Christianity. This denied the institutions of Church and State and called for nonresistance to evil. Thereafter he devoted himself to the elaboration and propagation of his credo, composing essays, tracts, and theological treatises, compiling works of edification, and writing thousands of letters. He did not abandon imaginative writing, but produced chiefly novels and plays with a purpose, parables like "How Much Land Does a Man Need?" and stories with a lesson, such as "After the Ball" and "Alyosha." Novelist and preacher, Tolstoy become the living conscience of Russia and a figure of immense prestige for the world at large.

Public acclaim went hand in hand with private harassments. The discrepancy between the voluntary poverty he preached and the arrangements insisted upon by his wife, as well as the fact that she was somewhat unbalanced, eventually made life at home intolerable to him. In the autumn of 1910 he secretly left Yasnaya, accompanied by a disciple who acted as both secretary and physician. He planned to go into seclusion either abroad or in the Caucasus, but three days after his departure was taken ill at a railway station, and within a week died in the apartment of the stationmaster.

# SEVASTOPOL IN DECEMBER, 1854

THE early dawn is just beginning to color the horizon above the Sapun Hill. The dark blue surface of the sea has already thrown off the gloom of night and is only awaiting the first ray of the sun to begin sparkling merrily. A current of cold misty air blows from the bay; there is no snow on the hard black ground, but the sharp morning frost crunches under your feet and makes your face tingle. The distant, incessant murmur of the sea, occasionally interrupted by the reverberating boom of cannon from Sevastopol, alone infringes the stillness of the morning. All is quiet on the ships. It strikes eight bells.

On the north side the activity of day is beginning gradually to replace the quiet of night: here some soldiers with clanking muskets pass to relieve the guard, there a doctor is already hurrying to the hospital, and there a soldier, having crept out of his dugout, washes his weather-beaten face with icy water and then turning to the reddening horizon says his prayers, rapidly crossing himself: a creaking Tartar cart drawn by camels crawls past on its way to the cemetery to bury the bloodstained dead with which it is loaded almost to the top. As you approach the harbor you are struck by the peculiar smell of coal-smoke, manure, dampness, and meat. Thousands of different objects are lying in heaps by the harbor: firewood, meat, gabions, sacks of flour, iron, and so on. Soldiers of various regiments, some carrying bags and muskets and others empty-handed, are crowded together here, smoking, quarreling, and hauling heavy loads onto the steamer which lies close to the wharf, its funnel smoking.

Private boats crowded with all sorts of people—soldiers, sailors, merchants, and women—keep arriving at the landing stage or leaving it.

"To the Grafskaya, your Honor? Please to get in!" Two or three old salts offer you their services, getting out of their boats.

You choose the one nearest to you, step across the half-decayed carcass of a bay horse that lies in the mud close to the boat, and pass on towards the rudder. You push off from the landing stage, and around you is the sea, now glittering in the morning sunshine. In front of you the old sailor in his camel-hair coat, and a flaxen-haired boy, silently and steadily ply the oars. You gaze at the enormous striped ships scattered far and wide over the bay, at the ships' boats that move about over the sparkling azure like small black dots, at the opposite bank where the handsome light-colored buildings of the town are lit up by the rosy rays of the morning sun, at the foaming white line by the breakwater and around the sunken vessels, the black tops of whose masts here and there stand mournfully out of the water, at the enemy's fleet looming on the crystal horizon of the sea, and at the foaming and bubbling wash of the oars. You listen to the steady sound of voices that reaches you across the water, and to the majestic sound of firing from Sevastopol which as it seems to you is growing more intense.

It is impossible for some feeling of heroism and pride not to penetrate your soul at the thought that you, too, are in Sevastopol, and for the blood not to run faster in your veins.

"Straight past the *Kistentin*,[1] your Honor!" the old sailor tells you, turning round to verify the direction towards the right in which you are steering.

"And she's still got all her guns!"[2] says the flaxen-headed boy, examining the ship in passing.

"Well, of course. She's a new one. Kornilov lived on her," remarks the old seaman, also looking up at the ship.

"Look where it's burst!" the boy says after a long silence, watching a small white cloud of dispersing smoke that has suddenly appeared high above the South Bay accompanied by the sharp sound of a bursting bomb.

"That's *him* firing from the new battery today," adds the old

---

[1] The vessel, the *Constantine*. Translators' note.
[2] The guns were removed from most of the ships for use on the fortifications. Translators' note.

seaman, calmly spitting on his hand. "Now then, pull away Míshka! Let's get ahead of that longboat." And your skiff travels faster over the broad swell of the roadstead, gets ahead of the heavy longboat laden with sacks and unsteadily and clumsily rowed by soldiers, and making its way among all sorts of boats moored there, is made fast to the Grafsky landing.

Crowds of gray-clad soldiers, sailors in black, and gayly-dressed women, throng noisily about the quay. Here are women selling buns, Russian peasants with samovars are shouting, "Hot sbiten!," [1] and here too on the very steps lie rusty cannon-balls, bombs, grapeshot, and cannon of various sizes. A little farther on is a large open space where some enormous beams are lying, together with gun carriages and sleeping soldiers. Horses, carts, cannon, green ammunition wagons, and stacked muskets, are standing there. Soldiers, sailors, officers, women, children, and tradespeople, are moving about, carts loaded with hay, sacks, and casks, are passing, and now and then a Cossack, a mounted officer, or a general in a vehicle. To the right is a street closed by a barricade on which some small guns are mounted in embrasures and beside which sits a sailor smoking a pipe. To the left is a handsome building with Roman figures engraved on its frontage and before which soldiers are standing with bloodstained stretchers. Everywhere you will see the unpleasant indications of a war camp. Your first impressions will certainly be most disagreeable: the strange mixture of camp-life and town-life—of a fine town and a dirty bivouac—is not only ugly but looks like horrible disorder: it will even seem to you that every one is scared, in a commotion, and at a loss what to do. But look more closely at the faces of these people moving about around you and you will get a very different impression. Take for instance this convoy soldier muttering something to himself as he goes to water those three bay horses, and doing it all so quietly that he evidently will not get lost in this motley crowd which does not even exist as far as he is concerned, but will do his job be it what it may—watering horses or hauling guns—as calmly, self-confidently, and unconcernedly as if it were all happening in Tula or Saransk. You will read the same thing on the face of this officer passing by in immaculate white gloves, on the face of the sailor who sits smoking on the barricade, on the faces of the soldiers waiting in the portico of what used to be the Assembly

---

[1] A hot drink made with treacle and lemon, or honey and spice. Translators' note.

Hall, and on the face of that girl who, afraid of getting her pink dress muddy, is jumping from stone to stone as she crosses the street.

Yes, disenchantment certainly awaits you on entering Sevastopol for the first time. You will look in vain in any of these faces for signs of disquiet, perplexity, or even of enthusiasm, determination, or readiness for death—there is nothing of the kind. What you see are ordinary people quietly occupied with ordinary activities, so that perhaps you may reproach yourself for having felt undue enthusiasm and may doubt the justice of the ideas you had formed of the heroism of the defenders of Sevastopol, based on the tales and descriptions and sights and sounds seen and heard from the North Side. But before yielding to such doubts go to the bastions and see the defenders of Sevastopol at the very place of the defense, or better still go straight into that building opposite which was once the Sevastopol Assembly Rooms and in the portico of which stand soldiers with stretchers. There you will see the defenders of Sevastopol and will see terrible and lamentable, solemn and amusing, but astounding and soul-elevating sights.

You enter the large Assembly Hall. As soon as you open the door you are struck by the sight and smell of forty or fifty amputation and most seriously wounded cases, some in cots but most of them on the floor. Do not trust the feeling that checks you at the threshold, it is a wrong feeling. Go on, do not be ashamed of seeming to have come to *look* at the sufferers, do not hesitate to go up and speak to them. Sufferers like to see a sympathetic human face, like to speak of their sufferings, and to hear words of love and sympathy. You pass between the rows of beds and look for a face less stern and full of suffering, which you feel you can approach and speak to.

"Where are you wounded?" you inquire hesitatingly and timidly of an emaciated old soldier who is sitting up in his cot and following you with a kindly look as if inviting you to approach him. I say "inquire timidly" because, besides strong sympathy, sufferings seem to inspire a dread of offending, as well as a great respect for him who endures them.

"In the leg," the soldier replies, and at the same moment you yourself notice from the fold of his blanket that one leg is missing from above the knee. "Now, God be thanked," he adds, "I am ready to leave the hospital."

"Is it long since you were wounded?"

"Well, it's over five weeks now, your Honor."

"And are you still in pain?"

"No, I'm not in any pain now; only when it's bad weather I seem to feel a pain in the calf, else it's all right."

"And how did it happen that you were wounded?"

"It was on the Fifth Bastion, your Honor, at the first *bondbarment*. I trained the gun and was stepping across to the next embrasure, when *he* hits me in the leg, just as if I had stumbled into a hole. I look—and the leg is gone."

"Do you mean to say you felt no pain the first moment?"

"Nothing much, only as if something hot had shoved against my leg."

"And afterwards?"

"And nothing much afterwards except when they began to draw the skin together, then it did seem to smart. The chief thing, your Honor, is *not to think*; if you don't think it's nothing much. It's most because of a man thinking."

At this moment a woman in a gray striped dress and with a black kerchief tied round her head comes up to you and enters into your conversation with the sailor. She begins telling you about him, about his sufferings, the desperate condition he was in for four weeks, and of how when he was wounded he stopped his stretcher-bearers that he might see a volley fired from our battery; and how the Grand Duke spoke to him and gave him twenty-five roubles, and how he had told them he wanted to go back to the bastion to teach the young ones, if he could not himself work any longer. As she says all this in a breath, the woman keeps looking now at you and now at the sailor, who having turned away is picking lint on his pillow as if not listening, and her eyes shine with a peculiar rapture.

"She's my missus, your Honor!" he remarks with a look that seems to say: "You must excuse her. It's a woman's way to talk nonsense."

You begin now to understand the defenders of Sevastopol, and for some reason begin to feel ashamed of yourself in the presence of this man. You want to say too much, in order to express your sympathy and admiration, but you can't find the right words and are dissatisfied with those that occur to you, and so you silently bow your head before this taciturn and unconscious grandeur and firmness of spirit—which is ashamed to have its worth revealed.

"Well, may God help you to get well soon," you say to him, and turn to another patient who is lying on the floor apparently awaiting death in unspeakable torment.

He is a fair-haired man with a puffy pale face. He is lying on his back with his left arm thrown back in a position that indicates cruel suffering. His hoarse breathing comes with difficulty through his parched, open mouth; his leaden blue eyes are rolled upwards, and what remains of his bandaged right arm is thrust out from under his tumbled blanket. The oppressive smell of mortified flesh assails you yet more strongly, and the feverish inner heat in all the sufferer's limbs seems to penetrate you also.

"Is he unconscious?" you ask the woman who follows you and looks at you kindly as at someone akin to her.

"No, he can still hear, but not at all well," and she adds in a whisper: "I gave him some tea to drink today—what if he is a stranger, one must have pity—but he hardly drank any of it."

"How do you feel?" you ask him.

The wounded man turns his eyes at the sound of your voice, but neither sees nor understands you.

"My heart's on fire," he mumbles.

A little farther on you see an old soldier who is changing his shirt. His face and body are a kind of reddish brown and as gaunt as a skeleton. Nothing is left of one of his arms. It has been amputated at the shoulder. He sits up firmly, he is convalescent; but his dull, heavy look, his terrible emaciation and the wrinkles on his face, show that the best part of this man's life has been consumed by his sufferings.

In a cot on the opposite side you see a woman's pale, delicate face, full of suffering, a hectic flush suffusing her cheek.

"That's the wife of one of our sailors: she was hit in the leg by a bomb on the 5th," [1] your guide will tell you. "She was taking her husband's dinner to him at the bastion."

"Amputated?"

"Yes, cut off above the knee."

Now, if your nerves are strong, go in at the door to the left; it is there they bandage and operate. There you will see doctors with pale, gloomy faces, and arms red with blood up to the elbows, busy

---

[1] The first bombardment of Sevastapol was on the 5th of October, 1854, Old Style, that is, the 17th of October, New Style. Translators' note.

at a bed on which a wounded man lies under chloroform. His eyes are open and he utters, as if in delirium, incoherent but sometimes simple and pathetic words. The doctors are engaged on the horrible but beneficent work of amputation. You will see the sharp curved knife enter the healthy white flesh; you will see the wounded man come back to life with terrible, heartrending screams and curses. You will see the doctor's assistant toss the amputated arm into a corner and in the same room you will see another wounded man on a stretcher watching the operation, and writhing and groaning not so much from physical pain as from the mental torture of anticipation. You will see ghastly sights that will rend your soul; you will see war not with its orderly beautiful and brilliant ranks, its music and beating drums, its waving banners, its generals on prancing horses, but war in its real aspect of blood, suffering, and death. . . .

On coming out of this house of pain you will be sure to experience a sense of relief, you will draw deeper breaths of the fresh air, and rejoice in the consciousness of your own health. Yet the contemplation of those sufferings will have made you realize your own insignificance, and you will go calmly and unhesitatingly to the bastions.

"What matters the death and suffering of so insignificant a worm as I, compared to so many deaths, so much suffering?" But the sight of the clear sky, the brilliant sun, the beautiful town, the open church, and the soldiers moving in all directions, will soon bring your spirit back to its normal state of frivolity, its petty cares and absorption in the present. You may meet the funeral procession of an officer as it leaves the church, the pink coffin accompanied by waving banners and music, and the sound of firing from the bastions may reach your ears. But these things will not bring back your former thoughts. The funeral will seem a very beautiful military pageant, the sounds very beautiful warlike sounds; and neither to these sights nor these sounds will you attach the clear and personal sense of suffering and death that came to you in the hospital.

Passing the church and the barricade you enter that part of the town where everyday life is most active. On both sides of the street hang the signboards of shops and restaurants. Tradesmen, women with bonnets or kerchiefs on their heads, dandified officers—everything speaks of the firmness, self-confidence, and security of the inhabitants.

If you care to hear the conversation of army and navy officers, enter the restaurant on the right. There you are sure to hear them talk about last night, about Fanny, about the affair of the 24th,[1] about how dear and badly served the cutlets are, and how such and such of their comrades have been killed.

"Things were confoundedly bad at our place today!" a fair beardless little naval officer with a green knitted scarf round his neck says in a bass voice.

"Where was that?" asks another.

"Oh, in the Fourth Bastion," answers the young officer, and at the words "Four Bastion" you will certainly look more attentively and even with a certain respect at this fair-complexioned officer. The excessive freedom of his manner, his gesticulations, and his loud voice and laugh, which had appeared to you impudent before, now seem to indicate that peculiarly combative frame of mind noticeable in some young men after they have been in danger, but all the same you expect him to say how bad the bombs and bullets made things in the Fourth Bastion. Not at all! It was the mud that made things so bad. "One can scarcely get to the battery," he continues, pointing to his boots, which are muddy even above the calves. "And I have lost my best gunner," says another, "hit right in the forehead." "Who's that? Mityuhin?" "No . . . but am I ever to have my veal, you rascal?" he adds, addressing the waiter. "Not Mityuhin but Abramov—such a fine fellow. He was out in six sallies."

At another corner of the table sit two infantry officers with plates of cutlets and peas before them and a bottle of sour Crimean wine called "Bordeaux." One of them, a young man with a red collar and two little stars on his cloak, is talking to the other, who has a black collar and no stars, about the Alma affair. The former has already been drinking and the pauses he makes, the indecision in his face—expressive of his doubt of being believed—and especially the fact that his own part in the account he is giving is too important and the thing is too terrible, show that he is diverging considerably from the strict truth. But you do not care much for stories of this kind, which will long be current all over Russia; you want to get quickly to the bastions, especially to that Fourth Bastion about which you have been told so many and such different tales. When anyone says: "I am going to the Fourth Bastion" he always betrays a slight

[1] The 24th October O.S. = 5th November N.S., the date of the Battle of Inkerman. Translators' note.

agitation or too marked an indifference; if anyone wishes to chaff you, he says: "You should be sent to the Fourth Bastion." When you meet someone carried on a stretcher and ask, "Where from?" the answer usually is: "From the Fourth Bastion." Two quite different opinions are current concerning this terrible bastion [1]: that of those who have never been there and who are convinced it is a certain grave for any one who goes, and that of those who, like the fair-complexioned midshipman, live there and who when speaking of the Fourth Bastion will tell you whether it is dry or muddy, whether it is cold or warm in the dugouts, and so forth.

During the half-hour you have spent in the restaurant the weather has changed. The mist that spread over the sea has gathered into dull gray moist clouds which hide the sun, and a kind of dismal sleet showers down.and wets the roofs, the pavements, and the soldiers' overcoats.

Passing another barricade you go through some doors to the right and up a broad street. Beyond this barricade the houses on both sides of the street are unoccupied: there are no signboards, the doors are boarded up, the windows smashed, here a corner of the wall is knocked down and there a roof is broken in. The buildings look like old veterans who have borne much sorrow and privation; they even seem to gaze proudly and somewhat contemptuously at you. On the road you stumble over cannon-balls that lie about, and into holes made in the stony ground by bombs and full of water. You meet and overtake detachments of soldiers, Cossacks, officers, and occasionally a woman or a child; only it will not be a woman wearing a bonnet, but a sailor's wife wearing an old cloak and soldiers' boots. After you have descended a little slope farther down the same street you will no longer see any houses, but only ruined walls amid strange heaps of bricks, boards, clay, and beams, and before you, up a steep hill, you see a black untidy space cut up by ditches. This space you are approaching is the Fourth Bastion. . . . Here you will meet still fewer people and no women at all, the soldiers walk briskly by, there are traces of blood on the road, and you are sure to meet four soldiers carrying a stretcher and on the stretcher probably a pale yellow face and a bloodstained overcoat. If you ask, "Where is he wounded?" the bearers without looking at you will answer crossly, "in the leg" or "in the arm" if the man is not severely wounded, or

[1] Called by the English the 'Flagstaff Bastion.' Translators' note.

will remain sternly silent if no head is raised on the stretcher and the man is either dead or seriously wounded.

The whiz of cannon-ball or bomb near by impresses you unpleasantly as you ascend the hill, and the meaning of the sounds is very different from what it seemed to be when they reached you in the town. Some peaceful and joyous memory will suddenly flash through your mind; self-consciousness begins to supersede the activity of your observation: you are less attentive to all that is around you and a disagreeable feeling of indecision suddenly seizes you. But silencing this despicable little voice that has suddenly made itself heard within you at the sight of danger—especially after seeing a soldier run past you laughing, waving his arms, and slipping downhill through the yellow mud—you involuntarily expand your chest, raise your head higher, and clamber up the slippery clay hill. You have climbed only a little way before bullets begin to whiz past you to the right and left, and you will perhaps consider whether you had not better walk inside the trench which runs parallel to the road; but the trench is full of such yellow liquid stinking mud, more than knee deep, that you are to choose the road, especially as *everybody* does so. After walking a couple of hundred yards you come to a muddy place much cut up, surrounded by gabions, cellars, platforms, and dugouts, and on which large cast-iron cannon are mounted and cannon-balls lie piled in orderly heaps. It all seems placed without any plan, aim, connection, or order. Here a group of sailors are sitting in the battery; here in the middle of the open space, half sunk in mud, lies a shattered cannon; and there a .foot-soldier is crossing the battery, drawing his feet with difficulty out of the sticky mud. Everywhere, on all sides and all about, you see fragments of bombs, unexploded bombs, cannon-balls, and various traces of an encampment, all sunk in the liquid, sticky mud. You think you hear the thud of a cannon-ball not far off and you seem to hear the different sounds of bullets all around, some humming like bees, some whistling, and some rapidly flying past with a shrill screech like the string of some instrument. You hear the dreadful boom of a shot that sends a shock all through you and seems most terrible.

"So this is the Fourth Bastion! This is that terrible, truly dreadful spot!" So you think, experiencing a slight feeling of pride and a strong feeling of suppressed fear. But you are mistaken, this is not the Fourth Bastion yet. This is only Yazonovsky Redoubt—comparatively a very safe and not at all dreadful place. To get to the Fourth Bastion you must turn to the right along that narrow trench where a foot-soldier has just passed, stooping down. In this trench you may again meet men with stretchers and perhaps a sailor or a soldier with a spade. You will see the mouths of mines, dugouts into which only two men can crawl, and there you will see the Cossacks of the Black Sea battalions changing their boots, eating, smoking their pipes, and, in short, living. And again you will see the same stinking mud, the traces of camp life and cast-iron refuse of every shape and form. When you have gone some three hundred steps more you will come out at another battery—a flat space with many holes, surrounded with gabions filled with earth, and cannons on platforms, and the whole walled in with earthworks. Here you will perhaps see four or five soldiers playing cards under shelter of the breastworks, and a naval officer, noticing that you are a stranger and inquisitive, will be pleased to show you his "household" and everything that can interest you. This officer sits on a cannon rolling a yellow cigarette so composedly, walks from one embrasure to another so quietly, talks to you so calmly and with such an absence of affectation, that in spite of the bullets whizzing around you oftener than before you yourself grow cooler, question him carefully and listen to his stories. He will tell you (but only if you ask) about the bombardment on the 5th of October; will tell you that only one gun of his battery remained usable and only eight gunners of the crew were left, and that nevertheless he fired all his guns next morning, the 6th. He will tell you how a bomb dropped into one of the dugouts and knocked over eleven sailors; from an embrasure he will show you the enemy's batteries and trenches which are here not more than seventy-five to eighty-five yards distant. I am afraid though, that when you lean out of the embrasure to have a look at the enemy the whiz of the flying bullets will hinder you from seeing anything, but if you do see anything you will be much surprised to find that this whitish stone wall—which is so near you and from which puffs of white smoke keep bursting—is the enemy: *he*, as the soldiers and sailors say.

It is even very likely that the naval officer from vanity, or merely for a little recreation, will wish to show you some firing. "Call the gunner and crew to the cannon!" and fourteen sailors—their hob-nailed boots clattering on the platform, one putting his pipe in his pocket, another still chewing a rusk—will quickly and cheerfully man the gun and begin loading. Look well into these faces and note the bearing and carriage of these men. In every wrinkle of that tanned face with its high cheekbones, in every muscle, in the breadth of those shoulders, the thickness of those legs in their enormous boots, in every movement, quiet, firm, and deliberate, can be seen the chief characteristic of the strength of the Russian—his simplicity and obstinacy.

Suddenly the most fearful roar strikes not only your ears but your whole being and makes you shudder all over. It is followed by the whistle of the departing ball, and a thick cloud of powder-smoke envelops you, the platform, and the black moving figures of the sailors. You will hear various comments made by the sailors concerning this shot of ours and you will notice their animation, the evidences of a feeling you had not perhaps expected: the feeling of animosity and thirst for vengeance which lies hidden in each man's soul. You will hear joyful exclamations: "It's gone right into the embrasure! It's killed two, I think. . . . There, they're carrying them off!" "And now *he's* riled and will send one this way," someone remarks; and really, soon after, you will see before you a flash and some smoke; the sentinel standing on the breastwork will call out "Can-n-non!" and then a ball will whiz past you and bury itself in the earth, throwing out a circle of stones and mud. The commander of the battery will be irritated by this shot and will give orders to fire another and another cannon, the enemy will reply in like manner, and you will experience interesting sensations and see interesting sights. The sentinel will again call "Cannon!" and you will have the same sound and shock, and the mud will be splashed around as before. Or he will call out "Mortar!" and you will hear the regular and rather pleasant whistle—which it is difficult to connect with the thought of anything dreadful—of a bomb; you will hear this whistle coming nearer and faster towards you, then you will see a black ball, feel the shock as it strikes the ground, and will hear the ringing explosion. The bomb will fly apart into whizzing and shrieking fragments, stones will rattle in the air, and you will be bespattered with mud.

At these sounds you will experience a strange feeling of mingled pleasure and fear. At the moment you know the shot is flying towards you, you are sure to imagine that it will kill you, but a feeling of pride will support you and no one will know of the knife that cuts at your heart. But when the shot has flown past without hitting you, you revive and are seized, though only for a moment, by an inexpressibly joyful emotion, so that you feel a peculiar delight in the danger—in this game of life and death—and wish the bombs and balls to fall nearer and nearer to you.

But again the sentinel in his loud gruff voice shouts "Mortar!" Again a whistle, a fall, an explosion; and mingled with this last you are startled by a man's groans. You approach the wounded sailor just as the stretchers are brought. Covered with blood and dirt he presents a strange, scarcely human, appearance. Part of his breast has been torn away. For the first few moments only terror and the kind of feigned, premature, look of suffering, common to men in this state, appear on his mud-besprinkled face, but when the stretcher is brought and he himself lies down on it on his healthy side you notice that his expression changes. His eyes shine more brightly, his teeth are clenched, he raises his head higher with difficulty, and when the stretcher is lifted he stops the bearers for a moment and turning to his comrades says with an effort, in a trembling voice, "Forgive me, brothers!" [1] He wishes to say more, something pathetic, but only repeats, "Forgive me, brothers!" At this moment a sailor approaches him, places the cap on the head the wounded man holds up towards him, and then placidly swinging his arms returns quietly to his cannon.

"That's the way with seven or eight every day," the naval officer remarks to you, answering the look of horror on your face, and he yawns as he rolls another yellow cigarette.

So now you have seen the defenders of Sevastopol where they are defending it, and somehow you return with a tranquil heightened spirit, paying no heed to the balls and bombs whose whistle accompanies you all the way to the ruined theater. The principal thought you have brought away with you is a joyous conviction of the strength of the Russian people; and this conviction you have gained not by looking at all those traverses, breastworks, cunningly interlaced trenches, mines, cannon, one after another, of which you could make nothing; but from the eyes, words, and actions—in short from seeing what is called the "spirit"—of the defenders of Sevas-

---

[1] "Forgive me" and "farewell" are almost interchangeable expressions in Russian. Translators' note.

topol. What they do is all done so simply, with so little effort, that you feel convinced that they could do a hundred times as much. . . . You understand that the feeling which actuates them is not that petty ambition or forgetfulness which you yourself experienced, but something more powerful, which has made them able to live so quietly under the flying balls, exposed to a hundred chances of death besides the one all men are subject to—and this amid conditions of constant toil, lack of sleep, and dirt. Men could not accept such terrible conditions of life for the sake of a cross, or promotion, or because of a threat: there must be some other and higher motive power.

It is only now that the tales of the early days of the siege of Sevastopol are no longer beautiful historical legends for you, but have become realities: the tales of the time when it was not fortified, when there was no army to defend it, when it seemed a physical impossibility to retain it and yet there was not the slightest idea of abandoning it to the enemy—of the time when Kornílov, that hero worthy of ancient Greece, making his round of the troops, said, "Lads, we will die, but will not surrender Sevastopol!" and our Russians, incapable of phrase-making, replied, "We will die! Hurrah!" You will clearly recognize in the men you have just seen those heroes who gladly prepared for death and whose spirits did not flag during those dismal days, but rose.

The evening is closing in. Just before setting, the sun emerges from behind the gray clouds that covered the sky and suddenly lights up with its bright red glow the purple clouds, the greenish sea with the ships and boats rocking on its broad even swell, the white buildings of the town, and the people moving in the streets. The sound of some old valse played by a military band on the boulevard is carried across the water and mingles strangely with the sound of firing on the bastions.

                                                                    1855

# THREE DEATHS

## I

I T WAS autumn. Two carriages were driving at a rapid trot along the highroad. In the foremost sat two women. One was a lady, thin and pale; the other, her maid, was plump, with shining, red cheeks. Her short, coarse hair stood out under her faded hat; her red hand, in a torn glove, kept hurriedly putting it tidy; her high bosom, covered with a tapestry kerchief, was eloquent of health; her quick, black eyes watched out of the window the fields flying past, then glanced timidly at her mistress, then shifted uneasily about the corners of the carriage. Just before the maid's nose swung the lady's hat, hanging from the rack above; on her lap lay a puppy. Her feet were kept from the floor by the boxes that stood on the carriage floor, and could be faintly heard knocking on them through the shaking of the springs and the rattling of the windows.

With her hands clasped on her knees and her eyes closed, the lady swayed feebly to and fro on the cushions that had been put at her back, and with a slight frown she coughed inwardly. On her head she wore a white nightcap, and a light blue kerchief was tied on her soft, white neck. A straight parting, retreating under her cap, divided her fair, pomaded, exceedingly flat hair, and there was a dry, death-like look about the whiteness of the skin of this wide parting. The faded, yellowish skin hung loose on her delicate and beautiful features, and was flushed on her cheeks. Her lips were dry and restless, her eyelashes were thin and straight, and her cloth travelling cloak fell in straight folds over her sunken bosom. Though her eyes were closed, the lady's face expressed fatigue, irritation, and habitual suffering. A footman was dozing on the box, one elbow on the rail of the seat. The driver, hired from the posting-station, shouted briskly to the four sturdy, sweating horses, and looked round now and then at the other driver, who called to him from behind on the coach. Smoothly and rapidly the wheels made their broad, parallel tracks along the chalky mud of the road. The sky was gray and cold; a damp mist was falling over the fields and the road. The carriage was close, and smelt of eau de Cologne and dust. The sick woman stretched her head back and slowly opened her eyes. Her large, handsome, dark eyes were very bright.

"Again," she said, her beautiful, thin hand nervously thrusting away a corner of the maid's cloak which was just brushing against her knees, and her mouth twitched painfully. Matryosha gathered up her cloak in both hands, lifted it up on her lap, and edged further away. Her blooming face flushed bright red. The sick woman's fine dark eyes kept eager watch on the servant's actions. She leaned with both hands on the seat and tried to raise herself, so as to be sitting higher up; but her strength failed her. Her mouth twitched and her whole face worked with an expression of helpless, wrathful irony. "You might at least help me! . . . Ah, you needn't! I can do it myself, only be so good as not to lay your bundles, bags, or whatever they are behind me, please! You had better not touch me if you're so awkward!"

The lady shut her eyes, and rapidly raising her eyelids again glanced at the maid. Matryosha was staring at her and biting her red underlip. A heavy sigh rose from the sick woman's chest, but changed to a cough before it was uttered. She turned away, frowning, and clutched at her chest with both hands. When the cough was over, she closed her eyes again and sat without stirring. The carriage and the coach drove into a village. Matryosha put her stout arm out from under her kerchief and crossed herself.

"What is it?" asked the lady.

"A station, madam."

"What do you cross yourself for, I ask?"

"A church, madam."

The sick woman turned towards the window, and began slowly crossing herself, her great eyes fastened on the big village church as the carriage drove by it.

The two carriages stopped together at the station. The sick woman's husband and the doctor got out of the other carriage and came up to her.

"How do you feel?" asked the doctor, taking her pulse.

"Well, how are you, my dear—not tired?" asked her husband, in French. "Wouldn't you like to get out?"

Matryosha, gathering up her bundles, squeezed into a corner so as not to be in their way as they talked.

"Just the same," answered the lady. "I won't get out."

Her husband stayed a little while beside the carriage, then went into the station-house. Matryosha got out of the carriage and ran on tiptoe through the mud to the gates.

"If I am ill, it's no reason you shouldn't have your lunch," the invalid said with a faint smile to the doctor, who was standing at the carriage window.

"None of them care anything about me," she added to herself, as soon as the doctor had moved with sedate step away from her and run at a trot up the steps of the station-house. "They are all right, so they don't care. O my God!"

"Well, Eduard Ivanovich," said her husband, meeting the doctor and rubbing his hands, with a cheery smile. "I've ordered the case of wine to be brought in. What do you say to a bottle?"

"I shouldn't say no," answered the doctor.

"Well, how is she?" the husband asked with a sigh, lifting his eyebrows and dropping his voice.

"I have told you she can't possibly get as far as Italy; if she reaches Moscow it will be a wonder, especially in this weather."

"What are we to do! O my God! my God!" The husband put his hand over his eyes. "Put it here," he added to the servant who brought in the case of wine.

"You should have kept her at home," the doctor answered, shrugging his shoulders.

"But tell me, what could I do?" protested the husband. "I did everything I could, you know, to keep her. I talked to her of our means, and of the children whom we should have to leave behind, and of my business—she won't hear a word of anything. She makes plans for her life abroad as though she were strong and well. And to tell her of her position would be the death of her."

"But death has hold of her already, you ought to know it, Vasily Dmitrich. A person can't live without lungs, and the lungs can't grow again. It's distressing and terrible, but what's one to do? My duty and yours is simply to see that her end should be as easy as possible. It's the priest who is needed now."

"O my God! But conceive my position, having to speak to her of the last sacrament. Come what will, I can't tell her. You know how good she is."

"You must try, all the same, to persuade her to wait till the roads are frozen," said the doctor, shaking his head significantly, "or we may have a disaster on the road."

"Aksyusha, hey, Aksyusha!" shrieked the stationmaster's daughter, flinging a jacket over her head, and stamping on the dirty back steps of the station; "let's go and have a look at the lady from Shirkin; they say she's being taken abroad for her lungs. I've never seen what people look like in consumption."

Aksyusha darted out at the doorway, and arm in arm they ran by the gate. Slackening their pace, they walked by the carriage, and peeped in at the lowered window. The sick woman turned her head towards them, but noticing their curiosity, she frowned and turned away.

"My gra-a-cious!" said the stationmaster's daughter, turning her head away quickly. "Such a wonderful beauty as she was, and what does she look like now. Enough to frighten one, really. Did you see, did you see, Aksyusha?"

"Yes, she is thin!" Aksyusha assented. "Let's go by and get another look at her, as though we were going to the well. She turned away before I'd seen her properly. I am sorry for her, Masha!"

"And the mud's awful!" answered Masha, and both ran back to the gate.

"I've grown frightful, it seems," thought the invalid. "Ah, to make haste, to make haste to get abroad, then I shall soon be better!"

"Well, how are you, my dear?" said her husband, still munching as he came up to the carriage.

"Always that invariable question," thought the sick woman, "and he goes on eating too!"

"Just the same," she muttered through her teeth.

"Do you know, my dear, I'm afraid the journey will be bad for you in this weather, and Eduard Ivanovich says so too. Hadn't we better turn back?"

She kept wrathfully silent.

"The weather will change, and the roads perhaps will be hard, and that would make it better for you; and then we would all go together."

"Excuse me. If I hadn't listened to you long ago, I should be in Berlin by now and should be quite well."

"That couldn't be helped, my angel; it was out of the question, as you know! But now, if you would wait for a month, you would be ever so much better. I should have settled my business, and we could take the children."

"The children are quite well, and I am not."

"But consider, my dear, with this weather if you get·worse on the road . . . there, at any rate, you're at home."

"And if I am at home? . . . To die at home?" the sick woman answered hotly. But the word "die" evidently terrified her; she bent an imploring, questioning look upon her husband. He dropped his eyes and did not speak. The sick woman's mouth puckered all at once like a child's, and tears dropped from her eyes. Her husband buried his face in his handkerchief, and walked away from the carriage without speaking.

"No, I am going," said the sick woman, lifting her eyes towards heaven, and she fell to whispering disconnected words. "My God, what for?" she said, and the tears flowed more freely. For a long while she prayed fervently, but there was still the same pain and tightness on her chest. The sky, the fields, and the road were just as gray and cheerless; and the same autumn mist, neither thicker nor clearer, hung over the mud of the road, the roofs of the huts, the carriage and the sheepskin coats of the drivers, who were greasing and harnessing a carriage, chatting together in their vigorous, merry voices.

## II

The horses were put in the shafts; but the driver lingered. He went into the drivers' hut. It was hot and stifling, dark and oppresive in the hut; there was a smell of human beings, baking bread, and cabbage, and sheepskins. There were several drivers in the room; the cook was busy at the stove; on the top of the stove lay a sick man wrapped in sheepskins.

"Uncle Fyodor! hey, Uncle Fyodor!" said the driver as he came into the room. He was a young fellow, in a sheepskin coat with a whip stuck in his belt, and he was addressing the sick man.

"What do you want Fedya for, you windbag?" one of the drivers interposed. "They are waiting for you in the carriage."

"I want to ask him for his boots; I've worn mine out," answered the young fellow, tossing back his hair and straightening the gloves in his belt. "Is he asleep? Hey, Uncle Fyodor?" he repeated, going up to the stove.

"What?" a weak·voice was heard in reply, and a thin face with a red beard bent over from the stove. A big, wasted, white hand, covered with hair, pulled up a coat on the bony shoulder in the dirty shirt. "Give me a drink, brother; what do you want?"

The young man handed him a dipper of water.

"Well, Fedya," he said, hesitating, "you won't be wanting your new boots now; give them to me; you won't be going out, you know."

Pressing his weary head to the shining dipper, and wetting his scanty, hanging mustaches in the turbid water, the sick man drank feebly and eagerly. His tangled beard was not clean, his sunken, lusterless eyes were lifted with an effort to the young man's face. When he had finished drinking he tried to lift his hand to wipe his wet lips, but he could not, and he wiped them on the sleeve of the coat. Without uttering a sound, but breathing heavily through his nose, he looked straight into the young man's eyes, trying to rally his strength.

"Maybe you've promised them to someone already?" said the young man; "if so, never mind. The thing is, it's soaking wet outside, and I've to go out on a job; and I said to myself, why, I'll ask Fedya for his boots, he'll not need them, for sure. If you are likely to need them yourself, say so."

There was a gurgle and a rattle in the sick man's throat; he bent over and was choked by a deep, stifling cough.

"He need them!" the cook cried out in sudden anger, filling the whole hut with her voice. "He's not got off the stove these two months! Why, he coughs fit to split himself; it makes me ache inside simply to hear him. How could he want boots? He won't wear new boots to be buried! And time he was, too, long ago—God forgive me the sin! Why, he coughs fit to split himself. He ought to be moved into another hut, or somewhere! There are hospitals, I've heard say, for such in the town; he takes up the whole place, and what's one to do? One hasn't room to turn round. And then they expect me to keep the place clean!"

"Hi, Seryoga! go and take your seat; the gentry are waiting," the stationmaster shouted at the door.

Seryoga would have gone away without waiting for an answer, but the sick man's eyes, while he was coughing, had told him he wanted to answer.

"You take the boots, Seryoga," said he, stifling the cough and taking breath a minute. "Only buy me a stone when I die, do you hear?" he added huskily.

"Thanks, uncle, so I'll take them; and as to the stone, ay, ay, I'll buy it."

"There, lads, you hear?" the sick man managed to articulate, and again he bent over and began choking.

"All right, we heard," said one of the drivers. "Go along, Seryoga, or the overseer will be running after you again. The lady from Shirkin is ill."

Seryoga quickly pulled off his torn boots, which were much too large for him, and thrust them under a bench. Uncle Fyodor's new boots fitted his feet perfectly, and Seryoga went out to the carriage looking at them.

"What grand boots! let me grease them for you," said a driver with the greasepot in his hand, as Seryoga got on the box and picked up the reins. "Did he give them you for nothing?"

"Why, are you jealous?" answered Seryoga, getting up and shaking down the skirts of his coat about his legs. "Hi, get up, my darlings!" he shouted to the horses, brandishing the whip, and the two carriages, with their occupants, boxes, and baggage, rolled swiftly along the wet road, and vanished into the gray autumn mist.

The sick driver remained lying on the stove in the stifling hut. Unrelieved by coughing, he turned over on the other side with an effort, and was quiet. All day till evening, men were coming and going and dining in the hut; there was no sound from the sick man. At nightfall, the cook clambered up onto the stove and reached across his legs to get a sheepskin. "Don't you be angry with me, Nastasya," said the sick man; "I shall soon clear out of your place."

"That's all right, that's all right; why, I didn't mean it," muttered

Nastasya. "But what is it that's wrong with you, uncle? Tell me about it."

"All my inside's wasted away. God knows what it is."

"My word! and does your throat hurt when you cough!"

"It hurts me all over. My death is at hand—that's what it is. Oh, oh, oh!" moaned the sick man.

"Cover your legs up like this," said Nastasya, pulling a coat over him as she crept off the stove.

A night-light glimmered dimly all night in the hut. Nastasya and some ten drivers lay on the floor and the benches asleep, and snoring loudly. The sick man alone moaned faintly, coughed, and turned over on the stove. Towards morning he became quite still.

"A queer dream I had in the night," said the cook, stretching next morning in the half-light. "I dreamed that Uncle Fyodor got down from the stove and went out to chop wood. 'Nastasya,' says he, 'I'll split you some'; and I says to him, 'How can you chop wood?' and he snatches up the axe and starts chopping so fast, so fast that the chips were flying. 'Why,' says I, 'you were ill, weren't you?' 'No,' says he, 'I'm all right,' and he swings the axe, so that it gave me quite a fright. I screamed out and waked up. Isn't he dead, perhaps? Uncle Fyodor! Hey, uncle!"

Fyodor made no sound in reply.

"May be he is dead. I'll get up and see," said one of the drivers who was awake.

A thin hand, covered with reddish hairs, hung down from the stove; it was cold and pale.

"I'll go and tell the overseer. He's dead, seemingly," said the driver.

Fyodor had no relations—he had come from distant parts. The next day he was buried in the new graveyard beyond the copse, and for several days after Nastasya told every one of the dream she had had, and how she had been the first to discover that Uncle Fyodor was dead.

## III

Spring had come. Streams of water hurried gurgling between the frozen dung-heaps in the wet streets of the town. The people moving to and fro were gayly dressed and gayly chattering. Behind the fences of the little gardens the buds on the trees were swelling, and their branches rustled faintly in the fresh breeze. Everywhere there was a running and a dripping of clear drops. . . . The sparrows chattered incoherently, and fluttered to and fro on their little wings. On the sunny side, on fences, trees, and houses, all was movement. There was youth and gladness in the sky and on the earth and in the heart of man. In one of the principal streets there was straw lying in front of a large house; in the house lay the dying woman who had been hastening abroad.

At the closed door of her room stood the patient's husband and her cousin, an elderly woman; on a sofa sat a priest with downcast eyes, holding something wrapped up in his stole. In a corner an old lady, the patient's mother, lay in an armchair, weeping bitterly. Near her stood a maid holding a clean pocket-handkerchief in readiness for the old lady when she should ask for it. Another maid was rubbing the old lady's temples with something and blowing on her gray head under her cap.

"Well, Christ be with you, my dear," said the husband to the elderly woman who was standing with him at the door; "she has such confidence in you, you know so well how to talk to her; go in, and have a good talk with her." He would have opened the door; but the cousin restrained him, put her handkerchief several times to her eyes, and shook her head.

"Come, now, I don't look as if I had been crying, I think," she said, and opening the door herself, she went into the sickroom.

The husband was in great excitement, and seemed utterly distraught. He walked towards the old lady, but stopped short a few paces from her, turned, walked about the room, and went up to the priest. The priest looked at him, raised his eyebrows heavenwards, and sighed. His thick, grizzled beard turned upwards too, and then sank again.

"My God! my God!" said the husband.

"There is nothing one can do," said the priest, and again his brows and his beard were elevated and drooped again.

"And her mother here!" the husband said, almost in despair. "She will never be able to bear this! She loves her, she loves her so that she . . . I don't know. If you, father, would attempt to soothe her and to persuade her to go out of this room."

The priest rose and went to the old lady.

"True it is, that none can sound the depths of a mother's heart," said he; "but God is merciful."

The old lady's face began suddenly twitching, and she sobbed hysterically.

"God is merciful," the priest went on, when she was a little calmer. "In my parish, I must tell you, there was a man ill, much worse than Marya Dmitryevna, and a simple artisan cured him with herbs in a very short time. And this same artisan is in Moscow now, indeed. I told Vasily Dmitryevich—he might try him. Any way, it would be a comfort to the sick woman. To God all things are possible."

"No, she can't live," said the old lady; "if it could have been me, but God takes her." And her hysterics grew so violent that she fainted.

The sick woman's husband hid his face in his hands, and ran out of the room.

The first person that met him in the corridor was a boy of six, who was running at full speed after a little girl younger than himself.

"Shouldn't I take the children to see their mamma?" asked the nurse.

"No, she doesn't want to see them. It upsets her."

The boy stood still for a moment, staring intently into his father's face, then suddenly kicking up his foot, with a merry shriek he ran on.

"I'm pretending she's my black horse, papa!" shouted the boy, pointing to his sister.

Meanwhile in the next room the cousin was sitting by the sick woman's bedside, and trying by skillfully leading up to the subject to prepare her for the idea of death. The doctor was at the other window mixing a draught.

The sick woman, in a white dressing-gown, sat propped up with pillows in bed, and gazed at the cousin without speaking.

"Ah, my dear," she said, suddenly interrupting her, "don't try to prepare me. Don't treat me as a child. I am a Christian. I know all about it. I know I haven't long to live; I know that if my husband would have listened to me sooner, I should have been in Italy, and perhaps, most likely indeed, should have been quite well. Everyone told him so. But it can't be helped, it seems that it was God's will.

We are all great sinners, I know that; but I put my trust in God's mercy: He will forgive all, surely, all. I try to understand myself. I, too, have sinned greatly, my dear. But, to make up, how I have suffered. I have tried to bear my sufferings with patience. . . ."

"Then may I send for the priest, my dear? You will feel all the easier after the sacrament," said the cousin. The sick woman bowed her head in token of assent. "God forgive me, a sinner!" she murmured.

The cousin went out and beckoned to the priest.

"She is an angel!" she said to the husband with tears in her eyes. The husband began to weep; the priest went in at the door; the old lady was still unconscious, and in the outer room there was a complete stillness. Five minutes later the priest came out, and taking off his stole smoothed back his hair.

"Thank God, the lady is calmer now," he said; "she wants to see you."

The cousin and the husband went in. The sick woman was weeping quietly, gazing at the holy picture.

"I congratulate you, my dear," said her husband.

"Thank you! How happy I am now, what unspeakable joy I am feeling!" said the sick woman, and a faint smile played about her thin lips. "How merciful is God! Is it not true? Is He not merciful and almighty?" And again with eyes full of tears she gazed at the holy picture in eager prayer.

Then suddenly something seemed to recur to her mind. She beckoned her husband to her.

"You never will do what I ask," she said in a weak, irritable voice.

Her husband, craning his neck forward, listened submissively.

"What is it, my dear?"

"How often I've told you those doctors don't know anything; there are plain women healers, who work cures. . . . The priest told me . . . an artisan . . . send for him."

"For whom, my dear?"

"My God, he won't understand anything!" . . .

And the sick woman frowned and covered her eyes. The doctor went up and took her hand. The pulse was growing perceptibly weaker and weaker. He made a sign to the husband. The sick woman noticed this gesture and looked round in alarm. The cousin turned away, and burst into tears.

"Don't cry, don't torture yourself and me," said the sick woman. "That destroys all the calm left me."

"You are an angel!" said the cousin, kissing her hand.

"No, kiss me here, it's only the dead who are kissed on the hand. My God! my God!"

The same evening the sick woman was a corpse, and the corpse lay in a coffin in the drawing-room of the great house. The doors of the big room were closed, and in it a deacon sat alone, reading the Psalms of David aloud in a rhythmic, nasal tone. The bright light of the wax candles in the tall silver candlesticks fell on the pale brow of the dead woman, on the heavy, waxen hands and the stonelike folds of the shroud, that jutted up horribly at the knees and toes. The deacon read on rhythmically without taking in the meaning of his own words, and the words echoed and died away strangely in the still room. From time to time the sounds of children's voices and the tramp of their feet came from a far-away room.

" 'Hidest thou thy face, they are troubled,' " the psalm-reader boomed; " 'thou takest away their breath, they die and return to their dust. Thou sendest forth thy spirit, they are created; and thou renewest the face of the earth. The glory of the Lord shall endure for ever.' "

The face of the dead woman was stern and solemn. Nothing stirred the pure, cold brow and the firmly set lips. She was all attention. But did she even now understand those grand words?

## IV

A month later a stone chapel was raised over the dead woman's grave. But there was still no stone over the driver's grave, and there was nothing but the bright green grass over the mound, which was the only sign of a man's past existence.

"You will be sinning, Seryoga," the cook at the station said one day, "if you don't buy a stone for Fyodor. You were always saying it was winter, but now why don't you keep your word? I was by at the time. He's come back once already to ask you for it; if you don't buy it, he'll come again and stifle you."

"Why, did I say I wasn't going to?" answered Seryoga; "I'll buy a stone as I said I would; I'll buy one for a silver rouble and a half.

I've not forgotten, but it must be fetched, you know. As soon as I've a chance to go to the town I'll buy it."

"You might put a cross up anyway," put in an old driver, "or else it's a downright shame. You're wearing the boots."

"Where's one to get a cross? You wouldn't cut one out of a log of firewood?"

"What are you talking about? You can't hew it out of a log. You take an axe and go early in the morning into the copse; you can cut a cross there. An aspen or something you can fell. And it'll make a fine wooden monument too. Or else you'll have to go and stand the forester a drink of vodka. One doesn't want to have to give him a drink for every trifle. The other day I broke a splinter-bar; I cut myself a first-rate new one, and no one said a word to me."

In the early morning, when it was hardly light, Seryoga took his axe and went into the wood. Over all lay a chill, even-colored veil of still-falling dew, not lighted up by the sun. The east was imperceptibly growing clearer, reflecting its faint light on the arch of sky covered with fine clouds. Not a blade of grass below, not a leaf on the topmost twig stirred. The stillness of the forest was only broken at intervals by the sound of wings in a tree or a rustle on the ground. Suddenly a strange sound, not one of nature's own, rang out and died away on the edge of the forest. But again the sound was heard, and began to be repeated at regular intervals near the trunk of one of the motionless trees. One of the treetops began shaking in a strange way; its sappy leaves whispered something; and a warbler that had been perched on one of its branches fluttered round it twice, and uttering a whistle and wagging its tail, settled on another tree.

The sound of the axe was more and more muffled, the sappy, white chips flew out on the dewy grass, and a faint crackling sound followed each blow. The tree shuddered all over, bowed, and quickly stood up straight again, trembling in dismay on its roots. For a moment all was still, but again the tree bent; a crack was heard in its trunk, and with a snapping of twigs its branches dropped, and it crashed down with its top on the damp earth. The sounds of the axe and of steps died away. The warbler whistled and flew up higher. The branch in which it had caught its wings shook for a little while in all its leaves, then became still like the rest. The trees displayed their motionless branches more gladly than ever in the newly opened space.

The first beams of the sun, piercing the delicate cloud, shone out in the sky and darted over the earth. The mist began rolling in waves in the hollows; the dew glittered sparkling on the green grass; the translucent clouds turned white, and floated in haste across the blue sky. The birds flitted to and fro in the thickets and twittered some happy song, like mad things. The sappy leaves whispered joyously and calmly on the treetops, and the branches of the living trees, slowly, majestically, swayed above the fallen dead tree.

1859

# POLIKUSHKA

## I

"IT'S AS you're pleased to command, madam, only I'm sorry for the Dutlovs! They're all—every one of them—good lads; but since there's not a house-serf to send, one of them's bound to go," said the bailiff. "As it is, everyone's pointing to them. It's as your honor wills, of course."

And he shifted his right hand over his left, holding both before his stomach, bent his head on the other side, drew in his thin lips, almost with a smack, turned up his eyes, and sank into silence, with the unmistakable intention of remaining silent a long while and hearing without comment all the nonsense his mistress would be sure to say upon the subject.

He was a bailiff, a serf, a close-shaven man in a long coat, of the peculiar bailiff cut, who was standing one autumn evening before his mistress with his report. Receiving the report consisted from the lady's point of view in listening to the accounts of past agricultural operations and giving directions for future ones. From the point of view of Yegor Mihailovich, the bailiff, the presentation of the report was a ceremonial that consisted of standing evenly on both bandy legs, in a corner, with his face to the sofa, listening to all sorts of irrelevant chatter, and leading the mistress by various devices to the point of saying quickly and impatiently, "Very well, very well," to all Yegor Mihailovich's suggestions.

At that moment the question was the furnishing of conscripts. Three had to be sent from Pokrovskoe. Two were unmistakably pointed out by the very finger of Fate, by the conjunction of domestic, moral, and financial considerations. As regards them, there could be no hesitation nor dispute on the part of the mir, on the part of their mistress, or on the part of public opinion. The third was the subject under discussion. The bailiff wanted to save Dutlov, who had three lads in his household eligible, and to send the family house-serf Polikushka, who had a very bad reputation, and had more than once been guilty of stealing bags, harness, and hay. The mistress, who had often petted Polikushka's ragged children, and was attempting to reform his morals by exhortations from the gospel, did not want to give him up. At the same time, she had no ill-will towards the Dutlovs, whom she did not know, and had never noticed. But for some reason she was unable to grasp the fact that, if Polikushka did not go, Dutlov must go, and the bailiff hesitated to explain this point in so many words to her. "Oh, I don't wish the Dutlovs to be unhappy!" she said with feeling. "If you don't wish it, then pay the three hundred roubles in lieu of a recruit," was the answer that ought to have been made to that. But policy forbade it.

And so Yegor Mihailovich remained standing quietly, leaned a little towards the doorpost, and fell to gazing at his mistress's lips moving, at the ruche in her cap dancing up and down, together with her shadow on the wall under the picture. But he did not feel it in the least necessary to penetrate to the meaning of her remarks. The lady talked a long while, and said a great deal. He felt a twitching impulse to yawn behind his ears, but he adroitly changed this nervous quiver into a cough, covering his mouth with his hand, and affecting to clear his throat. Not very long ago I saw Lord Palmerston sitting with his hat on, while a member of the Opposition thundered against the ministry; then, suddenly rising, he replied in a three hours' speech to every point his adversary had made. I saw this, and did not marvel at it, because I had seen something like it a thousand times over between Yegor Mihailovich and his mistress. Either because he was afraid of dropping asleep, or because it struck him that she was getting very much wrought up, he shifted the weight of his person from the left leg to the right, and began with the time-honored formula with which he used always to begin:—

"It's as you will, madam, only, only—the mir is meeting before the countinghouse now, and one must make an end. In the order it says they must take recruits to the town before Intercession. And of the peasants it's the Dutlovs that all point to, and no one else. The mir cares nothing for your interests; it's all one to them if we do ruin the Dutlovs. I know, to be sure, what a struggle they've had.

Why, ever since I've been bailiff, they've always been living in poverty. The old man's gone on, only reckoning on his younger nephews growing up to be a help, and now we must make it hard for them again. But I, as your honor's well aware, care for your property as for my own. It's a pity, madam; it's as you're pleased to command! They're no kith nor kin to me, and I've taken nothing from them—"

"Oh, I never thought of such a thing, Yegor," put in his mistress, and she suspected at once that he had been bribed by the Dutlovs.

"Only it's the best homestead in all Pokrovskoe—God-fearing, hard-working peasants. The old man was for thirty years church elder, never touches a drop, nor used a bad word, goes to church" (the bailiff knew what sop would be acceptable); "and what's the chief thing I'd like to report to you, he has only two sons, the others are nephews. The mir pitches on him, but in reality he ought to be reckoned among the two-men households. Others with three sons have divided into separate households in their foolishness, and now they're right enough, while these have to suffer for their prudence."

Here his mistress failed to grasp anything; she had no notion what "separate households" and "two-men households" meant in this connection. She simply heard the sound of the bailiff's voice, and looked at the nankeen buttons on his coat; the top one he probably did not often button, so it was quite firmly on; but a middle one was dragged out and hanging loose, and ought to have been sewed on long ago. But as we are all aware, for purposes of conversation, especially on matters of business, it is not at all necessary to understand what is said to you—the only thing necessary is to remember what you want to say yourself. And that the lady did on this occasion.

"How is it you won't understand me, Yegor Mihailovich?" she said. "I don't in the least desire a Dutlov to be sent for a soldier. I should have thought you might judge from what you know of me, that I do all I can to assist my peasants, and don't desire their unhappiness. You know that I'm ready to make every sacrifice to escape from this melancholy necessity, and not to let either Dutlov go or Horyushkin." (I don't know whether it occurred to the bailiff that to escape from this melancholy necessity there was no need to make *every* sacrifice, the sacrifice of three hundred roubles would be sufficient; but that reflection easily might have occurred to him.) "But one thing I tell you plainly, that I won't let Polikey go on any account. After that affair with the clock, when he confessed of himself to me, and wept and swore that he would reform, I talked a long while to him, and saw that he was touched and sincerely penitent." ("Well, she's off now!" thought Yegor Mihailovich, and he began scrutinizing the marmalade which had been put in her glass of water —orange or lemon was it? "Bitter it's sure to be," he thought.) "Here it's seven months since then, and he's never once been tipsy, and his conduct is excellent. His wife told me that he's become a different man. And how would you have me punish him now when he's reformed? And besides, wouldn't it be inhuman to send a man who has five children and only he to keep them? No; you'd better not talk to me about that, Yegor."

And the lady took a sip from the glass. Yegor Mihailovich watched the progress of the water down her throat, and then replied shortly and dryly:

"Then your orders are to fix upon Dutlov?"

His mistress flung up her hands.

"How is it you can't understand me? Do I want to make the Dutlovs miserable? Do you suppose I have anything against them? God is my witness that I'm ready to do anything for them." (She glanced at the picture on the wall, but bethought herself that it was not God. "Well, that's no matter, though," she thought. It was strange again that she did not stumble upon the idea of the three hundred roubles.) "But what am I to do? Do I know how and why? I can't know that. Well, I rely upon you, you know what I want. You act so that all may be content according to law. What's one to do? They're not the only ones, all have their painful moments. Only Polikey can't be sent away. You understand that would·be a horrid thing for me to do."

She would have gone on longer—she was so deeply stirred; but at that moment a maidservant came into the room.

"What is it, Dunyasha?"

"A peasant has come, bid me ask Yegor Mihailovich if it is his orders the meeting's to wait," said Dunyasha, and she glanced wrathfully at Yegor Mihailovich. ("Ugh, that bailiff!" she thought, "upsetting the mistress; now she won't let us get to sleep till two o'clock again.")

"You can go then, Yegor," said the lady. "Do the best you can."

"Yes, ma'am." He said no more now of Dutlov. "And whom do you bid me send to the gardener for the money?"

"Is Petrusha not yet back from the town?"

"No, ma'am."

"Can't Nikolay go?"

"Father's laid up with lumbago," said Dunyasha.

"Wouldn't your honor desire me to go myself tomorrow?" asked the bailiff.

"No; you're wanted here, Yegor." The lady pondered.

"How much is it?"

"Four hundred and sixty-two roubles."

"Send Polikey!" said the lady, glancing resolutely at the face of Yegor Mihailovich.

Yegor Mihailovich, without parting his teeth, drew his lips back, as though he smiled, and the expression of his face did not change.

"Yes, ma'am."

"Send him to me."

"Yes, ma'am," and Yegor Mihailovich went off to the counting-house.

## II

Polikey, being a man of no importance, and of tarnished reputation, and coming, too, from another village, had had no chance of obtaining privileges through the housekeeper or the butler, through the bailiff or the lady's-maid, and his "corner" was of the very poorest, although he and his wife and children made a family of seven. The "corners" had been built by the late master in this way. In a stone hut twenty-three feet square a Russian stove was placed in the center; all round it was the "collidor" (as the house-serfs called it), and at each angle a "corner" was partitioned off with boards. Space was consequently not plentiful, especially in Polikey's corner, which was nearest the door. The conjugal·couch with quilted counterpane and cotton chintz pillows, the hanging cradle with the baby, the three-legged table at which the cooking and the washing were done, and on which all the household goods were put, and at which Polikey himself did his work (he was a horse-doctor), tubs, clothes, fowls, a calf, and the seven of themselves filled up the whole "corner"; and they could not have stirred had not the common stove offered them one quarter of its surface on which things and persons could impartially be laid, and had it not been possible, too, to find an outlet on the steps. That, though, was hardly possible; in October it was cold, and their winter clothes consisted of a solitary sheepskin for the seven; but then the children could keep warm by running, and the grown-up folks by work, and both could creep onto the stove where the warmth rose to forty degrees Centigrade.

It must be terrible, one imagines, to live in such conditions, but it did not trouble them—one could get on all right. Akulina washed and mended for her husband and children, spun and wove and bleached her linen, cooked and baked in the common oven, quarreled and gossiped with the neighbors. There were not only monthly rations enough for the children, but litter for the cow as well. Kindling wood was free, and food for the beasts too. Hay too from the stable sometimes came their way. There was a strip of kitchen garden. Their cow had calved; they had their own chickens. Polikey worked in the stables, looked after two colts, and bled the horses and cattle; cleaned their hoofs, cured them of worms, and applied an ointment of his own invention, and a few coppers and provisions were bestowed on him for this. There were leavings of the oats too to be picked up. In the village there was a peasant who regularly, every month, gave him twenty pounds of mutton for two measures of oats. One could have got on well enough if there had been nothing to trouble the heart. But trouble there was, and plenty of it for all the family. Polikey had been in his youth in another village at a stud stable. The stable-keeper into whose hands he came was the greatest thief in the whole district; at last he was sent away to a penal settlement. From this stable-keeper Polikey received his training; and owing to his youth, he had grown so used to "these trifles," that he couldn't give them up even when he'd have been glad to. He was a young man, and weak; he had no father or mother, and no one to teach him. Polikey liked drink, and did not like anything lying about in the wrong place. Whether it was a rope or a pad, or a lock or a bolt, or something of more value, Polikey Ilyich found a place for everything. There were people everywhere who would take these articles and pay for them in spirits or money, according to agreement. Such wages are the easiest earned, as the people say; no apprenticeship nor labor—nothing is needed—and if once you try it, you never care for other work after. There's only one drawback to such gains: though everything's to be had cheap and without toil, and the life's pleasant as a rule, all of a sudden this line of business will come to grief through ill-disposed folk, and one has to pay for everything, and may find life a burden.

That was just what happened with Polikey. Polikey had married; God had given him good luck; his wife, the cowherd's daughter, had turned out a healthy, clever, hard-working woman, had borne him children, each finer than the last. Polikey still stuck to his line of business, and all went well. All at once a mischance befell him, and he was caught. And caught for the merest trifle; he had popped away some leather reins at a peasant's. They found them, beat him, reported it to the mistress, and began to keep an eye on him. A second and a third time he was caught. Folk began to cry shame on him, the bailiff threatened sending him for a soldier, the mistress reprimanded him, his wife began crying and fretting. . . . Everything went utterly wrong! He was a good-natured fellow, and no harm in him, only weak, liked a drop of drink, and had made such a habit of this sort of thing that he could not give it up anyhow. Sometimes his wife would start rating at him, even beating him when he came home drunk, and he'd cry. "Unlucky fellow I am," he would say. "What can I do? Blind my eyes, but I'll give it up, I will." A month later you'd see him leaving home again, going off drinking, and staying away for two days. "He must have got the money from somewhere for his spree," folks reasoned. His last exploit was with the countinghouse clock. There was in the countinghouse an old clock hanging on the wall; it hadn't gone for a long while. He chanced to go into the countinghouse alone; he took a fancy to the clock, carried it off, and disposed of it in the town. As ill-luck would have it, the shopkeeper to whom he sold the clock happened to be related by marriage to one of the house-serfs, and he came to the village for a feast-day, and told them about the clock. Folks began making inquiries, just as though it were anybody's concern. The bailiff in particular did not like Polikey. And they found the culprit. They reported it to the mistress. The mistress sent for Polikey. He fell at her feet at once, and with feeling, touchingly, made a full confession, as his wife had told him to do. He carried out all her instructions very well. The mistress began reasoning with him, talked away, preached away; talked of God, and of virtue, and of the future life, and of his wife, and of his children, and reduced him to tears. The mistress said—

"I forgive you; only promise me you will never do it again."

"I never will; may I sink into the ground, may my guts burst if I do!" said Polikey, and he wept pathetically.

Polikey went home, and lay on the stove, bellowing like a calf all day. Since then nothing had once been traced to Polikey. But his life had not been a gay one; folks looked on him as a thief, and as the time for levying recruits drew near, everyone began to point to him.

Polikey was a horse-doctor, as already stated. How he had all at once become so no one knew, and he less than anyone. In the stud stables, under the man who had been sent to a settlement, he had performed no duty except clearing the dung out of the horse-boxes, sometimes rubbing down the horses, and bringing water. There he could not have learnt his art. Then he had been a weaver; then he had worked in the garden, weeding paths; then, as a punishment, he had been sent to the brickyard; then, being allowed to go off on payment of a fixed sum a year to his master, he went into service as house-porter to a merchant. So there too he could not have had practice in his art. But the last time he came home a belief gradually somehow gained ground in his extraordinary, in fact, almost supernatural, knowledge of the veterinary art. He let blood—once, and a second time—then laid a horse on its back, and probed something in its leg, then insisted on the horse being placed in a trave and began cutting its frog till the blood came, in spite of the struggles and even screams of the horse, and said that this meant "letting off the under-hoof blood." Then he explained to the peasant that it was essential to take blood from both veins "for greater ease," and began tapping with a mallet on his blunt lancet. Next he bound a bandage made of the selvedge of his wife's kerchief round the belly of the porter's horse. Finally he took to sprinkling all sorts of sores with vitriol, wetting them with liquid out of a bottle, and sometimes giving internally what he thought fit. And the more horses he tortured and did to death, the more they believed in him, and the more horses were brought to him.

I feel that it's not quite for us gentlefolks to laugh at Polikey. The means to which he resorted to inspire confidence were exactly the same as those which have been effectual with our fathers and with us, and will be so with our children. The peasant lies with his belly on the head of his solitary nag, who is not merely his chief wealth, but almost one of his family, and gazes with faith and horror at Polikushka's significantly puckered-up face, and his thin arms with the sleeves tucked up, as he purposely squeezes the very spot that is painful, and boldly cuts into the living flesh, with the private reflection, "Here goes, come what may!" while he puts on an air of knowing where is blood and where pus, which is a tendon and which a blood vessel, holding in his teeth a healing rag or a bottle of vitriol. The peasant, watching him, cannot conceive that Polikushka's hand is raised to cut in ignorance. Himself he could not do that. And as soon as the incision is made, he cannot face the self-reproach of having given the poor beast to be cut up for nothing. I don't know how it may be with you, reader, but in my dealings with a doctor, torturing at my request those dearest to my heart, I have had precisely the same experience. The lancet and the mysterious whitish bottle of corrosive sublimate, and the words, "the staggers," "farcy," "let blood," "matter," and so on, are they not much the same as "neurosis," "rheumatism," "organisms," and so on? *Wage du zu irren und zu träumen*—that does not apply so much to poets as to doctors and to veterinary surgeons.

### III

On the same evening, while the village meeting buzzed round the countinghouse in the still October darkness, choosing the recruits, Polikey was sitting on the edge of the bed, pounding with a bottle on the table a medicine of which he knew nothing to cure a horse ailment of which he knew as little. It contained corrosive sublimate, sulphur, Glauber's salts, and a herb which Polikey had gathered, having suddenly decided that this herb would be very good for a broken-winded horse, and fancying it would not be amiss to give it also for other ailments. The children were already lying down—two on the stove, two in the bed, and one in the hanging cradle, at which Akulina was sitting busy with her yarn. A candle-end, a relic of some candles from the mistress's house that had been left lying about, stood in a wooden candlestick in the window; and that her husband might not break off from his important occupation, Akulina got up to snuff it with her fingers. There were independent spirits who considered Polikey a poor sort of doctor and a poor sort of man. Others, and they were the majority, regarded him as not much of a man, but a great master in his own line. Akulina, although she often scolded and even beat her husband, believed him to be incontestably the best horse-doctor and the best man in the world. Polikey sprinkled some simple on the palm of his hand. (He never made use of scales, and would allude ironically to Germans, who use them. "This," he would say, "is not an apothecary's!") Polikey weighed his simple in his hand, and shook it; but it seemed too little to him, and he scattered in ten times as much. "I'll put it all in; it'll pick 'em up better," he said to himself. Akulina looked round quietly at the voice of her lord and master, expecting some command; but seeing that the matter did not concern her, she shrugged her shoulders. "He's a deep one! How does he come by it all?" she thought, and took up her spinning again. The paper from which the drug was shaken fell under the table. Akulina did not let that pass unnoticed.

"Anyutka!" she called. "See what father's lost; pick it up."

Anyutka drew her thin, bare legs from under the old gown that served her as a quilt, crept like a kitten under the table, and picked up the paper.

"Here, daddy," she said, and dived into the bed again with her frozen little feet.

"Why are you pushing me?" whined her younger sister, lisping in a sleepy voice.

"I'll give it you!" said Akulina, and both heads vanished under the old gown.

"Three silver roubles he'll give," said Polikey, corking the bottle. "I shall cure the horse. Cheap, too," he added. "Brain-racking work, I say! . . . Akulina, run round and ask Nikita to lend me a pinch of tobacco. I'll pay him back tomorrow."

And Polikey took out of his trousers a limewood pipe, once painted, with sealing-wax at the mouthpiece, and began filling it.

Akulina left her spindle and went out without coming into collision with anything, which was a feat of some difficulty. Polikey opened a cupboard, put the bottle in it, and raised to his lips an empty flask, but there was no spirit left in it. He groaned; but when his wife brought the tobacco, and he had filled up his pipe, lighted it, and sat down on the bed, his face beamed with the pride and satisfaction of a man who has completed his day's work. Whether he was thinking how next day he would catch hold of the horse's tongue and pour into its mouth that amazing mixture, or whether he was reflecting that when a man's an indispensable person no one will refuse him anything—Nikita had just sent him the tobacco—anyway he was in good spirits. Suddenly the door, which hung on one hinge, was flung back, and into their "corner" came a maid from *up yonder* —not the second maid, but the third, the little one who was kept for errands. *Up yonder*, as everyone knows, always means the master's house, even though it be downhill. Aksyutka (that was the girl's name) always flew like a bullet; and as she ran, her arms hung straight and swung like a pendulum in time with her rapid movement, not at her sides, but in front of her person. Her cheeks were always rosier than her pink dress; her tongue always moved as rapidly as her legs. She flew into the room, and clutching for some reason at the stove, began swaying to and fro; and as though she were in such haste that she seemed to try to bring out two or three words at once, she suddenly articulated breathlessly, addressing Akulina:

"Mistress gave orders for Polikey Ilyich to come this minute up yonder; she gave orders . . ." She stopped, and drew a deep breath. "Yegor Mihailovich has been with the mistress; they've been talking of the recruits, mentioned Polikey Ilyich . . . Avdotya Mikolavna sent word to come this minute. Avdotya Mikolavna sent word" (again a sigh) "he's to come this minute."

For half a minute Aksyutka stared at Polikey, at Akulina, at the children, who peeped out from under the quilt, snatched up a nutshell which was lying on the stove, flung it at Anyutka, and articulating once more, "To come this minute," she flew like a whirlwind out of the room, and the pendulums swung with their usual rapidity across the line of her flight.

Akulina rose again and got her husband his boots—they were wretched, torn, soldiers' boots—took his coat from the stove and gave it to him, without looking at him.

"Ilyich, won't you change your shirt?"

"No," said Polikey.

Akulina did not once glance at his face while he was putting on his boots and his coat, and she did well not to glance at him. Polikey's face was pale, his lower jaw was twitching, and in his eyes there was that tearful, meek, profoundly unhappy expression which is only seen in good-natured, weak, sinful persons. He combed his hair and would have gone out, but his wife stopped him and tucked in a tape of his shirt, which was hanging out on his coat, and put on his cap.

"What, Polikey Ilyich, is it the mistress is wanting you?" they heard the voice of the carpenter's wife asking behind the screen. The carpenter's wife had only that morning had an intensely unpleasant scene with Akulina over a pot of lye, which the Polikey children had upset in her place, and she was at once delighted to hear that Polikey was summoned to the mistress: it was sure to be for no good. Moreover, she was a subtle, diplomatic lady, with an evil tongue. No one knew better than she did how to take the shine out of anyone with a word; such, at least, was her own conviction about herself.

"I suppose they want to send to town for some purchases," she went on. "I imagine that they choose a trustworthy man, and so they're sending you. You might buy me a quarter of a pound of tea there, Polikey Ilyich."

Akulina suppressed her tears, and her lips tightened into an expression of fury. She could have pulled the nasty hair of that wretch, the carpenter's wife. But as she glanced at her children and thought that they would be left fatherless, and she a soldier's widow, she forgot the spiteful carpenter's wife, hid her face in her hands, sat down on the bed, and her head sank into the pillows.

"Muvver, you're squashing me," lisped the little girl, pulling the covering from under her mother's elbows.

"I wish you were all dead! For sorrow I brought you into the world!" cried Akulina, and the whole "corner" was filled with her sobs, to the glee of the carpenter's wife, who had not yet forgotten the lye spilt that morning.

## IV

Half an hour passed by. The baby began to cry. Akulina got up and fed it. She was not crying now; but with her still handsome, thin face propped in her hand, she sat quietly with her eyes on the burnt-down candle, and pondered the question why she had married, why so many soldiers were wanted, and how, too, she was to pay out the carpenter's wife.

She heard her husband's steps; she wiped away the traces of her tears and got up to make way for him. Polikey came in as bold as brass, flung his cap on the bed, drew a long breath, and began undoing his belt.

"Well, why did she send for you?"

"H'm . . . of course! Polikushka's the least of men; but when there's business to be done, then who's wanted? Polikushka."

"What sort of business?"

Polikey was in no haste to reply; he lighted his pipe and spat.

"I'm to go to the merchant's to fetch some money."

"To fetch money?" asked Akulina.

Polikey chuckled and wagged his head.

"A clever one she is, too, with words. . . . 'You,' says she, 'were under observation because you were an untrustworthy man, but I trust you more than any other.' " (Polikey spoke loudly, so that the neighbors might hear.) " 'You promised me to reform,' says she, 'so here's the first proof that I trust you; set off,' says she, 'to the merchant, take the money, and bring it here.' I says, 'Madam,' says I, 'we are all your serfs, and bound, as we would·serve God, to serve you, so I feel that I would do anything for your welfare, and from no duty could I cry off; what you command, that I do, since I am your slave.' " (Again he smiled that peculiar smile of a weak, good-natured, and guilty man.) " 'So,' says she, 'you'll do it faithfully? You understand,' says she, 'that your fate depends on it?' 'Could I fail to understand that I must do everything? If they have slandered me, why, there's none that can't be blamed; but I never could, I do believe, ever have a thought against your welfare.' . . . So, to be sure, I talked to her, till my lady became quite soft. 'You,' says she, 'shall be my chief man . . . ' " (He paused, and again the same smile lingered on his face.) "I know just how to talk to them. When I was away working for hire, didn't I come across queer customers! But only let me come to talk to them. I'd soften them till they would be like silk."

"And is it a lot of money?" asked Akulina.

"Fifteen hundred roubles," Polikey responded carelessly.

She shook her head.

"When are you to go?"

"Tomorrow, she said. 'Take any horse you like,' says she, 'go to the countinghouse, and set off in God's name.' "

"Praise be to Thee, O Lord!" said Akulina, getting up and crossing herself. "God help you, Ilyich," she added in a whisper, that they might not hear on the other side of the partition, and pulling him by the sleeve of his shirt, "Ilyich, listen to me! For Christ's sake, I beseech you, kiss the cross when you set off, that you won't let a drop of anything pass your lips."

"As if I would drink with all that money about me!" he snorted.

"But, I say, there was someone playing away smartly on the piano there, grand!" he added, pausing and chuckling. "The young lady, no doubt. I stood like this before the old lady, at the whatnot; while the young lady there, through the door, didn't she rattle up and down the piano, and dash it off in fine style. I should like to play, upon my word I should. I know I could do it, that I could. I'm a smart chap at such things. Give me a clean shirt for tomorrow."

And they went to bed happy.

## V

Meanwhile the meeting in front of the countinghouse was going on noisily. It was no jesting matter that was in question. The peasants were almost all present; and while Yegor Mihailovich was with their mistress, they put their caps on, more voices were suddenly audible in the general buzz, and the voices were louder. The roar of bass voices, broken now and then by a breathless, husky, shrill speech, filled the air; and that roar floated across, like the sound of a booming sea, to the windows of the mistress, who was sensible of a nervous uneasiness at that sound, like the feeling before the outbreak of a violent storm. It was a feeling between dread and dislike. She kept fancying that now the voices were growing louder and noisier, and that something was happening. "As though they couldn't do it all quietly, peaceably, without strife and shouting," she thought, "according to the Christian law, in brotherly love and meekness."

Many voices were speaking at once, but Fyodor Rezun, the carpenter, shouted loudest. He was the head of a household with two sons, and was attacking the Dutlovs. Old Dutlov was defending himself; he stepped out in front of the crowd, behind which he had at first been standing; and waving his arms and pulling his beard, he talked with such frequent snufflings in his throat and nose, that it would have been hard for him to make out himself what he was saying. His children and nephews, strapping fellows, stood huddled behind him, and old Dutlov suggested the hen in the game of "Hawk and Chickens." The hawk was Rezun, and not Rezun only, but all the heads of families with two sons and fathers of only sons, almost all the meeting, in fact, pouncing down on Dutlov. The point was that Dutlov's brother had, thirty years before, been sent for a soldier, and so Dutlov wished to be excused from taking his turn with the families which had three members of military age, but wanted his brother's service to be reckoned, and said that his family should be put on a par with those which had only two eligible sons, and that the third recruit should be chosen by lot from among all those families. There were four other families with three men eligible for recruits in them besides Dutlov's. But one was the village elder, and he had been exempted by the mistress; from another family a recruit had been sent at the last levy; from the remaining two families two recruits had been chosen, and one of them had not even come to the meeting, though his wife was standing mournfully behind the others, blankly awaiting some turn in her fortunes. The father of the other chosen recruit, red-haired Roman, in a torn smock, though he was not poor, stood leaning against the steps with downcast head, and did not open his mouth, only now and then gazing intently at anyone who was talking loudly, and then looking down again. His whole figure was eloquent of misery. Old Semyon Dutlov was a man to whom anyone who had the slightest acquaintance with him would have readily intrusted hundreds and thousands of roubles. He was a steady, God-fearing, responsible man; he was, moreover, the church elder. All the more striking was his violent excitement at this moment.

Rezun, the carpenter, was, on the contrary, a tall, black-haired, drunken, turbulent man, bold and particularly clever in disputes and discussions at village meetings, at bazaars, with workmen, merchants, peasants, and gentry alike. Now he was self-possessed and sarcastic; and with all his superior height, all the force of his loud voice and oratorical talent, he overpowered the husky church elder, who was completely thrown out of the steady groove he always moved in. Among others taking part in the discussion was a roundfaced, squat, youngish fellow, with a square head and curly beard, Garaska Kopylov, one of the regular talkers of the younger generation, who followed Rezun's lead. He was always conspicuous for his abrupt speech, and had already gained a certain weight at the village meetings. Then there was Fyodor Melnichny, a long, thin, yellow-faced, stooping peasant, young too, with a scanty beard and little eyes, always bitter and gloomy, always seeing the bad side of everything, and often bewildering the meeting by his unexpected and disconnected questions and remarks. Both these speakers were on the side of Rezun. Besides these, there were two chatterboxes. who put in their word continually; one with a good-natured face and a bushy flaxen beard, Hrapkov, who was always beginning, "But, my dear fellow!" and the other, a little man, with a birdlike countenance, Zhidkov, who also began with an invariable preface, "It follows, my lads!" addressing everyone, and talking away without rhyme or reason. Both of these were first on one side and then on the other, but no one heeded them. There were others of the same sort, but these two who kept mincing through the crowd and shouting louder than all, to the alarm of the mistress, were listened to less than any; intoxicated with the noise and shouting, they gave themselves up entirely to the pleasure of letting their tongues wag.

There were many more peasants of different sorts: gloomy, decorous, indifferent, or depressed. There were peasant-women, too, behind the men, with sticks in their hands, but of all of them, please God, I will tell another time. The bulk of the crowd consisted of peasants, who stood at the meeting, as they did in church, talking in a whisper behind the others of domestic matters, of when they would cart home the faggots in the copse, or waiting in silence for the racket to be over. There were rich ones, too, whose prosperity the meeting could neither increase nor detract from. Such was Yermil, with his broad, shiny face, whom the peasants nicknamed Fat Belly, because he was rich. Such, too, was Starostin, whose face wore a complacent expression of power. "You may talk all you like," it seemed to say, "but no one can touch me. I've four sons, but not one of them will they take." Now and then some bold spirit, like Kopylov and Rezun, would try to pick a quarrel with them, and they answered, but calmly and firmly, with a sense of their own security.

If Dutlov was like the hen in the game of "Hawk and Chickens," his lads did not quite suggest chickens; they did not fidget uneasily, nor cackle, but stood calmly behind him. The elder, Ignat, was thirty years old; the second, Vasily, was married too, but not suitable for a recruit; the third, Ilyushka, the nephew, who had only just been married, a pink-and-white young fellow in a smart sheepskin (he used to go out as a driver), stood watching the people, and sometimes scratching his head under his hat, as though it were all no concern of his, though he it was whom the hawks were trying to pounce upon.

"For that matter, my grandfather also was a soldier," said one, "and so I'll cry off the lots too."

"There's no law like that, brother! Last levy they took Miheichev, and his uncle hadn't come home yet."

"You've neither father nor uncle that served the Czar," Dutlov was saying at the same time. "No, and you yourself have served neither your masters nor your mir. You do nothing but drink, and your children have parted from you because there's no living with you; so, you point to others. But I was village constable ten years; I've been elder; twice I've been burned out—no one helped me; and just because in our house it's all peaceable and decent, am I to be ruined? Give me back my brother. He's dead out there, for sure. Judge truly, in God's way, Orthodox folk, and be not led astray by a drunkard's ravings."

At precisely the same moment Garaska was saying to Dutlov:

"You talk about your brother, but he wasn't sent by the mir, but the masters sent him for his debauchery; so he's nothing for you to get off by."

Garaska had not finished when the lank, bilious Fyodor Melnichny, stepping forward, began:

"Yes, the gentry send whom they please, and then the mir may choose. The mir has decreed for your son to go; and if you don't like it, ask the mistress. She'll maybe send me, singlehanded as I am, to shave my head and leave my children. That's your law!" he said bitterly, and waving his arm again, he went back to his former position.

Red-haired Roman, whose son had been chosen, lifted his head, and brought out, "Yes, that's so, that's so!" and sank back onto the step in vexation.

But these were not all the voices that were speaking at once. Besides those who, standing in the background, were talking of their own affairs, the chatterboxes, too, did not forget to do their part.

"To be sure, Orthodox folk," said little Zhidkov, repeating Dutlov's words, "we must judge like Christians. Like Christians, to be sure, my lads, we must judge."

"We must decide according to our conscience, my good friend," put in the simple-hearted Hrapkov, repeating the words of Kopylov, and pulling Dutlov by his sheepskin; "that was a matter of the master's will, and not the decision of the mir."

"True! So it was, sure," said others.

"Who's a drunkard raving?" retorted Rezun. "Did you give me

drink, eh? or is your son, who's been picked up by the roadside, going to reproach me for drinking? Come, lads, we must come to a decision. If you want to spare Dutlov, you'd best pitch on a lad out of a family of two, or an only son, while you're about it; and he'll make a laughingstock of us."

"It's for a Dutlov to go. Why talk about it?"

"We all know it's for those that have three sons to draw the lots first," said voices.

"We've still to see what the mistress's orders are. Yegor Mihailovich was saying they meant to send a house-serf," said a voice.

This remark checked the dispute a little, but soon it flickered up again, and again passed into personalities.

Ignat, of whom Rezun had said that he had been picked up by the roadside, began to make out that Rezun had stolen a saw from some traveling carpenters, and had almost beaten his wife to death when he was drunk.

Rezun replied that he beat his wife both drunk and sober, and even so never beat her enough, and made everyone laugh thereby. But about the saw, he became suddenly offended, stepped closer up to Ignat, and asked:

"Who stole it?"

"You stole it!" the sturdy Ignat answered boldly, stepping still nearer to him.

"Who stole it? Wasn't it you?" shouted Rezun.

"No, you!" shouted Ignat.

After the saw they passed to the theft of a horse, to a sack of oats, to a certain strip of vegetable garden, to a certain dead body; and the two peasants said such awful things of each other that, if a hundredth part of their accusations had been true, they ought both by law to have been sent to Siberia at least.

Old Dutlov meanwhile had chosen another line of defense. He did not like his son's shouting. Stopping him, he said, "Shame—give over, I tell you!" and himself began to argue that families of three were not only those who had three sons living together, but those families which had broken up too; and he referred too to Starostin.

Starostin smiled faintly, cleared his throat, and stroking his beard with the manner of a well-to-do peasant, answered that the mistress's will had decided that. His son must have deserved it if the order was to pass him over.

As to divided families, Garaska too shattered Dutlov's arguments, observing that families ought never to have been allowed to break up, as it was in the old master's time; but that after the summer was over, there was no picking raspberries; that, as it was, you couldn't draft the only man left in a family.

"Is it to please themselves that they broke up? Why utterly ruin them now?" cried the voices of members of divided families, and the regular chatterboxes joined those voices.

"You buy a recruit, if you don't like it; you can afford it," said Rezun to Dutlov.

Dutlov wrapped his coat about him despairingly, and stood behind the other peasants.

"You've counted my money, it seems," he remarked angrily. "Let's see what Yegor Mihailovich will say when he comes from the mistress."

## VI

Yegor Mihailovich did in fact come out of the house at that moment. One cap after another was lifted over the heads, and as the bailiff approached one head after another uncovered—bald, at the top and in front, gray, grizzled, red, black, or flaxen—and gradually the voices subsided, till at last all was perfectly still. Yegor Mihailovich stood on the steps, and made a sign that he was going to speak. In his long coat, with his hands thrust awkwardly into his front pockets, in a factory-made forage cap, pulled down in front, Yegor Mihailovich stood firmly, his legs wide apart, and in his elevated position towered above those mostly old and mostly handsome bearded heads, raised and turned towards him. He looked very different from the way he had looked before his mistress. He was majestic.

"Here, lads, is the mistress's decision. It's not her pleasure to give up any of the house-serfs; but whomever you choose among yourselves, he will go. This time we need three; by rights, two and a half, but the half will have to go in advance. It's all the same; if not now, it would be next time."

"To be sure, that's a fact!" said voices.

"In my judgment," continued Yegor Mihailovich, "for Horyushkin and Mityuhin's Vaska to go, is God's own will."

"And so it is, indeed!" said voices.

"The third must be a Dutlov, or else one out of the families with two sons. What do you say?"

"Dutlov," said voices. "The Dutlovs have three!"

And again little by little the shouting began, and again it came back to the strip of garden, and to certain pieces of sacking stolen from the mistress's yard. Yegor Mihailovich had managed the estate now for twenty years, and was a shrewd and experienced man. He stood awhile, listened for a quarter of an hour, and suddenly commanded all to be silent, and bade the Dutlovs draw lots which of the three they would send. The lots were cut. Hrapkov began to draw them out of a hat in which they were shaken, and he drew Ilyushka's. All were silent.

"Mine, is it? Show it here," said Ilyushka in a breaking voice.

All were silent. Yegor Mihailovich bade them bring on the morrow the recruit's money, seven copecks from each family, and announcing that all was at an end, dismissed the meeting. The crowd moved off, putting on their caps round the corner, with a hum of talk and footsteps. The bailiff stood on the steps, looking after the retreating figures. When the younger Dutlovs had gone round the corner, he beckoned to the old man, who had of his own accord lingered, and went with him into the countinghouse.

"I'm sorry for you, old man," said Yegor Mihailovich, sitting down in an arm-chair before the table; "it was your turn. Will you buy your nephew off or not?"

The old man glanced significantly at Yegor Mihailovich without replying.

"There's no getting out of it," Yegor Mihailovich said in reply to his look.

"And glad we'd be to buy him off, but we haven't the money to do it, Yegor Mihailovich! Two horses died in the summer, and then there was my nephew's wedding. It seems our fate would have it so . . . because we live honestly. It's very well for him to talk." (He meant Rezun.)

Yegor Mihailovich rubbed his face with his hand and yawned. He was unmistakably weary of the business, and it was time for his tea.

"Ah, old man, don't fall into sin!" he said. "Look well under your floor. Maybe you'll find the old silver roubles to make up the four hundred. I'd buy you such a substitute, a perfect wonder! The other day a man offered himself—"

"In the city?" asked Dutlov.

"Why, will you buy him?"

"And I'd be glad to, before God, but—"

Yegor Mihailovich cut him short sternly.

"Well, then, listen to me, old man; mind Ilyushka doesn't do himself a mischief, and produce him at once when I send for him—either today or tomorrow. You produce him, you will have to answer for him; but if, God forbid, anything were to happen to him, I shall take your elder son to be shaved for a soldier. You hear?"

"But can't any of the families of two furnish a recruit, Yegor Mihailovich? Why, it's unfair," he said after a pause, "when my brother's dead a soldier, to take the son, too. Why should such a calamity fall on me?" he said, almost weeping, and ready to fall at his feet.

"Come, go along, go along," said Yegor Mihailovich; "there's nothing can be done, it's the law. Keep an eye on Ilyushka; you must answer for him."

Dutlov went homewards, mournfully flicking at the clods of the road with a limewood switch.

## VII

Next day, early in the morning, there stood at the steps of the house-serfs' quarters the cart in which the bailiff used to drive about on his rounds, with a big-boned bay gelding, for some unknown reason called Drum, in the shafts. In spite of the rain and hail and the cold wind, Anyutka, Polikey's eldest daughter, was standing barefoot at the horse's head, in obvious alarm, holding him a long way off with one hand on the bridle, while with the other she kept on her head the yellow-green wadded jacket, which the family used as quilt, cloak, headdress, carpet, overcoat for Polikey, and in many other ways. A great bustle was going on within. It was still dark; the morning light of the rainy day faintly glimmered in at the window, pasted up here and there with paper. Akulina had left her baking in the oven for a while, and also her children, of whom the smaller ones were shivering in bed, as their covering had been taken to be used as a garment, and in its place they had been given only their mother's head shawl. Akulina was busy getting her husband ready for the journey. His shirt was clean. His boots, which, as the saying goes, were begging for porridge, caused her particular anxiety. To begin with, she took off her own solitary pair of thick woolen stockings and gave them to her husband; and secondly, out of a saddle cloth, which had been lying about in the stable, and been brought to their hut by Polikey a couple of days before, she had contrived to make inner soles in such a way as to stop up the holes, and to keep Polikey's feet from getting wet. Polikey, seated with his feet on the bedstead, was engrossed in twisting his belt round so that it should not look like a dirty cord. And the cross, lisping little girl in a cloak, which even when put on over her head still tripped up her feet, had been dispatched to Nikita to beg the loan of a cap. The bustle was increased by house-serfs coming in to ask Polikey to buy for them in the town—needles for one, tea for another, olive oil for a third, tobacco for a fourth, and sugar for the carpenter's wife, who had already managed to have the samovar ready—and to propitiate Polikey, had brought him in a jug a decoction which she called tea. Though Nikita refused to lend the cap, and it was necessary to get his own into a fit state, that is, to poke in the stuffing that had burst and was hanging out, and with a veterinary needle to sew up the hole; though the boots with the saddle-cloth patches would not at first go on his feet; though Anyutka got frozen and let Drum go, and then Mashka had to put on the cloak to take her place, and then Mashka had to take off the cloak, and Akulina herself went to hold Drum—in the end Polikey had at last put on all the clothing of the family, leaving only one jacket and a pair of slippers, and fully equipped, seated himself in the cart, wrapped himself up, arranged the hay, once more wrapped himself up, picked up the reins, wrapped himself still more compactly, as very sedate persons do, and started.

His little boy, Mishka, running out onto the steps, begged for a ride. The lisping Mashka too began begging, "Let me wide and I sall be warm wivout a cloak"; and Polikey pulled up Drum, smiled his weak smile, while Akulina sat the children in beside him; and bending over to him, besought him in a whisper to remember his oath and not to touch a drop on the way. Polikey took the children as far as the smithy, put them down, muffled himself up again, again set his cap straight, and drove off alone at a steady little trot, his

cheeks quivering with the jolting, and his feet knocking on the bark
lining of the cart. Mashka and Mishka ran barefoot home down the
slippery hillside with such swiftness and such shrieks, that a dog,
running from the village to the serfs' quarters, stared at them; and
suddenly putting its tail between its legs, fled home barking, at which
the heirs of Polikey redoubled their shrieks.

It was miserable weather, the wind cut his face, and something
like snow and rain and hail at once beat persistently in Polikey's
face and on his bare hands, which he stuffed, holding the chilly reins,
up the sleeves of his coat. The wet sleet blew on the leather cover of
the horse-collar too, and on the head of old Drum, who twitched his
ears and blinked.

Then the snow suddenly ceased, and it cleared in an instant;
bluish snow clouds could be seen distinctly; and the sun began as
it were to peep out, but uncertainly and cheerlessly, like the smile of
Polikey himself. In spite of that, Polikey was plunged in agreeable
reflections. He whom they'd wanted to deport to a settlement, whom
they threatened to send for a soldier, whom everyone who was
not too lazy abused and beat, whom they always shoved into the
worst place—he was driving now to receive a *sum of money*, and a
large sum, too, and the mistress trusted him, and he was driving in the
bailiff's cart with Drum, with whom the mistress drove out sometimes, driving like some upper servant, with leather straps and reins.
And Polikey sat up straighter, set the stuffing in his cap right, and
wrapped himself up once more. If Polikey supposed, however, that
he looked exactly like some well-to-do innkeeper, he was in error.
It is true, indeed, as everyone knows, that men who do business in
tens of thousands drive about in carts with leather harness, but that's
not the same thing. A man with a beard, in a blue or a black long
coat, comes along driving a horse and sitting alone on the box—you
just have to look whether the horse is sleek, whether he's well fed
himself, how he's sitting, how the horse is harnessed, what the tires
of the wheels are like, how the man is belted, and you can see at
once whether the man does business in hundreds or in thousands.
Any man of experience would only have had to look close at Polikey,
at his hands, at his face, at his beard that he had lately let grow, at
his belt, at the hay carelessly flung into the cart, at thin Drum, at the
worn tires, to see at once that this was a poor serf driving and not
a merchant, not a drover, not an innkeeper, and that he didn't do

business in thousands, or in hundreds, or even in tens of roubles. But Polikey did not think so. He was in error, and the error was an agreeable one. He was to carry back fifteen hundred paper roubles in his bosom. If he liked, he could turn Drum's head towards Odessa instead of homewards, and drive off God knows where. Only that he would not do, but would faithfully bring the money to his mistress, and would tell people that he'd had to bring larger sums than that.

On reaching a tavern, Drum began pulling at the left rein, slackening his pace, and turning towards it. But Polikey, although he had the money given him to make purchases with, cracked the whip at Drum and drove by. He did the same thing too at another tavern, and towards midday got out of the cart, and opening the gate of the inn at which all his mistress's people used to stop led in the horse, unharnessed the cart, gave the horse some hay, dined with the innkeeper's workmen, not omitting to mention what important business he had come about, and went off with the letter in his cap to the gardener's.

The gardener, who knew Polikey, read the letter, and with evident doubt questioned him, whether he really had been told to take the money. Polikey would have liked to resent this, but did not know how to, and simply smiled his smile. The gardener read the letter again and handed him the money. Polikey took the money, put it in his bosom, and went back to the tavern. Neither beer-house nor gin-shop—nothing tempted him. He was conscious of an agreeable tension in all his being, and more than once he stopped at shops with tempting wares—boots, coats, caps, cotton goods, and things to eat. And after stopping a little while, he walked away with an agreeable feeling, "I can buy it all, but see, I'm not doing it." He went to a bazaar for the things he had been commissioned to buy, got everything, and discussed the price of a fur coat, for which he was asked twenty-five roubles. The salesman, staring for some reason at Polikey, did not believe that he could buy it; but Polikey pointed to his bosom, saying he could buy up all the shop if he liked, and asked to try on the cloak, fingered it, stroked it, blew into the fur, even smelt at it, and at last with a sigh took it off.

"The price doesn't suit me. If you'd say fifteen roubles, then . . . ," said he. The shopkeeper angrily flung the coat across a table, while Polikey went out, and in excellent spirits made his way to the inn. After supper, and after having given water and oats to Drum, he climbed up on the stove, and pulling out the envelope, looked at it a long while, and asked a man who could read to read to him the address and the words, "With enclosure of a thousand, six hundred and seventeen roubles in notes." The envelope was made of plain paper, the seal was of brown wax, with anchors on it; one big one in the middle, four at the corners; there was a drop of sealing wax on the side. Polikey gazed at all this and studied it, and even felt the sharp edges of the notes. He felt a sort of childish pleasure in knowing there was so much money in his hands. He thrust the envelope into the lining of his cap, put the cap under his head, and lay down. But even in the night he waked up several times and felt the envelope. And every time finding the envelope in its place, he had an agreeable sensation in realizing that here was he, Polikey, disgraced, degraded, taking such a sum, and bringing it faithfully— more faithfully than if the bailiff himself had brought it.

## VIII

About midnight the innkeeper's servants and Polikey were waked by a knocking at the gate and the shouting of peasants. It was the recruits who were being brought from Pokrovskoe. There were ten men: Horyushkin, Mityuhin, and Ilya (Dutlov's nephew), a couple of men to replace them in case of accident, the village elder, old Dutlov, and three peasants who drove them. A night light was burning in the hut; the cook was asleep on the bench under the holy images. She jumped up and began lighting a candle. Polikey, too, waked, and stooping over from the top of the stove, began looking at the peasants as they came in. They all came in, crossed themselves, and sat down on the benches. They were all quite self-possessed, so that no one could have said which were the recruits and which were their escorts. They greeted the people in the hut, chatted merrily, and asked for something to eat. Some, it is true, were silent and depressed; but others were exceptionally lively, having unmistakably been drinking. Among the latter was Ilya, who had never drunk before.

"Well, lads, will you sup or go to sleep?" asked the elder.

"Supper!" answered Ilya, throwing open his overcoat and settling himself on a bench. "Send for some vodka."

"Enough of your vodka!" the elder dropped casually, and he turned again to the others. "Just take a bite of bread, lads. Why wake the folk up?"

"Give me vodka!" repeated Ilya, not looking at anyone in particular, and speaking in a tone that suggested that he would not easily give way.

The peasants followed the elder's advice, got their bread out of the cart, ate a little, and asked for some rye-beer, and lay down, some on the stove, and some on the floor.

Ilya kept repeating at intervals, "Give us some vodka; I tell you, vodka!" Suddenly he caught sight of Polikey. "Polikey, hey, Polikey! You here, my dear fellow? I'm going for a soldier, you see; I've said the last goodbye to my mother and my wife. . . . How she did wail! They've sent me for a soldier. . . . Stand us some vodka."

"No money," answered Polikey; "but still, please God, they may reject you," added Polikey, to comfort him.

"No, brother, I'm like a clean birch-tree; I've never had any disease. What chance of my being rejected? What better soldier could the Czar want?"

Polikey began to tell a story about how a peasant had given the doctor a bribe, and he had got him off for it.

Ilya moved nearer the stove and became talkative.

"No, Polikey, it's all over now, and I don't want to stay myself. Uncle's sent me off. Do you suppose he couldn't have bought me off? No, he grudged his son, and he grudged his money. They're giving me up. . . . Now, I don't care to stay myself." (He talked softly, confidentially, under the influence of subdued sadness.) "The only thing is, I'm sorry for mother; she's simply broken-hearted! And my wife too; they've simply ruined the poor wench for nothing; she's done for now—a soldier's wife, that's all you can say. Better not have married. What did they marry me for? They're coming tomorrow."

"But why did they bring you away so early?" asked Polikey; "there was nothing heard about it, and now all of a sudden you're off."

"They're frightened, d'ye see, I might do myself some mischief," answered Ilyushka, smiling. "No fear, I'll not do anything. I shall be all right even as a soldier, only it's mother I'm sorry for. Why did they marry me?" he said softly and dejectedly.

The door opened, shut with a slam, and old Dutlov, shaking his cap, walked in in his immense basketwork shoes, which were like boats on his feet.

"Afanasy," said he, crossing himself and addressing the inn-keeper's man, "haven't you a lantern for me to put the oats out by?"

Dutlov did not glance at Ilya, and began quietly lighting a candle end. His gloves and whip were stuffed into his belt, and his smock was carefully belted; he looked as collected as though he had come with a train of loaded carts; his toil-worn face looked as simple, quiet, and worried about his affairs as usual.

Ilya, seeing that his uncle had ceased speaking, again let his eyes rest gloomily on the bench, and began again, addressing the elder:

"Give us some vodka, Yermila. I want drink."

His voice was gloomy and wrathful.

"Drink at this·time?" answered·the elder, sipping his cup. "Don't you see folks have eaten and lain down, and why are you making a row?"

The word "row" obviously suggested an idea to Ilya.

"Elder, I'll make mischief if you don't give me vodka!"

"If you'd just make him listen to reason," said the elder to Dutlov, who had lighted his candle, but was standing still, evidently to hear what would come next; and was looking askance with com-miseration at his nephew, as though marvelling at his childishness.

Ilya, looking down, said again:

"Give me vodka; I'll make mischief."

"Give over, Ilya!" said the elder mildly, "give over. Really now, it will be better."

But he had hardly uttered these words when Ilya jumped up, struck his fist into the window, and shouted with all his might, "You wouldn't listen, so there you are!" and rushed to the other window to smash that one too.

Polikey, in the twinkling of an eye, rolled over twice and hid himself in the furthest corner of the stove, so that he frightened all the cockroaches. The elder flung down his spoon and ran up to Ilya. Dutlov slowly put down the candle, untied his belt, and shaking his head and clucking with his tongue, he went up to Ilya, who was by now struggling with the elder and the innkeeper's man, who would not let him get near the window. They had caught hold of him by his arms, and held him, it seemed, firmly; but as soon as Ilya saw his uncle with his belt, his strength seemed redoubled, he tore himself away and, with rolling eyes, stepped with clenched fists up to Dutlov.

"I'll kill you; don't come near me, brute! You've been the ruin of me; you with your ruffianly sons, you've ruined me. Why did you marry me? . . . Don't come near me, I'll kill you."

Ilyushka was terrible. His face was purple, his eyes were wild, his entire healthy young body was shaking as though in a fever. He seemed to wish to, and was really able to, kill all the three peasants who were moving upon him.

"You are drinking your own brother's blood, bloodsucker!"

There was a flash of anger in Dutlov's ever-serene face. He took a step forward.

"If you won't obey of yourself . . ." he said suddenly. With inexplicable energy he caught hold of his nephew by a sudden movement, rolled with him on the ground, and with the help of the elder began to bind his hands. They were struggling for five minutes. At last Dutlov, with the peasant's assistance, got up, pulling Ilya's hands away from his coat, at which he was clutching; he got up himself, then lifted Ilya up with his hands tied behind him, and seated him on the bench in a corner.

"I told you it would be the worse for you!" he said, still breathing hard from the struggle, and setting straight his shirt band. "Why sin? We shall all have to die. Put a cloak under his head," he added, turning to the innkeeper's man, "or else his head will ache." And he took up the candle, tied a bit of cord round his waist, and went out again to the horses.

Ilya, with ruffled hair, with a pale face and rumpled shirt, looked about the room, as though trying to remember where he was. The innkeeper's man collected the broken bits of window-pane and stuffed a coat into the window to prevent a draught. The elder sat down to his cup again.

"Ay, Ilyuha, Ilyuha! I'm sorry for you, truly. What can one do? Here's Horyushkin, he too a married man; there was no getting you off, it seems."

"It's to my uncle, that evil man, I owe my ruin!" Ilya repeated with intense fury. "He wouldn't give his own son. Mother told me, the bailiff bade him buy a recruit. He won't; he can't do it, he says.

Have my brother and I brought so little into the house? He's an evil man!"

Dutlov came into the hut, said his prayer to the holy pictures, took off his overcoat, and sat down with the elder. The servant gave him more rye-beer, and a spoon. Ilya was silent, and shutting his eyes, lay down on the cloak. The elder pointed to him without speaking and shook his head. Dutlov waved his hand.

"Do you suppose I'm not sorry? My own brother's son. And as if things weren't bad enough, they've made me out a scoundrel to him. It's been put into his head by his wife, I suppose—a sly wench, for all she's so young—that we've money, so that we could buy a recruit, and so here he brings it up against me. But how sorry I am for the lad!"

"Ah, a fine lad!" said the elder.

"But I can do nothing with him. Tomorrow I shall send Ignat to him, and his wife wanted to come."

"Send them; it'll do him good," said the elder, and he got up and climbed on the stove. "What is money? Money's dust and ashes."

"If one had the money, who would grudge it?" said one of the workmen, lifting up his head.

"Ah, money, money! Many a sin comes from it," Dutlov responded. "Nothing in the world brings so much sin as money, and it is said so in the Scriptures."

"All is said there," assented the workman. "And so a man told me; there was a merchant, he piled up a great deal of money, and did not want to leave anything behind; he so loved his money that he took it with him to the grave. When he came to die, all he bade them do was to lay his pillow with him in the coffin. They suspected nothing, and so they did. Then the sons began looking for his money; there was none anywhere. One son guessed that the money must be in the pillow. The matter was brought to the Czar—he allowed them to dig him up. And would you believe it? They opened the coffin; there was nothing in the pillow, but the coffin was full of maggots; so they buried it again. So that's what money brings!"

"To be sure, many a sin it brings," said Dutlov, and he got up and began saying his prayers.

When he had prayed, he looked at his nephew. He was asleep. Dutlov went up, took the belt off his hands, and lay down. The other peasant went off to sleep with the horses.

## IX

As soon as everything was still, Polikey climbed down stealthily, as though he were somehow guilty, and began making ready to.set off. For some reason he felt wretched at spending the night here with the recruits. The cocks were already crowing to one another more often. Drum had eaten all his oats, and was trying to get to the drinking-trough. Polikey harnessed him and led him past the peasants' carts. The cap with its contents was in safety, and the wheels of the cart rattled again along the half-frozen Pokrovskoe road. Polikey felt more at ease only when he had driven out of the town. Till then he kept fancying for some reason that he would hear pursuers behind him, that they would stop him, and tie his hands behind him, and take him next day to the recruiting station in Ilya's place. A chill ran down his back, half from cold, half from fright, and he kept urging Drum on. The first man to meet him was a priest, in a tall winter cap, walking with a one-eyed workman. Polikey felt still more uneasy. But outside the town this terror gradually passed away. Drum went at a walking pace; the road could be seen more distinctly in front. Polikey took off his cap and began feeling the money. "Should I put it in my bosom?" he thought; "I should have to undo my belt again. Let me get beyond the turning uphill, and I'll get out of the cart and set myself to rights. The cap's sewed up strongly at the top, and it couldn't come out through the lining. And I won't take my cap off till I get home." As he got down to the foot of the hill, Drum of his own accord galloped up the next hill, and Polikey, who was as eager as Drum to get home, did not hinder his doing so. Everything was right—so at least it seemed to him—and he abandoned himself to dreams of the gratitude of his mistress, of the five roubles she would give him, and of the joy of all at home. He took off his cap, felt the letter once more, stuck it more firmly on to his head, and smiled. The cloth of the cap was rotten, and just because Akulina had sewed it up so carefully where it was torn, it began to go at the other end; and the very movement by which Polikey, when he took the cap off, thought to thrust the letter further under the stuffing—that very action made a hole in the stuff and pushed the letter at one corner out of the cloth.

It began to get light; and Polikey, who had not slept all night, dozed. Pulling his cap lower down, and in so doing pushing the letter further out, Polikey, half asleep, began nodding his head against the side of the cart. He waked up near home. His first action was to clutch at his cap; it was sitting firmly on his head; he did not even take it off, feeling certain that the envelope was in it. He touched up Drum, set the hay in order, assumed once more the air of an innkeeper, and looking about him with dignity, rattled homewards.

Here was the kitchen, here the servants' wing, yonder the carpenter's wife carrying linen; yonder the countinghouse; and over there the mistress's house, where Polikey would prove immediately that he was a trustworthy and honest man. "Anyone may be slandered," he would say, and the mistress would reply, "Well, thank you, Polikey, here's three for yourself"—or may be five, or may be even ten roubles, and would tell them to give him some tea too, and may be a drop of vodka. And it wouldn't be half bad after being in the cold. For ten roubles we can have a spree on the holiday, buy boots; and pay back Nikita his four and a half roubles, for he's begun to be very troublesome.

A hundred paces from home, Polikey wrapped himself up again, set his belt straight and his collar, took off his cap, smoothed his hair, and without hurry thrust his hand under the lining. His hand fumbled about in the cap, more and more quickly; the other was thrust in there too, his face grew paler and paler, one hand was poked through. Polikey fell on his knees, stopped the horse, and began looking about the cart, the hay, the parcels, fumbling in his bosom, in his trousers; the money was nowhere.

"Heavens! What does it mean? What will happen?" he howled, clutching at his hair.

But then recollecting that he might be seen, he turned Drum's head round, pulled his cap down, and drove the astonished and disgusted Drum back along the road.

"I can't stand being driven by Polikey!" Drum must have been thinking. "For once in my life he has fed me and watered me at the right time, and only to deceive me so horribly. How I tried to race home! I'm tired, and I'd hardly got a whiff of our hay, and he drives me back."

"Get on, you devil's jade!" Polikey shrieked through his tears, standing up in the cart, tugging at Drum's mouth with the reins, and lashing him with the whip.

## X

The whole of that day no one in Pokrovskoe saw Polikey. The mistress made inquiries several times after dinner, and Aksyutka flew to Akulina. But Akulina said that he had not come; that doubtless the gardener had detained him, or something had gone wrong with the horse. "Hasn't it gone lame?" she said. "Last time Mihail was gone full twenty-four hours just the same; he had to come the whole way on foot!" And Aksyutka swung her pendulums back to the house again; while Akulina sought for causes for her husband's being detained, and tried to soothe her fears, but did not succeed. She had an ache at her heart, and no sort of work for the holiday on the morrow went well in her hands. She was the more worried because the carpenter's wife affirmed that she had seen with her own eyes "a man exactly like Polikey come into view, and then turn back again." The children, too, awaited their father with impatience and uneasiness, though on other grounds. Anyutka and Mashka were left without either cloak or overcoat, which articles had enabled them, if only by turns, to get out into the street; and so, wearing nothing but their frocks, they were forced to confine themselves to making circles with exaggerated speed round the house, occasioning thereby no little inconvenience to all the inhabitants of the servants' lodge in their comings and goings. Once Mashka darted into the lap of the carpenter's wife as she was carrying water; and though she roared beforehand on knocking against her knees, she still received a good cuffing about her curly head, and cried still louder. When she did not run up against anyone, she flew straight indoors, and, by means of a tub, clambered onto the stove.

Only the mistress and Akulina were genuinely anxious about Polikey individually; the children's anxiety related to the question of his wearing apparel. But Yegor Mihailovich, going with his report to his mistress, in reply to her question, "Hasn't Polikey come, and where can he be?" smiled as he answered, "I can't say," and was obviously pleased that his apprehensions were justified. "He ought to have come by dinnertime," he said significantly. All that day no one in Pokrovskoe knew anything about Polikey; only later it was learned that some neighboring peasants had seen him without a cap running along the road and asking every one, "Hadn't they found a letter?" Another man had seen him asleep by the wayside, near a cart and horse tied up to a post. "And I did think, too," this man said, "that he was drunk, and the horse had had no food or water for two days, so lean it looked."

Akulina did not sleep all night; she was listening all the time; but even in the night Polikey did not come. If she had been alone, or if she had had a cook and a housemaid, she would have been even more miserable. But as soon as the cocks had crowed for the third time, and the carpenter's wife was stirring, Akulina was obliged to get up and to set to work at the stove. It was a holiday; before daylight she must have her bread out, must make rye-beer, bake cakes, milk the cow, iron out frocks and smocks, wash the children, bring in water, and not let her neighbor keep the oven all to herself. Akulina, though she never ceased listening, set to work on those duties. Daylight came, the bells had begun ringing, the children were getting up, and still Polikey had not come. The day before had been like winter, the snow in patches covered the fields, the road, and the roofs; but now, as though for the holiday, it was fine, sunny and frosty, so that one could see and hear at a distance. But Akulina, standing at the stove, poking her head into its opening, was so busy with the baking of the cakes that she did not hear Polikey come in, and only found out from the children's shouts that her husband had returned. Anyutka, being the eldest, had greased her head and dressed herself without help. She wore a pink cotton dress, new but crumpled, a present from the mistress, which stood out as stiffly as the bark of a tree, and was the envy of all beholders. Her hair glistened, she had rubbed half a candle end on it; her slippers, though not new, were elegant. Masha was still in the old jacket and dirty, and Anyutka would not let her come near her for fear of getting soiled.

Mashka was out of doors when her father drove up with a sack. "Daddy's come," she shrieked, and dashed headlong in at the door past Anyutka, soiling her dress. Anyutka, laying aside her fears of getting dirty, at once proceeded to give Mashka a beating, while Akulina could not tear herself away from her work. She only shouted to the children, "Now, then, I'll thrash you all!" and looked round at the door. Polikey, with a sack in his hands, came into the entry, and at once made his way to his "corner." Akulina fancied that he was pale, and his face looked as though he were half crying, half smiling. But she hadn't time to make it out.

"Well, Polikey, is everything all right?" she called to him from the oven.

Polikey muttered something that she did not catch.

"Eh?" she cried. "Have you seen the mistress?" Polikey in his corner sat down on the bed, looked wildly round him, and smiled his guilty and intensely miserable smile. For a long time he made no answer.

"Polikey, why so long gone?" Akulina's voice called again.

"I gave the money to the mistress, Akulina. How she did thank me!" he said suddenly, and began still more uneasily looking about him and smiling. Two objects particularly caught his restless, feverishly wide-open eyes—the cord tied to the hanging cradle, and the baby. He went up to the cradle, and with his deft fingers began hurriedly untying the knot of the cord. Then his eyes rested on the baby; but at that moment Akulina came into the "corner" with a tray of cakes. Polikey quickly hid the cord in his bosom and sat down on the bed.

"How is it, Polikey, you don't seem like yourself?" said Akulina.

"I haven't slept," he answered.

Suddenly something flashed by the window, and in an instant the girl from up yonder, Aksyutka, darted in like an arrow.

"The mistress gave orders for Polikey Ilyich to come to her this minute," she said. "This minute, Avdotya Mikolavna said, this minute."

Polikey looked at Akulina, at the girl.

"Directly! What more does she want?" he said so simply, that Akulina was reassured. "Perhaps she wants to reward me. . . . Say I'll come directly."

He got up and went out. Akulina took a deep tub, set it on the bench, poured water in from the buckets standing at the door, and from a caldron of hot water on the stove, tucked up her sleeves, and tried the water.

"Come, Mashka, I'll wash you."

The cross, lisping little girl began to roar.

"Come, you dirty girl, I'll put a clean smock on you! Now then, none of your nonsense. . . . Come, I've your sister to wash too."

Polikey meanwhile had not followed the errand-girl to the mistress, but had gone to quite a different place. In the entry close to the wall was a steep ladder leading to the loft. Polikey, going out into the entry, looked round, and seeing no one, bending nearly double, climbed nimbly and quickly, almost running, up this ladder.

"What can be the meaning of Polikey's not coming?" said the mistress, impatiently turning to Dunyasha, who was combing her hair. "Where is Polikey? Why is it he doesn't come?"

Aksyutka again flew to the serfs' quarters, and again flew into the entry, and summoned Polikey to go to the mistress.

"But he went long ago," answered Akulina, who had finished washing Mashka, and at that moment had just put her suckling in the trough, and, in spite of his screams, was wetting his scanty locks of hair. The baby cried, puckering up its face, and tried to clutch at something with its helpless little hands.

With one large hand Akulina supported his fat, soft little back, all dimples, while with the other she washed him.

"Look and see if he's dropped asleep somewhere," she said, looking round with anxiety.

At that moment the carpenter's wife, with her hair uncombed and her bosom opened, went, holding up her petticoats, to the loft, to get down her clothes that were drying there. Suddenly a shriek of horror was heard in the loft; and, like one possessed, the carpenter's wife, with her eyes shut, came flying backwards on all fours, falling rather than running down the ladder.

"Polikey!" she shrieked.

Akulina let the baby drop out of her hands.

"Strangled himself!" roared the carpenter's wife.

Akulina ran into the entry, not noticing that the baby, rolling over like a ball, had its head in the water and its little legs in the air.

"On the beam . . . hanging," brought out the carpenter's wife, but she stopped short on seeing Akulina.

Akulina rushed to the ladder; and before they had time to prevent her she had run up, but with a fearful scream she fell down the ladder like a dead body, and would have been killed, if the people who ran in from everywhere had not been in time to catch her.

## XI

For some minutes it was impossible to distinguish anything in the general uproar. A crowd of people had gathered, all were shouting, all were talking, children and old women were crying. Akulina lay unconscious. At last some men, the carpenter, and the bailiff, who had come running, went up above; and the carpenter's wife for the twentieth time repeated her story: "thinking nothing, I went after my cape, looked round like this: what do I see?—a man; I stared; a cap lies beside him, turned inside out. Mercy! why, the legs are swinging! A cold shudder ran down me. To think of a man's hanging himself, and I must be the one to see him! How I flew down, I couldn't say myself. And a marvel it is how God's mercy preserved me. Truly, the Lord had mercy on me. To think of it; so steep, and such a height! It might have been my death."

The men who had gone up told the same story. Wearing nothing but his shirt and his breeches, Polikey was hanging from a beam by the very cord he had taken from the cradle. His cap, turned inside out, lay there too. His coat and cloak had been taken off, and were tidily folded up beside him. His feet reached the ground, but there were no signs of life.

Akulina came to herself and made a dash again towards the ladder, but they did not let her go.

"Mammy, Syomka's choked himself," the lisping child whined suddenly from the "corner." Akulina broke away again, and ran to the "corner." The baby lay quite still, face downwards, in the tub, and its legs were not kicking now. Akulina snatched him out, but the baby did not breathe or move. Akulina threw him on the bed, leaned on her hands, and broke into such a loud, piercing, and terrible peal of laughter, that Mashka, who at first laughed too, stopped up her ears and ran crying out into the entry. The neighbors thronged into the "corner" with weeping and wailing. They carried the baby out and began rubbing it, but it was useless. Akulina rolled on the bed and laughed, laughed so that horror came upon all who heard that laugh. Only seeing this heterogeneous crowd of men and women, old people and children, thronging the hut, could one conceive of the mass of folk of all sorts living in the serfs' quarters. Everyone fussed, everyone talked, many cried, and no one did anything. The carpenter's wife still found people who had not heard her story, and described anew what a shock her sensitive feelings had received, and how providentially she had been preserved from falling down the ladder. A little old footman, wearing a woman's jacket, described how, in the old master's days, a woman had drowned herself in the pond. The bailiff sent messengers to the village constable and to the priest, and picked out men to keep a watch on the place. The errand-girl Aksyutka, her eyes starting out of her head, kept peering up the opening into the loft; and though she saw nothing there, she could not tear herself away and go to her mistress. Agafya Mihailovna, a maid in the last mistress's time, wept and demanded tea to restore her shattered nerves. Old Granny Anna, with her practiced fat hands, reeking with olive oil, laid the little corpse out on the table. The women stood round Akulina and stared mutely at her. The children huddled in corners, peeped at their mother and fell to roaring, then subsided, peeped again, and huddled further away than ever. Boys and men crowded about the steps, and with scared faces gazed at the door and at the windows, seeing and understanding nothing, and asked each other what was the matter. One said that the carpenter had chopped off one of his wife's legs with an axe; another declared that the washerwoman had been brought to bed of triplets; a third asserted that the cook's cat had gone mad and bitten folks; but the truth gradually spread, and at last reached the mistress's ears, and it appears they had not even the wit to break it to her gently. Yegor in his coarse way had told her bluntly straight out, and so upset the lady's nerves that it was a long while before she could recover from the shock.

The crowd was beginning to grow calm; the carpenter's wife set her samovar, and was brewing the tea, which made outsiders, not invited to partake of it, feel it unseemly to linger longer. Boys had begun scuffling at the steps. Everyone knew by now what had happened; and crossing themselves, they began to separate, when suddenly the cry was heard, "The mistress, the mistress!" and they all crowded together and squeezed close to make way for her, but every one wanted too to see what she was going to do. The mistress, pale and tearful, crossed the threshold into the entry and into Akulina's "corner." Dozens of heads squeezed in and gazed in the doorway. One woman, big with child, was so crushed that she shrieked, but promptly took advantage of the very circumstance to gain a place in front. And who would not want to stare at the mistress in Akulina's "corner"? For the house-serfs it was precisely what the fireworks are at the end of an entertainment. It's sure to be worth seeing if they're letting off fireworks; and sure to be worth seeing if the mistress, in silk and lace, has gone into Akulina's "corner." The mistress went up to Akulina and took her by the hand; but

Akulina pulled it away. The old house-serfs shook their heads disapprovingly.

"Akulina!" said the mistress, "you have children, have pity on yourself."

Akulina laughed and got up.

"My children are all silver, all silver. . . . I don't keep paper money," she muttered, speaking rapidly. "I said to Polikey, don't take the paper, and now they've smeared you, smeared you with pitch, pitch and soap, madam. Any scabbiness you've got will disappear directly." And again she broke into loud laughter.

The mistress turned away and asked for the apothecary to come with mustard. "Bring some cold water!" she said and began looking for water herself; but catching sight of the dead baby, before whom old Granny Anna was standing, the mistress turned away, and all saw how she hid her face in her handkerchief and burst into tears. Granny Anna (it was a pity the mistress didn't see, she would have appreciated it—it was all done for her benefit too) covered the baby with a piece of linen, straightened his little arm with her fat deft hand; and so shook her head, so pursed up her lips, so sympathetically dropped her eyelids and sighed, that no one could help seeing the goodness of her heart. But the mistress did not see this, and indeed she was incapable of seeing anything. She burst into sobs, was overcome by nervous hysterics, and was supported out into the entry and led home. "And that was all that came of her visit!" many people reflected, and they began to disperse. Akulina still laughed and talked nonsense. She was led away into another room; they bled her and put mustard plasters on her, applied ice to her head. Yet she remained still understanding nothing, not weeping, but laughing, talking, and doing such things that the good folks who were looking after her could not restrain themselves, and laughed too.

## XII

The holiday was not a lively one in Pokrovskoe. In spite of the fine weather, people did not go out walking; the girls did not meet together to sing songs; the factory lads, who came over from the town, did not play on the accordion nor the balalaika, or flirt with the girls. They all sat in corners; and if they talked, they talked softly, as though some evil one was about and might hear them. In the daytime it was not so bad; but in the evening, when it got dark, the dogs began to howl, and then, as ill-luck would have it, a wind sprang up and howled in the chimneys, and such a panic came over all the inhabitants of the serfs' quarters that those who had candles lighted them before the holy pictures. Any who lived alone in a "corner" went in to neighbors to ask them to let them stay the night where there were more people, while those who had to go out to the sheds to feed the cattle would not go, and did not scruple to leave the cattle unfed that night. And the holy water, of which everyone kept a bottle, was all used up during that night. Many positively heard someone pacing heavily about the loft that night, and the blacksmith saw a snake fly straight to the loft.

In Polikey's "corner" there was no one: the children and the mad woman had been removed. There was only the dead baby lying there, and two old women watching over it, and a pilgrim woman, who, in the fervor of her piety, read the Psalter aloud, not over the baby, but simply as a tribute to the whole occasion. This was by the wish of the mistress. These old women and the pilgrim woman heard with their own ears how, as soon as they were through reading a section of the Psalter, a rafter would shake overhead and someone would groan. When the words, "Let God rise from the dead," were read, all became still again.

The carpenter's wife invited a crony of hers; and sitting up together, they drank, in the course of that night, all the tea she had laid in to last her a week. They, too, heard the beams creaking overhead, and a noise as though sacks were falling down. The peasant watchmen kept up the courage of the house-serfs, or they would have died of fright that night. The peasants lay in the entry on hay; and afterwards asserted that they too had heard wonderful things in the loft, though on the night itself they conversed very calmly together about the recruiting, munched bread, scratched themselves, and, worst of all, made the entry so reek of the peculiar peasant smell, that the carpenter's wife when she passed spat in disgust and abused them for it.

However that might be, the suicide was still hanging in the loft, and it seemed as though the evil one himself had spread huge wings over the serfs' quarters that night, making his power manifest, and coming closer than ever before to these people. So at least they all felt. I can't say whether this was true. I believe indeed that it was altogether untrue. I believe that if on that terrible night some brave man had taken a candle or a lantern, and crossing himself or even without crossing himself, had gone up into the loft, and slowly putting to flight the terrors of the night with the candle, and lighting up the beams, the sand, the flue-pipe covered with cobwebs, and the cape forgotten by the carpenter's wife, had made his way to Polikey; and if, mastering his terrors, he had raised the lantern to the level of the face, he would have seen the familiar, lean body bending lifelessly to one side, with the legs touching the ground (the cord had grown slack), the shirt collar unbuttoned and no cross to be seen under it, the head sunk on the breast, and the good-natured face with its open sightless eyes, and the meek, guilty smile and stern repose, and stillness over everything. In reality, the carpenter's wife, huddled up in the corner of her bed, with disheveled locks and scared eyes, describing how she heard the sacks falling, was a great deal more awful and terrible than Polikey, though his cross had been taken off and was lying on the beam.

*Up yonder*, that is, at the mistress's house, the same terror reigned as in the serfs' quarters. The old lady's room reeked of eau de Cologne and medicine. Dunyasha was melting yellow wax and making ointment. What the ointment was for precisely, I don't know; but I know it was always made when the mistress was unwell. And now she was so upset that she was quite ill. Dunyasha's aunt had come to stay the night with her to keep up her courage. There were four of them with the errand-girl in the maid's room talking softly together.

"Who's to go for the oil?" said Dunyasha.

"Not on any account, Avdotya Mikolavna—I'm not going!" the second maid answered resolutely.

"Nonsense! Aksyutka and you go together."

"I'll run alone, I'm not afraid of anything," said Aksyutka; but her heart failed her as she spoke.

"Well, run along, there's a good girl; ask Granny Anna for a glassful, and don't spill it as you bring it," Dunyasha said to her.

Aksyutka picked up her skirt with one hand; and though she was consequently unable to swing both arms, she swung one with twice the energy across her line of advance, and flew off. She was frightened; and she felt that if she were to see or hear anything whatever, even her own living mother, she would drop with terror. Shutting her eyes, she flew along the familiar path.

## XIII

"Is the mistress asleep, or not?" suddenly asked close to Aksyutka a peasant's deep voice. She opened her eyes, which had till then been closed, and saw a figure that seemed to her taller than the hut before her. She squealed, and whisked back so quickly, that her petticoat could not keep pace with her. In one bound she was on the steps, in another she was in the maid's room, and with a wild yell she flung herself on the bed. Dunyasha, her aunt, and the other maid were numb with terror; but before they had time to recover themselves, slow, heavy, and hesitating steps were heard in the passage and at the door. Dunyasha rushed in to her mistress, dropping the ointment; the second maid hid herself behind the skirts hanging on the wall; the aunt, a person of stronger will, would have held the door, but the door opened, and a peasant came into the room.

It was Dutlov, in his boats of shoes. Taking no notice of the girls' terror, he looked about for the holy picture; and not making out the little image in the left corner, crossed himself, bowing to the shelf with the teacups, laid his cap down on the window-sill, and thrusting his hand far under his coat, as though he wanted to scratch under his armpit, he took out the letter with the five brown seals, stamped with anchors. Dunyasha's aunt clutched at her chest; with effort she articulated:

"How you did terrify me, Semyon Naumych! I can't utter a wo-ord. I fairly thought the end had come."

"How could you?" protested the second girl, popping her head out from under the skirts.

"And you've upset the mistress too!" said Dunyasha, coming in at the door. "Why do you come creeping up the maids' staircase without asking leave? A regular peasant!"

Dutlov, making no apology, repeated that he wanted to see the mistress.

"She's not well," said Dunyasha.

At that moment Aksyutka went off into such an unseemly loud laugh that she had to stuff her head again into the pillows of the bed, from which, in spite of the threats of Dunyasha and her aunt, she could not remove it for a whole hour without bursting into laughter, as though something was exploding in her pink bosom and red cheeks. It struck her as so funny that they had all been so scared, and she hid her head again, and flapped her slipper, and writhed all over, as though she were in convulsions.

Dutlov stopped, looked at her attentively, as though he wanted to ascertain what was happening to her; but unable to discover what was wrong, he turned away, and continued speaking.

"To be sure, then, it's a matter of great importance," he said. "Only tell her that a peasant has found the letter with the money."

"What money?"

Before taking this message, Dunyasha read the address and cross-examined Dutlov as to where and how he had found the money, which Polikey was to have brought from town. After having learnt every detail, and thrust the errand-girl, still guffawing, out into the passage, Dunyasha went in to her mistress; but to her surprise, her mistress still would not see him, and said nothing coherent to Dunyasha.

"I know nothing about it, and I don't want to know," said the old lady. "What peasant or what money? I can see no one, and I want to see no one. Let him leave me in peace."

"What am I to do?" said Dutlov, turning the envelope over; "it's not a trifling sum. Is anything written on it?" he asked Dunyasha, who once more read him the address.

Dutlov still seemed incredulous. He had hoped that maybe the money did not belong to the mistress, and that the address had not been read him right, but Dunyasha confirmed the reading of it. He sighed, put the envelope in his bosom, and was about to leave.

"I suppose I must give it to the police officer," he said.

"Stay, I'll try again; I'll speak to her," Dunyasha stopped him, attentively watching the disappearance of the envelope into the peasant's coat. "Give the letter here."

Dutlov drew it out again, but did not at once put it into Dunyasha's outstretched hand.

"Say it was found on the road by Dutlov—Semyon."

"Oh, give it here!"

"I did think it was just—a letter, but a soldier read out to me that there was money in it."

"Oh, give it me!"

"I didn't even venture to go home, so as . . ." Dutlov began again, still not parting from the precious envelope. "So you report that to her."

Dunyasha took the envelope, and once more went in to her mistress.

"Oh, mercy, Dunyasha!" said her mistress in a reproachful voice; "don't talk to me about that money. If I but think of that little baby . . ."

"The peasant, madam, doesn't know to whom you'd order him to hand it," Dunyasha said again.

Her mistress broke open the envelope, shuddered as soon as she saw the money, and pondered.

"Horrible money! What evil it does!" she said.

"It's Dutlov, madam. Do you bid him go, or is it your pleasure to come out and speak to him? Is the money all safe?" inquired Dunyasha.

"I don't want this money; it's unlucky money. Think what it's done! Tell him to take it himself if he likes," the lady said suddenly, feeling for Dunyasha's hand. "Yes, yes, yes!" she repeated to the amazed Dunyasha; "let him take it altogether, and do what he likes with it."

"Fifteen hundred roubles," observed Dunyasha, smiling as though at a child.

"Let him take it, all of it!" her mistress repeated impatiently. "How is it you don't understand me? That money's unlucky; never speak to me of it! Let that peasant take what he found. Go along! There, do go now!"

Dunyasha went into the maid's room.

"Was it all there?" asked Dutlov.

"You count them yourself," said Dunyasha, giving him the envelope. "My orders are to hand it to you."

Dutlov put his cap under his arm, and bending forward, began counting the money.

"Have you no reckoning beads?"

Dutlov supposed that his mistress was so stupid that she could not reckon the money, and so had told him to do so.

"You can count it at home! It's for you—your money!" said Dunyasha angrily. " 'I don't want,' says she, 'to see it; give it to the man who brought it.' "

Dutlov, who was still in his stooping posture, fixed his eyes on Dunyasha.

Dunyasha's aunt fairly flung up her hands.

"My goodness gracious! What luck God's given you! My gracious goodness!

The second maid would not believe it.

"Why, you're joking, Avdotya Mikolavna, surely?"

"Joking, indeed! She told me to give it to the peasant. There, take your money, and get along, do," said Dunyasha, not disguising her annoyance. "One man's sorrow is another's luck!"

"It's no joking matter, fifteen hundred roubles!" said the aunt.

"More," put in Dunyasha. "Well, now you can put up a ten-copeck candle to Saint Nicholas," said Dunyasha sarcastically. "Why, are you struck silly? And a good thing if it had been a poor man, but he has a lot of his own."

Dutlov at last grasped that it was not a joke, and began to put together and fold up in the envelope the notes he had unfolded to count; but his hands shook, and he kept glancing at the maids to assure himself it was not a joke.

"Why, he hardly knows what he's doing, he's so pleased," said Dunyasha, affecting to feel none the less contemptuous both of the peasant and the money. "Let me put them up for you."

And she would have taken the notes; but Dutlov would not give them her. He crumpled up the notes, stuffed them still further into his bosom, and took up his cap.

"Are you glad?"

"I don't know what to say! Why, really . . ."

He could not finish; he waved his hand, grinned, and, almost crying, went out.

The bell rang in the old lady's room.

"Well, have you given them to him?"

"Yes."

"Well, was he very much pleased?"

"He's quite beside himself."

"Oh, fetch him in. I'll ask him how he found them. Fetch him here; I can't come out."

Dunyasha ran and found the peasant in the entry. Without waiting to put on his cap, he had pulled out his purse, and was bending down, untying it, while he held the notes in his teeth. He fancied, perhaps, that the money was not quite his own till he had it in his purse. When Dunyasha called him, he was panic-stricken.

"What is it, Avdotya—Avdotya Mikolavna? Does she want to

take them back? If only you'd stand up for me, for God's sake, and I'll bring you some honey."

"I dare say!"

Again the door was opened, and the peasant was led in to see his mistress. He felt anything but cheerful. "Oh, she's going to take it back!" he thought, as he walked through the room, lifting his whole leg high up as though getting through high grass, and trying not to make a noise with his bast shoes. He did not take in, did not even see anything around him. He walked by a looking-glass, saw flowers of some sort, saw a peasant in bast shoes lifting his feet high, a gentleman with an eyeglass painted on the wall, some sort of green tub, and something white. . . . And behold that something white began talking; it was his mistress. He could make out nothing of what she said; he simply stared with round eyes. He did not know where he was, and saw everything in a sort of fog.

"Is that you, Dutlov?"

"Yes, madam. Just as it was, I never touched it," said he. "I'm not glad at having found it, so help me God! How I've worn out the horse!"

"Well, you're in luck!" she said, with a smile of supercilious good-nature. "Take it, take it for yourself!"

He could only roll his eyes blankly.

"I'm glad that you've got the money. God grant it has come when it was wanted! Well, are you glad?"

"Glad! Oh, so glad, ma'am! I'll always be praying to God for you! I'm so glad that, thank God, our lady's alive. That's all I had to do with it."

"How did you find it?"

"To be sure, we can always try our best for our lady, not but . . ."

"He's in a regular muddle, madam," said Dunyasha.

"I'd taken my nephew, the recruit, to town. I was driving back, and on the road I found it. Polikey must have dropped it by accident."

"Well, you can go, you can go, my good man! I'm glad you found it."

"So glad, ma'am!" said the peasant.

Afterwards he recollected that he had not thanked her, and that he had not behaved properly. The old lady and Dunyasha smiled while he stepped back again as though through high grass and with difficulty refrained from breaking into a trot. He still kept fancying they would stop him and take the notes back.

## XIV

On getting into the fresh air, Dutlov moved off the road to the lime-trees, untied his sash so as to get at his purse more easily, and began putting away the notes. His lips twitched and worked, though he did not utter a sound. After putting away the money and fastening his belt, he crossed himself and walked away along the path, staggering like a drunken man, so absorbed was he in the thought that surged in his brain. Suddenly he saw the figure of a peasant coming to meet him. He called; it was Yefim, who was walking round the serfs' quarters with an oak cudgel, as a watchman.

"Ah, Uncle Semyon!" Yefimka cried joyfully, coming closer. (Yefimka had been feeling scared all alone.) "Well, have you been seeing the recruits off, uncle?"

"Yes. And what are you doing?"

"Why, they've set me here to watch over Polikey, who's hanged himself?"

"Where is he?"

"Yonder, in the loft, they say he's hanging," answered Yefimka, pointing with his stick in the darkness towards the roof of the hut. Dutlov looked in that direction; and though he saw nothing, he puckered his brows, screwed up his eyes, and shook his head.

"The constable has come," said Yefimka; "the coachman was saying so. They're going to take him away at once. It's a fearful thing at night, uncle! I won't go at night—not for anything—if they tell me to go up to the loft. Yegor Mihailovich may kill me, but I won't go."

"A sin it is, a sin indeed!" Dutlov repeated, evidently for the sake of doing the proper thing, without in the least thinking of what he was saying, and he would have gone on his way. But the voice of Yegor Mihailovich stopped him.

"Hi, watchman, come here!" Yegor Mihailovich shouted from the step.

Yefimka called back in reply.

"But who is there with you?"

"Dutlov."

"You come too, Semyon."

As he came closer into the light of the lantern carried by the coachman, Dutlov made out Yegor Mihailovich and an undersized functionary in a cap with a cockade and a cloak; it was the district constable.

"Here's the old man who will come with us," said Yegor Mihailovich, on seeing him.

The old man felt qualms; but there was no getting out of it.

"And you, Yefimka, you're a bold young fellow, run up into the loft where he hanged himself, and set the ladder straight for his Honor to get up."

Yefimka, who had been most unwilling to go into the hut, ran towards it, his bast shoes stumping like logs of wood.

The constable struck a light and lit a pipe. He lived two versts away, and had only lately been cruelly reprimanded by the police captain for drunkenness, and was therefore just now in a very fever of zeal. He arrived on the scene at ten o'clock in the evening, and insisted on viewing the body without delay. Yegor Mihailovich asked Dutlov what brought him there. On the way Dutlov told the bailiff about finding the money and what the mistress had done. Dutlov said that he was coming to ask Yegor Mihailovich's sanction. The bailiff, to Dutlov's horror, asked for the envelope and examined it. The constable, too, took the envelope into his hands and shortly and dryly inquired into details.

"Come, the money's lost!" thought Dutlov, and he even began to apologize for his part in the affair. But the constable gave him back the money.

"Well, the peasant's in luck!" said he.

"It's come just right for him," said Yegor Mihailovich; "he's just taken his nephew for a recruit; now he'll buy him out."

"Oh," said the constable, and he went on in front.

"You'll buy out Ilyushka, won't you?" said Yegor Mihailovich.

"Buy him out? Will the money be enough? And maybe it's too late."

"That's for you to decide," said the bailiff, and both of them followed the constable.

They reached the serfs' hut, in the porch of which the stinking watchmen were waiting with a lantern.

Dutlov walked behind them.

The watchmen had a guilty air, possibly due only to a conscious-ness of the odor they had introduced into the place, for they had done no harm. Everyone was silent.

"Where is he?" asked the constable.

"Here," whispered Yegor Mihailovich. "Yefimka," he added, "you're a bold young chap, go on ahead with a lantern."

Yefimka had already put the board straight in the loft, and seemed to have lost all fear. Taking two or three steps at a time, he clambered up in front with a cheerful face, looking round to light the way for the constable, who was followed by Yegor Mihailovich. When they were out of sight, Dutlov, who had put one foot on the first step, sighed and stopped short. Two minutes passed, their steps died away in the loft; they had, doubtless, reached the body.

"Uncle, he's calling you!" Yefimka shouted through the hatch.

Dutlov went up. The constable and Yegor Mihailovich stood in the light of a lantern behind a rafter with only the upper part of their bodies visible; behind them stood someone else with his back turned. It was Polikey. Dutlov climbed over the beam and stood still, cross-ing himself.

"Turn him round, lad!" said the constable. No one moved.

"Yefimka, you're a bold young chap!" said Yegor Mihailovich.

The bold young chap strode across the beam; and turning Polikey round, stood beside him, looking with the most cheerful expression from Polikey to the authorities, as a showman exhibiting an albino or Julia Pastrana * looks from the public to the monster he is showing them, ready to execute all the wishes of the spectators.

"Turn him again!"

Polikey was turned again, with a slight swing of the arms and a scrape of the foot on the sand.

"Lift him; take him down!"

"Is it your order to cut him down, Vasily Borisovich?" asked Yegor Mihailovich. "Give me an axe, mates!"

The watchmen and Dutlov had to be told twice before they fell to. The bold young chap dealt with Polikey as though he were a sheep's carcass. At last they cut the rope, took down the body, and covered it up. The constable said that the doctor would come next day, and dismissed them all.

* A Mexican dancer, exhibited as half-woman half-monkey.—Ed.

# XV

Dutlov walked homewards, moving his lips. At first he felt uneasy; but, as he got nearer the village, this feeling passed away, and the feeling of gladness sank more and more deeply into his heart. In the village he heard sounds of singing and drunken voices. Dutlov never drank, and now he went straight home. It was late when he walked into the hut. His old wife was asleep. The elder son and the grandsons were asleep on the stove, the second son in the storeroom. Ilyushka's wife was the only one awake. In her dirty working-day smock, bareheaded, she sat on the bench wailing. She did not come out to open the door to her uncle, but only went on more vigorously with her crying and lamenting as he entered the hut. In the opinion of the old mother, her lament was an exceedingly fine and creditable performance, in spite of the fact that at her age she could not have had much practice.

The old woman got up and began getting supper for her husband. Dutlov drove Ilyushka's wife away from the table. "Enough, enough!" he said. Aksinya got up, and lying down on the bench, did not cease wailing. Without uttering a word, the old woman laid the table and cleared it again. The old man too did not say a word. Having said a prayer, he belched, washed his hands, and taking his reckoning frame from a nail went off to the storeroom. There he and the old woman first whispered together for a while, then the old woman went out, and he began rattling the reckoning beads. At last he closed the lid of a chest with a bang, and crept down into the cellar under the floor. He was a long while busily engaged in the storeroom and the cellar. When he came back to the living-room it was all dark—the splinter was not burning. The old woman, by day usually so quiet and unobtrusive, lay stretched out near the stove, and filled the whole hut with her snoring. The noisy young wife too was asleep, and her breathing could not be heard. She had fallen asleep on the bench, just as she was, without undressing or putting anything under her head.

Dutlov said his prayers, then looked at Ilyushka's wife, shook his head, put out the splinter he had lighted, clambered onto the stove, and lay down beside his little grandson. In the darkness he dropped his bast shoes down from the stove and lay down on his back, looking at the crossbeam, over the stove, which was faintly visible above his head, and, listening to the cockroaches rustling over the walls, to the sighs, to the snoring, to the scratching of one foot against another, and to the sounds of the cattle in the yard. For a long while he could not get to sleep; the moon rose, it grew lighter in the room, he could see Aksinya in the corner, and something which he could not clearly distinguish; he could not see whether it was a cloak his son had forgotten, or a tub the women had set there, or someone standing there. Whether he were dozing or not, he looked more intently again. . . . Apparently the spirit of darkness, who had driven Polikey to his fearful deed, and whose proximity the serfs had been aware of that night, had winged his way to the village, to Dutlov's hut, where lay the money *he* had used for Polikey's ruin. Anyway Dutlov felt *him* there, and Dutlov was ill at ease. He could neither sleep nor get up. Seeing something which he could not make out clearly, he thought of Ilyushka with his hands tied, thought of the face of Aksinya and her fine lament, thought of Polikey with his swaying wrists. Suddenly it seemed to the old man that someone passed by the window. "What's that? Could it be the village elder coming with a notice?" he thought. "How did he open the door?" wondered the old man, hearing steps in the entry, "or didn't the old woman put up the bar when she went out into the entry?" The dog howled in the back yard, and *he* walked about the passage, as the old man told afterwards, as though *he* were looking for the door, passed it by, began fumbling about the wall again, stumbled against a tub and it clattered. And again *he* fumbled about as though feeling for the handle. Then *he* got hold of the handle. A shiver ran down the old man. Then *he* pulled at the handle and entered in the shape of a man. Dutlov knew that it was *he*. He wanted to make the sign of the cross, but could not. *He* went up to the table on which there lay a cloth, pulled it off, flung it on the floor, and started climbing onto the stove. The old man became aware that *he* had taken the shape of Polikey. *He* grinned, *his* arms dangled. *He* climbed onto the stove, threw himself straight on the old man, and began strangling him.

"My money!" cried Polikey.

"Let me go, I won't do it," Semyon tried to say, and could not.

Polikey was crushing him with all the weight of a mountain of stone, pressing on his chest. Dutlov knew that if he were to repeat a prayer, *he* would let him go, and he knew what prayer he ought to recite, but could not utter it. His grandson was sleeping beside him. The boy screamed shrilly and began to cry—his grandfather was squeezing him against the wall. The child's cry freed the old man's lips. "Let God rise from the dead," articulated Dutlov. *He* pressed a little less hard. "And may His enemies be scattered," mumbled Dutlov. *He* got off the stove. Dutlov heard his two feet thud on the floor. Dutlov went on repeating prayers he knew; he repeated them all in succession. *He* went towards the door, passed by the table, and slammed the door so that the hut shook. Yet everyone slept on except the old man and his grandchild. The grandfather repeated his prayers, trembling all over, while the child cried as he dropped asleep and clung to the old man.

Everything was quiet again. The grandfather lay without stirring. The cock crowed on the other side of the wall just at Dutlov's ear. He heard the hens beginning to stir, heard the young cock trying to crow like the old one and failing. Something moved at the old man's feet. It was the cat; she leapt on her soft pads from the stove to the floor, and began mewing at the door. The grandfather got up, raised the window; it was dark and muddy in the street; he saw the shafts of the cart close to the window. Crossing himself, he went out barefoot to the horses. It was evident that the Evil One had come to them too. The mare, standing in the lean-to beside a tub of chaff, had caught her leg in the halter, and spilt the chaff. With her leg lifted and her head turned, she was waiting for her master. The colt was rolling in the dung-heap. The old man put him on his legs, freed the mare from the halter, set the food for her, and went back into the hut.

The old woman had got up and lighted a splinter. "Wake the lads," he said, "I'm going to town," and lighting a wax taper at the icon lamp, he crept with it into the cellar. When he came back, there were fires alight, not at Dutlov's only, but at all the neighbors'. The lads had got up and were already making ready. The women were coming in and out with pails and tubs of milk. Ignat was getting one cart out, while the second son was greasing the other. The young wife was not wailing now, but was sitting in the hut on a bench, dressed and with a kerchief on her head, waiting till it would be time to start for the town to say goodbye to her husband.

The old man seemed particularly severe. To no one did he say a single word; he put on his new long coat, fastened his belt, and with all Polikey's money in his bosom he went to see Yegor Mihail-ovich.

"Don't you dawdle!" he shouted to Ignat, who was turning the wheel round on the greased axle of the tilted cart. "I'll come in a minute. Have everything ready!"

The bailiff was only just up and was drinking his tea; he was going to town himself to deliver the recruits.

"What is it?" he asked.

"Yegor Mihailovich, I want to buy off the lad. Do help me! You said last night that you knew of a substitute in the town. Tell me how it's done—we are ignorant."

"Why, have you changed your mind?"

"Yes, Yegor Mihailovich; I feel for him; he's my brother's son. However he may behave, I feel for him. It's the cause of much sin, this money! So be so good and tell me how to do it," he said, bowing low.

As he always did on such occasions, Yegor Mihailovich smacked his lips for a long while without speaking, with an air of profound thought. Then, having considered the matter, he wrote two notes and told him how and what to do in the town.

When Dutlov returned home, the young wife had already set off with Ignat, and the potbellied roan mare stood at the gate all ready harnessed. Dutlov broke a switch out of the hedge, seated himself on the box, and set off. He drove the mare so violently that she quickly lost her belly and Dutlov did not look at her for fear of being moved by her plight. He was fretted by the fear of being somehow late, of Ilyushka's being sent off as a soldier, and the devil's money being left on his hands.

I will not attempt to describe all Dutlov's proceedings that morning; I will only say that he was particularly lucky. The man for whom Yegor Mihailovich had given him a letter had in readiness a volunteer who had already spent twenty-three roubles of the money he was to get as a substitute, and had been passed by the medical board. The man who was disposing of him wanted four hundred silver roubles for him, while the purchaser, a tradesman, had for the last three weeks persisted in begging him to come down to three hundred. Dutlov concluded the bargain in a couple of words. "Will you take three hundred and twenty-five?" he asked, holding out his hand with an expression by which it was obvious at once that

he was ready to give more. The man drew back his hand and persisted in asking four hundred. "Won't you take three hundred and
twenty-five?" repeated Dutlov, grasping the bargainer's right hand
in his left, and threatening to clap his right hand down on it. "Won't
you? . . . Well, God be with you!" he added suddenly, bringing
his hand down on the man's hand and turning away with a swing
of his whole person. "It seems it has to be so; take three hundred
and fifty then. Get out the discharge. Bring in the young fellow.
And now for the earnest-money. Here are two red notes. Is it
enough?"

And Dutlov undid his belt and got out the money.

Though the man did not draw back his hands, he still seemed
somehow not to agree; and, without accepting the earnest-money,
went on saying that Dutlov should wet the bargain and bear the
expense of entertaining the volunteer.

"Beware of sin," Dutlov repeated, thrusting the money upon
him; "we must all die!" he repeated, in a tone so mild, edifying, and
convincing, that the man said, "So be it, then!" clapped hands together once more, and began praying. "God give you luck!" he said.

They waked up the volunteer, who was still sleeping off his
drinking-bout of the previous day. For some unknown reason they
looked him carefully over, and all went off to the board. The
volunteer was in good spirits; he asked for rum to clear his head,
and Dutlov gave him money to get some. His courage failed him
only when they were entering the hall of the recruiting board. For
a long while the elder man in his blue greatcoat, and the volunteer
in his short, sheepskin coat, his eyebrows lifted and his eyes staring,
were standing about in the entrance-hall; a long while they whispered
together, asked permission to go somewhere, looked for someone,
took off their caps and bowed to each copying-clerk in turn, and
listened with an air of profundity to the decision delivered by the
clerk they knew personally. All hope of completing the business
that day was abandoned, and the volunteer had begun to regain his
cheerfulness and easy manners, when Dutlov caught sight of Yegor
Mihailovich, at once attached himself to him, and began imploring
his aid and bowing to him. Yegor Mihailovich helped him to such
good purpose, that by three o'clock the volunteer, to his great dis-
comfort and surprise, was brought before the board; and to the
general satisfaction, as it seemed, of everyone, from the guards to

the president, he was undressed, shaved, dressed again, and allowed to depart. And five minutes later Dutlov had counted out the money, received the discharge, and taking leave of the volunteer and his master, set off on his way to the lodgings where the recruits from Pokrovskoe were staying. Ilyushka and his young wife were sitting in the corner of the tavern kitchen; and as soon as the old man entered, they ceased talking, and stared at him with a look at once submissive and hostile. The old man—as always—said a prayer, unfastened his belt, took out a paper, and called into the hut his elder son Ignat and Ilyushka's mother, who was in the yard.

"Beware of sin, Ilyushka," said he, going up to his nephew. "Last night you said such a word to me. . . . Do you think I am not sorry for you? I remember how my brother bade me care for you. If I had had the power, would I have let you go? God has sent me luck, and I have not grudged it you. Here is the paper," he said, laying the discharge on the table, and carefully spreading it out with his stiff, crooked fingers.

All the Pokrovskoe peasants, the innkeeper's workmen, and even a crowd of outsiders, came running into the hut from the yard. All guessed what was going on, but no one interrupted the old man's solemn discourse.

"Here it is, the paper! Four hundred roubles I have given for it. Don't reproach your uncle."

Ilyushka got up, but was silent, not knowing what to say. His lips quivered with excitement; his old mother went up to him sobbing, and would have flung herself on his neck, but slowly and peremptorily the old man held her back by the arm and went on speaking.

"You said a word to me yesterday," the old man repeated once more; "with that word you stabbed me to the heart. Your father, as he lay dying, gave you into my charge; you've been to me like my own son; and if I've wronged you in any way, well, we all live in sin. That's so, good Christian folk, eh?" He turned to the peasants standing round. "Here's your own mother too and your young wife, and here is the discharge for you. The money, I don't regret it! As for me, forgive me, for Christ's sake."

And turning up the skirt of his coat, he dropped deliberately on his knees, and bowed down before Ilyushka and his wife. In vain did the young people try to restrain him; not before he had touched the ground with his head did he get up; then, shaking himself, he sat down on the bench. Ilyushka's mother and wife howled with delight. Words of approval were heard in the crowd. "That's the true, the godly way, indeed!" said one. "What is money? You can't buy a man for money!" said another. "What happiness!" said a third, "a righteous man, that's what he is!" Only the peasants who were to go as recruits said nothing, and slipped quietly out into the yard.

Two hours later the Dutlovs' two carts were driving out of the outskirts of the town. In the first cart, drawn by the roan mare with its sides pinched and its neck sweating, sat the old man and Ignat. In the back of the cart rattled strings of pots and of fancy bread. In the second cart, which no one was driving, the young wife sat sedately and happily beside her mother-in-law, both with kerchiefs on their heads. The young wife was holding a flask under her apron. Ilyushka sat swaying to and fro on the front seat, with his back to the horse. With a flushed face he was bending forward biting into a roll and talking incessantly. The voices, the rumble of the cart on the pavement, the snorting of the horses, all mingled into a general note of merriment. The horses, swishing their tails, moved at a more rapid trot as they recognized the way home. No one who walked or drove by them could help looking round at the merry family party.

Just as they drove out of the town the Dutlovs overtook a party of recruits. A group of them were standing in a ring round a tavern. One recruit wore his gray forage-cap pulled back on the nape of his neck; and with the unnatural expression given a man by the fore part of his head being shaven close, was jauntily strumming on a balalaika. Another, without a cap on his head, held a flask of vodka in one hand, while he danced in the middle of the ring. Ignat stopped the horse and got down to tighten the traces. All the Dutlovs stared with curiosity, approval, and amusement at the man who was dancing. The recruit seemed to see no one, but he was aware that the public admiring him had grown larger, and this gave him fresh energy and skill. He danced briskly. His brows were knitted, his flushed face was rigid, his mouth wore a fixed smile, which by now had lost all meaning. It seemed as though all the energies of his soul were bent on moving one foot after the other with the utmost possible speed, now on the toe and and now on the heel. Sometimes he would suddenly stop short, winking to the player of the balalaika, and the latter would begin striking all the strings more briskly than ever and even tapping on the case with his knuckles. The recruit would stop; but even when he stood still, he looked as if he were dancing all over. Then suddenly he would begin moving slowly, shaking his shoulders, and all at once would leap into the air, and with a wild shriek come down in a squatting position and start to throw out first one leg and then the other. The boys laughed, the women shook their heads, the men smiled approvingly. An old sergeant stood unmoved beside the dancer with an expression that seemed to say, "That seems a monstrous fine thing to you, but we know it all so well." The balalaika player was evidently tired; he looked round lazily, striking a false chord. All of a sudden he tapped the case with his fingers, and the dance was over.

"Hi, Alyoha!" said the musician to the dancer, pointing to Dutlov. "Yonder's your sponsor! . . ."

"Where? Ah, my dear good friend!" cried Alyoha; he was the recruit Dutlov had purchased as a substitute. With weary legs, stumbling forwards, and lifting a flask of vodka over his head, he came up to the cart. "Mishka, a glass!" he shouted. "Master! my dear good friend! This is a pleasure, really!" he cried, lurching tipsily against the cart, and he began offering vodka to the peasants and the women. The men drank some, the women refused. "My dears, what present can I make you all?" cried Alyoha, embracing the old woman.

A woman selling eatables was standing in the crowd. Alyoha caught sight of her, snatched her tray from her, and poured its contents into the cart.

"Never fear; I'll pa-a-ay, damn you!" he wailed in a tearful voice, and at once pulled out of his trousers a pouch with money in it, and flung it to Mishka.

He stood with his elbows on the cart and looked with wet eyes at the party sitting in it.

"Which is the mother?" he asked. "You, eh? I must give her a present too."

He pondered an instant and felt in his pocket; then pulled out a new kerchief folded up, took off the sash he wore under his soldier's cloak, hurriedly removed a red scarf from his neck, crumpled them all up together, and thrust them into the old woman's lap.

"There's an offering for you!" he said, in a voice which grew more and more subdued.

"What for? Thanks, my dear! Why, what a good-natured lad 'tis!" said the old woman, addressing old Dutlov, who had come up to their cart.

Alyoha sank into complete silence and stupefaction, and his head drooped lower and lower, as though he were falling asleep.

"It's for you I'm going, for you I'm perishing!" he said. "That's why I give you presents too."

"I dare say he's got a mother too," said someone in the crowd. "Such a good-natured lad!"

Alyoha raised his head.

"I've a mother," he said, "and a father too. They've all cast me off. Listen, old mother," he added, taking Ilyushka's mother by the hand. "I've made you a present. You listen to me, for Christ's sake. Go to Vodnoe village, ask there for old Mother Nikonova—she's my own mother, d'ye see?—and tell that same old woman, Mother Niko-nova—the third hut from the end, with the new well—tell her that Alyoha, her son . . . that is . . . Musician, strike up!" he shouted.

Muttering something, he began dancing again and dashed the flask with the rest of the vodka on the ground.

Ignat got into the cart and was about to drive away.

"Goodbye, God bless you!" said the old woman, wrapping her cloak round her.

Alyoha stopped all at once.

"You go to the devil!" he shouted, shaking his clenched fist at them. "Your mother be . . .!"

"O Lord," said Ilyushka's mother, crossing herself.

Ignat urged on the mare, and the carts rattled on again. The recruit Alyoha remained standing in the middle of the road, and shaking his clenched fists, with a look of fury on his face, abused the peasants with all the violence he was capable of.

"What did you stop for? Go on! Devils, cannibals!" he shouted, "you won't escape me! . . . Devils, low clodhoppers!"

At these words his voice broke, and he fell flat on the ground just where he stood.

Soon the Dutlovs got out into the open country, and looking back, saw no more of the crowd of recruits. After driving five versts further at a walking pace, Ignat got down from the cart, where his father had dropped asleep, and walked alongside Ilyushka's cart.

The two of them together emptied the flask of vodka they had brought from the town. Soon after, Ilyushka began singing; the women joined in with him. Ignat shouted gayly at the horse in tune with the song. A cheerful-looking posting-chaise came flying along to meet them. The driver called briskly to his horses as he passed the two festive carts; the postilion looked round and winked at the flushed faces of the men and the women, who were swaying in time to their merry song in the cart.

1863

# HOW MUCH LAND DOES A MAN NEED?

An ELDER sister came to visit her younger sister in the country. The elder was married to a tradesman in town, the younger to a peasant in the village. As the sisters sat over their tea talking, the elder began to boast of the advantages of town life: saying how comfortably they lived there, how well they dressed, what fine clothes her children wore, what good things they ate and drank, and how she went to the theater, promenades, and entertainments.

The younger sister was piqued, and in turn disparaged the life of a tradesman, and stood up for that of a peasant.

"I would not change my way of life for yours," said she. "We may live roughly, but at least we are free from anxiety. You live in better style than we do, but though you often earn more than you need, you are very likely to lose all you have. You know the proverb, 'Loss and gain are brothers twain.' It often happens that people who are wealthy one day are begging their bread the next. Our way is safer. Though a peasant's life is not a fat one, it is a long one. We shall never grow rich, but we shall always have enough to eat."

The elder sister said sneeringly:

"Enough? Yes, if you like to share with the pigs and the calves! What do you know of elegance or manners! However much your good man may slave, you will die as you are living—on a dung-heap —and your children the same."

"Well, what of that?" replied the younger. "Of course our work is rough and coarse. But, on the other hand, it is sure, and we need not bow to anyone. But you, in your towns, are surrounded by temptations; today all may be right, but tomorrow the Evil One may tempt your husband with cards, wine, or women, and all will go to ruin. Don't such things happen often enough?"

Pahom, the master of the house, was lying on the top of the stove and he listened to the women's chatter.

"It is perfectly true," thought he. "Busy as we are from childhood tilling mother earth, we peasants have no time to let any nonsense settle in our heads. Our only trouble is that we haven't land enough. If I had plenty of land, I shouldn't fear the Devil himself!"

The women finished their tea, chatted a while about dress, and then cleared away the tea-things and lay down to sleep.

But the Devil had been sitting behind the stove, and had heard all that was said. He was pleased that the peasant's wife had led her husband into boasting, and that he had said that if he had plenty of land he would not fear the Devil himself.

"All right," thought the Devil. "We will have a tussle. I'll give you land enough; and by means of that land I will get you into my power."

## II

Close to the village there lived a lady, a small landowner who had an estate of about three hundred acres. She had always lived on good terms with the peasants until she engaged as her steward an old soldier, who took to burdening the people with fines. However careful Pahom tried to be, it happened again and again that now a horse of his got among the lady's oats, now a cow strayed into her garden, now his calves found their way into her meadows—and he always had to pay a fine.

Pahom paid up, but grumbled, and going home in a temper, was rough with his family. All through that summer, Pahom had much trouble because of this steward, and he was even glad when winter came and the cattle had to be stabled. Though he grudged the fodder when they could no longer graze on the pasture-land, at least he was free from anxiety about them.

In the winter the news got about that the lady was going to sell her land and that the keeper of the inn on the highroad was bargaining for it. When the peasants heard this they were very much alarmed.

"Well," thought they, "if the innkeeper gets the land, he will worry us with fines worse than the lady's steward. We all depend on that estate."

So the peasants went on behalf of their commune, and asked the lady not to sell the land to the innkeeper, offering her a better price for it themselves. The lady agreed to let them have it. Then the peasants tried to arrange for the commune to buy the whole estate, so that it might be held by them all in common. They met twice to discuss it, but could not settle the matter; the Evil One sowed discord among them and they could not agree. So they decided to buy the land individually, each according to his means; and the lady agreed to this plan as she had to the other.

Presently Pahom heard that a neighbor of his was buying fifty acres, and that the lady had consented to accept one half in cash and to wait a year for the other half. Pahom felt envious.

"Look at that," thought he, "the land is all being sold, and I shall get none of it." So he spoke to his wife.

"Other people are buying," said he, "and we must also buy twenty acres or so. Life is becoming impossible. That steward is simply crushing us with his fines."

So they put their heads together and considered how they could manage to buy it. They had one hundred roubles laid by. They sold a colt and one half of their bees, hired out one of their sons as a laborer and took his wages in advance; borrowed the rest from a brother-in-law, and so scraped together half the purchase money.

Having done this, Pahom chose out a farm of forty acres, some of it wooded, and went to the lady to bargain for it. They came to an agreement, and he shook hands with her upon it and paid her a deposit in advance. Then they went to town and signed the deeds; he paying half the price down, and undertaking to pay the remainder within two years.

So now Pahom had land of his own. He borrowed seed, and sowed it on the land he had bought. The harvest was a good one, and within a year he had managed to pay off his debts both to the lady and to his brother-in-law. So he became a landowner, plowing and sowing his own land, making hay on his own land, cutting his own trees, and feeding his cattle on his own pasture. When he went out to plow his fields, or to look at his growing corn, or at his grass-meadows, his heart would fill with joy. The grass that grew and the flowers that bloomed there seemed to him unlike any that grew elsewhere. Formerly, when he had passed by that land, it had appeared the same as any other land, but now it seemed quite different.

## III

So Pahom was well contented, and everything would have been right if the neighboring peasants would only not have trespassed on his cornfields and meadows. He appealed to them most civilly, but they still went on: now the communal herdsmen would let the village cows stray into his meadows, then horses from the night pasture would get among his corn. Pahom turned them out again and again, and forgave their owners, and for a long time he forbore to prosecute anyone. But at last he lost patience and complained to the District Court. He knew it was the peasants' want of land, and no evil intent on their part, that caused the trouble, but he thought:

"I cannot go on overlooking it or they will destroy all I have. They must be taught a lesson."

So he had them up, gave them one lesson, and then another, and two or three of the peasants were fined. After a time Pahom's neighbors began to bear him a grudge for this, and would now and then let their cattle onto his land on purpose. One peasant even got into Pahom's wood at night and cut down five young lime trees for their bark. Pahom passing through the wood one day noticed something white. He came nearer and saw the stripped trunks lying on the ground, and close by stood the stumps where the trees had been. Pahom was furious.

"If he had only cut one here and there it would have been bad enough," thought Pahom, "but the rascal has actually cut down a whole clump. If I could only find out who did this, I would pay him out."

He racked his brains as to who it could be. Finally he decided: "It must be Semyon—no one else could have done it." So he went to Semyon's homestead to have a look round, but he found nothing, and only had an angry scene. However, he now felt more certain than ever that Semyon had done it, and he lodged a complaint. Semyon was summoned. The case was tried, and retried, and at the end of it all Semyon was acquitted, there being no evidence against him.

Pahom felt still more aggrieved, and let his anger loose upon the elder and the judges.

"You let thieves grease your palms," said he. "If you were honest folk yourselves you would not let a thief go free."

So Pahom quarreled with the judges and with his neighbors. Threats to burn his buildings began to be uttered. So though Pahom had more land, his place in the commune was much worse than before.

About this time a rumor got about that many people were moving to new parts.

"There's no need for me to leave my land," thought Pahom. "But some of the others might leave our village and then there would be more room for us. I would take over their land myself and make my estate a bit bigger. I could then live more at ease. As it is, I am still too cramped to be comfortable."

One day Pahom was sitting at home when a peasant, passing through the village, happened to call in. He was allowed to stay the night, and supper was given him. Pahom had a talk with this peasant and asked him where he came from. The stranger answered that he came from beyond the Volga, where he had been working. One word led to another, and the man went on to say that many people were settling in those parts. He told how some people from his village had settled there. They had joined the commune, and had had twenty-five acres per man granted them. The land was so good, he said, that the rye sown on it grew as high as a horse, and so thick that five cuts of a sickle made a sheaf. One peasant, he said, had brought nothing with him but his bare hands, and now he had six horses and two cows of his own.

Pahom's heart kindled with desire. He thought:

"Why should I suffer in this narrow hole, if one can live so well elsewhere? I will sell my land and my homestead here, and with the money I will start afresh over there and get everything new. In this crowded place one is always having trouble. But I must first go and find out all about it myself."

Towards summer he got ready and started. He went down the Volga on a steamer to Samara, then walked another three hundred miles on foot, and at last reached the place. It was just as the stranger had said. The peasants had plenty of land: every man had twenty-five acres of communal land given him for his use, and anyone who had money could buy, besides, at a rouble an acre as much good freehold land as he wanted.

Having found out all he wished to know, Pahom returned home as autumn came on, and began selling off his belongings. He sold his land at a profit, sold his homestead and all his cattle, and withdrew from membership of the commune. He only waited till the spring, and then started with his family for the new settlement.

## IV

As soon as Pahom and has family reached their new abode, he applied for admission into the commune of a large village. He stood treat to the elders and obtained the necessary documents. Five shares of communal land were given him for his own and his sons' use: that is to say—one hundred and twenty-five acres (not all together, but in different fields) besides the use of the communal pasture. Pahom put up the buildings he needed, and bought cattle. Of the communal land alone he had three times as much as at his former home, and the land was good corn-land. He was ten times better off than he had been. He had plenty of arable land and pasturage, and could keep as many head of cattle as he liked.

At first, in the bustle of building and settling down, Pahom was pleased with it all, but when he got used to it he began to think that even here he had not enough land. The first year, he sowed wheat on his share of the communal land and had a good crop. He wanted to go on sowing wheat, but had not enough communal land for the purpose, and what he had already used was not available; for in those parts wheat is only sown on virgin soil or on fallow land. It is sown for one or two years, and then the land lies fallow till it is again overgrown with prairie grass. There were many who wanted such land and there was not enough for all; so that people quarreled about it. Those who were better off wanted it for growing wheat, and those who were poor wanted it to let to dealers, so that they might raise money to pay their taxes. Pahom wanted to sow more wheat, so he rented land from a dealer for a year. He sowed much wheat and had a fine crop, but the land was too far from the village—the wheat had to be carted more than ten miles. After a time Pahom noticed that some peasant-dealers were living on separate farms and were growing wealthy; and he thought:

"If I were to buy some freehold land and have a homestead on it, it would be a different thing altogether. Then it would all be nice and compact."

The question of buying freehold land recurred to him again and again.

He went on in the same way for three years, renting land and sowing wheat. The seasons turned out well and the crops were good, so that he began to lay money by. He might have gone on living contentedly, but he grew tired of having to rent other people's land every year, and having to scramble for it. Wherever there was good land to be had, the peasants would rush for it and it was taken up at once, so that unless you were sharp about it you got none. It happened in the third year that he and a dealer together rented a piece of pasture-land from some peasants; and they had already plowed it up, when there was some dispute and the peasants went to law about it, and things fell out so that the labor was all lost.

"If it were my own land," thought Pahom, "I should be independent, and there would not be all this unpleasantness."

So Pahom began looking out for land which he could buy; and he came across a peasant who had bought thirteen hundred acres, but having got into difficulties was willing to sell again cheap. Pahom bargained and haggled with him, and at last they settled the price at fifteen hundred roubles, part in cash and part to be paid later. They had all but clinched the matter when a passing dealer happened to stop at Pahom's one day to get a feed for his horses. He drank tea with Pahom and they had a talk. The dealer said that he was just returning from the land of the Bashkirs, far away, where he had bought thirteen thousand acres of land, all for a thousand roubles. Pahom questioned him further, and the tradesman said:

"All one need do is to make friends with the chiefs. I gave away about one hundred roubles' worth of silk robes and carpets, besides a case of tea, and I gave wine to those who would drink it; and I got the land for less than a copeck an acre." And he showed Pahom the title-deeds, saying:

"The land lies near a river, and the whole prairie is virgin soil."

Pahom plied him with questions, and the tradesman said:

"There is more land there than you could cover if you walked a year, and it all belongs to the Bashkirs. They are as simple as sheep, and land can be got almost for nothing."

"There now," thought Pahom, "with my one thousand roubles, why should I get only thirteen hundred acres, and saddle myself with a debt besides? If I take it out there, I can get more than ten times as much for the money."

## V

Pahom inquired how to get to the place, and as soon as the tradesman had left him, he prepared to go there himself. He left his wife to look after the homestead, and started on his journey taking his man with him. They stopped at a town on their way and bought a case of tea, some wine, and other presents, as the tradesman had advised. On and on they went until they had gone more than three hundred miles, and on the seventh day they came to a place where the Bashkirs had pitched their tents. It was all just as the tradesman had said. The people lived on the steppes, by a river, in felt-covered tents. They neither tilled the ground, nor ate bread. Their cattle and horses grazed in herds on the steppe. The colts were tethered behind the tents, and the mares were driven to them twice a day. The mares were milked, and from the milk kumiss was made. It was the women who prepared kumiss, and they also made cheese. As far as the men were concerned, drinking kumiss and eating mutton, and playing on their pipes, was all they cared about. They were all stout and merry, and all the summer long they never thought of doing any work. They were quite ignorant, and knew no Russian, but were good-natured enough.

As soon as they saw Pahom, they came out of their tents and gathered round their visitor. An interpreter was found, and Pahom told them he had come about some land. The Bashkirs seemed very glad; they took Pahom and led him into one of the best tents, where they made him sit on some down cushions placed on a carpet, while they sat round him. They gave him some tea and kumiss, and had a sheep killed, and gave him mutton to eat. Pahom took presents out of his cart and distributed them among the Bashkirs, and divided the tea amongst them. The Bashkirs were delighted. They talked a great deal among themselves, and then told the interpreter to translate.

"They wish to tell you," said the interpreter, "that they like you, and that it is our custom to do all we can to please a guest and to repay him for his gifts. You have given us presents, now tell us which of the things we possess please you best, that we may present them to you."

"What pleases me best here," answered Pahom, "is your land. Our land is crowded and the soil is exhausted; but you have plenty of land and it is good land. I never saw the like of it."

The interpreter translated. The Bashkirs talked among themselves for a while. Pahom could not understand what they were saying, but saw that they were much amused and that they shouted and laughed. Then they were silent and looked at Pahom while the interpreter said:

"They wish me to tell you that in return for your presents they will gladly give you as much land as you want. You have only to point it out with your hand and it is yours."

The Bashkirs talked again for a while and began to dispute. Pahom asked what they were disputing about, and the interpreter told him that some of them thought they ought to ask their Chief about the land and not act in his absence, while others thought there was no need to wait for his return.

## VI

While the Bashkirs were disputing, a man in a large fox-fur cap appeared on the scene. They all became silent and rose to their feet. The interpreter said, "This is our Chief himself."

Pahom immediately fetched the best dressing-gown and five pounds of tea, and offered these to the Chief. The Chief accepted them, and seated himself in the place of honor. The Bashkirs at once began telling him something. The Chief listened for a while, then made a sign with his head for them to be silent, and addressing himself to Pahom, said in Russian:

"Well, let it be so. Choose whatever piece of land you like; we have plenty of it."

"How can I take as much as I like?" thought Pahom. "I must get a deed to make it secure, or else they may say, 'It is yours,' and afterwards may take it away again."

"Thank you for your kind words," he said aloud. "You have much land, and I only want a little. But I should like to be sure which bit is mine. Could it not be measured and made over to me? Life and death are in God's hands. You good people give it to me, but your children might wish to take it away again."

"You are quite right," said the Chief. "We will make it over to you."

"I heard that a dealer had been here," continued Pahom, "and that you gave him a little land, too, and signed title-deeds to that effect. I should like to have it done in the same way."

The Chief understood.

"Yes," replied he, "that can be done quite easily. We have a scribe, and we will go to town with you and have the deed properly sealed."

"And what will be the price?" asked Pahom.

"Our price is always the same: one thousand roubles a day."

Pahom did not understand.

"A day? What measure is that? How many acres would that be?"

"We do not know how to reckon it out," said the Chief. "We sell it by the day. As much as you can go round on your feet in a day is yours, and the price is one thousand roubles a day."

Pahom was surprised.

"But in a day you can get round a large tract of land," he said.

The Chief laughed.

"It will all be yours!" said he. "But there is one condition: If you don't return on the same day to the spot whence you started, your money is lost."

"But how am I to mark the way that I have gone?"

"Why, we shall go to any spot you like, and stay there. You must start from that spot and make your round, taking a spade with you. Wherever you think necessary, make a mark. At every turning, dig a hole and pile up the turf; then afterwards we will go round with a plow from hole to hole. You may make as large a circuit as you please, but before the sun sets you must return to the place you started from. All the land you cover will be yours."

Pahom was delighted. It was decided to start early next morning. They talked awhile, and after drinking some more kumiss and eating some more mutton, they had tea again, and then the night came on. They gave Pahom a feather-bed to sleep on, and the Bashkirs dispersed for the night, promising to assemble the next morning at daybreak and ride out before sunrise to the appointed spot.

## VII

Pahom lay on the feather-bed, but could not sleep. He kept think-ing about the land.

"What a large tract I will mark off!" thought he. "I can easily do thirty-five miles in a day. The days are long now, and within a circuit of thirty-five miles what a lot of land there will be! I will sell the poorer land, or let it to peasants, but I'll pick out the best and farm it. I will buy two ox-teams, and hire two more laborers. About a hundred and fifty acres shall be plowland, and I will pasture cattle on the rest."

Pahom lay awake all night, and dozed off only just before dawn. Hardly were his eyes closed when he had a dream. He thought he was lying in that same tent and heard somebody chuckling outside. He wondered who it could be, and rose and went out, and he saw the Bashkir Chief sitting in front of the tent holding his sides and rolling about with laughter. Going nearer to the Chief, Pahom asked: "What are you laughing at?" But he saw that it was no longer the Chief, but the dealer who had recently stopped at his house and had told him about the land. Just as Pahom was going to ask, "Have you been here long?" he saw that it was not the dealer, but the peasant who had come up from the Volga, long ago, to Pahom's old home. Then he saw that it was not the peasant either, but the Devil himself with hoofs and horns, sitting there and chuckling, and before him lay a man barefoot, prostrate on the ground, with only trousers and a shirt on. And Pahom dreamt that he looked more attentively to see what sort of a man it was that was lying there, and he saw that the man was dead, and that it was himself! He awoke horror-struck.

"What things one does dream," thought he.

Looking round he saw through the open door that the dawn was breaking. "It's time to wake them up," thought he. "We ought to be starting."

He got up, roused his man (who was sleeping in his cart), bade him harness; and went to call the Bashkirs.

"It's time to go to the steppe to measure the land," he said.

The Bashkirs rose and assembled, and the Chief came too. Then they began drinking kumiss again, and offered Pahom some tea, but he would not wait.

"If we are to go, let us go. It is high time," said he.

## VIII

The Bashkirs got ready and they all started: some mounted on horses, and some in carts. Pahom drove in his own small cart with his servant and took a spade with him. When they reached the steppe, the morning red was beginning to kindle. They ascended a hillock (called by the Bashkirs a *shikhan*) and dismounting from their carts and their horses, gathered in one spot. The Chief came up to Pahom and stretching out his arm towards the plain:

"See," said he, "all this, as far as your eye can reach, is ours. You may have any part of it you like."

Pahom's eyes glistened: it was all virgin soil, as flat as the palm of your hand, as black as the seed of a poppy, and in the hollows different kinds of grasses grew breast-high.

The Chief took off his fox-fur cap, placed it on the ground and said:

"This will be the mark. Start from here, and return here again. All the land you go round shall be yours."

Pahom took out his money and put it on the cap. Then he took off his outer coat, remaining in his sleeveless undercoat. He unfastened his girdle and tied it tight below his stomach, put a little bag of bread into the breast of his coat, and tying a flask of water to his girdle, he drew up the tops of his boots, took the spade from the man, and stood ready to start. He considered for some moments which way he had better go—it was tempting everywhere.

"No matter," he concluded, "I will go towards the rising sun."

He turned his face to the east, stretched himself, and waited for the sun to appear above the rim.

"I must lose no time," he thought, "and it is easier walking while it is still cool."

The sun's rays had hardly flashed above the horizon, before Pahom, carrying the spade over his shoulder, went down into the steppe.

Pahom started walking neither slowly nor quickly. After having gone a thousand yards he stopped, dug a hole, and placed pieces of turf one on another to make it more visible. Then he went on; and now that he had walked off his stiffness he quickened his pace. After a while he dug another hole.

Pahom looked back. The hillock could be distinctly seen in the sunlight, with the people on it, and the glittering tires of the cart-wheels. At a rough guess Pahom concluded that he had walked three miles. It was growing warmer; he took off his undercoat, flung it across his shoulder, and went on again. It had grown quite warm now; he looked at the sun, it was time to think of breakfast.

"The first shift is done, but there are four in a day, and it is too soon yet to turn. But I will just take off my boots," said he to himself.

He sat down, took off his boots, stuck them into his girdle, and went on. It was easy walking now.

"I will go on for another three miles," thought he, "and then turn to the left. This spot is so fine, that it would be a pity to lose it. The further one goes, the better the land seems."

He went straight on for a while, and when he looked round, the hillock was scarcely visible and the people on it looked like black ants, and he could just see something glistening there in the sun.

"Ah," thought Pahom, "I have gone far enough in this direction, it is time to turn. Besides I am in a regular sweat, and very thirsty."

He stopped, dug a large hole, and heaped up pieces of turf. Next he untied his flask, had a drink, and then turned sharply to the left. He went on and on; the grass was high, and it was very hot.

Pahom began to grow tired: he looked at the sun and saw that it was noon.

"Well," he thought, "I must have a rest."

He sat down, and ate some bread and drank some water; but he did not lie down, thinking that if he did he might fall asleep. After sitting a little while, he went on again. At first he walked easily: the food had strengthened him; but it had become terribly hot and he felt sleepy, still he went on, thinking: "An hour to suffer, a lifetime to live."

He went a long way in this direction also, and was about to turn to the left again, when he perceived a damp hollow: "It would be a pity to leave that out," he thought. "Flax would do well there." So he went on past the hollow, and dug a hole on the other side of it before he turned the corner. Pahom looked towards the hillock. The heat made the air hazy: it seemed to be quivering, and through the haze the people on the hillock could scarcely be seen.

"Ah!" thought Pahom, "I have made the sides too long; I must make this one shorter." And he went along the third side, stepping faster. He looked at the sun: it was nearly halfway to the horizon, and he had not yet done two miles of the third side of the square. He was still ten miles from the goal.

"No," he thought, "though it will make my land lopsided, I must hurry back in a straight line now. I might go too far, and as it is I have a great deal of land."

So Pahom hurriedly dug a hole, and turned straight towards the hillock.

## IX

Pahom went straight towards the hillock, but he now walked with difficulty. He was done up with the heat, his bare feet were cut and bruised, and his legs began to fail. He longed to rest, but it was impossible if he meant to get back before sunset. The sun waits for no man, and it was sinking lower and lower.

"Oh, dear," he thought, "if only I have not blundered trying for too much! What if I am too late?"

He looked towards the hillock and at the sun. He was still far from his goal, and the sun was already near the rim.

Pahom walked on and on; it was very hard walking but he went quicker and quicker. He pressed on, but was still far from the place. He began running, threw away his coat, his boots, his flask, and his cap, and kept only the spade which he used as a support.

"What shall I do," he thought again, "I have grasped too much and ruined the whole affair. I can't get there before the sun sets."

And this fear made him still more breathless. Pahom went on running, his soaking shirt and trousers stuck to him and his mouth was parched. His breast was working like a blacksmith's bellows, his heart was beating like a hammer, and his legs were giving way as if they did not belong to him. Pahom was seized with terror lest he should die of the strain.

Though afraid of death, he could not stop. "After having run all that way they will call me a fool if I stop now," thought he. And he ran on and on, and drew near and heard the Bashkirs yelling and shouting to him, and their cries inflamed his heart still more. He gathered his last strength and ran on.

The sun was close to the rim, and cloaked in mist looked large, and red as blood. Now, yes now, it was about to set! The sun was quite low, but he was also quite near his aim. Pahom could already see the people on the hillock waving their arms to hurry him up. He could see the fox-fur cap on the ground and the money on it, and the Chief sitting on the ground holding his sides. And Pahom remembered his dream.

"There is plenty of land," thought he, "but will God let me live on it? I have lost my life, I have lost my life! I shall never reach that spot!"

Pahom looked at the sun, which had reached the earth: one side of it had already disappeared. With all his remaining strength he rushed on, bending his body forward so that his legs could hardly follow fast enough to keep him from falling. Just as he reached the hillock it suddenly grew dark. He looked up—the sun had already set! He gave a cry: "All my labor has been in vain," thought he, and was about to stop, but he heard the Bashkirs still shouting, and remembered that though to him, from below, the sun seemed to have set, they on the hillock could still see it. He took a long breath and ran up the hillock. It was still light there. He reached the top and saw the cap. Before it sat the Chief laughing and holding his sides. Again Pahom remembered his dream, and he uttered a cry: his legs gave way beneath him, he fell forward and reached the cap with his hands.

"Ah, that's a fine fellow!" exclaimed the Chief. "He has gained much land!"

Pahom's servant came running up and tried to raise him, but he saw that blood was flowing from his mouth. Pahom was dead!

The Bashkirs clicked their tongues to show their pity.

His servant picked up the spade and dug a grave long enough for Pahom to lie in, and buried him in it. Six feet from his head to his heels was all he needed.

1886

# AFTER THE BALL

"—And you say that a man cannot, of himself, understand what is good and evil; that it is all environment, that the environment swamps the man. But I believe it is all chance. Take my own case . . ."

Thus spoke our excellent friend, Ivan Vasilyevich, after a conversation between us on the impossibility of improving individual character without a change of the conditions under which men live. Nobody had actually said that one could not of oneself understand good and evil; but it was a habit of Ivan Vasilyevich to answer in this way the thoughts aroused in his own mind by conversation, and to illustrate those thoughts by relating incidents in his own life. He often quite forgot the reason for his story in telling it; but he always told it with great sincerity and feeling.

He did so now.

"Take my own case. My whole life was molded, not by environment, but by something quite different."

"By what, then?" we asked.

"Oh, that is a long story. I should have to tell you about a great many things to make you understand."

"Well, tell us then."

Ivan Vasilyevich thought a little, and shook his head.

"My whole life," he said, "was changed in one night, or, rather, morning."

"Why, what happened?" one of us asked.

"What happened was that I was very much in love. I have been in love many times, but this was the most serious of all. It is a thing of the past; she has married daughters now. It was Varinka B——."

Ivan Vasilyevich mentioned her surname. "Even at fifty she is re-markably handsome; but in her youth, at eighteen, she was exquisite —tall, slender, graceful, and stately. Yes, stately is the word; she held herself very erect, by instinct as it were; and carried her head high, and that together with her beauty and height gave her a queenly air in spite of being thin, even bony one might say. It might indeed have been deterring had it not been for her smile, which was always gay and cordial, and for the charming light in her eyes and for her youthful sweetness."

"What an entrancing description you give, Ivan Vasilyevich!"

"Description, indeed! I could not possibly describe her so that you could appreciate her. But that does not matter; what I am going to tell you happened in the forties. I was at that time a student in a provincial university. I don't know whether it was a good thing or not, but we had no political clubs, no theories in our universities then. We were simply young and spent our time as young men do, studying and amusing ourselves. I was a very gay, lively, careless fellow, and had plenty of money too. I had a fine horse, and used to go tobogganing with the young ladies. Skating had not yet come into fashion. I went to drinking parties with my comrades—in those days we drank nothing but champagne—if we had no champagne we drank nothing at all. We never drank vodka, as they do now. Evening parties and balls were my favorite amusements. I danced well, and was not an ugly fellow."

"Come, there is no need to be modest," interrupted a lady near him. "We have seen your photograph. Not ugly, indeed! You were a handsome fellow."

"Handsome, if you like. That does not matter. When my love for her was at its strongest, on the last day of the carnival, I was at a ball at the provincial marshal's, a good-natured old man, rich and hospitable, and a court chamberlain. The guests were welcomed by his wife, who was as good-natured as himself. She was dressed in puce-colored velvet, and had a diamond diadem on her forehead, and her plump, old white shoulders and bosom were bare like the portraits of Empress Elizabeth, the daughter of Peter the Great.

"It was a delightful ball. It was a splendid room, with a gallery for the orchestra, which was famous at the time, and consisted of serfs belonging to a musical landowner. The refreshments were mag-nificent, and the champagne flowed in rivers. Though I was fond of champagne I did not drink that night, because without it I was drunk with love. But I made up for it by dancing waltzes and polkas till I was ready to drop—of course, whenever possible, with Varinka. She wore a white dress with a pink sash, white shoes, and white kid gloves, which did not quite reach to her thin pointed elbows. A disgusting engineer named Anisimov robbed me of the mazurka with her—to this day I cannot forgive him. He asked her for the dance the minute she arrived, while I had driven to the hairdresser's to get a pair of gloves, and was late. So I did not dance the mazurka with her, but with a German girl to whom I had previously paid a little attention; but I am afraid I did not behave very politely to her that evening. I hardly spoke or looked at her, and saw nothing but the tall, slender figure in a white dress, with a pink sash, a flushed, beaming, dimpled face, and sweet, kind eyes. I was not alone; they were all looking at her with admiration, the men and women alike, although she outshone all of them. They could not help admiring her.

"Although I was not nominally her partner for the mazurka, I did as a matter of fact dance nearly the whole time with her. She always came forward boldly the whole length of the room to pick me out. I flew to meet her without waiting to be chosen, and she thanked me with a smile for my intuition. When I was brought up to her with somebody else, and she guessed wrongly, she took the other man's hand with a shrug of her slim shoulders, and smiled at me regretfully.

"Whenever there was a waltz figure in the mazurka, I waltzed with her for a long time, and breathing fast and smiling, she would say, 'Encore'; and I went on waltzing and waltzing, as though unconscious of any bodily existence."

"Come now, how could you be unconscious of it with your arm round her waist? You must have been conscious, not only of your own existence, but of hers," said one of the party.

Ivan Vasilyevich cried out, almost shouting in anger: "There you are, moderns all over! Nowadays you think of nothing but the body. It was different in our day. The more I was in love the less corporeal was she in my eyes. Nowadays you see legs, ankles, and I don't know what. You undress the women you are in love with. In my eyes, as Alphonse Karr said—and he was a good writer—'the one I loved was always draped in robes of bronze.' We weren't like you; we tried to veil her nakedness, like Noah's good-natured son. Oh, well, you can't understand."

"Don't pay any attention to him. Go on," said one of them.

"Well, I danced for the most part with her, and did not notice how time was passing. The musicians kept playing the same mazurka tunes over and over again in desperate exhaustion—you know what it is towards the end of a ball. Papas and mammas were already getting up from the card-tables in the drawing-room in expectation of supper, the menservants were running to and fro bringing in things. It was nearly three o'clock. I had to make the most of the last minutes. I chose her again for the mazurka, and for the hundredth time we danced across the room.

" 'The quadrille after supper is mine,' I said, taking her to her place.

" 'Of course, if I am not carried off home,' she said, with a smile.

" 'I won't give you up,' I said.

" 'Give me my fan, anyhow,' she answered.

" 'I am so sorry to part with it,' I said, handing her a cheap white fan.

" 'Well, here's something to console you,' she said, plucking a feather out of the fan, and giving it to me.

"I took the feather, and could only express my rapture and gratitude with my eyes. I was not only pleased and gay, I was happy, delighted; I was good, I was not myself but some being not of this earth, knowing nothing of evil. I hid the feather in my glove, and stood there unable to tear myself away from her.

" 'Look, they are urging father to dance,' she said to me, pointing to the tall, stately figure of her father, a colonel with silver epaulettes, who was standing in the doorway with some ladies.

" 'Varinka, come here!' exclaimed our hostess, the lady with the diamond *ferronnière* and with shoulders like Elizabeth, in a loud voice.

"Varinka went to the door, and I followed her.

" 'Persuade your father to dance the mazurka with you, *ma chère.* —Do, please, Peter Valdislavovich,' she said, turning to the colonel.

"Varinka's father was a very handsome, well-preserved old man. He had good color, mustaches curled in the style of Nicholas I, and white whiskers which met the mustaches. His hair was combed over his temples and a bright smile, like his daughter's, was on his lips and in his eyes. He was splendidly set up, with a broad military chest, on which he wore some decorations, and he had powerful shoulders and long slim legs. He was that ultramilitary type produced by the discipline of Emperor Nicholas I.

"When we approached the door the colonel was just refusing to dance, saying that he had quite forgotten how; but at that instant he smiled, swung his arm gracefully around to the left, drew his sword from its sheath, handed it to an obliging young man who stood near, and smoothed the suède glove on his right hand.

" 'Everything must be done according to rule,' he said with a smile. He took the hand of his daughter, and stood one-quarter turned, waiting for the music.

"At the first sound of the mazurka, he stamped one foot smartly, threw the other forward, and, at first slowly and smoothly, then buoyantly and impetuously, with stamping of feet and clicking of boots, his tall, imposing figure moved the length of the room. Varinka swayed gracefully beside him, rhythmically and easily, making her steps short or long, with her little feet in their white satin slippers.

"All the people in the room followed every movement of the couple. As for me I not only admired, I regarded them with enraptured sympathy. I was particularly impressed with the old gentleman's boots. They were not the modern pointed affairs, but were made of cheap leather, square-toed, and evidently built by the regimental cobbler. In order that his daughter might dress and go out in society, he did not buy fashionable boots, but wore homemade ones, I thought, and his square toes seemed to me most touching. It was obvious that in his time he had been a good dancer; but now he was too heavy, and his legs had not spring enough for all the beautiful steps he tried to take. Still, he contrived to go twice round the room. When at the end, standing with legs apart, he suddenly clicked his feet together and fell on one knee, a bit heavily, and she danced gracefully around him, smiling and adjusting her skirt, the whole room applauded.

"Rising with an effort, he tenderly took his daughter's face between his hands. He kissed her on the forehead, and brought her to me, under the impression that I was her partner for the mazurka. I said I was not. 'Well, never mind. Just go around the room once with her,' he said, smiling kindly, as he replaced his sword in the sheath.

"As the contents of a bottle flow readily when the first drop has been poured, so my love for Varinka seemed to set free the whole force of loving within me. In surrounding her it embraced the world. I loved the hostess with her diadem and her shoulders like Elizabeth, and her husband and her guests and her footmen, and even the engineer Anisimov who felt peevish towards me. As for Varinka's father, with his homemade boots and his kind smile, so like her own, I felt a sort of tenderness for him that was almost rapture.

"After supper I danced the promised quadrille with her, and though I had been infinitely happy before, I grew still happier every moment.

"We did not speak of love. I neither asked myself nor her whether she loved me. It was quite enough to know that I loved her. And I had only one fear—that something might come to interfere with my great joy.

"When I went home, and began to undress for the night, I found it quite out of the question. I held the little feather out of her fan in my hand, and one of her gloves which she gave me when I helped her into the carriage after her mother. Looking at these things, and without closing my eyes I could see her before me as she was for an instant when she had to choose between two partners. She tried to guess what kind of person was represented in me, and I could hear her sweet voice as she said, 'Pride—am I right?' and merrily gave me her hand. At supper she took the first sip from my glass of champagne, looking at me over the rim with her caressing glance. But, plainest of all, I could see her as she danced with her father, gliding along beside him, and looking at the admiring observers with pride and happiness.

"He and she were united in my mind in one rush of pathetic tenderness.

"I was living then with my brother, who has since died. He disliked going out, and never went to dances; and besides, he was busy preparing for his last university examinations, and was leading a very regular life. He was asleep. I looked at him, his head buried in the pillow and half covered with the quilt; and I affectionately pitied him—pitied him for his ignorance of the bliss I was experiencing. Our serf Petrusha had met me with a candle, ready to undress me, but I sent him away. His sleepy face and tousled hair seemed to me so touching. Trying not to make a noise, I went to my room on tiptoe and sat down on my bed. No, I was too happy; I could not sleep. Besides, it was too hot in the rooms. Without taking off my uniform, I went quietly into the hall, put on my overcoat, opened the front door and stepped out into the street.

"It was after four when I had left the ball; going home and stopping there awhile had occupied two hours, so by the time I went out it was dawn. It was regular carnival weather—foggy, and the road full of water-soaked snow just melting, and water dripping from the eaves. Varinka's family lived on the edge of town near a large field, one end of which was a parade ground: at the other end was a boarding-school for young ladies. I passed through our empty little street and came to the main thoroughfare, where I met pedestrians and sledges laden with wood, the runners grating the road. The horses swung with regular paces beneath their shining yokes, their backs covered with straw mats and their heads wet with rain; while the drivers, in enormous boots, splashed through the mud beside the sledges. All this, the very horses themselves, seemed to me stimulating and fascinating, full of suggestion.

"When I approached the field near the house, I saw at one end of it, in the direction of the parade ground, something very huge and black, and I heard sounds of fife and drum proceeding from it. My heart had been full of song, and I had heard in imagination the tune of the mazurka, but this was very harsh music. It was not pleasant.

" 'What can that be?' I thought, and went towards the sound by a slippery path through the centre of the field. Walking about a hundred paces, I began to distinguish many black objects through the mist. They were evidently soldiers. 'It is probably a drill,' I thought.

"So I went along in that direction in company with a blacksmith, who wore a dirty coat and an apron, and was carrying something. He walked ahead of me as we approached the place. The soldiers in black uniforms stood in two rows, facing each other motionless, their guns at rest. Behind them stood the fifes and drums, incessantly repeating the same unpleasant tune.

" 'What are they doing?' I asked the blacksmith, who halted at my side.

" 'A Tatar is being beaten through the ranks for his attempt to desert,' said the blacksmith in an angry tone, as he looked intently at the far end of the line.

"I looked in the same direction, and saw between the files something horrid approaching me. The thing that approached was a man, stripped to the waist, fastened with cords to the guns of two soldiers who were leading him. At his side an officer in overcoat and cap was walking, whose figure had a familiar look. The victim advanced under the blows that rained upon him from both sides, his whole body plunging, his feet dragging through the snow. Now he threw himself backward, and the sergeants who led him thrust him forward. Now he fell forward, and they pulled him up short; while ever at his side marched the tall officer, with firm and nervous pace. It was Varinka's father, with his rosy face and white mustache.

"At each stroke the man, as if amazed, turned his face, grimacing with pain, towards the side whence the blow came, and showing his white teeth repeated the same words over and over. But I could only hear what the words were when he came quite near. He did not speak them, he sobbed them out,—

" 'Brothers, have mercy on me! Brothers, have mercy on me!' But the brothers had no mercy, and when the procession came close to me, I saw how a soldier who stood opposite me took a firm step forward and lifting his stick with a whirr, brought it down upon the man's back. The man plunged forward, but the sergeants pulled him back, and another blow came down from the other side, and again from this side and then from the other. The colonel marched beside him, and looking now at his feet and now at the man, inhaled the air, puffed out his cheeks, and breathed it out between his protruded lips. When they passed the place where I stood, I caught a glimpse between the two files of the back of the man who was being punished. It was something so vivid, wet, red, unnatural, that I could hardly believe it was a human body.

" 'My God!' muttered the blacksmith.

"The procession moved farther away. The blows continued to rain upon the writhing, falling creature; the fifes shrilled and the drums beat, and the tall imposing figure of the colonel moved alongside the man, just as before. Then, suddenly, the colonel stopped, and rapidly approached a man in the ranks.

" 'I'll teach you to hit him gently,' I heard his furious voice say. 'Will you pat him like that? Will you?' and I saw how his strong hand in the suède glove struck the weak, bloodless, terrified soldier for not bringing down his stick with sufficient strength on the red back of the Tatar.

" 'Bring new sticks!' he cried, and looking round, he saw me. Assuming an air of not knowing me, and with a ferocious, angry frown, he hastily turned away. I felt so utterly ashamed that I didn't know where to look. It was as if I had been detected in a disgraceful act. I dropped my eyes, and quickly hurried home. All the way I had the drums beating and the fifes whistling in my ears. And I heard the words, 'Brothers, have mercy on me!' or 'Will you pat him? Will you?' My heart was full of physical disgust that was almost sickness. So much so that I halted several times on my way, for I had the feeling that I was going to be really sick from all the horrors that possessed me at that sight. I do not remember how I got home and got to bed. But the moment I was about to fall asleep I heard and saw again all that had happened, and I sprang up.

" 'Evidently he knows something I do not know,' I thought about the colonel. 'If I knew what he knows I should certainly grasp —understand—what I have just seen, and it would not cause me such suffering.'

"But however much I thought about it, I could not understand the thing that the colonel knew. It was evening before I could get to sleep, and then only after calling on a friend and drinking till I was quite drunk.

"Do you think I had come to the conclusion that the deed I had witnessed was wicked? Oh, no. Since it was done with such assurance, and was recognized by everyone as indispensable, they doubtless knew something which I did not know. So I thought, and tried to understand. But no matter, I could never understand it, then or afterwards. And not being able to grasp it, I could not enter the service as I had intended. I don't mean only the military service: I did not enter the civil service either. And so I have been of no use whatever, as you can see."

"Yes, we know how useless you've been," said one of us. "Tell us, rather, how many people would be of any use at all if it hadn't been for you."

"Oh, that's utter nonsense," said Ivan Vasilyevich, with genuine annoyance.

"Well; and what about the love affair?"

"My love? It decreased from that day. When, as often happened, she looked dreamy and meditative, I instantly recollected the colonel on the parade ground, and I felt so awkward and uncomfortable that I began to see her less frequently. So my love came to naught. Yes; such chances arise, and they alter and direct a man's whole life," he said in summing up. "And you say . . ."

Written, 1903—published posthumously, 1911.

# ALYOSHA

ALYOSHKA was the younger brother. He had been nicknamed "Pot" because his mother had once sent him to carry a pot of milk to the deacon's wife, and he had stumbled and broken it. His mother had given him a beating and the boys began to tease him about "the pot." "Alyoshka the Pot" they called him, and the nickname stuck.

Alyoshka was a skinny fellow, with large ears. They stuck out like wings, and he had a big nose. "Alyoshka's nose is like a dog on a hillock," the boys would call after him.

There was a school in the village, but Alyosha had no head for learning; beside, he had no time to study. His elder brother was in town working for a merchant, so Alyosha began to help his father at a very early age. He was only six when he started going out with his little sister to watch the cow and the few sheep in the pasture, and a little later he looked after the horses by day as well as by night, while they grazed in the fields. At twelve he had begun to plow and to drive the cart. He was not strong, but he was able. He was always cheerful. The boys made fun of him; he either said nothing or laughed with them. If his father scolded him, he listened in silence, and as soon as the scolding was over, he would smile and go on with his work.

Alyosha was nineteen when his brother was drafted. So his father had him take his brother's place with the merchant as a porter. He was given his brother's old boots, his father's cap and coat, and was taken to town. Alyosha was delighted with his clothes, but the merchant was not pleased with his appearance.

"I thought you would give me a man in Semyon's place," said

the merchant, eyeing Alyosha, "and you've brought me a runt. What good is he to me?"

"He can do everything. He can hitch horses and drive a cart, he's a glutton for work; he only looks spindly, but he's a tough one."

"Well, I'm not sure."

"One thing, he never talks back. And he just eats up work."

"Well, what can I do? Leave him here."

So Alyosha remained with the merchant.

The merchant's family was not a large one: it included his wife, his old mother, a married son with little education who was in his father's business, a younger son who had finished school and studied at the university, but, having been expelled, was living at home, and a daughter who still went to school.

At first they did not take to Alyosha—he was loutish, was badly dressed, was rough-spoken and unmannerly; but they soon got used to him. He did the work even better than his brother had done, and he actually never talked back. Whatever he was ordered to do, he did willingly and quickly, going from one task to another without a pause. And so here, even as at home, all manner of chores were heaped upon his shoulders. And the more he did, the more work everyone found for him to do. The mistress, the master's mother, his daughter, his son, the shop assistant and the cook, all sent him hither and yon, all demanded services from him. You never heard anything but: "Alyosha, run an errand for me," or "Alyosha, do this," or "What, have you forgotten, Alyosha?" and "Mind you, don't forget, Alyosha!" And Alyosha ran, looked after this and that, forgot nothing, managed to do everything, and kept smiling.

He soon wore out his brother's boots, and the master scolded him for going about with his bare toes sticking out of the holes, and ordered other boots bought for him in the market. The boots were new and Alyosha was delighted with them, but his feet were the same, and by the end of the day they ached with so much running about and he was annoyed. And then he was afraid that his father, coming to town to fetch his wages, would be put out to find that the merchant had deducted the cost of the boots.

In winter Alyosha got up before daybreak. He would chop wood, sweep the yard, feed and water the horse and cow. Then he would light the stoves, black the boots, brush the master's clothes, and heat the samovar, which it was his duty to keep bright. Then the shop assistant would summon him to move the goods or the cook would set him to knead the dough and clean the pots. Then he was sent to town on various errands: to deliver a note, to fetch the daughter from school, to buy oil for the old woman. "Where have you been dawdling, damn you?" one or another would say to him. Or it would be: "Why should you trouble? Alyosha will go, Alyosha! Hey, Alyosha!" and Alyosha went.

He ate his breakfast on the run, and he hardly ever managed to be around when dinnertime came. The cook scolded him for failing to show up with the others. Nevertheless she was sorry for him and would save something hot for his dinner and supper. Work piled up on him particularly before and during holiday time, but Alyosha liked holidays, especially because he got tips then. Not much money certainly, perhaps some sixty copecks in all; but it was his very own, that he could spend as he pleased. Alyosha never so much as set eyes on his wages. His father would come, take them from the merchant, and only scold Alyosha for wearing out his boots so fast.

When he had saved up two roubles in tips, he bought himself a red knitted jacket on the cook's advice, and when he put it on, he was so happy that his mouth gaped in a perpetual grin.

Alyosha had little to say, and when he spoke he did so abruptly and briefly. When ordered to do anything or asked if he could do it, he always answered unhesitatingly, "Sure I can," and set to work at once.

He did not know any prayers: he had forgotten those his mother had taught him. But he prayed just the same, morning and evening— he prayed with his hands, crossing himself.

Thus Alyosha lived for a year and a half, and when the second year was drawing to a close a most extraordinary event took place in his life. This event was the amazing discovery that, in addition to the relations existing between human beings because they want to make use of you, there are also relations of a quite different kind: not that they want you to black their boots, or to carry a package or hitch up the horses, but just that they want you around, as you are, so that they may look after you and be tender towards you, and that he, Alyosha, was wanted just that way.

He learned this through Ustinya, the cook. She was an orphan, a young girl, and as hard-working as Alyosha. She began to feel sorry for Alyosha, and for the first time in his life Alyosha felt that he, he himself, not his services, was necessary to another human being. When his mother had been sorry for him, he had not paid any attention to it, he took it for granted, it was just as though he were sorry for himself. But here he suddenly noticed that Ustinya, a perfect stranger, was sorry for him; she would leave some porridge with butter in a pot for him and would sit watching him while he ate it, her chin propped on her bare arm with its sleeve tucked up. And he would look at her, she would laugh, and he too would laugh.

This was so novel and strange that at first it frightened Alyosha. He felt that it would prevent him from performing his services as well as before. But he was glad all the same, and when he looked at the trousers that Ustinya had mended for him, he shook his head and smiled. Often while at work or while running an errand he thought of Ustinya and would say admiringly: "Oh, that Ustinya!" Whenever she could, she helped him, and he helped her. She told him about her life, how she had lost her parents, how an aunt had taken her in, how she had been given a situation in town, how the master's son had tried to lead her astray and how she had sent him about his business. She liked to talk and he liked to listen to her. He had heard it said that peasants who worked in town often got to marry cooks. One day she asked him if he was soon to be married off. He said he didn't know, but he didn't care to have a wife from the village.

"Well, have you found a girl that suits you?"

"I would marry you. Would you be willing?"

"Look at the fellow. They call him 'Pot,' but he has managed to speak up," she said, slapping him on the back with a towel. "Why shouldn't I?"

At Shrovetide Alyosha's father came to town for the lad's wages. The merchant's wife had gotten wind of the fact that Alyosha was thinking of marrying Ustinya, and she did not like it. "She will become pregnant, and what good will she be with a baby?" She spoke to her husband about it.

The merchant handed the old man Alyosha's wages.

"How's the boy getting on?" he asked. "I told you, he wasn't one to talk back."

"You're right about the back talk, but he has gotten a foolish notion into his head. He wants to marry the cook. Now, I won't have married servants. It doesn't suit me."

"Well, who would have thought the fool would get such a notion into his head?" cried the old man. "But don't worry. I'll tell him to drop this nonsense."

He made his way into the kitchen and sat down at the table waiting for his son. Alyosha was out on an errand and came back out of breath.

"I thought you were a decent boy, but now what's this you've taken into your head?" said the old man.

"I? Nothing."

"How—nothing? You're thinking of getting married. I'll marry you off when the time comes, and I'll find the right kind of wife for you, not a town slut."

The father had a great deal to say. Alyosha stood before him and sighed. When the old man had finished, Alyosha smiled.

"Well, I can drop it."

"That's better!"

When his father had gone, and he was left alone with Ustinya, he told her what the old man had said (there was no need for it, though, for she had listened at the door).

"It's all come to nothing. D'you hear? He got angry. He put his foot down."

Ustinya cried quietly into her apron.

Alyosha clicked his tongue.

"Can't disobey. I figure we'll have to give it up."

In the evening when the mistress called him to close the shutters, she said to him:

"Well, are you going to mind your father? Will you give up that nonsense of yours?"

"Looks that way," said Alyosha with a laugh, and then burst into tears.


From that day on Alyosha no longer spoke to Ustinya about marriage, and his life was what it had been earlier.

One day in Lent the shop assistant told Alyosha to clear the snow from the roof. Alyosha climbed onto the roof and cleared all the snow away. Then he started loosening up the ice in the gutters, when his foot slipped and he fell off the roof with his shovel in his hands. As ill luck would have it, he fell not into the snow, but on the sheet of iron covering the cellar door. Ustinya and the master's daughter came running up to him.

"Are you hurt, Alyosha?"

"Hurt, indeed! It's nothing."

He tried to raise himself, but could not, and began to smile. He was taken into the lodge. The doctor's assistant came, examined him, and asked him where it hurt him.

"It hurts all over, but that's nothing. I'm only afraid the master will be angry. Word ought to be sent to father."

Alyosha lay in bed for two days, and on the third day they sent for the priest.

"Well, are you going to die?" asked Ustinya.

"What do you think? Can we live forever? Some day we must make an end," Alyosha said briefly in his usual way. "Thank you, Ustinya, for having been kind to me. It's a good thing they didn't let us marry. What would have been the use? Now all's well."

When the priest came, Alyosha prayed only with his hands and his heart, which held this thought: As it is well with a man in this world if he is obedient and does no one any harm, so it will be well with him in the world beyond.

He spoke little. He only kept asking for a drink of water, and there was a puzzled expression in his eyes.

He looked round wonderingly, stretched himself, and died.

Written, 1905—published posthumously, 1911

# Anton Chekhov . . . 1860–1904

CHEKHOV was born the year before the Emancipation at Taganrog, a sleepy town on the Sea of Azov inhabited chiefly by Greeks. The third child in a family of six, he was the son of a grocer and the grandson of a serf. The atmosphere at home was both strict and sordid, the boy clerking for his father when he should have been playing or doing his homework. He was still at school when his father went bankrupt and the family moved away, leaving young Anton to fend for himself in Taganrog. At nineteen he followed his parents to Moscow, where he studied medicine. He had begun writing even earlier, and now he contributed sketches to the newspapers and humorous weeklies to help support himself and his family. In 1884 he published at his own expense a thin volume of skits and took his degree. For a few years he practiced medicine in good earnest. He called it his "lawful wife," and literature his "mistress." As time went by, it was to the latter that he came to give his full devotion. The strenuous work of a physician was difficult, too, for a man who at twenty-six showed symptoms of advanced tuberculosis.

In his early thirties he was an esteemed as well as a popular author: he had to his credit several books of short stories, many of them in a serious vein, which had previously appeared in the leading monthlies, had put on a play or two, and was the recipient of the Pushkin Prize from the Academy of Sciences. He was now able to buy a small estate and to gratify his taste for travel. It was not, however, as a tourist that he went to Sakhalin in the summer of 1890, but to study the penal colony there. The result of his investigation was a book which dealt impressively with the cruel facts, but had little practical effect. Although he was not politically minded, he had for some time been in the liberal camp, having ceased to contribute to the reactionary paper, *Novoye Vremya*, in which he had frequently appeared. During one of his trips to western Europe he became interested in the Dreyfus affair, siding with the defendant, which led to his break with the editor of *Novoye Vremya*, until then a close friend. Another gesture that endeared Chekhov to the opposition was his resignation, in 1902, from the Academy of Sciences, of which he was an honorary member, in protest against the annulment—under government pressure—of the election thereto of the radical Maxim Gorky.

At the turn of the century Chekhov's collected works were brought out in ten volumes. Altogether he wrote some six hundred short stories and a dozen plays. Most of the plays were written for the Moscow Art

Theater, with which he was associated from its inception in 1898 and with which his name is inextricably linked. He could not be in Moscow during the season, however, since the progress of his pulmonary disease forced him to winter in the Crimea, where he had built a villa near Yalta. The same unhappy circumstance separated him for long intervals from his wife, the actress, Olga Knipper, whom he married in 1901 (in 1943 she received the Stalin Prize for her contribution to the art of the theater). On his forty-fourth birthday, which coincided with the opening night of *The Cherry Orchard*, Chekhov's friends and admirers arranged a public celebration of the twenty-fifth anniversary of his career as a writer. Less than six months later he died at a health resort in the Black Forest.

# SMALL FRY

"HONORED SIR, Father and Benefactor!" a petty clerk called
Nevyrazimov was writing a rough copy of an Easter congratulatory
letter. "I trust that you may spend this Holy Day even as many more
to come, in good health and prosperity. And to your family also
I . . ."

The lamp, in which the kerosene was getting low, was smoking
and smelling. A stray cockroach was running about the table in
alarm near Nevyrazimov's writing hand. Two rooms away from the
office Paramon the porter was for the third time cleaning his best
boots, and with such energy that the sound of the blacking-brush
and of his expectorations was audible in all the rooms.

"What else can I write to him, the rascal?" Nevyrazimov wondered, raising his eyes to the smutty ceiling.

On the ceiling he saw a dark circle—the shadow of the lampshade.
Below it was the dusty cornice, and lower still the wall, which had
once been painted a bluish muddy color. And the office seemed to
him such a place of desolation that he felt sorry, not only for himself, but even for the cockroach.

"When I am off duty I shall go away, but he'll be on duty here
all his cockroach-life," he thought, stretching. "I am bored! Shall I
clean my boots?"

And stretching once more, Nevyrazimov slouched lazily to the
porter's room. Paramon had finished cleaning his boots. Crossing himself with one hand and holding the brush in the other, he was standing at the open windowpane, listening.

"They're ringing," he whispered to Nevyrazimov, looking at him
with eyes intent and wide open. "Already!"

Nevyrazimov put his ear to the open pane and listened. The Easter chimes floated into the room with a whiff of fresh spring air. The booming of the bells mingled with the rumble of carriages, and above the chaos of sounds rose the brisk tenor tones of the nearest church and a loud shrill laugh.

"What a lot of people!" sighed Nevyrazimov, looking down into the street, where shadows of men flitted one after another by the illumination lamps. "They're all hurrying to the midnight service. . . . Our fellows have had a drink by now, you may be sure, and are strolling about the town. What a lot of laughter, what a lot of talk! I'm the only unlucky one, to have to sit here on such a day. And I have to do it every year!"

"Well, nobody forces you to take the job. It's not your turn to be on duty today, but Zastupov hired you to take his place. When other folks are enjoying themselves you hire yourself out. It's greediness!"

"Devil a bit of it! Not much to be greedy over—two roubles is all he gives me; a necktie as an extra. . . . It's poverty, not greediness. And it would be jolly, now, you know, to be going with a party to the service, and then to break the fast. . . . To drink and to have a bit of supper and tumble off to sleep. . . . One sits down to the table, there's an Easter cake and the samovar hissing, and some charming little thing beside you. . . . You drink a glass and chuck her under the chin, and it's first-rate. . . . You feel you're somebody. . . . Ech-h-h! . . . I've made a mess of things! Look at that hussy driving by in her carriage, while I have to sit here and brood."

"We each have our lot in life, Ivan Danilich. Please God, you'll be promoted and drive about in your carriage one day."

"I? No, brother, not likely. I shan't get beyond a 'titular,' not if I try till I burst. I'm not an educated man."

"Our General has no education either, but . . ."

"Well, but the General stole a hundred thousand before he got his position. And he's got very different manners and deportment from me, brother. With my manners and deportment one can't get far! And such a scoundrelly surname, Nevyrazimov! It's a hopeless position, in fact. One may go on as one is, or one may hang oneself . . ."

He moved away from the window and walked wearily about

the rooms. The din of the bells grew louder and louder. . . . There was no need to stand by the window to hear it. And the better he could hear the bells and the louder the roar of the carriages, the darker seemed the muddy walls and the smutty cornice and the more the lamp smoked.

"Shall I hook it and leave the office?" thought Nevyrazimov.

But such a flight promised nothing worth having. . . . After coming out of the office and wandering about the town, Nevyrazimov would have gone home to his lodging, and in his lodging it was even grayer and more depressing than in the office. . . . Even supposing he were to spend that day pleasantly and with comfort, what had he beyond? Nothing but the same gray walls, the same stopgap duty and complimentary letters. . . .

Nevyrazimov stood still in the middle of the office and sank into thought. The yearning for a new, better life gnawed at his heart with an intolerable ache. He had a passionate longing to find himself suddenly in the street, to mingle with the living crowd, to take part in the solemn festivity for the sake of which all those bells were clashing and those carriages were rumbling. He longed for what he had known in childhood—the family circle, the festive faces of his own people, the white cloth, light, warmth . . . ! He thought of the carriage in which the lady had just driven by, the overcoat in which the head clerk was so smart, the gold chain that adorned the secretary's chest. . . . He thought of a warm bed, of the Stanislav order, of new boots, of a uniform without holes in the elbows. . . . He thought of all those things because he had none of them.

"Shall I steal?" he thought. "Even if stealing is an easy matter, hiding is what's difficult. Men run away to America, they say, with what they've stolen, but the devil knows where that blessed America is. One must have education even to steal, it seems."

The bells died down. He heard only a distant noise of carriages and Paramon's cough, while his depression and anger grew more and more intense and unbearable. The clock in the office struck half-past twelve.

"Shall I write a secret report? Proshkin did, and he rose rapidly."

Nevyrazimov sat down at his table and pondered. The lamp in which the kerosene had quite run dry was smoking violently and threatening to go out. The stray cockroach was still running about the table and had found no resting-place.

"One can always send in a secret report, but how is one to make it up? I should want to make all sorts of innuendoes and insinuations, like Proshkin, and I can't do it. If I made up anything I should be the first to get into trouble for it. I'm an ass, damn my soul!"

And Nevyrazimov, racking his brain for a means of escape from his hopeless position, stared at the rough copy he had written. The letter was written to a man whom he feared and hated with his whole soul, and from whom he had for the last ten years been trying to wring a post worth eighteen roubles a month, instead of the one he had at sixteen roubles.

"Ah, I'll teach you to run here, you devil!" He viciously slapped the palm of his hand on the cockroach, who had the misfortune to catch his eye. "Nasty thing!"

The cockroach fell on its back and wriggled its legs in despair. Nevyrazimov took it by one leg and threw it into the lamp. The lamp flared up and spluttered.

And Nevyrazimov felt better.

1885

# THE BEGGAR

"KIND sir, be so good as to notice a poor, hungry man. I have not tasted food for three days. . . . I have not a five-copeck piece for a night's lodging. . . . I swear by God! For five years I was a village schoolmaster and lost my post through the intrigues of the Zemstvo. I was the victim of false witness. I have been out of a place for a year now."

Skvortsov, a Petersburg lawyer, looked at the speaker's tattered dark blue overcoat, at his muddy, drunken eyes, at the red patches on his cheeks, and it seemed to him that he had seen the man before.

"And now I am offered a post in the Kaluga province," the beggar continued, "but I have not the means for the journey there. Graciously help me! I am ashamed to ask, but . . . I am compelled by circumstances."

Skvortsov looked at his galoshes, of which one was shallow like a shoe, while the other came high up the leg like a boot, and suddenly remembered.

"Listen, the day before yesterday I met you in Sadovoy Street," he said, "and then you told me, not that you were a village schoolmaster, but that you were a student who had been expelled. Do you remember?"

"No-o. No, that cannot be so!" the beggar muttered in confusion. "I am a village schoolmaster, and if you wish it I can show you documents to prove it."

"That's enough lies! You called yourself a student, and even told me what you were expelled for. Do you remember?"

Skvortsov flushed, and with a look of disgust on his face turned away from the ragged figure.

"It's contemptible, sir!" he cried angrily. "It's a swindle! I'll hand you over to the police, damn you! You are poor and hungry, but that does not give you the right to lie so shamelessly!"

The ragged figure took hold of the door-handle and, like a bird in a snare, looked round the hall desperately.

"I . . . I am not lying," he muttered. "I can show documents."

"Who can believe you?" Skvortsov went on, still indignant. "To exploit the sympathy of the public for village schoolmasters and students—it's so low, so mean, so dirty! It's revolting!"

Skvortsov flew into a rage and gave the beggar a merciless scolding. The ragged fellow's insolent lying aroused his disgust and aversion, was an offence against what he, Skvortsov, loved and prized in himself: kindliness, a feeling heart, sympathy for the unhappy. By his lying, by his treacherous assault upon compassion, the individual had, as it were, defiled the charity which he liked to give to the poor with no misgivings in his heart. The beggar at first defended himself, protested with oaths, then he sank into silence and hung his head, overcome with shame.

"Sir!" he said, laying his hand on his heart, "I really was . . . lying! I am not a student and not a village schoolmaster. All that's mere invention! I used to be in the Russian choir, and I was turned out of it for drunkenness. But what can I do? Believe me, in God's name, I can't get on without lying—when I tell the truth no one will give me anything. Telling the truth one may die of hunger and freeze without a night's lodging! What you say is true, I understand that, but . . . what am I to do?"

"What are you to do? You ask what are you to do?" cried Skvortsov, going close up to him. "Work—that's what you must do! You must work!"

"Work. . . . I know that myself, but where can I go to get work?"

"Nonsense. You are young, strong, and healthy, and could always find work if you wanted to. But you know you are lazy, pampered, drunken! You reek of vodka like a pothouse! You have become false and corrupt to the marrow of your bones and fit for nothing but begging and lying! If you do graciously condescend to take work, you must have a job in an office, in the Russian choir, or as a billiard-marker, where you will have a salary and have nothing to do! But how would you like to undertake manual labor? I'll be bound, you

wouldn't be a house porter or factory hand! You are too genteel
for that!"

"What things you say, really . . ." said the beggar, and he gave
a bitter smile. "How can I get manual work? It's rather late for me
to be a shopman, for in trade one has to begin from a boy; no one
would take me as a house porter, because I am not of that class.
. . . And I could not get work in a factory; one must know a
trade, and I know nothing."

"Nonsense! You always find some justification! Wouldn't you
like to chop wood?"

"I would not refuse to, but the regular wood-choppers are out
of work now."

"Oh, all idlers argue like that! As soon as you are offered anything you refuse it. Would you care to chop wood for me?"

"Certainly I will. . . ."

"Very good, we shall see. . . . Excellent. . . . We'll see!"

Skvortsov, in nervous haste, and not without malignant pleasure,
rubbing his hands, summoned his cook from the kitchen.

"Here, Olga," he said to her, "take this gentleman to the shed
and let him chop some wood."

The beggar shrugged his shoulders as though puzzled, and irresolutely followed the cook. It was evident from his demeanor
that he had consented to go and chop wood, not because he was
hungry and wanted to earn money, but simply from shame and
*amour propre*, because he had been taken at his word. It was clear,
too, that he was suffering from the effects of vodka, that he was
unwell, and felt not the faintest inclination to work.

Skvortsov hurried into the dining-room. There from the window
which looked out into the yard he could see the woodshed and everything that happened in the yard. Standing at the window, Skvortsov
saw the cook and the beggar come by the back way into the yard
and go through the muddy snow to the woodshed. Olga scrutinized
her companion angrily, and perking her elbow unlocked the woodshed and angrily banged the door open.

"Most likely we interrupted the woman drinking her coffee,"
thought Skvortsov. "What a cross creature she is!"

Then he saw the pseudo-schoolmaster and pseudo-student seat
himself on a block of wood, and, leaning his red cheeks upon his
fists, sink into thought. The cook flung an axe at his feet,

spat angrily on the ground, and, judging by the expression of her mouth, began abusing him. The beggar drew a log of wood towards him irresolutely, set it up between his feet, and diffidently drew the axe across it. The log toppled and fell over. The beggar drew it towards him, breathed on his frozen hands, and again drew the axe along it as cautiously as though he were afraid of its hitting his galosh or chopping off his fingers. The log fell over again.

Skvortsov's wrath had passed off by now; he felt sore and ashamed at the thought that he had forced a pampered, drunken, and perhaps sick man to do hard, rough work in the cold.

"Never mind, let him go on . . ." he thought, going from the dining-room into his study. "I am doing it for his good!"

An hour later Olga appeared and announced that the wood had been chopped.

"Here, give him half a rouble," said Skvortsov. "If he likes, let him come and chop wood on the first of every month. . . . There will always be work for him."

On the first of the month the beggar turned up and again earned half a rouble, though he could hardly stand. From that time forward he took to turning up frequently, and work was always found for him: sometimes he would sweep the snow into heaps, or clear up the shed, at another he used to beat the rugs and the mattresses. He always received thirty to forty copecks for his work, and on one occasion an old pair of trousers was sent out to him.

When he moved, Skvortsov engaged him to assist in packing and moving the furniture. On this occasion the beggar was sober, gloomy, and silent; he scarcely touched the furniture, walked with hanging head behind the furniture vans, and did not even try to appear busy; he merely shivered with the cold, and was overcome with confusion when the men with the vans laughed at his idleness, his feebleness, and the ragged coat that had once been a gentleman's. After the removal Skvortsov sent for him.

"Well, I see my words have had an effect upon you," he said, giving him a rouble. "This is for your work. I see that you are sober and not disinclined to work. What is your name?"

"Lushkov."

"I can offer you better work, not so rough, Lushkov. Can you write?"

"Yes, sir."

"Then go with this note tomorrow to my colleague and he will give you some copying to do. Work, don't drink, and don't forget what I said to you. Goodbye."

Skvortsov, pleased that he had put a man in the path of rectitude, patted Lushkov genially on the shoulder, and even shook hands with him at parting. Lushkov took the letter, departed, and from that time forward did not come to the backyard for work.

Two years passed. One day as Skvortsov was standing at the ticket-office of a theater, paying for his ticket, he saw beside him a little man with a lambskin collar and a shabby cat's-skin cap. The man timidly asked the clerk for a gallery ticket and paid for it with copeks.

"Lushkov, is it you?" asked Skvortsov, recognizing in the little man his former wood-chopper. "Well, what are you doing? Are you getting on all right?"

"Pretty well. . . . I am in a notary's office now. I earn thirty-five roubles."

"Well, thank God, that's capital. I rejoice for you. I am very, very glad, Lushkov. You know, in a way, you are my godson. It was I who shoved you into the right way. Do you remember what a scolding I gave you, eh? You almost sank through the floor that time. Well, thank you, my dear fellow, for remembering my words."

"Thank you too," said Lushkov. "If I had not come to you that day, maybe I should be calling myself a schoolmaster or a student still. Yes, in your house I was saved, and climbed out of the pit."

"I am very, very glad."

"Thank you for your kind words and deeds. What you said that day was excellent. I am grateful to you and to your cook, God bless that kind, noble-hearted woman. What you said that day was excellent; I am indebted to you as long as I live, of course, but it was your cook, Olga, who really saved me."

"How was that?"

"Why, it was like this. I used to come to you to chop wood and she would begin: 'Ah, you drunkard! You God-forsaken man! And yet death does not take you!' and then she would sit opposite me, lamenting, looking into my face and wailing: 'You unlucky fellow! You have no gladness in this world, and in the next you will burn in hell, poor drunkard! You poor sorrowful creature!' and she always went on in that style, you know. How often she upset herself, and how many tears she shed over me I can't tell you. But what affected me•most—she chopped the wood for me! Do you know, sir, I never chopped a single log for you—she did it all! How it was she saved me, how it was I changed, looking at her, and gave up drinking, I can't explain. I only know that what she said and the noble way she behaved brought about a change in my soul, and I shall never forget it. It's time to go up, though, they are just going to ring the bell."

Lushkov bowed and went off to the gallery.

1885

# MISERY

"To whom shall I tell my grief?"

THE twilight of evening. Big flakes of wet snow are whirling lazily about the street lamps, which have just been lighted, and lying in a thin soft layer on roofs, horses' backs, shoulders, caps. Iona Potapov, the sledge-driver, is all white like a ghost. He sits on the box without stirring, bent as double as the living body can be bent. If a regular snowdrift fell on him it seems as though even then he would not think it necessary to shake it off. . . . His little mare is white and motionless too. Her stillness, the angularity of her lines, and the sticklike straightness of her legs make her look like a halfpenny gingerbread horse. She is probably lost in thought. Anyone who has been torn away from the plow, from the familiar gray landscapes, and cast into this slough, full of monstrous lights, of unceasing uproar and hurrying people, is bound to think.

It is a long time since Iona and his nag have budged. They came out of the yard before dinner-time and not a single fare yet. But now the shades of evening are falling on the town. The pale light of the street lamps changes to a vivid color, and the bustle of the street grows noisier.

"Sledge to Vyborgskaya!" Iona hears. "Sledge!"

Iona starts, and through his snow-plastered eyelashes sees an officer in a military overcoat with a hood over his head.

"To Vyborgskaya," repeats the officer. "Are you asleep? To Vyborgskaya!"

In token of assent Iona gives a tug at the reins which sends cakes of snow flying from the horse's back and shoulders. The officer gets into the sledge. The sledge-driver clucks to the horse, cranes his neck like a swan, rises in his seat, and more from habit than necessity brandishes his whip. The mare cranes her neck, too, crooks her sticklike legs, and hesitatingly sets off. . . .

"Where are you shoving, you devil?" Iona immediately hears shouts from the dark·mass shifting to and fro before him. "Where the devil are you going? Keep to the r-right!"

"You don't know how to drive! Keep to the right," says the officer angrily.

A coachman driving a carriage swears at him; a pedestrian crossing the road and brushing the horse's nose with his shoulder looks at him angrily and shakes the snow off his sleeve. Iona fidgets on the box as though he were sitting on thorns, jerks his elbows, and turns his eyes about like one possessed, as though he did not know where he was or why he was there.

"What rascals they all are!" says the officer jocosely. "They are simply doing their best to run up against you or fall under the horse's feet. They must be doing it on purpose."

Iona looks at his fare and moves his lips. . . . Apparently he means to say something, but nothing comes but a sniff.

"What?" inquires the officer.

Iona gives a wry smile, and straining his throat, brings out huskily: "My son . . . er . . . my son died this week, sir."

"H'm! What did he die of?"

Iona turns his whole body round to his fare, and says:

"Who can tell! It must have been from fever. . . . He lay three days in the hospital and then he died. . . . God's will."

"Turn round, you devil!" comes out of the darkness. "Have you gone cracked, you old dog? Look where you are going!"

"Drive on! drive on! . . . " says the officer. "We shan't get there till tomorrow going on like this. Hurry up!"

The sledge-driver cranes his neck again, rises in his seat, and with heavy grace swings his whip. Several times he looks round at the officer, but the latter keeps his eyes shut and is apparently disinclined to listen. Putting his fare down at Vyborgskaya, Iona stops by a restaurant, and again sits huddled up on the box. . . . Again the wet snow paints him and his horse white. One hour passes, and then another. . . .

Three young men, two tall and thin, one short and hunchbacked, come up, railing at each other and loudly stamping on the pavement with their galoshes.

"Cabby, to the Police Bridge!" the hunchback cries in a cracked voice. "The three of us, . . . twenty copecks!"

Iona tugs at the reins and clucks to his horse. Twenty copecks it not a fair price, but he has no thoughts for that. Whether it is a rouble or whether it is five copecks does not matter to him now so long as he has a fare. . . . The three young men, shoving each other and using bad language, go up to the sledge, and all three try to sit down at once. The question remains to be settled: Which are to sit down and which one is to stand? After a long altercation, ill-temper, and abuse, they come to the conclusion that the hunchback must stand because he is the shortest.

"Well, drive on," says the hunchback in his cracked voice, settling himself and breathing down Iona's neck. "Cut along! What a cab you've got, my friend! You wouldn't find a worse one in all Petersburg. . . ."

"He-he! . . . he-he! . . ." laughs Iona. "It's nothing to boast of!"

"Well, then, nothing to boast of, drive on! Are you going to drive like this all the way? Eh? Shall I give you one in the neck?"

"My head aches," says one of the tall ones. "At the Dukmasovs' yesterday Vaska and I drank four bottles of brandy between us."

"I can't make out why you talk such stuff," says the other tall one angrily. "You lie like a brute."

"Strike me dead, it's the truth! . . ."

"It's about as true as that a louse coughs."

"He-he!" grins Iona. "Me-er-ry gentlemen!"

"Tfoo! the devil take you!" cries the hunchback indignantly. "Will you get on, you old plague, or won't you? Is that the way to drive? Give her one with the whip. Hang it all, give it her well."

Iona feels behind his back the jolting person and quivering voice of the hunchback. He hears abuse addressed to him, he sees people, and the feeling of loneliness begins little by little to be less heavy on his heart. The hunchback swears at him, till he chokes over some elaborately whimsical string of epithets and is overpowered by his cough. His tall companions begin talking of a certain Nadyezhda Petrovna. Iona looks round at them. Waiting till there is a brief pause, he looks round once more and says:

"This week . . . er . . . my . . . er . . . son died!"

"We shall all die, . . ." says the hunchback with a sigh, wiping his lips after coughing. "Come, drive on! drive on! My friends, I simply cannot stand crawling like this! When will he get us there?"

"Well, you give him a little encouragement . . . one in the neck!"

"Do you hear, you old plague? I'll make you smart. If one stands on ceremony with fellows like you one may as well walk. Do you hear, you old dragon? Or don't you care a hang what we say?"

And Iona hears rather than feels a slap on the back of his neck.

"He-he! . . ." he laughs. "Merry gentlemen. . . . God give you health!"

"Cabman, are you married?" asks one of the tall ones.

"I? He-he! Me-er-ry gentlemen. The only wife for me now is the damp earth. . . . He-ho-ho! . . . The grave, that is! . . . Here my son's dead and I am alive. . . . It's a strange thing, death has come in at the wrong door. . . . Instead of coming for me it went for my son. . . ."

And Iona turns round to tell them how his son died, but at that point the hunchback gives a faint sigh and announces that, thank God! they have arrived at last. After taking his twenty copecks, Iona gazes for a long while after the revelers, who disappear into a dark entry. Again he is alone and again there is silence for him. . . . The misery which has been for a brief space eased comes back again and tears his heart more cruelly than ever. With a look of anxiety and suffering Iona's eyes stray restlessly among the crowds moving to and fro on both sides of the street: can he not find among those thousands someone who will listen to him? But the crowds flit by heedless of him and his misery. . . . His misery is immense, beyond all bounds. If Iona's heart were to burst and his misery to flow out, it would flood the whole world, it seems, but yet it is not seen. It has found a hiding-place in such an insignificant shell that one would not have found it with a candle by daylight. . . .

Iona sees a house-porter with a parcel and makes up his mind to address him.

"What time will it be, friend?" he asks.

"Going on for ten. . . . Why have you stopped here? Drive on!"

Iona drives a few paces away, bends himself double, and gives himself up to his misery. He feels it is no good to appeal to people.

But before five minutes have passed he draws himself up, shakes his head as though he feels a sharp pain, and tugs at the reins. . . . He can bear it no longer.

"Back to the yard!" he thinks. "To the yard!"

And his little mare, as though she knew his thoughts, falls to trotting. An hour and a half later Iona is sitting by a big dirty stove. On the stove, on the floor, and on the benches are people snoring. The air is full of smells and stuffiness. Iona looks at the sleeping figures, scratches himself, and regrets that he has come home so early. . . .

"I have not earned enough to pay for the oats, even," he thinks. "That's why I am so miserable. A man who knows how to do his work, . . . who has had enough to eat, and whose horse has had enough to eat, is always at ease. . . ."

In one of the corners a young cabman gets up, clears his throat sleepily, and makes for the water-bucket.

"Want a drink?" Iona asks him.

"Seems so."

"May it do you good. . . . But my son is dead, mate. . . . Do you hear? This week in the hospital. . . . It's a queer business. . . ."

Iona looks to see the effect produced by his words, but he sees nothing. The young man has covered his head over and is already asleep. The old man sighs and scratches himself. . . . Just as the young man had been thirsty for water, he thirsts for speech. His son will soon have been dead a week, and he has not really talked to anybody yet. . . . He wants to talk of it properly, with deliberation. . . . He wants to tell how his son was taken ill, how he suffered, what he said before he died, how he died. . . . He wants to describe the funeral, and how he went to the hospital to get his son's clothes. . . . He still has his daughter Anisya in the country. And he wants to talk about her too. . . . Yes, he has plenty to talk about now. His listener ought to sigh and exclaim and lament. . . . It would be even better to talk to women. Though they are silly creatures, they blubber at the first word.

"Let's go out and have a look at the mare." Iona thinks. "There is always time for sleep. . . . You'll have sleep enough, no fear. . . ."

He puts on his coat and goes into the stables where his mare is standing. He thinks about oats, about hay, about the weather. . . . He cannot think about his son when he is alone. . . . To talk about him with someone is possible, but to think of him and picture him is insufferable anguish. . . .

"Are you munching?" Iona asks his mare, seeing her shining eyes. "There, munch away, munch away. . . . Since we have not earned enough for oats, we will eat hay. . . . Yes, . . . I have grown too old to drive. . . . My son ought to be driving, not I. . . . He was a real cabman. . . . He ought to have lived. . . ."

Iona is silent for a while, and then he goes on:

"That's how it is, old girl. . . . Kuzma Ionich is gone. . . . He said goodbye to me. . . . He went and died for no reason. . . . Now, suppose you had a little colt, and you were own mother to that little colt. . . . And all at once that same little colt went and died. . . . You'd be sorry, wouldn't you? . . ."

The little mare munches, listens, and breathes on her master's hands. Iona is carried away and tells her all about it.

1886

# VANKA

VANKA ZHUKOV, a boy of nine, who had been for three months apprenticed to Alyahin the shoemaker, was sitting up on Christmas Eve. Waiting till his master and mistress and their workmen had gone to midnight service, he took out of his master's cupboard a bottle of ink and a pen with a rusty nib, and, spreading out a crumpled sheet of paper in front of him, began writing. Before forming the first letter he several times looked round fearfully at the door and the windows, stole a glance at the dark icon, on both sides of which stretched shelves full of lasts, and heaved a broken sigh. The paper lay on the bench while he knelt before it.

"Dear Grandfather, Konstantin Makarych," he wrote. "I am writing you a letter. I wish you a happy Christmas, and all blessings from God Almighty. I have neither father nor mother, you are the only one left me."

Vanka raised his eyes to the dark icon on which the light of his candle was reflected, and vividly recalled his grandfather, Konstantin Makarych, who was night watchman to a family called Zhivarev. He was a thin but extraordinarily nimble and lively little old man of sixty-five, with an everlastingly laughing face and drunken eyes. By day he slept in the servants' kitchen, or made jokes with the cook; at night, wrapped in an ample sheepskin, he walked round the grounds and tapped with his little mallet. Old Kashtanka and Eel, so called on account of his dark color and his long body like a weasel's, followed him with hanging heads. This Eel was exceptionally polite and affectionate, and looked with equal kindness on strangers and his own masters, but had not a very good reputation. Under his politeness and meekness was hidden the most Jesuitical cunning. No one knew better how to creep up on occasion and snap at one's legs, to slip into the storeroom, or steal a hen from a peasant. His hind legs had been nearly pulled off more than once, twice he had been hanged, every week he was thrashed till he was half dead, but he always revived.

At this moment Grandfather was, no doubt, standing at the gate, screwing up his eyes at the red windows of the church, stamping with his high felt boots, and joking with the servants. His little mallet was hanging on his belt. He was clasping his hands, shrugging with the cold, and, with an aged chuckle, pinching first the housemaid, then the cook.

"How about a pinch of snuff?" he was saying, offering the women his snuffbox.

The women would take a sniff and sneeze. Grandfather would be indescribably delighted, go off into a merry chuckle, and cry:

"Tear it off, it has frozen on!"

They give the dogs a sniff of snuff too. Kashtanka sneezes, wriggles her head, and walks away offended. Eel does not sneeze, from politeness, but wags his tail. And the weather is glorious. The air is still, fresh, and transparent. The night is dark, but one can see the whole village with its white roofs and coils of smoke coming from the chimneys, the trees silvered with hoarfrost, the snowdrifts. The whole sky spangled with gay twinkling stars, and the Milky Way is as distinct as though it had been washed and rubbed with snow for a holiday. . . .

Vanka sighed, dipped his pen, and went on writing:

"And yesterday I had a wigging. The master pulled me out into the yard by my hair, and whacked me with a boot-stretcher because I accidentally fell asleep while I was rocking their brat in the cradle. And a week ago the mistress told me to clean a herring, and I began from the tail end, and she took the herring and thrust its head in my face. The workmen laugh at me and send me to the tavern for vodka, and tell me to steal the master's cucumbers for them, and the master beats me with anything that comes to hand. And there is nothing to eat. In the morning they give me bread; for dinner, porridge; and in the evening, bread again; but as for tea, or soup, the master and mistress gobble it all up themselves. And I am put to sleep in the passage, and when their wretched brat cries I get no sleep at all, but have to rock the cradle. Dear Grandfather, show the divine mercy, take me away from here, home to the village. It's more than I can bear. I bow down to your feet, and will pray to God for you forever. Take me away from here or I shall die."

Vanka's mouth worked, he rubbed his eyes with his black fist, and gave a sob.

"I will powder your snuff for you," he went on. "I will pray for you, and if I do anything you can thrash me like Sidor's goat. And if you think I've no job, then I will beg the steward for Christ's sake to let me clean his boots, or I'll go for a shepherd-boy instead of Fedka. Dear Grandfather, it is more than I can bear, it's simply no life at all. I wanted to run away to the village, but I have no boots, and I am afraid of the frost. When I grow big I will take care of you for this, and not let anyone annoy you, and when you die I will pray for the rest of your soul, just as for my mammy's.

"Moscow is a big town. It's all gentlemen's houses, and there are lots of horses, but there are no sheep, and the dogs are not spiteful. The lads here don't come caroling at Christmas with the star, and they don't let anyone go into the choir, and once I saw in a shop window fishing-hooks for sale, fitted ready with the line and for all sorts of fish, awfully good ones—there was even one hook that would hold a forty-pound sheatfish. And I have seen shops where there are guns of all sorts, after the pattern of the master's guns at home, so that I shouldn't wonder if they are a hundred roubles each. . . . And in the butchers' shops there are grouse and woodcocks and fish and hares, but the shopmen don't say where they shoot them.

"Dear Grandfather, when they have the Christmas tree at the big house, get me a gilt walnut, and put it away in the green trunk. Ask the young lady Olga Ignatyevna, say it's for Vanka."

Vanka gave a tremulous sigh, and again stared at the window. He remembered how his grandfather always went into the forest to get the Christmas tree for his master's family, and took his grandson with him. It was a merry time! Grandfather made a noise in his throat, the forest crackled with the frost, and mimicking them Vanka chortled too. Before chopping down the Christmas tree, Grandfather would smoke a pipe, slowly take a pinch of snuff, and laugh at frozen Vanka. . . . The young fir trees, covered with hoarfrost, stood motionless, waiting to see which of them was to die. Wherever one looked a hare flew like an arrow over the snowdrifts. . . .

Grandfather could not refrain from shouting: "Hold him, hold him . . . hold him! Ah, the bobtailed devil!"

When he had cut down the Christmas tree, Grandfather used to drag it to the big house, and there set to work to decorate it. . . . The young lady, who was Vanka's favorite, Olga Ignatyevna, was the busiest of all. When Vanka's mother Pelageya was alive, and a servant in the big house, Olga Ignatyevna used to give him goodies and, having nothing better to do, taught him to read and write, to count up to a hundred, and even to dance a quadrille. When Pelayega died, Vanka had been transferred to the servants' kitchen to be with his grandfather, and from the kitchen to the shoemaker's in Moscow.

"Do come, dear Grandfather," Vanka went on with his letter. "For Christ's sake, I beg you, take me away. Have pity on an unhappy orphan like me; here everyone knocks me about, and I am fearfully hungry; I can't tell you what misery it is, I am always crying. And the other day the master hit me on the head with a last, so that I fell down. My life is wretched, worse than any dog's. . . . I send greetings to Alyona, one-eyed Yegorka, and the coachman, and don't give my concertina to anyone. I remain, your grandson, Ivan Zhukov. Dear Grandfather, do come."

Vanka folded the sheet of writing-paper twice, and put it into an envelope he had bought the day before for a copeck. . . . After thinking a little, he dipped the pen and wrote the address:

*To Grandfather in the village.*

Then he scratched his head, thought a little, and added: *Konstantin Makarych.* Glad that he had not been prevented from writing, he put on his cap and, without putting on his little greatcoat, ran out into the street as he was in his shirt. . . .

The shopmen at the butcher's, whom he had questioned the day before, told him that letters were put in postboxes, and from the boxes were carried about all over the earth in mail-carts with drunken drivers and ringing bells. Vanka ran to the nearest postbox, and thrust the precious letter in the slit. . . .

An hour later, lulled by sweet hopes, he was sound asleep. . . . He dreamed of the stove. On the stove was sitting his grandfather, swinging his bare legs, and reading the letter to the cooks. . . .

By the stove was Eel, wagging his tail.                    1886

# EASTER EVE

I WAS standing on the bank of the river Goltva, waiting for the ferryboat from the other side. At ordinary times the Goltva is a humble stream of moderate size, silent and pensive, gently glimmering from behind thick reeds; but now a regular lake lay stretched out before me. The waters of spring, running riot, had overflowed both banks and flooded both sides of the river for a long distance, submerging vegetable gardens, hayfields and marshes, so that it was no unusual thing to meet poplars and bushes sticking out above the surface of the water and looking in the darkness like grim solitary crags.

The weather seemed to me magnificent. It was dark, yet I could see the trees, the water and the people. . . . The world was lighted by the stars, which were scattered thickly all over the sky. I don't remember ever seeing so many stars. Literally one could not have put a finger in between them. There were some as big as a goose's egg, others tiny as hempseed. . . . They had come out for the festival procession, every one of them, little and big, washed, renewed and joyful, and every one of them was softly twinkling and beaming. The sky was reflected in the water; the stars were bathing in its dark depths and trembling with the quivering eddies. The air was warm and still. . . . Here and there, far away on the further bank in the impenetrable darkness, several bright red lights were gleaming. . . .

A couple of paces from me I saw the dark silhouette of a peasant in a tall hat, with a thick knotted stick in his hand.

"How long the ferryboat is in coming!" I said.

"It is time it was here," the silhouette answered.

"You are waiting for the ferryboat, too?"

"No, I am not," yawned the peasant—"I am waiting for the illumination. I should have gone, but, to tell you the truth, I haven't the five copecks for the ferry."

"I'll give you the five copecks."

"No; I humbly thank you. . . . With that five copecks put up a candle for me over there in the monastery. . . . That will be more interesting, and I will stand here. What can it mean, no ferryboat, as though it had sunk in the water!"

The peasant went up to the water's edge, took the rope in his hands, and shouted: "Ieronim! Ieron-im!"

As though in answer to his shout, the slow peal of a great bell floated across from the further bank. The note was deep and low, as from the thickest string of a double bass; it seemed as though the darkness itself had hoarsely uttered it. At once there was the sound of a cannon shot. It rolled away in the darkness and ended somewhere in the far distance behind me. The peasant took off his hat and crossed himself.

"Christ is risen," he said.

Before the vibrations of the first peal of the bell had time to die away in the air a second sounded, after it at once a third, and the darkness was filled with an unbroken quivering clamor. Near the red lights fresh lights flashed, and all began moving together and twinkling restlessly.

"Ieron-im!" we heard a hollow prolonged shout.

"They are shouting from the other bank," said the peasant, "so there is no ferry there either. Our Ieronim has gone to sleep."

The lights and the velvety chimes of the bell drew one towards them. . . . I was already beginning to lose patience and grow anxious, but behold at last, staring into the dark distance, I saw the outline of something very much like a gibbet. It was the long-expected ferry. It moved towards us with such deliberation that if it had not been that its lines grew gradually more definite, one might have supposed that it was standing still or moving to the other bank.

"Make haste! Ieronim!" shouted my peasant. "The gentleman's tired of waiting!"

The ferry crawled to the bank, gave a lurch and stopped with a creak. A tall man in a monk's cassock and a conical cap stood on it, holding the rope.

"Why have you been so long?" I asked, jumping upon the ferry.

"Forgive me, for Christ's sake," Ieronim answered gently. "Is there no one else?"

"No one. . . ."

Ieronim took hold of the rope in both hands, bent himself to the figure of a mark of interrogation, and gasped. The ferryboat creaked and gave a lurch. The outline of the peasant in the tall hat began slowly retreating from me—so the ferry was moving off. Ieronim soon drew himself up and began working with one hand only. We were silent, gazing towards the bank to which we were floating. There the illumination for which the peasant was waiting had begun. At the water's edge barrels of tar were flaring like huge camp fires. Their reflections, crimson as the rising moon, crept to meet us in long broad streaks. The burning barrels lighted up their own smoke and the long shadows of men flitting about the fire; but further to one side and behind them from where the velvety chime floated there was still the same unbroken black gloom. All at once, cleaving the darkness, a rocket zigzagged in a golden ribbon up the sky; it described an arc and, as though broken to pieces against the sky, was scattered crackling into sparks. There was a roar from the bank like a far-away hurrah.

"How beautiful!" I said.

"Beautiful beyond words!" sighed Ieronim. "Such a night, sir! Another time one would pay no attention to the fireworks, but today one rejoices in every vanity. Where do you come from?"

I told him where I came from.

"To be sure . . . a joyful day today. . . ." Ieronim went on in a weak sighing tenor like the voice of a convalescent. "The sky is rejoicing and the earth and what is under the earth. All the creatures are keeping holiday. Only tell me, kind sir, why, even in the time of great rejoicing, a man cannot forget his sorrows?"

I fancied that this unexpected question was to draw me into one of those endless religious conversations which bored and idle monks are so fond of. I was not disposed to talk much, and so I only asked:

"What sorrows have you, father?"

"As a rule only the same as all men, kind sir, but today a special sorrow has happened in the monastery: at mass, during the reading of the Bible, the monk and deacon Nikolay died."

"Well, it's God's will!" I said, falling into the monastic tone. "We must all die. To my mind, you ought to rejoice indeed. . . . They say if anyone dies at Easter he goes straight to the kingdom of heaven."

"That's true."

We sank into silence. The figure of the peasant in the tall hat melted into the line of the bank. The tar barrels were flaring up more and more.

"The Holy Scripture points clearly to the vanity of sorrow, and so does reflection," said Ieronim, breaking the silence; "but why does the heart grieve and refuse to listen to reason? Why does one want to weep bitterly?"

Ieronim shrugged his shoulders, turned to me and said quickly:

"If I died, or anyone else, it would not be worth notice, perhaps; but, you see, Nikolay is dead! No one else but Nikolay! Indeed, it's hard to believe that he is no more! I stand here on my ferryboat and every minute I keep fancying that he will lift up his voice from the bank. He always used to come to the bank and call to me that I might not be afraid on the ferry. He used to get up from his bed at night on purpose for that. He was a kind soul. My God! how kindly and gracious! Many a mother is not so good to her child as Nikolay was to me! Lord, save his soul!"

Ieronim took hold of the rope, but turned to me again at once.

"And such a lofty intelligence, your honor," he said in a vibrating voice. "Such a sweet and harmonious tongue! Just as they will sing immediately at early matins: 'Oh, lovely! oh, sweet is Thy voice!' Besides all other human qualities, he had, too, an extraordinary gift!"

"What gift?" I asked.

The monk scrutinized me, and as though he had convinced himself that he could trust me with a secret, he laughed good-humoredly.

"He had a gift for writing hymns of praise," he said. "It was a marvel, sir; you couldn't call it anything else! You will be amazed if I tell you about it. Our Father Archimandrite comes from Moscow, the Father Subprior studied at the Kazan academy, we have wise monks and elders, but, would you believe it, no one could write them; while Nikolay, a simple monk, a deacon, had not studied anywhere, and had not even any outer appearance of it, but he wrote them! A marvel! a real marvel!" Ieronim clasped his hands and, completely forgetting the rope, went on eagerly:

"The Father Subprior has great difficulty in composing sermons;

when he wrote the history of the monastery he worried all the brotherhood and drove a dozen times to town, while Nikolay wrote canticles! Hymns of praise! That's a very different thing from a sermon or a history!"

"Is it difficult to write them?" I asked.

"There's great difficulty!" Ieronim wagged his head. "You can do nothing by wisdom and holiness if God has not given you the gift. The monks who don't understand argue that you only need to know the life of the saint for whom you are writing the hymn, and to make it harmonize with the other hymns of praise. But that's a mistake, sir. Of course, anyone who writes canticles must know the life of the saint to perfection, to the least trivial detail. To be sure, one must make them harmonize with the other canticles and know where to begin and what to write about. To give you an instance, the first response begins everywhere with 'the chosen' or 'the elect.' . . . The first line must always begin with the 'angel.' In the canticle of praise to Jesus the Most Sweet, if you are interested in the subject, it begins like this: 'Of angels Creator and Lord of all powers!' In the canticle to the Holy Mother of God: 'Of angels the foremost sent down from on high,' to Nikolay, the Wonder-Worker, 'An angel in semblance, though in substance a man,' and so on. Everywhere you begin with the angel. Of course, it would be impossible without making them harmonize, but the lives of the saints and conformity with the others is not what matters; what matters is the beauty and sweetness of it. Everything must be harmonious, brief and complete. There must be in every line softness, graciousness and tenderness; not one word should be harsh or rough or unsuitable. It must be written so that the worshipper may rejoice at heart and weep, while his mind is stirred and he is thrown into a tremor. In the canticle to the Holy Mother are the words: 'Rejoice, O Thou too high for human thought to reach! Rejoice, O Thou too deep for angels' eyes to fathom!' In another place in the same canticle: 'Rejoice, O tree that bearest the fair fruit of light that is the food of the faithful! Rejoice, O tree of gracious spreading shade, under which there is shelter for multitudes!' "

Ieronim hid his face in his hands, as though frightened at something or overcome with shame, and shook his head.

"Tree that bearest the fair fruit of light . . . tree of gracious spreading shade . . ." he muttered. "To think that a man should find words like those! Such a power is a gift from God! For brevity he packs many thoughts into one phrase, and how smooth and complete it all is! 'Light-radiating torch to all that be . . .' comes in the canticle to Jesus the Most Sweet. 'Light-radiating!' There is no such word in conversation or in books, but you see he invented it, he found it in his mind! Apart from the smoothness and grandeur of language, sir, every line must be beautified in every way; there must be flowers and lightning and wind and sun and all the objects of the visible world. And every exclamation ought to be put so as to be smooth and easy for the ear. 'Rejoice, thou flower of heavenly growth!' comes in the hymn to Nikolay the Wonder-Worker. It's not simply 'heavenly flower,' but 'flower of heavenly growth.' It's smoother so and sweet to the ear. That was just as Nikolay wrote it! exactly like that! I can't tell you how he used to write!"

"Well, in that case it is a pity he is dead," I said; "but let us get on, father, or we shall be late."

Ieronim started and ran to the rope; they were beginning to peal all the bells. Probably the procession was already going on near the monastery, for all the dark space behind the tar barrels was now dotted with moving lights.

"Did Nikolay print his hymns?" I asked Ieronim.

"How could he print them?" he sighed. "And, indeed, it would be strange to print them. What would be the object? No one in the monastery takes any interest in them. They don't like them. They knew Nikolay wrote them, but they let it pass unnoticed. No one esteems new writings nowadays, sir!"

"Were they prejudiced against him?"

"Yes, indeed. If Nikolay had been an elder perhaps the brethren would have been interested, but he wasn't forty, you know. There were some who laughed and even thought his writing a sin."

"What did he write them for?"

"Chiefly for his own comfort. Of all the brotherhood, I was the only one who read his hymns. I used to go to him in secret, that no one else might know of it, and he was glad that I took an interest in them. He would embrace me, stroke my head, speak to me in caressing words as to a little child. He would shut his cell, make me sit down beside him, and begin to read. . . ."

Ieronim left the rope and came up to me.

"We were dear friends in a way," he whispered, looking at me

with shining eyes. "Where he went I would go. If I were not there
he would miss me. And he cared more for me than for anyone, and
all because I used to weep over his hymns. It makes me sad to remember. Now I feel just like an orphan or a widow. You know, in
our monastery they are all good people, kind and pious, but . . .
there is no one with softness and refinement, they are just like
peasants. They all speak loudly, and tramp heavily when they walk;
they are noisy, they clear their throats, but Nikolay always talked
softly, caressingly, and if he noticed that anyone was asleep or praying he would slip by like a fly or a gnat. His face was tender, compassionate. . . ."

Ieronim heaved a deep sigh and took hold of the rope again.
We were by now approaching the bank. We floated straight out of
the darkness and stillness of the river into an enchanted realm, full
of stifling smoke, crackling lights and uproar. By now one could
distinctly see people moving near the tar barrels. The flickering of
the lights gave a strange, almost fantastic, expression to their figures
and red faces. From time to time one caught among the heads and
faces a glimpse of a horse's head motionless as though it were cast in
copper.

"They'll begin singing the Easter hymn directly," said Ieronim,
"and Nikolay is gone; there is no one to appreciate it. . . . There
was nothing written dearer to him than that hymn. He used to take
in every word! You'll be there, sir, so notice what is sung; it takes
your breath away!"

"Won't you be in church, then?"

"I can't; . . . I have to work the ferry. . . ."

"But won't they relieve you?"

"I don't know. . . . I ought to have been relieved at eight;
but, as you see, they don't come! . . . And I must own I should
have liked to be in the church. . . ."

"Are you a monk?"

"Yes . . . that is, I am a lay-brother."

The ferry ran into the bank and stopped. I thrust a five-copeck
piece into Ieronim's hand for taking me across, and jumped on land.
Immediately a cart with a boy and a sleeping woman in it drove
creakily onto the ferry. Ieronim, with a faint glow from the lights
on his figure, pressed on the rope, bent down to it, and started the
ferry back. . . .

I took a few steps through mud, but a little farther walked on a soft freshly trodden path. This path led to the dark monastery gates, that looked like a cavern, through a cloud of smoke, through a disorderly crowd of people, unharnessed horses, carts and chaises. All this crowd was rattling, snorting, laughing, and the crimson light and wavering shadows from the smoke flickered over it all. . . . A perfect chaos! And in this hubbub the people yet found room to load a little cannon and to sell cakes. There was no less commotion on the other side of the wall in the monastery precincts, but there was more regard for decorum and order. Here there was a smell of juniper and incense. They talked loudly, but there was no sound of laughter or snorting. Near the tombstones and crosses people pressed close to one another with Easter cakes and bundles in their arms. Apparently many had come from a long distance for their cakes to be blessed and now were exhausted. Young lay brothers, making a metallic sound with their boots, ran busily along the iron slabs that paved the way from the monastery gates to the church door. They were busy and shouting on the belfry, too.

"What a restless night!" I thought. "How nice!"

One was tempted to see the same unrest and sleeplessness in all nature, from the night darkness to the iron slabs, the crosses on the tombs and the trees under which the people were moving to and fro. But nowhere was the excitement and restlessness so marked as in the church. An unceasing struggle was going on in the entrance between the inflowing stream and the outflowing stream. Some were going in, others going out and soon coming back again to stand still for a little and begin moving again. People were scurrying from place to place, lounging about as though they were looking for something. The stream flowed from the entrance all round the church, disturbing even the front rows, where persons of weight and dignity were standing. There could be no thought of concentrated prayer. There were no prayers at all, but a sort of continuous, childishly irresponsible joy, seeking a pretext to break out and vent itself in some movement, even in senseless jostling and shoving.

The same unaccustomed movement is striking in the Easter service itself. The altar gates are flung wide open, thick clouds of incense float in the air near the candelabra; wherever one looks there are lights, the gleam and splutter of candles. . . . There is no reading; restless and light-hearted singing goes on to the end without ceasing.

After each hymn the clergy change their vestments and come out to burn incense, which is repeated every ten minutes.

I had no sooner taken a place, when a wave rushed from in front and forced me back. A tall thick-set deacon walked before me with a long red candle; the gray-headed archimandrite in his golden miter hurried after him with the censer. When they had vanished from sight the crowd squeezed me back to my former position. But ten minutes had not passed before a new wave burst on me, and again the deacon appeared. This time he was followed by the Father Subprior, the man who, as Ieronim had told me, was writing the history of the monastery.

As I mingled with the crowd and caught the infection of the universal joyful excitement, I felt unbearably sore on Ieronim's account. Why did they not send someone to relieve him? Why could not someone of less feeling and less susceptibility go on the ferry? "Lift up thine eyes, O Sion, and look around," they sang in the choir, "for thy children have come to thee as to a beacon of divine light from north and south, and from the east and from the sea. . . ."

I looked at the faces; they all had a lively expression of triumph, but not one was listening to what was being sung and taking it in, and not one was "holding his breath." Why was not Ieronim released? I could fancy Ieronim standing meekly somewhere by the wall, bending forward and hungrily drinking in the beauty of the holy phrase. All this that glided by the ears of people standing by me he would have eagerly drunk in with his delicately sensitive soul, and would have been spellbound to ecstasy, holding his breath, and there would not have been a man happier than he in all the church. Now he was plying to and fro over the dark river and grieving for his dead friend and brother.

The wave surged back. A stout smiling monk, playing with his rosary and looking round behind him, squeezed sideways by me, making way for a lady in a hat and velvet cloak. A monastery servant hurried after the lady, holding a chair over our heads.

I came out of the church. I wanted to have a look at the dead Nikolay, the unknown canticle writer. I walked about the monastery wall, where there was a row of cells, peeped into several windows, and, seeing nothing, came back again. I do not regret now that I did not see Nikolay; God knows, perhaps if I had seen him I should have lost the picture my imagination paints for me now. I imagine

that lovable poetical figure, solitary and not understood, who went
out of nights to call to Ieronim over the water, and filled his hymns
with flowers, stars and sunbeams, as a pale timid man with soft, mild,
melancholy features. His eyes must have shone, not only with intelligence, but with kindly tenderness and that hardly restrained childlike
enthusiasm which I could hear in Ieronim's voice when he quoted to
me passages from the hymns.

When we came out of church after mass it was no longer night.
The morning was beginning. The stars had vanished and the sky was
a morose grayish blue. The iron slabs, the tombstones and the buds
on the trees were covered with dew. There was a sharp freshness in
the air. Outside the precincts I did not find the same animated scene
as I had beheld in the night. Horses and men looked exhausted,
drowsy, scarcely moved, while nothing was left of the tar barrels but
heaps of black ash. When anyone is exhausted and sleepy he fancies
that nature, too, is in the same condition. It seemed to me that the
trees and the young grass were asleep. It seemed as though even the
bells were not pealing so loudly and gayly as at night.  The restlessness was over, and of the excitement nothing was left but a pleasant
weariness, a longing for sleep and warmth.

Now I could see both banks of the river; a faint mist hovered
over it in shifting masses. There was a harsh cold breath from the
water. When I jumped onto the ferry, a chaise and some two dozen
men and women were standing on it already. The rope, wet and as
I fancied drowsy, stretched far away across the broad river and in
places disappeared in the white mist.

"Christ is risen! Is there no one else?" asked a soft voice.

I recognized the voice of Ieronim. There was no darkness now to
hinder me from seeing the monk. He was a tall narrow-shouldered
man of five-and-thirty, with large rounded features, with half-closed
listless-looking eyes and an unkempt wedge-shaped beard. He had an
extraordinarily sad and exhausted look.

"They have not relieved you yet?" I asked in surprise.

"Me?" he answered, turning to me his chilled and dewy face
with a smile. "There is no one to take my place now till morning.
They'll all be going to the Father Archimandrite's to break the fast
directly."

With the help of a little peasant in a hat of reddish fur that looked
like the little wooden tubs in which honey is sold, he threw his

weight on the rope; they gasped simultaneously, and the ferry started.

We floated across, disturbing on the way the lazily rising mist. Everyone was silent. Ieronim worked mechanically with one hand. He slowly passed his mild lusterless eyes over us; then his glance rested on the rosy face of a young merchant's wife with black eyebrows, who was standing on the ferry beside me silently shrinking from the mist that wrapped her about. He did not take his eyes off her face all the way.

There was little that was masculine in that prolonged gaze. It seemed to me that Ieronim was looking in the woman's face for the soft and tender features of his dead friend.

1886

# AGAFYA

During my stay in the district of S. I often used to go see the watchman Savva Stukach, or simply Savka, in the kitchen gardens of Dubovo. These kitchen gardens were my favorite resort for so-called "mixed" fishing, when one goes out without knowing what day or hour one may return, taking with one every sort of fishing tackle as well as a store of provisions. To tell the truth, it was not so much the fishing that attracted me as the peaceful stroll, the meals at no set time, the talk with Savka, and being for so long face to face with the calm summer nights. Savka was a young man of five-and-twenty, well grown and handsome, and as strong as a flint. He had the reputation of being a sensible and reasonable fellow. He could read and write, and very rarely drank, but as a workman this strong and healthy young man was not worth a farthing. A sluggish, over-powering sloth was mingled with the strength in his muscles, which were strong as cords. Like everyone else in his village, he lived in his own hut, and had his share of land, but neither tilled it nor sowed it, and did not work at any sort of trade. His old mother begged alms at people's windows and he himself lived like a bird of the air; he did not know in the morning what he would eat at midday. It was not that he was lacking in will, or energy, or feeling for his mother; it was simply that he felt no inclination for work and did not recognize the advantage of it. His whole figure suggested unruffled serenity, an innate, almost artistic passion for living carelessly, never with his sleeves tucked up. When Savka's young, healthy body had a physical craving for muscular work, the young man abandoned himself completely for a brief interval to some free but nonsensical pursuit, such as sharpening skates not wanted for any

612

special purpose, or racing about after the peasant women. His favorite attitude was one of concentrated immobility. He was capable of standing for hours at a stretch in the same place with his eyes fixed on the same spot without stirring. He never moved except on impulse, and then only when an occasion presented itself for some rapid and abrupt action: catching a running dog by the tail, pulling off a woman's kerchief, or jumping over a big hole. It need hardly be said that with such parsimony of movement Savka was as poor as a mouse and lived worse than any homeless outcast. As time went on, I suppose he accumulated arrears of taxes and, young and sturdy as he was, he was sent by the commune to do an old man's job—to be watchman and scarecrow in the kitchen gardens. However much they laughed at him for his premature senility he did not object to it. This position, quiet and convenient for motionless contemplation, exactly fitted his temperament.

It happened I was with this Savka one fine May evening. I remember I was lying on a torn and dirty sackcloth cover close to the shanty from which came a heavy, fragrant scent of hay. Clasping my hands under my head I looked before me. At my feet was lying a wooden fork. Behind it Savka's dog Kutka stood out like a black patch, and not a dozen feet from Kutka the ground ended abruptly in the steep bank of the little river. Lying down I could not see the river; I could only see the tops of the young willows growing thickly on the nearer bank, and the twisting edges, gnawed away as it were, of the opposite bank. At a distance beyond the bank on the dark hillside the huts of the village in which Savka lived lay huddling together like frightened young partridges. Beyond the hill the afterglow of sunset still lingered in the sky. One pale crimson streak was all that was left, and even that began to be covered by little clouds as a fire with ash.

A copse with alder-trees, softly whispering, and from time to time shuddering in the fitful breeze, lay, a dark blur, on the right of the kitchen gardens; on the left stretched the immense plain. In the distance, where the eye could not distinguish between the sky and the plain, there was a bright gleam of light. A little way off from me sat Savka. With his legs tucked under him like a Turk and his head hanging, he looked pensively at Kutka. Our hooks with live bait on them had long been in the river, and we had nothing left to do but to abandon ourselves to repose, which Savka, who was never exhausted and always rested, loved so much. The glow had not yet quite died away, but the summer night was already enfolding nature in its caressing, soothing embrace.

Everything was sinking into its first deep sleep except some night bird unfamiliar to me, which indolently uttered a long, protracted cry in several distinct notes like the phrase, "Have you seen Ni-ki-ta?" and immediately answered itself, "Seen him, seen him, seen him!"

"Why is it the nightingales aren't singing tonight?" I asked Savka.

He turned slowly towards me. His features were large, but his face was open, soft, and expressive as a woman's. Then he gazed with his mild, dreamy eyes at the copse, at the willows, slowly pulled a whistle out of his pocket, put it in his mouth and whistled the note of a hen-nightingale. And at once, as though in answer to his call, a land-rail called on the opposite bank.

"There's a nightingale for you . . . " laughed Savka. "Drag-drag! drag-drag! just like pulling at a hook, and yet I bet he thinks he is singing, too."

"I like that bird," I said. "Do you know, when the birds are migrating the land-rail does not fly, but runs along the ground? It only flies over the rivers and the sea, but all the rest it does on foot."

"Upon my word, the dog . . ." muttered Savka looking with respect in the direction of the calling land-rail.

Knowing how fond Savka was of listening, I told him all I had learned about the land-rail from sportsmen's books. From the land-rail I passed imperceptibly to the migration of the birds. Savka listened attentively, looking at me without blinking, and smiling all the while with pleasure.

"And which country is most the bird's home? Ours or those foreign parts?" he asked.

"Ours, of course. The bird itself is hatched here, and it hatches out its little ones here in its native country, and they only fly off there to escape being frozen."

"It's interesting," said Savka. "Whatever one talks about it is always interesting. Take a bird now, or a man . . . or take this little stone; there's something to learn about all of them. . . . Ah, sir, if I had known you were coming I wouldn't have told a woman to come here this evening. . . . She asked to come today."

"Oh, please don't let me be in your way," I said. "I can lie down in the wood. . . ."

"What next! She wouldn't have died if she hadn't come till tomorrow. . . . If only she would sit quiet and listen, but she always wants to be slobbering. . . . You can't have a good talk when she's here."

"Are you expecting Darya?" I asked, after a pause.

"No . . . a new one has asked to come this evening . . . Agafya, the signalman's wife."

Savka said this in his usual passionless, somewhat hollow voice, as though he were talking of tobacco or porridge, while I started with surprise. I knew Agafya. . . . She was quite a young peasant woman of nineteen or twenty, who had been married not more than a year before to a railway signalman, a fine young fellow. She lived in the village, and her husband came home there from the line every night.

"Your goings on with the women will lead to trouble, my boy," said I.

"Well, may be, . . ."

And after a moment's thought Savka added:

"I've said so to the women; they won't heed me. . . . They don't trouble about it, the silly things!"

Silence followed. . . . Meanwhile the darkness was growing thicker and thicker, and objects began to lose their contours. The streak behind the hill had completely died away, and the stars were growing brighter and more luminous. . . . The mournfully monotonous chirping of the grasshoppers, the call of the land-rail, and the cry of the quail did not destroy the stillness of the night, but, on the contrary, gave it an added monotony. It seemed as though the soft sounds that enchanted the ear came, not from birds or insects, but from the stars looking down upon us from the sky. . . .

Savka was the first to break the silence. He slowly turned his eyes from black Kutka and said:

"I see you are dull, sir. Let's have supper."

And without waiting for my consent he crept on his stomach into the shanty, rummaged about there, making the whole edifice tremble like a leaf; then he crawled back and set before me my vodka and an earthenware bowl; in the bowl there were baked eggs, lard scones made of rye, pieces of black bread, and something else. . . . We had a drink from a little crooked glass that wouldn't stand, and then we fell upon the food. . . . Coarse gray salt, dirty, greasy cakes, eggs tough as india-rubber, but how nice it all was!

"You live all alone, but what lots of good things you have," I said, pointing to the bowl. "Where do you get them from?"

"The women bring them," mumbled Savka.

"What do they bring them to you for?"

"Oh . . . from pity."

Not only Savka's menu, but his clothing, too, bore traces of feminine "pity." Thus I noticed that he had on, that evening, a new woven belt and a crimson ribbon on which a copper cross hung round his dirty neck. I knew of the weakness of the fair sex for Savka, and I knew that he did not like talking about it, and so I did not carry my inquiries any further. Besides there was not time to talk. . . . Kutka, who had been fidgeting about near us and patiently waiting for scraps, suddenly pricked up his ears and growled. We heard in the distance repeated splashing of water.

"Someone is coming by the ford," said Savka.

Three minutes later Kutka growled again and made a sound like a cough.

"Shsh!" his master hissed at him.

In the darkness there was a muffled thud of timid footsteps, and the silhouette of a woman appeared out of the copse. I recognized her, although it was dark—it was Agafya. She came up to us diffidently and stopped, breathing hard. She was breathless, probably not so much from walking as from fear and the unpleasant sensation everyone experiences in wading across a river at night. Seeing near the shanty not one but two persons, she uttered a faint cry and fell back a step.

"Ah . . . that is you!" said Savka, stuffing a scone into his mouth.

"Ye-es . . . I," she muttered, dropping on the ground a bundle of some sort and looking sideways at me. "Yakov sent his greetings to you and told me to give you . . . something here. . . ."

"Come, why tell stories? Yakov!" laughed Savka. "There is no

need for lying; the gentleman knows why you have come! Sit down;
you shall have supper with us."

Agafya looked sideways at me and sat down irresolutely.

"I thought you weren't coming this evening," Savka said, after
a prolonged silence. "Why sit like that? Eat! Or shall I give you a
drop of vodka?"

"What an idea!" laughed Agafya. "Do you think you have got
hold of a drunkard? . . . "

"Oh, drink it up. . . . Your heart will feel warmer. . . . There!"

Savka gave Agafya the crooked glass. She slowly drank the
vodka, ate nothing with it, but drew a deep breath when she had
finished.

"You've brought something," said Savka, untying the bundle and
throwing a condescending, jesting shade into his voice. "Women
can never come without bringing something. Ah, pie and potatoes.
. . . They live well," he sighed, turning to me. "They are the only
ones in the whole village who have got potatoes left from the
winter!"

In the darkness I did not see Agafya's face, but from the movement of her shoulders and head it seemed to me that she could not
take her eyes off Savka's face. To avoid being the third person at
this tryst, I decided to go for a walk and got up. But at that moment
a nightingale in the wood suddenly uttered two low contralto notes.
Half a minute later it gave a tiny high trill and then, having thus
tried its voice, began singing. Savka jumped up and listened.

"It's the same one as yesterday," he said. "Wait a minute."

And, getting up, he went noiselessly to the wood.

"Why, what do you want with it?" I shouted out after him,
"Stop!"

Savka shook his hand as much as to say, "Don't shout," and
vanished into the darkness. Savka was an excellent sportsman and
fisherman when he liked, but his talents in this direction were as completely thrown away as his strength. He was too slothful to do
things in the routine way, and vented his passion for sport in useless
tricks. For instance, he would catch nightingales only with his hands,
would shoot pike with a fowling piece, he would spend whole hours
by the river trying to catch little fish with a big hook.

Left alone with me, Agafya coughed and passed her hand several
times over her forehead. . . . She began to feel a little drunk from
the vodka.

"How are you getting on, Agasha?" I asked her, after a long silence, when it began to be awkward to remain mute any longer.

"Very well, thank God. . . . Don't tell anyone, sir, will you?" she added suddenly in a whisper.

"That's all right," I reassured her. "But how reckless you are, Agasha! . . . What if Yakov finds out?"

"He won't find out."

"But what if he does?"

"No . . . I shall be at home before he is. He is on the line now, and he will come back when the mail train brings him, and from here I can hear when the train's coming. . . ."

Agafya once more passed her hand over her forehead and looked away in the direction in which Savka had vanished. The nightingale was singing. Some night bird flew low down close to the ground and, noticing us, was startled, fluttered its wings and flew across to the other side of the river.

Soon the nightingale was silent, but Savka did not come back. Agafya got up, took a few steps uneasily, and sat down again.

"What is he doing?" she could not refrain from saying. "The train's not coming in tomorrow! I shall have to go away directly."

"Savka," I shouted. "Savka."

I was not answered even by an echo. Agafya moved uneasily and sat down again.

"It's time I was going," she said in an agitated voice. "The train will be here directly! I know when the trains come in."

The poor woman was not mistaken. Before a quarter of an hour had passed a sound was heard in the distance.

Agafya kept her eyes fixed on the copse for a long time and moved her hands impatiently.

"Why, where can he be?" she said, laughing nervously. "Where has the devil carried him? I am going! I really must be going."

Meanwhile the noise was growing more and more distinct. By now one could distinguish the rumble of the wheels from the heavy gasps of the engine. Then we heard the whistle, the train crossed the bridge with a hollow rumble . . . another minute and all was still.

"I'll wait one minute more," said Agafya, sitting down resolutely. "So be it, I'll wait."

At last Savka appeared in the darkness. He walked noiselessly on the crumbling earth of the kitchen gardens and hummed something softly to himself.

"Here's a bit of luck; what do you say to that now?" he said gaily. "As soon as I got up to the bush and began taking aim with my hand it left off singing! Ah, the bald dog! I waited and waited to see when it would begin again, but I had to give it up."

Savka flopped clumsily down to the ground beside Agafya and, to keep his balance, clutched at her waist with both hands.

"Why do you look cross, as though your aunt were your mother?" he asked.

With all his soft-heartedness and good-nature, Savka despised women. He behaved carelessly, condescendingly with them, and even stooped to scornful laughter of their feelings for himself. God knows, perhaps this careless, contemptuous manner was one of the causes of his irresistible attraction for the village Dulcineas. He was handsome and well built; in his eyes there was always a soft friendliness, even when he was looking at the women he so despised, but the fascination was not to be explained by merely external qualities. Apart from his happy exterior and original manner, one must suppose that the touching position of Savka as an acknowledged failure and an unhappy exile from his own hut to the kitchen gardens also had an influence upon the women.

"Tell the gentleman what you have come here for!" Savka went on, still holding Agafya by the waist. "Come, tell him, you good married woman! Ho-ho! Shall we have another drop of vodka, friend Agasha?"

I got up and, threading my way between the plots, I walked the length of the kitchen garden. The dark beds looked like flattened-out graves. They smelt of dug earth and the tender dampness of plants beginning to be covered with dew. . . . A red light was still gleaming on the left. It winked genially and seemed to smile.

I heard a happy laugh. It was Agafya laughing.

"And the train?" I thought. "The train has come in long ago."

Waiting a little longer, I went back to the shanty. Savka was sitting motionless, his legs crossed like a Turk, and was softly, scarcely audibly humming a song consisting of words of one syllable something like: "Out on you, fie on you . . . I and you." Agafya, intoxicated by the vodka, by Savka's scornful caresses, and by the stifling warmth of the night, was lying on the earth beside him, pressing her face convulsively to his knees. She was so carried away by her feelings that she did not even notice my arrival.

"Agasha, the train has been in a long time," I said.

"It's time—it's time you were gone," Savka, tossing his head, took up my thought. "What are you sprawling here for? You shameless hussy!"

Agafya started, took her head from his knees, glanced at me, and sank down beside him again.

"You ought to have gone long ago," I said.

Agafya turned round and got up on one knee. . . . She was unhappy. . . . For half a minute her whole figure, as far as I could distinguish it through the darkness, expressed conflict and hesitation. There was an instant when, seeming to come to herself, she drew herself up to get upon her feet, but then some invincible and implacable force seemed to push her whole body, and she sank down beside Savka again.

"Bother him!" she said, with a wild, guttural laugh, and reckless determination, impotence, and pain could be heard in that laugh.

I strolled quietly away to the copse, and from there down to the river, where our fishing lines were set. The river slept. Some soft, fluffy-petaled flower on a tall stalk touched my cheek tenderly like a child who wants to let one know it's awake. To pass the time I felt for one of the lines and pulled at it. It yielded easily and hung limply—nothing had been caught. . . . The further bank and the village could not be seen. A light gleamed in one hut, but soon went out. I felt my way along the bank, found a hollow place which I had noticed in the daylight, and sat down in it as in an armchair. I sat there a long time. . . . I saw the stars begin to grow misty and lose their brightness; a cool breath passed over the earth like a faint sigh and touched the leaves of the slumbering osiers. . . .

"A-ga-fya!" a hollow voice called from the village. "Agafya!"

It was the husband, who had returned home, and in alarm was looking for his wife in the village. At that moment there came the sound of unrestrained laughter: the wife, forgetful of everything, sought in her intoxication to make up by a few hours of happiness for the misery awaiting her next day.

I dropped asleep.

When I woke up Savka was sitting beside me and lightly shaking my shoulder. The river, the copse, both banks, green and washed, trees and fields—all were bathed in bright morning light. Through the slim trunks of the trees the rays of the newly risen sun beat upon my back.

"So that's how you catch fish?" laughed Savka. "Get up!"

I got up, gave a luxurious stretch, and began greedily drinking in the damp and fragrant air.

"Has Agasha gone?" I asked.

"There she is," said Savka, pointing in the direction of the ford.

I glanced and saw Agafya. Disheveled, with her kerchief dropping off her head, she was crossing the river, holding up her skirt. Her legs were scarcely moving. . . .

"The cat knows whose meat it has eaten," muttered Savka, screwing up his eyes as he looked at her. "She goes with her tail hanging down. . . . They are sly as cats, these women, and timid as hares. . . . She didn't go, silly thing, in the evening when we told her to! Now she will catch it, and they'll flog me again at the peasant court . . . all on account of the women. . . ."

Agafya stepped upon the bank and went across the fields to the village. At first she walked fairly boldly, but soon terror and excitement got the upper hand; she turned round fearfully, stopped and took breath.

"Yes, you are frightened!" Savka laughed mournfully, looking at the bright green streak left by Agafya in the dewy grass. "She doesn't want to go! Her husband's been standing waiting for her for a good hour. . . . Did you see him?"

Savka said the last words with a smile, but they sent a chill to my heart. In the village, near the furthest hut, Yakov was standing in the road, gazing fixedly at his returning wife. He stood without stirring, and was as motionless as a post. What was he thinking as he looked at her? What words was he preparing to greet her with? Agafya stood still a little while, looked round once more as though expecting help from us, and went on. I have never seen anyone, drunk or sober, move as she did. Agafya seemed to be shriveled up by her husband's eyes. At one time she moved in zigzags, then she moved her feet up and down without going forward, bending her knees and stretching out her hands, then she staggered back. When she had gone another hundred paces she looked round once more and sat down.

"You ought at least to hide behind a bush . . ." I said to Savka. "If the husband sees you . . ."

"He knows, anyway, who it is Agafya has come from. . . . The women don't go to the kitchen garden at night for cabbages— we all know that."

I glanced at Savka's face. It was pale and puckered up with a look of fastidious pity such as one sees in the faces of people watching tortured animals.

"What's fun for the cat is tears for the mouse . . ." he muttered.

Agafya suddenly jumped up, shook her head, and with a bold step went towards her husband. She had evidently plucked up her courage and made up her mind.

1886

# THE WITCH

IT WAS approaching nightfall. The sexton, Savely Gykin, was lying in his huge bed in the hut adjoining the church. He was not asleep, though it was his habit to go to sleep at the same time as the hens. His coarse red hair peeped from under one end of the greasy patchwork quilt, made up of colored rags, while his big unwashed feet stuck out from the other. He was listening. His hut adjoined the wall that encircled the church and the solitary window in it looked out upon the open country. And out there a regular battle was going on. It was hard to say who was being wiped off the face of the earth, and for the sake of whose destruction nature was being churned up into such a ferment; but, judging from the unceasing malignant roar, someone was getting it very hot. A victorious force was in full chase over the fields, storming in the forest and on the church roof, battering spitefully with its fists upon the windows, raging and tearing, while something vanquished was howling and wailing. . . . A plaintive lament sobbed at the window, on the roof, or in the stove. It sounded not like a call for help, but like a cry of misery, a consciousness that it was too late, that there was no salvation. The snowdrifts were covered with a thin coating of ice; tears quivered on them and on the trees; a dark slush of mud and melting snow flowed along the roads and paths. In short, it was thawing, but through the dark night the heavens failed to see it, and flung flakes of fresh snow upon the melting earth at a terrific rate. And the wind staggered like a drunkard. It would not let the snow settle on the ground, and whirled it round in the darkness at random.

Savely listened to all this din and frowned. The fact was that he knew, or at any rate suspected, what all this racket outside the window was tending to and whose handiwork it was.

"I know!" he muttered, shaking his finger menacingly under the bedclothes. "I know all about it."

On a stool by the window sat the sexton's wife, Raïssa Nilovna. A tin lamp standing on another stool, as though timid and distrustful of its powers, shed a dim and flickering light on her broad shoulders, on the handsome, tempting-looking contours of her person, and on her thick plait, which reached to the floor. She was making sacks out of coarse hempen stuff. Her hands moved nimbly, while her whole body, her eyes, her eyebrows, her full lips, her white neck were as still as though they were asleep, absorbed in the monotonous, mechanical toil. Only from time to time she raised her head to rest her weary neck, glanced for a moment towards the window, beyond which the snowstorm was raging, and bent again over her sacking. No desire, no joy, no grief, nothing was expressed by her handsome face with its turned-up nose and its dimples. So a beautiful fountain expresses nothing when it is not playing.

But at last she had finished a sack. She flung it aside, and, stretching luxuriously, rested her motionless, lackluster eyes on the window. The panes were swimming with drops like tears, and white with short-lived snowflakes which fell on the window, glanced at Raïssa, and melted. . . .

"Come to bed!" growled the sexton. Raïssa remained mute. But suddenly her eyelashes flickered and there was a gleam of attention in her eye. Savely, all the time watching her expression from under the quilt, put out his head and asked:

"What is it?"

"Nothing. . . . I fancy someone's coming," she answered quietly.

The sexton flung the quilt off with his arms and legs, knelt up in bed, and looked blankly at his wife. The timid light of the lamp illuminated his hirsute, pockmarked countenance and glided over his rough matted hair.

"Do you hear?" asked his wife.

Through the monotonous roar of the storm he caught a scarcely audible thin and jingling monotone like the shrill note of a gnat when it wants to settle on one's cheek and is angry at being prevented.

"It's the post," muttered Savely, squatting on his heels.

Two miles from the church ran the posting road. In windy weather, when the wind was blowing from the road to the church, the inmates of the hut caught the sound of bells.

"Lord! fancy people wanting to drive about in such weather," sighed Raïssa.

"It's government work. You've to go whether you like or not." The murmur hung in the air and died away.

"It has driven by," said Savely, getting into bed.

But before he had time to cover himself up with the bedclothes he heard a distinct sound of the bell. The sexton looked anxiously at his wife, leapt out of bed and walked, waddling, to and fro by the stove. The bell went on ringing for a little, then died away again as though it had ceased.

"I don't hear it," said the sexton, stopping and looking at his wife with his eyes screwed up.

But at that moment the wind rapped on the window and with it floated a shrill jingling note. Savely turned pale, cleared his throat, and flopped about the floor with his bare feet again.

"The postman is lost in the storm," he wheezed out, glancing malignantly at his wife. "Do you hear? The postman has lost his way! . . . I . . . I know! Do you suppose I . . . don't understand?" he muttered. "I know all about it, curse you!"

"What do you know?" Raïssa asked quietly, keeping her eyes fixed on the window.

"I know that it's all your doing, you she-devil! Your doing, damn you! This snowstorm and the post going wrong, you've done it all—you!"

"You're mad, you silly," his wife answered calmly.

"I've been watching you for a long time past and I've seen it. From the first day I married you I noticed that you'd bitch's blood in you!"

"Tfoo!" said Raïssa, surprised, shrugging her shoulders and crossing herself. "Cross yourself, you fool!"

"A witch is a witch," Savely pronounced in a hollow, tearful voice, hurriedly blowing his nose on the hem of his shirt; "though you are my wife, though you are of a clerical family, I'd say what you are even at confession. . . . Why, God have mercy upon us! Last year on the Eve of the Prophet Daniel and the Three Young Men there was a snowstorm, and what happened then? The mechanic came in to warm himself. Then on St. Alexey's Day the ice broke on the river and the district policeman turned up, and he was chatting with you all night . . . the damned brute! And when he came out in the morning and I looked at him, he had rings under his eyes and his cheeks were hollow! Eh! During the August fast there were two storms and each time the huntsman turned up. I saw it all, damn him! Oh, she is redder than a crab now, aha!"

"You didn't see anything."

"Didn't I! And this winter before Christmas on the Day of the Ten Martyrs of Crete, when the storm lasted for a whole day and night—do you remember?—the marshal's clerk was lost, and turned up here, the hound. . . . Tfoo! To be tempted by the clerk! It was worth upsetting God's weather for him! A drivelling scribbler, not a foot from the ground, pimples all over his mug and his neck awry! If he were good-looking, anyway—but he, phew! he is as ugly as Satan!"

The sexton took breath, wiped his lips and listened. The bell was not to be heard, but the wind banged on the roof, and again there came a tinkle in the darkness.

"And it's the same thing now!" Savely went on. "It's not for nothing the postman is lost! Blast my eyes if the postman isn't looking for you! Oh, the devil is a good hand at his work; he is a fine one to help! He will turn him round and round and bring him here. I know, I see! You can't conceal it, you devil's bauble, you heathen wanton! As soon as the storm began I knew what you were up to."

"Here's a fool!" smiled his wife. "Why, do you suppose, you thick-head, that I make the storm?"

"H'm! . . . Grin away! Whether it's your doing or not, I only know that when your blood's on fire there's sure to be bad weather, and when there's bad weather there's bound to be some crazy fellow turning up here. It happens so every time! So it must be you!"

To be more impressive the sexton put his finger to his forehead, closed his left eye, and said in a singsong voice:

"Oh, the madness! oh, the unclean Judas! If you really are a human being and not a witch, you ought to think what if he is not the mechanic, or the clerk, or the huntsman, but the devil in their form! Ah! You'd better think of that!"

"Why, you are stupid, Savely," said his wife, looking at him compassionately. "When father was alive and living here, all sorts of people used to come to him to be cured of the ague: from the village, and the hamlets, and the Armenian settlement. They came almost every day, and no one called them devils. But if anyone once a year comes in bad weather to warm himself, you wonder at it, you silly, and take all sorts of notions into your head at once."

His wife's logic touched Savely. He stood with his bare feet wide apart, bent his head, and pondered. He was not firmly convinced yet of the truth of his suspicions, and his wife's genuine and unconcerned tone quite disconcerted him. Yet after a moment's thought he wagged his head and said:

"It's not as though they were old men or bandy-legged cripples; it's always young men who want to come for the night. . . . Why is that? And if they only wanted to warm themselves— But they are up to mischief. No, woman; there's no creature in this world as cunning as your female sort! Of real brains you've not an ounce, less than a starling, but for devilish slyness—oo-oo-oo! The Queen of Heaven protect us! There is the postman's bell! When the storm was only beginning I knew all that was in your mind. That's your witchery, you spider!"

"Why do you keep on at me, you heathen?" His wife lost her patience at last. "Why do you keep sticking to it like pitch?"

"I stick to it because if anything—God forbid—happens tonight . . . do you hear? . . . if anything happens tonight, I'll go straight off tomorrow morning to Father Nikodim and tell him all about it. 'Father Nikodim,' I shall say, 'graciously excuse me, but she is a witch.' 'Why so?' 'H'm! do you want to know why?' 'Certainly. . . .' And I shall tell him. And woe to you, woman! Not only at the dread Seat of Judgment, but in your earthly life you'll be punished, too! It's not for nothing there are prayers in the breviary against your kind!"

Suddenly there was a knock at the window, so loud and unusual that Savely turned pale and almost dropped backwards with fright. His wife jumped up, and she, too, turned pale.

"For God's sake, let us come in and get warm!" they heard in a trembling deep bass. "Who lives here? For mercy's sake! We've lost our way."

"Who are you?" asked Raïssa, afraid to look at the window.

"The post," answered a second voice.

"You've succeeded with your devil's tricks," said Savely with a wave of his hand. "No mistake; I am right! Well, you'd better look out!"

The sexton jumped onto the bed in two skips, stretched himself on the feather mattress, and sniffing angrily, turned with his face to the wall. Soon he felt a draught of cold air on his back. The door creaked and the tall figure of a man, plastered over with snow from head to foot, appeared in the doorway. Behind him could be seen a second figure as white.

"Am I to bring in the bags?" asked the second in a hoarse bass voice.

"You can't leave them there." Saying this, the first figure began untying his hood, but gave it up, and pulling it off impatiently with his cap, angrily flung it near the stove. Then taking off his great-coat, he threw that down beside it, and, without saying good evening, began pacing up and down the hut.

He was a fair-haired, young postman wearing a shabby uniform and black rusty-looking high boots. After warming himself by walking to and fro, he sat down at the table, stretched out his muddy feet towards the sacks and leaned his chin on his fist. His pale face, reddened in places by the cold, still bore vivid traces of the pain and terror he had just been through. Though distorted by anger and bearing traces of recent suffering, physical and moral, it was handsome in spite of the melting snow on the eyebrows, mustaches, and short beard.

"It's a dog's life!" muttered the postman, looking round the walls and seeming hardly able to believe that he was in the warmth. "We were nearly lost! If it had not been for your light, I don't know what would have happened. Goodness only knows when it will all be over! There's no end to this dog's life! Where have we come?" he asked, dropping his voice and raising his eyes to the sexton's wife.

"To the Gulyaevsky Hill on General Kalinovsky's estate," she answered, startled and blushing.

"Do you hear, Stepan?" The postman turned to the driver, who was wedged in the doorway with a huge mailbag on his shoulders. "We've got to Gulyaevsky Hill."

"Yes . . . we're a long way out." Jerking out these words like a hoarse sigh, the driver went out and soon after returned with another bag, then went out once more and this time brought the post-man's sword on a big belt, of the pattern of that long flat blade with which Judith is portrayed by the bedside of Holofernes in cheap woodcuts. Laying the bags along the wall, he went out into the outer room, sat down there and lighted his pipe.

"Perhaps you'd like some tea after your journey?" Raïssa in-quired.

"How can we sit drinking tea?" said the postman, frowning. "We must make haste and get warm, and then set off, or we shall be late for the mail train. We'll stay ten minutes and then get on our way. Only be so good as to show us the way."

"What an infliction it is, this weather!" sighed Raïssa.

"H'm, yes. . . . Who may you be?"

"We? We live here, by the church. . . . We belong to the clergy. . . . There lies my husband. Savely, get up and say good evening! This used to be a separate parish till eighteen months ago. Of course, when the gentry lived here there were more people, and it was worth while to have the services. But now the gentry have gone, and I need not tell you there's nothing for the clergy to live on. The nearest village is Markovka, and that's over three miles away. Savely is on the retired list now, and has got the watchman's job; he has to look after the church. . . ."

And the postman was immediately informed that if Savely were to go to the General's lady and ask her for a letter to the bishop, he would be given a good berth. "But he doesn't go to the General's lady because he is lazy and afraid of people. We belong to the clergy all the same . . ." added Raïssa.

"What do you live on?" asked the postman.

"There's a kitchen garden and a meadow belonging to the church. Only we don't get much from that," sighed Raïssa. "The old skin-flint, Father Nikodim, from the next village, celebrates here on St. Nicholas' Day in the winter and on St. Nicholas' Day in the summer, and for that he takes almost all the crops for himself. There's no one to stick up for us!"

"You are lying," Savely growled hoarsely. "Father Nikodim is a saintly soul, a luminary of the Church; and if he does take it, it's the regulation!"

"You've a cross one!" said the postman, with a grin. "Have you been married long?"

"It was three years ago the last Sunday before Lent. My father was sexton here in the old days, and when the time came for him to die, he went to the Consistory and asked them to send some unmarried man to marry me that I might keep the place. So I married him."

"Aha, so you killed two birds with one stone!" said the postman, looking at Savely's back. "Got wife and job together."

Savely wriggled his leg impatiently and moved closer to the wall. The postman moved away from the table, stretched, and sat down on the mail-bag. After a moment's thought he squeezed the bags with his hands, shifted his sword to the other side, and lay down with one foot touching the floor.

"It's a dog's life," he muttered, putting his hands behind his head and closing his eyes. "I wouldn't wish a wild Tatar such a life."

Soon everything was still. Nothing was audible except the sniffing of Savely and the slow, even breathing of the sleeping postman, who uttered a deep prolonged "h-h-h" at every breath. From time to time there was a sound like a creaking wheel in his throat, and his twitching foot rustled against the bag.

Savely fidgeted under the quilt and looked round slowly. His wife was sitting on the stool, and with her hands pressed against her cheeks was gazing at the postman's face. Her face was immovable, like the face of someone frightened and astonished.

"Well, what are you gaping at?" Savely whispered angrily.

"What is it to you? Lie down!" answered his wife without taking her eyes off the flaxen head.

Savely angrily puffed all the air out of his chest and turned abruptly to the wall. Three minutes later he turned over restlessly again, knelt upon the bed, and with his hands on the pillow looked askance at his wife. She was still sitting motionless, staring at the visitor. Her cheeks were pale and her eyes were glowing with a strange fire. The sexton cleared his throat, crawled on his stomach off the bed, and going up to the postman, put a handkerchief over his face.

"What's that for?" asked his wife.

"To keep the light out of his eyes."

"Then put out the light!"

Savely looked distrustfully at his wife, put out his lips towards the lamp, but at once thought better of it and clasped his hands.

"Isn't that devilish cunning?" he exclaimed. "Ah! Is there any creature slyer than womenkind?"

"Ah, you long-skirted devil!" hissed his wife, frowning with vexation. "You wait a bit!"

And settling herself more comfortably, she stared at the postman again.

It did not matter to her that his face was covered. She was not so much interested in his face as in his whole appearance, in the novelty of this man. His chest was broad and powerful, his hands were slender and well formed, and his graceful, muscular legs were much comelier than Savely's stumps. There could be no comparison, in fact.

"Though I am a long-skirted devil," Savely said after a brief interval, "they've no business to sleep here. . . . It's government work; we shall have to answer for keeping them. If you carry the letters, carry them, you can't go to sleep. . . . Hey! you!" Savely shouted into the outer room. "You, driver. . . . What's your name? Shall I show you the way? Get up; postmen mustn't sleep!"

And Savely, thoroughly roused, ran up to the postman and tugged him by the sleeve.

"Hey, your Honor, if you must go, go; and if you don't, it's not the thing. . . . Sleeping won't do."

The postman jumped up, sat down, looked with blank eyes round the hut, and lay down again.

"But when are you going?" Savely pattered away. "That's what the post is for—to get there in good time, do you hear? I'll take you."

The postman opened his eyes. Warmed and relaxed by his first sweet sleep, and not yet quite awake, he saw as through a mist the white neck and the immovable, alluring eyes of the sexton's wife. He closed his eyes and smiled as though he had been dreaming it all.

"Come, how can you go in such weather!" he heard a soft feminine voice. "You ought to have a sound sleep and it would do you good!"

"And what about the post?" said Savely anxiously. "Who's going to take the post? Are you going to take it, pray, you?"

The postman opened his eyes again, looked at the play of the dimples on Raïssa's face, remembered where he was, and understood Savely. The thought that he had to go out into the cold darkness sent a chill shudder all down him, and he winced.

"I might sleep another five minutes," he said, yawning. "I shall be late, anyway. . . ."

"We might be just in time," came a voice from the outer room. "All days are not alike; the train may be late for a bit of luck."

The postman got up, and stretching lazily began putting on his coat.

Savely positively neighed with delight when he saw his visitors were getting ready to go.

"Give us a hand," the driver shouted to him as he lifted up a mailbag.

The sexton ran out and helped him drag the postbags into the yard. The postman began undoing the knot in his hood. The sexton's wife gazed into his eyes, and seemed trying to look right into his soul.

"You ought to have a cup of tea . . ." she said.

"I wouldn't say no . . . but, you see, they're getting ready," he assented. "We are late, anyway."

"Do stay," she whispered, dropping her eyes and touching him on the sleeve.

The postman got the knot undone at last and flung the hood over his elbow, hesitating. He felt it comfortable standing by Raïssa.

"What a . . . neck you've got! . . . " And he touched her neck with two fingers. Seeing that she did not resist, he stroked her neck and shoulders.

"I say, you are . . ."

"You'd better stay . . . have some tea."

"Where are you putting it?" The driver's voice could be heard outside. "Lay it crossways."

"You'd better stay. . . . Hark how the wind howls."

And the postman, not yet quite awake, not yet quite able to shake off the intoxicating sleep of youth and fatigue, was suddenly overwhelmed by a desire for the sake of which mailbags, postal trains . . . and all things in the world, are forgotten. He glanced at the door in a frightened way, as though he wanted to escape or hide himself, seized Raïssa round the waist, and was just bending over the lamp to put out the light, when he heard the tramp of boots in the outer room, and the driver appeared in the doorway. Savely peeped in over his shoulder. The postman dropped his hands quickly and stood still as though irresolute.

"It's all ready," said the driver. The postman stood still for a moment, resolutely threw up his head as though waking up completely, and followed the driver out. Raïssa was left alone.

"Come, get in and show us the way!" she heard.

One bell sounded languidly, then another, and the jingling notes in a long delicate chain floated away from the hut.

When little by little they had died away, Raïssa got up and nervously paced to and fro. At first she was pale, then she flushed all over. Her face was contorted with hate, her breathing was tremulous, her eyes gleamed with wild, savage anger, and, pacing up and down as in a cage, she looked like a tigress menaced with red-hot iron. For a moment she stood still and looked at her abode. Almost half of the room was filled up by the bed, which stretched the length of the whole wall and consisted of a dirty feather-bed, coarse gray pillows, a quilt, and nameless rags of various sorts. The bed was a shapeless ugly mass which suggested the shock of hair that always stood up on Savely's head whenever it occurred to him to oil it. From the bed to the door that led into the cold outer room stretched the dark stove surrounded by pots and hanging clouts. Everything, including the absent Savely himself, was dirty, greasy, and smutty to the last degree, so that it was strange to see a woman's white neck and delicate skin in such surroundings.

Raïssa ran up to the bed, stretched out her hands as though she wanted to fling it all about, stamp it underfoot, and tear it to shreds. But then, as though frightened by contact with the dirt, she leapt back and began pacing up and down again.

When Savely returned two hours later, worn out and covered with snow, she was undressed and in bed. Her eyes were closed, but from the slight tremor that ran over her face he guessed that she was not asleep. On his way home he had vowed inwardly to wait till next day and not to touch her, but he could not resist a biting taunt at her.

"Your witchery was all in vain: he's gone off," he said, grinning with malignant joy.

His wife remained mute, but her chin quivered. Savely undressed slowly, clambered over his wife, and lay down next to the wall.

"Tomorrow I'll let Father Nikodim know what sort of wife you are!" he muttered, curling himself up.

Raïssa turned her face to him and her eyes gleamed.

"The job's enough for you, and you can look for a wife in the forest, blast you!" she said. "I am no wife for you, a clumsy lout, a slugabed, God forgive me!"

"Come, come . . . go to sleep!"

"How miserable I am!" sobbed his wife. "If it weren't for you, I might have married a merchant or some gentleman! If it weren't for you, I should love my husband now! And you haven't been buried in the snow, you haven't been frozen on the highroad, you Herod!"

Raïssa cried for a long time. At last she drew a deep sigh and was still. The storm still raged without. Something wailed in the stove, in the chimney, outside the walls, and it seemed to Savely that the wailing was within him, in his ears. This evening had completely confirmed him in his suspicions about his wife. He no longer doubted that his wife, with the aid of the Evil One, controlled the winds and the post sledges. But to add to his grief, this mysteriousness, this supernatural, weird power gave the woman beside him a peculiar, incomprehensible charm of which he had not been conscious before. The fact that in his stupidity he unconsciously threw a poetic glamor over her made her seem, as it were, whiter, sleeker, more unapproachable.

"Witch!" he muttered indignantly. "Tfoo, horrid creature!"

Yet, waiting till she was quiet and began breathing evenly, he touched her head with his finger . . . held her thick plait in his hand for a minute. She did not feel it. Then he grew bolder and stroked her neck.

"Leave off!" she shouted, and prodded him on the nose with her elbow with such violence that he saw stars before his eyes.

The pain in his nose was soon over, but the torture in his heart remained.

1886

# VOLODYA

At FIVE o'clock one Sunday afternoon in summer, Volodya, a plain, shy, sickly-looking lad of seventeen, was sitting in the arbor of the Shumihins' country villa, feeling dreary. His despondent thoughts flowed in three directions. In the first place, he had next day, Monday, an examination in mathematics; he knew that if he did not get through the written examination on the morrow, he would be expelled, for he had already been two years in the sixth form and had two and three-quarter marks for algebra in his annual report. In the second place, his presence at the villa of the Shumihins, a wealthy family with aristocratic pretensions, was a continual source of mortification to his *amour-propre*. It seemed to him that Madame Shumihin looked upon him and his *maman* as poor relations and dependents, that they laughed at his *maman* and did not respect her. He had on one occasion accidentally overheard Madame Shumihin, in the veranda, telling her cousin Anna Fyodorovna that his *maman* still tried to look young and got herself up, that she never paid her losses at cards, and had a partiality for other people's shoes and tobacco. Every day Volodya besought his *maman* not to go to the Shumihins', and drew a picture of the humiliating part she played with these gentlefolk. He tried to persuade her, said rude things, but she—a frivolous, pampered woman, who had run through two fortunes, her own and her husband's, in her time, and always gravitated towards acquaintances of high rank—did not understand him, and twice a week Volodya had to accompany her to the villa he hated.

In the third place, the youth could not for one instant get rid of a strange, unpleasant feeling which was absolutely new to him. . . . It seemed to him that he was in love with Anna Fyodorovna,

635

the Shumihins' cousin, who was staying with them. She was a vivacious, loud-voiced, laughter-loving, healthy, and vigorous lady of thirty, with rosy cheeks, plump shoulders, a plump round chin and a continual smile on her thin lips. She was neither young nor beautiful—Volodya knew that perfectly well; but for some reason he could not help thinking of her, looking at her while she shrugged her plump shoulders and moved her flat back as she played croquet, or after prolonged laughter and running up and down stairs, sank into a low chair, and, half closing her eyes and gasping for breath, pretended that she was stifling and could not breathe. She was married. Her husband, a staid and dignified architect, came once a week to the villa, slept soundly, and returned to town. Volodya's strange feeling had begun with his conceiving an unaccountable hatred for the architect, and feeling relieved every time he went back to town.

Now, sitting in the arbor, thinking of his examination next day, and of his *maman*, at whom they laughed, he felt an intense desire to see Nyuta (that was what the Shumihins called Anna Fyodorovna), to hear her laughter and the rustle of her dress. . . . This desire was not like the pure, poetic love of which he read in novels and about which he dreamed every night when he went to bed; it was strange, incomprehensible; he was ashamed of it, and afraid of it as of something very wrong and impure, something which it was disagreeable to confess even to himself.

"It's not love," he said to himself. "One can't fall in love with women of thirty who are married. It is only a little intrigue. . . . Yes, an intrigue. . . ."

Pondering on the "intrigue," he thought of his uncontrollable shyness, his lack of mustache, his freckles, his narrow eyes, and put himself in his imagination side by side with Nyuta, and the juxtaposition seemed to him impossible; then he made haste to imagine himself bold, handsome, witty, dressed in the latest fashion.

When his dreams were at their height, as he sat huddled together and looking at the ground in a dark corner of the arbor, he heard the sound of light footsteps. Someone was coming slowly along the avenue. Soon the steps stopped and something white gleamed in the entrance.

"Is there anyone here?" asked a woman's voice.

Volodya recognized the voice, and raised his head in a fright.

"Who is here?" asked Nyuta, going into the arbor. "Ah, it is you, Volodya? What are you doing here? Thinking? And how can you go on thinking, thinking, thinking? . . . That's the way to go out of your mind!"

Volodya got up and looked in a dazed way at Nyuta. She had only just come back from bathing. Over her shoulder there was hanging a sheet and a rough towel, and from under the white silk kerchief on her head he could see the wet hair sticking to her forehead. There was the cool damp smell of the bathhouse and of almond soap still hanging about her. She was out of breath from running quickly. The top button of her blouse was undone, so that the boy saw her throat and bosom.

"Why don't you say something?" said Nyuta, looking Volodya up and down. "It's not polite to be silent when a lady talks to you. What a clumsy seal you are though, Volodya! You always sit, saying nothing, thinking like some philosopher. There's not a spark of life or fire in you! You are really horrid! . . . At your age you ought to be living, skipping, and jumping, chattering, flirting, falling in love."

Volodya looked at the sheet that was held by a plump white hand, and thought. . . .

"He's mute," said Nyuta, with wonder; "it is strange, really. . . . Listen! Be a man! Come, you might smile at least! Phew, the horrid philosopher!" she laughed. "But do you know, Volodya, why you are such a clumsy seal? Because you don't devote yourself to the ladies. Why don't you? It's true there are no girls here, but there is nothing to prevent your flirting with the married ladies! Why don't you flirt with me, for instance?"

Volodya listened and scratched his forehead in acute and painful irresolution.

"It's only very proud people who are silent and love solitude," Nyuta went on, pulling his hand away from his forehead. "You are proud, Volodya. Why do you look at me like that from under your brows? Look me straight in the face, if you please! Yes, now then, clumsy seal!"

Volodya made up his mind to speak. Wanting to smile, he twitched his lower lip, blinked, and again put his hand to his forehead.

"I . . . I love you," he said.

Nyuta raised her eyebrows in surprise, and laughed.

"What do I hear?" she sang, as prima donnas sing at the opera when they hear something awful. "What? What did you say? Say it again, say it again. . . ."

"I . . . I love you!" repeated Volodya.

And without his will having any part in his action, without reflection or understanding, he took half a step towards Nyuta and clutched her by the arm. Everything was dark before his eyes, and tears came into them. The whole world was turned into one big, rough towel which smelt of the bathhouse.

"Bravo, bravo!" he heard a merry laugh. "Why don't you speak? I want you to speak! Well?"

Seeing that he was not prevented from holding her arm, Volodya glanced at Nyuta's laughing face, and clumsily, awkwardly, put both arms round her waist, his hands meeting behind her back. He held her round the waist with both arms, while, putting her hands up to her head, showing the dimples in her elbows, she set her hair straight under the kerchief and said in a calm voice:

"You must be tactful, polite, charming, and you can only become that under feminine influence. But what a wicked, angry face you have! You must talk, laugh. . . . Yes, Volodya, don't be surly; you are young and will have plenty of time for philosophizing. Come, let go of me; I am going. Let go."

Without effort she released her waist, and, humming something, walked out of the arbor. Volodya was left alone. He smoothed his hair, smiled, and walked three times to and fro across the arbor, then he sat down on the bench and smiled again. He felt insufferably ashamed, so much so that he wondered that human shame could reach such a pitch of acuteness and intensity. Shame made him smile, gesticulate, and whisper some disconnected words.

He was ashamed that he had been treated like a small boy, ashamed of his shyness, and, most of all, that he had had the audacity to put his arms round the waist of a respectable married woman, though, as it seemed to him, neither his age nor anything in his outward appearance, nor his social position gave him any right to do so.

He jumped up, went out of the arbor, and, without looking round, walked into the recesses of the garden furthest from the house.

"Ah! only to get away from here as soon as possible," he thought, clutching his head. "My God! as soon as possible."

The train by which Volodya was to go back with his *maman* was at eight-forty. There were three hours before the train started, but he would with pleasure have gone to the station at once without waiting for his *maman*.

At eight o'clock he went to the house. His whole figure was expressive of determination: what would be, would be! He made up his mind to go in boldly, to look them straight in the face, to speak in a loud voice, regardless of everything.

He crossed the terrace, the big hall and the drawing-room, and there stopped to take breath. He could hear them in the dining-room, drinking tea. Madame Shumihin, *maman*, and Nyuta were talking and laughing about something.

Volodya listened.

"I assure you!" said Nyuta. "I could not believe my eyes! When he began declaring his passion and—just imagine!—put his arms round my waist, I should not have recognized him. And you know he has a way with him! When he told me he was in love with me, there was something brutal in his face, like a Circassian."

"Really!" gasped *maman*, going off into a peal of laughter. "Really! How he does remind me of his father!"

Volodya ran back and dashed out into the open air.

"How could they talk of it aloud!" he wondered in agony, clasping his hands and looking up to the sky in horror. "They talk aloud in cold blood . . . and *maman* laughed! . . . *Maman!* My God, why didst Thou give me such a mother? Why?"

But he had to go to the house, come what might. He walked three times up and down the avenue, grew a little calmer, and went into the house.

"Why didn't you come in in time for tea?" Madame Shumihin asked sternly.

"I am sorry, it's . . . it's time for me to go," he muttered, not raising his eyes. "*Maman*, it's eight o'clock!"

"You go alone, my dear," said his *maman* languidly. "I am staying the night with Lili. Goodbye, my dear. . . . Let me make the sign of the cross over you."

She made the sign of the cross over her son, and said in French, turning to Nyuta:

"He's rather like Lermontov . . . isn't he?"

Saying goodbye after a fashion, without looking anyone in the face, Volodya went out of the dining-room. Ten minutes later he was walking along the road to the station, and was glad of it. Now he felt neither frightened nor ashamed; he breathed freely and easily.

About half a mile from the station, he sat down on a stone by the side of the road, and gazed at the sun, which was half hidden behind a barrow. There were lights already here and there at the station, and one green light glimmered dimly, but the train was not yet in sight. It was pleasant to Volodya to sit still without moving, and to watch the evening coming little by little. The darkness of the arbor, the footsteps, the smell of the bathhouse, the laughter, and the waist—all these rose with amazing vividness before his imagination, and all this was no longer so terrible and important as before.

"It's of no consequence. . . . She did not pull her hand away, and laughed when I held her by the waist," he thought. "So she must have liked it. If she had disliked it she would have been angry. . . ."

And now Volodya felt sorry that he had not had more boldness there in the arbor. He felt sorry that he was so stupidly going away, and he was by now persuaded that if the same thing happened again he would be bolder and look at it more simply.

And it would not be difficult for the opportunity to occur again. They used to stroll about for a long time after supper at the Shumihins'. If Volodya went for a walk with Nyuta in the dark garden, there would be an opportunity!

"I will go back," he thought, "and will go by the morning train tomorrow. . . . I will say I have missed the train."

And he turned back. . . . Madame Shumihin, *maman*, Nyuta, and one of the nieces were sitting on the veranda, playing vint. When Volodya told them the lie about missing the train, they were uneasy that he might be late for the examination next day, and advised him to get up early. All the while they were playing he sat on one side, greedily watching Nyuta and waiting. . . . He already had a plan prepared in his mind: he would go up to Nyuta in the dark, would take her by the hand, then would embrace her; there would be no need to say anything, as both of them would understand without words.

But after supper the ladies did not go for a walk in the garden, but went on playing cards. They played till one o'clock at night, and then broke up to go to bed.

"How stupid it all is!" Volodya thought with vexation as he got into bed. "But never mind; I'll wait till tomorrow . . . tomorrow in the arbor. It doesn't matter. . . ."

He did not attempt to go to sleep, but sat in bed, hugging his knees and thinking. All thought of the examination was hateful to him. He had already made up his mind that they would expel him, and that there was nothing terrible about his being expelled. On the contrary, it was a good thing—a very good thing, in fact. Next day he would be as free as a bird; he would put on ordinary clothes instead of his school uniform, would smoke openly, come out here, and make love to Nyuta when he liked; and he would not be a schoolboy but "a young man." And as for the rest of it, what is called a career, a future, that was clear; Volodya would go into the army or the telegraph service, or he would go into a chemist's shop and work his way up till he was a dispenser. . . . There were lots of callings. An hour or two passed, and he was still sitting and thinking. . . .

Towards three o'clock, when it was beginning to get light, the door creaked cautiously, and his *maman* came into the room.

"Aren't you asleep?" she asked, yawning. "Go to sleep; I have only come in for a minute. . . . I am only fetching the drops. . . ."

"What for?"

"Poor Lili has got spasms again. Go to sleep, my child, your examination's tomorrow. . . ."

She took a bottle of something out of the cupboard, went to the window, read the label, and went away.

"Marya Leontyevna, those are not the drops!" Volodya heard a woman's voice, a minute later. "That's lily of the valley, and Lili wants morphine. Is your son asleep? Ask him to look for it. . . ."

It was Nyuta's voice. Volodya turned cold. He hurriedly put on his trousers, flung his coat over his shoulders, and went to the door.

"Do you understand? Morphine," Nyuta explained in a whisper. "There must be a label in Latin. Wake Volodya; he will find it."

*Maman* opened the door and Volodya caught sight of Nyuta. She was wearing the same loose wrapper in which she had gone to bathe. Her hair hung loose and disordered on her shoulders, her face looked sleepy and dark in the half-light. . . .

"Why, Volodya is not asleep," she said. "Volodya, look in the cupboard for the morphine, there's a dear! What a nuisance Lili is! She always has something the matter."

*Maman* muttered something, yawned, and went away.

"Look for it," said Nyuta. "Why are you standing still?"

Volodya went to the cupboard, knelt down, and began looking through the bottles and boxes of medicine. His hands were trembling, and he had a feeling in his chest and stomach as though cold waves were running all over his inside. He felt suffocated and giddy from the smell of ether, carbolic acid, and various drugs, which he quite unnecessarily snatched up with his trembling fingers and spilled in so doing.

"I believe *maman* has gone," he thought. "That's a good thing . . . a good thing. . . ."

"Will you be quick?" said Nyuta, drawling.

"In a minute. . . . Here, I believe this is morphine," said Volodya, reading on one of the labels the word "morph . . ." "Here it is!"

Nyuta was standing in the doorway in such a way that one foot was in his room and one was in the passage. She was tidying her hair, which was difficult to put in order because it was so thick and long, and looked absent-mindedly at Volodya. In her loose wrap, with her sleepy face and her hair down, in the dim light that came into the white sky not yet lit by the sun, she seemed to Volodya captivating, magnificent. . . . Fascinated, trembling all over, and remembering with relish how he had held that exquisite body in his arms in the arbor, he handed her the bottle and said:

"How wonderful you are!"

"What?"

She came into the room.

"What?" she asked, smiling.

He was silent and looked at her, then, just as in the arbor, he took her hand, and she looked at him with a smile and waited for what would happen next.

"I love you," he whispered.

She left off smiling, thought a minute, and said:

"Wait a little; I think somebody is coming. Oh, these school-boys!" she said in an undertone, going to the door and peeping out into the passage. "No, there is no one to be seen. . . ."

She came back.

Then it seemed to Volodya that the room, Nyuta, the sunrise and himself—all melted together in one sensation of acute, extraordinary, incredible bliss, for which one might give up one's whole life and face eternal torments. . . . But half a minute passed and all that vanished. Volodya saw only a fat, plain face, distorted by an expression of repulsion, and he himself suddenly felt a loathing for what had happened.

"I must go away, though," said Nyuta, looking at Volodya with disgust. "What a wretched, ugly . . . fie, ugly duckling!"

How unseemly her long hair, her loose wrap, her steps, her voice seemed to Volodya now! . . .

" 'Ugly duckling,' . . ." he thought after she had gone away. "I really am ugly . . . everything is ugly."

The sun was rising, the birds were singing loudly; he could hear the gardener walking in the garden and the creaking of his wheelbarrow . . . and soon afterwards he heard the lowing of the cows and the sounds of the shepherd's pipe. The sunlight and the sounds told him that somewhere in this world there is a pure, refined, poetical life. But where was it? Volodya had never heard a word of it from his *maman* or any of the people round about him.

When the footman came to wake him for the morning train, he pretended to be asleep. . . .

"Bother it! Damn it all!" he thought.

He got up between ten and eleven.

Combing his hair before the looking-glass, and looking at his ugly face, pale from his sleepless night, he thought:

"It's perfectly true . . . an ugly duckling!"

When *maman* saw him and was horrified that he was not at his examination, Volodya said:

"I overslept myself, *maman*. . . . But don't worry, I will get a medical certificate."

Madame Shumihin and Nyuta waked up at one o'clock. Volodya heard Madame Shumihin open her window with a bang, heard Nyuta go off into a peal of laughter in reply to her coarse voice. He saw the door open and a string of nieces and other toadies (among the latter was his *maman*) file into lunch, caught a glimpse of Nyuta's freshly washed laughing face, and, beside her, the black brows and beard of her husband the architect, who had just arrived.

Nyuta was wearing a Little Russian dress which did not suit her at all, and made her look clumsy; the architect was making dull and vulgar jokes. The rissoles served at lunch had too much onion in them—so it seemed to Volodya. It also seemed to him that Nyuta laughed loudly on purpose, and kept glancing in his direction to give him to understand that the memory of the night did not trouble her in the least, and that she was not aware of the presence at table of the "ugly duckling."

At four o'clock Volodya drove to the station with his *maman*. Foul memories, the sleepless night, the prospect of expulsion from school, the stings of conscience—all roused in him now an oppressive, gloomy anger. He looked at *maman's* sharp profile, at her little nose, at the raincoat which was a present from Nyuta, and muttered:

"Why do you powder? It's not becoming at your age! You make yourself up, don't pay your debts at cards, smoke other people's tobacco. . . . It's hateful! I don't love you . . . I don't love you!"

He was insulting her, and she rolled her little eyes in alarm, clapped her little hands, and whispered in horror:

"What are you saying, my dear! Good gracious, the coachman will hear! Be quiet or the coachman will hear! He can overhear everything."

"I don't love you . . . I don't love you!" he went on breathlessly. "You've no soul and no morals. . . . Don't dare to wear that raincoat! Do you hear? Or else I will tear it into rags. . . ."

"Control yourself, my child," *maman* wept. "The coachman can hear!"

"And where is my father's fortune? Where is your money? You have wasted it all. I am not ashamed of being poor, but I am ashamed of having such a mother. . . . When my schoolfellows ask questions about you, I always blush."

In the rain they had to pass two stations before they reached the town. Volodya spent all the time on the little platform between two carriages and shivered all over. He did not want to go into the compartment because there the mother he hated was sitting. He hated himself, hated the ticket collectors, the smoke from the engine, the cold to which he attributed his shivering. And the heavier the weight on his heart, the more strongly he felt that somewhere in the world, among some people, there was a pure, honorable, warm, refined life, full of love, affection, gayety, and serenity. . . . He felt this and was so intensely miserable that a passenger, after looking in his face attentively, actually said: "You have the toothache, I suppose?"

In town *maman* and Volodya lived with Marya Petrovna, a lady of noble rank, who had a large flat and let rooms to boarders. *Maman* had two rooms, one with windows and two pictures in gold frames hanging on the walls, in which her bed stood and in which she lived, and a little dark room opening out of it in which Volodya lived. Here there was a sofa on which he slept, and, except that sofa, there was no other furniture; the rest of the room was entirely filled up with wicker baskets full of clothes, cardboard hatboxes, and all sorts of rubbish, which *maman* preserved for some reason or other. Volodya prepared his lessons either in his mother's room or in the "common room," as the large room in which the boarders assembled at dinnertime and in the evening was called.

On reaching home he lay down on his sofa and put the quilt over him to stop his shivering. The cardboard hatboxes, the wicker baskets, and the other rubbish, reminded him that he had not a room of his own, that he had no refuge in which he could get away from his mother, from her visitors, and from the voices that were floating up from the "common room." The satchel and the books lying about in the corners reminded him of the examination he had missed. . . . For some reason there came into his mind, quite inappropriately, Mentone, where he had lived with his father when he was seven years old; he thought of Biarritz and two little English girls with whom he ran about on the sand. . . . He tried to recall to his memory the color of the sky, the sea, the height of the waves, and his mood at the time, but he could not succeed. The English girls flitted before his imagination as though they were living; all the rest was a medley of images that floated away in confusion. . . .

"No; it's cold here," thought Volodya. He got up, put on his overcoat, and went into the "common room."

There they were drinking tea. There were three people at the samovar: *maman*, an old lady with tortoiseshell pince-nez, who gave music lessons; and Avgustin Mihailych, an elderly and very stout Frenchman, who was employed in a perfumery factory.

"I have had no dinner today," said *maman*. "I ought to send the maid to buy some bread."

"Dunyasha!" shouted the Frenchman.

It appeared that the maid had been sent out somewhere by the lady of the house.

"Oh, that's of no consequence," said the Frenchman, with a broad smile. "I will go for some bread myself at once. Oh, it's nothing."

He laid his strong, pungent cigar in a conspicuous place, put on his hat and went out. After he had gone away *maman* began telling the music teacher how she had been staying at the Shumihins', and how warmly they welcomed her.

"Lili Shumihin is a relation of mine, you know," she said. "Her late husband, General Shumihin, was a cousin of my husband. And she was a Baroness Kolb by birth—"

"*Maman*, that's false!" said Volodya irritably. "Why tell lies?"

He knew perfectly well that what his mother said was true; in what she was saying about General Shumihin and about Baroness Kolb there was not a word of lying, but nevertheless he felt that she was lying. There was a suggestion of falsehood in her manner of speaking, in the expression of her face, in her eyes, in everything.

"You are lying," repeated Volodya; and he brought his fist down on the table with such force that all the crockery shook and *maman's* tea was spilt. "Why do you talk about generals and baronesses? It's all lies!"

The music teacher was disconcerted, and coughed into her handkerchief, affecting to sneeze, and *maman* began to cry.

"Where can I go?" thought Volodya.

He had been in the street already; he was ashamed to go to his schoolfellows. Again, quite incongruously, he remembered the two little English girls. . . . He paced up and down the "common room," and went into Avgustin Mihailych's room. Here there was a strong smell of ethereal oils and glycerine soap. On the table, in the window, and even on the chairs, there were a number of bottles, glasses, and wineglasses containing fluids of various colors. Volodya took up from the table a newspaper, opened it and read the title *Figaro*. . . . There was a strong and pleasant scent about the paper. Then he took a revolver from the table. . . .

"There, there! Don't take any notice of it." The music teacher was comforting *maman* in the next room. "He is young! Young people of his age never restrain themselves. One must resign oneself to that."

"No, Yevgenya Andreyevna; he's too spoilt," said *maman* in a singsong voice. "He has no one in authority over him, and I am weak and can do nothing. Oh, I am unhappy!"

Volodya put the muzzle of the revolver to his mouth, felt something like a trigger or spring, and pressed it with his finger. . . . Then he felt something else projecting, and once more pressed it. Taking the muzzle out of his mouth, he wiped it with the lapel of his coat, looked at the lock. He had never in his life taken a weapon in his hand before. . . .

"I believe one ought to raise this . . ." he reflected. "Yes, it seems so."

Avgustin Mihailych went into the "common room," and with a laugh began telling them about something. Volodya put the muzzle in his mouth again, pressed it with his teeth, and pressed something with his fingers. There was the sound of a shot. . . . Something hit Volodya in the back of his head with terrible violence, and he fell on the table with his face downwards among the bottles and glasses. Then he saw his father, as in Mentone, in a top-hat with a wide black band on it, wearing mourning for some lady, suddenly seize him by both hands, and they fell headlong into a very deep, dark pit.

Then everything was blurred and vanished.

1887

# A FATHER

"I ADMIT I have had a drop. . . . You must excuse me. I went
into a beer-shop on the way here, and as it was so hot I had a couple
of bottles. It's hot, my boy."

Old Musatov took a nondescript rag out of his pocket and wiped
his shaven, battered face with it.

"I have come only for a minute, Borenka, my angel," he went on,
not looking at his son, "about something very important. Excuse me,
perhaps I am hindering you. Haven't you ten roubles, my dear, you
could let me have till Tuesday? You see, I ought to have paid for
my lodging yesterday, and money, you see! . . . None! Not to save
my life!"

Young Musatov went out without a word, and began whispering
on the other side of the door with the landlady of the summer villa
and his colleagues who had taken the villa with him. Three minutes
later he came back, and without a word gave his father a ten-rouble
note. The latter thrust it carelessly into his pocket without looking
at it, and said:

"*Merci.* Well, how are you getting on? It's a long time since
we met."

"Yes, a long time, not since Easter."

"Half a dozen times I have been meaning to come to you, but
I've never had time. First one thing, then another. . . . It's simply
awful! I am talking nonsense, though. . . . All that's nonsense! Don't
you believe me, Borenka. I said I would pay you back the ten roubles
on Tuesday—don't believe that either. Don't believe a word I say.
I have nothing to do at all, it's simply laziness, drunkenness, and I
am ashamed to be seen in such clothes in the street. You must excuse

648

me, Borenka. Here I have sent the girl to you three times for money and written you piteous letters. Thanks for the money, but don't believe the letters; I was telling fibs. I am ashamed to rob you, my angel; I know that you can scarcely make both ends meet yourself, and feed on locusts, but my impudence is too much for me. I am such a specimen of impudence—fit for a show! . . . You must excuse me, Borenka. I tell you the truth, because I can't see your angel face without emotion."

A minute passed in silence. The old man heaved a deep sigh and said:

"You might treat me to a glass of beer, perhaps."

His son went out without a word, and again there was a sound of whispering on the other side of the door. When, a little later, the beer was brought in, the old man seemed to revive at the sight of the bottles and abruptly changed his tone.

"I was at the races the other day, my boy," he began telling him, assuming a scared expression. "We were a party of three, and we pooled three roubles on Frisky. And, thanks to that Frisky, we got thirty-two roubles each for our rouble. I can't get on without the races, my boy. It's a gentlemanly diversion. My virago always gives me a dressing over the races, but I go. I love it, and that's all about it."

Boris, a fair-haired young man with a melancholy immobile face, was walking slowly up and down, listening in silence. When the old man stopped to clear his throat, he went up to him and said:

"I bought myself a pair of boots the other day, Father, which turn out to be too tight for me. Won't you take them? I'll let you have them cheap."

"If you like," said the old man with a grimace, "only for the price you gave for them, without any cheapening."

"Very well, I'll let you have them on credit."

The son groped under the bed and produced the new boots. The father took off his clumsy, rusty, evidently secondhand boots and began trying on the new ones.

"A perfect fit," he said. "Right, let me keep them. And on Tuesday, when I get my pension, I'll send you the money for them. That's not true, though," he went on, suddenly falling into the same tearful tone again. "And it was a lie about the races, too, and a lie about the pension. And you are deceiving me, Borenka. . . . I feel your generous· tactfulness. I see through you! Your boots are too small, because your heart is too big. Ah, Borenka, Borenka! I understand it all and feel it!"

"Have you moved into new lodgings?" his son interrupted, to change the conversation.

"Yes, my boy. I move every month. My virago can't stay long in the same place with her temper."

"I went to your lodgings, I meant to ask you to stay here with me. In your state of health it would do you good to be in the fresh air."

"No," said the old man, with a wave of his hand, "the woman wouldn't let me; and I shouldn't care to, myself. A hundred times you have tried to drag me out of the pit, and I have tried myself, but nothing came of it. Give it up. I must stick in my filthy hole. This minute, here I am sitting, looking at your angel face, yet something is drawing me home to my hole. Such is my fate. You can't draw a dung-beetle to a rose. But it's time I was going, my boy. It's getting dark."

"Wait a minute then, I'll come with you. I have to go to town today myself."

Both put on their overcoats and went out. When, a little while afterwards, they were driving in a cab, it was already dark, and lights began to gleam in the windows.

"I've robbed you, Borenka!" the father muttered. "Poor children, poor children! It must be a dreadful trouble to have such a father! Borenka, my angel, I cannot lie when I see your face. You must excuse me. . . . What my depravity has come to, my God! Here I have just been robbing you, and put you to shame with my drunken state; I am robbing your brothers, too, and put them to shame, and you should have seen me yesterday! I won't conceal it, Borenka. Some neighbors, a wretched crew, came to see my virago; I got drunk, too, with them, and I blackguarded you poor children for all I was worth. I abused you, and complained that you had abandoned me. I wanted, you see, to touch the drunken hussies' hearts, and pose as an unhappy father. It's my way, you know: when I want to screen my vices I throw all the blame on my innocent children. I can't tell lies and hide things from you, Borenka. I came to see you as proud as a peacock, but when I saw your gentleness and kind heart, my tongue clave to the roof of my mouth, and it upset my conscience completely."

"Hush, Father—let's talk of something else."

"Mother of God, what children I have!" the old man went on, not heeding his son. "What wealth God has bestowed on me! Such children ought not to have had a black sheep like me for a father, but a real man with soul and feeling! I am not worthy of you!"

The old man took off his cap with a button at the top and crossed himself several times.

"Thanks be to Thee, O Lord!" he said with a sigh, looking from side to side as though seeking an icon. "Remarkable, exceptional children! I have three sons, and they are all alike. Sober, steady, hardworking, and what brains! Cabman, what brains! Grigory alone has brains enough for ten. He speaks French, he speaks German, and talks better than any of your lawyers—one is never tired of listening. My children, my children, I can't believe that you are mine! I can't believe it! You are a martyr, my Borenka—I am ruining you, and I shall go on ruining you. . . . You give to me endlessly, though you know your money is thrown away. The other day I sent you a pitiful letter. I described how ill I was, but you know I was lying—I wanted the money for rum. And you give to me because you are afraid to wound me by refusing. I know all that, and feel it. Grisha's a martyr, too. On Thursday I went to his office, drunk, filthy, ragged, reeking of vodka like a cellar. . . . I went straight up, such a figure, I pestered him with my nasty talk, while his colleagues and superiors and petitioners were standing round. I have disgraced him for life. And he wasn't the least confused, only turned a bit pale, but smiled and came up to me as though there were nothing the matter, even introduced me to his colleagues. Then he took me all the way home, and not a word of reproach. I rob him worse than you. Take your brother Sasha now, he's a martyr too! He married, as you know, a colonel's daughter of an aristocratic circle, and got a dowry with her. . . . You would think he would have nothing to do with me. No, brother, after his wedding he came with his young wife and paid me the first visit—in my hole. . . . Upon my soul!"

The old man gave a sob, and then began laughing.

"And at that moment, as luck would have it, we were eating grated radish with kvass and frying fish, and there was a stink enough in the flat to make the devil sick. I was lying down—I'd had a drop; my virago bounced out at the young people with her face crimson. . . . It was a disgrace in fact. But Sasha rose superior to it all."

"Yes, our Sasha is a good fellow," said Boris.

"The most splendid fellow! You are all pure gold, you and Grisha and Sasha and Sonya. I worry you, torment you, disgrace you, rob you, and all my life I have not heard one word of reproach from you, you have never given me one cross look. It would be all very well if I had been a decent father to you—but as it is! You have had nothing from me but harm. I am a bad, dissipated man. . . . Now, thank God, I am quieter and I have no strength of will; but in former days when you were little, I had determination, will. Whatever I said or did, I always thought it was right. Sometimes I'd come home from the club at night, drunk and ill-humored, and scold your poor mother for spending money. The whole night I would be railing at her, and think it the right thing too; you would get up in the morning and go to school, while I'd still be venting my temper upon her. Heavens! I did torture her, poor martyr! When you came back from school and I was asleep you didn't dare to have dinner till I got up. At dinner again there would be a flare-up. I dare say you remember. I wish no one such a father; God sent me to you for a trial. Yes, for a trial! Hold out, children, to the end! Honor thy father, and thy days shall be long. Perhaps for your noble conduct God will grant you long life. Cabman, stop!"

The old man jumped out of the cab and ran into a tavern. Half an hour later he came back, cleared his throat in a drunken way, and sat down beside his son.

"Where's Sonya now?" he asked. "Still at boarding-school?"

"No, she left in May, and is living with Sasha's mother-in-law now."

"There!" said the old man in surprise. "She is a jolly good girl! So she is following her brother's example. . . . Ah, Borenka, she has no mother, no one to rejoice over her! I say, Borenka, does she—does she know how I am living? Eh?"

Boris made no answer. Five minutes passed in profound silence. The old man gave a sob, wiped his face with a rag, and said:

"I love her, Borenka! She is my only daughter, you know, and in one's old age there is no comfort like a daughter. Could I see her, Borenka?"

"Of course, when you like."

"Really? And she won't mind?"

"Of course not. She has been trying to find you so as to see you."

"Upon my soul! What children! Eh, cabman? Arrange it, Borenka darling! She is a young lady now, *delicatesse, consommé*, and all the rest of it in a refined way, and I don't want to show myself to her in such an abject state. I'll tell you how we'll contrive to work it. For three days I will keep away from spirits, to get my filthy, drunken phiz into better order. Then I'll come to you, and you shall lend me for the time some suit of yours; I'll shave and have my hair cut, then you go and bring her to your flat. Will you?"

"Very well."

"Cabman, stop!"

The old man sprang out of the cab again and ran into a tavern. While Boris was driving him to his lodging he jumped out again twice, while his son sat silent and waited patiently for him. When, after dismissing the cab, they made their way across a long, filthy yard to the "virago's" lodging, the old man put on an utterly shame-faced and guilty air, and began timidly clearing his throat and clicking with his lips.

"Borenka," he said in an ingratiating voice, "if my virago begins saying anything, don't take any notice . . . and behave to her, you know, affably. She is ignorant and impudent, but she's a good baggage. There is a good, warm heart beating in her bosom!"

The long yard ended, and Boris found himself in a dark entry. The swing door creaked, there was a smell of cooking and a smoking samovar. There was a sound of harsh voices. Going through the passage into the kitchen, Boris could see nothing but thick smoke, a line with washing on it, and the chimney of the samovar through a crack of which golden sparks were dropping.

"And here is my cell," said the old man, stooping down and going into a little room with a low-pitched ceiling, and an atmosphere unbearably stifling from the proximity of the kitchen.

Here three women were sitting at the table regaling themselves. Seeing the visitors, they exchanged glances and left off eating.

"Well, did you get it?" one of them, apparently the "virago" herself, asked abruptly.

"Yes, yes," muttered the old man. "Well, Boris, pray sit down. Everything is plain here, young man—we live in a simple way."

He bustled about in an aimless way. He felt ashamed before his son, and at the same time apparently he wanted to keep up before the women his dignity as cock of the walk, and as a forsaken, unhappy father.

"Yes, young man, we live simply with no nonsense," he went on muttering. "We are simple people, young man. . . . We are not like you, we don't want to keep up a show before people. No! . . . Shall we have a drink of vodka?"

One of the women (she was ashamed to drink before a stranger) heaved a sigh and said:

"Well, I'll have another drink on account of the mushrooms. . . . They are such mushrooms, they make you drink even if you don't want to. Ivan Gerasimich, offer something to the young gentleman—perhaps he will have a drink!"

The last word she pronounced in a mincing drawl.

"Have a drink, young man!" said the father, not looking at his son. "We have no wine or liqueurs, my boy, we live in a plain way."

"He doesn't like our ways," sighed the "virago."

"Never mind, never mind, he'll have a drink."

Not to offend his father by refusing, Boris took a wineglass and drank in silence. When they brought in the samovar, to satisfy the old man, he drank two cups of disgusting tea in silence, with a melancholy face. Without a word he listened to the virago dropping hints about there being in this world cruel, heartless children who abandon their parents.

"I know what you are thinking now!" said the old man, after drinking more and passing into his habitual state of drunken excitement. "You think I have let myself sink into the mire, that I am to be pitied; but to my thinking, this simple life is much more normal than your life. . . . I don't need anybody, and . . . and I don't intend to eat humble pie. . . . I can't endure a wretched boy's looking at me with compassion."

After tea he cleaned a herring and sprinkled it with onion, with such feeling that tears of emotion stood in his eyes. He began talking again about the races and his winnings, about some Panama hat for which he had paid sixteen roubles the day before. He told lies with the same relish with which he ate herring and drank. His son sat on in silence for an hour, and began to say goodbye.

"I don't venture to keep you," the old man said, haughtily. "You must excuse me, young man, for not living as you would like!"